Pr

Maria Isabel Pita is al...
If you're unfamiliar wi...
effortlessly between the past and present, while indestructible true love weaves its eternal spell on her characters' minds and souls.
— *Marilyn Jaye Lewis*

Ah, can Pita write! Her prose is graceful and flowing without a hint of sloppiness, and her tone is delicate, playful yet serious... as an author she pulls you in with her words, and makes you want to continue reading... she doesn't hold back, just as she didn't hold back in her non-fiction. She shows it all.
— *Romance Divas*

Dreams of Anubis is a compellingly erotic tale unveiled in one of the world's most romantic and mystical lands... Ms. Pita brings together both a sensually historic plot and a contemporary Egypt... her elegant style of writing pulls at your senses and allows you to live the moment through her characters. The language flows beautifully, the characters are well drawn, the plot is exciting and always fresh and riveting, and the setting is romantic. I highly recommend *Dreams of Anubis* for anyone with a love of erotic romance with a touch of magic and mysticism.
— *Just Erotic Romance Reviews*

A nice respite from many of the 'cookie cuter' erotic romances out there... it will leave you impressed and applauding Ms. Pita's literary talents and incredible imagination.
— *Cupid's Library Reviews*

Maria Isabel Pita has to be, hands down, one of America's top erotica writers today... What makes this novel great is what it isn't... much of today's erotica has had to sell itself on extreme BDSM and violence against women that makes the ordinary person cringe. Ms. Pita manages to take us on an erotic journey with her characters as they explore each other both physically and mentally to discover that perhaps there is such a thing as a soul mate. Not only the gentle side of love but also the hot sizzling sex scenes in the book are written with such skill that it's almost naughty for the reader to form a picture in the mind's eye. Take a glass of your favorite wine on a lazy afternoon and I'm sure that you'll not put it down until either the book or the bottle of wine is finished...
— *Rudolf Spoerer*

Cat's Collar —
Three Erotic Romances

Maria Isabel Pita

CAT'S COLLAR – Three Erotic Romances
Copyright ©2005 by Magic Carpet Books, Inc.
All Rights Reserved

No part of this book may be reproduced,
stored in a retrieval system, or transmitted in any form,
by any means, including mechanical, electronic,
photocopying, recording or otherwise, without
prior written permission from the publisher and author.

First Magic Carpet Books, Inc. edition October 2005

Published in 2005

Manufactured in the United States of America
Published by Magic Carpet Books, Inc.

Magic Carpet Books, Inc.
PO Box 473
New Milford, CT 06776

Library of Congress Cataloging in Publication Date

CAT'S COLLAR – Three Erotic Romances
by Maria Isabel Pita
$16.95 / $20.95

ISBN# 0-9766510-0-9
Book Design: P. Ruggieri

Table of Contents

Dreams of Anubis   7

Rituals of Surrender   203

Cat's Collar   407

Dreams of Anubis

DEDICATION

To Stinger, now and always

Prologue

My life-long friend, Caroline Jordan, was working in Cairo, Egypt. She had found what I considered the dream job—photographing mastabas in Saqqara for an Egyptologist writing a book on the Old Kingdom burial ground. Yet I was the one who had loved ancient Egypt since I was a little girl.

At approximately five-years-old, I'd accompanied my mother to a public library, where I'd wandered through the maze of bookshelves pulling volumes out at random. I remember one particularly dark and heavy tome was too much for me, and falling from my grasp it landed open at my feet. I know now that I was looking at a black-and-white photograph of an Egyptian bas-relief, but at the time all I could do was feel. I eagerly ran to find my mother, dragged her by the hand back to the book lying on the floor, and pointing down at it cried, 'Home!'

During the long plane rides from Boston to Cairo, I passed the time lost in colorful daydreams, and by the time we landed, I felt stiff as a butterfly born in a jar. It had taken me fifteen hours and twenty-two years to finally make it to Egypt. I was so excited that the throbbing, teeming chaos of the airport didn't surprise me; it seemed natural, like an extension of my racing pulse.

It took me another small eternity to get through Customs, but at last my blue passport was imprinted with a circular red hieroglyph, and stepping through the gate I spotted my friend almost at once. Her long pale arm was swaying like a branch over a darkly heaving sea of native heads.

'Carol!' I cried.

'Mary, over here!'

Dreams of Anubis

'Carol!' I threaded my way to her through the tapestry of races crowding the airport. There seemed to be people from all over the world there, which was not surprising since it was the middle of winter and the height of the tourist season.

'You look great!' I cried over the roar of voices as we quickly hugged each other. 'But how can you manage to still be as pale as a ghost in Egypt?'

'We'll talk in the car,' she said, relieving me of one of my carry-on bags, the smaller and lighter one.

Following her, I paused to stare up in awe at the two stone colossi who sat smiling peacefully over the teeming masses at their feet as if looking serenely into the past. 'Carol, where's the baggage claim?' I asked anxiously.

'Right over there.' She indicated a wall where native men clad in the traditional *galabiyya* were lifting suitcases out of a dark hole and quite literally tossing the luggage back into a waiting crowd.

'Oh, my God,' I exclaimed, 'that one's mine!' just as a black suitcase hit the floor with an ominous thud, and burst open like a giant seed. Immediately a crowd of Egyptian men descended upon the colorful petals of my clothing and undergarments, passionately caressing everything back into place, and clearly enjoying the task. Then one of these men sat on top of my suitcase to force it closed. Carol purposefully grabbed the handle, and he leapt to his feet, grinning at me.

'Don't worry, Mary,' she said, 'my maid will wash and iron everything for you in the morning.' She gestured to a more sober looking native to help carry the suitcase out for us.

'Your maid,' I repeated numbly.

Her chauffeur was waiting for us outside in a big blue Chevrolet that easily became king of the road. Once again I was sealed away in an air-conditioned technological cocoon and the land I had dreamed of seeing all my life remained as unreal as a film playing on the window screens. The broad avenue we followed away from the airport might have been anywhere in the world if not for the colossal statue of Ramses II that loomed over us at an intersection. Then we turned right and suddenly there was an explosion of life. Our American boat now shared the road with a tumultuous sea of pedestrians and assorted vehicles. We appeared to be passing through a marketplace, where black clouds of flies hovering over food stalls matched the robes of the women strolling by. Some of them balanced large, heavy urns on their heads while their hips swayed with a slow, timeless rhythm offering a mysterious counterpoint to the chaos of life around them. Usually it was not so much a matter of driving as of squeezing between things, and the trickling flow of traffic wasn't helped by donkeys pulling heavily loaded carts while flicking centuries away with their tails as casually as flies.

'And I thought rush hour in Boston was bad,' I remarked.

'We'll be out of it soon,' Carol assured me placidly, sitting in the backseat beside me. 'You cut your hair, Mary.' She finally noticed. 'It looks nice, very Old Kingdom.'

Her apartment was located in a foreign residential area of Cairo free of any noisy street life, and took up the entire ninth floor of a white building surrounded by palm trees.

'Well, it sure beats your attic in Newton,' I grumbled.

'Well, normally us lowly archeologists can't afford such a nice place, but Simon has a friend in U.S. A.I. D. who's away for a year, and he was nice enough to let me borrow it.'

'You're not an archeologist,' I snapped. 'Oh, God, I need a shower…'

'I'm afraid you'll be a little disappointed with the water pressure, Mary. I recommend a bath.'

'That'll be wonderful. Thank you. Who's Simon?' I asked belatedly; my mental synapses were functioning on emergency power.

'My boss.'

'Oh.' I glanced beyond the unimaginatively furnished modern living room into the more traditional and even more boring dining room. 'Wine?' I asked hopefully.

Carol avoided my eyes. 'I tried to buy things you would like, Mary, but I couldn't afford what the Commissary charges for wine.'

'Oh, well,' I said bravely, and would have shrugged if my shoulders hadn't felt so heavy.

'You poor thing, come on, it took me a whole week to recover from the jet-lag. Here, I put some towels out for you.' She showed me where everything was

Dreams of Anubis

in the spacious bathroom—the soap, the shampoo and conditioner, the body lotions and scented powders—like a golden-haired angel giving me a quick tour of paradise. 'I spend more time in here than in any other room. The air is so dry outside it's heaven soaking in a bath at night. How would you like a dirty martini? Hard liquor is a lot cheaper at the Commissary, and you can set your glass right here where I usually put my tea cup.'

Thirty minutes later, I could not have felt much better if my fairy godmother had tapped me on the shoulder with the wand of my olive-tipped crystal stirrer. Sipping the ice-cold vodka from an inverted glass pyramid, I ranked the martini as one of civilization's greatest achievements while contemplating the wonderful days to come. I gazed down at my breasts, which I'm proud to say are completely natural. I've never done anything to them except watch them grow and shape themselves into the tender buds crowning my torso now. More than one man has commented on what perfect handfuls they are, just big enough to cup and weigh and get a good luscious grip on. When I was younger I had wondered if my aureoles and nipples were a bit too big, a little too exuberantly fertile in relation to the rest of my gently swelling mounds. That was until men praised them with moaning, hungry attention; delighting in the generous rosy nipples, as they'd gently catch them between their teeth.

I set the fragile tulip of my martini glass carefully down on the rim of the tub and paid full attention to my breasts swelling like twin half moons out of the sky-blue water. Instead of the traditional boring bubbles, I had chosen mineral rocks from one of the many jars available to me. Carol's bathrooms always made me think of an alchemist's laboratory. In my friend's mind, every benign substance on earth should be translatable into the pleasure it gives her skin at the end of the day when she ritually soaks all her cares away in a hot and fragrant bath. Usually I prefer showers, but I was on vacation now, relaxing and deliberately letting myself become aroused by the sight of my naked body.

I sank a little deeper into the water's hot embrace, grateful for the pillow cushioning my shoulders and the back of my neck as I stretched my long legs out in the tub's delightfully accommodating dimensions. The curves of my figure were only slightly distorted by the clear blue liquid washing over them and imbuing my skin with a sapphire's glistening radiance, except that my body was infinitely more precious. It was true I had made a gift of it to more than a few men, but none of them had been worthy of me in the end, and I had taken myself back without feeling I had lost anything except a little time. I think that for a while I was actually in love with every man I fucked. Yet it was really only lust, sexual infatuation, physical obsession, whatever you wanted to call it. It wasn't love, true love, in which I still fervently believed despite so many profound disappointments.

I settled more comfortably against the pillow watching both my hands lightly caressing the insides of my thighs, and smiled to myself hearing again a chorus of men's voices in my head all saying, 'You have great legs, Mary'. Whenever I looked in the mirror now, I didn't just see what my own critical eyes told me, I saw the way men had touched and kissed and caressed my body with their hands, lips, tongues, and erect cocks. Remembering how passionately they had possessed me, how rock-hard they had become just holding me, telling me how beautiful I was better than any mirror ever could.

I was teasing myself, letting a sweet ache kindle in my pussy for something more than the gentle lapping of hot water as my hands kept slowly stroking my thighs around it. It was a luscious torment working my sex up to the moment when I would touch it, gently and tentatively at first, before a deepening excitement inevitably made me start boldly stroking myself. I didn't like to use dildos when I masturbated. My vagina was offended by the cold, lifeless feel of plastic, a pathetic substitute for the warm, thrusting energy of a real live penis. I preferred enjoying the soft fullness of my labial lips as my fingertips gently parted them, and then relishing the slick tightness of my pussy as I gently penetrated myself. I used two, sometimes three fingers knowing this divinely silky sensation was what a man's erection experienced sliding in and out of me.

My vulva was frustratingly stimulated and sensitized by the mineral-rich currents lapping against it, and I finally took mercy on it by slipping my right hand between my legs. I caught my breath from the shock of pleasure it gave me just to touch the heart of my labia, that wonderfully sensitive spot just over the entrance to the dark hungry hole in my flesh. The puckered lips of my sex were

Dreams of Anubis

in full, sensitive bloom, and I realized my mental and emotional excitement at being in Egypt, the land of all my most sensual fantasies, had mysteriously aroused my body, too. I was exquisitely open to anything in every sense, and when I grazed my clitoral hood with the tip of my forefinger, I gasped when I felt how firm my skin's magical button was. All it would take was the relentless pressure of my rhythmically moving fingertips to send me over the edge.

I closed my eyes, and more swiftly than I believed possible, it was as if my soul began magically slipping out of the confines of my skin, escaping my skeleton's cage on a climax's invisible wings. As I came, in my mind's eye I saw a colorful falcon soaring against a vivid blue sky above the phallic trunks of palm trees, between which I glimpsed a distant pyramid rising up out of the desert's hot flesh glowing a molten gold... my clitoris burning and dissolving into the most divine sensation possible...

'My God,' I breathed, opening my eyes, and for a timeless moment I wasn't sure where I was. My gaze first landed on a plant belonging in a tropical garden beside a pool tiled in lapis-lazuli blue...but I realized a few disappointed heartbeats later that I was actually inside a bathroom.

'Wow,' I whispered, awed by the powerful orgasm I had just given myself. No doubt my body's jetlagged exhaustion had contributed to making the pleasure almost blindingly intense, but I had seen something as I came, an image as sharp and detailed as a photograph flashing in my brain as though squeezed out of my deepest memory by the muscles contracting within me. My orgasm had come with a vision much more distinctly real than the fantasies I excited myself with when I masturbated. I couldn't explain it, but I had always suspected my sensuality and my imagination were intimately related, and my body was finally in the embrace of a sacred atmosphere, sitting in a bath in an ancient land I had daydreamed about ever since I could remember.

I sighed happily and reached for my martini. I sipped it appreciatively; draining my glass down to the last drop while wonderfully romantic possibilities lapped in and out of my mind as pleasantly as the sky-blue water around my body...I was in Egypt!

Chapter One

The next morning I could have cared less that I was in Egypt. My head felt as heavy as a stone from the pyramid, and Carol's quiet knock was easy to ignore.

'Get up, Mary,' she urged through the door, 'we have to leave soon.'

'Okay,' I groaned, 'but please just let my lie in one of the mastabas and sleep all day.'

'Would you prefer coffee or tea?'

'Coffee!'

A short while later, I felt a bit better, but not much.

'You'll be fine,' Carol assured me.

'Really? I thought it took you a week to recover.'

'Oh, it did, but you're stronger than I am.' She meant less sensitive. 'Anyway, you can take it easy today. Simon wants us to finish the mastaba we're working in, then I'll be free to show you the sights. Here.' She handed me a large thermos. 'Now, let's go, Hamud's waiting for us downstairs.'

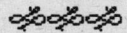

Hamud, Carol's chauffeur, was still in the same short-sleeved blue shirt and brown polyester pants he had been wearing yesterday when he picked us up at the airport, and I met the woman who laundered them on the way down the stairs. His wife was the maid, and Carol explained to her by way of a mixture of English, Arabic and sign language that all my clothes required washing and ironing. The woman's broad smile smoothed a few

Dreams of Anubis

wrinkles from her leathery skin, and she nodded with such fervor I was sure she had not understood a word.

We had to walk around a sleeping family – a father and a mother and two young children—to get to the car. They were lying beneath a group of palm trees on the decorative island in front of the building and looked quite peaceful in the cool morning with their arms wrapped protectively around each other.

The crisp air helped clear my head, and I actually felt a stab of excitement as Hamud opened the back door for us with a good-natured grin.

Once again, we drove through a tumultuous sea of life, and then, at last, I got my first look at the Nile. Hamud floored the accelerator and we flew south along the east bank, the silver water on our right flowing north towards the Delta and the Mediterranean.

I felt as though we were driving back into the past. Apart from a few isolated housing complexes Carol informed me were U.S. A.I.D. projects and that resembled dried-out honeycombs, there were nothing but green and brown fields on our left where robed figures bent towards the earth in the eternal dance of sowing and reaping…time seemed to slow down…and to press against my heart like the head of an invisible lover lying contentedly against me after centuries of lovemaking…

I was jolted out of my reverie when Hamud abruptly turned right onto a narrow bridge.

'You'll be able to see the Step Pyramid soon,' Carol informed me, breaking our dreamy silence.

We entered a forest of date palms. The ancient Egyptians made wine from dates, and it was so easy for me to picture tanned young men in scanty white loincloths climbing up the slender trunks. Then we drove through a miserable little village where Hamud was forced to slow down as a small herd of naked children surrounded the car.

'Baksheesh!' they shrieked. 'Baksheesh!'

I did not have any Egyptian money on me yet, and passing this way every morning, Carol had hardened herself to the scene. Her waist-length blonde hair firmly braided, she looked straight ahead, and not a muscle in her aristocratic face twitched when I heard what distinctly sounded like curses hurled after us along with equally harmless pebbles.

I could not help myself; a lecture began forming in my mind like a storm cloud. 'The Old Kingdom Nomarch of this province would have been horrified by these living conditions!' Hamud jumped as my indignant voice thundered through the car's contented silence. 'Thousands of years ago those children would have had a much better life.'

Carol glanced at me with an abstracted little smile, and I could not tell if she was listening to me or lost in a daydream. I knew my friend had long ago learned to tune me out when she wanted to.

I didn't care. 'A Nomarch was personally responsible for every individual in his domain just like a father,' I went on fervently. 'Each of his subjects was as much a part of him as his own vital organs. Everyone played a different role in sustaining the living body of the province, and their well-being was a reflection of the Nomarch's own physical and spiritual health...'

'There it is,' Carol announced, sounding relieved.

Nearly invisible on the trembling haze of the horizon, Zoser's Step Pyramid was distinguishable from the flesh-colored desert only by its geometric purity. I stared at it in awe, and watched in fascination as the sand inexorably crept up around the palm trees. It wasn't long before the desert took over completely and we found ourselves at the foot of a rocky cliff studded with signs.

I gripped Hamud's bony shoulder. 'Stop, please.' I stepped out into the beautiful morning and just stood there for a full minute savoring the fact that I was really here at last. An arrow indicated that the mastaba of Ptah-Hotep, author of the famous maxims, lay straight ahead to the west, while the eternal home of the handsome nobleman, Ti, was to be found to the north. I was so excited these great men were still here in a mysterious sense that my exhaustion evaporated. I got back into the car. 'Let's go,' I said eagerly.

His dark eyes shining at me through the rearview mirror, Hamud rewarded my reverence for his country's history by burning rubber up the winding slope, throwing Carol and me into each other's arms, a sight that brought the teeth out in his grin. He must have driven this way a thousand times before, because I

Dreams of Anubis

swear he did not look at the road once. We crunched to a stop in a flat open space where two tourist buses lay abandoned in the soft morning sunshine in front of an amazingly modern-looking wall.

'Shukron, Hamud,' I said breathlessly, enunciating my first Arabic word in order to thank him.

'Sa-eeda,' Carol added briskly. 'Ba-dayn.'

'What did you just say to him?' I asked curiously.

'"Good-bye" and "later".'

'Well, that's specific.'

'It's specific enough for Egypt, believe me.'

Still grinning lasciviously at his success in getting Carol and me to hold on to each other in response to his prowess behind the wheel, Hamud drove off and my friend and I approached the wall. Its dark golden stone was made vividly three-dimensional by a pattern of recesses and projections that could easily have placed it in the twenty-first century. I was wearing white shorts and a short-sleeved white shirt in order to reflect the sun and expose as much of my pale skin to its tanning rays as was decent.

'Isn't it beautiful, Mary?' She finally showed some real emotion. 'I can understand why Victorian architects came to Egypt for inspiration and to get away from that awful cluttered style that was so popular back then. Only the first twelve feet up is the original wall,' she added in a clipped, academic tone. 'The rest was restored.' She had always been good at recording information, and I assumed this little speech had been edited from a longer one delivered by her employer.

Behind the enclosure wall that stretched for miles around the burial ground but only a fragment of which remains, Zoser's pyramid rose step by crumbling step into the cloudless sky.

'What mastaba are you working in now, Carol?' I asked, my excitement building.

'Oh just a small one, but it's lovely. I like it better than some of the big famous ones, maybe because it belonged to a princess.'

We passed through the opening in the wall and found ourselves in a shadowy antechamber where the stone ceiling had been carved to simulate bunches of logs roped together. But it was the false doors to the left and right of the entrance that I found truly haunting. Carved to look as if they had just begun to open, they were symbolic entrances to another dimension as impossible for the mortal mind to conceive of as it is for the body to step into solid rock. Directly ahead of us stretched a long pillared hall.

'Simon says it's ridiculous to think the Egyptians used engaged columns because they didn't know free-standing columns could withstand vertical stress,' Carol informed me. 'He says there are so many innovations in Saqqara there's no reason they couldn't have used freestanding columns if they'd really wanted to.'

'Whatever,' I replied. I had no idea what she was talking about and nor did she, which for the first time made me wonder what Simon looked like. That he had managed to impress these abstract facts on my friend's visually oriented brain was significant. Carol was a photographer and a painter; her perception and experience of the world lay entirely within the framework of images. I was the verbal, philosophical one. Physically, we were opposites as well. I have shoulder-length black hair and honey-brown eyes while Carol resembles a living doll with her waist-length blonde mane and traditional big baby-blue's.

Sunlight streamed down between the columns in hazy rays that struck me as wordless sentences my heart could almost mysteriously understand. I had done a lot of reading on the plane in between daydreaming, so I knew the columns were carved to look like bunches of reeds tied together, and that the distance between them gradually narrows as the colonnade progresses west, creating an impression of great distance. We moved silently as ghosts across the sand towards a door of pure white light at the end, but when we passed through it we found ourselves in another hot and empty section of desert, not in the magically fertile fields of the next world.

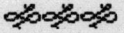

How Carol found the particular mastaba she was working in is beyond me. She must have charted her way by counting sand dunes as I wandered behind her, enthralled by the desert's featureless haze and the lovely

Dreams of Anubis

violet color shimmering above the horizon like a veil separating this harsh world from a softer, more flowing dimension not yet broken up into space and time, shape and sound. The silence was so intense I could almost hear it—a subliminal hollow, haunting sound like the wind blowing through the shell of my skull. The lifeless emptiness pressed against my senses in a strangely arousing way, and as I paused to fully experience it, in that instant Carol disappeared. I staggered across the deep sand in the direction I had last seen her, and was relieved to catch sight of her just below me as I crested a hill, that was steeper than I had thought. Distances and appearances were obviously deceptive in the desert, where there were no landmarks to judge them by. We passed the sights of several ongoing excavations—deep pits in the sand it would have been disturbingly easy to fall into. None of the doggedly patient archeologists responsible for them were in evidence, but clearly Saqqara had not yet yielded up all its treasures.

Infinitely glad to be free of my administrative position in a Beacon Hill law firm for nearly a month, I once again found myself regretting I had not studied Egyptology as I had dreamed of doing when I was a little girl. Walls covered with ancient hieroglyphs were profoundly more interesting than modern legal forms.

Up and down we went over increasingly rocky dunes, during which time we both paused to take several long sips from our thermoses. I had never experienced such dry air before, yet despite the sun's relentlessly penetrating rays, the temperature was ideal.

'We're almost there,' Carol announced as we reached the summit of another steep incline.

I ran my fingers through my hair. Thanks to the desert's natural blow dryer, it was incredibly soft and straight. Carol skipped gracefully down the hill, but preoccupied as I was with the paradoxical cosmetic benefits of a deadly environment, I tripped near the top and gathered so much momentum on the way down that I could not stop myself from running straight into a man's arms.

Seemingly unsurprised by my abrupt and passionate embrace, he detached me from him gently and smiled. 'Hello,' he said, and I might have been looking straight through his skull at the sky his eyes were so intensely blue.

'Hello!' I gasped, letting go of him as I regained my balance. 'I'm so sorry!'

'It was my pleasure. Have you come to help with the work?'

'No, I'm on vacation.'

His smile disappeared. 'Then I suggest you stay out of the way.'

'Um, Simon,' Carol said hesitantly, 'this is Mary, you know, my friend from Boston. I told you she was coming, remember?'

Now I knew exactly why she had learned so much about ancient Egypt.

'Oh, yes, nice to meet you, Mary,' Simon said, staring into my eyes as if they were dark pools into which he tossed the coins of these polite words, while making a silent wish. Then he turned away and disappeared into a rock outcropping that I realized must be a mastaba.

Carol stared after him. 'He likes you, Mary. I knew he would.'

'Likes me? He thinks I'm a stupid little tourist! I should have offered to help.'

'Don't worry about it,' she said, and followed her employer into the tomb.

Anxious not to interfere with their work, I paused in the pleasantly cool little corridor at the entrance to the mastaba. Smiling figures the size of my fingers moved in procession towards the burial chamber in row upon row of bas-reliefs still glowing with life after centuries. Much of the original paint remained, especially the red-brown tone of flesh and the ghostly white of dresses and loincloths.

Losing myself in vivid scenes of daily life, I was especially captivated by a boat depicted over a row of tiny pyramids—a stylized rendering of the river's surface—beneath which a variety of fish were carved in exquisitely realistic detail. My eyes ensnared by the scenes bursting with life around me, I set the thermos down and let my purse slip from my shoulder onto the sand. Whatever more literal-minded Egyptologists think, I could not believe these bas-reliefs were merely simple representations of daily activities, and they could not possibly be the ancient Egyptians' crudely literal conception of paradise either, for some of life's more pleasurable activities were obviously missing.

I stood there staring at one of the walls trying to find words for my own theory. I focused on a perfectly proportioned young man carrying the entire hind leg of a cow in his arms, part of the delectable fare being offered to the deceased. It

Dreams of Anubis

was as if the whole world was being laid before her piece by piece, a process during which she asserted her sensual connection with nature as well as her spirit's mastery over it. The giant baskets of fruit being carried towards the burial chamber might be meant to represent her emotions, the fish in the river her thoughts…

Looking away from a cat clutching a duck in its jaws, I suddenly found myself studying a pair of very fine, life-size brown legs. I suffered the impression that one of the young men carved on the wall had been released from his stone spell and made real before me as my eyes traveled slowly up to his bare chest, and lingered there appreciatively before moving up to his smile.

'Hi,' he said, revealing a bright crescent of teeth.

'Hi,' I echoed, peering at him closely. I was able to tell now that he was wearing ragged shorts, not a loincloth.

He offered me his hand. 'You must be Carol's friend, Mary. I'm Steve.'

I was very pleased by his firm grip. 'Nice to meet you, Steve.'

He glanced at the bas-reliefs I had been studying. 'Beautiful, aren't they?'

'Totally beautiful,' I agreed fervently.

'When did you arrive? Have you been to the Cairo Museum yet?'

'No, I just flew in yesterday afternoon.'

'You're going to love Egypt, Mary. Well, excuse me.' He slipped past me on his way out of the tomb.

For a wonderful moment I had mistaken his shining skin for a spiritual aura, but I realized now it was merely a thick coat of sunscreen. Wondering if it was Playgirl Magazine who was financing this expedition, I followed the procession of bas-reliefs deeper into the mastaba.

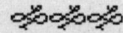

Carol's photographic equipment resembled a lunar module just landed on the otherworldly sand of the silent tomb. Silver light-stands reared their black hooded heads around the camera that was focused on one small section of wall.

Cat's Collar - Three Erotic Romances

Staying away from the sensitive equipment, I examined the bas-reliefs on the opposite wall while Simon and Carol took an astronomically long time setting up just one shot. I must admit, I found it difficult to concentrate on the tomb paintings with such an exquisite three-dimensional representation of the male form occupying the same space with me, and not a very large space at that. If I had known Egyptologists could look like Simon and Steve, nothing would have stopped me from getting my degree. I kept casting surreptitious glances over my shoulder at my friend and her employer. He was dressed just like the traditional Great White Hunter, in khaki shorts and a matching short-sleeved button-down shirt, an adventurous style somewhat marred by clean white socks and very cushy-looking sneakers. He was bent over the camera, which gave me a very good view of his...let's just say trekking through the desert every day hadn't hurt his physique, which was already very nice to begin with. He was tight and tan everywhere, and either he had bought stock in Coppertone or he had been blessed with a magical gene that enabled his fair skin to turn golden instead of red beneath the sun, a stunning contrast to his Nordic-blond hair and blue eyes.

I wondered how Carol was able to concentrate on her work, yet I wasn't surprised she hadn't told me how attractive her boss was. I loved her dearly, but ever since grade school she had done her best to keep me away from any boy she was interested in. I wondered what had prompted her to tell me that Simon liked me. Was she jealous of sharing his attention? I would definitely have to have a talk with her when we got back to the apartment, because if she wanted Simon to do more than sign her paycheck, then I would somehow have to control how attracted I was to him. I don't normally run straight into the arms of a man I've never met (although of course I hadn't meant to). The fact that he was an Egyptologist as well as stunningly handsome added up to the very annoying fact that I could not concentrate on bas-reliefs I had waited all my life to see.

We were in one of the very early mastabas, and it had clearly belonged to a woman. As she was brought the world piece-by-piece, she looked incredibly peaceful, happy and assured of her immortality. The clean, form-fitting lines of her ankle-length dress and her casually pulled back hair also struck me as strangely contemporary, as if I were looking at a princess of the twenty-second or twen-

Dreams of Anubis

ty-third century rather than at a girl who lived thousands of years ago. Her image was considerably larger than those of the people bringing her offerings, yet I could barely make her out on the pale stone wall in her tight white dress. She was holding a lotus flower up to her smiling face, inhaling its fragrance—a metaphor for the soul's ability to bloom inside one body and then another and another, each one decaying like a seed in the eternal rhythm of flowering.

'Amazing,' Simon suddenly murmured in my ear, 'I thought only horses fell asleep on their feet.'

The princess's smile seemed to deepen as I kept my eyes fixed on her face. 'I wasn't asleep,' I replied serenely.

'You know, if you put your hair up in a ponytail like that, you would look like her, Mary.' He sounded perfectly serious.

I smiled, pleased he was testing me like this. 'I would very much like to believe there is an eternal energy inside me which clothes itself in different forms,' I stated matter-of-factly, still looking at the princess. 'However, I didn't come to Egypt to shop for my soul's old dresses. I don't think I was Cleopatra or a high priestess of Isis in a past life, or anything like that.' I turned my head and looked him straight in the eye. 'If that's what you're thinking.'

A smile flickered across his thin mouth like energy traveling down a wire. 'I stand corrected, Mary,' he apologized in his soft, even voice.

There was a series of lightning-like flashes as Carol finally took the same picture ten times.

The strobe-like flashes were reflected by the nerve-endings deep in my belly as Simon's hand reached up and lightly held my arm, ostensibly to steady me during the brief technological storm. But he was staring deep into my eyes again in a way that made my emotions feel like hieroglyphs he could read and appreciate.

'Simon, I'm ready to set up the next shot,' Carol declared plaintively.

'Mm,' he said, continuing to hold my eyes for a few steady moments that had the opposite effect on my pulse. Then he turned back to his work with a light, almost apologetic squeeze of my shoulder.

Hurrying out of the mastaba, I nearly collided with the walking bas-relief, Steve, on his way back in.

'Off to see some more tombs?' he asked cheerfully.

'Yep.'

'Well, I recommend you start with the one behind and to the right of this one. It's gorgeous.'

'Thanks, I'll do that.'

The princess's mastaba was indeed part of a small group—the first townhouses were tombs. Still suffering from jetlag, I really didn't have the energy to do them justice today, so I decided to take a nap in one of them for a while. I followed painted processions into an empty burial chamber, and settled down in a nice cool corner. Praying no tourists would disturb my rest, I beat my purse into a relatively comfortable pillow and spread myself across the soft, cool sand. The only part of me that wasn't tired were my lips, which curved upwards as my eyes closed...

'Meow?'

'Go away,' I mumble, 'can't you see I'm resting?'

'Purrrrrrrrrr...'

My smile deepening, I open my eyes, and giggle in surprised delight as a cat's cold little nose touches the tip of mine in greeting. 'E'Ahmose, my love...' I sit up and take the big feline in my arms. 'There, are you happy now, baby?'

'Purrr...purrr...purrr...'

'You knew I wasn't asleep anyway because you're the wisest and most beautiful of cats, aren't you?' I set him down on the floor at my feet, admiring the way his supple body pours out of my arms like molten gold. 'Now go catch some mice, and if you're a good boy and keep the kitchens perfectly clean, I promise I'll take you fowling soon, perhaps on the next full moon.'

He listens intently as I speak, sitting perfectly still as though posing for a statue, then casually lowers his handsome head to lick one of his angular shoulders before turning away in the direction of the eastern garden, and the path that will take him to the kitchens.

It is true I had not been asleep, although I had been dreaming. My heart feels perched on the vines of my veins like a bird on the verge of taking wing; whenever I see him, my heart seems to flutter joyfully right into his hands. I cannot

Dreams of Anubis

possibly rest when I know he is coming, when I know that any moment now I will see his tall figure approaching along the western path, more alive and more beautiful than anything else growing in my garden. There is no comparing the parts of his body to other parts of nature; a perfect man such as my Priest of Anubis is the most beautiful thing in the world, the form of Ptah-Hotep himself, shaper of all creation. I feel as though I am embracing the god when I am with my lover. When I sink to my knees before him, it is Min's very phallus I worship as I give thanks for the divine sensations he fills me with when I bathe his shaft with my tongue and polish it with my lips, while cradling his heavy ballsack, filled with the white gold of his seed, reverently in my hands.

As I get up off the couch, I admire my almond-colored toenails—ten silvery half moons I have often seen rising over the desert slopes of his bare shoulders when he lifts my legs up against his chest to thrust as deeply as possible into my warm and yielding flesh. In those moments we are Nut and her consort Geb in reverse, with the feminine sky lying below the masculine earth, the weight of his rock-hard muscles pressing me down into the soft pillows making it hard for me to breathe, and yet nothing on earth feels better than his body beating against mine, his cool balls slapping against my wet heat—the sound of the river lapping against the shore as the juices of my pleasure rise into full flood around him.

I pace the floor with restless excitement as colorful fish dart beneath me between blossoming lotuses and thick green papyrus plants. I like the feel of the painted tiles against my bare feet, but they do nothing to cool the intoxicating expectation flowing through my blood like warm spiced wine as I await the arrival of E-Ahmose, High priest of Anubis, leader of the Winged Sandals—and my lover, now and forever. I raise a polished gold mirror in the shape of the lunar disc before my face from which Hathor's cow ears sprout at the base, happy to know the Nile will flood countless more times before my skin dries out and my reflection fails to please me. My golden-brown irises shine like sunlit honey framed by my coal-darkened eyes, and my smiling lips are those of a woman in full bloom. It seems I am always smiling since I met my beloved E'Ahmose, Born of the Moon.

As though invoked by my thoughts, he appears silhouetted against a sky the deep red color of my lips, as if all the goddesses deem his powerful silhouette worthy of their combined sensual kiss. I set the mirror down carefully, afraid of dropping it, for the sight of him always makes me feel strangely weak. Then I realize that both E'Ahmose's are approaching my bedroom—my cat returning with a dead gift in his jaws for me, and my lover with a living gift hidden in his moon-white loincloth, a gift that will rise to heavenly dimensions the instant I sink to my knees to worship it.

'Oh E'Ahmose!' I say fervently, at once addressing the man striding down the garden path who cannot yet hear me, and my devoted feline who has just laid an inert mouse at my feet. 'Thank you, my sweet little boy, but you must take that away at once. My lord approaches, and it would be very rude to greet him with something dead.'

As though he understands perfectly, E'Ahmose the cat retrieves his prize and dashes out of the room again into the eastern garden, just as my Priest of Anubis steps inside from the west.

I approach him slowly, so he can appreciate the sight of my naked body, which is how he likes me to wait for him. I dismissed my servant when she came around earlier to light the lamps, so I cannot see the face of the man silhouetted against the burning twilight, but I know him as I have never known another. He is the lord of my heart, for it is our love for each other that makes my heart light as the feather that will be weighed against Maat, goddess of truth, after my death. It is our love for each other that is the very nature of eternity, for if we cannot always be together I have no desire to live forever.

'Nefermun,' he says my name quietly, coming to meet me in the center of the room.

I raise my face to his for the caress of his greeting, closing my eyes to better absorb the warmth of his skin as for a blessed instant his palm hovers just above my features before lightly caressing my cheek down to the side of my neck, where his hand comes to rest. 'E'Ahmose,' I whisper, planting my hands on his bare chest in order to feel him, and to brace myself as our lips meet. When I was a little girl, I asked my father if statues had tongues hidden behind their stone lips. He replied, 'One day you will find out' and now I know that every smile holds the secret of what it is like to kiss someone you love. It is like being a child again running around and playing, but infinitely better, because below our energetically wrestling tongues are two adult bodies straining against each other aching to merge and become one. 'Oh E'Ahmose!' I say his precious name again breathlessly. 'It's not possible, and yet it's true, that I love you even more today than I did yesterday.'

'Sweet Nefermun, it's not possible and yet it's true,' he unhooks the jackal-headed broach holding his loincloth closed, 'that I am even harder for you this evening than I was last night.'

We both laugh quietly as he lets the stiff white linen fall to the floor at our feet so that we stand naked together in the newborn night. The western sky is no longer visible between the leaves of the date palms; darkness has fallen and the first jewels of Nut's black dress shine above the trees as I sink to my knees before him. His erect penis is so magnificent it mysteriously takes my breath away before I even fill my mouth with its demanding dimensions. Even though it looks just as rigid, this is no cold stone phallus rising out of a statue but a living cock that is at once firm and tender against the welcoming caress of my tongue. Letting it slip all the way out of my mouth again, I kiss its crown, and am rewarded with a glimmer of semen reminding me of the stars in the sky and the mysterious fact that his pleasure is everything to me.

'Oh, Nefermun, I have no need to build a tomb,' he grips the base of his erection with one hand, 'for I wish to be buried inside your mouth forever.' He guides himself slowly between my devoted lips.

I moan with joy and also from the effort it costs me to help him fulfill his deepest desire. Yet every night my throat opens up around him more easily. I experience a thrill of pride each time my lips kiss his groin as I swallow him whole. I squeeze my eyes closed to better relax the muscles of my neck as he holds himself inside me for a few excitingly arduous moments. Then, very slowly, he slips out of the loving seal of my lips, and grasping my arms, pulls me swiftly back up to my feet.

I turn away towards the couch blessed by Hathor where we always make love.

He stops me. 'No,' he commands, 'right here.' He reaches down and clutches the backs of my thighs.

'My lord!' I gasp as he lifts me up off the floor, forcing my arms to cling to him, my legs tight around his hips.

'I want you to pleasure yourself, Nefermun. I want you to use me as you would the god Himself. Do not be afraid. I want all your servants to hear you scream with pleasure, for you are my one true love, now and forever!'

He thrusts this declaration into me with such force there can be absolutely no doubt inside me that he means every word, and the pleasure I experience as he rams the indelible proof of his love into my body is almost unbearable. I cling to him, holding on to him for all I am worth, as he moves my hips swiftly up and down over his erection, relentlessly probing my innermost flesh, over and over again. He strokes his full length into my tight depths, savoring the dewy kiss of my labial lips, lifting me almost all the way off him before stabbing into me again.

'Oh, yes, my lord, yes!' I cry shamelessly, and then moan, 'E'Ahmose?' because for some reason he is trying to pull away from me and I don't want him to stop, I never want him to stop...

'Mary, wake up, you're dreaming.'

The climax inexorably building between my thighs was about to carry me away when I opened my eyes, and suddenly the intense pleasure ebbed, leaving me stranded on dry sand inside a lifeless mastaba.

'Are you awake now?' Simon asked warily.

My heart sank as I looked into the clear daylight of Simon's eyes abruptly replacing the sight of a star-filled night and another man. 'Oh...' I quickly slipped my arms from around the Egyptologist's neck. 'I'm sorry.' I sat back awkwardly.

'That must have been some nightmare,' he said, remaining crouched before me on the floor of the mastaba. 'You were gasping and moaning, and when I tried to wake you up, you wouldn't let go of me for anything.'

'It wasn't a nightmare,' I murmured, brushing sand off my legs.

'Oh, no?' His right eyebrow arched like the top of a question mark as a curious dimple appeared in his cheek below it. 'What was it, then?'

I beat my purse back into shape. 'Just a dream.' I was too dazed to understand why all I was feeling was an intense disappointment.

Dreams of Anubis

He rose and offered me his hand so I could brace myself on it as I got up. He seemed to realize I was feeling strangely weak and needed his help.

'You have a bad case of jetlag, Mary.'

I shrugged.

'Are you hungry?'

'Yes,' I said even though I still wasn't feeling anything except a disappointment so profound all my thoughts and feelings were sucked into an emotional black hole such as I had never known.

'Then let's go grab some lunch.'

Chapter Two

Carol, Simon and I had lunch in a large open-air tent in the middle of the desert, sharing the shade beneath the white canopy with busloads of tourists. We ate the surprisingly tasty gourmet hummus, lettuce and cucumber sandwiches Simon produced from his battered backpack, and drank the local soda, which tasted like polluted water with a truckload of sugar dumped into it. It did nothing to assuage my thirst, but I drank it anyway. Carol, however, wisely ordered boiling water and added her own herbal tea bag. The living bas-relief, Steve, was not present, having vanished on yet another errand.

I didn't care that Carol was probably sick and tired of hearing about Saqqara; I shamelessly pumped Simon for his knowledge, and he obviously didn't mind.

'Saqqara is an Arabic term which comes from the Egyptian Sokar,' he was saying.

'The one who fashioned man,' I threw in eagerly. The vivid dream I had enjoyed while napping in a mastaba was beginning to fade, and I wasn't really making an effort to hold on to it. I couldn't deal with the pain of something that had been so intensely wonderful not being real.

'Sokar is the hawk-headed version of the god Ptah,' he went on as though I hadn't spoken, 'reflecting one of the chief triads of the capital of Memphis, Ptah, Sokar and Nefertum. The Necropolis was a true city of the dead. What is known as Saqqara today is just the area containing Zoser's funerary complex, but originally it stretched over thirty miles all along the western bank.'

I sighed, 'I love the Old Kingdom!'

'Saqqara is full of tombs and funerary structures from all periods of Egypt's history,' he pointed out. 'There are even some early Christian remains here.'

Dreams of Anubis

'But that's awful!' I exclaimed, my jetlag taking the form of inflated sentimentality. 'If people in later dynasties took over older tombs, what was the point then? Didn't they just expect someone to do that to them in a few hundred years?'

'Saqqara was built in the third dynasty,' Simon continued, once again ignoring my outburst. 'It's the oldest stone complex in the world besides the pyramids at Giza.' He glanced at Carol—a sober person condemned to sit at a table with two ancient Egyptian addicts.

'Go on,' she said indulgently, 'Mary's really into this.' She attempted to smile, but it was more like her lips curdled in her creamy complexion.

I gathered my courage and told Simon how I felt about the offerings so meticulously depicted in mastabas—that they stood for aspects of the natural world the deceased was expressing his, or her, union with, and his, or her, power over at the same time. I couldn't tell whether his eyes narrowed as I spoke because he thought I was being a flake or because the sun was bothering him.

'I agree, Mary, that what is represented in the early tombs, especially those of the king, are symbolic stages of transformation,' he answered carefully. 'Just like a caterpillar dies to its former state inside the cocoon and emerges as a winged creature of light, so did the king rise from his tomb. The Egyptians made extensive use of this kind of symbolism. You're right,' he admitted finally, 'the scenes of daily life in the mastabas we're documenting are in fact scenes of transformation. But brought up as we are with a rationalist view of the world, it's difficult to know exactly what each scene symbolizes.' He gazed out at the desert. 'It's a fascinating challenge.'

'Uh-huh.' I propped my chin in my hands and gazed at him happily. 'That's exactly how I feel.'

'The tombs of the kings are completely spiritual.' He continued staring past me as he spoke. 'They describe, in metaphorical form, the processes experienced by the disembodied soul in its journey to resurrection. Represented are all the different stages of transformation.'

There was nothing even I could think to say after that, but there was no need, for Simon continued.

Cat's Collar - Three Erotic Romances

'A temple or a pyramid imposes its meaning on us through complex factors,' he leaned over the table towards me, 'which are ultimately reducible to numbers and mathematics.' His long fingers played with the wrapping from his straw, which in my eyes was transformed from a meaningless strip of paper into a snake's mystically shed skin as I remembered the way those same fingers had wrapped around my arm in the tomb. 'You see,' he went on earnestly, his thoughts seeming to brace themselves on my wide-eyed fascination, 'we can't help but respond to the harmonies and proportions controlling their mass. With sculptures and friezes it's different, yet even these were carefully planned according to harmonic and geometric laws, and this is essentially what we respond to when we look at ancient Egyptian art. Yet the symbolic meaning, the actual motivating force behind the work, is lost to us. We're essentially dealing with an alien culture whose symbols correspond to nothing we know. Artists are all that remain now of this way of perceiving the world.' He glanced at Carol again.

'Oh I don't really know what I'm doing,' she stated with admirable humility and annoying vagueness.

'So, do you think the great Imhotep was a real man, Simon?' I was far from finished with him yet. 'Or is he just a legendary creation made up of different figures from the Old Kingdom?'

He stared sharply into my eyes. 'Why do you ask, Mary?'

'Um...' His penetrating stare nearly made me forget my question. 'Why not?'

He sat back. 'The legendary Imhotep,' he began in a detached, lecture-like tone completely different from the one in which he had been speaking only a moment ago, 'prototype of man as creative genius. His titles included that of Sage, Architect, High Priest, Astronomer and Doctor. He was deified by the Egyptians and two-thousand years later usurped by the Greeks for their own prototype healer, Asclepius, founder of medicine.'

'But that doesn't answer my question,' I reminded him, intrigued by his reaction.

He smoothed his hair away from his forehead so forcefully the dark-blonde strands shone like molten gold poured over the stone of his skull. 'The nineteen twenty-four excavation put flesh on the legend,' he declared, almost sounding angry. 'A pedestal of a statue of Zoser was found, and on it Imhotep is mentioned with all his titles, Chancellor of the King of Lower Egypt, Administrator of the Great Palace, Hereditary Lord, the High Priest of Heliopolis, Imhotep the Builder, the Sculptor and the maker of stone vases.'

I laughed. 'Well, I guess that last title gives it away then, Imhotep was a real man.'

He pushed his chair away from the table and stood up. 'Back to work,' he said. 'I'd like to get as much done this afternoon as possible, Carol, so you and your friend can spend the next few days together sightseeing.'

My stomach a sloshing bog of cheap cola, I nevertheless rose with alacrity. 'I'd like to help if I may, Simon.'

'That's okay, Mary, you go ahead and take another nap. I can recommend an even cozier little mastaba, and I have a blanket in the car I'd be happy to lend you.'

'Thanks, but I'm wide awake now...although I had the most incredibly vivid dream this morning.'

'I know. It was so vivid you nearly dragged me into it. That's what you get for sleeping in an Egyptian tomb.'

Without thinking I declared, 'I'd like to spend a whole night in one!'

'I might be able to arrange that.'

The way he looked at me threatened to dissolve my insides, and made me self-consciously aware of my panties clinging to my wet sex. We were walking side-by-side, but now I paused, letting him go on ahead while I waited for Carol to catch up with me.

'See?!' she whispered ambiguously, and I slipped into the backseat of the Egyptologist's beat-up little white car while she took her usual place up front.

Simon glanced back at me. 'I was serious when I said I could arrange your spending a night in a tomb, Mary.'

'You're allowed to do that?' I made a supreme effort to sound only mildly interested.

'A little baksheesh goes a long way here in Egypt,' he stated bluntly.

'I imagine. Um...so what is Steve doing now?' I quickly changed the subject in an effort to control my pulse. 'He's been running around all morning.'

'He's just mapping the area,' Simon said dismissively. 'How would you two ladies like to see the Sound and Light Show at the pyramids tonight?'

'We'd love too,' I declared without consulting Carol.

'Good. I'll pick you both up at six.'

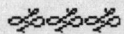

I spent most of the rest of the afternoon sleeping deep inside the same mastaba hoping to return to the intensely vivid dream I had had, but only nonsensical images paraded through my subconscious that left me feeling strangely groggy mentally even as the rest of me felt physically refreshed. It was a bit disturbing how natural it felt to wake up in a tomb, and I smiled dreamily up at the faded bas-reliefs embracing me, until discomfort made me realize the clasp on my purse was creating a seal-like imprint in my cheek.

I found Carol alone in the princess's mastaba packing up her gear. There was no sign of Simon or Steve, and I was relieved. I was sure I didn't look my best at the moment, and my brain wasn't functioning at full capacity. I imagined if the princess in whose mastaba I was standing was abruptly resurrected in the twenty-first century that she would feel very much as I did in those moments—profoundly at home and yet strangely lost and unable to think straight. I could see everything so clearly, every little carving on the wall, every little smiling figure. What seemed unreal to me and was already fading from my memory was my job and my life (or lack thereof) back in Boston. The dream I had had in the mastaba that morning felt infinitely more real. Apparently, I was suffering from a case of jetlag so severe it bordered on the mystical.

'Did you enjoy your nap?' Carol asked me, and then added before my mental synapses had a chance to communicate with my vocal chords, 'Simon's already left.'

'I gathered as much,' I replied. 'Can we go now, too?'

'As soon as I'm finished packing up my stuff.'

Hamud was parked out in front of the entrance waiting for us.

'Carol, please tell him not to drive like a maniac, my head's already spinning.'

Dreams of Anubis

'Why don't you tell him?'
'Because I don't know how to say, "don't drive like a maniac" in Arabic.'
'Neither do I.'

My friend and I were clearly not getting along at the moment and I didn't need to be able to think straight to know why.

Hamud carefully helped Carol store her gear in the trunk, and then she and I both slipped into the backseat, slumping against the exquisitely comfortable leather. During the long drive we were as silent as two recently exhumed and beautifully preserved mummies. I was grateful Hamud didn't speak much English and that my Arabic was next to non-existent, which meant I didn't feel compelled to make polite conversation with him.

Once back in her spacious apartment, Carol said generously, 'You can have the bathroom first.'

'Oh no, that's okay, you go first,' I offered just as magnanimously. 'And please take your time; don't rush on my account, I know how much you love your long meditative soaks.'

'Okay, thanks.'

I wanted to ask her exactly how she felt about Simon, but I couldn't get the words out. The question seemed too blunt, and I suppose part of me was afraid of the answer. If she had her heart set on him, then I would simply have to remember I was returning to the United States in a few weeks and forget about him, even though already he felt like the ideal man for me.

Hamud's wife had indeed washed and ironed the entire contents of my suitcase, which was empty now and tucked away in a corner of the guestroom. My dresses and blouses were hanging in the closet and my shirts, shorts and socks were all neatly folded in the dresser drawers. Hamud's hard-working spouse had also unpacked all my make-up and jewelry, which was laid out on top of the dresser as neatly as a museum exhibit. I did not doubt curiosity had prompted her to do a bit more than her job required, and I certainly didn't mind. In fact, her interest in me made me feel curiously rich as I stared at my reflection in the mirror. Millions of women the world over can afford inexpensive cosmetics and gems made of colored paste, but beauty is an asset that cannot be earned; it's something you're born with. And yet, I thought, staring intently into my eyes, maybe I did earn it, in a past life...

I had not been lying when I told Simon I did not believe I was actually a reincarnated Egyptian princess, although enough men, and even women, had remarked I looked like Cleopatra enough times to encourage such a delusion on my part. Yet ever since I had that experience in the library as a little girl, I flirted with the idea of past lives, specifically a past life, or lives, in ancient Egypt. I had felt an instant, inexplicable affinity with that black-and-white bas-relief the moment I laid eyes on it. At the tender age of five, I was in no intellectual position to flirt with the concept of past existences; my emotional reaction was hauntingly real and rationally inexplicable. I must have come across the names E'Ahmose and Nefermun in some book once and they had surfaced in my dream. E'Ahmose, Born of the Moon, High Priest of Anubis...my subconscious had been amazingly specific; I had never had such a vivid, detailed dream in my life. Even now I could hardly bare to think about it because the sadness I had experienced when I woke was still there like a thorn in my heart—a thorn I could do nothing about except ignore.

I changed the subject in my head by wondering what Simon's personal beliefs were. I was at once nervous and excited that we were having dinner with him tonight after the Sound and Light Show, to which he had so kindly offered to accompany us. I was nervous because I was much too attracted to him, especially considering how little time I had to get to know him, and because he was strictly off-limits if Carol was interested in him. It wasn't just a matter of friendship ethics, for she had three months head-start and would be staying in Cairo...but I was wasting time with these catty thoughts, and I had a very important task before me—deciding what to wear on my first real night in Egypt.

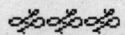

The spectacle at the pyramids would have been a serious disappointment if Simon had not been there. I was elegantly and daringly clad in a form-fitting, long-sleeved violet dress with a scoop neck that only fell to

Dreams of Anubis

mid-thigh, and black knee-high boots. Around my neck I was wearing a genuine scarab beetle amulet on a gold chain that I considered my good luck charm, and all my essentials were tucked into a small black designer purse shaped like a crescent moon. The night was more than cold enough to encourage my appreciation of the archaeologist's warm body sitting next to mine. He had diplomatically placed himself between Carol and me on one of the foldout chairs behind the Mina House hotel in the makeshift auditorium full of a reverently hushed international crowd. The sun had set while Hamud drove us to the lobby of the hotel at the foot of the pyramids where Simon was waiting for us. Now, finally, a wave of darkness descended over the audience and a phosphorescent tide of red, yellow and green lights flooded the Sphinx's enigmatic smile. Behind it, the Great Pyramid soared straight up into the darkness of space, the spotlights trained on it barely able to grasp its full mass. Its dimensions filled my heart to bursting, but not just with the sentimental pleasure of at last achieving my life-long dream of experiencing the Great Pyramid in person. The feeling that possessed me was much fuller and deeper. Staring at the only remaining wonders of the ancient world, I was filled with a wonderful sense of hope and certainty. It was as though I was beholding incontrovertible physical evidence that there is indeed a divine dimension to human existence. The two more 'modest' pyramids rose one after the other behind it as the lights shone over them. Originally, all three structures had been covered by a layer of limestone that would have made them shine as brightly as lighthouses in a sea of sand.

The Sound and Light Show at Giza still managed to be an impressive spectacle despite unimaginative translations of ancient texts recited over loud speakers. There is enough speculation concerning the construction of the pyramids for me to feel that no one really knows exactly how the Egyptian's managed to build them, and I fully intended to ask Simon what he thought about it. I also wanted to query him about the Egyptologist John Anthony West's theory that the Sphinx is much older than previously believed; that the erosion marks on its body were made by water rather than sand, which would link its mysterious smile with the legends of Atlantis.

Cat's Collar - Three Erotic Romances

I was intensely aware of Simon's warm presence beside me the whole time, especially when he shifted in his seat and his shoulder brushed mine, and at some point during the show, I found the courage to glance at him. I expected to see his slightly bored profile, but instead I caught him gazing down at me. He immediately looked away, but it was too late; I had seen a speculative look in his eyes that made me feel faint with happiness. Soon after what I already considered a landmark moment in my personal history, the audio shut off with a disenchanting crackle and a blessedly non-psychedelic light flooded the open space behind the Mina House. Wearing high-heeled boots forced me to concentrate on my footing as we slowly followed the rest of the crowd back into the hotel, and helped bring me down to earth a little, enough for me to remember the increasingly distressing fact that I would only be in Egypt a few weeks. And I still had to have that little, but extremely major, talk with Carol about her beautiful boss. Back at the apartment, we had both been too busy getting ready for our evening out, and in the car we were both reluctant to talk about anything significant since we didn't really know just how much English Hamud understood. However, the fact that my friend's glorious blonde hair was still neatly restrained in a braid worthy of a nineteenth century schoolteacher was a good sign, because whenever Carol was interested in a man she let her hair down.

Despite the ghastly Egyptian cola, I had enjoyed our lunch in the open-air tent more than I relished our dinner in the four-star hotel dining room. Once again, I could have been anywhere in the world, and I found myself wishing the management had opted for an ancient Egyptian banquet hall décor. However, there was something to be said for not sharing Simon's attention with a bunch of naked dancing girls, and it was impossible to picture Carol in a black wig dripping with perfume as the scented wax cone on top of her head gradually melted.

Simon recommended some local specialties to me, including a dip made of ground eggplant and spices. He politely asked me questions about my life in Boston, and volunteered a little information about himself in the process. I was not at my most eloquent, half hypnotized as I was by the symmetry of his features beneath a tan that looked very much like a layer of gold applied by the finest artisan. His eyes were the stunning final touch, especially when the can-

Dreams of Anubis

dlelight hit them as he looked intently at me while I answered one of his questions. But what truly made his regard so devastating was the mind behind it—an Egyptologist's mind, a mind obsessed with ancient Egypt just like mine. As I picked daintily at chunks of lamb swimming in a delicious yogurt-cucumber sauce, I reminded myself to occasionally look at Carol and break my trance-like contemplation of her employer. Fortunately, he had no problem carrying the conversation while I chewed and admired his broad shoulders. I was infinitely pleased if not surprised that he wasn't married, as most women would find it difficult to set up housekeeping in tombs. I learned he had been in Egypt for nearly a year now, the lucky recipient of a major grant, but I couldn't quite tell if those were faint wrinkles around his eyes or squint lines.

'Excuse me a moment,' he said, and left the table, ostensibly in search of the men's room.

I looked at Carol.

'Yes,' she sighed, 'I know.'

'God,' I took another long, bracing sip of white wine, 'how can you stand it?'

'I couldn't stand it,' she agreed, sipping her herbal tea, 'so I just got it over with.'

I almost choked on a piece of pita bread.

'Look, we would only have wasted a bunch of time and energy wondering what it would have been like, so we just got it over with.'

I asked slowly, 'You got what over with?'

'We slept together, okay? Now we can work together without any tension and just be friends.'

'Right.' I felt irrationally betrayed.

'Look, Mary, don't be upset, we're not each other's type. It just had to happen, it was inevitable, but you're much more-'

'Are you all right, Mary?' Simon slipped back into his seat intently studying my face again.

'Oh I'm fine, thank you.'

'You look like you might be coming down with a touch of pharaoh's revenge,' he observed.

'Oh it's worse than that,' Carol said breezily.

'I'm fine,' I repeated firmly.

'Well, I'm glad to hear it,' Simon said. 'We wouldn't want you wasting any time in bed.'

⸙⸙⸙

The Khan el-Khalili Bazaar—the dark and timeless bowels of the city of Cairo—proved to be a labyrinth of lamp-lit alleys littered with merchandise overflowing from a myriad of tiny shops.

Simon had kindly exchanged some of my American money at the hotel for Egyptian currency, and there was a precious moment when his fingers brushed mine as he handed me the colorful bills. We had both drunk wine with dinner, our coordination wasn't at its best, so I tried not to make too much of it. Ever since Carol's revelation, I was trying to remain detached from this man, who was suspiciously too much like a dream come true for me.

Strolling leisurely through the bazaar's exotic maze, we passed dozens of jewelry shops selling reproductions of ancient Egyptian pieces that probably looked good to the average tourist but did not fool me. The faces of the gods and goddesses forming the center of elaborate pectoral pendants wore sour expressions nothing like the profoundly peaceful smiles found on ancient originals. The personalities of the modern artisans were revealed in the often-harsh casts of the deities' features and their discontented frowns, which completely failed to capture the profoundly positive ancient Egyptian spirit. All my life I had gotten into countless arguments with people who insisted people in the time of the pharaohs were morbid because they were obsessed with death, and I had tried my best (usually not very patiently) to make them understand the Egyptians were obsessed with life and all its pleasures, and therefore had no desire to give it up.

Carol stopped to inspect a cart loaded with bundles of dried herbs and what looked like every kind of incense known to man. Simon had apparently talked himself out at dinner, because he walked silently between us looking a bit bored. After all, he must have been to the bazaar dozens of times already. Or perhaps

Dreams of Anubis

he was distracted by his thoughts; there was a slightly preoccupied air about him. His shoulder brushed mine as he turned away from the aromatic cart, obviously realizing it was going to be a while before Carol finished inspecting it, and the contact triggered something inside me.

'You know, people make the mistake of thinking the Egyptians drew the human figure the way they did because they didn't know how to do it right,' I said, pursuing my thoughts out loud. . 'But I read a fascinating book once that said they drew the body the way they did in order to capture the essence of each feature and present an essentially whole picture of the human being... I mean they drew the shoulders facing forward beneath a profile in which the eye was also fully visible while the torso was turned sideways, because that way we see the person in his entirety all at once. Their use of perspective attempted to conquer the limits of time and space. Do you know what I mean?'

He opened his mouth to speak just as Carol thrust a stick of incense beneath his nose to get his opinion on it, and he ended up responding to both our queries by sneezing.

'Bless you!' my friend and I cried in chorus.

'Thank you.' He sniffed. 'Mm, that's...interesting, Carol.' He said, and then facing me with his body, he turned his profile on me. 'It's a damned uncomfortable perspective if you ask me.' His one eye winked.

Considering the distraction, I forgave him this irreverent response to my enlightened observation.

Carol waved the same stick of incense in my face. 'Doesn't it smell delicious, Mary?'

I took a step back. 'Jesus, that's one potent stick.'

'Damn right it is,' Simon murmured, brushing past me. 'Come on, Carol.' He pulled her away from the cart by her braid. 'You don't need any more incense. When my friend returns to his apartment, I'm going to have a hell of a time trying to explain what you've been doing in there.'

I trailed behind them, gazing admiringly at Simon's broad shoulders, narrow waist and long legs. In his white shirt and shorts he was as tall as an ancient Egyptian nobleman in white linen, an effect marred only by his blond hair. He and Carol turned into a shop that sold what appeared to be footrests—large red cushions embroidered with eighteenth dynasty dancing girls in gilded thread—while I chose to remain out in the cool alleyway. A strip of sky showed between the awnings, but the golden glow of the lamps strung between them washed out the stars. I should have known better than to just stand there all by myself, however; a crowd of merchants immediately surrounded me. As each one gestured passionately for me to follow him to his cart, I attempted to escape by diving between the choppy waves of their dark robes. I waited for Simon to rescue me, but there was no sign of him.

'No…la, shukron,' I said. 'No, la…la la!' I sounded as if I was about to break out into song as I fervently repeated the Arabic word for 'no'. The tide of merchants ebbed away reluctantly, and I quickly entered the shop of footstools in search of Carol and her boss. The small space was empty except for the owner, who swooped towards me like a vulture in his black robe. I turned and hurried back out into the alley. At a loss as to where my companions could have gone, I glanced into the dark space between two shops just in time to see two luminous heads coming together and the tendons in Simon's arms standing out like serpents as he pressed my friend's slender body hard against his.

Without thinking, I ran from the sight.

My hurt indignation carved its way through groups of tourists and eager vendors who did their best to intercept me, and how hard my heart was beating told me it was at least a full minute before I finally stopped to catch my breath. I went for long jogs in Boston three days a week, but never after dinner and wine through dark, lamp-lit alleys wearing high-heeled boots. I had always possessed a flare for the dramatic, and in the back of my mind I hoped Simon had observed me run off and would follow me. Obviously, I had seen too many romantic movies, because naturally he wasn't following me; he had been too busy kissing Carol to even notice me. Once again I was in the eye of a storm of shopkeepers, one of whom abruptly grabbed my arm and began forcibly leading me somewhere.

I clutched my purse close to my body and tried to remember more of the Arabic words Carol had taught me. 'Ana mish…eis,' I said breathlessly. 'I don't want any,' I translated for my own benefit. 'Ana mish eis,' I repeated, to no effect. My captor shoved me up a short flight of steps, reached past me to open the door, and gave me another encouraging shove. I turned around to give this unbelievably fascist merchant a piece of my mind, but he was gone and had closed the trailer door behind me.

I turned around again. I was standing in a tiny perfume shop. Cushioned seats ran along both walls in front of a glass display case full of colorful little vials that made me think of miniature genie bottles. The exotic trailer was empty, and I turned back towards the door with the intention of opening it.

'Good evening, my lady,' a cultured male voice said from behind me.

I whirled around again. 'I don't want any,' I cried. 'Mafish!' I was developing a nice little vocabulary, for all the good it did me. Then the robed figure behind the counter flung off his hood and I found myself at a loss for words in any language.

'I believe you have it backwards, love.' His deep voice was lightened by a sophisticated English accent. He slipped out from behind the counter and approached me. 'You have something I want.'

'I do?' I asked hopefully.

He took my flushed and confused face in his large hands. 'Yes,' he said quietly, 'I suspect you do.' There was a deeply serious expression in his slate gray-green eyes as he caressed both my cheeks with his thumbs very much like a sculptor assessing the quality of my bone structure, and I suffered the impression he was mysteriously determining my worth. I opened my mouth with the idea of saying something, but was distracted by the pale crescent of a scar just below his own mouth that gave him a dangerous aura. Part of me knew I should be worried to suddenly find myself completely alone in a pungent trailer with a total stranger boasting a scar on his face. Yet it was beginning to feel wonderfully natural to run into strikingly handsome men in Egypt, so I simply accepted what was happening. He had the most remarkable eyes, and it wasn't just because his pupils were rimmed in gold…there was something very familiar about the way they looked at me…

'My lady,' he whispered fervently, and suddenly kissed me softly on the lips.

It was not just a paralyzing blend of shock and pleasure (or was it that the pleasure was shocking?) that kept me from pulling away, I simply couldn't; I had absolutely no desire to pull away from him. On the contrary, I was magnetically drawn to this total stranger. While we spoke, I had been standing as close to him as I possibly could, trying to fight an irrational but almost irresistible desire to fall into his arms. It was an intense relief when he kissed me, as though I had been waiting forever for his lips to press against mine like this again.

He pulled back to observe my reaction, and a gratified smile I might have found humiliating had I been thinking straight, turned his firm mouth up at the corners. Caressing the sleek black hair on both sides of my face, he kept my head reverently in his hands, making me feel precious as an ancient bust he had just unearthed. 'What do you know about it?' he whispered.

'Know about what?' I whispered back. He was dressed like a native Egyptian in a traditional white galabiyya. At first I had thought his black hair was cut short, but now I realized it was actually long and pulled back in a ponytail. I wondered if he had tired of the long winters back home in England and come to sunny Egypt to run a cozy little perfume shop, but I dismissed the possibility at once because there was absolutely nothing retired looking about this man. He wanted something, and I found myself hoping I had it to give.

'Don't you remember?' He looked searchingly down into my eyes.

'Remember what?' I asked even though it sounded silly, because if I remembered I wouldn't need to ask what I had forgotten.

'Your dreams.'

'Yes, actually, I do.' I didn't even think to wonder why a complete stranger was asking me about my dreams in the heart of the Khan el-Khalili bazaar since for some reason it felt perfectly natural. 'I had a particularly vivid dream today, as a matter of fact, when I was taking a nap inside a mastaba.'

He glanced at the door to the trailer. 'We don't have much time,' he warned quietly, and then suddenly laughed as though what he had said was extremely funny.

The naked joy in his smile struck me as a bright light reaching into the darkest corners of my mind, illuminating something I had always known but had only just realized. 'There's no such thing as time,' I declared happily because it was the only way I could translate the wonderful feeling suddenly possessing me into words.

Dreams of Anubis

'Most people don't realize that.'

'Well, I'm not most people.'

'No,' he agreed fervently, reaching for my hand, 'you're not.' He led me over to the counter.

For a highly confused and disappointed moment I thought he was going to try and sell me some perfume, and that our encounter had only been some kind of mercantile foreplay found only in Egypt, so I was both relieved and surprised when he grabbed me by the waist and lifted me up onto the glass surface. My short dress hiked shamelessly up my thighs, nearly exposing the black lace bikini panties my dinner with a sexy Egyptologist had inspired me to wear beneath it.

'I love these boots,' he told me, sinking to one knee before me like an old-fashioned cobbler cradling the backs of my high-heels in his hands as though admiring his work.

'Thank you...hey, what are you doing?' I leaned back against the counter even as I made an effort to keep my thighs modestly pressed together, but it was impossible simply because I didn't really want to. It wasn't his hands gripping my boots that were spreading my legs as much as my own shameless yet irresistible desire to open myself to this man.

'Just having a little taste, love, don't be afraid,' he urged, caressing the smooth black leather up to my knees and gently shoving them even further apart. 'Tell me your name.'

'Mary!' I gasped, desperately trying to control my pussy's sudden wanton hunger in the face of my usual modest behavior and in his face, the proximity of which was making my sex so hot and wet, my panty was clinging to my labial lips in a dangerously tantalizing way; teasing me with the wicked knowledge that what I really wanted was to feel his strikingly handsome features between them.

'Mary...' He savored my name on his tongue before glancing up at my face. 'May I?'

I didn't respond, riveted by his intensely earnest expression and by how much I wanted to feel it between my legs.

'Time is a man-made concept, and as a result,' he indicated the door behind him with a slight tilt of his head, 'we don't have much of it now. All I ask, Mary, is a taste of what's to come.'

I inclined my head in wordless ascent.

He reached up beneath what there was of my dress and gripped the edges of my panties, holding my eyes the whole time in a way that was both reassuring and hypnotic.

I lifted my hips off the cool glass and let him slide the skimpy lace garment over my knees, down my boots, and off. He kept bracing me on his stare as he exposed my pussy, not letting me look away shyly, forcing me to face what was happening in a way that excited me even more. It had been a long time since I'd been so intensely turned on that I couldn't control myself.

'Oh my God,' I breathed, scarcely able to believe the sight of a complete stranger's face framed by my bare thighs as he draped them over his strong shoulders. But it was truly happening, and I sighed, 'Oh yes!' watching the lips on his face touch the lips of my sex, which were much wetter and fuller as I was so aroused by this wickedly daring encounter. I couldn't believe I was letting a man whose name I didn't even know lick my pussy. A man who could conceivably be dangerous was eating me out with a violent skill that even as it frightened my mind also literally thrilled me to the core of my being.

I leaned back against the counter to brace myself, and watching his head working between my legs, I began longing to take hold of it and caress the sleek dark hair that I could now see fell all the way down his back.

'Who are you?' I gasped, not really expecting or wanting an answer because his mouth and his tongue were doing something much more important than talking. The need my brain felt to hear his name was nowhere near as important as the pleasure his absolute wordless attention was giving me. And even though it made no sense, somehow everything about him felt more familiar than all my other lovers combined. Was it him, or was he so perfect because I didn't know anything about him and it was actually only my own fantasies that were wreaking such divine havoc on me? No, it was definitely him because oral sex had never felt so unbelievably good to me no matter what I was daydreaming about at the time.

Dreams of Anubis

'Mm!' he moaned, and the deep vibration of his satisfaction against my vulva contributed another layer to the ecstasy of his tongue diving in and out of my hot hole. I had never experienced such a hard, thrusting tongue and it was starting to drive me wild with the desire to ride it. I edged my hips forward on the counter in a breathless effort to impale myself on his tongue's thick, rigid energy, crying out softly as its gloriously agile hardness penetrated me as deeply as possible, and then licked my vulva soothingly, as though apologizing for not being a penis by treating me to sensations distinct from the pleasures a cock could offer. And when his firm lips caught my aching clit between them, I forgot my delicious frustration and succumbed to a sweet, sharp, almost unbearable pleasure as he toyed with my swollen seed, alternating between flicking the tip of his tongue against it and slowly circling it.

'Oh my God,' I repeated helplessly, because it didn't seem possible that a man I didn't know at all knew exactly how to please me. He seemed magically in touch with the current of my delight. It was as if he had sensed it ebb slightly when he sucked directly on my clitoris and knew that indirect pressure and stimulation were what would direct the rush of exquisite feelings inside me into the irresistible undertow of an orgasm. Of all the things I couldn't believe about this encounter, the most unbelievable was the fact that I felt myself coming. My pussy seemed to be dissolving in his mouth, the whirlpool of a climax forming around his spiraling tongue threatening to suck my awareness of everything into the tumultuous depths of uncontrollable vaginal spasms as I climaxed.

'Oh yes!' I cried breathlessly. 'Yes…yes…oh my God…' I closed my eyes and flung my head back as an orgasm broke between my thighs, flooding my pelvis before crashing through my blood with such power I nearly fell back across the counter as my elbows buckled. Even after the searing ecstasy dimmed, my sex kept throbbing contentedly, and I could hardly stand it as he continued lapping up my juices, the deep, gratified sounds rising from his throat only adding to my blissful torment.

'Smooth as alabaster,' he said approvingly, running the tip of a finger down between the full bloom of my labial lips glistening with the sticky sap of my climax, 'and soft as a flower.' His mouth shiningly anointed with my body's delicate musty scent, he smiled up at me. 'I like it that you shave, Mary.' My thighs were still resting on his shoulders; I couldn't seem to move, I was feeling so beautifully relaxed. 'I want you to always keep yourself smooth for me like this.'

I had to bite my lip to keep from asking, 'Does that mean I'm going to see you again?' A nameless stranger had just eaten me alive, yet my only concern was that he would vanish forever as suddenly and mysteriously as he had appeared. 'All right,' I said instead.

'Did you like that?'

'Are you kidding?' I replied an instant before I realized he was teasing me.

He laughed quietly as he gently brushed my legs off his shoulders and stood up, my black lace panties in his hand. 'I'm going to keep these,' he told me, lifting them to his face and inhaling the unique fragrance of my pussy still clinging to them thanks to how excited he had gotten me before he slipped them off. 'To remind me of you until we meet again, Mary.'

'Aren't you going to tell me your name?' I asked finally, sitting up straight and attempting to smooth my dress down over my thighs, which were still subliminally quivering.

'You know my name, Mary.' He glanced behind him at the trailer door again.

'No I don't, you never told me.'

He gave me a long, sober look. 'Yes, you do,' he insisted quietly, 'you just don't realize it yet.'

'But...'

There was suddenly the sound of a commotion outside.

He stashed my panties in his robe, and slipping a strong arm around my waist lifted me off the counter so that my boots barely touched the floor as he held me against him. I could scarcely breathe he was holding me so tightly, and I wondered if (I hoped) he would kiss me again, but all he did was stare deep into my eyes while stroking my hair away from my face. 'Remember your dreams, Mary,' he urged quietly, and suddenly I was standing alone on trembling legs inside a trailer full of exotic glass perfume vials in the middle of Cairo trying to wrap my brain around the exhilarating pleasure I had just experienced, the aftermath of which was still making my whole body feel deliciously weak.

Dreams of Anubis

The trailer door burst open.

'Jesus, Mary, there you are! Why the hell did you run off like that?' Simon demanded. 'We've been looking everywhere for you.'

I wasn't surprised he had found me sooner than later; a trail of grinning merchants had undoubtedly pointed the way for him. I glanced over my shoulder at the softly swaying curtains behind which my mysterious British sheik had vanished, feeling bereft. 'I thought you and Carol wanted to be alone,' I replied sulkily.

'Was someone in here with you?' he asked accusingly.

I didn't reply, but I have always had a very expressive face.

Brushing past me abruptly, he too slipped behind the glass counter, and vanished between the curtains.

I held my breath, wanting very much to learn the identify of the stranger whose sensually eloquent lips and tongue had made such a beautiful impression on my pussy. I did not, however, want him and Simon in the same room; an explosive combination that I feared would destroy my chances with the Egyptologist if he realized what had just, literally, gone down between me and the handsome Brit. So when Carol's boss returned a moment later, alone, I was at once disappointed and relieved. I let out my breath in a long, languid sigh, strangely glad my mysterious friend had made good his escape.

Simon came to stand before me, and gripping both my arms stared searchingly down into my eyes. 'Who was here with you, Mary?' he demanded to know.

'I have no idea,' I replied, gratified to be able to protect the robed stranger even while telling the absolute truth.

'Was he an Egyptian?'

'No, actually, he sounded British.'

Simon's grip on my arms tightened almost painfully. 'What did he say to you?'

'Why do you want to know?'

'Just answer my question, Mary.'

'He said I had something he wanted...' I couldn't speak for a moment, breathlessly remembering how his tongue had swirled around the glowing jewel of my clitoris. 'Then he asked me how much I knew about it. And for some reason, he called me "my lady".' I glanced pointedly at his hands clutching my arms to indicate this was no way to treat a lady, and he let go of me self-consciously. 'And he also asked me if I remembered my dreams. I have no idea why, but he was extremely…pleasant.' My sex lips were still tingling from how extremely pleasant he had been to them.

'Did he say anything else?'

'Yes, just before he left he told me to remember my dreams,' I confessed.

'Mary!' Carol exclaimed, appearing in the doorway with what looked like a small crowd of native men in gleeful pursuit, their combined curiosity lapping like an intangible wave against the trailer. 'What's the matter with you?' she gasped, catching her breath. 'Why did you run off like that?'

I didn't answer. I was too busy enjoying both the consternated and possessive way I fancied Simon was looking at me, and being deliciously haunted by the stranger's kisses, both on my mouth and the lips of my pussy, both of which had opened for him willingly.

'Let's get the hell out of here,' Simon said.

Chapter Three

I opened my eyes. The blinds in the guestroom were closed, but the golden light framing each one told me the sun had been up for a while now. Freed of her photographic duties for a few days, Carol was sleeping in (and would remain entombed all morning unless I forcibly exhumed her) whereas only the lingering exhaustion of crossing half a dozen time zones had enabled me to rest so deeply for so long. Simon's blond head immediately rose into my mind as I sat up, flooded with excitement, just as the handsome Englishman's compelling eyes pulled like moons on my blood.

Remembering the mysterious sheik I had encountered in the bazaar the night before, I fell back against the pillows again, overwhelmed by the shamelessly wicked memory. My body came fully awake remembering the unexpected gift of ecstasy his lips and tongue had so generously given me, but my brain was still trying to shift into working gear. As I lay there in the comfortable guest bed, I got absolutely nowhere trying to understand what in the world was going on. Where had he come from? How had he known I was in that trailer? Then I remembered the man I had believed to be a rudely determined shopkeeper practically shoving me into the perfume shop, and wondered whether or not it was possible my British sheik had had me brought to him. Yet none of it made any sense, none of it except the incredible sensation his lips had made against mine when he kissed me, and the indescribably wonderful sensation his mouth had made when his dark head was buried between my legs.

I had run away from the sight of Simon and Carol embracing in a dark alley, ending up in that sweet-smelling little trailer by accident. Or had I? The stranger had said I knew who he was, but there was no way on earth I would have forgot-

Dreams of Anubis

ten him if we had met before. Maybe—and this thought caused me to squirm against the soft mattress in distress—this had been his poetic way of not telling me his name since he never planned on seeing me again, my juicy pussy only an idle passing treat for him. Yet he had asked me for a taste of what was to come, and told me to always keep myself shaved for him, all of which seemed to promise I would see him again. I fervently hoped I would, but it still did not explain why he had asked me about my dreams and urged me to remember them.

Finally, I gave up trying to make sense of the encounter and decided it was time to exchange memories and daydreams for reality, which meant getting out of bed. I walked over to the window and opened the blinds. As I had suspected, it was a bit too late for an outing to the Cairo Museum, which is lit strictly by sunlight. By the time Carol and I made it there, it would be mid afternoon and the place would be closing at sunset. The Cairo Museum required at least one whole day to appreciate. I intended to spend hours wandering its crowded halls, and because the display rooms are illuminated only by daylight, it is necessary to get an early start. I also wasn't quite ready for the pyramids yet as I already had two wonders of the world on my mind this morning—a mysterious dark-haired Englishman and a blond American Egyptologist.

I turned away from the window and the blue sky beyond it, and noticed an envelope lying on the table beneath it. For some reason, I stood staring at it for almost a full minute. It was so worn around the edges and darkened by almost sinister-looking stains it looked as though it had been around the world ten times at least. I wondered if it perhaps belonged to Carol's maid (an old love letter from Hamud she carried with her everywhere?) as I picked it up gingerly between a thumb and forefinger. There was nothing written on either side. The envelope had never been mailed, or even addressed to anyone, but I could tell there was something inside it. I raised the loose tattered flap and withdrew a single photograph.

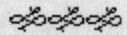

'But I can't read hieroglyphs,' Carol mumbled in protest to my request, rubbing her sleep-swollen eyes with the back of her hands in a way that made me think of a cat taking a very thorough bath. Her hair fell straight as gilded tent flaps around her face between which her eyes peered out at me resentfully, for I had committed the grievous sin of awakening her.

'Oh come on,' I insisted. 'You must have developed some feel for hieroglyphs. After all, they're lovely little pictures, right up your alley, and you've been photographing them for over three months now.' I got up off the edge of her bed and ruthlessly pulled up the blinds.

She wailed like an affronted vampire as she covered her face with both hands.

I sat down beside her again. 'Wake up, Carol, and take it one character at a time, please. What does this feather stand for?' I pointed at the photograph. 'We know we're looking at a name because the hieroglyphs are enclosed in a cartouche. You do know what a cartouche is?'

'Of course I know what a cartouche is.' She uncovered one eye and studied the picture with a sullen frown. 'I think that's an I,' she said finally, 'and that's an M…I need to make some tea…'

I held her down. 'Not until you decipher this for me.'

'Mary, I can't,' she protested desperately. 'Why don't you…?' she yawned cavernously. 'Why don't you ask Simon what it says?'

'Because, don't you get it, Carol? Something strange is going on. I think Simon might be up to something he hasn't told you about.'

'What?'

I wondered myself what I meant; I had not been fully conscious of my suspicion until I voiced it out loud. 'Carol, think. Are you sure you didn't take this picture for him and just forgot about it?'

Her facial muscles got their first exercise of the day in a look of indignation. 'I remember every photograph I take, Mary.'

'So, where did this one come from then? It wasn't in the guestroom yesterday morning, which means your maid must have put the envelope on the table when she was going through my stuff. And I didn't notice it until this morning because yesterday I was too busy getting ready to go to the Sound and Light Show with Simon. And I was too, um, distracted when we got back from the bazaar last night and went straight to bed.'

Dreams of Anubis

'Well it's definitely not one of my photographs.' She snatched the print from me and scowled at it. 'It's not even in focus.'

'That's true, but who cares? Just tell me whose name is in the cartouche, please.'

'Mary, I told you, I can't read hieroglyphs, I really can't.' She handed me back the photo and slipped out of bed.

'Carol, I have to tell you something,' I said, and told her about my encounter with the British sheik in the perfume shop, for the moment omitting the fact that he had kissed me and then gone down on me, very skillfully. 'He didn't admit it, but I have a feeling Simon knows who the man is and what he meant when he said I had something he wanted…I think your boss is up to something,' I concluded with a flash of intuition. I wasn't sure if the idea upset or intrigued me, but in either case it made Simon seem even sexier than he already was, and made my illicit encounter with a mysterious stranger feel even more excitingly dangerous.

Carol opened a drawer and quickly slipped into a pair of cut-off denim shorts, and then selected a T-shirt to go with them that even the Salvation Army would have shunned. 'You trust some stranger you met for a minute in the bazaar more than the respectable Egyptologist I've been working with for months?'

'Don't forget, Carol, Simon is a stranger to me, too. I've only known him for a day.'

'Well I know him very well, and he would never—what exactly are you accusing him of anyway?'

I suddenly recalled the snake-like tendons in Simon's arms as he pressed her slender body against his in the dark alley. 'Nothing,' I snapped. 'Forget it.' I hurried back to my bedroom, taking the photograph with me. I set it back down on the table where I had found it and began making the bed. Or rather, I started throwing pillows around in frustration.

Carol appeared in the hall and watched me from the safety of the doorway. 'Mary, what's wrong with you?'

'Nothing. I'm happy for you, really.'

'You don't need to make the bed. What are you happy about?'

'I saw you and Simon in the alley,' I admitted finally, and abandoning the bed pretended to search for something I vitally needed in the dresser.

'Oh that.' She flung her hair behind her back. 'I told you, Mary, we're just friends, but he still thought I might be a little upset if he…anyway, I told him I wasn't jealous and we hugged, that's all.'

I stared at her over my shoulder in the mirror. 'He thought you might be upset if he what?' My reflection held its breath.

'Oh stop acting so insecure.' She turned away in disgust. 'You know perfectly well he likes you.'

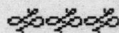

My body adequately fortified by a cup of coffee with cream and sugar, two pieces of whole grain toast with butter, and two eggs over-easy, my spirits were soaring dangerously as Carol and I lay facedown on the plush carpet in her living room. We were once again examining the photograph that had inexplicably materialized in the guestroom.

'Are you sure the first two letters are an I and an M?' I queried, finding it hard now to concentrate on the blurry cartouche as I kept seeing the way Simon's eyes had looked when he entered the perfume shop, blue and hard as lapis-lazuli…

'No, but I'm pretty sure they are.' Holding the photograph in one hand, resting her chin in the other, her knees bent and her ankles crossed, Carol resembled a living hieroglyph herself. 'And this little maze-like box here…that's an H sound, I think.'

'I, M, H…Imhotep? There are four more letters, so it very well could say Imhotep, especially if the photo was taken in Saqqara…Carol, this could say Imhotep! Weren't you listening to our conversation at lunch yesterday? Didn't you notice the way Simon reacted when I asked him about Imhotep?'

'Not really. Don't you find him just a little boring the way he goes on and on? But I guess you're interested in what he's saying. I've learned to tune him out.'

I snatched the photograph out of her hand and sat up, staring at it intently.

Dreams of Anubis

It was a close-up of a stone fragment containing the bas-relief of a cartouche, yet there was nothing else in the picture except rubble, and even though I studied it carefully, I could not tell if what I was seeing were small pebbles or large rocks, which made it impossible to determine the cartouche's size. There was no doubt, however, that the exquisitely carved hieroglyphs dated from the Old Kingdom. The last two characters in the cartouche were a half circle and a rectangle standing on one end. 'Carol,' I whispered, 'if this really says Imhotep, do you know what it could mean?'

'What?' She almost sounded bored.

'Don't you see?' I glanced around the living room, a chill traveling down my spine. 'This cartouche could mark the entrance to Imhotep's tomb, the tomb every Egyptologist dreams of finding.'

'Mary, there was absolutely nothing in your room before you got here,' she informed me abruptly. 'I know because I cleaned it myself.'

Her domestic thoroughness had always inspired me with a reluctant awe. 'And when you clean, Carol, you clean.'

'That's right. I even polished the insides of the dresser drawers for you.'

'Wow.' I would have to remember to appreciate this later when I was dressing. 'Thanks.'

'In other words,' she went on, quickly following the trail of her thoughts lest they get away from her, as they often did, 'unless Azi brought the photo with her-'

'Azi?'

'Hamud's wife. Unless she brought the photo with her and left it in your room for some completely inexplicable reason, the envelope must have been in your suitcase and she found it there when she was taking all your clothes out to wash and iron them.'

'In my suitcase,' I repeated blankly. 'How could it have been in my suitcase? It's not my envelope.'

'The airport, Mary! Somebody must have dropped the envelope in the airport and one of the men who helped put your stuff back in your suitcase when it burst open thought it was yours. It's just some stupid tourist's picture.'

This was a highly disappointing, if logical, conclusion and I could not suppress the feeling that there was something wrong with her reasoning. 'Or someone deliberately put the envelope in my suitcase,' I suggested, for this train of thought was decidedly much more entertaining, and also more in keeping with the mysterious sheik's remark in the perfume shop, that I had something he wanted. 'Carol, that beautiful Englishman was dressed like a native,' I went on excitedly. 'It could be he was one of the men in the airport who…no.' I shook my head, dismissing the idea at once.

'Why not?' she asked eagerly, her interest in the conversation resurrecting.

'Because, he's too tall and his shoulders are too broad and none of the native men around my suitcase in the airport were that well-built.'

'Oh…was he really that attractive?'

'Yes,' I sighed, 'he was striking! He had long black hair pulled back in a ponytail, and his eyes were so intense, I mean, the way he looked at me, and there was this gold rim around his pupils—I've never seen eyes like his. His irises were the most unique color, somewhere between gray and dark-green…and he kissed me.'

'He what?'

'Oh, it was just a polite little peck on the lips.'

I looked away, knowing it was only a matter of time before I told her everything, but I was resisting the temptation a little longer. I had never done anything so daring before—I had never been so impulsively wicked—and I was not in the mood for a lecture on the dangers inherent in such wanton behavior. I also didn't want any bad vibes ruining the strangely pure memory of a handsome stranger orally worshipping me in the dark heart of an ancient bazaar. Because the truth was I couldn't remember a man ever making me feel so beautiful and so precious.

'Mary,' Carol's big round eyes evoked pictures of the earth taken from outer space, 'do you realize you could easily have gotten raped running off like that by yourself?'

'Raped?' I repeated incredulously, and then laughed nervously, a little unsettled that the possibility had not even occurred to me. 'He only kissed me,' I lied, looking down at the photograph again without seeing it. 'I let him kiss me…'

'You let a complete stranger kiss you? Was it exciting?' she asked in one breath.

Dreams of Anubis

'I can't stop thinking about him,' I admitted. 'I also wish I knew what he meant when he said that I have something he wants. He asked me how much I knew about it. Do you think it could have something to do with this photograph?'

'Mary, we have no idea who this man is. He could be dangerous.'

I smiled wistfully. 'Yes…'

'This is serious,' she insisted sternly. 'If you see him again–'

'He went down on me.'

Her pupils dilated into black holes as she stared at my face, and at the soft, reminiscent smile I made no artificial effort to suppress. 'Excuse me?' she said tightly.

I rephrased it. 'He licked my pussy,' I said, enjoying her shock and deliberately stoking it.

'He licked your pussy,' she repeated.

'Yes, and he made me come. I never knew oral sex could be so devastatingly effective. I mean, I've come that way before, but never so fast and so…intensely, there's no other word for it.'

My friend let out a Banshee-like shriek and flung herself at me. 'Are you crazy?' She grabbed me by the shoulders and made a literal effort to shake some sense into me. 'You let a strange man you just met go down on you?'

'Yes!' I laughed, gratified by her dramatic reaction.

She fell back across the carpet clutching her chest as if shot in the heart, and then abruptly sat up again in a parody of resurrection. 'Tell me everything,' she commanded. 'Right now! I can't believe you didn't tell me this last night when we got home.' She seemed more offended by the fact that I had failed to confide in her than by my sinful behavior.

'I'm sorry, but I was exhausted.'

'He made you come?'

'And then some!'

'I don't believe you,' she concluded abruptly. 'You're making this up. What's his name?'

'I don't know, he didn't tell me. When I asked him, he said I knew who he was, and when I said I didn't, he insisted I did and that I just didn't remember yet. And just before he left, he urged me to remember my dreams.'

'Why would a complete stranger talk about your dreams and go down on you?' she asked more calmly.

'I have no idea, but it felt so natural at the time, so right. I can't describe it. I know it doesn't really make any sense in retrospect, but somehow it made sense at the time, and he made me feel so good, Carol, so beautiful and sensual...' my voice trailed away.

'You weren't afraid?' she asked quietly, a strangely reverent tone in her own voice now.

'I don't think so, maybe for a second, but only because I thought I should be afraid, but not because I actually was. He lifted me up onto the glass counter and knelt before me...he was so beautiful, Carol, his face and the way he looked at me. He said he just wanted a taste of what was to come, so...so I let him pull off my panties.'

'Oh, my God.' She closed her eyes as if she couldn't bear to face what I was saying, either that or she was trying to picture it.

'I know that objectively it seems like an incredibly dangerous thing I did, having a sexual encounter with a total stranger in the middle of a strange city at night,' I admitted, 'but obviously nothing bad happened, on the contrary, it was so strangely beautiful that if I don't see him again—' I couldn't even conceive of the thought.

'Oh, my God,' she repeated, opening her eyes. 'You're already falling in love with him and you don't even know his name. Mary, you're not thinking straight.' She sounded genuinely concerned now. 'You know absolutely nothing about him except that he likes to go down on girls he just met.'

'No,' I said firmly, 'he went down on me because—because there was something special between us, I could feel it!'

'Oh, Mary.' She rolled her eyes.

'You weren't there, Carol,' I insisted angrily. 'You didn't even see him, much less feel what I did.'

'You're falling in love with him because he gave you a really great orgasm and because you know nothing about him so he's the perfect fantasy, but you were

Dreams of Anubis

really lucky, Mary, he could easily have turned out to be—'

The phone rang, blessedly interrupting her moral tirade as we both gasped and leapt to our feet, then giggled self-consciously at our melodramatic reaction.

Carol's 'Hello?' as she picked up the receiver was slightly suspicious, but then I saw her body relax. 'Oh, hi,' she purred, and her husky voice told me there was a man on the other end of the line. 'Well, I don't know,' she said, glancing over at me, 'I'll ask her. Mary, Simon wants to know if we'd like to camp out in a tomb tonight.'

By way of reply, I covered my heart with both hands and stared at her with the wide, beseeching eyes of a painted sarcophagus.

'Yes, she says that would be lovely.'

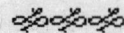

Once again Hamud dropped us off at Saqqara, but this time he only took us as far as that glorious rock-face studded with signs pointing in the direction of different mastabas. From there, Carol and I set off on foot in the direction of the nobleman Ti's eternal resting place, although to the Egyptians this term would have been anathema; the idea of resting for all eternity would have scared them to death. It was more as if we were making our way to Ti's eternal party house, although that is also an erroneous way to describe the ancient Egyptian belief in an afterlife since they were not merely superficial hedonists. These were the nature of my thoughts as I walked a few steps behind my friend. Packing for our night in a tomb had been lots of fun. We were both hunched beneath backpacks stuffed to bursting with absolute essentials such as toilet paper; sweaters and sweatpants (because the temperature drops dramatically in the desert after sunset); a first aid kit just in case one of us got bitten (by what I did not care to ask); make-up, since I couldn't very well have the girls on the tomb walls looking better than I did; and so on. It was four o'clock in the afternoon when we started across the featureless sand in what I sincerely hoped was truly the direction of Ti's mastaba.

It wasn't long before all I could see through the dark windows of my sunglasses was a featureless brightness in every direction, and the unearthly silence began pressing against my heart like another burden. It was extremely surreal to come upon two headless robed statues dating from the Greco-Roman period that suddenly rose up against the sky as if from the depths of my own subconscious. Whatever monument they had once adorned had long since vanished or been buried beneath the sand, and the silence was so absolute I felt as though I were moving through a dream landscape rather than through objective space. It was as if the desert horizon formed the borders of my mind, which made the bleached white statues seem a haunting part of my own imagination-filled skull.

'Carol,' I said, and was startled by the way my voice filled the world, 'I have to rest for a second. I'm thirsty again.' I blamed lingering jetlag for my testiness, but I knew it was only an excuse; I was feeling tense for a myriad of other reasons, not the least of which was how exciting nearly every second of my stay in Egypt had been so far. That was not the problem, certainly, the problem was that I would have to go home soon, back to boring days at work that all flowed monotonously into each other like the desert's featureless haze.

Carol didn't seem to hear because she trudged on, her long legs making swift progress across the deep sand.

I hurried to catch up with her, stumbled, and fell in curious slow motion. The fall was like one in a dream in that it seemed to go on forever, and then abruptly I found myself on my hands and knees facing slightly to the right of Carol's relentless course. At first I thought what I was seeing had to be a mirage created by the projector-like glare of the sun on its slow way down and by my eyelids blinking swiftly to get sand out of my eyes. I stared, and stared, waiting for the vision to vanish, but it refused to do so. Brushing sand off my knees, elbows and hands, I stood up and approached it curiously.

'Carol,' I cried, 'wait up, there's something…oh, my God!' I dumped my backpack behind me and fell to my knees again.

Carol strode impatiently towards me. 'Mary, what are you doing? I thought you were in good shape. You can't keep resting or we'll never…oh, my God!' She shed her own backpack and knelt beside me. 'Oh my God,' she repeated, 'it's Steve!'

Dreams of Anubis

'We have to do something,' I declared brilliantly.

'But what if he's hurt?' She made to touch him, then snatched her hand back. 'If we move him we could make him worse.'

'Obviously he's hurt,' I snapped. 'He's not out here sunbathing.'

Steve lay on his stomach with his arms bent around his dark head, one of his cheeks resting against the sand, a soft smile deepening the one corner of his mouth I could see. Like yesterday, all he was wearing were cut-off shorts, socks and sneakers. 'Maybe he collapsed from sunstroke,' I suggested, admiring his long tanned back.

'Oh no, he's used to the sun.'

'Hmm...let's try to give him some water. Maybe he's dehydrated.'

'No, he's used to-'

'He can't be that used to it or he wouldn't be lying out here unconscious!'

He was wearing lotion all over his body, and the sun glittered off the sand stuck to the oil in a way that made his skin shine like gold mixed with bronze. He was so perfectly still he might have been a fallen statue, and suddenly fear lapped like cold water against my heart. 'He is breathing, isn't he, Carol?'

She rested the back of her hand beneath his nose as we both held our own breath. 'Yes,' she sighed, and for a few seconds we were both too relieved to do anything. Then my friend somehow managed to free herself from the spell his helpless beauty had wrought upon our strained systems. Beginning at his ankles, she began caressing him slowly. 'I don't think anything's broken,' she diagnosed uncertainly.

Tearing my eyes away from his slender, but strong and muscular, thighs, I fished the thermos out of my backpack and quickly filled the cap. I noticed my hands were shaking slightly as I baptized the smiling mouth with a thin stream of the blessedly cold water. But he did not react as in the movies, by immediately stirring to life and appreciatively licking his lips. He did not react at all.

'We've got to get him out of the sun,' Carol stated urgently.

'Right,' I agreed. 'But how? He's too heavy for us to carry.'

'We'll just have to drag him.'

'Drag him?'

'Can you come up with a better idea, Mary?'

'Go for help?'

'We're almost at Ti's mastaba. If we can get him there and out of the sun, then one of us can stay with him while the other one goes for help. I'll go. You won't be able to find Simon.'

'Okay, let's do it.'

We slipped our backpacks on again, and then very gently turned Steve over onto his back.

'You take his feet,' Carol instructed, 'and I'll grab him under the arms. Maybe that way we can lift him a little.'

We could not lift him. After only a few feet, we abandoned the idea and simply dragged him. Standing at his head, Carol took one of his hands, I grasped the other one, and together we pulled him along behind us like a living sleigh. I hated straining his muscles like that, and the way his head fell back terrified me that we would break his neck, but at least only his legs, and his very nice tight backside, came into contact with the hot sand.

I'm really not sure how we made it all the way to the tomb. It seems the body does indeed produce extra amounts of adrenaline in an emergency. 'He's an idiot for not wearing a shirt in this climate,' I gasped. 'What was he thinking?'

'We're almost there,' Carol assured me for the tenth time.

'Almost where? There isn't anything for...oh!' I was suddenly looking straight down into a courtyard.

'Look out,' she warned belatedly.

'Falling in would be the easiest way to get him down there,' I observed. The alternative was a long, narrow flight of steps on the other side of a gaping hole in the sand.

'I'll get the boab guarding the tomb to carry him down.' Literally dropping Steve, she ran around the pit and down the steps into the courtyard. I watched her disappear into the mastaba, and waited with Steve, hot and breathless for all the wrong reasons.

A moment later, Carol raced across the courtyard again and back up the steps, followed more slowly by a native man on whose dark face lazy suspicion battled with

Dreams of Anubis

greed as he anticipated the large tip this special service would entail. He asked no questions, however. He simply bent over, draped Steve over one of his skinny shoulders, the strength of which surprised me, and carefully descended the stairs with him.

Walking at the rear of this strange procession, I was reminded of the ones depicted on mastaba walls. If I had been an Old Kingdom princess, I would definitely have liked for my loving relatives to offer me young men like Steve in addition to cows' legs and baskets of fish.

It was wonderful stepping out of the sun into the cool and shadowy mastaba, and I shed my backpack with a heart-felt groan in the chamber at the end of a long corridor. Then I suffered a pleasant shock when I saw the handsome face staring out at me through a small rectangular opening in the back wall.

Ti's smile was so enigmatically alive, it took my brain a second to register it was only a statue I was seeing. He stood within a small sealed chamber behind the wall known as a serdab, gazing out from another dimension at all the loved ones who desired to commune with his Ba, the human-headed bird symbolizing his soul.

'Stay with him while I go get help,' Carol said briskly. 'And see if you can't get him to wake up and drink some water. But don't let him drink too much or he'll go into shock.' She ran back down the corridor and the native man hurried after her with the unmistakable gleam of baksheesh in his eyes. He had spread Steve out in the center of the chamber, and it was my impression he would have dropped him like a sack if Carol and I had not been watching him like hawks.

Once again, I sank to my knees beside the young Egyptologist's inert body. I gazed down at his smooth, hairless chest, perhaps a little longer than was necessary, and then moved my gaze down to the sunken valley of his stomach wondering how I should go about trying to rouse him. Should I slap him? Should I shake him gently by the shoulders? Yet if being dragged across hot sand had not revived him, I doubted any more subtle methods would work.

Trying not to enjoy myself too much, I straddled him and tentatively slapped one of his cheeks. His head fell to one side, but that was the only reaction I got from him...I think. It was probably only my imagination that his body grew a little firmer beneath me, meaning the bulge in his shorts swelled and stiffened slightly against my own soft crotch. Tempted to tentatively rub myself against him and test my theory, I quickly got up, feeling guilty. I could not make it a habit to give in to every sinful temptation that came my way.

I pulled my thermos out of my backpack, and crouching beside Steve again poured a little water over his cheek, then a little more over his chest, slowly caressing it into his warm and oily skin. I continued my delicate libations, kneeling beside him like Isis trying to revive Osiris, after she had traveled the lengths of the earth gathering together the pieces of his body the evil Set had scattered to make it impossible for her to resurrect her beloved consort. She had found all the pieces except for one. I glanced down at Steve's shorts. Whatever was wrong with him, at least a crocodile hadn't eaten that vital piece of his anatomy.

I relaxed into a cross-legged position and looked up at a section of the bas-reliefs carved around me. I could tell right away this particular scene depicted the nobleman Ti and his wife. Behind them stretched fields of wild game and cattle, and a table before them was laid out with a delectable assortment of food and drink.

Rising, I approached their smiling figures. Because I was in his tomb, Ti was twice the size of his wife. He was seated on a chair while she knelt at his feet, her arms wrapped around one of his legs even as her face and torso looked away from his body, ostensibly in the direction of his immortality. I desperately longed to feel that way about a man, yet so far it had remained only a romantic dream. None of the men I dated had even remotely inspired such love and devotion in me.

A soft moan penetrated the stillness of the chamber.

I quickly knelt beside Steve again, and held my breath as his head turned slowly from side to side. I glimpsed the gleam of his irises as he nearly reached the surface of consciousness, but then I sensed him sink back into the comfortable peace of oblivion again. I sighed in frustration and sat back on my heels. The room I was trapped in with a young man who resembled a statue of Ti escaped from his serdab, felt oppressively timeless. His pulse and mine were the only measure of time's passage, and already I felt as though I had been alone with him for hours even though it had only been minutes.

Steve was so motionless I had to reassure myself again he was breathing by resting a finger just above his upper lip and feeling his warm exhalations bathe my skin. And as I did, I suffered the haunting impression that all the other

Dreams of Anubis

brown male chests depicted around me were also rising and falling, so slowly their movement was nearly invisible.

Suddenly the procession of little reddish-brown figures circling the chamber struck me as a reflection of my own blood cells flowing through my body, the mastaba's separate chambers symbolizing my different vital organs. However, in this particular mastaba there was only one other room besides the one in which I was now, plus the serdab, from which Ti continued regarding me so enigmatically. If I remembered correctly, the space Steve and I were in was the sacrificial chapel. Strikingly realistic effigies of Ti once stared through three rectangular slits in the western wall, now only one statue remains, a replica of the original in the Cairo museum, the shining black stones used for his eyes giving him a marvelously life-like stare.

I glanced down at the bare chest I was kneeling beside, and then back up at Ti's firm brown torso depicted all around me. Steve's head was turned away, and his black hair could easily have belonged to an ancient Egyptian nobleman's. I looked over at the serdab and Ti's secretly smiling face, then back down at Steve's neck and broad shoulders. If I took off his shorts, I could easily make myself believe it was Ti's body lying before me and that the eyes of his Ba statue were challenging the priestess of Isis inside me to revive him, to bring him back to life with the mysterious powers of my female sexuality.

Abandoning myself to the fantasy, in the back of my mind justifying my actions with the thought that they might actually help rouse Steve from his dangerous stupor as nothing else had, I planted my hands on his warm chest and slowly caressed his pecs. They were almost as hard as a statue's, but his skin was tender, alive, inviting my nails to scratch it lightly and leave ghostly trails that gradually faded away. I found myself straddling him again, less carefully and hesitantly this time, encouraged by the haunting way Ti's smile seemed to deepen as my pulse accelerated. I ran my hands down to his firm belly, which was also vulnerably soft, appreciating the low-cut shorts that enabled me to penetrate the vulnerable little space of his navel with my fingertip and make a crescent-like imprint around it with my nail as I pressed it gently but firmly into his skin.

He did not make a sound or move a muscle in response to my gently vicious probe, and yet I realized he did, in a way, as I became even more stimulatingly aware of the bulge in his crotch between my legs. I bit my lip, hesitating for an instant before obeying Ti's smiling command to rub my pussy against his growing hard-on, for in my imagination Ti's virile ancient soul was magically possessing the inert body of the young man lying below me. I immediately felt frustrated by all the layers of cloth separating my hungry hole from the stiff fullness I distinctly felt pressing against my vulva now and insinuating itself between my labial lips through our shorts. I moaned, allowing all my weight to sink down against the buried erection that I was bringing fully to life without his even knowing it, and leaning forward slightly to brace myself against his chest, I began rubbing myself against it selfishly.

'Oh yes,' I whispered, because the top button on his shorts was in just the right place to give my clit an excitingly hard kiss every time I moved my hips up and down against him, and my panties provided a teasingly effective friction that told me I could come like this if I wanted to.

I was sorely tempted to take myself all the way. It would be so easy with Ti's metaphysical voyeurism caressing my imagination, combined with the memory of the handsome Englishman's tongue flicking with devastating skill against my clitoris, which was already swelling with the promise of an orgasm taking divine root between my thighs. Whatever the conscious Steve might think about it, his body was obviously enjoying what I was doing with him, and I wondered if my intimate caress was causing the synapses in his brain to flash a sexy dream on the screen of his closed eyelids.

It certainly couldn't hurt to stimulate him like this. And after thinking all day about what had happened the night before in the bazaar, I was more than ready for the momentary reprieve and relief of a climax.

I rode the timelessly handsome young man beneath me with concentrated abandon, working myself to a pitch by alternately gazing down at his black hair and broad shoulders, then over at Ti's supernaturally sexy smile, merging them in my fantasy until for a few stunning instants they actually seemed to become one in my body.

The intensity of my pleasure was reflected by my breathless silence as I climaxed, my vaginal muscles contracting as ecstasy expanded within me. I was sure Steve would turn his head and look up at me, that the subliminal vibrations of my orgasm had been powerful enough to penetrate his psyche. But nothing happened except that his penis remained frustratingly stiff against my hot wet pussy.

Telling myself I had done all I could for him, I waited until my legs could comfortably support me again before I got up to resume my examination of the exquisite bas-reliefs.

I noticed that quite a few scenes involved the capture and taming of wild animals, which according to John Anthony West, one of the more inspired Egyptologists, symbolized the human spirit imposing a sense of order and meaning over the chaotic impulses of nature and the flesh. Continuing on in this vain, Ti's banquet table could be seen as being rich with the emotions he had learned to master, his soul a field sown with the belief in a divine harvest of life's experiences. In this light, the artwork around me was effectively a complex equation for immortality.

I went and stood directly in front of the serdab. 'What were you really like?' I asked Ti's smiling face, my voice reverently quiet. 'Were you as naïve and idealistic as a child, or were you strong and wise like the man I've always dreamed of?' Perhaps like the man in the bazaar last night, I thought, before I forced myself to stop thinking about him. 'Yet I feel as though you're still waiting for something, as if the eternity you believed in depends on what becomes of humanity itself. Maybe an afterlife doesn't just happen any more than life does. Maybe we have to build it ourselves with the energy of our desire.'

'I don't have any damned energy left to desire anything,' Ti's lips magically spoke without moving, his voice hoarse from the centuries that it had remained buried in his throat, 'except a drink of water, please.'

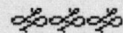

'Steve, that's enough,' I protested gently. 'It's bad for you to overdo it. Just sip it.'

He paid me not the slightest heed; the thermos gradually rose until it was almost perpendicular with the ceiling as he guzzled the water.

'You should know better than to walk around in the desert without a shirt on,' I scolded him, my compassion for him all but dried up.

He finally set my cooler down, and collapsed back across the sand again.

'Steve?' I asked, concerned. His eyes were closed, but his smile told me he was awake, and aware of my hands gripping his shoulders. 'What happened to you?'

His uncanny resemblance to Ti vanished when his eyes opened again. His irises were the vivid green of spring leaves, a delicate color not found in Egypt's tougher foliage. 'Nothing happened to me,' was his infuriating reply.

'Excuse me, nothing? I suppose that's why we found you lying unconscious in the middle of the desert.'

He shrugged, and then winced in pain. 'How did I get here?' He sounded only mildly curious.

'Carol and I dragged you here, and it wasn't easy.'

'Carol?' He raised his head for a moment and looked around. 'Where is she?'

'She went to get help, naturally.'

'Help?' His shoulder-length hair formed a black halo across the white sand. 'What for?' With the typical stubbornness of his sex, he was pretending nothing was wrong with him, but I could sense his exhaustion as his eyes closed again.

'Steve, you could have died out there,' I said soberly. 'What happened to you?'

'Don't worry about it, Mary, I'm all right now.'

'Yes, but if we hadn't found you, you wouldn't be all right, not at all. Could your misfortune possibly have something to do with Imhotep's tomb?'

His eyes flew open. 'What?'

I smiled. 'Well, for some reason, Steve, I'm in possession of a photograph that—'

'You have it?' He sat up abruptly, and my surprise enabled him to push me back across the sand and straddle me just as I had him.

The pleasant shock, as well as the considerable weight of his hard muscles, took my breath away.

He grabbed both my wrists, and pinned them down over my head as he

Dreams of Anubis

leaned over me. 'Where did you get it, Mary?' he asked quietly, his hair raining sand down into my face.

'Ouch!' I squeezed my eyes shut reluctantly, because his broad shoulders were quite an inspiring view.

'Tell me, Mary,' he whispered coaxingly in my ear.

'I didn't get it anywhere, it just appeared in my room at Carol's place.'

'Please tell me you haven't shown it to anyone, Mary.'

'I haven't shown it to anyone,' I said obediently, 'except Carol, of course.'

Apparently his relief was so great that he kissed me. 'Where is it now?' he asked, his lips moving against mine. 'Tell me...' He thrust his tongue between my lips as if he could wrestle the answer out of me.

'Mary!' Carol shrieked.

Steve rolled off me as suddenly as if the sound of her voice was a gunshot mortally wounding him.

'I see she managed to revive him,' Simon commented dryly. He strode into the chamber and yanked me to my feet, not very gently.

'Baksheesh!' The mastaba's native guard had returned with them. 'Baksheesh!' he demanded from the doorway.

Carol turned to settle our account with him as Steve got carefully to his feet. 'Mary has the photograph,' he informed Simon.

'I know, Carol told me.'

'I—'

Simon cut her off. 'What happened to you, Steve?'

Wincing in pain, Ti's look-alike bent over and gingerly caressed the backs of his sunburned calves. 'I ran into some friends,' he replied absently, increasingly engrossed in his skin's budding misery. He was beginning to realize just what his body had been through while his consciousness was on sabbatical. 'I guess it upset them that I didn't have much to say.'

'I didn't—' Carol tried a second time to make a vital point, but this time she was interrupted by a man staggering into the sacrificial chamber looking as though he had just crossed the entire Sahara on foot.

'Where's the patient?' the newcomer gasped, removing his safari hat to caress his bald scalp as if to make sure it's egg-like surface hadn't cracked from the strain.

I assumed he was a doctor, even though of all the people in the mastaba he was the only one who looked in need of medical attention. I stepped up to Carol. 'You didn't what?' I whispered.

'I didn't tell Simon about the photograph,' she whispered back.

'Then he knew I had it?'

'Where's the patient?' the little bald man asked again, a bit hysterically. He was beginning to suspect his arduous race across the sand had been for nothing.

'I'm here,' Steve groaned. 'My lovely saviors burned the skin off my legs.'

With a gratified 'Humph!' the doctor hurried over to inspect him.

'Well, so much for our cozy night in a tomb,' I declared.

'Lost your nerve already?' Simon taunted.

'No, but someone just tried to kill—'

'Quiet, Mary.' He glanced at the doctor. The man was conferring with Carol, who had efficiently pulled out her little first aid kit to assist him. Standing perfectly still between them, Steve truly resembled a statue wearing a relieved smile on his lips as the doctor began applying a soothing balm to his back like the artist's finishing coat of paint.

Simon abruptly grabbed my arm and pulled me out into the corridor. 'Don't be silly, Mary, no one tried to kill Steve.' He led me into the smaller chamber.

'But—'

'No buts.'

'But how did you know about the photograph, and that I had it?'

'Where is it now?' In typical male fashion, he parried my question with one of his own. However, I was expected to provide an answer even though he had not.

'It's back at the apartment,' I lied impulsively; it was actually in my backpack.

'Good,' he said firmly, 'keep it there.'

'Does the cartouche in the picture mark the entrance to Imhotep's tomb?' I whispered eagerly.

'Yes, I believe it does,' he admitted, frowning at the wall behind me. 'That's the problem.'

'My God, you discovered Imhotep's tomb?!'

Dreams of Anubis

He put a hand over my mouth. 'Would you kindly lower your voice, Mary?'

'Sorry,' I mumbled against his palm. His skin was slightly rough and salty, and I didn't think I had ever tasted anything quite so delicious. Then there was the added spice of his face so close to mine, and his penetrating stare stirring up all sorts of feelings inside me.

He uncovered my mouth, and gripped both my arms the way he had in the perfume shop. 'Getting around like a little butterfly, aren't you?' he accused, and pulled me roughly against him.

I was lost in his crushing embrace and in the joy of his tongue suddenly leading mine around and around in a breathless dance.

'Ahem?'

I had no idea how long the doctor had been standing in the doorway watching us, but with my blood singing, his flushed little frame made me think of the dwarf-god, Bes, whom the ancient Egyptians had associated with music and childbirth.

'I believe my work is done here,' he said.

I was forced to rediscover gravity when Simon released me abruptly. 'We're sorry to have troubled you, sir.' He pulled a wad of colorful bills out of his back pocket that made me think of dried flower petals.

'Oh I couldn't possibly…' Bes eyed the money greedily.

'I insist.' Simon shoved the paper garishly decorated with Sphinx heads and pyramids into the doctor's hand. 'Just don't mention this little incident to anyone, please. The local authorities can be so trying, you know.'

'Oh but of course.' Bes smiled. 'Mention what?'

Chapter Four

I never would have thought I could be so happy and comfortable in a tomb. We were sitting against a wall of Ti's courtyard gazing meditatively at the fire burning in its center, and the Chardonnay we were drinking that was soaking deliciously into my tired muscles made staring up at the sky feel like looking up at a divine vineyard. I could not believe how many stars there were, all of them glistening like juicy grapes making our sun and earth just one vintage in a multitude of intoxicatingly beautiful and exciting worlds. Carol and I had brought the basic necessities, but Simon provided a small world of luxuries.

Shortly after the doctor departed, three native men (one of whom looked distinctly familiar when he grinned at me) paid a visit to the mastaba like the Three Kings stripped of all their finery, and among the wonderful gifts they unwrapped for us were several bottles of wine accompanied by canned delicacies such as smoked oysters and chicken liver Pâté.

When I was feeling so good that I was nearly incapable of speech, Simon began answering the questions I did not have the energy to ask him out loud. He seemed able to read my mind, however, and I hung on his every word because it kept me from falling asleep. We were sharing a blanket, and the side of me resting against him felt wonderfully warm while the other half of me shivered in the rapidly dropping temperature. I could hear Carol talking quietly with Steve on Simon's other side, his profile looming large as a colossi's from my cozy position beneath his arm, and I hoped she was feeling as good as I was.

'I've had my man, Halaf, watching you ever since you got here, Mary,' Simon informed me, 'and it's a good thing too, or I wouldn't have found you so quickly at the bazaar when you ran away, foolish girl.'

I was trying not think about the man I had met as a result of my foolishness, not to mention the pleasure my impulsive act had resulted in. 'Halaf...he was just here, wasn't he, the tall one of the three who delivered this wonderful wine and everything else? I thought he looked familiar. After he helped put everything back in my suitcase at the airport he sat on top of it grinning like a maniac.'

Simon chuckled. 'Yes, that was him.'

With my free hand, I lifted the paper cup to my lips. To my chagrin, I discovered it was empty again.

'Need a refill?' He reached for the bottle, careful not to disturb the exquisite cuddle we had achieved as he did so.

'Thank you,' I said as he filled my cup nearly to overflowing.

'My pleasure, Mary.'

'So...' It was an effort to speak, but I wanted to take advantage of his confidential mood. 'So you had Halaf slip the photograph into my suitcase. Why?'

'Because I needed a good place to hide it.'

'Halaf deliberately threw my suitcase half way across the airport so it would burst open?' I was too tired to feel indignant. I did not question why Simon had chosen me as the photo's recipient since at the moment I was not opposed to him choosing me for anything he desired.

'I'm sorry Mary, but my stuff, and Steve's too, would inevitably have been searched by interested parties once the rumor got out.'

'So you put me in danger instead?' I asked mildly, still not able to find it in me to be angry with him thanks to the conciliatory wine flowing through my veins.

'I told you, Mary,' he said patiently, 'there's no danger.'

'But someone roughed Steve up, didn't they? They left him lying unconscious in the desert, and if Carol and I hadn't found him, he might have-'

'Don't be silly. It would take a hell of a lot more than that to kill Steve. They were merely trying to intimidate us into revealing the location of the tomb, because even if they got a hold of the rumored photograph, it wouldn't tell them anything. There's no way they can determine the mastaba's location from the picture. However, ownership of the photo is important for claiming first excavation rights, so I made sure there wasn't a negative. I borrowed Carol's Polaroid when she wasn't looking, and then Steve and I re-buried the evidence. Actually, I really don't know what possessed me to give you the photo. It was an odd inspiration. I couldn't put it in a safe deposit box, or anywhere else similarly practical, because Egyptian archaeologists watch us like vultures just waiting to move in on a kill. If even one of them got a look at that picture the Antiquities Department would be all over us like jackals. Then Carol told me about her friend who was coming to visit her from Boston, and I thought that's it, no one will suspect a stupid little tourist.'

'Excuse me?'

'I didn't know you at the time, Mary.'

His apology was very effective—another long, lingering kiss in which his tongue pointed out all sorts of fascinating new twists to an age-old activity. I had to admit, Simon Taylor was an excellent kisser. He was so good I wouldn't have been surprised to learn he had a PhD in the subject. I was tired, and relaxed by decadently good food and wine, a condition that made kissing the sexy Egyptologist who had been gracious enough to arrange a night in a tomb for me feel like the perfect pastime, even if in the back of my mind I couldn't stop thinking about another man…'But I'm staying with Carol,' I somehow remembered what we had been talking about when he let me up for air, 'and she works for you.'

'True. However, there's very tight security around her building, and in the unlikely event anyone dared to break into her apartment, they would concentrate on her possessions and not yours. Anyway, I told you, it was an odd inspiration. I'm not normally so impulsive. Some strange intuition must have told me,' his arm tightened around my shoulders, 'I would want you intimately involved in all my affairs.'

This statement turned my head towards his again for another session of mouth-to-mouth stimulation, as the wine and his heavy arm around me drowned all the frustration I had been feeling remembering my mysterious sheik from the bazaar. Part of me felt anxious wondering if I would ever see him again, while another part of me did not doubt for a second that I would.

'Who was the man in the perfume shop, Simon?' I asked as casually as I possibly could. 'He seems to know I have the photograph. He said I had something he wanted, and asked me how much I knew about it, and I got the impression last night that you knew who he was.'

'I do.'

I waited breathlessly for him to volunteer more information, but suddenly he seemed content to just sip his wine. 'Well, who is he?' I couldn't quite disguise my impatient eagerness.

'How long were you alone with him, Mary?'

I squirmed beneath his arm in frustration that he was fighting my question with another question again. 'Who was I alone with?' I countered.

'A rich bastard.'

'He's rich?' I asked in surprise, because in the twenty-four hours I had spent thinking about the strikingly attractive stranger from the bazaar I had not once speculated about his profession or financial standing. There was something about him that had seemed above all such concerns, and I couldn't explain way, but I was sure I would have continued to feel this way about him even if Simon had told me he was a beggar.

'He's obscenely rich. Does that appeal to you, Mary?'

I wasn't so tipsy that I couldn't tell the question was a test. 'I could care less,' I replied truthfully.

He rewarded me for not being a materialistic girl with another academically perfect merging of our lips that scored big with the nerve-endings in my belly as his tongue's thrusting, surging skill made me wonder what it would be like to have him kissing me at the same time that his stiff cock plunged in and out of my pussy.

I moaned and looked searchingly up into his light eyes when he finally pulled his head back.

'I'm sorry I put you in this position, Mary,' he said soberly. 'It was stupid to involve you like this. I could easily have found a much more rational hiding place for the photograph, but it was such an unexpected monumental discovery, I guess I wasn't thinking straight. And when Carol mentioned her friend who was coming to visit from the States, I don't know, I just—'

'It's all right, Simon, I don't mind,' I assured him, because if he hadn't put me in this position by slipping the photograph into my suitcase, the nameless Englishman would not have put me in the position he did on the glass counter. 'Yet how did that man who was with me in the trailer know I have the photograph?' I was glad to have another objective excuse to ask about him.

'Because that bastard has a way of knowing everything. I wouldn't be surprised if half of Cairo was on his unofficial payroll.'

I was not happy that despite my cleverly detached questioning, the only name I could still give my beautiful sheik was "bastard".

'And yet the mere rumor of this discovery has the vultures circling already, Mary. Steve and I didn't breathe a word of it to anyone, not even Carol knew about it until today, and yet somehow rumors started flying around, and that bastard's the eye of the storm, I'm sure of it.'

'Would you please stop calling him a bastard.' This was no way to refer to a man so admirably skilled in the age-old art of cunnilingus. 'I'm sure he has a name, and if he's so interested in the discovery of a mastaba, then that means he's an Egyptologist, too?'

'He's not.' Simon replied shortly. 'He's just rich enough to be able to make a hobby of Egyptology, and he's only one nuisance in my life right now. Do you know what will happen when it's made public that the entrance to Imhotep's mastaba has been discovered? All hell will break loose here, that's what, and I want to finish my book on Saqqara before that happens. I won't be able to hold them back much longer, though.'

'Why can't you include Imhotep's mastaba in your book?' I suggested brilliantly. 'Wouldn't that be the crowning glory?'

'Because, Mary, proper excavation of Imhotep's eternal resting place will take nearly as long as he's been dead, and Egypt will jealously horde all the initial glory for itself. I'd be surprised if they even let Steve and I work on it that much even though we discovered it.'

'How did you discover it?' I asked excitedly. 'I can understand why you're feeling frustrated, but you must be thrilled, too, aren't you?'

'Oh yes, I'm thrilled,' he made it sound like a medical condition he had been cured of long ago by a heavy dose of reality, 'and the discovery was an accident, of course. All the really good ones are. I'll spare you the boring details.'

'I wouldn't find them boring,' I protested, but without much conviction. 'If I wasn't so sleepy,' I added more honestly.

'What, tired already?' he teased. 'I thought you might like to join me in a nocturnal exploration of Ti's burial chamber.'

'Oh, that would be lovely!' I struggled to convey my mental excitement to my legs, without success. 'But I can't seem to move...'

He chuckled. 'Lovely isn't exactly the adjective I'd use to describe it.' His arm slipped from around me as he slipped the blanket we were sharing off his shoulder and stood up. His back was to the fire as he stood facing me, and his tall silhouette might have been Ti's magical Shade reaching down for my hand.

I set my cup down, and let him pull me up towards Nut's beautiful starry womb, shedding the blanket like a shroud. 'But why didn't you even tell Steve I had the photograph?' It suddenly occurred to me to ask. Steve and Carol were also sharing a blanket, and they ignored us as we got up.

'Because, if he didn't know where it was, he couldn't tell anyone else, could he?'

'Simon, I—'

'No more questions, Mary.' He took my hand and led me past the dying fire.

'But I have to—'

'I said drop it.'

'I can't drop it, I really have to go to the bathroom.' Standing had made me fully aware of my pressing need.

'That's where we're headed,' he said, and laughed softly when I hesitated. 'Don't worry, the desert's big enough for both of us.' He switched on a flashlight as we walked past the fire across the courtyard, and then let me walk up the steps ahead of him, half hypnotizing me with the undulating pool of light he kept focused at my feet. At the top of the stairs, he gave me a playful shove, and I started off alone into the pitch-black darkness.

I had stuffed some toilet paper into one of the pockets of my shorts earlier, and I was glad for my forethought now when I judged I had wandered off far enough. I pulled my shorts and panties down and squatted as I gazed up at the heavens. My urine was hot and pungent in contrast to the cold night air, and the countless stars winking down at me were stimulating company. I had known since I was a little girl that the earth's sun is only one of a multitude of suns, and tonight I found this fact more thrilling than ever, not only because I could actually see and feel that it was true, but because I was sure I had found him at last. The man I had been waiting for all my life was here in Egypt, there was no doubt about it in my heart, and it was entirely possible I had met him last night at the bazaar. And yet here I was getting ready to spend the night with another man, a handsome, intelligent Egyptologist who seemed absolutely perfect for me. If I started dating Simon, I could possibly arrange to stay in Egypt somehow, and if we were married, I could live in Egypt. He had said it would take years to excavate Imhotep's mastaba, and I could be part of the incredible excitement surrounding this historic discovery, sharing my days and nights with a man who shared my same passion for ancient Egypt. It was such a perfect daydream that for a few seconds I actually managed to forget the sensual gift another man had given me last night in the bazaar as a promise of things to come...

I wiped myself clean, pulled my panties and shorts back up, and buried the scrap of tissue in the sand. There was no point deciding between Simon and the nameless stranger tonight. I had time, thank the gods. I had only just arrived in Egypt, yet already I had been here long enough to know that things would unfold as they were meant to. Here in this ancient land coincidences felt like part of a mysterious choreography intimately related to everything I had ever thought and felt and dreamed. And right now all I knew for certain was that the nameless man from the bazaar had given me very good advice—I had to remember my dreams, in every sense, and trust that they would come true, although how, and with whom, I could not yet know.

I rejoined Simon at the top of the steps leading down into the mastaba. He was holding the flashlight towards the ground, and to me it looked as though the golden disc of the sun had fallen worshipfully at his feet.

'Feel better?' he asked quietly.

'Yes, thank you. I'm ready for the burial chamber now.'

'Are you sure?'

Dreams of Anubis

His undertone told me I could expect to encounter a lot more than an empty sarcophagus down there. 'I'm sure,' I replied quietly.

Back down in the courtyard, Steve was encouraging the fire back to a more passionate life while Carol remained huddled beneath their blanket, her knees drawn up against her chest in an effort to ward off the desert chill. I tried to catch her eye, but she was looking at Steve, and I couldn't blame her. The way the muscles of his back rippled as he stoked the flames was rather engrossing, especially when I compared the sight to the cold black hole Simon was leading me towards.

'You first,' he said.

'Oh no, you first.'

His flashlight revealed worn steps descending almost at a right angle deep into the earth. Without hesitation, he started down them.

I followed carefully behind him. His shoulders blocked the light, so I descended mostly by feel, tentatively clinging to him the whole way down. We had only gone a few feet into the darkness before I found myself longing for the fire we had left behind, very much like a disembodied soul must miss its warm, pulsing heart. In a matter of seconds, the absolute darkness of this secret place—deliberately dug far from the sacrificial chamber where Ti's life-like form still stands within the serdab—made the comforts and pleasures of the courtyard feel distressingly, almost impossibly, far away.

It was a relief when we finally reached level ground, but there wasn't much else to feel good about. Until Simon grasped my hand, and his firm grip sent reassuring warmth through my whole body. I sensed he was not in the least bit nervous, and I found this mysterious inner male strength intensely attractive. We just stood there hand in hand for a moment, our eyes gradually adjusting as he thrust the beam of his flashlight into the pitchy gloom. The edge of the light revealed a massive structure looming against a far wall and I assumed this was Ti's sarcophagus.

'Was Ti encased in eight different coffins like Tutankhamun?' I asked, whispering respectfully.

Simon didn't answer as he led me deeper into this haunting wound inflicted in the earth by Ti's stubborn desire to live forever.

Cat's Collar - Three Erotic Romances

I made nervous conversation, anxiously wondering just how far he was planning to take us down here, in more ways than one. 'I don't believe the Egyptians mummified themselves because they wanted to keep using the same body.'

'Then why do you think they did it?' He laid the flashlight down on the thick rim of the sarcophagus.

'I don't know.' I clutched myself as I shivered.

'Are you cold, Mary?'

'Yes a little.'

The steady beam of light flowing parallel to us gilded the edges of his silhouette and made it look like the darkness itself had taken form. A stab of fear intensified my excitement in a way I had only experienced the night before in the bazaar. And now I shivered again, this time from the thrill of desire that coursed down my spine to the dark opening between my thighs I could never see, only feel.

'Then brace yourself,' he warned quietly, grasping my wrists and gently forcing my arms out of their unconscious mummy-like pose over my chest. He raised them up over my head, and before I could wonder what he was doing, he reached down and pulled my shirt off. 'I want you,' he whispered, carelessly dropping my clothes onto the packed earth, and impatiently tugging my zipper down with a ripping sound that echoed sinisterly in the ancient tomb. 'Do you want me, Mary?'

'Yes…' I wasn't wearing a bra, and my naked breasts looked so flawlessly pale and firm in the darkness they might have been made of alabaster.

'Then I'm going to take you.'

'Yes,' I repeated helplessly, glad he wasn't giving me time to think about what was happening. It would be foolish for me to remain loyal to a nameless stranger, and yet I was irrationally tempted to do so, which made Simon's commanding attitude come as a relief.

He genuflected before me. 'Are you sure?' he asked even as he slid my shorts and panties down my legs.

By way of response, I stepped out of them, looking down at the dim light of his blond hair and remembering a dark head in a similar position. I wasn't sure, but I

Dreams of Anubis

think a stab of disappointment became hopelessly confused with how much it inevitably excited me to have a handsome man's face so close to my sex lips. I didn't appreciate the careless way he abandoned my new white cotton panties to the black dirt of a centuries-old grave, yet I was grateful for the powerful current of his desire which made it easy for me let go of my heavy thoughts and just go with the sensual flow, submerging my body in these timelessly arousing moments deep in the earth.

'Oh Mary...' He grabbed me by the waist as his mouth fell hungrily on one of my nipples, making me gasp from the stimulating contrast between his warm lips and the frigid crypt. I surrendered to the supple arch of my spine by tossing my head back as he pressed me firmly against him while passionately suckling one of my breasts.

I was overwhelmed by a small storm of sensations that sent a hot flash of arousal down my body, instantly making the space between my legs warm and wet. His mouth was hot and alive compared to the cold still air of the burial chamber, and my naked skin pressed against his slightly rough jeans as he clutched my slender waist with hard, possessive fingers made me even more aware of how soft and vulnerable my young body was surrounded by timeless earth and unyielding stone.

I moaned as he transferred his attentions to my other achingly firm nipple, but I wasn't so much responding to the sweet pleasure of having my breasts so thoroughly appreciated as to the feel of my body, braced on the comfortable modern pedestals of my sneakers, willingly going completely limp in his hands. I deliberately didn't do anything except passively let him worship the lush charms of my flesh as he literally held me up with his hands and his mouth. I was seriously turning myself on imagining that stripped of all defenses my slender body was supported only by the irresistible force of his lust. His fingers digging into my skin promised that his cock would be just as hard and unrelenting as it thrust me into ecstasy's otherworldly dimension.

'Oh Mary!' he repeated eloquently.

I didn't respond, not wanting to break the submissive trance I was letting myself fall into; my back arched as I offered my breasts up to his deliciously devouring appetite, my head thrown back so all I saw were my own rousing dark fantasies.

He planted his hand against my upper back and straightened me up to face him. 'You're so fucking beautiful,' he said accusingly.

I moaned feeling bereft as he suddenly let go of me, but it was only so he could open his pants. I held my breath waiting to see what would emerge, and the pale shaft of his stiff penis as he pulled it out was all I could have hoped for. The mere sight of it made the hole between my legs feel even deeper and darker, desperately in need of his almost luminous erection to fill it and show me all the beautiful sensations buried within me.

'There's nowhere to lie down,' he said in a threatening undertone that made me shiver it got me so hot inside despite how cold my skin was. 'What do you suggest?' He stroked himself slowly, clearly enjoying the feel of my eyes on his cock.

Shivering again, I hugged myself in anticipation of feeling his long, thick erection sliding into my tight pussy, and because it was much more exciting not knowing how he would put it inside me, I didn't answer.

'Turn around and bend over,' he ordered quietly, correctly interpreting my silence to mean it was his decision, 'and brace yourself on the edge of the sarcophagus.'

I didn't care that the stone scraped my skin a little. It was a small price to pay for the intense turn-on of being helplessly naked in such rough surroundings as I bent at the waist and gripped the edge of Ti's eternal resting place. I was surprised by how much it excited me that we weren't in a safe comfortable bedroom lying on a nice soft bed with silk sheets caressing our skins. In this impenetrably dark tomb all we had was each other, our two bodies embraced by elements hostile to our flesh bringing us more intensely together.

'Mm, yes, that's a good girl,' he murmured as I felt him step up tightly behind me. 'Arch your back just a little more,' he urged, resting his hand on the base of my spine and pushing down on it gently. 'That's it. Are you on the pill?'

'Yes,' I whispered.

'I'm glad, because I would hate not being able to feel you, and I want to feel you, Mary. More than anything right now I want to feel your pussy caressing every inch of my cock all the way down to my balls.'

I whimpered in an agony of anticipation as he caressed the cool moons of my

Dreams of Anubis

ass cheeks with his warm hands, making me almost painfully aware of my wet, begging pussy made to wait for his penis. At last he began penetrating me, but so slowly I could hardly stand it. The teasing sensation of his head lodged between the lips of my sex gradually became the deepening pleasure of his hard-on forcing my clinging depths open around it, his rigid cock suffusing my belly with a penetrating warmth like a solid shaft of light magically illuminating the secret shrine between my thighs. When he was finally all the way in, it felt so good I moaned in protest as he remained buried motionless inside me for what felt like a small eternity.

'Oh yes…' he whispered, and pulled out all the way to start thrusting into me hard and fast. After his initial control he drove into me, beating his hips against my ass as though his life depended on it, making my arms strain against the sarcophagus as every time he plunged I felt as though he was granting my body its deepest wish. 'You like it like this, don't you, Mary?'

I was in no position to argue.

'Do you like my cock inside you?' He rammed the question into me.

'Oh yes!' I gasped. He banged me from behind with such force that even my clitoris, technically left out in the cold, trembled in response to his virile onslaught, making the experience almost overwhelmingly pleasurable for me.

Sustaining his relentless rhythm, he demanded, 'Tell me how much you like it.'

'Oh God, I love it,' I obeyed breathlessly, 'I love it!'

It was true. I loved the sensation of his erection surging up into my body and granting me the blessed feeling of being full of a real man. Keeping my legs straight to help brace me as I held on to the edge of the sarcophagus, my back arched receptively to offer my slick pussy up to his deep, hard thrusts. It was an exercise I could have sustained forever.

'You have such a sweet little pussy, Mary, so tight and yet so deep, I can shove my cock all the way up inside you like this…'

I cried out from the excruciating pleasure as he illustrated his point and I felt the cool kiss of his balls on my hot vulva.

'I ram my dick all the way up into your sweet little slit and still barely touch bottom.'

'Oh God that feels so good, don't stop,' I begged, 'please!'

'Does it feel like I'm going to stop, Mary? Does my cock feel like it's anywhere near ready to stop fucking you?'

'No...' I groaned as he pulled out of me slowly, allowing me to relish the full rigid length of his erection as my innermost flesh seemed to swell worshipfully open around it. And then I whimpered from the torturous ecstasy as he plunged all the way into me again. His penis was so thick and rigid and planted so deep inside my flesh the fulfillment was excruciating, and yet there was still enough mysterious room left inside me to accommodate the thought of another man.

'Oh yes, yes!' I cried shamelessly, forgetting to respect Ti's ghost as Simon's hips started pumping again and the impression his hard-on made inside me became confused with the memory of a dark-haired stranger's head buried between my thighs.

'Mm, yes, Mary, come for me...'

'I can't...'

'You,' he stabbed into me accusingly, 'can't?'

'I have to touch myself!'

'I see.' He pulled out of me abruptly. 'Come here, baby.'

I obeyed him a little stiffly, straightening up and turning around to face him. For some reason it excited me that he was still fully clothed and I was completely naked except for my shoes and socks. It was perversely arousing to have my tender breasts and open sex exposed in a cold stone tomb while the naked soles of my feet were still protected by my sneakers, reassuring symbols of the fact that I could walk out of there whenever I wanted to; comfortable reminders that my body wasn't really the helpless vulnerable plaything of unseen forces that might be penetrating me in the form of Simon's powerfully virile silhouette.

He pulled me into the shelter of his arms. 'This is turning you on, isn't it?' he whispered, holding me close against him.

'Yes,' I confessed. 'I guess I have a kinky streak.'

'Well this is the first time I've ever had sex in a crypt, too, in case you're wondering.'

I wasn't, all I was wondering was if I would ever see the mysterious sheik

Dreams of Anubis

from the bazaar again, and fully admitting this to myself while standing naked in another man's arms, I heaved a sad, frustrated sigh.

'I'm not finished with you yet,' he warned quietly. 'We're not leaving this tomb until I feel you come fully to life.'

He grasped one of my hands and led me in the direction the flashlight was pointing, its faint yellow light washing over what looked like a broken column. 'Sit on this and lie back,' he instructed.

The surface looked smooth enough, and just conceivably wide enough for me to obey him. I lifted myself gingerly up onto the pedestal, aroused by how cold and hard the stone was against my soft ass, and I was even more enticingly aware of my tender wet pussy lips as the bottom of my pouting little pudenda kissed the edge.

'Lie back,' he urged as I hesitated, stroking himself again even though his erection did not look in the slightest danger of diminishing.

I obeyed him with the thrill of longing to feel his cock stabbing me again. I was perched on the very edge of the broken column that was digging into my ass cheeks, and with my spread legs bent at the knees, the tips of my sneakers just barely touched the ground. My body felt excitingly soft and vulnerable lying against the totally unyielding surface, and any discomfort I felt was washed away by a flood of anticipation as I watched a broad-shouldered silhouette gilded by the light behind him step forcibly between my thighs.

I was infinitely glad he didn't say anything, which enabled my imagination to take off as I lifted my hand and touched myself, pressing the tips of two of my fingers against my clitoris. I caressed myself as only I know how watching a rock-hard shadow penetrating me, and as it slowly filled me, pleasure fully possessed me. The silence in the chamber was absolute beyond our excited breathing, and the soft wet sound of his balls slapping against me as he gripped the backs of my thighs, raising them around him so he could dive fast and hard into my juicing hole. I willed him not to speak—to remain a tall anonymous silhouette embodying the tomb's eternal penetrating power—as the soul of my flesh began rising between my legs, spreading the divine wings of an orgasm through my pelvis as his stone-stiff erection stabbed me over and over again relentlessly, sinking deep into my weeping pussy before pulling out again almost all the way, until I imagined that the pleasure of his full length rending me open would kill me as I started coming around it.

'Oh yes, Mary, come with me.'

I barely heard his voice as a soaring climax left my naked body lying across the cold stone; a willing sacrifice to the ecstasy dispersing all my thoughts in an upsurge of pure joy.

※※※※

Emerging from Ti's burial chamber, part of me concentrated on my footing, while the rest of me dwelled breathlessly on the things I had learned about myself clinging to the edge of a sarcophagus while being violently fucked from behind.

It was going to be hard to live with the knowledge that I was a lot kinkier than I had believed, judging from my morbid fantasy in the crypt that my helpless young body was being possessed by irresistible unseen forces embodied in Simon's forceful silhouette. I had imagined an Egyptologist would have sensitive, skilled hands (I had seen all those National Geographic specials in which archaeologists brushed dirt off long-buried artifacts with mind-numbing patience) but I had never suspected they would have such equally hard-digging erections that would help me unearth feelings and sensations I had not realized my emotions and my body were capable of.

Deep in languorous thoughts about the last timeless hour that would live in my memory forever, I collided with Simon when he suddenly stopped dead at the top of the stairs. Without turning around, he reached behind him, gripped one of my shoulders, and applied a pressure that indicated he wanted me to stay down in the tomb. Much as I had enjoyed everything he had done to me there, I was not willing to submit to this particular inexplicable desire of his, so I was relieved when he muttered, 'Too late' and completed his ascent up into the fresh night air with me following right behind him.

At first glance, I thought the three Egyptian men who had earlier delivered our hedonistic supplies had returned to take away the evidence of our decadence, but then I realized there were at least half-a-dozen native men crouched around the fire. As we emerged from the crypt, they stared at Simon and me as grimly as if we were actually rising from the dead, and their sober expressions made my light-headed sensual contentment feel so sinful I began to worry we had violated some sacred Moslem law by making love in a tomb. I sensed they all knew what had just taken place down in Ti's sacred resting place, and I was torn between feeling profoundly ashamed and elatedly wicked. Then I ceased being aware of anyone or anything else as a figure strode out of the mastaba like my best nightmare.

'Good evening,' my mysterious stranger from the bazaar said in a deep, quiet voice that carried effortlessly around the courtyard and seemed to echo in my very bones.

Tonight my handsome sheik from the perfume shop was wearing Western clothing that did a much better job of showing off his breathtakingly broad shoulders tapering down into narrow hips and long, strong legs. His full-sleeved white shirt was tucked into tight black pants, which in turn disappeared into knee-high black leather boots, and everything fit him so perfectly I found I could not fit anything else into my mind looking at him.

He strode right up to me as I stared at him with a relief that was mingled equally with disbelief, because this was the last place I had expected him to show up. Completely ignoring Simon's presence beside me, he reached down for one of my hands and holding it gently, raised it slowly to his lips. 'Allow me to introduce myself, Mary.'

In the shadows ebbing and flowing over his features like an amorphous tide controlled by the hissing fire, the scar beneath his mouth attracted me like the crescent moon with its sensually dangerous mystery. 'Sir Richard Gerald Ashley, at your service.'

'He's carrying a gun,' Carol suddenly announced in a tight voice.

I glanced over my shoulder, and saw my friend and Steve still huddled beneath a blanket, but apparently it wasn't just the cold they were protecting each other from now.

'It's a very small gun, just a toy, really,' Richard protested without taking his eyes off me or letting go of my hand. 'Very useful, however, against scorpions and,' he finally looked at Simon, 'other vermin.'

As if he had not heard or even seen him, Simon walked away in the direction of the fire, effectively abandoning me. The men who were crouched around the flames all leapt to their feet as he approached, but he simply strolled past them as if they too were invisible.

'Listen to me, Mary.' Richard slipped a heavy arm around my shoulders and drew me slightly away from everyone. 'I don't know what Simon has told you, but I'm sure it's not the truth, at least not all of it.'

There was an urgency below the surface of his calm voice that captured my attention even as I tried not to enjoy the weight of his arm too much, or the feel of his firm, muscular body against mine. 'So let me tell you what I know, Mary. I know your boyfriend is holding up the progress of Egyptology for his own selfish purposes—'

'He's not my boyfriend,' I interrupted him with what I felt was a very important fact.

He flashed me a smile that literally made me feel weak in the knees, which were already a little tired from my trudging across deep sand with a heavy backpack and from my recent erotic exercise down in the tomb. 'I'm glad to hear that, Mary, but you should never interrupt me.'

'I'm sorry.'

'Simon, the man whom I'm sure would very much like to be your boyfriend, is deliberately burying evidence that could throw immeasurable light on the field of Egyptology. He believes Imhotep's tomb is his to do with as he pleases, which I don't need to tell you is not the case whether he discovered it or not.'

'He doesn't believe that,' I argued even though in a sense I agreed with what he was saying. But I felt guilty about betraying Simon with my thoughts, so I reluctantly slipped out from beneath Richard's arm. It was more difficult pulling my hand out of his, however, like deliberately letting go of something I had always desired. 'Simon only wants to be able to finish his book on Saqqara without being—'

Dreams of Anubis

'Ah, so he has found the entrance. I was sure it wasn't just a rumor this time.'

'I didn't say...I...'

'Don't worry, love, you haven't betrayed him. I know about the photograph, and I would like to see it, if I may.'

'Why were you dressed like an Egyptian at the bazaar?'

This question helped me skirt the issue of the photograph, which would put me in the impossible position at the moment of choosing between him and Simon. I also wanted to know more about this man who felt so hauntingly familiar to my body even though there was no chance we had met before last night.

'Because I find it easier to mingle with the natives when dressed like one,' he replied, staring earnestly down into my eyes. He was standing as close as he possibly could to me, and I was letting him because I wanted him that close. 'The local culture is much more interesting when you truly open yourself to its unique pleasures,' he added softly.

I forced myself to take a step back, a little disconcerted by his penetrating regard and by the fact that I felt myself falling strangely against gravity up into his eyes. 'Is that how you found out I had the photograph,' I made an effort to organize my thoughts and continue the conversation so I wouldn't keep thinking about how good it had felt when his tongue was wordlessly circling my clitoris, 'because your disguise lets you in on all the good local gossip?'

My feelings were in turmoil. My brain wanted to mistrust him because Simon obviously didn't like him, and yet everything he said struck me as completely reasonable, not to mention the magnetic physical attraction I felt for him that made it almost impossible for me to think straight. I wondered if it was my body, so strangely and irresistibly drawn to his that was seducing my mind into believing whatever, and then another distressing possibility prompted me to demand, 'Did you have something to do with Steve's little accident? Were you trying to get a hold of—'

'I had nothing to do with whatever happened to Steve.' His mouth hardened and I suffered the impression that he was disappointed I had felt it necessary to ask him such a question. 'If I had wanted to steal the photograph, Mary, rest assured I would not have made such a mess of it.'

'I'm sorry,' I said quickly, 'I didn't mean to imply...I mean, I don't believe you're a thief, Richard, not at all.'

'Thank you.' While it lasted his smile made my heart feel wonderfully light. 'However, there are other interested, and much less ethical, parties than myself who would stop at nothing to claim such a momentous discovery for themselves. And also please remember, Mary, that it was Simon who started this little game. He was a fool to think he could keep such an important find a secret for very long.'

It hit me then that the man I had just made love to was not the man I was standing so close to now and had no desire to move away from. Perhaps Simon was a bit foolish, not just for thinking he could keep the discovery of Imhotep's tomb a secret, but because he had left me alone with an attractive, eloquent man whose low opinion of him was beginning to feel distressingly justified.

I looked behind me. Richard's native companions were squatting comfortably around the fire again talking amongst themselves, and Simon, I was shocked to discover, was sitting back against the mastaba wall comfortably wrapped in the blanket we had been sharing earlier. I couldn't believe it, and his complete detachment suddenly made me feel as if I were dreaming; it just didn't seem possible after everything we had done together down in Ti's burial chamber.

Richard followed my gaze. 'How do you suppose he would react if I made off with you, Mary? Would he fight me for you, I wonder? Shall we test him?' Before I could respond, he swept me off my feet into his arms. 'My poor love, you look exhausted. What you need is a nice soft bed.'

I opened my mouth to protest, and discovered the rest of me had absolutely no desire to do so.

He carried me back towards the fire, whispering, 'Let's see if you're more important to him than that precious photograph, shall we?' He raised his voice challengingly. 'Mr. Taylor, I'll make a bargain with you. I'll let you have Mary, for the moment, if you'll let me take a look at that photograph.'

'Sorry,' Simon's apology drifted amiably across the courtyard, 'but I don't have it.'

'I know. Mary has it, but considerate young woman that she is, she won't let me see it without your permission.'

Dreams of Anubis

Comfortable as I was in Richard's arms, the silence with which Simon greeted this proof of my loyalty made me squirm indignantly. How dare he put me in this position? It didn't matter that I was finding it quite stimulating…

'I don't respond to coercion, Sir Ashley,' Simon replied at last. 'You can wait along with everyone else for the discovery to become public. That's assuming, of course, there is a discovery worth mentioning and it's not just another pedestal.'

'Simon, aren't you going to tell him to put me down?!'

'Why don't you ask him to put you down yourself, Mary?'

This was not the point, and yet he did have a point, and I was so furious with him for undermining my self-esteem by treating me so nonchalantly after fucking me so passionately that I couldn't think straight. I had to show him just how much his indifferent attitude was hurting me, or at least would have been hurting me if I hadn't felt so good in Richard's arms.

'The photo is right over there, Sir Ashley,' I said politely, 'so if you'll kindly put me down I'll…hey, stop them!' Clearly understanding English better than they let on, Richard's native companions immediately leapt to their feet and converged on our supplies like a pack of starving dogs.

Simon finally showed some emotion as he too rose abruptly. 'Mary!' he exclaimed, the blanket hanging from his shoulders like a kingly cape. 'You lied to me.' He sounded stunned. 'You told me you didn't have the photo with you.'

'Simon, I…' I didn't know what to say.

'Bass!' Richard's thunderous command magically dispersed the cloud of white robes from around my possessions. 'Mary,' he set me down gently, 'I don't want them pawing at your things. Would you please be good enough to fetch the photograph for me yourself?'

'You're only going to look at it, Richard? You're not going to take it?'

'I give you my word.'

One of the Egyptians impatiently kicked a fallen log back into the blaze as I reflected on the dancing, potentially destructive flames for a long moment before finally walking over to my backpack, and slipping the photograph out from inside a zippered pocket. Then I counted to three and made a wild dash for the fire. Two of Richard's men attempted to intercept me, but I changed course and the sand cushioned my fall as with an eager hiss a flame licked the photograph painfully from of my fingertips. I watched the cartouche of Imhotep's tomb dissolve in a black wave, and then dozens of hands reached for me at once like a monstrous centipede landing on top of me.

'Get away from her!' Simon yelled.

'Mafish!' Sir Ashley's angry Arabic command was more effective. I was released at once, but the minute I got to my feet, Richard swept me up into the safety of his arms again even though they also felt dangerously good around me. 'That was beautifully dramatic of you, love. Still, I wish you hadn't done it. You've burned the only evidence of a potentially great discovery.'

He began walking towards the steps leading out of the mastaba's courtyard, his long stride unhindered by my weight. 'Nevertheless, the photograph is of no consequence anymore. The discovery will become public soon enough, and it has already led me to a far greater treasure.'

'Where the hell are you going with her?' Simon demanded, finally coming back to life. 'You can't kidnap an American citizen, Richard, put her down.'

'Who said anything about kidnapping her?' Sir Ashley replied without bothering to look back. 'She's coming with me quite willingly. Aren't you, Mary?'

'It won't work.' Simon sounded infuriatingly calm. 'I'm not telling you where the tomb is, so put her down or I'll have you arrested.'

'Arrested for what, for stealing her heart?' Richard started climbing the steps with me still cradled in his arms, forming the head of a procession of men that made me feel like a sacred offering, except that we were headed out of the mastaba where I was leaving a part of my heart in the form of a handsome Egyptologist I had just made passionate love with.

I craned my neck to look back down into the fire-lit courtyard, crying, 'Simon?'

'Don't be afraid, Mary,' he called up to me, 'he can't hurt you.'

'You're in much better hands now, love,' Richard assured me soberly.

It became so dark as we climbed towards the desert floor that all I could see were stars winking mischievously, or meaningfully, in his eyes, it was impossible to tell which. 'But you can't just take me!'

Dreams of Anubis

'I can't?' He sounded almost genuinely surprised that I would question is ability to do anything.

'No, you can't,' I insisted, yet I wasn't making the slightest effort to get away from him. In fact, I had my arms wrapped around his neck. I told myself I couldn't hope to fight him, so there was no point in doing so, but I knew this was a flimsy excuse for how happy he made me feel.

'I have no intention of letting you get away, Mary.'

I kept staring up the dark space where I knew his eyes were and at the stars burning in his gaze. They seemed to form hieroglyphic constellations my soul understood, and they told me he meant what he said.

'So...' I took a deep breath, 'you're going to hold on to me until Simon tells you where he found the entrance to Imhotep's tomb?' I was suddenly afraid that I was only a means to an end to him and that I was imagining everything else between us.

He did not answer as we reached level ground and I felt the dessert spread its majestic silence all around us.

'He won't tell you, Richard. He knows you can't keep me away from him. He won't tell you where the tomb is,' I insisted, more hurt than I cared to admit by the possibility that a major archeological discovery was all he was really interested in.

'Mary,' he lifted me up and set me down on a smooth, hard surface even my inexperienced bottom immediately realized was a saddle, 'don't you understand yet?' He helped me spread my legs and get one of them over the pommel so I was perched comfortably on the horse's back. 'It's you I'm after.'

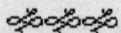

Despite the awe-inspiring beauty of a sky so full of stars it made me realize what I had been missing all my life living beneath the light pollution of a modern city, I was too confused and overwhelmed by recent events to really appreciate the sight. I was also scared of falling off the magnificent creature flexing its powerful muscles between my thighs. I had never ridden a horse before, and pounding at full gallop across the desert was a rough way to lose my equestrian virginity. I was very glad to have the white fence of

Richard's arms around me as I leaned back against his solid warmth and clung to the pommel for all I was worth.

I had no idea where he was taking me, all I knew was that with every muffled beat of the horse's hooves I was farther away from Simon and all the incredible feelings and sensations he had unearthed in my flesh and psyche deep in a tomb. Naturally, I hadn't expected him to give in to Richard and reveal the location of Imhotep's tomb, but I didn't see why he couldn't at least have tried to prevent another man from carrying me away right under his nose.

He should have done something! He should have done something! He should have done something!

The damning statement beat through my head in rhythm with the horse's hooves. All I could see were stars above me, and Richard's rippling sail-like sleeves around me. The cold wind keened in my ears and made my face feel as if it were carved out of stone even as all the muscular life supporting me kept the rest of me comfortably warm.

My friends back at the office in Boston would certainly think I was making it up if I told them I had been abducted on horseback and whisked across the Sahara by a beautiful armed Englishman. I couldn't even picture myself telling the tale, perhaps because I had absolutely no desire ever to return to the fluorescent sterility of my office in the Prudential Tower. Just thinking about it was ruining the adventure, so I put incredulous co-workers out of my mind and immersed myself in the tumultuous present, where multitudes of stars overhead were an audience focused entirely on me and my life, which from the moment I landed in Egypt started becoming truly interesting.

'Where are you taking me, Richard?' I cried over the roar of the wind. 'To your gilded tent in an oasis?'

He laughed at my little joke, and the vibration of his chest against my back blending with the horse's surging motion between my legs was quite stimulating. In fact, it was just a bit too stimulating. My pussy was feeling even more sensitive than usual after Simon's rampant strokes down in Ti's eternal home, and with my legs spread open across the horse's surging muscles, my labia was responding to the hard, relentless caress of the saddle in a highly debilitating way. Unable to get a grip on anything with my feet, I had no choice but to tighten my thighs around the saddle in order not to slip off as I held on to the pommel for dear life—which had the effect of bringing the wickedly arched front of the saddle directly into contact with my clitoris. The unyielding pressure of the hard leather vibrating directly between my thighs was uncomfortable one moment and intensely exciting the next, as I struggled to reconcile my mind's opinion that it would be dangerous to give in to the pleasure with my body's insidiously sweet insistence that ecstasy is welcome under any circumstances.

'Richard, are we almost there?' I cried.

'No, we have a ways to go yet.' He didn't need to shout over the wind; he responded directly in my ear, and his deep voice flowing through me on his warm breath stoked the delight smoldering between my legs. 'Aren't you enjoying the ride?'

'Oh yes, I'm enjoying it too much!'

He chuckled again, and once more the vibration of his hard body pressed against mine contributed to the hot havoc between my legs.

'Oh God,' I moaned, 'can't we stop for a minute?'

'No, we cannot,' he said, and flicked the reigns so the horse picked up its pace.

My grip tightened convulsively on the pommel, which had the effect of jamming it directly against my clit in a deliciously painful way.

'Why are you fighting it, Mary?' His quietly reasonable yet deeply seductive tone seemed to rise straight out of my own soul. 'Let yourself go.'

'I can't let go, I'll fall!'

'You know what I mean, Mary, just let yourself go.' A commanding edge entered his voice that mysteriously sharpened the delight cutting up through my pelvis. 'Do it, Mary, I want to feel you trembling with pleasure against me. I won't let you fall, trust me.'

I could no longer resist what was happening. The sight of the stars burning overhead was becoming wonderfully confused with the feel of my own smoldering blood cells as the promise of a climax ignited the haunting branches of my veins. Suddenly I couldn't understand why I was fighting the effects of the rhythmic pounding against my vulva, and as the pleasure ascended inside me, I lost my fear of falling because even though I couldn't explain it I trusted this man implicitly.

'Oh yes, Mary, I can feel how close you are…look, can you see them, directly ahead and just slightly to the right of us on the horizon?'

I looked, and the sight became confused with the pleasure peaking inside me.

'Come now, Mary…'

My body obeyed him, and yet I somehow managed to keep my eyes open during the orgasm's devastating throes so as not to lose sight of the three pyramids of Giza silhouetted on the horizon. For a few physically transcendent moments my heart beat faster than the horse's hooves, and as it fluttered back down to a deeply relaxed and contented pace, I watched the pyramids slowly growing and swallowing more and more stars with their haunting dimensions. The sight filled me with a sense of well being so profound that my brain, desperately fishing for words to describe it, failed utterly.

'Good girl,' Richard murmured in my ear, then he didn't speak again as we approached the only remaining wonders of the ancient world. Now that I had given into the erotic pressure of the saddle against my pussy, it ceased to bother me and I settled comfortably back against him, relaxing my grip on the pommel somewhat as I settled into the horse's rhythm instead of fighting it out of fear of falling.

When we finally reached the base of the smallest pyramid we slowed to a swift trot, and I could only admire the confident way Sir Ashley maneuvered the horse over the rocky terrain as I heard his native minions clattering less elegantly behind us. And as we rode beneath it, the great pyramid's shadow darkened my mind in a mystical way I find it hard to explain now. The feel of Richard's arms around me deepened into a timeless embrace in which I forgot his name, which I had only just learned anyway, and it was as though I even forgot what my own name was supposed to be because names didn't matter at all, they were superficial and temporary and what we felt when we were together was destined to last forever…

I jolted back into my own tired and bemused identity as Mary Fallon, legal secretary enjoying an unbelievably eventful vacation in Egypt, when the horse trotted casually to a stop.

Dreams of Anubis

Behind me, Richard dismounted, and I literally fell out of the saddle and down into his arms. After that, I have a vague memory of lights washing over my closed eyelids in warm waves accompanied by murmuring voices, and then of being laid across a wonderfully soft surface my entire being sank into gratefully.

Chapter Five

In the morning, when I awoke to my naked body lying in a king size bed, my sore muscles were too grateful to permit me to worry about it just yet. According to my body's cat-like perceptions, it was better to be lying on a soft mattress beneath clean cotton sheets than wrapped in a sand-filled blanket on the hard ground.

I opened my eyes, but I didn't move for a while; I just enjoyed lying there, going over everything I had experienced in the last twenty-four hours. I had backpacked across the desert, dragged a well-developed young man into a tomb, made love in a dark crypt and been whisked away on horse back by an English lord beneath a universe burgeoning with stars. To think I had worried about missing my workouts at the gym while I was on vacation! And those were just the last twenty-four hours; even more incredible things had happened to me since I arrived in the land of the pharaohs.

Tentatively, I raised my head from out of a bower of pillows, and found myself face to face with a smiling alabaster bust of one of Akhenanton's many daughters. She looked as happy as I realized I was feeling even though she would have had reasons to be concerned about her future, just as I did. She did not look at all worried about the fact that her father had thrown Egypt into chaos by replacing the worship of multiple gods with one Supreme Being. I, on the other hand, was trying not to worry about the fact that Richard's appearance in the mastaba last night had thrown my feelings into chaos by making it obvious I wasn't ready to devote myself to one man, not yet. I liked and admired Simon to no end, and my head said he was the perfect mate for me, yet the two times I had encountered Richard I felt as though every cell in my body was flung into

Dreams of Anubis

orbit around him through irresistible magnetic laws of attraction I could not explain away, much less ignore.

The quality of the silence in the room told me I was alone, so I sat up.

Sky-blue curtains hung over floor-length windows. The sun penetrated the fine material in a luminous haze through which the white silhouettes of eighteenth dynasty dancing girls were visible, their hips swaying gently in the breeze from a central air-conditioner. On the nightstand opposite the one occupied by one of the heretic pharaoh's daughters sat a lamp I recognized as a copy of one found in Tutankhamun's tomb. It was shaped like three lotus blossoms growing out of a central stem, and the almost translucent white alabaster was undoubtedly a breath-taking sight in a dark room when it was lit from within. And it was no lifeless museum copy either. I could tell from where the stone became slightly more opaque at the base that it was actually filled with oil. Apparently, the room was decorated in the New Kingdom style, which was lovely, but I preferred Old Kingdom purity and boldness of line. The artistic style of Egypt's earliest dynasties was hard and confident, an arousing balance of physical sensuality and metaphysical conviction. In other words, I was not going to let myself be girlishly impressed by Sir Richard Ashley's seductive accommodations.

After making use of the bathroom (which thankfully was completely modern) I examined the rest of my beautiful room with restless delight.

A gilded wooden chest sat at the foot of the bed. Every inch of it was carved with exquisitely colorful bas-reliefs also dating from the eighteenth dynasty, and still exhibiting some of the stylistic decadence instigated by Akhenaten even though the artist had ostensibly returned to the traditional style. It occurred to me that if I could find my clothes I could get dressed and leave, but I deliberately postponed looking for them. After all, Simon was probably still in the desert with Steve and Carol, not to mention that he had done nothing to prevent Richard from literally riding away with me, so he deserved to worry about me a little. Besides, I couldn't find a phone in the room, which meant there was no way I could call him even if I knew where to reach him. Apart from the bed, there wasn't a single modern object; even the nightstands were gilded shrines. There were two beautiful chairs made of a dark, gold-edged wood, their backs carved into figures of eternity—a handsome man with one leg bent beneath him in a deep genuflection and a large ankh, symbol of life, hanging from one of his outstretched arms. He was smiling peacefully despite the fact that he was clutching a snake in each hand, the two serpents rising stiffly on either side of him and curving above him to rest their heads on the solar and lunar discs.

After I had finished taking an appreciative inventory of my room, I began waking up to my situation. I couldn't be sure exactly what Simon's feelings were for me. There was no doubt about the fact that we had shared intense pleasure down in an ancient burial chamber, but sexual chemistry did not a relationship make, and in three weeks I was supposedly flying back to the States. Then there was the disconcerting knowledge that it was probably Richard who had undressed me last night, and I suspected my exhausted body had innocently enjoyed his warm caresses as he pulled off my shirt, then my shorts and panties...

This was the thought I had been avoiding since I woke up. How could I possibly have slept through a man carrying me up to his room, laying me on a bed and taking off all my clothes? It was true I had had an exhausting day and night, but I had never been so tired that I could sleep through the experience of someone handling my body. No matter how tired and sleepy I was, or how gentle he had been, I should have felt what Richard was doing to me and been aware of what was happening. I had not behaved in such a relaxed and unconsciously trusting fashion with another person since I was a baby and my father rocked me in his arms before laying me in my cradle, and I could not even begin to understand how it had happened to me now as a grown woman with an almost complete stranger.

I got back into bed, taking refuge from my thoughts—which were both strangely disturbing and exciting—inside the sheets' protective cocoon. My brain felt sluggish as a caterpillar heavy with the imminent glory of its metamorphosis into a winged being no longer subject to earthly laws. Whether they wanted to or not, certain caterpillars were meant to transcend their nature, and I sensed something akin to this happening inside Mary Fallon. The change inside me had begun the other night in the heart of the Kahn el-Khalili bazaar when a robed man I recognized before I even saw his face entered a perfume shop. I couldn't put my finger on the feelings Richard had awoken in my heart,

Dreams of Anubis

but they were there, and they were growing. The vivid sensual dream I had had when napping in a mastaba haunted me like a butterfly's wings in which part of me sensed a pattern that kept eluding my rational waking mind. Nevertheless, as I lay in bed in that modern hotel room decorated with ancient art, I became aware of the subtle but somehow undeniable fact that a mysterious new sense was blooming inside me...

Or maybe it was just the opposite, maybe I was losing my senses, abandoning myself to wanton excess here in this exotic land, breaking out of my snowy New England cocoon and flitting from man to man just like a wild butterfly. Perhaps Simon was right and I was sexually out of control.

But I didn't want to think about the bastard who had not lifted a finger to help me last night. How could he let another man carry away a woman he had just made passionate love to in a tomb? His behavior was so incomprehensible that I flung the sheets off me angrily and got out of bed again.

I had to wrestle with two dancing girls to get the curtains open.

My breath caught. The city of Cairo stretched out below me as far as my eyes could see, the domed spires of mosques, delicate and colorful as the distended throats of male frogs showing off, lending a unique quality to the urban sprawl. And even through the glass I could hear the faint insect-like drone of millions of people and terrible traffic.

The much louder sound of the doorknob being turned made me jump. For an instant I considered draping a curtain around me, but whoever was on the other side of the door paused just long enough to give me time to run back to the bed, and pull the sheets up over my chest as I sat up against the headboard.

Sir Richard Gerald Ashley entered the room wearing a smile on his lips that tripped up my heartbeats because his mouth looked so much like the one on the handsome figure of eternity.

'Good morning, my lady,' he said cheerfully, as he casually seated himself on the edge of the bed facing me. He was wearing a black silk ankle-length robe tied at the waist. The portion of his chest I could see was covered with a sparse bush slightly darker than his long hair, which he had not bothered to pull back in a ponytail yet, and its soft flow behind and over his shoulders made them look even stronger and broader.

'Good morning,' I replied sulkily, trying to hide how much his appearance affected me by deliberately refusing to call him 'my lord'.

His smile vanished as he reached for me abruptly and yanked the bed sheet out of my grasp. 'So beautiful,' he murmured, gazing intently at my naked breasts. 'Just as I always imagined them.'

I raised the sheet defiantly back up to my chin. 'It isn't a good morning.'

'And why is that, dear?'

'You know why.' I stared back at him helplessly.

'Because I spared you a cold and uncomfortable night in a tomb with a man who doesn't really care for you?'

'Whether he does or not,' the casual way he stabbed me with this statement seriously hurt, but I kept my voice under control, 'I shouldn't be here right now and you know it, so I'm not going to argue with you, Richard.'

'Excellent, then we can have breakfast. I imagine you must be starving.' He rose. 'There's a dress in the closet. You may put it on if you like, although I would be delighted if you didn't. I'll be back in a minute.' He left.

The dress he referred to was long and sleeveless and made of nearly transparent white linen. I had just finished slipping it on when he returned leaving the door open behind him so two native men could wheel in a table laden with silver serving platters. They kept their eyes lowered, careful not to look at me as they positioned the table, and then set the two chairs carved with figures of eternity at each end. There was a crisp flutter of robes as they hurried out of the room, closing the door very quietly behind them.

'Mary, if you please.' Richard pulled one of the chairs out for me, his smile deepening as he gazed at me with an appreciation that was at once relaxed and possessive.

Beneath his regard my nipples got so hard they threatened to poke through the linen, which revealed my rosy aureoles like flowers blooming beneath a soft morning mist. Resisting the urge to cross my arms over my breasts, which would have contributed to my Egyptian appearance, I seated myself with all the slow,

Dreams of Anubis

unhurried dignity of an ancient queen. 'I normally have a light breakfast,' I informed him somewhat haughtily.

'But you're not living your normal life at the moment, are you,' he pointed out, taking his place across from me. He then uncovered the platters one by one, and watching him casually set the silver lids down on the carpet, I thought of a god creating a domed city. He had ordered a traditional breakfast, and it took all my self-control not to look too interested as my sense of smell was assaulted by the sinfully delicious aroma of eggs over-easy accompanied by thick slices of bacon, hash browns and French bread still hot from the oven. There were little porcelain containers of butter and strawberry preserves, a glass pitcher of orange juice, a pot of coffee, what looked like real heavy cream, and a bowl of sugar cubes I thought would make ideal building blocks for an ant pyramid.

'Eat up, Mary you don't have to pretend with me.'

'What do you mean by that?'

'I mean you don't have to feign a lady-like appetite. I respect all your hungers, and the more intense they are, the better.'

I couldn't help but smile at this remark as I began filling my plate with gusto, because the truth is, I was starving.

'Coffee?' he inquired.

'Yes, please. But I'm surprised you didn't order tea, being a Brit.'

'Personally, I prefer coffee.'

'I'm sorry, I should have known there wasn't anything trite about you, Richard.'

'Thank you, Mary, that's very perceptive of you.'

'You sound surprised.'

'Not at all, on the contrary, it's to be expected.'

I had to swallow a decadent mouthful of runny egg yolks before repeating, 'Expected? How can you expect anything from me, Richard? You don't even know me.'

'I know you very well, Mary.'

'But we've only met twice,' I reminded him, trying not to think about how well we had gotten to know each other the first time in the bazaar, but that had only been our bodies.

'Are you sure about that, Mary?' he asked quietly, gazing into my eyes over the gilded horizon of his porcelain coffee cup.

I looked away. 'You forgot to include a hairbrush in your stage props.' I deflected his profound question with a sarcastic observation, and immediately hated myself for it. Yet part of me was overwhelmed by how fast everything was happening and how intense it was. 'Or is it that I don't need a hairbrush because you want me to shave my head like an ancient Egyptian noble woman and wear a wig?'

'You can have—'

'Aha! You were about to say "you can have anything you desire", weren't you, which would be very disappointingly trite of you, Richard.'

'No, I wasn't about to say that,' he replied placidly, and sipped his coffee before continuing. 'I was about to say that you can have only what it pleases me to give you.'

'Oh.' I picked up my knife and started buttering my bread to hide how much I liked the sound of that. 'Well then, my lord, can I please have a toothbrush and some dental floss as well?'

'Certainly, my lady, especially if they will encourage you to smile more. You really are incredibly beautiful when you smile.'

'Unfortunately, your actions don't usually prompt me to smile, Richard.'

'But they have made you cry out with pleasure,' he reminded me.

I looked away shyly.

'If my actions do not make you smile, Mary, it's because you take them the wrong way. There's more than one way to perceive the same thing, and then there's a level of perception above all others that captures the full picture.'

'Like ancient Egyptian wall paintings.' I looked at him again eagerly.

'Exactly. And what does that tell you?'

'It tells me that intuition, inspiration, is the key, maybe the only key, to a higher level of perception.'

'Very good.' He set his empty cup down. 'So, forget for a moment what your brain tells you about me as a result of certain circumstances involving an arrogant Egyptologist and other distracting, but ultimately irrelevant, factors. What does your much more inspired intuitive sense say about me, Mary?'

Dreams of Anubis

I wiped my lips with the cloth napkin, my eyes fixed on the inverted pyramid of chest visible between the nocturnal folds of his robe. 'It tells me…'

'Go on, love, I know how you feel, I just want to hear you say it…you have to say it in order to fully realize it and accept it.'

'But that's just it,' I braced myself by looking into his eyes, 'I don't know what I feel.'

'Yes, you do, you just don't know what to think about what you feel, but we always know how we feel.'

'That's true.' I glanced across the room at the lovely face of Akhenaten's daughter. Whatever had happened to her in life, her soft, secret smile afforded me a glimpse into a dimension of being transcending every possible concern. Her smile was the visible expression of the absolute faith she had in her eternal nature, which made her perfectly comfortable with her body since her true self did not share in its limitations only in its pleasures.

'I feel like I know you, Richard,' I stated matter-of-factly, meeting his intensely serious and beautiful eyes again. 'My body knows you somehow. I just want to fall into your arms every time I see you!'

※※※

An hour later, after I had brushed my teeth, enjoyed a long hot shower, brushed my hair until it was sleek and straight as an ancient Egyptian queen's, dabbed lotus oil on the back of my wrists and applied genuine black kohl to my eyelids, I felt ready for anything.

The girl gazing back at me from the mirror could easily have lived five thousand years ago. She was beautiful and intelligent, deeply spiritual yet also intensely sensual, and she had equal rights with men under the law…well, to a certain extent anyway. Even though she could own property, an ancient Egyptian woman could also be property, meaning a man was only allowed one wife, but he could have as many concubines as he could afford. Nevertheless, it had taken centuries for women to be treated with the same respect they had enjoyed in the Egypt of the pharaohs.

Cat's Collar - Three Erotic Romances

I spent a little more time than was necessary in the small bathroom's shrine to the pleasures of the flesh. I was avoiding the conversation Richard had interrupted after my passionate confession by stating that we would continue it later after I had refreshed myself. I knew whatever he said would constitute a devastating assault on all my psychological defenses, and despite how irresistibly drawn I was to him part of me was still compelled to mistrust him because Simon did. Carol's boss was a down-to-earth scientist who had worked hard to get where he was. Sir Richard Ashley had probably been born with a silver spoon in his mouth with which he fed himself whatever fantasies pleased him. The suspicion gnawed at me that maybe he believed his soul had been around since the beginning of time because being wealthy he had too much time on his hands and didn't know what to do with himself in the present. Yet I was assuming a lot; he could also have made his own fortune. Not to mention that when I looked into his eyes the last thing I saw was a spoiled and deluded man—what and who I saw actually took my breath away.

He was waiting for me when I finally opened the bathroom door, pausing shyly on the threshold. The beautiful objects before me might have belonged to me thousands of years ago, and I suffered a feeling akin to déjà vu but much more powerful. It was as if this room were a tomb I had never left and my life back in Boston was only a dream I was having while I waited; waited to come alive again as who I really was.

'Mary,' Richard whispered, and it hit me that Simon would be content with my mind and my body but that this man was after my very soul.

He looked enthroned where he sat in one of the 'eternity' chairs. He had placed it in front of the gently swaying dancing girls, and positioned the other chair facing his at a slight angle. I got the impression he was granting me an audience, and it suddenly made me acutely aware of my barefoot and unadorned state. I was dressed like a servant or a very poor man's concubine without shoes or jewelry, yet this humiliating fancy was wiped out of my mind by the look in his eyes as I approached him. My skin was still slightly damp from the shower, and judging from his expression the fine linen clung to my body in all the right places. My nipples were standing at attention again, and there was nothing I could do about the way the dress got caught between my thighs as I walked, making me vulnerably aware of my labia's soft, slick lips as I seated myself. I gripped the chair's gilded arms and planted my feet side-by-side on the carpet, very conscious of the fact that I would have looked just like an Egyptian statue if I had bothered to smile.

'Since you have forbidden me to express any trite sentiments, Mary, I will not tell you again how beautiful you look.' The sash holding his robe closed had loosened somewhat and exposed more of his chest. 'You are an exceedingly rare vintage, Mary. I saw it in your eyes the other night at the bazaar. I've learned to glimpse a woman's soul in her eyes the way I judge a wine by the depth of its color,' his gaze traveled slowly down my figure, 'and by its legs.' He smiled softly as he looked at my face again. 'Your soul has been around for a long time, Mary, aging through wooden coffins the way a fine wine matures in oak barrels, and I have no intention of letting your intoxicating power go to waste.'

'I like that metaphor,' I replied guardedly. 'Or is it an analogy?'

'It was a compliment.'

I couldn't resist returning his smile. 'And not at all trite,' I observed.

'How much do you know about ancient Egypt?' he asked me abruptly.

'How much do you know, Richard?'

'A great deal. Are you familiar with the term Winged Sandals?'

'Aren't they what Hermes wore? But that's Greek mythology.'

'Full of entertaining stories, but a pathetic excuse for a religion, don't you think?'

'Absolutely.'

'Winged Sandals, Mary, were worn by the priests and priestesses of Anubis, although not literally, of course, it was simply the title given to people who possessed the ability to leave their bodies.'

'Really?'

'Really.' He did a good job of imitating my blunt American exclamation. 'It referred specifically to their ability to dream true dreams.'

'What do you mean by true dreams?' I was interested against my will, and tempted to tell him about the dream I had had while taking a nap in a mastaba, but I stopped myself. I didn't want to make this too easy for him. I wanted him to do his best to convince me of something my heart was beginning to believe even while my brain kept struggling to put it into words.

'Let's just say the priests and priestesses of Anubis were able to meet with each other on another plane of existence, or another frequency of being, if you prefer more modern terms. It's incorrect, however, to call it an out-of-body experience, because in reality we possess several bodies composed of varying degrees and concentrations of energy. The soul is as much a body as our flesh-and-blood vehicle, only it is much more sensual and powerful, to put it as simply as possible.'

'So, what you're saying is that the priests and priestesses of Anubis met on another frequency of being where everything is as fluid as it is in our dreams?'

'With the difference, Mary, that they were able to control what happened to them there. It was often their duty to help people whose unconscious fears manifested in unsavory ways while they were asleep, a time when even the most unimaginative human being becomes an infinitely creative artist. Whether they remember their dreams or not, everyone has an active nightlife.'

'You mean these priests and priestesses would enter other people's dreams?'

'They would meet them there. Yes.'

'And meet each other there too?'

'Yes. Imagine the possibilities.'

I was silent for a moment as I did so.

The sash of his robe came undone as he brought his left ankle up to rest on his right knee, and even though knew I was staring shamelessly, I couldn't raise my eyes from what I could now see hanging between his thighs.

'Is something wrong, love?'

'For Christ's Sake, Richard, I can see...you know.' I looked over at Akhenaten's daughter to avoid staring at the rather insultingly relaxed part of his anatomy he was deliberately exposing to me.

'The hypocrisy of our so-called normal social relationships is ridiculous, Mary. People have to learn to be more honest with each other. Does it really bother you that you can see my penis?'

Dreams of Anubis

'Yes, it does.' I stared indignantly into his eyes.

'Why?'

'Because!'

'That's not an answer.'

'Because it's not polite, Richard.'

'And why is that?'

'Oh, stop it, you know perfectly well it's not acceptable normal behavior.'

'I rarely find normal behavior acceptable in any sense.'

'Granted, but perfect honesty is a dangerous policy, Richard. We can't just do or say whatever we please if it's going to hurt someone else.'

'And how am I hurting you by just sitting here? Is there something about the male sexual organs you find offensive?' Leaning back in his 'throne' he uncrossed his legs and stretched them out before him. The robe got caught between them and almost fully revealed one of his strong thighs.

'It's not right,' I argued tightly, even though his beautifully large and shapely organ was no longer visible.

'You didn't answer my question.'

'No, there's nothing about the male sexual organs I find offensive.'

'Then is it my penis in particular that makes you uncomfortable, or that you didn't like the look of for some reason?'

'Of course not, it's beautiful…I mean…'

He gave me that breathtaking smile of his again. 'I'm actually doing you an honor by letting you see my most private parts, Mary. I want you to see them.' He lowered his voice. 'I want to feel your eyes caressing me. Our sexuality is a perfectly natural—'

'Now that's trite.'

He frowned slightly. 'Nothing could be more trite than Simon's behavior last night. He got what he wanted, and then…' He shrugged. There was no need for him to say more. 'First of all,' he went on after what for me was a painfully awkward moment, 'you should know that what you and your friends were doing in Ti's mastaba is illegal. I don't know who Simon had to bribe to get permission, but obviously camping out in a national treasure is against the law. Smoke from the fire you built in the courtyard can damage the paintings, and so on. Simon must be friendly with some rather corrupt members of the Antiquities Department to have gotten away with it. He obviously wanted to impress you. Either that or he has a kinky streak and prefers cold crypts to comfortable hotel rooms—No, don't say anything yet, please let me finish first. God knows I have nothing against kinky streaks, but I don't think one should be allowed to risk damaging priceless works of art just to indulge in them. Secondly, I didn't threaten anyone with a gun. Your friend observed one on my person and made unwarranted assumptions that I was going to use it to intimidate either Simon or Steve into revealing the location of the mastaba. Thirdly, I told you I had no intention of stealing the photograph, and I meant it. However, you denied me the chance to keep my word by burning it first. There, I trust you're a little less confused now about what happened. I wanted to give you the chance to correct the mistake I feel you're making by becoming involved with a man whose methods and morals are extremely questionable. I also wished to get to know you better, and I'm sorry if I misread your feelings last night. I sensed it was your desire to come with me. You're free to leave at anytime if that's what you wish.'

'It's not what I wish,' I murmured, staring down at my lap.

'I know it's not,' he said gently. 'But I get the feeling you need more time to think about things. I have some business to take care of. I can only hope you'll still be here when I get back, Mary. I'm sure you will be.'

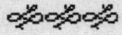

Richard left me alone again to ponder his words. It was wise of him, for the more I thought about what he had said, the more the handsome Egyptologist shrank in my esteem. I assumed I was in a suite at the Mina House hotel where my host had done a little redecorating with reproductions of ancient Egyptian pieces worth a small fortune in themselves. His Victorian ancestors had probably started an illegal collection of Egyptian antiquities. Simon might have corrupt connections, but Richard had enough money to be emotionally corrupt in every sense.

Dreams of Anubis

Lying despondently across the bed, I began to understand what it felt like to be a royal mummy in her lovely tomb. I couldn't have been more paralyzed if I had been bound from head to toe in resin-dipped strips of cloth.

Most of me longed to stay with Richard and explore the mystical connection he was obviously implying we had, but another part of me wanted to return to Simon and our very real promising relationship. My tired muscles were also appreciating just relaxing for a while. Despite the recurring questions that seemed to be all the royal embalmers had left of my brain—Does Simon really care about me? Can I trust Richard even though he's decadently rich and I know nothing about him?—I dozed off.

I must have slept for a long time. When I woke, I sensed the day drawing to a close sooner than I had expected as the room swiftly darkened.

I discovered only the bathroom was wired up to the twenty-first century when I got up and tried to find a light switch, which explained the oil in the alabaster lamp and the black box of matches I discovered lying behind it. I couldn't find a papyrus with instructions on how to light it, but it turned out I didn't need one. The matches were long and the wicks floating in the dark oil sparked eagerly to life. The princess's smile also came hauntingly to life in the flickering illumination, her alabaster skin pale as a ghost's. The lotus lamp shone more and more beautifully as the shadows deepened around it, and gazing at it, I began seeing the lamp as a symbol of my own stubbornly positive heart surrounded by all the doubts and fears inevitably cast by the troubled world in which I lived.

Who did Richard think he was anyway? If I wanted to make a mistake by getting involved with Simon—and so far it had been quite a stimulating error—it was my own damn business. Sir Ashley wasn't my father, and he couldn't justify his interference in my personal life by saying he was my friend, either. We had only met twice, for Christ's sake!

Seated on the edge of the bed, I glanced down at my hands clenched tightly in my lap, and suddenly I knew beyond a shadow of a doubt that I was somewhere else. I was someone else as for a subliminal instant the electrical synapses in my brain rearranged themselves and my pulse flew out of the branches of Mary Fallon's veins before fluttering back down into a whole other self.

My back straightened into the regal spine of a woman who knows time is circular because her own blood cells are the nature of time itself, and when the bedroom door opened suddenly, I rose and ran joyfully into the arms of the man who entered the room.

'Mary!' he whispered. 'I knew you would feel it, I knew it.' He stroked my hair. 'My beautiful one.'

His caress made my brain feel like a stone carried away on feelings too deep for words. It was a long moment before I reluctantly remembered that I was clinging to a rich Englishman, not an ancient priest of Anubis, and my arms slipped sadly from around him. I saw that his broad shoulders were set off by a short-sleeved white shirt, his black pants merged with the darkness, and his belt buckle glinted like fangs as he drew me towards the bed. 'How do you feel?' he asked gently.

'Stunned…I mean, I've had déjà vu before, but that was…my God!'

'Yes, I know, it's me, Nefermun,' he whispered, his breath warm against my temple, 'don't you feel it?'

'Yes.'

His strong arm around my shoulders inexorable as the law of gravity, I sat down on the edge of the bed again. He stood facing me, and I watched in a contented trance as he unbuckled his belt and unzipped his pants.

'These are a lot harder to get out of than a linen loincloth,' he remarked, and I heard myself laugh quietly with him. 'Remember your dream, Mary?'

I looked up at his face, and the firm shadows of his features softly carved by the lotus lamp seemed to fill all the empty spaces inside me.

'Yes, I remember,' I said, and reached up with both hands so he could cradle the sacred gift of his penis in my cupped palms as he pulled it out of his pants. He was only partially erect, which gave me a chance to savor the warm tenderness of his smooth, circumcised skin over the unyielding strength of his stiffening length. Remembering the drop of semen that had glistened from the rift in his head and reflected the rising stars in my dream, I grasped the base of his shaft boldly with one hand, relishing how rigid it already was in my grasp. The elastic of his underwear was shoving his balls directly up beneath his cock, and I lifted it up out of my way to lick the delicate fullness of his scrotum, noticing with appreciation that it was shaved. I heard both surprise and pleasure in his moan, and deeply gratified by the sound, I immediately slid his erection into my mouth, sucking on his head for a second to moisten my lips and make it easier to slip their tight ring down his full length.

'Oh Mary,' he whispered.

I sensed him deliberately resist the urge to take hold of my head with his hands. Instead he kept his arms relaxed at his sides as his penis grew even harder against my soft tongue. I remembered my dream and the way I had caressed my lover's head with the back of my throat, a skill no man had inspired me to develop in this life until now, for no other cock had ever tasted so good to me. The flavor of his semen was just right, as though it had been made especially for my tongue and taste buds. So many times in the past the flavor of a man's bodily juices had deterred me from wanting to please him this way for too long, but Richard's pre-cum was the mysterious foam on the intoxicating pleasure I took in swallowing his erection whole over and over again. Every time the bulbous tip of his rigid shaft sank down towards my virgin neck, the satisfaction I experienced in burying all of him inside me was much greater than the slight discomfort.

'Oh yes, you do remember, Mary.' His voice was as soft as his cock was hard.

I moaned in disappointment as he stepped back, sliding out of my devoted mouth. He shoved his pants and underwear down his legs, then just stood there looking at me.

Without even thinking, I sank to my knees before him, pulling off the black leather sandals he was wearing before tugging his pants all the way off him. I didn't just toss them aside; I laid them carefully down beside his sandals. Even though they were not a ritually blessed loincloth, they still belonged to him and therefore deserved my respect as symbols of the flesh his soul had chosen to wear in this world. Then, I stood before him and caressed the white shirt up his chest, savoring the complimentary contrasts of his tender flesh and the hard muscles beneath it. His skin was warm beneath the crisp coolness of his chest hair, which was just enough to give him all the exciting feel of a man without interfering with my kiss as I planted my mouth between the gentle swell of his pecs.

I felt his heart beat beneath my lips, then he finished the job of pulling his shirt up over his head. Before he could toss it away, I took it from him and spread it neatly over his pants. He was completely naked now, and I seated myself on the edge of the bed again to take him in. As with his features, the proportions of his body struck a chord of perfection deep inside me. His broad shoulders and chest tapered down to an ideally slender waist and hips supported by strong, long legs that were just the right pedestal for the crowning glory of his fully erect penis.

'You're so beautiful,' I told him.

'Now it's your turn to take off your dress and show yourself to me, Mary.'

I obeyed him gladly, enjoying the caress of the delicate material as I pulled it up over my head. I draped it beside his clothes on the floor, and then stood at once proudly and shyly before him. He had already seen my naked sex close up at the bazaar, but this was the first time I felt the warm touch of his eyes on my breasts, and all the rest of me.

'You are even more beautiful,' he said. 'Lie back across the bed, my love.'

My love…the words seemed to give me a delicious shove across the firm mattress and make it easy for me to get comfortable against the pillows. He joined me on the bed by crawling onto it on all fours like a sleek, powerful animal; a jackal with a long black snout and sharp, gilded ears—

—I cry out in terror, and then whimper in intensely confused relief when instead of sharp teeth sinking into my skin I see a man's ringed hands gently grasp my ankles and spread my legs. It is a Priest of Anubis kneeling between my thighs, and his erection promises me as much pleasure as I can bear. Then I look up past his broad shoulders and see his shaved skull gleaming in the lamplight.

'E'Ahmose!' I sigh.

'Nefermun.'

He spreads his body over mine without letting our skins touch, the strong columns of his arms rising on either side of my breasts as he gazes down at my face.

I grasp his cock like a dagger in my hand and arch my back, lifting my hips off the bed, urgently begging him to stab me with his full, rending length.

'No,' he says firmly.

Dreams of Anubis

I let go of his beautiful rod knowing I have done wrong, that it is not my place to force his entry into my achingly empty passage. He will determine the moment and the pace of the penetration knowing that the longer he makes me wait the more receptively open I become to him and all his desires. So I distract myself by caressing his shoulders and breathing in the scent of his warm skin, a stimulating combination of maleness and the oils he uses to shave, as well as to anoint his skin when serving the god in the sacred heart of the temple only he is allowed to enter. And like the divine altar, the space between my legs is always mysteriously burning for him, especially when he is inside me and stoking my need for him almost unbearably.

'Oh yes,' I breathe, 'thank you, my lord!' as he finally grants the moist lips of my opening the promising kiss of his head. But then he seems content to remain planted there, enjoying the desperately juicing embrace of the entrance to my flesh.

'Oh E'Ahmose, you are being very cruel tonight.'

I fling my arms up over my head so as not to grasp the firm cheeks of his ass and push his fleshly column down to the very foundations of my being.

'And you are enjoying it, my love,' he lets me have a teasing bit more of his erection, 'as you enjoy everything I do to you.'

'Please, my lord,' I beg, writhing my hips against the leopard-skin and subjecting myself to the sweet torture of his rampant cock stuffing the mouth of my hole and stirring up my lust for his full length even more.

'Stop that, Nefermun,' he chides me sternly, but even in the dark chamber I can see the smile in his eyes, 'or I shall make you wait until the next full moon to feel the ray of my love inside you.'

'I can only hope my lord will not be so cruel to his devoted consort and priestess.'

'Your hopes and dreams are as dear to my heart, Nefermun, as the silent voice of the god, so I will give you what you want now, and ask only that you savor the blessing of our union without moving, so that you can fully experience your innermost self merging with mine on every level.'

'Yes, my lord,' I whisper, but then almost forget my promise when he begins sinking inside me and the longed for pleasure scatters my thoughts like so many grains of wheat drifting away on an ever-deepening fulfillment.

'Open your eyes, Nefermun and look into mine.'

I obey him, and the ecstasy becomes even more profoundly intense when his penetrating stare merges with the experience of his erection slowly stabbing me. When he is fully submerged between my thighs, he bends his arms and opens his mouth over mine, thrusting his tongue between my lips in time with his body beginning to beat against me, so that it is all I can do to consciously observe the overwhelming sensation of our becoming one with each other.

I wrap my arms around his chest and pull him down on top of me, loving the powerful weight of his body and the feel of his warm, tender skin over the implacable heart of his manhood pumping between my legs.

I gasp when the feel of long hair flowing down his back surprises me.

'Don't speak!' His whisper is timeless as the wind echoing through the ages in the spiraling shell of my ear.

I don't feel the need to understand what is happening. His driving energy is all I care about as my awareness of everything becomes almost wholly concentrated in my sex. My thoughts are replaced by the sensation of my vaginal muscles contracting and expanding around him in the most intimate caress possible, enabling me to thoroughly experience the full length and breadth of his cock breaching my tight yet welcomingly wet depths. And every time I tighten my inner muscles the exercise tugs on my clitoris, sensitizing it to the rhythmic friction of his thrusts opening me up. His erection just barely brushes my glowing seed as he digs deep and hard into my cleft, determined to wrest the earth-shattering bloom of a mutual climax from our flesh. I can feel my body beginning an ascent that is exactly the same even though every time I close and open my eyes I see a different room around us and feel a different surface beneath us.

He pulls out of me abruptly. 'Turn around,' he commands.

Without hesitation I roll over on the soft skin and gladly offer this virile priest the smoldering shrine of my pussy from behind. Kneeling and spreading my legs, I arch my back as deeply as possible, thrusting my ass up into his hands so he can brace himself by clutching my soft cheeks as he plunges back inside me. But when I bury my face in the animal skin, breathlessly accepting his

Dreams of Anubis

aggressive thrusts, it is Richard's voice I hear behind me, 'Oh yes, Mary…yes…' for in this position his cock slides effortlessly into my slick passage all the way down to his balls. Long hair or a smoothly shaved skull, a thin mouth or full lips, it doesn't matter. The only thing that matters is how good it feels as he channels all his strength into possessing me, until his erection finds the divine core of ecstasy buried deep in our flesh by the grace of the gods and that only he has the power to access for both of us. 'Come with me!' he commands.

I reach down beneath me, find the swollen bud of my clitoris and obey him instantly, my cries of pleasure harmonizing with his groans as his cock pulses deep between my thighs and suffuses my belly with the uniquely fulfilling warmth of his cum.

He remained buried inside me for a long moment after the wave of our pleasure ebbed, leaving us breathing hard on the soft shore of the bed, on which the sensual animal skin had been replaced by sterile white sheets. The great loss I experienced as he finally pulled out was assuaged by the knowledge that I would feel him inside me again. I knew now that we had been meant to come together like this for longer than I could literally remember, and I could only hope we would be able to continue feeling each other like this forever.

'Come here,' he said tenderly.

I sat up, and found myself falling languidly and comfortably into his arms as he lay back against the pillows, cradling my head comfortably on his shoulder. 'Tell me what you just felt, Mary, and what you saw.'

'It was only my imagination, I'm sure,' I mumbled, loving the sensation of his warm, strong body lying pressed against mine. 'I have a very vivid imagination!'

'I'm sure you do, but it wasn't your imagination this time.' He used the firm but gentle tone of an adult addressing an uncertain child. 'Now tell me what you believe you only imagined.'

'I saw you, and a man who wasn't you, and yet it was you, he just didn't look like you do now.' I knew my grammar was hopelessly sloppy, but that seemed irrelevant in light of what I was trying to describe. 'His head was shaved and he was a priest, a priest of Anubis because I saw a jackal…'

'Yes,' he whispered, 'a wearer of the Winged Sandals.' Sliding lower on the bed, he turned on his side to face me, his arms coming around me as his eyes looked straight into mine. Tiny golden lotus blossoms floated in his irises, reflecting the alabaster lamp. 'And in the past he found you the same way I found you now.'

'And how did you find me now?' I asked softly, knowing the answer but scarcely believing it.

'I found you through dreams, my love.'

'You mean you're psychic?'

'I am when I'm dreaming. We all are, we just don't remember it, usually.'

The golden lotuses floating in his dark stare affected my blood like moons stirring up my desires again in a way I had thought possible only in dreams. 'Richard…' There was so much I wanted to ask him I found I couldn't put a single question into words.

'Yes?'

'Do you love me?'

'You know I do,' he planted his lips against mine, 'Nefer-marymun.'

Chapter Six

I helped my priest of Anubis put his clothes back on as best I could. He had to handle his tight black pants, but I found the ritual of assisting him in donning his clothes again strangely pleasurable and relaxing. The act helped create a bridge between the devastating pleasure we had just experienced together, and whatever was to come next. I was at once relieved and slightly disappointed that the only thing he had planned for the moment was dinner. After he watched me slip back into my dress, he took my hand and led me out of the tomb-like room into his own adjoining suite. The lotus lamp we left burning behind us was lovely, but there's nothing like electricity to steady the nerves, and my mystically shadowed brain needed all the light it could get.

'Are we eating downstairs in the dining room?' I ventured to ask, but since he had not provided me with a less revealing garment, I rather doubted it.

'A dining room crowded with tourists is hardly the place to talk about the real Egypt, Mary.'

This man had a way of saying 'no' I could only admire. 'I'm all ears,' I declared, which was not true, for he had just made me intensely aware of other more intimate parts of my body. Now that I had seen and felt him naked, he looked better to me than ever, and I watched him hungrily as he seated himself in a delicate chair resembling a sugary confection, that amazingly enough supported his considerable muscular weight. He picked up the white gilded receiver of a French phone and proceeded ordering dinner from room service in as much detail as a pharaoh commanding a legion of cooks, his black pants such a stunning contrast to the room's airy blue-and-white décor that I felt slightly disoriented. It was as though the door between our two bedrooms was a portal in

Dreams of Anubis

time through which we had traveled centuries in the second it took us to cross the threshold from ancient Egypt to Edwardian England.

I leaned back against the dresser, growing increasingly light-headed. Looking around the room, I suffered the disconcerting impression that nothing in it was actually solid. Everything appeared to be really there, edges were sharp and focused, but somehow I knew it was only because I was aware of them. When I looked away the blue-and-white tones would dissolve into formless waves of energy again. I had read somewhere that electrons act as particles when they're being observed, but at all other times they behave like waves.

'Dilwaatee minfadlak.' Richard slammed the receiver down with satisfaction.

I nearly jumped out of my present skin.

He looked over at me tenderly. 'Come here.' He patted his dark lap. 'Why are you so far away? We have a lot to talk about.'

That was the understatement of centuries. I was bound to him like a patient to a doctor since only he could possibly explain to me what had just happened between us. 'I would prefer to stand for the moment, thank you,' I said. 'My head feels like it's about to disconnect from my shoulders and fly away like a Ba bird.'

He laughed. 'You're quite a lovely bird.'

'I wasn't referring to British slang.'

'I know that,' he said patiently. 'You were referring to the fact that Egyptians often depicted the soul as a bird with a human head.'

'I'm sorry, of course I knew you knew that, I just feel very weird...I don't feel like myself.'

'No pun intended?' He sounded serious, but his eyes were smiling.

I returned the smile with my lips, but my confusion was growing exponentially and inevitably making me anxious.

'Please, my love, come here.' He patted his thighs again with both hands, his brows furrowing slightly as if he couldn't possibly think of any reason why I would refuse.

Before I knew it, I found myself perched on his firm thighs with my wrists resting on his strong shoulders as I held on to the excitingly strong yet tender column of his neck. 'What did you mean when you said you found me through dreams,

Richard? Is that how you knew I'd be in the bazaar the other night?' I met his earnest stare with my own, once again admiring the golden rim around his pupils that made me think of sunflowers growing in the heart of his irises, which were that inscrutably beautiful color between slate-gray and the deepest green possible.

'I thought you remembered your dreams, Mary.'

'Yes, but up until recently, they've only been dreams that had nothing to do with my real life.'

He shifted my weight on his lap, not because I was too heavy for him but to hold me even closer. 'Until recently?' he prompted, his expression neutral, but I could sense how much he wanted to hear what I was about to say.

'Until I arrived in Egypt. But I think you knew that.'

'I think I did, I just didn't know whether you remembered. I hoped you did.'

'Richard…' I said weakly, because his hand slowly caressing the side of my thigh was making it difficult for me to concentrate.

'Yes, my love?'

'Was that you?' His rhythmic caress was hypnotizing me. 'Was that you in the dream I had in the mastaba?'

'You mean the dream in which you were lying on a leopard-skin couch with your favorite cat in a room open to a garden on both sides and I came to you?'

'Silhouetted against the sunset…'

'Yes, I suppose I was, since I came in from the western garden.'

I asked breathlessly, 'And what did I call you?'

His mouth tilted subtly up at both ends, giving his smile the enigmatic cast of an ancient statue. 'You called me E'Ahmose, which means Born of the Moon. You named your cat after me, my beloved Nefermun.'

I planted my lips against his, the only possible response to undeniable proof that he had entered the profoundly intimate space of my dreams with the same effortless power his erection penetrated my flesh. His tongue thrust civilly but demandingly into my mouth, and I felt both of us pouring our souls into the kiss through the strong, supple, sensitive and agile muscle buried beneath our lips. So many things were expressed without words, swiftly and magically, while at the same time so many urgent, passionate questions were asked in this kiss, that I finally let go of the confused shipwreck of my rational thoughts and surrendered to the overwhelming knowledge I was in love with this man. I was drowning in him, utterly losing myself as I let go of the fear that what I felt between us wasn't real but only a deluded desire to believe in true love and that it lasts forever.

I surfaced reluctantly from our deep and complex kiss. 'Do you expect me to believe all this?' I gasped. 'How did you even know I was in Egypt? Are you playing with me, Richard?'

'Let's see, which question would you like me to answer first? I'll start with the last one, which is a clear indication that Mary Fallon is still fighting Nefermun. I am not playing with you, and you know it. A dream told me you were in Egypt. I didn't know what your name was, or exactly when you would be arriving, or even what you actually looked like, but I knew you were coming to Egypt. You told me so yourself. And after that it was pure choreography that helped bring us together, all with the first step of Simon's wild inspiration to stash the photograph in your luggage. Obviously he was being influenced by forces beyond his control that meant for us to come together again.'

'What do you mean I told you I was coming to Egypt? How could I have told you if I didn't even know you?'

'Our souls have met countless times before in dreams. I know you don't remember, but you did tell me, or rather, Nefermun did.'

'But my name is Mary.'

'I'm sure you've read Shakespeare.'

'"What's in a name"?'

'Actually, more than you realize,' he blithely contradicted himself. 'You need to answer to Nefermun again to truly be yourself, Mary.'

Even though it made me feel strangely off balance again to do so, I let go of his neck and got up off his lap. 'Nefermun,' I echoed, tasting the syllables on my tongue and trying not to like them so much. 'She's who you're in love with, not me.'

'You're being ridiculous.'

A blend of anger, impatience and disappointment darkened his expression for a moment that made me feel foolish indeed, for this was not the sort of reaction I wanted to inspire in him. There was a perversely stubborn and suspicious streak in me, bred by a number of previous disappointing relationships with men that had nothing to do with how I really felt about love, or about this man in particular. 'That was not Nefermun talking, was it?' I asked by way of apology.

'No,' he stood up, 'it wasn't.' He pulled me into his arms and let me feel the hard bulge between his thighs pressing into my soft belly as he spoke. 'The way I see on the other side is more complete than my waking consciousness, Mary, and yet it's also not quite so defined, or definite, I don't know how else to express it. It'll take time to try and describe it to you. But for now, just answer me this. Do you normally let total strangers kiss you,' he was referring to our meeting in the bazaar, 'and go down on you?'

'Of course not! But nothing that's happened to me since I arrived in Egypt has been normal.'

'Thank the gods for that, hmm?'

He was teasing me, but his supernatural interpretation of the chemistry between us was too serious for me to respond lightheartedly. 'How can I believe this, Richard?' I begged to know. 'How can I really believe my dreams aren't just my imagination, and that it's not just a coincidence you had a similar dream? How do I know— I didn't want to ask this, but I had to. 'How do I know I didn't mutter in my sleep last night when you carried me up here?'

He let go of me. 'Are you accusing me of lying to you?'

His mouth was so hard I suddenly understood the meaning of pharaoh's crook and flail—I had just been in the wonderful crook of his embrace, now his frown felt like a flail applied directly to the haunting muscle of my heart. 'No,' I said meekly.

'That's what you implied, that I learned the details of the dream you had in the mastaba from your sleepy mutterings last night and used them to seduce you into believing we had dreamed together.'

I was appalled, because that was exactly what my statement had implied, and yet I didn't really believe that about him at all. 'Perhaps,' I looked earnestly up into his eyes, 'I should make more of an effort to behave like Nefermun for a change. Whether or not I really am her reincarnation is another matter altogether. The point is she's much more like I imagine myself being. I'm beginning to realize there are aspects of Mary Fallon that I don't really like that I was never really aware of before and that I should stop indulging and identifying with. Nefermun feels a lot wiser, and a lot less stressed out. Um, does that make any sense?'

He drew me into his arms again and held me close, laying my cheek against his chest and resting his hand on my head. 'It makes perfect sense, Nefermun. And remember, the only proof you need of anything is how you feel deep down in the very heart of your soul, forget what your rational mind or the rest of the world tell you that you should feel.'

'Yes!' I sighed.

'Now stop thinking about it,' he urged gently, 'and let's just relax together for a while and enjoy the lovely dinner I've ordered for us. I think you'll appreciate the wine I've selected to go with it.' He let go of me and turned towards a door I assumed led out into the corridor.

Right on cue, there was a polite knock. I hadn't heard a sound outside in the hall. Maybe his hearing was keener than mine, or maybe…I'd never actually known a person who possessed any kind of extra-sensory perception, and I couldn't help wondering how it worked. What was his range, so to speak? And more importantly, how was it possible for me to resist a man who could sense what I was thinking and play my feelings like an instrument?

He went to open the door, and two native men promptly wheeled in a couple of tables. Richard spoke to them in Arabic, and I gathered something he had ordered was missing. A second later I discovered what it was when another man literally ran into the room cradling a black bucket of ice containing a bottle of white wine. He set down his precious cargo on one of the tables, and I swear it was not my imagination that he winked at me before he left because I thought I recognized him. The other two waiters hung around for a moment while Richard made sure everything he had ordered had been prepared to his specifications, then they too left the room without ever once looking at me. I might have been a ghost for all the attention they paid me.

My emotions were suddenly a sickeningly mixed brew. Battling with the elation the appearance of one of Simon's native assistants naturally aroused in me was annoyance. I had been bottled up in a room all day long like a genie in her bottle, yet at the moment I had no desire to leave and return to my insultingly cool-headed Egyptologist. I couldn't be sure, but I suspected he was spying on me through his hired hand, making sure I was all right, which I suppose I should have found flattering, but instead it only made me more anxious than I already was. I did not doubt the bottle Richard had ordered was expensive, and now a wild thought ruined how eagerly I had been anticipating a glass of wine. I wasn't sure it was safe to drink. What if Simon actually believed Richard was keeping me here against my will and his smiling lackey had slipped something in the wine that would render my host sleepy enough to let me get away? It was a totally crazy idea, but then again I was in Egypt, where anything seemed to be possible, and the fact was, the bottle had already been opened. (I wasn't thinking straight enough to consider the fact that if the wine had indeed been spiked with something that it would have the same effect on me, hence defeating Simon's purposes, whatever they might be.)

'Come, Mary,' Richard said, smiling over at me from beside the feast awaiting us.

'It looks wonderful,' I declared even though nothing was visible except the covered silver serving platters like the domed rooftops of a city famous for its culinary arts. I didn't know what to do. The bottle was already in his hand. 'Does the hotel usually open your wine bottles for you?' I asked. 'I mean, shouldn't they bring it up to your room sealed, then open it and let you taste and approve the vintage?' I seated myself watching him pour a small amount of the wine into his glass.

'That would be the proper procedure,' he agreed. 'But I'm sure it's fine.'

I held my breath as he took a sip. Surely his cultivated palate would detect a foreign substance?

'Mm, very nice…I'd like to propose a toast.' Apparently satisfied with the quality of the vintage, he filled both our glasses. 'To us,' he intoned soberly, 'and to every other us we've ever been and ever will be.' He raised his glass and waited for me to follow suit.

I did so, but the instant the crystal rim touched his lips, I leaned over the table and passionately knocked the glass out of his hand.

Dreams of Anubis

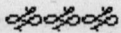

After dinner, Richard rewarded me for my loyalty with heavy golden bracelets inlaid with lapis-lazuli. He slipped them onto my arms, and for a moment they felt a little too much like shackles I had perversely chosen over freedom, but only for a moment. However, my gesture had not pleased him at first since he had believed it my rude response to his romantic toast, and the look in his eyes after I knocked the glass out of his hand is one I prefer to forget. When I quickly and breathlessly explained to him there was a chance the wine was drugged, he laughed and kissed me on my highly imaginative forehead. 'I don't think so, love,' he assured me. 'Simon is simply making sure you're here with me and that you're all right. It's common knowledge I have a Suite in the Mina House.'

When he was finished with me, I stood motionless as a mannequin displaying a style that was popular millenniums ago and which is still fashionable with women whenever they want to dress up dramatically and exotically. The full-length mirror he positioned me in front of made it quite clear that I made a beautiful Egyptian princess. An exquisite copy of a belt I recognized from a book on Middle Kingdom jewelry made of tiny golden fish linked together swam around my hips, and draped over my chest and shoulders was an amazingly light collar composed of red-and-blue faience beads. I held my breath as my host suddenly genuflected before me, but it was only to slip gilded sandals on my feet that matched the thick bracelets on my arms. Then standing behind me again, he gently placed a golden filigree crown on my head carved in the form of a delicate vine decorated with tiny carnelian flowers.

'Are we going to a costume party?' I heard myself ask dryly as I pretended not to be impressed with Nefermun's beauty. I knew it was my body, Mary Fallon's body, reflected in the glass, but it was an ancient soul I glimpsed staring back at me with a depth of confidence and a profound sensual ease I did not possess in this life except in my fantasies.

'Yes, as a matter-of-fact we are.' Richard stood with his hands lightly gripping my bare upper arms and his eyes holding mine in the mirror. 'A private party.' His white shirt could have been made of the finest linen, and his long dark hair resting on his broad shoulders before flowing down his back was certainly Egyptian enough.

I managed to keep my voice steady. 'This is just a little strange, Richard.'

'I sense Mary Fallon and Nefermun at each other's throats, and Mary is afraid of losing a part of herself in awakening another, but there's no need to be afraid, trust me.'

I clung to his voice, which was both infinitely soft and firm, listening to what he had to say for all I was worth, whoever I was.

'Nefermun is an ancient priestess. Mary Fallon's personality was shaped by the twentieth century, and so she believes her rational mind is to be worshipped above all her other feelings and perceptions. But pure reason is a limited, fear-ridden deity, my love, and I know your heart is pure and powerful enough to see past the pragmatic, money-worshipping culture into which you happened to be born this time around. Do you understand what I'm saying to you, Nefer-mary-mun?'

'Yes!' I whispered fervently. 'You make complete sense to me, Richard. Your mystical beliefs strike me as totally logical.'

'That's because they are, logic of a higher order. Do you like your new name, Nefer-marymun?'

'Yes, it feels right.'

'Mm...' He pressed his hard-on against me, cradling it in the small of my back. 'You feel right, just right.' He turned me to face him abruptly, his possessive grip tightening on my arms. 'Nefer-marymun,' he whispered.

'E-Ahmose.'

I savored the ancient name on my modern tongue and liked how sweet and familiar it tasted. Our breaths wrestled together for a moment before his lips pinned mine down and slowly parted, teasing me with the promise of his tongue and another deep, spiraling kiss. Then I was distracted from our silent conversation by the feel of his hand lifting my dress up in front, and slipping between my legs. I moaned into his mouth as he cradled my soft, sleek pussy in his hard palm, feeling my naked sex lips bloom eagerly against the pressure of his skin. I sincerely hoped that what lay in his future was touching me like this again and again forever. I cried out softly as he thrust his index finger into the moist heart of my vulva while at the same time gently crushing my clitoris beneath his thumb. The summit of my mound was caught in the vice of his grip. The pleasure was almost painfully intense as his hard thumb rubbed up and down against my clit, his finger penetrating me rhythmically.

'Oh God, stop,' I begged.

'Why?' he whispered against my cheek. 'Doesn't it feel good?'

'Oh yes, too good...'

He laughed. 'How can anything feel too good, Nefer-marymun?'

'I don't know!' I wrapped my arms around his neck and clung to him. The sharp ecstasy cutting up through my pelvis made me feel as though he was lifting me off the floor in the devastatingly powerful cradle of his thumb and forefinger.

'I want you to come for me again, my love. Soon you'll learn to come without touching yourself,' he promised. 'The more times we come together and you let go of all your tensions, the more sensitive your clitoris will grow until it learns to respond to the subtle friction of my cock as much as to the slightest touch.'

'Oh God,' I groaned, loving what he was saying as much as what he was doing, though I still felt it was too much pleasure too fast for my body to handle. Then I let out a small scream when the door leading out into the hall crashed against the wall as someone kicked it open.

Simon's man cut a menacing figure in a long black robe, and there was something threateningly sinister about the white crescent of teeth he flashed Richard.

E'Ahmose, Priest of Anubis, did not react as I expected him to by pulling his hand out from between my legs and letting my dress fall around my ankles. Instead he behaved as though we had not even been interrupted.

'Richard,' I gasped, 'there's a man—'

'You're going to come for me, Mary,' he said calmly.

I glanced over at the intruder, whose initial defiant grin was dimming to a look of disbelief as he eyed my naked thighs and Richard's hand working between them.

I had never been in such a position before, and something strange was happening inside me. I realized with a shock that it was seriously turning me on to be skillfully fondled by one man while another man watched. Our observer's stare penetrated me at the very heart of the pleasure I was feeling from Richard's relentless caress. My defenses collapsed around me. Overwhelmed by how strangely aroused I grew when we were no longer alone, I climaxed.

'Mm, yes, that's it,' Richard purred in my ear as I came in his palm burying my face in his neck so as not to witness my own wanton behavior.

He pulled his hand out from between my legs, and as he took a decisive step back, my arms slid reluctantly from around him.

His eyes held mine as he slipped his glistening index finger between his lips and sucked off my juices before facing the man standing motionless in the doorway, as if paralyzed by what he had just witnessed. Richard crossed his arms over his chest and regarded our dumbfounded audience with an expression that appeared passive, but the contained power I sensed in his absolute control thrilled me.

'It appears Simon is not man enough to come for you himself, Mary,' he observed, his voice ominously civil. 'But now his servant has, I think, a very meaningful message to deliver to his master.'

Suddenly the Egyptian seemed to fly into the room in his billowing black robes like a huge raven cawing angrily in Arabic.

I had no idea what the man was saying. Richard's voice captured all my attention as he drew me into the safe harbor of his arm and whispered urgently in my ear, 'Go, Nefer-marymun! Find your way back to your friend and your sexy Egyptologist and think about everything you've felt here with me, and everything I've said, then make your choice.'

'But I don't—'

He shoved me gently away from him. 'Go now.'

'But I don't want—'

Simon's man stepped between us.

Dreams of Anubis

'Richard, I can't leave like this!' I was referring to my scanty ancient attire, but especially to all the feelings he had stirred up inside me that beat like fists against my chest, in protest at being nipped in the bud like this.

'Go, Mary,' he insisted, his eyes beautifully hard, 'I'll come for you again when you've resolved the conflicts inside you and divested yourself of everything, and everyone, you really don't need or want.'

'But—'

'Go, my love, now.'

Nefermun obeyed E'Ahmose's command at once, overriding Mary Fallon's desire to linger uncertainly in the doorway. I knew in my heart that what he was telling me to do was necessary, but I didn't want to leave him, not now after what both his personalities—the powerfully erotic priest of Anubis and the romantically skilled Englishman—had made me feel in that bedroom lit only by an alabaster lotus lamp. But even as I ran impulsively down the corridor in search of an elevator, I knew I had felt a similar reluctance to separate myself from Simon after everything he had made me feel down in Ti's burial chamber. Nefermun might understand E'Ahmoses's logic and motives, but I, Mary Fallon, definitely resented Richard for essentially kicking me out of his room just after giving me a violent orgasm in front of another man. Nefermun might not mind that her nipples and pubic mound were enticingly visible through the finely pleated long white dress, but I certainly cared about exposing myself to all of Cairo like this.

I stopped to wait for the elevator. I had no desire to leave Richard, but if it was true he had loved me through the ages, then he would come for me again soon enough, just as he had said he would. Yet simply because we were in Egypt did not give him the right to behave as despotically as a pharaoh! Nevertheless, he was right. I had to make my mind up about Simon, and to do so it was necessary for me to see him again. My intense attraction to Richard could not be denied, but neither could my feelings for Simon.

I kept glancing back in the direction of Sir Ashley's suite expecting Simon's messenger to appear and lead me safely back to Carol's place, but the door-lined hallway was as still and silent as the corridor of a tomb. I wondered what had happened to him and wondered if I should be concerned about Richard, until I realized how foolish that was. My Priest of Anubis could take care of himself; it was Simon's servant I should have been concerned about, but I was too busy worrying about myself right now.

I let two empty cars come and go before I finally accepted the fact that no one was going to escort me home or anywhere else. I still had no idea what had become of Simon's man (maybe he'd flown out a window) and I was sorely tempted to return to Richard's room and demand he let me put on my normal clothes, yet Nefermun would not let me do it. I stood with my arms crossed over my chest as though posing for my own mummy, and I imagine my eyes looked as big and dark and profoundly uncertain as a Greco-Roman sarcophagus. I don't think I had ever appreciated the expression 'torn inside' as much as I did in those moments. But three times must be the charm, because when the elevator doors parted again I stepped into the thankfully empty car.

The whole way down I dreaded other guests would get on and that I would be unable to escape their incredulous stares, but I was spared this embarrassment. There was no way I could avoid being seen down in the lobby, however, and as the doors sighed open, I braced myself for peoples' reaction to my appearance. Forcing my arms down to my sides, I stepped stiffly out onto the polished marble floor. Fortunately, I was relatively familiar with the layout of the Mina House, having had dinner here with Simon and Carol, and I headed purposefully towards the entrance trying my best to avoid eye contact with anyone. Then I realized that although everyone I passed noticed me and often stopped to stare at me, no one actually seemed shocked by my appearance. In fact, everyone smiled when they saw me, and when they whispered amongst themselves, pointing in my direction, it was with a respectfully subdued, almost reverent, curiosity. Well, of course, I was in Egypt; they probably thought I was on my way to work somewhere playing Cleopatra.

Nefermun did not mind being the center of public attention, and so I let her take over, or rather I let her possess me as I walked confidently, I can almost say regally, across the slick stone floor in my gilded sandals, my back straight and proud. My stiff shoes made a delicate clicking sound, and I was amazed by how

Dreams of Anubis

well they fit me, which in turn led me to admire Sir Richard Ashley's powers of observation.

I had almost made it to the front doors when I was intercepted by a group of jovial Japanese businessmen who swarmed in on me hungrily, all of them wielding cameras that buzzed and clicked around me like insects capturing my image from every angle. It was impossible for me to shoo them away, and I saw no point in ruining their fun by crossing my arms over my chest and attempting to cover my nipples—which felt hard as stone against the veil-like dress—so I let them have their delighted fill of me. I painted the appropriate smile on my lips as flashes exploded in my face with the blinding power of suns going novae.

When they finally lost interest in me and walked laughingly and triumphantly towards the front desk to check in, I stumbled slightly on my way out the front doors. At last I found myself out in the cool night air, and even though it was heavily perfumed with car exhaust, it still tasted delicious to me after being cooped up inside all day in my tomb-like bedroom.

I was immediately surrounded again, this time by cabbies all dying to take me wherever on this earth—or beyond it by way of passionately reckless driving—I wanted to go. It was only then that it hit me like a block falling off the pyramid that I didn't have any money on me, American or Egyptian. I debated whether or not to run back up to Richard's room and demand cab fare. Charm alone, extensive as it was in my nearly transparent attire, wasn't enough to get me across the Nile to Carol's apartment, and yet the robed men eagerly orbiting me didn't seem at all concerned by my lack of a purse.

I shook my head. 'No money, sorry.' I raised my empty hands dramatically in front of me. 'Nothing. Mafish.'

They didn't seem to understand me, perhaps because I was wearing golden bracelets and a shimmering golden vine crowned my dark hair. I had assumed Richard adorned me with costume reproductions of ancient Egyptian jewelry, but I began to suspect I had underestimated his tastes and the value of his gifts when one of the drivers tried pulling one of my bracelets off, quite unconcerned about taking my whole arm with it if necessary. Since I was not about to let him have it, I found myself moving in the direction of the street and what I assumed was his cab, at which point he let go of me, grinning happily. That's when I realized he hadn't actually been trying to steal my jewelry; the gesture had been his rather primitive but admittedly effective way of letting me know I could pay my fare with the bracelet. Much as I hated to part with my lover's gift, Sir Ashley had given me no choice but to fend for myself as best I could, so I let myself be enthusiastically ushered (politely shoved) into the back seat of the small car. I forced myself to relax against the seat, and then clung to it as we shot away from the curb like a bullet released from a gun into Cairo's rushing bloodstream of traffic that glowed with the white and red cells of countless headlights.

'Ala-tool?' My chauffeur grinned back at me. 'Urrayib? Bi-eed, beautiful princess?'

I had to tell him where I wanted to go. The only problem was I had no idea since I didn't know Carol's address by heart. 'The American Embassy,' I improvised. They would be able to give me my friend's address, or at least her phone number so I could call her, and hopefully she would be home and be able to give my driver directions. I would tell the people at the embassy that Carol and I had been at a costume party and that she had left with someone else forgetting I didn't know the way back to her apartment. It was a lame story, but much more believable than the truth.

'American Embassy one bracelet,' my driver stated emphatically.

'Half a bracelet,' I haggled, 'and the other half when you get me to my friend's apartment.' I spoke slowly, praying he would understand me. 'I have to go to the embassy because I lost my friend's address.'

'Yes,' he nodded, 'embassy first to obtain address, then friend's apartment.'

'Exactly!' I was infinitely relieved he understood English.

'Beautiful princess's crown for whole journey!'

'Oh no, only one bracelet, and count yourself lucky.'

'Two bracelets,' he bargained cheerfully.

'One bracelet.'

'Oh very well, aywa!' He flung his hands up in mock exasperation as he agreed to my terms. The car swerved violently, leaving my organs floating in one spot as my skeleton shifted into another, yet my Egyptian driver appeared unaffected by the laws of gravity as he calmly took hold of the wheel again with one hand while at the same time lighting a cigarette with the other.

Now that business was taken care of, we sped along in a comfortable silence punctuated by the burning red tip of his cigarette rising and falling, rising and falling…Occasionally, he glanced at my face in the rear-view mirror, and my enigmatic smile as I thought about my new name, Nefer-marymun, must have made him feel as though he was transporting an ancient statue. It was dawning on me that Richard was perhaps attempting to escalate my transformation into Nefer-marymun by sending me out into the world without any of Mary Fallon's clothes or possessions, thereby forcing me to identify with my ancient self, whose mysterious strength I would have to call upon to help the nervous and stressed out legal secretary from Boston deal with such adverse circumstances. Nefer-marymun could handle a night alone in Cairo without any money or a passport, wearing only a transparent dress and priceless jewelry, because somehow she knew everything would be all right, she just had to help Mary believe that and stay calm.

The little car came to an abrupt stop beside a small guardhouse outside the gates of what I could only hope was the American Embassy.

My driver quickly got out to open the back door for me, and I caught him intently studying the effect of the cool night air on my nipples as I emerged. Once again, I crossed my arms over my chest. I wished Richard had been kind enough to provide me with a flail I could use to defend myself if necessary.

I found myself in a small antechamber furnished with a handful of very uncomfortable looking chairs. There was a wall directly across from me whose blank facade was broken by a screened window. Behind the fine metal web sat a young Egyptian man in uniform whose eyes widened in disbelief when he saw me appear before him like a vision from the ancient past, or a drunken hallucination, depending on whether or not he happened to have a bottle hidden in his desk. He shook his head swiftly back and forth like a wet dog, and rubbed his eyes like a sleepy child, but I refused to go away. Finally accepting the fact that I was real, he barked an order over his shoulder. Two more uniformed Egyptians immediately appeared behind him, and stared at me open-mouthed.

My driver stepped up beside me and began speaking rapidly in Arabic.

I fervently hoped he was explaining my situation to them, and careful not to uncross my arms, I tugged on his sleeve. 'I need my friend's address, my American friend's address. Her name is Caroline Jordan.'

'Could you please repeat that?' The man seated at the desk requested in perfect English.

I was so relieved I was going to be able to communicate that I relaxed my royal mummy's stance. 'I need my friend's address,' I repeated. 'Her name is Caroline Jordan. She lives in the foreign residential area...well, in one of them. We were at a costume party...'

He listened to my tall tale with a slight smile on his lips (I preferred not to think of it as a smirk).

'And the problem is she left with someone forgetting she hadn't written her address down for me,' I concluded.

'I see,' he said, and there was no question about the fact that he could see, that they could all see, my most intimate assets. 'And how do we know you are really a friend of this young woman?'

I had dreaded this question, for I had no way of proving it. 'Well, you can call her and ask her. I mean, she should be home by now.'

'Do you have her telephone number?'

'No, that's why I came here, because I don't have her address or her number.' My patience was beginning to wear as thin as my dress.

'Do you not carry a purse, miss...?'

'Fallon, Mary Fallon.'

'May I see your passport please, Miss Fallon?'

'No, you may not,' exasperation replaced my anxiety, 'because I don't have it. I don't have anything.' Nefermun wouldn't have needed a passport to travel through Egypt, I thought testily.

He glanced up at the men flanking him as if to say, 'Can you believe these crazy American girls?' before resuming his polite interrogation and lascivious examination of my nipples. 'Was your purse stolen, Miss Fallon? Do you need to file a report with the Tourist Police?'

Dreams of Anubis

These were perfectly reasonable questions, and yet I found I could not answer them. 'No, it wasn't stolen, I…I accidentally left it in a tomb, but my friend found it, and it's back at her apartment now, where I would very much like to be, so can you please—'

'I thought you said you were at a costume party.'

'Oh God, I was, it's a long story, believe me. Can you please just look up her number and call her for me? She'll verify who I am.'

Suddenly, an impatient stream of Arabic welled up out of my driver, who had obviously lost his patience with the embassy officials. I had no idea what he was saying, but I was hopeful his tirade would get me what I needed. Finally, one of the men behind the screen disappeared, and I endured an awkward moment avoiding two pairs of dark eyes boring through my dress until he returned a moment later carrying what looked like a thick phone directory.

The young man in charge flipped through it casually, deliberately taking his time. He would also have found what he was looking for a lot faster if he hadn't kept glancing at me, even though his eyes never made it up as far as my face. Finally, he picked up a pen and wrote something on a notepad. He tore off the bottom of the sheet, and slipped it beneath the screen.

My driver promptly snatched up the scrap of paper covered in swirling black lines I sincerely hoped were Carol's coordinates. He clutched the vital information to his chest, muttered something in Arabic to the officials, and grabbing my arm yanked me back outside.

Once again I found myself in the cockpit of a little Egyptian cab, and discovered it was time to pay my fare.

'I take bracelet now,' my escort stated firmly, 'then I deliver you safely to friend's house.'

I couldn't argue with him after how helpful he had been, so I slipped off one of the bracelets.

He snatched it out of my hand, and it vanished into the folds of his robe so swiftly I suspected some of his ancestors had been tomb robbers.

I recognized the foreign residential section the moment we entered it, and my heart began fluttering like a butterfly perching on all my nerve-endings in turn as Simon's sunny blonde head drew nearer. I hadn't realized how much I wanted to see him again, and I was dismayed by my elation, which Nefermun felt was a betrayal of Richard. Then a circumstantial net was flung over my pulse when I realized I was on my way to Carol's apartment, and that Simon would not even be there. I probably wouldn't even see him tonight, and yet I absolutely had to see him; I couldn't possibly wait until tomorrow. I had left my beautiful priest of Anubis, so I was going to see that damned Egyptologist tonight if it was the last thing Mary Fallon ever did. When she went to bed tonight, it would not be alone like a mummy retiring to her cold sarcophagus. 'No way!' I vowed out loud.

My driver jumped in surprise at my sudden outburst and his cigarette fell from between his fingers into the folds of his robe. He let go of the steering wheel, searching wildly for it with both hands, and as a result the little cab began veering from one side of the street to another like a drunk scarab beetle.

'Look out!' I cried, because we were headed straight for two palm trees and the space between them was definitely not wide enough to accommodate us.

The Egyptian triumphantly placed the cigarette's crumpled body back between his lips, and casually saved us both from a fiery death at the last possible moment.

Suddenly, it didn't seem so vital to me that I see Simon tonight; it would be enough if I managed to remain in the same dimension with both him and Richard—although I was sure E'Ahmose could find me in the next world should my cab driver end up taking me there.

A few minutes, and dozens of sultry daydreams later my kamikaze cabby announced, 'Beautiful princess's apartment!' as we screeched to a halt so abruptly I nearly dove into the front seat.

I quickly opened the door and stepped out onto the safe sidewalk. 'Shukron!' I gasped.

'Kuwayyis.' Grinning, he walked ahead of me towards the building and held open the glass door leading into the lobby.

'Shukron,' I said again, politely tying to get rid of him since I could find my own way from here, but he simply nodded enthusiastically, and I started up the stairs with him trailing on the heels of my gilded sandals. He escorted me all the way up to Carol's apartment, where he abruptly stepped in front of me and knocked loudly and peremptorily on the door demanding that whatever infidel lay behind it let the beautiful princess in at once. At least that's what I think he said; it was hard for me to make sense of his passionate mixture of Arabic and English, all I know is it sounded wonderfully dramatic. However, there was no response whatsoever from within the apartment.

'It's no use,' I told him. 'Either Carol isn't home or she's taking a nap, which would be just as bad. She sleeps like a fairytale princess and it would take a lot more than banging on the door, or a kiss from a handsome prince, to wake her.'

'Princess?' He looked astonished. 'Another princess inside?'

I laughed, trying the doorknob. It turned like a charm and I nearly tumbled into the living room.

By the time I found my balance and turned around to thank my driver for all his help, he had vanished as silently as a genie.

I closed, and carefully locked, the door behind me. It was still relatively early, yet the apartment was dark and silent as a tomb. Carol wasn't losing any sleep over the minor matter of her best friend being swept away on horseback across the desert by an armed man. It was more likely however that she was out with Steve. It was also possible she was out with both Steve and Simon. Or maybe she and her adorable boss were out alone together somewhere fondly hugging each other again in my absence.

I refused to pursue the catty thought. The truth is, I really didn't care where anyone was, because I suddenly became aware of a void inside me that had nothing to do with the empty apartment.

'E'Ahmose,' I whispered into the dark room filled with modern furniture that struck me as totally lifeless compared to the lovely objects I had been surrounded by all day. 'Oh, Richard,' I sighed, 'why did you make me leave you? So I would miss you? So I would realize how much you already mean to me?' Well, I had to admit it was working, and if this temporary separation deepened the bond between us, then I told myself the desolation I was suffering now was more than worth it.

I made my way down the hall by feel. Carol's bedroom door was closed and it appeared to be just as dark on the other side. I opened the door a crack and peered into the impenetrable gloom. 'Carol?' I called softly.

'Mary,' she replied at once sounding strangely breathless, 'you're back!'

'Yes, I am. May I turn on a light?'

'No!'

'Why not?'

'Because she's not alone,' an amused male voice replied.

'Oh, God, I'm sorry.' I quickly closed the door again and retreated down the hallway.

The guestroom was as dark and cold as a crypt, which felt just about right at the moment; I deliberately didn't turn on a light. Just able to make out the soft sarcophagus shape of the bed, I went and sat despondently on its edge. I was the one who had two men fighting for me, at least metaphorically, yet here I was sitting all alone with my beautiful sexy outfit going completely to waste.

A deep moan behind me made me leap off the mattress. 'Who's there?' I gasped, almost knocking over the lamp on the nightstand in my haste to switch it on.

For an instant I was half blinded, but I had no problem making out the body that suddenly sat bolt upright on the bed as though resurrected by the power of Re even in his humble form of an electric light bulb.

'Nefertari?' Simon's eyes were huge and strangely blank; his irises really might have been made of lapis-lazuli. 'The beautiful one has come back to me,' he muttered, reaching hesitantly towards me as though I was an apparition he couldn't actually hope to touch.

Only then did I realize he merely appeared to be conscious. Amused that my eloquent Egyptologist also talked in his sleep, I took hold of him by the shoulders. 'Simon, wake up.' I shook him gently.

His head fell forward, and then snapped back up again. 'Mary?' He gazed sleepily up at my face before his gaze traveled slowly down my body. 'Jesus,' he whispered, 'I must still be dreaming.'

'No, you're not,' I assured him, standing up straight so he could feast his eyes on me, especially on my firm breasts flatteringly outlined by the transparent linen.

Dreams of Anubis

He caught hold of one of my wrists, and pulled me down onto the bed with him. 'You must be a dream,' he muttered, crushing me passionately against him.

'Simon, I can't breathe.'

'But you don't need to breath, Mary, you're only a dream, and dreams don't breathe.'

'I'm not a dream,' I insisted, trying to push him away.

He relaxed his vice-like embrace, but refused to let go of me. 'If you're not a dream, why are you dressed like an ancient Egyptian princess?'

I wondered if he was still half asleep because his reasoning powers seemed a bit groggy. 'Sir Richard Gerald Ashley dressed me like this.' It titillated me to say the full name of his current incarnation, which was not as romantic as E'Ahmose, Born of the Moon, but still possessed a dignity worthy of how magnificently intelligent and beautiful he was, in my opinion.

Simon did not so much let go of me as push me away from him, and the look in his eyes told me he was wide awake finally. 'That bastard,' he said through his teeth.

'I don't have a problem with it,' I remarked lightly, admiring one of the gold bracelets I still had left. It was decorated with a geometric rendering of lotus blossoms formed by inlaid blue and red stones I could not identify but that were beautiful enough to be precious.

Simon snatched my wrist, and raising it between us studied the bracelet himself. 'He gave you this?'

'Yes, and my crown, too.' I touched the delicate vine reverently. 'And my belt.' I looked down at the little golden fish swimming around my hips. 'Isn't it beautiful? And my collar.' I caressed the controlled explosion of primary colors resting against my chest. 'And my sandals.' I extended one of my slender legs and displayed my gilded foot.

'Thanks for the inventory.'

'My pleasure. They look real, don't they?' I couldn't resist asking. He was an Egyptologist, so he should be able to tell. It wasn't the monetary value of the ancient-style jewels that interested me; I was looking for evidence of the value my so-called Priest of Anubis actually placed on our relationship. If he had showered me with costume jewelry, my faith in his timeless feelings for me would suffer a disappointing blow.

Simon studied my face for a moment, and I sensed him determine that my curiosity had nothing to do with money as he frowned down at my collar, and then rubbed one of the little fish dangling from my belt between his thumb and forefinger. 'They're either real or very good imitations, but I suspect they're real,' he concluded.

My respect for him deepened as he gave me a totally objective assessment of the valuable gifts another man had given me.

His shoulders slumped as though he was suddenly exhausted. 'He's rich as a pharaoh,' he added despondently, and his head fell heavily into his hands.

Respect naturally flowed into concern. 'Are you all right?' I asked, gently resting my hand on one of his thighs. He was wearing khaki slacks and a matching shirt that made him look every inch the handsome Anthropologist.

'I'm fine,' he muttered, then suddenly looked up at me askance. 'Why are you here, anyway?'

'Because this is Carol's apartment and I'm staying with her?'

He sat up again. 'Why didn't you stay with Richard?' he demanded bluntly.

'Did you send one of your men to spy on me?' I continued our tradition of answering each other's questions with more questions.

'I wanted to make sure you were all right. Obviously,' the ghost of a sneer touched his lips, 'there was no need for me to be concerned. I should have known it wasn't true.'

'That what wasn't true?'

'I thought you said money didn't mean anything to you, Mary.'

'It doesn't,' I insisted. 'I could care less that Richard is rich.' I winced. That was the second time in one night my grammar had left much to be desired.

'Then what is it about him you can't resist, the size of his dick?'

I slapped him.

He caressed his cheek gingerly. 'I'm sorry, Mary, that was way out of line. You have the right to see whoever you please.'

'Apology accepted,' I declared magnanimously.

Dreams of Anubis

He smiled. 'Thank you, princess.' Then he frowned again as he observed my erect nipples nearly poking through my dress. 'If it turned you on to slap me,' he said very quietly, 'please feel free to do it again.'

I glanced self-consciously down at my breasts. I couldn't say I minded how much attention they had received lately, but I was becoming a bit concerned about the constant state of arousal my body was experiencing since I'd landed in Egypt. It made resisting a handsome man's advances very difficult, and in this case impossible. When Simon grasped both my arms and pulled me to my feet, I meant to protest, but the lips on my face remained sealed as I felt the lips of my sex gape open willingly. He pushed me back against a wall, and the trace of anger in his lustful stare made me even wetter.

'So, how far did you go with him?' His voice remained dangerously quiet as he cupped my breasts in his hands through the dress and bounced them up and down slowly, almost as if weighing my character along with them.

'All the way,' I confessed, and cried out from the excruciating pleasure as he gave my soft mounds a punishing squeeze.

'Did you suck his cock?'

I met his eyes. 'Yes.'

He released me to unzip his pants. 'Then you won't mind sucking mine now, will you?'

I shook my head. 'No, please, Simon, I'm really tired.' This was true. I didn't have to tell him I just wasn't inspired to worship his penis as I had Richard's.

'You're tired, are you?' He didn't sound convinced, but he zipped his pants back up as though he were. 'Too tired to stand for a little while?' He reached down and deftly undid the clasp of my fish belt, letting it fall to the floor with a delicate ringing sound that echoed in my nerve-endings.

'No, I guess not,' I said, wondering what he had in mind.

I found out when he knelt before me and impatiently shoved my dress up my legs. The soft material formed a cloudy halo around my hips as I willingly spread my legs just far enough to accommodate his face between them. I couldn't believe another attractive man was eating me out hungrily, and yet my pussy had no problem accepting more stimulating attention. Holding my dress up out of his way, I stood motionless as a statue being worshipped. I watched his blond head for a while as it worked between my thighs, but then I just stared straight ahead into space like a true princess accepting the passionate devotion of one of her many subjects. His tongue was technically as agile as Richard's and yet somehow not as skilled because he wasn't as sensitive to the escalations and fluctuations of my pleasure. For a breathtaking moment his mouth would fondle my clitoris in just the right way, but then suddenly it would move on and the glorious current of a climax would ebb again, making his oral attention as frustrating as it was enjoyable.

Mary Fallon would have felt guilty about how long she was letting a man work on her like this, but Nefer-marymun was thoroughly and selfishly enjoying herself. I could see my reflection in the mirror over the dresser, and the delight lapping between my thighs felt like a fitting reward for how strikingly beautiful I looked, the blond head between my legs an infinitely more priceless gift than the jewels I was wearing. Then he abruptly brought his right hand into play, almost savagely thrusting two fingers up into my wildly juicing slit, and I saw the lovely statue in the glass come alive as I cried out in ecstasy.

He worked on me longer than any man ever had, and yet I couldn't come. Every time I felt the current of an orgasm rushing towards his sucking mouth and cresting tongue, it flowed disappointingly away again as I thought of Richard E'Ahmose, mysteriously more alive inside me than the physical pleasure another man was struggling to give me. Finally Simon stood up slowly in defeat, wiping his mouth on the back of his sleeve. I was so wet, I felt as though I had come close to drowning him without even climaxing.

'I'm sorry,' I murmured, letting my dress slip down my legs. 'But it's usually hard for me to come like that.' I kept telling him the truth, but only half of it. It was hard for me to come like that except with Richard.

'I enjoyed it very much, Mary.'

'Me too,' I said quickly.

'Yes,' he smiled ruefully, 'I know. But you warned me you were tired, and I still insisted on taking advantage of you. I'm the one who should be apologizing.'

Suddenly I wondered: what am I doing? I was blowing my chances with a handsome Egyptologist who was clearly interested in winning my affections, because I was perversely obsessed with a decadently rich Englishman obsessed with the occult. 'Oh Simon.' I slipped my arms around his chest and rested my cheek against his hard shoulder, 'I'm so confused.'

'Just give me a chance, Mary.'

I stepped back so I could look up at his face. 'Of course,' I said.

He returned my earnest regard with a long unreadable stare. 'We're both tired,' he concluded at last. 'Do you mind sharing your bed with me, or should I go sleep out on the couch?'

'Of course I don't mind.'

'Then take off your jewels princess, and let's hit the sack.'

Chapter Seven

The next day dawned bright and beautiful (nothing unusual in Egypt) and found me sitting at the dining room table with my chin in my hands half hypnotized by the twin serpents of Simon's lips as he talked, and talked and talked. This time he was wide awake, only now he was in danger of putting everyone else to sleep.

Still, he had put his tongue to such good use again that morning that part of me was feeling open to whatever he had to say. I had awakened as his golden head sank between my legs, and then it was as if the sun slowly rose inside me as I felt his warm tongue dipping and swirling. He quickly coaxed a sweet climax from my sleepy clitoris, in a sense catching it off guard before it had time to tense up in response to my thoughts of another man.

Now the four of us, Carol and Steve and Simon and I, were sitting around the polished mahogany table that belonged to the nameless American government worker who owned this generically furnished apartment. We had enjoyed a light breakfast of toast and preserves and were lingering over second helpings of coffee, which I had brewed good and strong—except for Carol, of course, who was drinking her proverbial tea.

I glanced at Steve, admiring his recuperative powers—I still hadn't seen him wearing a shirt. Carol wanted to hear all about my 'adventure' with Richard, but Simon obviously didn't, which is probably one reason he kept talking. If I hadn't found his subject matter so interesting, his evasiveness might have annoyed me.

While we prepared breakfast, Carol filled me in on what had happened after Richard carried me away on horseback. She confirmed that Simon had indeed sent his man to the Mina House to make sure Richard had taken me there. She

Dreams of Anubis

also thought it highly significant that her boss had not gotten any work done yesterday. 'Let me tell you, Mary,' she whispered conspiratorially over the toaster, 'ever since I started working for him, absolutely nothing has kept him away from Saqqara for even half a day. Once he had a fever and yet he and Steve still went out to work. He must really have feelings for you. He stayed here waiting for news of you all day. I think he was hoping you'd show up like you finally did, and I think he had one too many scotches because he fell asleep in the guestroom where you found him. Now, quick, tell me what happened with Richard!'

But I hadn't had time to comply with her request; bread doesn't take that long to toast and both Steve and Simon came to hover hungrily in the doorway.

'Advances in modern neurology prove the ancient Egyptians understood the workings of the nervous system,' Simon informed us now, staring deep into my eyes, 'as well as the different relationships between the areas of the brain and how they control all our bodily functions.'

'Is that so?' I prompted.

'Yes.' He spun his empty coffee cup around and around as he spoke like a miniature parody of a flying saucer. 'That's so, Mary.'

I had to bite my tongue to keep from saying, 'Nefer-marymun, if you please.'

Carol placidly sipped her Green Tea.

Steve's face and inevitably bare chest were now hidden behind the tiny black hieroglyphs of *The New York Times*.

'As modern studies progress in such areas as the psychological aspects of healing and the effects of sound-waves on the body,' Simon went on as if everyone were listening attentively, 'even the incantations used in ancient healing methods can receive serious consideration. Ultra-sound is commonly used in advanced surgery today. May I have some more coffee, please, Mary?'

'Certainly, Simon.' I smiled at him sweetly, picked up his cup and returned to the kitchen with it.

'I need more tea,' Carol declared, following me. 'Tell me!' she whispered. 'Did you sleep with Richard?'

I smiled beatifically as I refilled Simon's cup. 'What do you think?'

Unfortunately, he took his coffee black, because cream and sugar would have given us an excuse to linger in the kitchen.

'I think you definitely slept with him.'

'I think you're definitely right.'

'Mary!' She looked genuinely shocked. 'You're sleeping with two men at once?'

'I didn't plan on it,' I started back out to the dining room, 'it just happened.'

'What just happened?' Simon inquired suspiciously.

'Excuse me,' Carol said stiffly, and a moment later I heard the bathroom door close firmly behind her. I knew from past experience that she would not emerge from her humid haven for at least half an hour.

'Nothing,' I said, my smile and voice so sweet they more than made up for the lack of sugar in his coffee.

He stared fixedly at my face as I seated myself again. 'This process of gradual upgrading,' he continued where he had left off, 'has been taking place in every specialty within the field covered by Egyptology.'

'That's fascinating,' I said truthfully, yet it was also true that his monologue was starting to bore Nefer-marymun.

'Just how much the Egyptians and other ancient cultures knew about astronomy,' he seemed content to have only me for an audience, 'is finally being recognized by even the most conservative historians now.' A curl of his lip indicated what he thought of these academic turtles.

'Yes, I know, it's called Archeo Astronomy, isn't it?'

'Very good, Mary.' His passion for the subject kept him from sounding condescending. 'But what's even more interesting is that advances in high energy physics, molecular biology and even genetics can be applied to ancient creation myths which at first seem so alien and arbitrary.'

Steve snapped the Times down onto his lap. 'Get to the goddamned point,' he said, winking at me sympathetically as he folded the newspaper. 'You're putting the poor girl to sleep.'

'The point is, I believe there was once a great doctrine in which science, religion, philosophy and art were all fused into a grand synthesis,' Simon at

Dreams of Anubis

last came to his impressive conclusion. 'And I believe this fusion, and the mysterious power latent within it, was responsible for the temples and pyramids of ancient Egypt.'

'Amen.' Steve slammed the newspaper down on the table before him as though swatting a fly taking the form of a period finally punctuating Simon's endless speech. 'Now let's get down to business, shall we?' Impatiently, he smoothed his hair back away from his forehead, and I noted it was no longer full of sand. I couldn't help thinking that his bare chest was not very businesslike, but he folded his hands before him on the table as seriously as an executive vice president in a conference room.

'What the hell are we going to do about this bastard, Simon?' I could only assume he was referring to Sir Ashley. 'He knows we've discovered the entrance to Imhotep's mastaba. The crazy bastard's rich enough to dabble in whatever profession he pleases, and right now, unfortunately for us, it pleases him to be interested in ancient Egypt.'

'Which he seems to know a great deal about,' I remarked.

'Listen to her,' Simon said, 'she sounds as though she enjoyed her stay at the Mina House.' The fact that he was suddenly referring to me in the third person gave away how angry he was even though his expression and the tone of his voice were perfectly civil. 'I hear Sir Ashley has a suite on the top floor decorated with an extensive collection of ancient artifacts as well as more contemporary antiques. It must be lovely.'

Steve asked me quickly, 'Do you have any idea how he knew about the photograph, Mary?'

'Yes,' I replied, my stare locked with Simon's in the painful way fingers stick to ice, 'he dreamed about it.'

'What?' Steve sat back in his chair. 'He dreamed about it?'

'That's what he told me.'

'And you believed him?' Simon asked, but it sounded more like an accusation.

'He appears to be somewhat psychic,' I replied evasively.

He turned his head and stared out the living room window at the clear blue sky.

'He told me he sometimes has true dreams,' I added quietly, but it would have felt like betraying Richard to say more.

'Go on, Mary,' Simon urged while continuing to stare impassively out at the heavens. 'I know there's more, and there's no reason you shouldn't tell us.' He met my eyes again abruptly. 'Is there? It's not exactly a secret that Sir Ashley is interested in the occult, like so many of his wealthy British predecessors.'

'You're right, there's no reason I shouldn't tell you. After all, everyone believes whatever they want to.' I was talking fast, irritated that his skeptical attitude had the power to make me question all the fervent feelings I had experienced with Richard. 'Sir Ashley believes he was once a priest of Anubis and a wearer of the Winged Sandals,' I blurted.

'Winged sandals?' Steve repeated blankly.

'Yes, Winged Sandals,' Simon echoed. 'Interesting. And I suppose that you, Mary, are his long lost priestess?' His eyes shone like mirrors reflecting the sky, giving nothing away while making me see my poetic emotions as mere character flaws it was necessary for me to outgrow.

'That's what he would like me to believe,' I replied guardedly, and was humiliated by the realization that I had sunk completely back into Mary Fallon's rationally limited perceptions and forsaken Nefermun along with my deepest feelings, simply because I had no way of proving them. Yet even if there truly was something supernatural going on between Richard and me, Simon was the last person I wanted to be talking to about it.

'Let me get this straight, Mary.' He drained his third cup of coffee as though he needed every drop of caffeine to deal with Sir Ashley's deluded dreams. 'All day yesterday you sat in a room filled with copies of some of the treasures that might be found in an Egyptian tomb, and in the evening, Richard wined and dined you while very politely suggesting you had been lovers in a past incarnation, more specifically wearers of the Winged Sandals, and that dreams had led him to you again after countless centuries?'

I was aghast. Put that way, Richard's methods seemed so cheap and obvious that I felt my self-esteem plummeting into the dimples of the Egyptologist's

Dreams of Anubis

maddeningly superior smile. At least Mary Fallon did. Nefermun and Nefermarymun were both furious that someone was discussing Richard in such a disrespectfully judgmental fashion, blithely making light of his profound conviction in the immortality of the soul and the deathless power of love simply because they did not share in his beliefs.

'He left you there all day so you'd begin to feel like a mummy in her tomb,' Simon went on smugly, undoubtedly encouraged by my troubled expression. 'There wasn't any electricity, nothing modern in the room at all except the bed, and the central air-conditioner, of course. Am I correct?'

I nodded, too upset to speak.

'He hid your clothes and forced you to dress like an ancient Egyptian princess—'

'Excuse me, but he didn't force me to do anything.' I came back to life. 'I want to make that perfectly clear. He behaved like a perfect gentleman the entire time.' That wasn't exactly true, of course, but everything he'd done had pleased me and that was the truth.

'So you willingly left the mastaba with him?'

'Yes, I did.' I couldn't lie. 'Not that you were doing much to stop me,' I added petulantly. 'But you're right, he did all those things you described, and when it got dark I had to light a lotus flower lamp. And you know what? It was beautiful. I enjoyed every minute I spent at the Mina House.'

'And he showered you with jewels,' Simon reminded me. 'No woman ever born ever complained about that. They're beautiful copies of ancient pieces made of real gold and lapis-lazuli and other precious stones. You should see them, Steve. They're exquisite reproductions of Middle Kingdom pieces.'

'Well, what do you expect,' his assistant scoffed, 'the ass-hole's richer than pharaoh.'

And it seemed to me that these grant-dependent American anthropologists were decidedly jealous of the Englishman's financial independence.

Simon smoothed his hair back away from his face with both hands so forcefully it made his skull look gilded. There was a thin line of tension carved horizontally across the center of his forehead, and another smaller line was etched between his eyebrows, the only visible signs of the slight hangover he must have been suffering after drinking half a bottle of twelve-year-old scotch. Then suddenly he laughed, a harsh, disturbing sound.

'What's so funny?' I demanded.

'Carol, oh, Carol?' Steve called plaintively. 'Where are you, honey?'

'I'm sorry, Mary.' Simon's soul suddenly returned to his glassy eyes as his long fingers began fiddling awkwardly with his empty cup again.

'Sorry for what, for not doing anything to stop me from leaving the mastaba with Richard?'

His eyebrow arched again in that infuriatingly superior way. 'But I thought you said you went with him willingly, Mary?'

'I did.'

'Then there was no need to stop anyone, was there?'

'Oh, forget it! Is it true we were breaking the law by camping out in Ti's tomb?' I desperately changed the subject.

All the warmth vanished from his eyes again. 'You'd better decide right now what side you're on, sweetheart.'

I should have been prepared for the challenge, but I wasn't. I had been postponing the moment when I would have to choose between these two men and both of them had captured my imagination and my feelings in devastatingly exciting ways. But now the moment had come, and I couldn't seem to find my voice. I was looking directly into Simon's eyes, but I was seeing a dark room lit only by a golden lotus lamp and feeling the strong, bare arms of a man reaching for me as the sunset burned like the blood of all the gods behind him and my blood purred joyfully through my body as he kissed me...

'Shit,' Steve whispered, 'he got to her.'

'Mary?'

That was all Simon said, but the concern in his voice broke a mysterious dam inside me. With a wild rush of verbs and adjectives, I heard myself trying to describe the dream I had had in the mastaba and the mystical feelings and visions Richard inspired in me.

'He must have drugged her,' Steve concluded cynically.

Dreams of Anubis

I shook my head. 'No, he didn't, and I had the dream before I even met him.'

'The dream you were having in the mastaba when I woke you,' Simon remembered out loud.

'Yes.'

'Then he must have hypnotized you somehow.' Steve stubbornly insisted on believing Richard had coerced me into desiring him. 'Either that, or you have an overactive imagination that's easily influenced by—'

'Excuse me?' I snapped.

'Or it could have been a genuine mystical experience,' Simon conceded with suspicious good grace. 'But whether you and Richard were acquainted in a past life is irrelevant now, Mary.'

'That's right, because whoever he was in the past, if you believe in all that reincarnation crap,' Steve threw in with admirable objectivity, 'in the real life present, he's a bastard, plain and simple.'

'Reincarnation is not crap.' Carol had returned. She seated herself beside Steve again looking as fresh as a dew-covered lily with her long braided hair hanging in a thick stem down her back.

'Let's not get into a metaphysical discussion.' Simon crossed his arms and relaxed in his chair. 'Mary is simply trying to decide who to trust in the here and now.'

'I never said I didn't trust you, Simon, and Richard has a right to believe whatever he wants to.'

'What's going on here?' Carol demanded with unusual firmness. 'What did that man say to you, Mary?'

'I have a feeling he threw dirt, or more appropriately sand, at my personal and professional integrity,' Simon told her soberly—and he certainly was sober this morning.

'And you believed him?' Carol accused me.

'Look, they asked me how Richard knew about the photograph, and I told them, he dreamed about it, but I have no idea if he was lying or not.'

Nefermun angrily squeezed my heart as I said this, but I desperately wanted this conversation to end. I wasn't ready to choose between Simon and Richard, not yet; I needed more time to think, or more importantly, to feel.

'Some people really do have extra sensory perceptions,' I added, 'it's not impossible whether you care to believe it or not. And I certainly don't see how playing with my head could possibly help him steal your discovery of Imhotep's tomb, which is what I assume you think he's trying to do. Yet I don't see why he would even bother. He's not an Egyptologist, and you told me yourself the Antiquities Department will be all over the find once it's made public.'

'Or maybe he thinks he's the reincarnation of Imhotep and doesn't want us violating his eternal resting place.' Steve's sarcasm was so intense he almost sounded serious. 'Maybe he's deluded enough to imagine he has occult rights to the mastaba.'

'Yes, and maybe he's anxious for you to begin digging and it's the delay that's bothering him,' Carol elaborated as though her lover really were serious. 'Maybe he feels his powers will be enhanced once his mastaba comes to light.'

'Carol?' Steve waved his hand in front of her face. 'Earth to Carol.'

'This conversation is degenerating fast,' Simon observed.

I looked at him, and was surprised to sense he was disturbed, not about me, and my shifting sensual and emotional loyalties, but about something else, something he felt powerless to control. Maybe it was the hangover, but I didn't think so. I was already sensitive to what went on inside him, his thoughts and feelings were like waves beating against the shore of my awareness, and I sensed now that Carol's fancifully occult diagnosis actually bothered him. I remembered then what he had just been saying, that ancient Egypt was once a place where science, art and religion were a sensuous, powerful whole, and this would have been particularly true in the Old Kingdom, in which Imhotep's reputation was that of the wisest man of his time. If all aspects of life had at one time been a seamless whole, then wisdom would also have meant power, magical power of unimaginable proportions. Or perhaps it wasn't so unimaginable and this sundered union was still reflected in the Great Pyramid and all the feelings it still inspired in people.

I suddenly realized Simon and I were staring deep into each other's eyes, and the way his sky-blue irises shone above the horizon of his smile was all the proof I needed that he had been thinking very much the same thing I had.

Dreams of Anubis

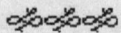

Carol and I were to be rather unceremoniously dropped off at the Cairo Museum, where Hamud would pick us up later that afternoon. Steve and Simon were returning to their work in Saqqara; sunburns and minor hangovers were not about to slow them down. They would return to Cairo in the evening, and the plan was that after they showered and changed we would all go out to dinner (not at the Mina House) and enjoy some of the city's more exotic nightlife (I refrained from mentioning even to Carol that it would be hard to top the exotic evening I had spent with Richard, a.k.a. E'Ahmose, in a bedroom filled with ancient works of art).

I doubted Simon would be in any condition to stay out late tonight—the line across his forehead had been deepening by the second—but it would be fun to watch him try. I was deliberately forcing myself to remain lighthearted. I knew where to find Richard and he knew where to find me, and if all else failed we could always meet up again in a dream. For now I was glad of the brief timeout I was being given. It is an understatement to say I was a bit overwhelmed by my experiences in the Mina House, and Simon's inexhaustible tongue had gone a long way to convincing me that it was in my best interests to honor his request and give him a chance. Nefermun was not so easily swayed, however, and my soul felt painfully torn. I knew the moment I met Simon that he was perfect for me, until Richard strode into my life in the bazaar and I was possessed by the feeling that we had always known, and desired, each other.

I really wasn't in the mood to visit the Cairo Museum, but I didn't say so because what I was in the mood for couldn't be expressed in mixed company. In my opinion, the long sunny afternoon would have been much better spent in a dark bedroom. The question was with whom. As Carol was quick to point out the second Steve and Simon were out of earshot, I couldn't sleep with two men forever. Maybe a tour of lifeless artifacts was just the thing I needed to cool my blood a little, which would hopefully help me think straight and decide once and for all who I wanted to be with, Simon or Richard-E-Ahmose.

The Cairo Museum is a vast, multi-story warehouse-like building depressingly lacking in atmosphere and brimming with treasures. Egyptian civilization lasted thousands of years, but in the Cairo Museum no distinction is made between the different eras and dynasties; beautiful Old Kingdom pieces sit next to decadent Roman imitations. The ground floor of the Victorian building is a veritable forest of statues. Amidst colossi with legs as thick as tree trunks and shoulders the size of boulders, sit smaller, amazingly life-like pieces. As Carol and I wove our way between them, I was particularly drawn to the sculpture of a scribe with his scroll open across his lap. The folds of his soft belly were accurately and humbly depicted, and his smile was so breathtakingly alive I seriously wanted to get to know him. I could feel his love for his work as a scribe, and it might almost have been the centuries unrolling in his lap as he looked up for a moment to rest his shining black eyes.

Carol and I wandered from room to room, admiring art while daydreaming about living, breathing pieces of work. I assumed she was thinking about Steve, and I had the binary suns of Richard and Simon forever in my mind...although with his long dark hair and mystical powers Richard was more like a mysterious black hole to which I was irresistibly drawn.

'You know, Carol,' I joined her in her contemplation of a poorly drawn papyrus of the Ptolomeic era, 'Sometimes I wonder about Lillith, Adam's first wife, you know, the one who got kicked out of paradise for some reason or other.'

She gave me her undivided attention, which was rare for her. 'Why?' she demanded as though her whole life depended on the answer.

I noticed that the armed security guard standing in the doorway was giving us both his undivided attention.

'I don't know...' My train of thought turned a conceptual corner and I almost lost track of it. 'I just can't help wondering why no one ever talks about her. You'd think the first real woman, the woman created by God at the same time as man who wasn't just part of his rib, you'd think she'd be important, wouldn't you? Lillith, the first real woman, got kicked out of paradise for some reason and

Dreams of Anubis

Adam was left with Eve, who wasn't his equal or his soul mate because she was made from his rib, and look what she ended up doing. I mean why is Lillith—?'

'Mary, what the hell are you trying to say?'

'Carol, do you realize there really haven't been any religious figures for women to identify with, at least not that I can think of, since the Egyptian goddess Isis, and the Christians cleaned her up immediately, adopting her as the Virgin Mary. They actually took ancient statues of Isis sitting with her baby Horus, the falcon god, and turned him into Jesus, but Isis was no virgin…although she did conceive Horus with Osiris after he was dead and she found all the pieces of his body the evil Set had scattered across the world except for his penis, but that doesn't make her virginal, just totally, magically, sensual.'

'You're seriously attracted to Richard, aren't you?' She translated my lame theological rambling into a succinct and significant fact.

'Very attracted. I've never been so literally drawn to a man in my life, and yet I'm afraid it might only be a physical—'

'You're incapable of only feeling something physical for a man and you know it, Mary. You always end up falling in love with the guys you sleep with.'

'Mm, yes, that is a problem.'

The security guard took another step towards us.

Carol moved over to a papyrus display case a little farther away from his smoldering interest. 'It's our genetic make-up,' she went on quietly. 'How quickly and intensely a woman gets attached to a man dates back to prehistoric times when men had to get as many women as possible pregnant to procreate the race, and women tied them down in order to raise these children and create a safe environment.'

'Working for an archaeologist is really bringing out your long-buried academic side, Carol, but I think you're suffering from a lobotomy of the imagination looking at the relationship between the sexes so, so naturalistically.' I had no idea if that was actually a word and I didn't care. 'The relationship between men and women is also metaphysical. The sun doesn't need the earth, but the earth and all its beauty wouldn't exist without the sun, and all that cosmic male-female principle stuff.'

'But what purpose would all that fiery burning power serve if it wasn't to create and sustain life?' my friend pointed out astutely. 'Men need and want women just as much as women need and want men.' She glanced over at the guard. 'Let's get out of here. He's getting up his nerve to talk to us and these papyruses aren't that interesting anyway.'

I followed her out of the room. 'So how was it with Steve?' I felt guilty about not asking her before, having been selfishly wrapped up in my own affairs.

'It was really great.'

'Would you care to elaborate? I'm your best friend, remember. What did you do together?'

'Well, everything, I guess.'

'Wow. So, are you just getting him out of your system like you did Simon or do you really like him?'

'I think I love him.'

'Really?'

'Yes!' she sighed.

Chapter Eight

We spent most of our time at the Cairo Museum in the jewelry room. I meditated for a good while on a colorful pectoral of Horus spread out on black cloth in which each tiny inlaid stone was a feather. The piece's stylized realism was strangely uplifting; it was both a detailed representation of a falcon and a symbolic image of the human soul. At its best, ancient Egyptian jewelry is visual poetry. Yet the beautiful pectoral struck me as dead lying inside a sealed glass case. The bird's outspread wings needed a heart beating beneath them to bring them to life. The necklace was meant to be worn against a man's chest, and I couldn't help imagining how good it would look framed by Richard's powerful pecs.

The fact did not escape me that it was not Simon's chest I pictured. I felt like a detective gathering evidence in the form of all my fleeting fantasies, trying to crack the case of which of the two men stalking my thoughts had truly captured my heart and not just my lust.

'Carol,' I whispered, 'I think those two guys over there have been following us.'

'Just ignore them.'

Was it my imagination, or did one of them look familiar? They were dressed in western clothing today, but that didn't mean they couldn't be two of Richard's servants. I could almost swear I had seen them crouching around the fire when Simon and I emerged from Ti's burial chamber. My pulse sped up at the possibility Richard was keeping an eye on me. 'Let's walk away and see if they follow us,' I suggested.

'Whatever.' She shrugged. 'Hamud will be here soon anyway.'

The two Egyptians did indeed follow us out of the jewelry room, but they were hard-pressed to keep up with us. Two slightly overweight men could not hope to match what Carol and I called our 'Boston walk', developed out of

Dreams of Anubis

necessity when traveling from a train station to our destination in wind-chill factors that often plummeted well below zero.

We ran up a long flight of stairs, competing with each other to see who was less out of breath at the top. 'You might as well see the Mummy Room while you're here.' Carol's voice was admirably steady after the exertion. 'You have to pay extra, so maybe they won't follow us in there.'

Beneath the glass roof lay rows of glass cases displaying mummies in varying stages of preservation or decay, depending on whether you see the glass as half full or half empty. Some were nothing but blackened skeletons, yet a few, horribly enough, retained a semblance of life.

'Carol, this is sick,' I muttered, sticking close to her fresh, living body. 'And here they come. I guess they consider us worth the price of admission.'

Our pursuers had the audacity to grin at us as they entered the Mummy Room.

I ignored them as I paused over the remains of Seti I, the best looking mummy ever found, in my opinion. I enjoyed a sobering moment of communion with the long dead pharaoh. In the presence of this once strikingly handsome man, I lost my sensual appetite for a few moments, which broke my stimulating connection with both Richard and Simon and left me standing alone beneath the blue sky, remembering the intense love in E'Ahmose's eyes when we were lying in each other's arms.

'Good bye, Seti,' I whispered, caressing the glass over his face. 'And thank you.'

'Hamud should be here by now,' Carol said, 'let's go.' We wove swiftly between the mummy cases, and it was fun racing each other down the stairs then across the main lobby into the sunlight.

I groped in my purse for my sunglasses, and slipping them on, I spotted the large blue Chevrolet waiting for us at the bottom of the steps, parked directly below us at the curb. 'I want to buy something in the gift shop,' I declared.

'Forget it,' Carol snapped. She knew I wasn't really interested in the little tourist trap. 'We're leaving.'

I shrugged, and followed her down to the car. Even if Richard was having me followed, there was no point in standing around waiting for his men to spot us again, so I slipped compliantly into the back seat.

Carol sat up front with the grinning Hamud, and glanced sternly at me over her shoulder. 'You have to decide between Richard and Simon right now, Mary.'

'Right this minute?'

Hamud gazed curiously at my face in the rear-view mirror.

I frowned back at him playfully. 'He didn't have to choose,' I pointed out. 'How many wives does he have anyway, two, three? So why can't a woman have two men?'

His gold tooth flashed in the sunlight. 'Room for one more,' he announced.

'Shut-up, Hamud,' Carol said fondly. 'Mary, you have so much in common with Simon. You seem perfect for each other. You're the only person I know who actually likes listening to him talk. I don't think you should risk blowing your chances with him by letting some crazy rich Englishman turn your head. I realize Simon is dirt poor but—'

'Carol, Richard is not crazy, and it's not about the money. You know me better than that.' I slumped down in the seat so I was no longer reflected in the rearview mirror. 'Would you tell your chauffeur to keep his eyes on the road, please.' Without him seeming to pay any attention to its progress, the big car was swerving like an enchanted snake through the basket-like metal weave of bumper-to-bumper traffic.

'You have to be careful, Mary.' Carol was working herself up into full lecture mode. 'I know you're on vacation, but how you behave now can affect the rest of your life.'

The temperature in the car was plummeting by the second; Hamud enjoyed basking in the air-conditioner's Arctic breeze.

'You know what you said this morning about Richard and Imhotep's tomb, Carol, that he was anxious for Simon to start digging because he feels his powers will be enhanced once this mastaba comes to light?'

'I have no idea where that idea came from,' she admitted, sounding proud of her occult reasoning powers.

'Well, wherever it came from, I think Simon took it seriously.'

'No way.'

'The look in his blue eyes after you suggested it, it was like catching a glimpse of the sky the way it looked thousands of years ago before the pollution of cynicism.'

Dreams of Anubis

'That's a beautiful image, Mary, I think you're in love with him.'

'He's not your normal academic Egyptologist.' I ignored her romantic conclusion. 'I get the feeling he's trying to decode Saqqara's symbolism, not just create a detailed record of the bas-reliefs in each mastaba for posterity. I'm beginning to suspect all those beautiful bas-reliefs are equations and that there's an actual power hidden inside them.'

We were driving along the Nile now and the pyramids were visible on the opposite bank, small and far away yet still awe-inspiring.

'I think Simon is worried that Richard believes in the synthesis he was talking about this morning,' I went on enthusiastically. 'I think they're actually both after the same thing, but in different ways.'

'Imhotep's mastaba, or you, Mary?'

I let my feelings purr around this question for a moment. 'No, it's more than Imhotep's mastaba. Richard doesn't believe he's Imhotep's reincarnation. He's not some New Age flake, trust me on this one. I know for a fact that he believes his name was E'Ahmose, which means Born of the Moon, and that he was a priest of Anubis. I really don't think he's lying about his psychic powers either. He says he has true dreams, and I believe him.'

'Because you desire him.'

'No, because he knew what I dreamed the other day when I fell asleep in the mastaba. He described the details of my dream to me exactly—but now you made me forget what I was going to say. Where was I?'

'I have no idea.'

'You suggested that Richard wants to tap into Imhotep's power once his mastaba is unearthed. Imhotep was high priest, he designed the entire Zoser complex at Saqqara, the Step Pyramid and everything.'

'I know, Mary,' she sighed, 'I work there. Richard wants to be a maker of stone vases, too?'

'What?'

'That's the only one of Imhotep's titles I remember Simon ranting on about because it sounded so funny coming after all those other pretentious ones.'

'Would you please be serious, Carol. I feel like I'm on the verge of understanding something very important here.' I was struggling to give birth to a theory straining the parameters of my rational mind. 'Imhotep designed the Zoser complex and built it himself,' I went on. 'High priest wasn't just a prestigious title given to someone who burned incense and chanted meaningless spells, not if the synthesis of art and science and religion Simon was talking about this morning really existed. A high priest of ancient Egypt would have commanded literal, physical forces because he fully understood who, and what, he was. He would have believed beyond a shadow of a doubt, he would have known in his being in a way we've lost the ability to know, that his soul was an indestructible energy and his physical body merely a garment his naked power had slipped on for a while. The gods of Egypt are all symbolic expressions of the different stages involved in pure energy, or the pure force of life, taking form and becoming matter. Modern physics is saying the same thing in different ways, and I think the Egyptians believed that the creation of the universe is directly related to the human soul and its development, which means—'

'We're home,' Carol announced, sounding infinitely relieved. 'You can finish telling me all this later.'

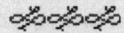

Back up in the guestroom, I was hit by a wave of restlessness that made the blank white walls of the modern room feel like an empty shell. I collapsed onto the edge of the bed, and fell heavily back across it to stop myself from calling a cab to take me to the Mina House hotel. Now that I had consciously made my choice, every second I spent away from my beautiful E'Ahmose felt like a century. And yet reason told me to keep my date with Simon, even if it was only to politely inform him that I was in love with Richard.

Carol was running a bath for herself, which meant I had more time on my hands than I knew what to do with until it was my turn to bathe and dress for dinner. I told myself I should enjoy the time alone, but it was impossible to relax feeling as though I had expensive champagne flowing through my body instead of blood. I was so intoxicatingly in love with Richard E'Ahmose the possibility of

Dreams of Anubis

choosing Simon instead felt like a silly hiccup I had indulged in. The truth was, part of me had known from the moment I saw Richard's face and heard his voice in the bazaar that my heart and soul were lost to this enigmatically sexy stranger, and only my ridiculously rational mind had continued considering Simon.

I rolled restlessly over onto my stomach remembering the last time I had done this, and the hot stab of desire I experienced between my thighs made me moan into the mattress. Then I heard Richard's deep voice in my head saying, 'Remember your dreams, Mary…' and suddenly I knew I had a possible way out of the cage-like guestroom, less alive than an ancient Egyptian tomb which had at least been decorated with vibrant scenes of life. I would take a nap. I would try to fall asleep and see if I could meet my Priest of Anubis again in a dream. I hadn't seen him last night after I went to bed, but Simon had been lying next to me, and my uncomfortable awareness of his naked body kept waking me up throughout the night. There was nothing to prevent me from falling into a deep sleep now.

I got up and quickly stripped off my clothes, including my panties. I felt it was important to completely open myself to the purely sensual dimension I was consciously seeking to explore. There was no avoiding the slightly gritty feel of the polyester comforter as I lay down again, but I closed my eyes determined to ignore this reminder that I was in the twenty-first century. I had thought it would be difficult to fall asleep since I was feeling so strangely on edge, so it was a pleasant surprise when I felt my limbs growing gratefully heavy, and sinking into the bed in the unmistakably delicious way I knew would soon drown the constant chatter in my head and enable the deepest parts of me to drift off.

A loud beating sound directly above me startled me into sitting up.

'Meooow!' E'Ahmose the cat yowls in frustration that all the birds have gotten away from him again.

I blink, dazzled by the light and all the vibrant colors suddenly surrounding me. Then I realize it is the spirit of the setting sun sparkling across the water trapped in my dark lashes as my vision slowly comes into focus. Tall papyrus stalks form natural dark-green columns on either side of the river, that narrows to an intimate channel here in the place where we like to come fowling. The excited feline looks like a living figurehead with this front paws perched on the prow of the boat, but it is the tall, tanned man through whose legs I am able to see my cat who captures all my attention. Only a short white loincloth interferes with the sinuous flow of his muscles even as it enhances the bronzed smoothness of his skin. His back is to me, but every cell in my body recognizes his as my blood seems to course more joyously down the haunting tributaries of my veins at the sight of him. I feel wonderfully relaxed where I lie across a Nile-blue cloth embroidered with tiny white gazelles leaping across it. The finely woven linen covers a thick grass mattress, and is littered with dark-gold cylindrical pillows made from a lion's skin stuffed with goose feathers.

'Come back to me, my lord,' I say plaintively, hungrily admiring his long, strong back.

'Just one last throw,' he replies, 'so my namesake does not die of frustration.'

I know he is referring to the excitedly taut figure of my cat at the head of our small boat, drifting with the current along the eastern shore as close as possible to dense marshes alive with nesting birds.

'If you do not aim your shaft at me soon,' I tease, squirming languidly, 'it is I who shall die of longing years before our eternal home is finished, and then what will you do with my body?'

About a dozen birds abruptly explode from the marshes and, my heart racing, I watch with pleasure as my lover casts his spear into the heart of the wildly beating flock with the controlled power I am forever longing to be the victim of. It seems a small but wholly fitting tribute to his cat-like speed and grace when one of the winged creatures drops straight down from the sky at his sandaled feet, his weapon thrust deep into its delicious little body. He just has time enough to pull the small spear out of the dead bird before the four-legged E'Ahmose sinks his fangs into what he obviously considers his rightful prey, and hauls it triumphantly away to his place at the head of the boat.

The tall, two-legged E'Ahmose turns towards me, smiling. 'There,' he declares, kneeling on our make-shift bed, 'that demanding animal of yours is satisfied for the moment, so now I can concentrate on the much more arduous task of satisfying you, my love. It will take more than one thrust to quiet your wild desires, Nefermun.' He spreads himself on top of me as he speaks, aligning his sex with mine, and he is so much taller that I find my face on a level with his heart, which feels just right since it is his presence in the world that puts a smile on my lips, and makes me glad to open my eyes every morning as I inhale the subtly invigorating scent of his naked body lying beside me.

'Oh my lord!' I hold on to him, suddenly afraid the gods will take him away from me as jealous punishment for worshipping their priest more than them. 'Promise you'll never leave me, E'Ahmose.'

'Sweet Nefermun,' he kisses my forehead, effortlessly banishing the demons of my frightened thoughts as he lifts his body slightly off mine to find the opening in my pleated garment, 'we will be together forever,' he parts my dress as I unpin his loincloth, 'in this world and in any other Re shapes for the pleasure of our flesh through the soul of the gods.'

I do not need to reach down and guide his erection, for his rigid length makes its way effortlessly into my tight channel. I sigh happily, raising my legs and wrapping them possessively around his hips as he begins thrusting hard, the full weight of his body pinning mine down beneath it. This evening there is no torturous savoring of the moment of union; his face buried in a lion-skin pillow, he penetrates me fast and furiously, concentrating on the divine exercise of driving his cock as deep into my body as possible even while pulling it almost all the way out, subjecting me to the exquisite agony of his head parting my labia and his rampant penis — solid as a god's golden phallus — rending me open time and time again. I love it when he possesses me like this, seemingly without a thought for my feelings, which inexplicably stokes my excitement almost more than when he is being a patient and considerate lover. I love the experience of his firm muscles straining against my soft curves trapped beneath them. I love the sensation of his balls slapping against my wet sex blending with the sound of the river lapping against the hull as I sense my flesh becoming deeper and deeper for him. And yet I am also his vessel contentedly riding the current of the pleasure I can give him simply by lying passively beneath him. Then I lift my legs high and spread them wide so as not to hinder the violent choppiness of his hips as I sense an orgasm carry his soul away like a powerful undertow leaving his gasping body lying motionless in my arms.

Chapter Nine

'Mary was saying something really strange in the car today,' Carol remarked at dinner that evening.

Simon looked even worse than I had expected he would; he could barely keep his eyes open, which made him look intensely angry, or maybe he *was* angry, with me, because he could sense I had already chosen Richard over him.

I nearly hadn't recognized Steve at first because he was wearing a shirt, and judging from his expression it had been hand-woven in a monastery of self-flagellating monks. The top three buttons were undone, yet he still kept tugging on the collar to get the starched rim away from the back of his sunburned neck.

Not surprisingly, neither Simon nor Steve reacted to Carol's vague statement. The former was enjoying his 'hair of the dog' with a vengeance, and the latter was too busy writhing like a caterpillar struggling to find a way out of its cocoon. And I for one was too busy missing Richard, or E'Ahmose, or was there a difference? The only way I had been able to console myself after I awoke from my second amazingly vivid dream of the man I had loved centuries ago was to choose a white dress for the evening that was the closest thing I owned to an ancient Egyptian gown. The halter top set off my shapely shoulders, and made a bra impossible, but I was no longer shy about showing off my lovely nipples. The dress clung gently to my curves and ended at mid thigh, enabling me to show off the legs so many men had admired in white high-heeled strap sandals. And since I didn't feel it was right to wear the jewelry Richard had given me while I was supposedly out on a date with another man, I hadn't adorned my body with anything at all. Only my nails were still sporting an expensive French manicure that I frowned down on now, thinking that the delicate almond polish

Dreams of Anubis

I had seen in my first dream might be more interesting.

'I love the way everyone just ignores me,' Carol declared petulantly.

'Sorry. What did you say, honey?' Steve made a noble effort to concentrate on something other than his physical misery.

'Oh never mind.' She pouted.

'She said "Mary said something very strange in the car today".' Simon said. 'Which means it probably made profound sense,' he found the energy to add.

'Thank you,' I chimed in. 'I rather think it did. I was just telling Carol that I don't believe your book is a mere documentation for posterity of Saqqara's bas-reliefs. I believe you're studying them the way a physicist would work on an equation. I think you're trying to decode their symbolic language because you believe the Egyptian's had access to a very real physical power resulting from the synthesis of art, science and religion that you were talking about this morning, a force mankind lost when it concentrated on developing the rational part of the brain that can't see how, on an invisible level, everything is a mysterious whole.'

His eyes opened almost all the way, but remained fixed on his drink. 'Now is not the time, Mary,' he said wearily.

'And why isn't it?'

'Because the show is about to begin.'

A milky spotlight suddenly spilled between the two rows of tables and a loud, rhythmically pulsing music burst out of hidden speakers, making further conversation impossible. There was the trill of a tambourine evocative of Hathor's sistrum, and then a vision sashayed into the light—a woman trailing golden gossamer-thin veils like hazy morning sunshine flowing over her green bra flowering with red tassels that danced against a snowy field of naked flesh. In her navel gleamed a dark-red jewel held magically in place as her belly undulated and rippled in enviably supple waves. Her luxurious black hair was pinned up away from her face but allowed to tumble freely down her back. Her unveiled features were heavily but tastefully made up, and her bone structure was strikingly beautiful.

After the inevitable stab of jealousy, I allowed myself to succumb to the dancer's spell. It was amazing how she could jiggle her hips and make a supple wave out of her soft yet toned belly, and coordinate these tantalizing displays of erotic skill with the graceful motion of her arms as well as the precise steps of her bare feet. It made me wish I possessed such athletic control of my torso so I could treat Richard in private to this enticing visual display of a woman's mysterious inner muscles. The firm control the dancer had over her undulating curves beneath the expressive arcs of her arms symbolically transformed her whole body into a woman's sexual organ rippling and contracting, yielding and tightening around a man's erect force while her lovely face smiled rapturously and her arms slipped lovingly around him. I was entranced by the spectacle of a professional belly dancer practicing her art, not in the way a man would be, but because it filled me with a sense of my own feminine power.

After her performance, the applause lasted a long time, during which I was surprised and annoyed to catch Simon and Steve whispering to each other, obviously deep in a conversation that had been going on for a while.

'I'm going to the Lady's Room,' Carol announced.

'I'll go with you,' I said. Richard would not have ignored the sensual dance, I was sure of that, and Simon plummeted another notch in my esteem because he obviously had.

'...From the Antiquities Department,' I heard Steve murmur as I got up to leave the table.

'Maybe, but they can't do anything,' Simon replied, looking smug. 'Even if they've heard the rumors, it's illegal to torture us to try and find out the location.'

'Yeah, but they'll be watching us like vultures, and the minute they figure out where the entrance is, they'll bury us in red tape and nationalist rights and hand it over to their own archaeologists on a silver platter.' Steve looked particularly handsome when he was angry. 'A few of them are sitting over there at the bastard's table right now. We'll never swing the excavation rights, never.'

I hurried after Carol, who had been born with a honing device for bathrooms; she always knew where to find them no matter where we were. 'Richard's here!' I whispered.

'What?' She stopped dead. 'Where?'

'Somewhere...oh, my God, there he is!'

Dreams of Anubis

'Mary, you're here with Simon. Remember?' The painful strength of her grip on my arm made me wonder why she hadn't gone into sculpting as well as painting and photography. 'Don't even look at him!'

'But he's so beautiful!'

'"The devil is a charming man",' she quoted glibly, literally dragging me towards the bathroom.

'I don't believe in the devil, Carol.'

'Which makes it all the easier for him to get you.'

'You don't believe in the devil either, for Christ's sake.'

'I know, but I have to say something to stop you from making a fool of yourself. Weren't you scared when he carried you off on horseback? You don't know anything about him except that he's rich.'

'And smart and handsome and great in bed and—'

'So is Simon.'

'Yes,' I wrenched my arm out of her grasp, 'you would know that, wouldn't you.'

I shoved open the bathroom door, frightening away the young Egyptian boy who had been standing just inside it serving as a living towel rack in exchange for baksheesh. When I stormed in, he raced out waving all the white flags of his towels in a terrified surrendering of space to the angry foreign woman.

I slammed into one of the stalls and began relieving myself not just of wine but of the ridiculous jealousy that had possessed me, especially considering the fact that it wasn't Simon I wanted. I knew it now beyond a shadow of a doubt. Twenty-four hours away from Richard had been almost more than I could stand, and my dream of E'Ahmose and Nefermun fowling and fooling around in the marshes was still so fresh and vivid in my mind it hurt. When I realized Richard was in the nightclub with me, the joy that suffused my whole being felt like my heart bursting free of all the minor doubts bandaging it. I had recognized the quality of the joy from my dreams—a happiness as subtle and yet as obvious and wonderful as the sunrise. It was Richard I wanted to spend the rest of my days with, Richard, handsome and intelligent and sensitive enough to consider the possibility that he had lived before. Simon was also extremely bright, and his theories about ancient Egypt were marvelously profound, but I felt there was something missing when I was with him. He believed magical things about ancient Egypt yet failed to apply it to the present and to his own life. He prided himself on the fact that he was a hard-working anthropologist and not just a rich eccentric like Sir Ashley.

Yet it seemed to me that unless you embraced the reality, the fact, of mystery as an undeniable aspect of life, you could never truly be a great scientist. Simon was a wonderful man (although I didn't agree with the selfish way he was covering up a monumental discovery) and Mary Fallon would probably have been happy with him, but my deepest self, Nefermun, would have remained unfulfilled. My true self, the woman I had always imagined being, the intensely sensual yet also deeply spiritual woman waiting curled up in my chest like a sleeping cat dreaming of what life could really be like with the right man, Nefer-marymun would never have been born. Nefer-marymun would never have had a chance to begin realizing herself if I had not met Sir Richard Gerald Ashely. And we would never have met at all if he had not seen me in a dream and traveled across the world to find me against all rational odds.

'Mary?' Carol called plaintively from an adjoining stall. 'Are you all right?'

'I'm fine,' I said cheerfully. We flushed in tandem, and smiled at each other as we washed our hands, forced to shake them dry as the living towel rack had fled. 'I've made my choice, Carol.'

She looked at my face in the mirror, her eyes wide with anticipation.

My smile deepened.

She sighed, 'Richard.'

'Yes. I know you think I hardly know him, but the truth is, part of me knows him better than anyone I've ever met before and I think than anyone I ever will meet. He's my destiny, Carol. I've never felt this way before. Things just got complicated because I happened to meet Simon first, and he seemed so perfect for me that my brain wouldn't let me shake that initial impression and take Richard seriously. You see, my mind mistrusted our irresistible attraction to each other. I thought maybe it was just a sexual thing, but that's because our bodies were responding to the mysterious magnetic attraction between our souls. I don't know if it's true or not, Carol, but with this man I can truly sense I've lived

Dreams of Anubis

before and that love really is forever, and that no matter how many times love changes form, it never dies.'

Her eyes were shining. 'I think I'm going to cry,' she warned.

'Oh Carol,' I slipped an arm around her shoulder, 'don't worry, Simon won't be that upset, he—'

She shrugged my arm off angrily. 'That's not why I'm crying!' She sniffed dramatically. 'It's just so beautiful!'

I laughed. 'It's a beautiful mess I've gotten myself into. That damned photograph complicated things even more. It's strange that my finding my soul mate is coinciding with the discovery of Imhotep's tomb.'

'I believe you love Richard, Mary, but are you sure you can trust him?'

'Carol, I could ask you the same thing. Are you sure you can trust your boss, and Steve for that matter?'

'Steve's the one we found lying unconscious in the desert, not Richard,' she reminded me sharply.

'He told me he had nothing to do with that.'

'And of course you believe him because he's your soul mate. But what are you going to do now? You came here with Simon tonight.'

'I know.' I bit my lip wondering what was the best way to handle the situation.

'You have to come back to the table with me, Mary, you can't be so rude as to—'

'I know,' I repeated. Now that my mind had finally caught up with my heart and soul, every second I spent away from my beloved E'Ahmose was torture, but Simon had already ordered my dinner and I liked and respected him too much to just blow him off. But when we emerged from the bathroom, it was Richard's seated figure my eyes were drawn to.

'Come on, Mary.'

'I'm coming,' I said, but I lingered in the corridor leading on one end to the bathrooms and on the other to the exit.

Richard was talking to the man seated beside him, but suddenly he turned his head and met my eyes as though he had felt the touch of my longing on his skin. Beneath his intent stare my knees began to feel weak, and I had no idea how I was going to convince them to carry me back to Simon instead.

When two black-robed men gently took hold of both my arms and began escorting me towards the exit, I was more relieved than anything. I had fully intended to do the right thing and return to Simon's table to politely break up with him, but it seemed the decision was being taken out of my hands, and I was glad. The moment I became aware of Richard's presence in the club, my body began suffering something akin to physical pain fighting the irresistible need to move towards him and fall into the orbit of his arms. And when our eyes met across the dark room, I knew he felt the same way about me.

I had no idea how he had communicated with his men so quickly, but there was no doubt in my mind or in my heart that it was two of his servants leading me out of the building. Outside, I saw people glance curiously at the young woman walking between two unusually large Egyptians in elegant black robes, but all I cared about was the fact that any moment now Richard and I would be together again. I did notice, however, that the door one of the men opened for me belonged to a long black limousine, and the bare skin of my arms and legs appreciated the exquisitely soft leather interior as I seated myself.

Only a few heartbeats later, the door opened again so Richard could slip in beside me. Almost at once, the gleaming vehicle flowed away from the curb as smoothly as a whale diving into the twisting currents of dark alleys as the lights of Cairo glimmered like moonlit foam behind us.

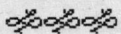

Beneath his black suit jacket my priest of Anubis was wearing a sleeveless white T-shirt tucked into black jeans, and the sight of his strong bare arms as he slipped off the jacket struck me as the hieroglyph spelling out how much I loved this man. He leaned forward in the seat to press a button in the space-age console before him, and a bottle of Champagne appeared as if by magic followed by two crystal flute glasses. The interior of the limousine was incredibly spacious; I think it was bigger than my living room back home. I gladly accepted the glass he offered me, and watched in appreciative silence

Dreams of Anubis

as he filled it with the glimmering liquid. My hand trembled slightly, but it wasn't the car's fault; the ride was so smooth we might have been flying away from the club on a magic carpet.

'Thank you, sir,' I said formally.

He touched his glass to mine. 'My pleasure, Nefer-marymun.'

I took a sip. 'Mm, this bottle must have cost your chauffeur's entire month's salary. It's divine.'

'A compliment and a criticism all wrapped up in one.' He chimed his glass against mine a second time. 'Neatly done.' He smiled.

'I wasn't criticizing you, Richard.'

'I know you weren't, you're just socially conscious. I respect that.'

'Were you born into money?'

'Yes, and as a consequence people tend to assume I was handed everything on a silver platter.'

'Were you?' I sipped my champagne contentedly; it was wonderful just getting to know him better.

'Yes, I suppose I was.' A shadow of concern dimmed his smile. 'Does that bother you?'

'Not at all. I don't believe character is determined by circumstances, not to the extent modern psychology would have us believe, anyway.'

He touched his glass to mine in a third toast. 'You're as wise as you are beautiful, Nefer-marymun.'

'Well, I'm getting there,' I said humbly, draining my glass.

He promptly refilled it, his slate-green eyes inscrutably dark in the limousine's luxurious twilight.

'Why, Sir Ashley,' I drawled with an exaggerated southern accent, 'I do believe you're trying to get me drunk.'

'Have you eaten yet tonight?'

'No.' I felt a stab of guilt. 'Simon had ordered me dinner, but...' I took a long, numbing swig of the fine champagne to forget about the man I had just left stranded in a restaurant along with my best friend and her date.

'Was I mistaken?' he asked quietly.

'Mistaken about what?'

'When our eyes met in the club, I sensed, I knew, you had made your choice, Mary.' He drained his own glass abruptly. 'Was I mistaken?' he asked again even more softly.

'No,' I whispered fervently. 'But I was planning to go back to Simon's table and tell him politely, somehow.'

'I sensed you were torn.' He refilled his glass. 'And I hope you'll forgive me for sparing you an uncomfortable scene that in my opinion wasn't necessary. Mr. Taylor doesn't really care about anyone except himself and his career. He'll be fine without you.'

'That's a bit harsh, don't you think?'

'Not at all, just the sad truth, and I'm glad you haven't eaten tonight. A ritual should always be performed when the gross process of digestion isn't interfering with higher functions.'

'Ritual?' My empty stomach contracted uncomfortably around the portentous word.

'Yes, my love, a sacred rite that will help Nefermun come fully to life inside you and enable you to truly begin living as Nefer-marymun.'

I discovered my throat was suddenly too tight to swallow the fine champagne. 'What exactly do you have in mind, Richard?'

'If it's all right with you, Mary, I'd like you to spend part of the night in a pyramid, the pyramid of Unas, to be precise.'

I laughed. 'Are you joking?'

'No, I'm not.'

I still couldn't quite make out the expression in his eyes, but I could sense my reaction had disappointed him somewhat. 'I'm sorry, Richard, it's just so…unexpected.'

'You should learn to expect the unexpected, my love, always. But it really shouldn't be so unexpected. The final stage of initiation for priests and priestesses of Anubis consisted of spending whole nights alone in the heart of a pyramid.'

'Alone? Did you say alone?'

'You're co cute.' Smiling indulgently, he caressed my cheek with the fingertips of his free hand in the way that made me feel infinitely precious. 'Don't be afraid, I'll be with you in the beginning, and at the end.'

'Richard, I—'

'Hush.' He gently placed his index finger over my lips. 'You know Nefermun wants this more than anything and that only Mary is getting the jitters.'

I looked deep into myself while gazing into his shadowed eyes and realized he was absolutely right, as usual.

'It was fun fowling in the marshes this afternoon, wasn't it?' he asked casually, and his smile deepened as I nearly dropped my glass.

'You were there?' I breathed.

'Yes. I'm so proud of you, Mary,' he added seriously, 'you've come so far so fast, no pun intended. You're so close to finding the key that will unlock abilities buried deep inside you. That's why I arranged for this ritual tonight, because you're ready.'

'Ready for what?'

'To slip on some Winged Sandals, my love.'

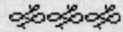

I discovered during the long ride to Saqqara that eating was not the only thing prohibited before an important ritual. We spent a good part of the journey kissing and caressing each other, but that was as far as Richard would allow us to go. He said we couldn't waste any of our vital energy ahead of time. His mystical logic made perfect sense to me, especially when his tongue was passionately explaining it to me without words, and wondering what exactly he had planned was getting me so wet my pussy felt hotter and deeper by the second. I moaned, desperate to feel his magnificent penis opening me up as it filled me completely, but for the moment I was content to settle for the hard hand he thrust between my thighs to cradle my smoldering sex.

'Please,' I begged, clinging to his shoulders and kissing the deliciously firm yet tender side of his neck.

'No,' he whispered, his breath hot on my temple as he pulled gently on my hair to lift my face up to his again, 'not yet.'

I gasped when he pressed the heel of his hand against the infinitely sensitive seed of my clitoris through my cotton panties, and began moving it up and down slowly. 'Do you like that?' he whispered in my ear.

'Oh yes, don't stop.'

'I can't let you come,' he warned.

I leaned slightly back in the seat and caressed his hard arm down to his wrist, pressing his hand even harder against my clit. 'But I want to come,' I said softly, longingly.

'You can't,' he insisted even as he kept moving his hand relentlessly against me, 'not yet.'

I felt increasingly desperate for him to take off my panties and at least slip some of his fingers inside me, but he knew if he went so far that I would climax around his penetrating digits, so he deliberately left the frustrating white bandage of my panties covering my aching sex even as he kept rubbing my clit with the heel of his palm, at once cruelly teasing me and thoroughly pleasing me.

'Oh God, stop,' I begged breathlessly. 'I'm going to come if you don't stop!'

'No, you won't.' He kept up his subtle rhythmic caressing of the crown of my sex where my pleasure was growing and swelling, threatening to reach a peak from which all my feelings would plunge into a shattering climax. 'I'm going to bring you to the edge, Mary, and you're going to hold yourself there.'

'Oh God, I can't.'

'Yes, you can.' His voice was as firm as the base of his hand beneath which he was expertly massaging and stimulating the divine little seed of my flesh. 'You're going to poise your body on the brink of pleasure, Nefer-marymun, and let the promise of it suffuse your entire being, not just your body.'

'Richard, I can't do it, I can't!' I flung my arms up over my head and held on to the back of the seat as I gazed down the length of his arm. It was so straight and hard I thought of the serpents the god of eternity grasped in his hands, and I felt the beginning of an orgasm licking my clit like a hot tongue threatening to fork through my veins as a searing pleasure. 'You're just too good!' I gasped. 'You know just how to do that.'

Dreams of Anubis

He laughed beneath his breath, but his voice was serious. 'When you're sure, absolutely sure you can't take anymore without coming, tell me and I'll stop.'

'All right,' I lied.

'I'm trusting you not to let yourself come, Nefer-marymun.' He looked into my eyes. 'It's important, and trust me, the pleasure you'll experience later will be more than worth the struggle now.'

'But I'm so wet...' My white panties were clinging to my labia like a thick mist coating a flower's rosy petals. A climax was inexorably taking root between my legs and sending delicate yet deliciously strong tendrils of ecstasy up through my pelvis.

'Mm, yes, you are, very wet,' he agreed. 'Your pussy is so hot and wet my big cock would sink all the way down inside you with just one good hard thrust.'

'Oh Richard...Richard!'

He pulled his hand out from between my legs.

'Oh nooo!' I wailed.

The limousine came to a stop.

'We're here, my love.' He smoothed my dress down over my thighs again. 'You did very well.'

'I hate you.' I pouted.

He laughed again quietly.

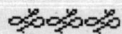

I carried my high-heeled sandals across the sand during the brief trek to the pyramid of Unas, legendary pharaoh of the Old Kingdom. Every inch of the interior of his pyramid is covered with hieroglyphs known as The Pyramid Texts, which in later dynasties came to be called The Book of Coming Forth By Day, better known now as The Book of the Dead. It was Unas who first used these complex hieroglyphic formulas to render himself immortal, and it was in the heart of his pyramid temple that Richard intended to perform our ritual. I still had no idea what he had planned, and I distracted myself from trying to imagine it with academic thoughts that soothed my nerves. It had always struck me as rather inaccurate to call pyramids tombs. Unas had had no intention of 'resting in peace' inside his burial chamber, which was actually more like a launch pad to eternity. The mummy that was left behind could be likened to the discarded stages of the first Apollo rockets, a necessary part of the mysterious vehicle of spiritual growth but one that was nevertheless expendable, although it was true that great care had to be taken in how it was discarded in order not to short-circuit the divine journey.

'What are you thinking, Nefer-marymun?' Richard's deep, quiet voice seemed to rise all the way up into the pulsing sky and fill the universe with his uniquely stimulating personality.

'Oh nothing,' I replied, 'just some crazy stuff about mummies and rockets.'

'What?' He laughed, squeezing my hand, which he had not let go of since we left the limousine and he began leading me across the sand.

I explained my thoughts to him, and somehow refrained from asking him what exactly the ritual we were about to perform would entail.

'That's all true,' he agreed, 'although it is a rather unwholesome mixing of metaphors.'

'Talking to you is so much fun, Richard.'

'Just talking to me?' he teased.

Finally, unable to contain my curiosity and anxiety a moment longer, I blurted, 'What are we going to do inside the pyramid? You mentioned something about spending part of the night in there?'

'Yes, that'll be part of it. You need to spend part of the night alone in a pyramid.'

'But I don't want you to leave me alone in there.' I had been hoping he really hadn't meant the alone part.

'Yes, you do.'

'No, I don't.'

'Forget for a moment what Mary Fallon thinks and ask Nefermun what she wants.'

I bit my lip to keep from retorting, 'But they're the same person!' knowing full well this was not exactly true, and much as I hated to admit it, after a few uncomfortable minutes of soul-searching, I realized he was right—Nefermun was looking forward to the haunting challenge of being left alone inside a pyramid at night.

Dreams of Anubis

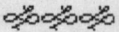

I suffered the nervous thrill of a conspirator when we arrived at the entrance to the pyramid of Unas and were greeted by two of Richard's servants, possibly the same two who had escorted me out of the nightclub. I couldn't help noticing their long black robes were finer than anything Simon's men ever wore. It was a strange moment for what I knew mentally to suddenly kick in as a visceral knowledge that the man I loved was filthy rich. I had never considered the size of a man's bank account when assessing his worth, so perhaps it was poetic justice that my soul mate just happened to be wealthy.

'Are you ready, my lady?' Sir Ashley asked me with an intense formality that launched a flock of butterflies in my belly.

'Yes, my lord.' I really liked the sound of that.

One of his men handed him a lantern. 'Hold on to my belt,' Richard instructed me, and I dutifully followed him into the pyramid.

When we emerged from the uncomfortably claustrophobic passage, I had to bite my tongue. Richard had pointed out to me that the fumes from the fire Simon had lit in the courtyard of Ti's mastaba could potentially damage the bas-reliefs, yet his servants had lit four bronze braziers supported on pedestals inside the burial chamber of Unas containing some of the oldest and most sacred hieroglyphs in Egypt. This was such a prime example of double standards that I couldn't keep my mouth shut. 'Richard, won't the fumes from these fires damage the priceless Pyramid Texts?'

'They're being sucked out through a small tunnel by that battery-powered fan over there.'

'Oh.' I smiled, very pleased that my ancient priest had not become a modern hypocrite.

'But it was good of you to ask, and I would not even have considered doing this if I didn't feel you were worth the time, trouble and risk.'

'Thank you.'

He came and stood before me. 'My pleasure.'

My arms slipped around his neck and I tilted my head back for his kiss.

He reached up and grasped my wrists, gently removing my arms from around him. 'You look beautiful in this dress, my love, nevertheless, it must come off.' He took me by the arm and led me over to the large sarcophagus.

I had seen the Pyramid Texts in books countless times, but in reality, and experienced as a whole, they were much more striking. Lovely, exquisitely rendered hieroglyphs still alive with traces of color covered every inch of the walls, so that we were literally embraced by magical incantations.

Richard pulled off his shirt, and I followed his cue by undoing the clasp on my halter top and exposing my breasts. He watched me slide my dress down my legs standing on the packed sand of the profoundly still chamber, the soft crackling of the flames in the braziers only enhancing the centuries-old, millenniums deep silence.

'No, I'll do that,' he said as I made to remove my white lace bikini panties.

He hooked his thumbs into the delicate elastic, and caressed the sides of my legs as he slowly pulled the skimpy garment down to my ankles, holding it open so I could step out of it in my high-heels.

I waited for him to compliment my legs, and was strangely pleased that he didn't. I could see the appreciation in his eyes, and that was more than enough. It was as if he knew that I knew I had great legs and had been told so countless times before, and his telling me now would be just another penny tossed into the fountain. In these uniquely special moments in the heart of a pyramid, his remaining silent before all my visible charms not only made him stand out from all my other lovers, it was somehow also proof that his feelings for me ran so deep there was no need for him to indulge my vanity.

'I want you to lie back on the sarcophagus, Mary, but first take your shoes off.'

I obeyed him, and he grasped me around the waist as he had in the bazaar, lifting me onto the edge.

I lay back across the stone lid of Unas's sarcophagus. Once again, I surrendered to the arousing sense of how soft and vulnerable my young flesh seemed surrounded by crushing layers of rock; rock that was in turn surrounded by the impenetrable darkness of a desert night trembling with a multitude of stars. And even while I couldn't see them, I felt those stars mysteriously reflected in all my nerve-endings. Part of me wanted to sit up anxiously, but I didn't, I just lay feeling wonderfully languid and relaxed against the cold, hard surface, enjoying the contrast of the warm light pulsing against my lids as I closed my eyes for a moment, then opened them again to gaze contentedly at one of the walls covered with hieroglyphs. I could scarcely believe I was looking at the famous Pyramid Texts, the earliest example of Egyptian funerary writing, and forever one of its finest.

'It's time.' The bare chest and arms that stepped into my field of vision certainly seemed to belong there. 'I'm pleased to see you don't appear at all nervous.' He regarded me soberly, and in the flickering lamplight his hair, which was only loosely pulled back, formed sleek black wings around his face. He placed a large, warm hand on my chest just above my breasts. Very slowly, barely touching me, he caressed my body down to the highly sensitized space between my navel and my clitoris. 'I want everything from you, Nefer-marymun.'

'You have everything, Richard.' I gazed hungrily up at his powerful torso. No elaborate pendant interfered with the clean lines of his chest, truly giving him the forceful aura of an Old Kingdom priest.

He leaned over me. 'Your body isn't all I want from you,' he whispered, his lips brushing my forehead, and when he suddenly cradled my warm, slick pussy in his hand, my moan of pleasure echoed around the ancient chamber. 'You're special enough to come with me into another dimension, my love. The physical consummation is only the beginning of equally vital levels of union to be realized between us. The experience I'm about to thrust you into is one you'll never forget.'

He removed his hand from between my thighs and took a step back. Then he retrieved his shirt, slipping it back on before picking up the lantern he had brought into the pyramid with him.

For a mere second, I felt myself turn into Mary again, my body tense against the unyielding stone. But Nefermun was anticipating the sacred challenge to come, and she kept Mary relatively calm.

The flickering light in the chamber darkened ominously when E'Ahmose walked over to one of the lamps and blew out the flame. 'I'll guide you by going ahead of you, my love,' he informed me cryptically, 'but you have to follow me yourself.' He spoke casually, as though we were merely planning a little car trip together.

'Richard, what are you doing?' I watched in growing trepidation as he moved to the opposite corner of the chamber and extinguished a second lamp. Now only two were left passionately fighting off the darkness. 'You didn't mention anything about leaving me alone in the dark, Richard,' I protested childishly.

'Don't be afraid, my love.' He repeated the endearment knowing it would soothe me as well as give me strength. 'Part of you recognizes this ritual of initiation. All priests and priestesses of Anubis had to go through this. It's necessary to immerse yourself in total darkness so the lines between your flesh and your soul are erased, which will help you become aware of your other, higher, senses.' He did not blow out the third flame but instead gently snuffed it out between his thumb and forefinger.

A host of restless menacing shadows was born around the last remaining lamp, and I don't think it was my imagination that they all appeared to be reaching for me like threatening fingers hungering for my dimly luminous flesh. 'Richard?!' I made a supreme effort not to let terror take complete hold of me.

He quickly returned to my side. 'The ability to dream true dreams is buried within you, Nefer-marymun.' His expression was kind but stern, and he did not touch me again. 'I'm going to help dig it out of you. What would otherwise take months might under these precise circumstances, and in this mystical place, take only a few hours. Your dreaming skills are not as developed as mine in this life so I'm appointing myself your teacher.' He turned away again and extinguished the last flickering lamp so the chamber was lit now only by his lantern.

'Richard, you're actually going to leave me alone here in the dark?' I was proud of how remarkably calm I sounded. 'Without any matches so I can relight the lamps, I mean, just in case?'

Dreams of Anubis

Keeping his distance, he looked over at me where I lay on top of the sarcophagus. 'You won't need to light them,' he assured me. 'You're perfectly safe in here. My men are outside the pyramid and I'll be close by, closer than you think. I'll be as close as your heart, my love. Use your pulse like wings to lift you out of your fear into the dimension of your true self, Nefer-marymun.' He bent over, preparing to enter the passage leading out of the room. 'Only your body is tied to its limitations,' he told me over his shoulder, 'the rest of you is absolutely free and as powerful as your imagination. I'm confident you'll find the door inside you that will bring you to me.' And with these final, impossibly positive words, he crouched into the passageway and left me alone in the dark.

Chapter Ten

I couldn't move a muscle I was so terrified of the absolute darkness. My feelings were running around each other like crazy and they felt just as real, or even more so, than my own skin now that I could no longer distinguish the borders between my inner and physical self.

I tried to forget the fact that the part of me named Mary Fallon slept with a nightlight back in her North End apartment. It was a lovely clear glass nightlight in the shape of an elegant seated cat. I thought of her as the Egyptian cat goddess Bastet, and she kept me safe at night by holding the darkness at bay, sort of like a metaphysical curtain hook draping gentle, luminously edged shadows around me.

Yet even when Bastet wasn't plugged in, the darkness back in Boston was never impenetrable thanks to street lamps. I had never known such a complete and utter blackness could exist as the one my beloved E'Ahmose plunged me into when he left with the lantern. The second he left I knew that I either panicked completely or stayed absolutely calm, because only one or the other extreme was possible in the black hole that sucked all my thoughts and feelings out of me until they seemed to sinisterly fill the room around my helpless body.

I would either come out of this experience a better, stronger person, or I would faint from terror and sleep through the ordeal, it was my choice. Richard was waiting for me in a dream, but I would never be able to meet him there if I simply passed out from fear. I had to be brave. I had to take a deep breath and force my tense limbs to relax against the stone. I had to tell the cowering child inside me that I was not in any danger just because a silent, lifeless blackness was pressing against my skin. I was in the heart of a pyramid alive with beautiful

Dreams of Anubis

hieroglyphs, hieroglyphs that guided the soul through all the necessary steps involved in becoming one with Re's eternal light and life.

I thought about the sun, I pictured it burning in the sky and tried to imagine its warmth caressing me the way Richard's hands caressed me. I could not let myself be mad at him for leaving me alone like this because I knew his intentions were good, and I was also genuinely concerned that any negative vibes I sent out would develop an objective life of their own around me. It seemed entirely possible to me that my thoughts could use the darkness to take form, so I had to keep my imagination as positive as possible.

No longer even dimly able to make out the borders of my flesh, I suffered the impression that my thoughts weren't imprisoned in my mind at all but were actually milling around me. It was an unnerving concept since I had seen too many horror movies in my life; my heart and soul were nowhere near as pure as an ancient Egyptian's would have been. I felt my brain perversely reigning over a veritable kingdom of nightmares swirling around me in an invisible psychological storm even as I tried to think calmly and rationally.

The air in the chamber was oppressively still and there wasn't even a whisper of sound, which made my quiet breathing seem unnaturally loud. The silence weighed as heavily as the inert hand of a mummy resting directly against my heart, my mind a Pandora's box abruptly flung open by the absolute absence of light and sound.

I can control this experience, I thought desperately, but my voice sounded impotently loud in my head. I didn't dare actually speak out loud for fear of calling attention to myself and encouraging one of the vague atrocities occupying the burial chamber with me to attack, which made me realize I was not really in control of myself at all. I knew for a fact that I was completely alone, yet I could not shake the horrible feeling that my vulnerably naked body had become the center of a demonic crowd.

I can control this, I repeated again with more determination. Darkness is not evil, I told myself sternly. And suddenly, in a blessed wave of remembering, Egyptian cosmology came to my rescue. A voice that was mine and yet stronger than mine recited words that seemed written in a luminous script before me:

Cat's Collar - Three Erotic Romances

Darkness is the primeval clay of the universe from which I can shape whatever I desire. My mind is the Lotus bud that rose from the dark primordial waters of Nun and flowered into the divine light and life of consciousness.

By leaving me alone in here without any means to rekindle the lamps, Richard had made it clear that if I wanted light, it would have to shine from inside me.

I don't remember exactly when I began sensing the hieroglyphs carved into the chamber walls subliminally supporting me. Picturing their hard, confident lines surrounding me somehow helped me get a grip on my irrational fears. They enabled me to reign in my wildly out of control feelings and focus my thoughts.

It just so happened I had read a translation of the Pyramid Texts on the plane from Boston, and now I 'entertained' myself by mentally reciting the fragment I remembered: *Draw the bolt! Open the door to heaven! Open for Unas! The doors are open over the fire of spirit...Arise Horus born of the flame...clearing the way that he may pass...*

This had to be the inner door Richard had referred to, the 'bolt' was fear, and until I found the strength to draw it, the way to heaven and the luminous flame of my invulnerable spirit was closed to me. Lying naked across the lid of a sarcophagus in a pitch-black burial chamber, my soul understood and appreciated this ancient invocation in a much more intimate and vital way than just casually reading it on a plane. All I had to do was lighten my heart by letting faith burn away the fears clogging my metaphorical arteries, or something like that.

At some point, I found myself not only forgiving Richard for leaving me here alone in the dark but actually thanking him for forcing me to face myself as I never had before. And remembering the way he loked at me banished the demons haunting me and filled me instead with a reassuring sense of his presence. Suddenly, the darkness was not a formless threat, it was the mysterious depth of his love embracing me.

'I love you, E'Ahmose,' I dared to whisper the truth out loud. 'I love you, Richard!'

Eventually, amazingly, I felt myself drifting off to sleep. He had promised he would lead the way into our shared dream, and I didn't want to keep him waiting too long...

Dreams of Anubis

I can feel the heat of the sand through my gilded sandals. My power is a presence surrounding my body and I am fully accompanied by it as I walk deeper into the temple. Re descending behind me caresses my bare shoulders with his penetrating heat, a little less ardently in the dry season. I am wearing only jeweled sandals and a pure white dress. I know the rite in which I am to participate is performed every cycle on the night the divine crook of the crescent moon first appears in the evening sky, and I am looking forward to it, as I look forward to everything with E'Ahmose...

I sensed myself shift restively against the cold stone on which I was lying, refusing to let go of the priestess walking through the temple merely to indulge a few minor physical discomforts...

Nefermun reaches the hall growing vast stone papyrus stalks where Re stretches long golden arms between the columns to caress the priests and priestesses of Anubis preparing to worship his dark spirit.

Vividly painted hieroglyphs bloom metaphysical vines all the way up to the star-covered ceiling as in a final flood of light, the god completes his circuit of the heavens and plunges into the black earth.

In the same instant every man in the hall spreads himself on his back across the stone floor covered with blood-red runners, while every woman lets her dress feint into a pool of moonlight next to the body of her lover.

I am one of these women, and for a few moments I gaze around me at my sisters. They are all beautiful in their own way, different garments of flesh and blood woven by Hathor, goddess of love. E'Ahmose lies still as Osiris beneath me as I admire all the lovely pairs of breasts exposed to the invigoratingly cool temple air. From small and pert to full and heavy, every firm yet luscious bosom is oiled to a golden perfection shining in the light from braziers being lit around us. Naked servants whose black skins blend with the darkness make it seem as though the flames spring to life of their own volition, and they walk away so silently on their bare feet the illusion is complete.

Priestesses never bear children, so all my sisters' bellies and hips are as taut as Khnum fashioned them on his potter's wheel, and to me it is obvious his hands lingered lovingly on the round cheeks of their buttocks, but especially on the ripe bud of flesh between their legs containing all the delights of earth.

I love looking at other women's bodies that are as sensually graceful as mine, knowing they are feeling very much the same things I am feeling. During the rite, our combined sensations will flood the space between the stone papyrus stalks in invisible yet irresistible currents of pleasure, lapping with a swiftly deepening power between our thighs. But only part of my attention is concentrated on my fellow priestesses, for most of it is devoted to the splendid sight of my priest's shaft surging straight up from the soft mound of his groin, and then to the sensation like no other of planting it inside me as I lower myself over him, my sandaled feet resting on either side of his hips. In this position, holding my back perfectly straight, I can feel the lips of my sex gaping open, and the tender petals protecting the darkly moist mouth of my flesh gladly accept the crown of his stiff penis, longer and thicker and harder than any vegetative stamen.

He does not move a muscle as I mount him, seemingly alive only in his erection, which becomes everything to me as it fills my belly. Continuing to hold my back straight with my arms crossed over my chest, I can tell from the soft cries rising around me that I am not the only one overwhelmed by the experience of slowly stabbing myself. I must sink all the day down around him, taking his hard cock so deep into my body the fulfillment is excruciating, as I crouch like a woman giving birth to the divine soul of ecstasy. We merge completely, then hold utterly still for a brief eternity.

Gasps of mingled effort and pleasure echo mine as all the other priestesses willingly impale themselves while opening their arms wide to spread the invisible wings of love over the inert men below them.

As Isis resurrected Osiris, we hold our torturously arousing positions until the temple floor seems to come to life, all the priests suddenly moving as one. There is no choreography now as every couple does as it pleases surrounded and observed by other beautiful bodies consecrated to the dark god Anubis.

The strong shoulders and chests of the other priests are all embracing me when E'Ahmose's beloved arms come around me. Yet he is mysteriously more than just one of the powerful physiques I see thrusting their erections deep into the holes of moaning priestesses. And as I watch them, the all-consuming sen-

Dreams of Anubis

sation of my lover possessing me from behind jackal-style is intensified to the point where all the gasping, groaning energy in the hall feels devastatingly concentrated between my own thighs.

My mouth opens in hungry sympathy observing a rampant penis penetrate a lovely upturned face held possessively in the man's hands. Then I see a couple only a column away who seem a reflection of E'Ahmose and me, and I find it intensely exciting watching the girl's breasts bobbing swiftly back and forth just like mine are doing as our lovers ram into us.

My Priest of Anubis is feeling vicious tonight, and I love every moment of his strong body beating against mine. My sex is slick as perfumed oil and hot as the pulsing flames when he grabs me by my finely braided hair, and makes me face in a different direction so we can watch other couplings together. The blessed suffering of his cock once again spearing me is almost more than I can bear, especially combined with the vision of another rock-hard column of flesh disappearing into the soft depths between two slender legs. It is the sound of the other priest's balls slapping against her helplessly juicing sex as he pumps in and out between her widespread thighs, and the sight of her delicate breasts quivering beneath the onslaught of his selfish thrusts, that make the shadowy temple vanish in a blinding flash of joy as the seed of divinity bursts open in my womb and for a few timeless moments I glimpse what paradise will feel like…

I moaned in protest against the cold stone, but the living temple slipped out of my grasp as I sank down into my heavy body again, descending from the higher realm of my dream into a dark and dreamless sleep.

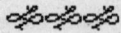

The sun rose abruptly in the heart of the pyramid and momentarily blinded me with its intense beauty.

'My love.' Richard set the lamp down on its stand and approached me. 'Do you remember the dream we shared, Nefer-marymun?' Naked hope shone in his eyes as he awaited my response.

'Yes, my lord,' I smiled, 'I believe I do.'

'Were we alone?' he prompted.

My smile deepened. 'Hardly. In fact, we were part of an orgy.'

With a triumphant grin, he slipped his arms beneath my body and lifted me up against his warm chest. 'It wasn't exactly an orgy.'

'No,' I agreed, 'it took place in a temple.'

'The instant after sunset, symbolically re-enacting Isis resurrecting Osiris.'

'Yes! And the amazing thing is,' I said earnestly, 'is how pure it felt. I mean, it didn't feel at all sinful to be making love in front of all those other couples.'

'I know.' He smiled indulgently as he kissed my lips and set me down on the floor of the burial chamber.

'It was so beautiful and exciting.' I was reluctant to leave the world of my vividly sensual dream and re-enter the pragmatic twenty-first century.

'Yes, it was,' he agreed soberly, picking my white dress up off the floor. 'And you'd better get used to feeling that way about everything now that we're together again.'

He handed me my garment and I slipped it on in a languid daze, lifting my hair up out of the way so he could snap the halter top against the nape of my neck. It sent a delicious chill down my spine when he kissed me lightly just between my shoulder blades, and I sighed happily.

'What time is it?' I asked, and then laughed because it seemed such a silly and irrelevant question standing in the heart of a pyramid with a man my soul had known for centuries.

'Does it matter?'

'Not at all.'

'It's two o'clock in the morning, time to get you back to my hotel room and into a hot bath with a glass of champagne to celebrate, then we'll have a snack before we go to bed and sleep all day.'

'That sounds wonderful. But I should really let Carol know where I am.'

'My men have already informed your friend that you're with me and perfectly safe.'

'She might not believe them,' I said doubtfully. 'I should call her.'

'Of course, you can call her from the hotel.'

Dreams of Anubis

'But I don't know her number.'

'I can obtain it for you.' He came and stood before me so I could slip my arms around him and look up into his eyes. 'I intend to give you all you desire, Mary, and I don't just mean that in a materialistic sense.'

'I know.' I felt my heart perching on his mouth like a bird freed from the cage of thinking true love was only a dream.

'It's a great responsibility being wealthy, Mary, but I know that together we can make the best use of our energy and resources in this world. Perhaps we can help others to dream together as we do.'

'Yes, without letting their cynical modern brains get in the way of their passionate ancient hearts.'

'It's not that simple, but I agree with the sentiment. The scientific mind and the poetic soul have to come together again. This re-unification has already begun with individuals like us, and is symbolized by the discovery of Imhotep's mastaba at this moment in time.'

I frowned. 'Why do Simon and Steve dislike you so much, Richard? I imagine they're jealous of your money, but it doesn't explain their intense animosity.'

'Well, they'll just have to get over it since I'll be helping to finance the dig once it's made public. The Antiquities Department is more than happy to accept my generous contribution.'

I pulled away from him. 'You are trying to take their discovery away from them!' I exclaimed in despair.

'Mary, think about what you're saying. Do you really believe that about me?'

I looked at his stern, handsome face and into his eyes, unfathomably dark in the fire-lit chamber. 'No,' I said with relief, 'that was definitely not Nefer-mary-mun talking. I'm sorry…. I love you, Richard.'

'And I've been waiting a long time to hear you say that, Mary.' He kissed my forehead tenderly. 'Simon Taylor is one of the brightest, most enlightened Egyptologists out there,' he said reasonably, 'and in exchange for my considerable financial gift, the Antiquities Department has agreed to grant my request that Simon and Steve be allowed to run the project. They'll be in charge of the find from beginning to end, which means there's no reason for them to keep the discovery secret for fear of losing it. Everyone knows about it already anyway. I would have told Simon straight out if I had thought he would believe me. Besides, I find the man extremely irritating and I've enjoyed watching him sweat a little. We'll never be friends, but I imagine he'll manage to be cordial to me in the future, even though now he'll have two reasons for resenting me.' He pulled me back into his arms again. 'If he thought I was wealthy before, it's nothing compared to how rich I am now that I have you, Nefer-marymun.'

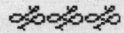

After we finally got out of bed the next day, I was loath to leave my Priest of Anubis, but it was necessary for me to return to Carol's apartment, and not just to collect my belongings. I felt compelled to apologize to her for disappearing on her the night before, after we emerged from the bathroom at the club. I had essentially saddled her with the task of explaining my vanishing act to Simon (not that he had probably needed an explanation) and worse still of dealing with his reaction to it.

That Richard's politely insistent servants had left me no choice in the matter was no excuse for abandoning my friend and date the way I had. I did not in the least regret my actions, but I was so happy that for a while I even entertained the idea of seeing Simon again and personally asking him to forgive me for being so rude by vanishing like a genie from the club (after which I ended up in the very plush bottle of Richard's limo). I quickly abandoned the idea, however. I would see Simon again soon enough when he finally deigned to announce his discovery of Imhotep's mastaba, at which time he would learn that he and Steve would be in charge of the excavation of the legendary tomb because the man I had chosen over him—the rich and handsome Sir Richard Gerald Ashley, more fondly known to me as E'Ahmose, Born of the Moon—was contributing a considerable sum to the project.

I would have plenty of opportunities to make it up to Simon, for I was not returning to Boston. My head was still spinning with the realization that I would be staying in Egypt indefinitely. I could never have dreamed that my last day at the office before my long-awaited vacation to the land of the pharaohs would be my last day of work ever. Richard had made it clear, as we sipped champagne in bed, that I was free to pursue my love of Egyptology in whatever way I saw fit because money was no longer a concern for me. This last fact I couldn't quite wrap my brain around yet. I had been on a budget for as long as I could remember, but being wealthy was a challenge I was more than happy to face with Nefermun's help.

Part of me felt it was perfectly natural to drink champagne until sunrise and then sleep most of the day, even as another part of me suffered the thrill of being wickedly decadent. I could sense these two sides of me had a long way to go before they would be fully reconciled with each other, but all I had to do was look into Richard's eyes to see the beautifully centered, sensually confident and fulfilled woman I would one day be in the magical world created by the horizon of his arms and his love for me. There was no rational explanation for the chemistry that had existed between us since the moment we met, or for the passionate love deepening between us. All I knew was that even since before I could remember I had been dreaming of, and waiting for, a man like him, and now that we had finally found each other, I felt my life was really beginning as Nefer-marymun.

That evening, my trip to Carol's apartment was very different. Richard had seen me off in his limo, in which I was to return to him after I had set things straight with my friend and packed all my things.

'Not that you'll really be needing them,' he had remarked as he'd kissed my cheek outside the hotel. The car waited at the curb. 'I'll buy you everything you need and anything you want. I think Nefer-marymun will be needing two whole new wardrobes.'

'Two?' I asked giddily.

'Yes, one for public appearances and one for private festivities.'

I savored the promise all the way from the Mina House to the residential area of Cairo where Carol resided.

I knew I would find her at home because I had called before I left the hotel, and she greeted my quiet knock at the door with a scowl that almost managed to dispel the languid cloud of daydreams I drifted into the apartment on.

'You said you were coming back to the table last night,' she accused, making it a point to slam the door behind me.

'I fully intended to,' I defended myself wistfully, 'but…' I shrugged. 'Oh Carol.' I hugged her. 'I'm so happy!'

Her tense body resisted me for about half a second before she hugged me back fervently. 'And I'm really happy for you!'

'I know you are; you're just pretending to be mad at me.' I grasped her hand and led her towards the guest bedroom. 'Come in here with me while I pack so I can tell you all about it. I spent half the night in King Unas's pyramid lying naked on the sarcophagus!'

'What?' She snatched her hand away. 'Why?'

'So the skills I possessed as a wearer of the Winged Sandals would hopefully come back to me more quickly —priests and priestesses of Anubis were initiated in pyramids—and it worked! I deliberately met Richard in a dream, only he wasn't Richard, he was E'Ahmose, and—'

'Mary, stop, you're not making any sense.'

'And wait till you hear what I have to tell you about Imhotep's tomb.'

Epilogue

'Ahmose the cat jumps on my back. I gasp in surprise and open my eyes because I am lying naked on the couch and his claws are sharp. But I need not have worried, for he always keeps them carefully sheathed when he is being affectionate with me, and his soft paws actually feel good as he walks down my legs to curl up in the accomodating hollow formed by the back of my knees. Smiling, I close my eyes again.

'You know you can't stay there very long, you silly cat,' I murmur affectionately, and my smile deepens as the subtle vibration of his contented purr provides me with a soothing little massage.

The increasingly warm spot created by his heavy body makes me even more appreciative of the cool breeze wafting in from the garden. The sun is slowly setting and I am doing one of my favorite things—relaxing in the late afternoon twilight. Usually I am awaiting my lover, who always joins me for refreshments before dinner and our invariably stimulating nights together, but whenever possible we spend the whole day with each other, and this is one of those special times when he is already here with me, spread out on his back across his own couch reading the latest details of the tomb's progress.

I open my eyes again just for the pleasure of looking at him. His profile is beautifully stern when he's concentrating, and the sight of his soft, generous penis resting on his naked lap makes me want to take it into my mouth and hold it there contentedly, letting him rest the papers on my loving head as he continues reading.

It is not lost to me that my cat and I have much in common in that we spend most of our time sensually expressing our devotion to our master, and are both as happy with our lives as any living creatures have a right to be.

Setting his business aside abruptly, my lover remarks, 'That cat of yours is quite ingenious.'

'What do you mean?'

'He is making sure I cannot spread your legs and claim your affections for myself as he knows I love to do.'

I laugh. 'Yes, he is very possessive, isn't he?'

'I cannot possibly blame him.'

I feel E'Ahmose the cat raise his head off my calf sensing a challenge, then his hot, heavy weight is lifted off my knees when he leaps off the couch, wisely retreating as his namesake rises and approaches me. I turn languidly over onto my back, and smile up at the beautiful man who seats himself beside me.

'Do you know how much I love you?' he asks quietly.

'As much as I love you, I hope,' I reply happily.

He returns my smile as we look earnestly into each other's eyes for a few timeless moments, then he glances at the blue circle of water out in the garden. 'I believe it's time for a glass of wine and a little fun in the Jacuzzi,' he concludes. 'Then, much as I know you enjoy supervising all the chopping and stirring in the kitchen as my cooks prepare the delicious recipes you come up with, I want to take us out to dinner tonight. And after that, I feel it's time we climbed the pyramid and behaved very wickedly at the top in front of the entire city. What do you think, Nefer-marymun?'

'I think it sounds like a plan,' I sit up so I can slip my arms fervently around him, 'my lord.'

The End

Rituals of Surrender

Author's Note

One etymology of the word Druid derives it from "dru-wid" meaning "knower of oak trees" but "deru" also means truth and can also be interpreted as "knower of the truth". It is believed Druid priests fashioned wands from the wood of oak trees that had been struck by lightning, and everyone knows they met in the dark hearts of forests, but for the most part Druids remain a class of men and women shrouded in romance and mystery...

Prologue

A cigarette burning between his fingers, a man wearing a black leather jacket lightly caressed the moist rim of his scotch glass and exhaled a stream of smoke as he smiled sadly. Then he raised the glass to his lips and took a sip of the dark-gold spirit, his eyes never leaving the face of a young woman seated only a few feet away from him in the intimate restaurant. Votive-like candles trembled in the center of each round table covered with a pure white cloth and he was using his as an ashtray.

Maia frowned. 'We need a new candle,' she observed, 'this one's nearly dead.' For some reason this seemingly insignificant detail made her somewhat cross. She was a grown woman of twenty-three, yet whenever she went out to dinner with her parents, a part of her felt like a little girl again, pouting and frustrated that none of her dreams of love and adventure had come true, at least not yet.

'My dear, you have innocently stumbled upon a serious philosophical issue here,' her father replied gravely. 'Would it be right to end its struggling life prematurely or should we let it burn out to its natural end?'

The man in black leather sitting by himself smiled as though he could hear this conversation, and raised a free hand to caress shoulder-length dark-brown hair away from his strong jawed, fine-featured face set with intensely blue eyes. Then with the ball of his thumb, he idly traced a faint white scar just below his thin lower lip as he took a final drag off his cigarette, and casually tossed its remains into the flame.

The resulting sparks captured Maia's attention. Suddenly, she couldn't

Rituals of Surrender

understand how she had failed to notice this man before, a man who made her intensely aware of her own mysterious melancholy as he got up to go. This strikingly handsome man dressed entirely in black seemed to embody all her deepest, darkest feelings, and his leaving did not make her feel better, on the contrary...

Chapter One

Stoneshire Hospital's Emergency Room was never crowded. State-of-the-art medical facilities were housed inside a Victorian factory that had been gutted, its rotting wooden beams replaced with a less vulnerable metal skeleton. Nevertheless, the centuries-old town refused to outgrow its narrow winding streets and quaint historic buildings.

The hospital's elegant waiting room boasted large chairs upholstered in burgundy leather, softened by years of comforting the stressed bodies of people waiting for news of their loved ones, a far cry from the cold plastic slap to your backside suffered in most modern hospitals. Large potted plants helped soothe eyes strained by the inevitable fluorescent light, and encouragingly hot fragrant tea was brought around by quietly sympathetic nurses wearing traditional white knee-length outfits.

Stoneshire's Chief Resident, Eric Christianson, was personally responsible for the waiting room's aesthetic charm; the furniture had come from his family estate, which he was aching to get rid of. Lately, the endless, lifeless rooms surrounding him at night felt disturbingly like cancer cells threatening his altruistic health, yet for some reason he couldn't bring himself to sell the place.

The thunder-filled night they brought in the old woman and her niece – a strikingly lovely creature in her early twenties – he had just slipped off his lab coat and was reluctantly preparing to drive to his palatial home through the storm. He was almost relieved to be spared another lonely night in his study as the paramedics quickly informed him that a tree had fallen across the victims' car. One of the elderly female's knees was crushed beyond repair. The young woman appeared unharmed yet she was unconscious, and Eric immediately suspected she might be suffering from serious internal bleeding. After only a few

Rituals of Surrender

minutes with her, he was able to staunch the flow of her life's blood, thereby saving her life, but a heavy tree branch had struck her womb with such force no life would ever be able to take root inside her.

Eric had done everything he could for her, but Maia Wilson's vital signs were still fluctuating dangerously. It was a desperate, unorthodox impulse that caused him to dismiss his nurses and to bend over the young woman's unresponsive body. He whispered passionately in her ear like a lover, begging her to hold on to life, pleading with her to let him save her, fervently urging her to stay alive.

Even though he definitely should have been, he was not surprised when her pulse suddenly grew stronger and a warm hint of color returned to her snowy cheeks. Not yet daring to hope, he gently raised one of her marble-white eyelids and shone a light into her deep brown iris, but it was as though a tiny round sun moved instead of the dark cloud obscuring it, because she remained unconscious.

Dr. Christianson was exhausted and frustrated, but at least he had not lost his lovely patient, who uncannily evoked the legend of Sleeping Beauty as she smiled peacefully in her unnatural sleep. Her parents were still out in the waiting room (they had been there for over twenty-four hours) and his smile as he approached them was reassuring if also somewhat abashed. He was feeling just a little guilty about the unorthodox way he was going about the desired end of saving their daughter's life.

'How is she?' Peter Wilson demanded, anxiety making his voice sound uncharacteristically harsh.

'She's still unconscious,' Eric informed Maia's father reluctantly, 'but as I said, she's stopped bleeding internally and all her vital signs have stabilized. She's very weak, naturally, and she's still not responding to stimulus, but her strength seems to be returning gradually. I've done every possible test and there's no evidence at all that she was injured anywhere except...' He glanced at the dark leaf of a plant brushing against his white sleeve. 'She won't be able to have children,' he concluded bluntly, 'but other than that, she should be perfectly healthy.' *If she ever decides to wake up*, he thought despondently. As a scientist, he both respected and resented mysteries he could not solve if they were ones that thwarted him in some way.

'But then why is she still unconscious?' Stella Wilson pleaded to know, clinging to her husband's arm. They were a strikingly attractive couple; it was easy to see where their daughter had gotten her looks.

'I don't know,' Eric admitted softly, studying the plant intently. 'It could be shock, some sort of psychological defense mechanism against the trauma she suffered... she slipped into the safety of unconsciousness to escape the pain and she's not ready to come out yet.' He was taken aback by his intuitive diagnosis and somewhat concerned by how casually he expressed it, with absolutely no scientific evidence to back him up.

'I see.' Surprisingly, Maia's father apparently found the explanation reasonable and convincing. 'What about my sister, Carol? Is she still in stable condition?'

'Oh yes, no need to worry about Carol. She's heavily sedated, of course, and I'm afraid she'll need a cane to walk from now on, but she will be able to walk, she won't require a wheelchair. Don't worry, please, I fully intend to stay by Maia's side until she comes around. She's not in a coma, not in the traditional sense... you see, I believe she can hear me. When I spoke to her...' He thrust his hands in his pockets and cleared his throat decisively. 'When I spoke to her, her vital signs responded.'

'You spoke to her and she heard you?' Stella's hand resembled a bird's claw clinging to the solid branch of her husband's arm. 'What did you say to her, doctor?' She sounded fascinated.

'Nothing, really.' He cleared his throat again self-consciously wishing there was something in his pockets he could hold onto. 'I simply urged her not to give up.'

'Please,' Peter slipped a supportive arm around his wife's shoulders, 'tell us what you said to her.'

Eric glanced over at the plant again knowing it wouldn't judge him no matter what he thought or did. 'Well, I said, "I want you to live for me".' Looking

Rituals of Surrender

back at Maia's parents, he tried very hard to sound as though he was only reciting his grocery list as he went on. 'I said, "don't fight me, you know you want to live, you're so beautiful, you have to hold on", and so on.' Attempting to look innocently relaxed, he ran the fingers of his right hand through his silver-blonde hair even while his other hand clenched into a fist inside his lab coat.

Stella gazed fervently up at her husband. 'Then what Drew said is true, Maia is–'

'Thank you, doctor,' Peter cut her off abruptly. 'We know she's in good hands.'

After two final introspective drags, Drew Landson killed his cigarette and then gazed down at its broken body for a moment before at last meeting the eyes of the man and woman seated before him. 'You both know,' he began quietly, 'that there's no such thing as an accident or a coincidence.'

'This is too much!' Peter struck the table with his fist, but made no impression on the snowy plain of the cloth. Even the candle kept burning steadily in its glass sphere as though mocking the uncontrolled heat of his anger. There was so much pain written on the lines of his face as he focused on the small flame that he might have been watching the distant tower of his castle burn beneath an enemy's torch.

'Please, dear.' Stella spread the soft, pale roots of her fingers over her husband's rock-hard fist. 'You heard what the doctor said, there's no rational explanation for Maia's condition, it's as though she's being held–'

'There's always a rational explanation!' Her husband's chin dug into his chest as he closed his eyes and struggled to gain control of himself.

Drew sat back in his chair holding Stella's eyes, their thoughts in such perfect harmony they might as well have been caressing each other beneath the table. They were meeting in the restaurant where only last Sunday evening he had seen Maia for the first time having dinner with her parents. Their eyes had met, and he had felt the sparks literally fly between them as he tossed his cigarette into the flame. And because of this, because of the desire and longing he had felt her touch him with, he was in the position to reach out to her now, because her beauty had evoked the same intense response in him...

'I am extremely upset,' Peter muttered tightly in an oblique apology for his emotional outburst.

'Your emotions have their roots in the limits of your perceptions,' Drew stated mildly. 'Why don't you try actually thinking about what Maia is experiencing for a change instead of selfishly dwelling on what you're going through? For all we know, she's enjoying herself. In the dream she's living now, she has absolutely no awareness of her body lying in a hospital bed, and you need to stop thinking about her that way, too. Her soul is very much alive and well in another dimension, or another frequency of being, or however you want to think about it, and in whatever adventure she's living out, I suspect it's you, her parents, who are dead. In her psyche, she has to accept the fact of a car crash, but instead of the victims being herself and her aunt, Carol, I imagine she thinks you both were in the crash, and since she can't communicate with you, in her mind it's her parents who were killed in a fatal accident. I'm just speculating here because I haven't gone in yet, but I'm assuming since Carol was involved in the trauma with her that Maia imagines herself living with her aunt now, instead of with you. Her personal history will be slightly different in her subconscious fantasy, but other than that, she'll be completely herself, and I mean *completely*, much more herself than she is normally in so-called real life.'

'What do you mean?' Stella breathed in wonder.

'I mean her deepest self, all her most intense longings and desires, will have full reign in her dream. You say she's an artist?'

'Yes, she's a painter,' her mother said proudly. 'Her work is haunting, full of standing stones and blood-red sunsets and women lying across altars…'

'Jesus!' Peter heaved a deep sigh. 'All right, man, what do we do?' The rational and Christian portions of his brain surrendered abruptly. 'Just tell us what we have to do to help Maia.'

'It's the soul's delicate organs of fear and desire, hope and despair that we're dealing with here,' Drew responded matter-of-factly. 'We have to read the events and come up with a diagnosis. I'm relatively certain Maia has entered the haunting sensual world of her paintings.'

'We trust you, Drew.' Stella handed him the intangible yet infinitely heavy gift of their hope. 'Just tell us what to do.'

Rituals of Surrender

'I will try my absolute hardest to help you.' His charismatic smile was broad enough to contain several meanings, but it dimmed almost at once as his face resumed a respectful lack of expression. 'First things first,' he stated briskly, and draining his glass of scotch rose abruptly. 'I have to sleep in her bedroom tonight, in her bed.'

Peter locked himself in the library, to Stella's mingled relief and dismay. She longed for the solace of his presence, but his negative attitude in the face of the unknown was no comfort at all to her. She was grateful Drew had given her the nearly impossible task of digging up an ashtray in a house where no one had smoked cigarettes for years. At least the search kept her from stalking around the telephone, very much like a panther walking on two legs in her form-fitting black dress; she was desperately fighting the hunger she felt for constant news of her daughter. Doctor Christianson would call her as soon as there was any change in Maia's condition.

Stella finally found what she was looking for in the bottom drawer of a wooden cupboard hidden away in a back hallway. She held the round clay object reverently in both hands, treating it like an archaeologist unearthing an ancient relic. Maia had made this ashtray for her father in kindergarten when he still smoked. A crude, heavy little sphere the dark-gray of stone, its entire surface was covered with the mysterious spirals of her childish fingerprints, which had grown as she aged yet never changed. Inevitably, Stella found herself comparing the rough childish art project with a Celtic artifact, and she smiled for the first time in over forty-eight hours as she pressed it against her heart. The object's earthy appearance, combined with the pure love that had shaped it, reassured her that she was doing the right thing with Drew, whom she knew would be very pleased with her discovery.

He was perched at the foot of Maia's single bed looking slowly around him when Stella entered her daughter's bedroom. The sight of his black jacket spread across the blue-and-white quilt made her heart skip for an instant it looked so much like a big black bird with its wings spread wide, and she paused anxiously in the doorway, at once questioning and understanding why she had put her daughter's life in this man's hands. He was wearing a sleeveless black T-shirt that fully exposed his powerful arms, and as she watched him, he abruptly leaned forward as though listening intently to something beyond the range of her own hearing.

'What is it?' she whispered, her heart racing.

He sat up again. 'Nothing.'

The casual smile he tossed her felt like a boomerang momentarily carrying her fears away, but then the desire it hit her with made her feel even worse. 'I found what you wanted,' she told him, thrusting the ashtray towards him as though it was suddenly burning her hand.

He got up and quickly took it from her. 'This is perfect,' he murmured, caressing the rough surface imprinted with Maia's sensual identity in the form of her unique fingerprints. 'She made this for me.'

'She made it for her father,' Stella retorted weakly, for she was already half drugged by his heady aura of leather and male flesh irresistibly blended with his spiritual and physical self-assurance.

'Your daughter is testing your faith, my lady.' He set the ashtray gently down on the nightstand.

'You mean she deliberately chose to almost get herself killed,' she snapped, her husband's attitude inevitably rubbing off on her, 'and to never be able to have children of her own?'

'Stella,' he gently grasped one of her arms and urged her down onto the edge of the bed beside him. 'Without your blessing, it will be impossible for me to reach your daughter,' he trapped both her hands firmly between his while looking earnestly into her eyes, 'and your doubting rational mind is an utterly unacceptable chaperone on this blind date Fate has chosen to set up between Maia and me. So please do your best to relax and trust me. That's the most important thing you can do right now, because if you don't trust me and believe in me, neither will Maia.'

Red hair licked around the waxy pallor of her face as she lowered her head submissively. 'I trust you,' she sighed.

Chapter Two

The evening of May Day, the anniversary of her parents' death in an automobile accident, Maia Wilson drove to the cemetery where they were buried, their bodies lying eternally side-by-side in a single coffin. Another year had passed; the earth had made yet another full turn around the sun like a girl in a country dance, her vulnerable green eyes meeting her partner's penetrating regard as she raised such a lovely skirt of flowers in the Spring you could almost forget her skeletal legs.

Tears streaming down her face, Maia drove slowly along the path between the graves while stars appeared overhead as if in sympathy with her glistening cheeks. The last thing she expected to happen was for her engine to suddenly give a loud metallic cough, shudder ominously, and die.

A deafening silence settled around her as in her rearview mirror a pair of headlights shone indifferently on their way outside the cemetery gates. She was miles outside of Stoneshire surrounded by a crescent of woodland, all that remained of a once vast ancient forest. She had no way of getting home; it was much too far for her to walk, especially in the dark. She would be forced to take the dangerous option of flagging down a pair of anonymous headlights hoping they would stop for her and that there wouldn't be a rapist or a killer behind the wheel who would have her completely at his mercy...

She switched on her emergency lights. They flashed an urgent rhythm with her pulse, giving the deepening darkness a small, hopeful heart. She doubted, however, that anyone would notice her luminous plea for help, and she knew absolutely nothing about the inner workings of the metal shell that carried her around everywhere.

It seemed an absolute miracle when after only a few minutes a pair of head-

Rituals of Surrender

lights turned off the main road outside the gate and shone her way, effortlessly penetrating the night with sword-like shafts as the modern armor of another car pulled up just behind hers.

Maia gratefully opened her door and leaned out to watch a tall man's silhouette rimmed in gold approaching her, his blond hair catching the glow of his headlights so that his dark face seemed surrounded by a halo.

'What seems to be the trouble, miss?' he asked in a kind, quiet voice that instantly made her feel better.

'I don't know,' she replied, 'the engine just died.'

'I'll take a look at it for you.'

'Oh would you, please?' She stepped out of the car gratefully. 'Thank you so much!'

He walked back to his own vehicle to fetch something from the trunk, and it struck her that his small red sports car looked exactly like the one she had seen parked between the standing stones yesterday evening, its polished body shining beneath the setting sun making her think of a yoke inside the egg-shaped circle. She heard the trunk slam shut, then carefully stepped out of his way so he could walk past her. He lifted her hood, and holding it up with one hand he shone a flashlight into her vehicle's dark bowels. Above the small light his pale features rose out of the darkness like a cresting wave flooding her with feelings. Not only had someone come to her rescue out in the middle of nowhere, that someone was amazingly handsome. 'I think I saw your car parked at the standing stones last night,' she said impulsively, even though she really had no way of knowing if it had actually been his car. 'You know which stones I'm talking about, the small group just outside Stoneshire?'

'Yes, I know them,' he responded absently, neither denying or confirming her assumption as he concentrated on diagnosing her mechanical problem, lightly touching something here, then something there. In the dim halo of illumination cast by his flashlight, her car's organs were serpentine, evil looking things to her.

'Are you an archaeologist?' she asked him curiously.

He laughed briefly. 'No, I'm just interested in standing stones, that's all.'

'So am I,' she confessed.

'Isn't everyone? Well, I don't see a problem here. Why don't you try starting it again and see what happens.'

She slipped obediently back into the driver's seat, and was paradoxically disappointed when the engine rolled over just like normal, as though there had never been anything wrong with it at all, effectively killing her hopes of getting to know him better. She stepped back out of the car as he slammed the hood closed. 'I can't understand it,' she murmured, somewhat embarrassed and intensely distressed that he was going to drive out of her life again forever. 'I'm sorry to have troubled you.'

'It was no trouble at all,' he assured her, switching off the flashlight and plunging them into a darkness alleviated only by the distant stars. 'Nevertheless, you now owe me a favor.' The mating music of crickets punctuated his statement in a strangely sinister way.

'I do?' she asked both hopefully and anxiously.

'Yes, you do. My name is Christopher Thorn and you are now obliged to grant me whatever I request.'

'With pleasure... I mean...' But it was too late to slip a proper corset on her naked eagerness. 'My name is Maia Wilson.'

'It's a pleasure to meet you, Maia, and I would be honored if you would join me for dinner.'

It felt very strange being asked out to dinner by a featureless silhouette, yet what she had seen of his face was branded into her brain and there was no way she could pass up the opportunity to get to know him better. 'I would like that,' she replied, and felt wonderfully daring. Stoneshire wasn't exactly full of attractive eligible men and she had already dated (as well as almost immediately discarded) those who were.

'My place isn't far,' he said. 'You can follow me in your car. I'll keep you in sight just in case it stalls again.'

'But... but we just met...' She had believed they were to dine together in public. It was another thing entirely to enter the home of a man she didn't know at all.

'I understand, Maia, please don't be afraid. You can trust me. I won't do anything you don't want me to, and I mean that.'

She knew perfectly well she *should* be afraid, but there was something about him she was finding it absolutely impossible to resist. How instantly she had been attracted to him killed all her natural misgivings. She heard herself say, 'Okay, lead the way' even as part of her cringed in dread of what she was daring to do in defiance of everything she had ever been taught by everyone.

Back behind the wheel of her mysteriously moody car, Maia followed Christopher Thorn out of the graveyard. They took the main street for a few miles, then he turned onto a much narrower road flanked on both sides by ancient oak trees. Their headlights washing over the massive trunks turned them a ghostly gray color, illuminating lower branches so the darkness seemed to open its arms for her in a menacing illusion of welcome. She had never felt comfortable around large old trees, not since the accident years ago when an oak tree struck by lightning collapsed across the car she was in with her aunt, permanently crippling Carol in one knee and making it impossible for her niece to ever have children. Fortunately, Maia had never wanted to be a mother; paintings were all she desired to create.

Christopher's turn signal flashed a bright green and she followed him off onto several increasingly narrow roads, until she found herself in a pitch-black tunnel formed by tree branches embracing high above her. By now her nerves were sharp as restless kittens squirming in the basket of her belly. She was regretting having agreed to follow a strange man to his home in the middle of nowhere, but there was literally no going back now; they had made too many turns in a pitch-black darkness unrelieved by a single streetlight for her to be able to find her way home without his direction.

She was nearly breathless with panic when they at last pulled up in front of such a narrow two-story house it might have been made from a hollowed-out tree trunk. It was the only house in sight, the crescent of grass cleared out in front of it surrounded by an impenetrable forest.

Still refusing to really think about the dangerous thing she was doing, Maia got out of her car, then calmly preceded Christopher's silent silhouette onto a miniature porch framed by hanging vines. She stiffened when his hand suddenly reached past her, but it was only to open the unlocked black door.

She entered a room of highly polished wooden walls illuminated by a chandelier, and the ceiling was so high the black wrought iron chain from which it hung vanished into darkness. She caught her breath gazing up at the light fixture, for it was beautifully carved to resemble a winter-bare bush glimmering with dozens of warm golden lights. 'What a beautiful chandelier!' she exclaimed, for a moment forgetting all her fears. 'It looks like a bush covered with dew drops shining beneath the light of the rising sun. It's exquisite. Where on earth did you get it?'

He closed the door behind them. 'I made it,' he replied. Brushing past her, he walked over to a small wooden cabinet with doors carved in an intricate bas-relief of intertwined grapevines. He sank to one knee before it. 'Perhaps it's a little too obvious that I'm a carpenter.'

Above his kneeling form, elegant in a long-sleeved button-down burgundy shirt and black slacks, Maia spotted a steep, narrow stairway carved straight into the wall and suffered the impression that it led up into the darkly powerful branches of a tree. She could not shake the impression of being inside a hollowed out trunk as she walked over to a loveseat made from the slender barks of a silver birch tree, and covered with thick, sky-blue cushions impossible to resist. She hadn't meant to sink all the way back in the loveseat, but the way it was constructed made it impossible to merely perch tensely on its edge. She hadn't realized before how short her sleeveless white dress was, and she quickly covered her half bare thighs now with her red purse. Too small for all the things she was carrying, it sat in an awkward heart-shaped lump on her lap as her host approached her holding a bottle of red wine in one hand and two sparkling crystal glasses in the other. 'Does that mean you made everything in here yourself?' she asked in anxious wonder.

'Yes, it does.' He set the bottle down on a coffee table carved from a thick slab of wood that seemed to be floating just above the floor; she had to look to catch sight of the delicate black wrought iron legs actually holding it up. He seated himself beside her and handed her one of the empty glasses. 'What do you do for a living, Maia?' He reached for the bottle and poured wine for them both, politely beginning with her.

Rituals of Surrender

'I paint,' she said at once. 'But unfortunately that's not what I do to make ends meet. I work as a receptionist for a solicitor to pay the bills. What I love to do is paint though.'

'That's wonderful,' he stated earnestly. 'Money is inconsequential.' He held her eyes as he took a sip of wine. 'May I see your work sometime? I have a feeling I'd like it.'

'I think you would, especially if you're interested in standing stones. They're in most of my paintings.'

'Is that so? Would you care to describe one to me?'

'I don't know...' She bought herself some time by taking a long sip of wine, then gazed shyly down into her glass. His features were so perfectly proportioned it almost hurt her to look at them, maybe because she knew she would never be able to capture them on paper; she could never do justice to the haunting poetry of his bone structure. And his eyes... his eyes were such a clear blue she almost experienced a strange vertigo looking into them, as though the sky was falling in on her...

'Please, Maia,' he urged quietly, 'I would very much like to hear you describe one of your paintings.'

'Well, they're a bit strange,' she admitted, glancing up at him, and his seriously attentive expression encouraged her to go on. 'I haven't shown them to anyone, not even Carol... she's my aunt. I live with her.' She shifted anxiously against the deep cushion she was sinking into in such a way she was afraid she wouldn't ever want to get up... yet she absolutely had to go home later, she couldn't possibly stay here all night with a total stranger... 'I should call her and tell her I won't be home for supper tonight. She'll be expecting me.'

'I'm sorry, Maia, I don't have a phone.'

'Oh.'

'Don't worry about it, just drink your wine, she'll understand. And I promise you won't go hungry. In fact, you can have anything you like here.'

'Except a phone,' she pointed out.

He smiled as he took another sip of wine, apparently waiting for her to comply with his request and describe one of her paintings to him.

She bit her lip, but curiosity was too much for her. 'What I really want is for you to tell me what you were doing at the standing stones last night,' she blurted.

'I could show you,' he offered quietly. 'We could drive there after we finish our wine if you like, it's going to be a full moon tonight.'

His response to her query was so unexpected she started in surprise and embarrassingly bloodied the front of her dress with the delicious vintage. 'Oh my God!' she cried, so upset by the sight of the red stain spreading fatally across the pure white fabric that she didn't realize she had dropped her glass until she heard the fine crystal shatter against the floorboards. 'Oh my God,' she repeated helplessly and closed her eyes, unable to face the disaster she had made of such a promising evening. When she felt him gently grasp both her arms, part of her stiffened in dread, not so much of his intentions as of her own humiliating lack of self control.

'It's all right,' he whispered soothingly, 'I'm here, Maia.'

She sank willingly back against the cloud-deep cushions, knowing that her breathless whimpers as he lifted her dress sounded more like soft exclamations of pleasure than modest protests, and so did the way she moaned when he grasped both her slender thighs with his strong craftsman's hands and quickly spread her legs wide.

'I want you to live for me, Maia,' he whispered passionately in her ear, 'Don't fight me. You're so beautiful!'

She was shocked that he didn't bother to kiss her first. He simply ripped off her panties with a violent skill that dazed her, and swiftly slipped two fingers up inside her. For an instant his sudden penetration hurt so much she wanted to cry out in protest, but almost at once the firm, knowledgeable way he began exploring her as his thumb pressed on her mound just below her clitoris made her breathless with pleasure. It almost felt too good to believe the way his fingers flicked gently back and forth deep inside her sex.

'You're so beautiful, Maia. I want you to live for me, sweetheart, do it for me...'

She wanted to tell him that the slow, exploratory penetration of his fingers felt almost too good to bear, but she couldn't seem to find her voice. It had been wonderfully obvious to her from the moment he lifted her dress up out of his way that she was in a real man's hands at last. He was saving her from the crude pawing of the mere boys she had dated whom she had known from the beginning could never handle the depth and intensity of her feelings and win her heart or even her desire. Finally, she felt her body being used as it had always longed to be, and she was so excited she had to keep her eyes closed to endure it.

'Come on, baby...' He thrust his hard fingers even deeper into her tender, clinging pussy.

She felt her inner juices flowing shamelessly into his hand as she gasped and moaned and writhed against the cushion, shifting her hips as if compelled to escape the excruciating delight, but the actual effect of her sensual squirming was to shove her sex willingly up into his hand. He hadn't even kissed her and yet already he was finger-fucking her. She couldn't believe it, this wasn't the way a gentleman behaved on the first date, and yet the truth was his rough possessiveness aroused her like nothing else ever had. Then he gave the mysterious seal of approval to her budding ecstasy by pressing his mouth lightly against hers. He kissed her chastely at first, keeping his lips sealed as her tender pussy lips bloomed open around the digging stamens of his fingers, then at last his tongue reached for hers and began dancing with it, leading hers around and around and making her aware of the climax forming like a whirlpool deep in her hole. Her clitoris had found a magical harbor between his thumb and forefinger and a hot joy was flooding her body as it never had before, much more intensely than it did when she played with herself in the privacy of her bedroom. She had been afraid no man would ever know how to touch her the way she knew how to touch herself, and she was thrilled to experience him killing this fear inside her once and for all. The orgasm cresting between her thighs had all the devastating power of a tidal wave about to wash away everything she knew about sex like a frustratingly small town as it exposed the wildly beautiful landscape of all her fantasies. But right now it was too much for her the way his tongue kept playing with hers while his fingers plunged relentlessly in and out of her wet pussy, cradling her clitoris in the caressing folds of skin between his thumb and forefinger as he thrust his rigid digits up inside her body as far as they would go. She wanted to wait for his cock to come, but she couldn't take anymore; she had to surrender to the pleasure and climax in his hand, moaning breathlessly and gratefully up into his mouth thinking that at last she had found a real man, or rather that at last he had found her.

Chapter Three

Carol Wilson's entire body ached and psychologically she was feeling black-and-blue with fear and guilt. *She* had been driving the car in which Maia was injured, and the truth was she would rather have died herself than hurt her beloved niece. Peter and Stella had forgiven her, naturally, pointing out that the accident was in no way her fault, but she was finding it much more difficult to forgive herself. Yet it had all happened so fast; there was nothing she could have done to get away from that falling tree.

'Oh doctor, it was terrible!' She closed her eyes, but that only made her see the hellish scene even more vividly on the dark screen of her inner eyelids. 'There was this blinding flash of light in which I saw everything so clearly for an instant... the wet road shone like a silver snake winding between the trees... then it was as if the Devil's own pitchfork was flung straight in our path! I've never seen anything like it before in my life, doctor, and I hope I never do again! Three bolts of lightning, one right after the other, cut through that huge old tree like a knife through butter!'

'Don't keep dwelling on it, Ms. Wilson,' Eric urged, yet he had to admit the old woman painted a disturbingly sinister picture. 'Try and forget about it,' he insisted without much conviction.

Carol's eyes snapped opened. 'How in God's name can you ever forget something like that?' she demanded.

'I don't know. You just have to.' He was still trying to get up the nerve to tell her that her lovely niece had paid for her life with any she might have hoped to conceive in the future.

'My brother tells me you've stayed by Maia's side day and night, doctor. We all appreciate your help more than we can ever express, but you really should get some sleep, young man.' She knew his blue eyes were staring at her so intensely not because she was anything worth looking at anymore, but because he was on the verge of collapsing from exhaustion. 'If you don't get some rest you'll need a doctor yourself soon.'

'I'll be fine,' he replied a bit gruffly, haunted by two long nights spent watching over 'Sleeping Beauty', the nurses' inevitable nickname for Maia. He was growing both attached to, and angry with, the lovely, unresponsive body, and neither emotion was in any way respectable or productive.

Maia felt completely wiped out. She had never experienced such an intense orgasm in all her life, not even in her wildest dreams, and even after her heart stopped pounding and her blood stopped racing down her veins, resuming its normal pace coursing through her body, she couldn't seem to move. She was also reluctant to open her eyes because then she would have to face her incredibly wanton behavior, and the inevitable dimming of respect in Christopher's eyes as he regarded her in a less serious light. She was afraid how easily she had succumbed to his advances, not to mention how quickly and intensely she had climaxed, would make him think less of her.

'Maia, look at me,' he commanded gently.

She had no choice but to open her eyes, yet it cost her an immense effort of will to do so. She did not want to see her ruined dress or the shattered glass at her feet, and the memory of the intense pleasure she had suffered in his hands was still smoldering in her womb in a way that felt almost like the ghost of pain.

'What's wrong, Maia?' Her silence seemed to be upsetting him. 'Talk to me.'

She found the courage to meet his eyes, and the tender concern in them amazed her because it was a universe away from the sharp cynical glint she had expected to see as he planned to keep taking advantage of her easy virtue. 'Nothing's wrong,' she whispered, holding on to his expression as though it was a life raft in the turbulent sea of her feelings. She needed to know he approved of her intense sensual nature, and wouldn't respect her less for not holding anything back from a total stranger. 'It's just... it's just that I've never done anything like this before.'

He smiled as he gently brushed the hair away from her face with one hand. 'You've never done anything like *what* before, Maia?' His other arm was wrapped around her shoulders where he sat as close to her as possible on the yielding cushion.

'You know...' she hedged shyly, avoiding the sight of her ruined dress still hiked shamelessly up her thighs, but for some reason she didn't feel like pulling it back down modestly; she liked the fact that he could see her pouting pussy lips and feeling vulnerably open to whatever he might desire to do to her next. It excited her that he was still fully and elegantly dressed while she herself was a weak and helpless mess in his arms.

'You're not still a virgin.' It wasn't a question; he had probed her sex deeply and thoroughly enough to know her hymen had been ruptured before tonight.

'No, I'm not,' she admitted, 'but I've never... I've never come like that before.' She gazed earnestly up into his eyes, silently pleading with him to understand that she had barely known him two hours yet already he had made her experience sensations no other man had ever come close to arousing in her. 'And I've never accepted a dinner invitation from a total stranger, much less gone home with him,' she added fervently, praying he would read between the lines and hear what she was telling him – that he was special and she had started falling in love with him from the instant his features rose out of the darkness in the graveyard.

His contented smile deepened as he insinuated the tip of his thumb between her lips. 'You're being a very naughty girl tonight, aren't you, Maia?' he teased quietly, gradually forcing her to accept his whole thumb.

She moaned and sucked on his hard and slightly salty digit like a baby. It made her try to picture his cock still buried in his black slacks, and his penetrating stare told her he knew what she was thinking and that it both amused and pleased him. And the longer he made her suck on his thumb while staring down into her eyes, the more she longed to reach into his lap and feel the hard-on she hoped was waiting for her there, but for some reason she couldn't bring herself to touch him

Rituals of Surrender

so boldly. She was grateful when he took the decision out of her hands by grasping one of her wrists and resting her palm against his crotch. She gasped with pleasure at the rock-hard erection filling her grasp through his silky-soft pants.

'Would you like to feel me inside you, Maia?' He slipped his thumb out of her mouth so she could answer.

'Oh yes,' she whispered.

He laughed softly and stood up abruptly.

The suddenness of his motion made her catch her breath, then whimper in alarm as he grasped both her hands and pulled her to her feet. She was afraid of slipping on the wet floor, made even more treacherous by shards of broken glass. Red wine seeping into the wood looked disturbingly like freshly spilled blood, and she suddenly suffered a vivid flashback of the car's broken window through which tree branches thrust unhindered and cold rainwater poured into the front seat where she lay pinned down beneath the rough old arm…

He swept her up into his arms and carried her away from the wreck she had made of his living room. She wrapped her own arms gratefully around his neck and gazed trustingly up at his face. She could scarcely believe he was real, and it both thrilled and worried her to know that any moment now she was going to see his penis for the first time. Everything around her told her he was as talented and creative as he was physically attractive, yet if she didn't like his cock, if it wasn't big enough to satisfy her fantasies as well as her flesh, none of his good qualities would matter as much. It was terrible, yet it was true, and the suspense came close to killing her as he strode across the room with her cradled against him. She had thought he was going to carry her upstairs to his bed, but she discovered he had other plans for her when she felt a hard edge against her backside as he set her down carefully. He spread her legs and stood directly between them. 'Lie back,' he said.

She obeyed him, but moaned in disappointment that he wasn't going to undress her. It hurt her that he didn't want to see her naked body and couldn't be bothered to prime her for his penetrations by caressing her a little first. Then she stiffened against the hard wooden surface when she realized how wrong she was. 'What are you doing?' she gasped. 'No!'

'Relax, Maia, I'm not going to hurt you.' He gripped the edge of her dress over her chest, and began slicing through it with the small knife he had pulled out of his pants. He lifted the material away from her skin as he cut it all the way down to where it was crumpled around her thighs, then quickly reached up to nip through the spaghetti straps on her shoulders.

She learned in those moments that mixing dread and desire was seriously intoxicating as her body went limp and her pussy got so hot for him it burned straight through her ability to think. He peeled her dress open, fully exposing her curving, naked body to his eyes as he unzipped his fly. She lifted her head slightly, and literally held her breath in desperate anticipation as he pulled his cock out of his slacks. Her dark eyes widened as she absorbed the length and girth of his hard-on, and unconsciously she spread her legs even farther apart where they hung off the edge of the table. His penis was everything she could have hoped for, and there was as much relief as desire contained in her cry as he slipped his hands beneath her thighs and raised them forcefully up around him.

Suddenly, Maia couldn't believe what was happening, but even as her prim and proper mind closed itself to the shockingly wicked way she was behaving tonight, her pussy willingly opened up to the experience. He didn't make a sound as he penetrated her so patiently she thought it would drive her crazy even as she loved every overwhelming second. First he tormented her with the fullness of his head spreading her labial lips open around it and making her achingly aware of how empty she was without his cock filling her up. Then finally he began pushing his way into her, and her pussy seemed to weep with joy at how good his erection felt, as though the dimensions of his desire had been made especially to fulfill hers. He possessed her so slowly, she was aware of every nerve ending in her tight cleft clinging to his dick, and sensing that his pleasure was as breathtakingly acute as hers mysteriously burst the last proper dam inside her.

'Oh God, just fuck me!' she begged. 'Fuck me, please!'

His cool scrotum kissed her hot vulva as he lodged his enormous erection all the way inside her tight little pussy. 'Say my name,' he commanded, squeezing her thighs where they rested in his hands but otherwise not moving a muscle.

'Oh God, Chris, please…'

'Please what?' he teased cruelly, squeezing her thighs again.

Rituals of Surrender

She gasped as the slight pain intensified the tormenting pleasure of his erection kissing the mysterious heart of her flesh and nearly killing her with longing to be stabbed by him over and over again. 'Please fuck me, Chris, *please*!'

He pulled out of her.

She whimpered in distress at how empty she suddenly felt.

He thrust back inside her.

She cried out from the overwhelming satisfaction and continued crying out softly as he banged her mercilessly. The few young men she had been with until then had pumped awkwardly against her and come in a matter of minutes, but not Chris, and blended with her intense pleasure was joy and amazement at his virility mixed with the exciting fear that she wouldn't be able to handle it. Her heart and thoughts racing, she suspected the climax he had offered her as a gift before fucking her had served another purpose besides rendering her even more malleable to his will; it had made her sex wet and pliant enough to accept, and thoroughly enjoy, the onslaught of his almost painfully big cock making her aware of her innermost flesh as never before. No other man had made her so aware of the silky passage of her pussy clinging to him even while blooming open around his relentless penetrations. How beautiful he looked as he possessed her selfishly, almost violently, inexorably deepened her yielding ecstasy, which was mysteriously stoked by the intent expression on his face as he concentrated on driving his rigid penis as deep into her flesh as possible faster and harder. Yet his eyes were on her face and holding hers in a way that made her want him even more as she seemed to feel him thrusting deeper and deeper. Her breasts bounced wildly up and down beneath his onslaught and her lips parted as she panted in sympathy with his approaching orgasm. She had never truly enjoyed the taste of cum before, but gazing up at him as he approached his peak she was sure it was only because she had been eating in all the wrong places...

'Oh Maia,' he said breathlessly, and abruptly pulled out of her eagerly straining hole.

She moaned as he pumped his erection fervently over her body, tossing his head back with a groan as a stream of foam bathed her belly and formed a milky pool in her navel. She was grateful to him for not coming inside her since she had not told him yet it didn't matter; she could never get pregnant.

Chapter Four

'Let's see what we can prepare for this special young man,' Carol said cheerfully.

'I have no idea how old he is, auntie. He's so beautiful, he seems ageless.'

'Dear, when you're my age, everyone else is young.' The old woman's good-natured chuckle evoked a seasoned hen laying yet another egg.

Maia smiled fondly up at her aunt from her usual place at the kitchen table. Carol had filled her life with stories in which the nourishing yoke of a moral was always inevitably concealed in the round-about way in which she told the tales.

'You say he built his own home and everything in it? He must be amazingly talented and creative.'

'Yes, he is.' Maia stared down into the murky depths of her tea. 'I'm nervous about tonight,' she confessed.

'Why in heaven's name should you be nervous, dear? I'm doing all the cooking. Shall we have rack of lamb or a beef roast, what do you think?'

She shrugged indifferently.

Carol glanced at her in alarm. 'He's not a vegetarian, is he?'

'I don't know.' She remembered the violent way he had stabbed her with his erection as she lay naked across his kitchen table, the white peel of her dress spread open around her. 'No,' she shook her head, 'I really don't think he is.' She wished she could share her tumultuous feelings with Carol, but the poor old dear would be too shocked; she would be absolutely stunned to learn that her usually well-behaved niece had made love with a complete stranger last night, a

Rituals of Surrender

man she didn't know at all, except in the biblical sense now. It had not been like her to do what she did, but then Chris was like no other man she had ever met. He lived deep in the woods in a house like a hollowed out tree trunk and his blond hair was so soft and luminous it made her think of spun sunlight. She would almost be more surprised if he actually showed up at her house for dinner tonight than if she never saw him again. She half expected him to vanish forever like an enchanted being in a perverse fairytale after offering her a teasingly cruel glimpse into the mythical kingdom of great sex. What she had experienced with him last night was worlds away from the clumsy, groping frustration she had so often suffered in the front seats of cars after a mind-numbingly boring date invariably consisting of a disappointing dinner and a mediocre movie. She had wondered if getting her own flat would improve her love life. Maybe her life would miraculously become more exciting if she moved out of her aunt's house and got a place of her own. But the truth was that none of the men she had dated truly excited her, not mentally or physically, and if she stopped splitting the bills with Carol she would be obliged to seek full time employment at the solicitor's office where she was now fortunate enough to only work half days. This left her enough time and energy to paint, never mind that she would probably never be able to make a living off her strangely surreal and sensual landscapes. That wasn't important, all that mattered was the fact that art, at least, enabled her to experience a sense of magic and a mysteriously profound fulfillment sadly lacking from her day-to-day reality, not to mention her love life. She kept recalling the wonderful moment last night when she had felt her heart knight Chris her true love as he knelt before the wooden cabinet containing his spirits. She didn't want to dwell on what had happened on his love seat, and then later on his kitchen table, not while she was in the same room with Carol. She would think about it all again later upstairs in her bed...

Maia's thoughts felt like a car's windshield wipers in a downpour powerless against the rush of emotions this man aroused in her. He had asked her to spend the night with him, but had not insisted she do so when she told him Carol would be seriously worried about her if she didn't come home, and since he didn't have a telephone there was no way she could let her aunt know she was safe.

He had not argued with her, he had simply unbuttoned his shirt, shrugged it off and slipped it on her tenderly, gently lifting her arms and turning her around as though she was a life-sized doll. The dark-red shirt had been wonderfully warm from resting against his skin, and there had been something very comforting about the soft, cozy way it embraced her all the way home when she was alone in her dark little car again. She had not needed to ask him to give her directions back to the main highway; he had led her back there in his own car, and she had felt as though her heart was vanishing into darkness when he turned back onto the narrow, tree-shrouded roads winding confusingly back to his home. Fortunately, Carol had been asleep when she let herself in and so had not seen her niece wearing a man's shirt and nothing else except high-heels.

'Maia, sweetheart, where are you? You've been lost in daydreams all morning,' Carol observed as she limped efficiently around their small kitchen. 'Christopher isn't like all the other lads, is he?' Her voice betrayed a mixture of hope and concern. 'You're really taken with him, aren't you?'

I was taken by him all right, Maia thought, and yet again a debilitating desire flashed like lightning in her belly. 'Carol, do you remember our accident?' The question was rhetorical since every step her aunt took reminded her of that dreadful night. 'I still don't know what actually happened. I remember it was thundering and lightning and-'

'It doesn't matter now.' Carol said quickly, closing the refrigerator and leaning back against it. 'Go upstairs and get some rest while I straighten out this mess.' She glanced at the wreckage of dishes in the sink.

Normally, Maia would have offered to help, but this morning she simply rose, abandoning her cup of tea untouched, and climbed the stairs up to her room, where she lay back across her bed to once again relive the unbelievably naughty way she had behaved last night, and how much she had enjoyed it.

Dressed to receive their guest in a short red cotton dress with a V-neck and matching high-heels, her dark-brown hair falling in gentle waves half way down her back, Maia rejoined Carol later that evening. 'Can I help with anything?' she asked belatedly. Her aunt had apparently spent most of the day in the kitchen, but since Maia knew she loved to cook it didn't make her feel guilty.

'Well, let's see... you can break three eggs into that bowl for me, dear, that would help. I'm baking your favorite buttermilk biscuits.'

'Oh great, thank you.' She selected three eggs from the carton, then rested the fragile spheres on a green pot-holder so they wouldn't roll off the counter. She carefully cracked open the first one. 'Oh look,' she exclaimed, 'it's a double yoke!'

'Well, so it is, dear. That seems like a good omen for tonight, wouldn't you say?'

'Yes.' It meant Chris was her soul mate, he *had* to be, there were no other possible candidates in Stoneshire and he had made her feel things last night she had only fantasized were possible. 'But now I don't feel like scrambling them...'

'Oh they won't mind,' Carol replied brightly, 'not as long as you beat them together.'

Maia reluctantly picked up a fork and attempted to impale both yokes at once, but they kept slipping and sliding away together, so she was forced to decide which one would go first. Soon they were a single flowing whole, their liquid saffron cloud reflecting the vivid sunset outside the kitchen window, its dying luminosity scrambled by a lacy white curtain. She picked up another egg and, suddenly, she became disturbingly conscious of all the unknown forces surrounding the fragile illusion of their cozy little home just as her fingers gripped the delicate shell... it made her aware of how hungrily she was holding on to every instant of her life...

The doorbell rang just as she cracked the egg against the edge of the bowl. 'Oh my God, he's here,' she cried. 'He's early!'

'Indeed he is, but there's no need to panic,' Carol scolded her tenderly. 'Just rinse your hands off and go let him in.'

The countless possible greetings Maia had rehearsed all day vanished like shadows beneath his smile, forcing her to use her arms' silent sentences to tell him how relieved and happy she was to see him again. She felt as though they could have stood embracing in the dark foyer forever, but somehow they managed to separate into two bodies again and walk hand-in-hand into the dining room.

'Why did you leave me last night?' he whispered, giving her hand a reprimanding squeeze. 'Today was centuries long.'

'You sit here, please, Christopher.' Carol was at her most formal this evening.

He smiled as he obeyed her. 'Call me Chris.'

'Of course. It was very nice of you to bring a bottle of wine, Chris.'

'Can I help with anything, Carol?' Maia was compelled to ask before she seated herself on Chris's right side at the circular table.

'No thank you, dear, I have it all under control. There's tomato soup to start with and homemade buttermilk biscuits. I won't be a moment.' She pushed through the swinging wooden door dividing the kitchen from the dining room.

Chris immediately grasped Maia's hand, and laid it beneath his on the white table cloth. 'You wanted to say something to me before she walked in?' he prompted.

'I'm not sure... I forgot what it was...'

'Tell me.'

'Chris, please, you're cutting the circulation off in my fingers,' she whispered, glancing in the direction of the kitchen. 'You don't know you're own strength.'

'I know it very well, Maia.' But he released her hand in order to caress the knife at his place setting as though admiring the craftsmanship.

Watching the tip of his index finger stroke the full length of the silver, she was reminded of how devastatingly skilled it was. Never before had a man made her come with only his hand...

'Here we are.' Carol returned carrying a heavy steaming bowl she quickly placed in the center of the table. 'Help yourselves while I go get myself a glass of water and pull the biscuits out of the oven.'

Rituals of Surrender

Chris reached for the ladle. 'It smells divine, Carol.'

'No, thank you.' Maia covered her soup dish with one hand as he prepared to serve her.

'Why not?' he asked, smiling as though he knew the answer but wanted to hear it from her.

'I just don't want any... I haven't felt like myself all day, really.' She stared down into her empty bowl, studying the colorful wreath of flowers decorating the rim of the white stoneware.

'Maia is being a bad girl,' Chris informed Carol when she returned. 'Your niece doesn't even want to taste any of your delicious soup.'

'Why not, dear?' Her aunt sounded concerned. 'You love my tomato soup.'

Maia cried out when a cold wave of water suddenly drenched her breasts as her limping aunt inadvertently tripped on a warped wooden floor board.

'Oh my dear, I'm so sorry!' Carol set the tray of biscuits down on the table along with her now empty water glass. 'I've completely soaked you. You'll have to go upstairs and change, you can't eat in that wet–'

'It's all right, Carol, sit down, please, I'm fine,' Maia assured her, but shivered uncontrollably as Chris began drying her off with his white cloth napkin.

'You really *should* change your dress,' Carol insisted, hovering over her in concern and frowning slightly at the familiar way Chris was stroking her niece's pert breasts with the napkin. 'You'll catch your death...'

'I'm fine!' Maia snapped at her without meaning to. 'Now sit down, please, auntie,' she said more kindly.

'You see, Carol,' Chris dropped the napkin and quickly rose to pull his hostess's chair out for her, 'it's destiny that you partake of some wine this evening.'

'I suppose it is.' She politely twisted her shaken frown into a smile as she seated herself across from him.

'Let's light the candles to help dry Maia off,' he suggested, and proceeded to do so with the pack of matches he slipped out of his pocket. He was clad in a forest-green button-down shirt and dark-brown slacks that made him look even more handsome than Maia remembered him, if that was possible. Glad to put the embarrassing moment behind them, she rose to switch off the overhead light as he lit the candles, but when she resumed her seat, it dismayed her that Carol's lovingly prepared soup looked very much like a sinister cauldron of blood with three flames pulsing around it.

'Does it remind you of something?' Chris asked her, uncannily reading her mind as he began pouring them all some wine, beginning with her glass.

'Yes,' she admitted, feeling inexplicably somber.

'You see, Carol,' he said again as he proceeded to fill her glass, 'your niece and I have met before.'

'That's more than enough, thank you, Christopher... you mean before you helped her get her car started in the graveyard last night?'

'No, another time I helped her into the graveyard.'

'Excuse me?' Carol brought a wrinkled hand up to her right ear. 'My hearing isn't what it used to be. I don't think I heard you correctly.'

'Never mind.' He smiled indulgently and raised his glass. 'Cheers,' he said, and took an appraising sip of the dark-red vintage.

'Well,' Carol cleared her throat as though something was sticking in it, 'since Maia's not having any soup, I think I'll pass on it as well and go get the lamb out of the oven.' She rose again with difficulty. 'Excuse me, I won't be a moment.'

Maia impatiently watched her leave the room. 'What did you mean by that?' she demanded of Chris as soon as her aunt was out of earshot. 'I never saw you before last night. And why are you trying to scare her saying things like that? It sounded like you said you helped me *into* the graveyard, not *in* the graveyard. Why-?'

'Baby,' his tone was infinitely patient as he picked up her glass of wine and handed it to her, 'drink.'

Upset as she was by his behavior, which although oddly sinister was faultlessly polite, she could not resist obeying that tone in his voice or the look in his eyes reminding her of what he could make her feel... she sipped her wine obediently.

'You have to realize, Maia that you were just now symbolically baptized for sacrifice when Carol spilled water over you and I lit fire to help dry you off.'

'What are you talking about?' Her chest was suddenly so tight she could scarcely get the words out. 'You're starting to scare me, Chris.'

'You say there are standing stones in all your paintings, which means that whenever you drive by them you can feel the energy stored inside them, can't you, Maia?'

'I think so,' she agreed, desperately hoping he was going to explain his strange comments so she could feel good about him again and not be afraid of the power he already had over her.

'There's a Celtic saying, he who defies the spirit of reason places himself within reach of salvation.'

As if in a dream she heard herself add, 'But also exposes himself to the dangers of the sword-edge bridge.' The words welled out of her unbidden; she had no idea where they came from. The only explanation she could think of was that she had read them somewhere once and forgotten she knew them until he triggered her memory.

'Very good, Maia.' He leaned over to gently kiss her forehead. 'We've already started across the sword-edge bridge together.' He sat back in his chair again looking in the direction of the kitchen. 'Now we just have to get you out of here. You're coming with me tonight, sweetheart, and you're going to stay with me. After dinner I want you to go up to your room and pack a suitcase with all your essentials. We'll collect the rest of your things some other time.'

'But, Chris…'

'No buts, Maia.' He picked up his silver spoon and took a sip of the blood-red soup. 'Mm, this is wonderful.'

'Chris, I can't just leave with you tonight,' she protested in a conspiratorial whisper, glancing in the direction of the kitchen where Carol was taking her sweet time.

'Why not?' He held her eyes, the expression in his at once tender and challenging. 'You feel the connection between us, don't you, Maia?'

'Yes, Chris, but-'

'Then why waste time? You know perfectly well you want to leave here with me, so why not tonight?'

'If it was just up to me, Chris, I wouldn't hesitate, but Carol…' She glanced at the dividing wooden door again. 'Carol will be shocked.'

He shrugged, and concentrated on his soup again. 'Sometimes shock is a good thing,' he said lightly, and paused to swallow another hot red mouthful before adding, 'it wakes people up.'

'But what about my art supplies?'

'You'll bring those with you, of course. They're the most important thing you own, much more important than clothing. You won't really be needing that.' He smiled and winked at her.

She laughed even as her heart gave an anxious flutter. 'But I have so many canvasses and brushes and paints, not to mention my easel…'

'Maia,' his tone and the way he set his spoon down made it clear her hesitant attitude was beginning to make him impatient, 'it's only stuff, and my trunk is bigger than it looks. We'll take everything you need with us, and Carol will deal with it. It's not the end of the world, just of your life together, but you'll be beginning a new adventure with me. Isn't that what you want?'

'Yes,' she replied fervently, 'more than anything!'

He slipped his hand beneath the table and stroked her bare thigh. 'The sword-edge bridge is a fascinating place to be,' he stated cryptically, and squeezed her flesh possessively. 'You'll see.'

Chapter Five

Maia stared up at the full moon through the small window in Chris's proportionally small bedroom. The sun's clinging satellite was slowly sinking in a silky-black sky perspiring with stars as it gazed amorously down at his naked back where he lay sleeping beside her. It was strange how the marble-white light carving out the deep shadows of his muscles made his arms and shoulders look thicker and broader than they actually were. The earth's one and only moon was perched in the heavens cool as a queen surrounded by her court; all the stars visible at the edges of her royal-blue aura sparkled like infinitely wealthy lords and ladies covered from head to toe in jewels. Maia couldn't see her lover's face because it was turned away from her on his pillow, which he had bunched passionately up around his head like a cloud, and she found herself wondering at how inexplicably dark his hair looked in the otherworldly light that seemed to be forge the muscles in his body just for the pleasure she took in gazing down at them...

She concentrated on the moon's infinitely calm face in order not to remember Carol's politely concealed distress when her niece left the house with a man she had met only twenty-four hours ago, taking with her two suitcases and a large duffel bag full of art supplies. And as Maia stared at the moon without blinking, its luminous sphere became the bottom of a polished silver chalice into which the sun passionately poured its boundless energy without ever filling her... then she blinked a few times and the full moon struck her as the ghostly negative of a fingerprint belonging to every beautiful woman who had ever lived impressed on the universe at the moment of her birth, the shadow-lined sphere the soft round end of her own pale, mysteriously unique fingertip...

Rituals of Surrender

Maia realized she must have fallen asleep while gazing out the window because suddenly she was standing in front of her parents' tombstone, only it had grown much taller than she remembered it and sprouted a protective dome like a massive mushroom. She was rather pleased by its transformation, yet she hesitated to approach the narrow black opening in the solid white stem. The mushroom's head glowed like a perfect half moon, so she wasn't surprised to discover there wasn't really a door, only an impenetrably dark portal. Then she thought she glimpsed the soft glow of her mother's red hair inside, and the sight gave her the courage she needed to enter the hauntingly organic mausoleum.

The woman in whose body she had shaped herself lay beneath a stone sheet, the cold weight of which didn't seem to bother her because she was smiling peacefully, her head slightly raised by a marble pillow carved in the shape of a large open book, its blank pages dimly illuminating the circular room. All around Maia the shadows were thick and heavy as black velvet curtains slowly rising in whichever direction she focused, then swiftly falling again when she looked away. Glancing into one corner of the pitch-black crypt, she briefly made out smiling figures painted on the wall, their clothing impossibly bright in the absolute gloom. And then just beside her to the right appeared an exquisite little prayer room very much like the kind found in Medieval Cathedrals containing a beautiful statue of the Virgin Mary perched on a gilded globe of the world.

'Oh mummy,' she sighed, bending over to rest her head for an instant on the cold stone breasts of Stella's effigy. She longed to be comforted and loved without question, to know that no matter how badly she behaved her mother would always care for her. The tiny prayer room did not vanish even when she turned away from it, and looking back at it curiously, she realized the black serpent imprisoned beneath the Virgin's white toes was alive. With one upraised hand the Mother of God blessed the world while with the other hand she wantonly raised the hem of her sky-blue dress, smiling with secret pleasure as the evil serpent began sliding slowly up her shapely leg.

'Father!' Maia cried in horror.

'It's all right, sweetheart, don't be afraid, you're not alone....' A man's voice spoke directly in her head as she felt a reassuring warmth envelop her and safely cradle her within it, giving her the courage to watch the serpent twisting eagerly up to a snowy thigh. She held her breath, waiting for cruel fangs to pierce the Virgin's infinite tenderness and for red rivers of blood to run, but suddenly a passionate faith in the Lady's power possessed her as she felt her cheek pressed against an invisible yet mysteriously benevolent chest. Mary's blue skirt and white shift were the daylight sky filled with soft clouds, and as the serpent rose eagerly up into this heavenly atmosphere, she gasped in the throes of a sensation such as she had never known; a sensation that intensified almost unbearably when the tip of the black tail shuddered a victorious defeat between the Virgin's thighs and disappeared inside her…

Maia woke with a cry of mingled ecstasy and alarm as Chris rolled over and unconsciously pinned her down with a heavy arm. She couldn't move and the moon was no longer visible outside the window.

She was having very strange dreams lately, but this last one had been particularly vivid. She could still see her mother's red hair rippling like fire across the cold marble bed, and the Virgin letting herself be possessed by the serpent coiled submissively beneath her delicate white feet… She should have found the images rising out of her subconscious disturbing and shocking, but instead she realized with a soft groan of shame that they had made her pussy so warm and wet the pressure of Chris's arm across her breasts was seriously tempting her to wake him. In the morning, she would try and paint the scenes she had seen in the mushroom-shaped mausoleum of her dream, but right now she wasn't interested in symbols and metaphors; what she wanted was the undeniably real pleasure of Chris's cock inside her. They had only made love once so far, yesterday evening when he spread the feast of her naked body across his kitchen table, and carved her hungrily up with his erection as the hot juices of her pleasure flowed helplessly around him. When they arrived at his little house tonight with all the essentials she had been able to bring with her at such short notice (and with all her beloved art supplies, naturally) she had been expecting him to take her passionately in his arms and have his way with her as he had not been able to do in front of her aunt Carol, but he hadn't even kissed her. Leaving her possessions in his living room, he had simply taken her hand and led her upstairs. His unlit

Rituals of Surrender

narrow stairway seemed to spiral up and up for longer than seemed possible judging by the house's physical dimensions, and his bedroom had been just as impenetrably dark. She had been about to ask him to turn on a light when he told her to take off her clothes. She heard him doing the same, and had been too hurt and disappointed by his indifference to complain as she slipped casually into bed beside him as though they had been together forever.

Long after he fell asleep after a quiet 'Good night, Maia' she lay awake gazing restlessly up at the moon tormented by the awareness of his naked body lying so close to hers, and now her haunting dream was somehow making her want him even more. 'Chris?' she whispered, feeling it would drive her crazy if he didn't wake up and fuck her. 'Chris,' she repeated a little more loudly.

'Mm,' he said, his voice muffled by her hair. His face was buried in the side of her neck as he slept, but suddenly it slid purposefully down to one of her breasts.

She gasped when his lips latched on to one of her nipples, and moaned in delight as his tongue lapped her stiffening peak, suckling it like a sleepy baby. The pleasure traveled directly from her breast down to her sex as inexorably as a lit fuse smoldering in her sex, and she was so aroused already she knew all it would take was a few hard strokes of his cock for an orgasm to explode between her thighs and wipe out all the night's frustrations.

'Mm...' he said again, sounding more awake now, and she cried out hopefully as he fervently transferred his attentions to her other nipple. His insatiable hunger got the tips of her tits so rigid she felt the beginnings of a climax lick deep inside her belly like a hot forked tongue as he gently bit one.

'Oh Chris,' she breathed, 'please, I need you...' She wondered if he was going to make her beg him to fuck her again, and her mouth had opened to say the words when he abruptly slid beneath the sheet and thrust his whole body between her legs. Before she knew what was happening he had buried his face between her thighs and transferred the skilled attention of his tongue from her nipples to her clitoris.

'Oh yes,' she sighed gratefully, reaching down to lightly grasp his head in her hands. His hair was so soft it made her almost morbidly aware of the contrasting hardness of his skull. She was desperate to feel the rending length of his erection fully opening her up around it, yet the sensation of his features imprinting themselves on the yieldingly moist warmth of her labia was so sweet she didn't mind waiting.

In the past she had never taken much pleasure from oral sex, either in giving or receiving it, but she had been right to suspect that with Chris everything would feel miraculously different. The awkward, unfocused licks and uncomfortable groping fingers she had come to expect were tonight replaced by a concentrated yet effectively indirect attack on her clit. The flicking tip of his tongue and his suckling lips almost made her vaguely ashamed of the way her juices began pouring helplessly into his mouth, but she couldn't help herself; her sensual slot had never felt so bottomless, so in need of him to fill it, even if it was only with two of his fingers.

'Oh yes, yes…' she breathed, flinging her arms up over her head and clutching a pillow as she gently gripped the sides of his hard head with her soft thighs. She shifted her hips against the bed, seeking to position his penetrating fingers and orbiting tongue in just the right elusive spot that would send her hurtling along the blinding course of a climax. But he was teasing her; every time she felt her flesh poised on the speed of orgasmic light about to dissolve in timeless flashes of heart-pounding ecstasy, he shifted the stimulation of his tongue slightly and altered the rhythm of his fingers plunging into her cunt, cruelly delaying her release.

'Oh God, Chris, please,' she begged, 'I want to come, please…' She forgot about her lust for his cock; all she wanted now was to catch the pure joy cresting between her legs on the warm wave of his tongue and ride it to its crashing end in her blood.

He didn't respond to her plea verbally, but respond he did by suddenly pushing all her right buttons, sliding his fingers in and out of her pussy just hard and deep and fast enough as his tongue concentrated its assault on her clitoris, keeping her escalating ecstasy relentlessly on course. She lay breathlessly still on the soft launch pad of the mattress as her pleasure soared, then at last her body took off and she wasn't aware of anything anymore except his face between her thighs

Rituals of Surrender

and the sound of her cries as she climaxed more intensely than she ever had in her life. She didn't just come the way she did when she touched herself alone in her room; she came and came and came, her orgasm rushing into his mouth as though he had struck the elixir of life with his digging fingers and determined tongue. It almost scared her how long he was able to prolong her ecstasy as she selfishly rode his mouth, until she was thoroughly exhausted by the pleasure's unbelievable staying power.

It was a relief when he finally slipped out from beneath the sheet and lay down beside her again. He took her utterly relaxed body in his arms, and pulling her over onto her side held her close that way for a long time, until they fell asleep together.

Peter was offended by how much Drew appeared to be enjoying his breakfast, the yokes of his fried eggs bright as suns that had no place in the curtained dimness of a dining room where only black tea had been served for the last forty-eight hours.

'May we ask if you made any progress last night, *Merlin*?' Peter had decided this was an appropriately sarcastic nickname for someone whose command of the *Dragon's Breath* was exercised only through the poisonous smoke of cigarettes, a clear sign of physical weakness rather than of spiritual power.

'Dear, that's quite enough,' Stella said quietly but firmly. She had made her own decision – not to wear black anymore. After all, her daughter was not dead, she was merely sleeping, therefore, in an effort to reflect her positive attitude and her growing hope that Maia would make a full recovery, she had donned a form-fitting knee-length violet dress with long sleeves and a plunging neck-line.

Peter thought his wife's garment positively indecent considering the circumstances. 'Going to a party, love?' he asked her contemptuously, feeling oddly chastised by the smooth coolness of her deep cleavage.

She flinched at his tone even as she told herself it was only a temporary mix of fear and grief that made his eyes seem to glitter hatefully. 'Unlike you, dear,' her smile was strained as she paused to sip her tea from a cup decorated with colorful wreathes of flowers, 'I am attempting to maintain a positive attitude. You know perfectly well how I feel about the color violet, and I am not about to stop applying my beliefs when we need them most!' The porcelain saucer chimed defiantly against its matching plate like an urgent bell rung in the kingdom of the Fairies punctuating her faith-filled statement. The high-pitched sound was followed by the charged silence of an emotional storm brewing, and Drew added a sinister hissing sound to it as he lit a match.

'Aren't you afraid of getting lung cancer?' Peter demanded, and awaited a platitude on the negative nature of fear in response he could enjoy shooting down.

'It crosses my mind now and then,' Drew replied amiably, blithely continuing to ignore the tension in the room as he enjoyed a cigarette after his meal. 'I'll quit eventually,' he added wistfully, 'if I don't die first, of course.' A smile touched his lips. 'But in answer to your first question,' he sobered up, '*yes*, I believe I connected with Maia last night, very briefly, but it was a definite beginning.'

Stella's left hand flew up to her slender throat and clung to it as though this was the only way she could control the desperate anxiety in her voice as she spoke. 'How is she?'

Drew caressed the crescent-shaped scar below his lip. 'I can't very well tell you she's just fine,' he admitted, 'but she's definitely… active.' He studied the cigarette's slender form caught between the slightly rough tips of his fingers. 'Her soul feels much older than her twenty-three years… her essence is very deep and powerful.' He leaned towards Peter over the table even as he held Stella's eyes. 'What I'm saying is that, psychically, you can add at least two zeros to Maia's age. She's an old soul, and she's right at home in another dimension. I'm going to have a hell of a time convincing her to come back.'

Chapter Six

Maia lay in bed, comfortably propped up against some pillows, staring at the scaled down silhouette of a tree Chris had carved as a kind of bas relief into one of the oak walls in his bedroom. The shower hissed loudly inside his tiny bathroom. Listening to it, she was strangely aware of the water pipes coiling behind the walls like supple metal serpents, their fangs thrusting out in the handles of his sink, which she had seen for herself earlier were minimalist slivers of metal. She could not help but be impressed by a man who had designed every little detail of his home himself. Objects she herself had always taken for granted – the fixtures of a bathroom sink, for example – in her lover's house assumed intriguing organic qualities that were naturally aesthetic. There was so much she wanted to ask him about how and why he had built everything the way he had that she hadn't been able to figure out where to start.

Last night, her bare feet had relished the thick green carpet she hadn't been able to see in the darkness, but when she woke this morning and was confronted by the bare black arms of a tree's silhouette, the sight unsettled her so much she almost hadn't been able to enjoy it when, murmuring with sleepy lust, Chris rolled over into her arms and began exploring her naked body. Nothing had come of it, however, as she desperately needed to empty her bladder first, and when she returned to the bed, he declared it was his turn and disappeared into the bathroom. Now he was taking a leisurely shower while she studied his bedroom. It was very small and almost perfectly round; it could actually be a hollowed out tree trunk. The ceiling was so high, it was lost in darkness even with the bedside lamp turned on and with the humidly tarnished silver light of an

Rituals of Surrender

overcast day failing to penetrate into the room through the small window. Half the wall space was hidden behind tall bookshelves he must also have made himself because they conformed perfectly to the curving architecture, which had an odd effect on the leather-bound volumes, thrusting some out farther than others. Gazing at the spines, Maia verified her initial impression that most of her lover's books appeared old and worn enough to be first editions. She could make out texts on Astronomy and Physics and Biology on the top shelves, with poetry anthologies as well as works by individual poets just below them. Underneath the poetry were rows of novels, countless fictional realms sitting over heavy tomes on history and ancient cultures, with one whole bottom shelf devoted exclusively to Celtic culture and the legend of the Druids.

She would not have been so impressed by her lover's apparent erudition if it had not been so uniquely coupled with his skills as a craftsman (which also struck her as unusually artistic) not to mention with his physical beauty and with how skilled his hands were in other ways... his tongue was also extremely eloquent...

She sighed and stirred contentedly yet also restlessly against the deliciously comfortable feather pillows. It was so gray and gloomy outside she felt even less inclined to rise. She must have done something right in her life, because the universe had rewarded her with Christopher Thorn, a totally unique man who transcended even all her fantasies of the perfect lover.

She frowned gazing at the black bas relief of the tree directly across from her. She told herself it didn't matter that he could be strangely cold and detached sometimes, like last night, for example, when he had gone to sleep without even kissing her. Of course, he had more than made up for it later when he gave her another intense climax by going down on her. Still, she would have liked for him to cuddle her a little this morning before spending such a long time in the shower by himself, especially since she had believed he was only getting up to relieve himself as she had; she had expected him to come back to bed.

She sighed again, pouting. Didn't all new lovers shower together in the morning? Yet it was silly and superficial of her to expect Chris to behave normally when that was precisely the last thing she wanted him to do. So far, *normal* had bored her nearly to death in men. Therefore, she had to take the good with the bad and consider herself lucky, which she definitely was to have met someone like him in dreary old Stoneshire.

At last she heard the water shut off in the bathroom.

'Well, what do you think?' Chris emerged almost at once followed by a cloud of steam drying his water-darkened blond hair with a light-blue towel.

Maia stared at him, wide-eyed. He was completely naked and the perfection of his body aroused the artist in her even more than the woman. He looked like a Renaissance sketch of the ideal man fully fleshed out by the strokes of a master, a master whose brush had been slightly tainted with red paint; his pale skin had been beaten into an unnatural rosy hue by the hot shower. 'Think about what?' she asked lamely. His cotton bed sheet was decorated with blazing autumn leaves. She pulled it shyly up to just beneath her naked breasts and they looked cool and white as snow against the vivid colors.

'What do you think of my bedroom?' He lowered the towel and shook his wet head over her like a puppy coming in out of the rain. 'Wake up,' he commanded, wrapping the wet towel around his lean hips.

'I love your room,' she said fervently. 'I love your whole house. I feel like I'm inside a giant tree.'

'I know.' He sat on the edge of the bed beside her. 'That's what I want it to feel like.'

'How did you do *that*?' she asked, looking over at the bas relief of the tree.

'It's a different kind of wood from the rest of the house.'

'I can see that, but how did you do it?'

'It wasn't easy, believe me; it involved lots of exact measurements. I built the whole room around it, not the other way around. The wood came from an oak that was struck by lightning three time in one night, and obviously I used only the charred pieces of wood.' He stood up and approached the branching silhouette.

Maia watched him thinking how his blue towel looked like a fragment of the sky and wondering when he was going to kiss her good morning. Once again she found his behavior disappointingly casual and friendly. She would have liked for him to be more passionate and loving. She felt the need to be reassured that she had done the right thing essentially moving in with him after only knowing him for twenty-four hours.

'It's my closet,' he announced.

She gasped in astonishment when he casually pushed open the trunk of the tree and a row of shirts and pants appeared that gave the silhouette a disturbingly impressive depth.

'You see, Maia, I believe my soul has worn as many bodies as this.' He smiled at her over his shoulder as he stood proudly in front of his considerable wardrobe.

'I don't doubt it has,' she agreed, very pleased with his comment, for she had always thought of her body as a dress her ageless soul would slip off at the end of her life's long day.

He stepped into his sinister closet, and emerged a moment later holding a short-sleeved button-down shirt the same color as his towel, and a pair of stiff blue-jeans. 'I think we can expect a visitor soon,' he said, tossing his clothes onto the bed.

'A visitor?' she repeated, feeling like a queen spotting an invader on the horizon; she was loath to surrender her sensually rich and fledgling intimacy with him.

He walked over to her again. 'Don't be so distressed, love.' He mussed her hair affectionately. 'Our guest won't stay long. He's just dropping in to see my work.'

'Well, if he doesn't like it, he has absolutely no taste,' she declared.

He laughed. 'Your faith in me will not go unrewarded, young lady.' He unwrapped the towel from around his hips again and let it fall to the floor. 'I think my baby needs her bottle.' He held her face with one hand while with the other hand he gently insinuated his soft penis into her mouth. 'There you are, drink your protein like a good girl. It tastes good, doesn't it?'

She moaned and the bed sheet slipped down into her lap as she sat up to eagerly align her face with his hips.

'Yes, that's a good girl, it's all yours, Maia, so suck on it, suck on it and make it hard... that's it, I want you to have every last drop.'

No man had ever talked to her before while she went down on him, and she discovered now that words excited her as much as the possessive way he stroked her hair with both hands, smoothing it away from her face so it wouldn't interfere with the smooth passage of his stiffening cock sliding in and out between her soft, full lips. She had never really enjoyed giving head before, and she closed her eyes with a slight grimace expecting not to like the taste of his semen. His dick was getting so big and rigid between her soft lips she had to keep opening her mouth wider as she adjusted his burgeoning dimensions against her tongue. She moaned again, this time anxiously when she realized he was casually reaching for her throat as though it, too, had been made especially to caress and please him. She knew she was not very good at fellatio, much less at deep-throating, and opening her eyes again she tried to tell him this with a desperate, pleading glance up at his face.

'It's all right,' he slipped the fingers of both hands through her dark hair to take control of her head, 'you can handle it, Maia. Not only can you handle it, you're going to love sucking my cock, trust me.'

It amazed her that she believed him, maybe because the flavor of his pre-cum was so clean and subtle there was nothing about it she found distasteful, and this was such an intense relief her jaw relaxed around him, giving him full entry into her inexperienced orifice.

'Oh yes,' he whispered, managing to get his erection all the way into her mouth for an excruciating moment that made her squeeze her eyes closed again as they watered from the effort she had to make not to gag on his swollen glans. 'Mm, that's good, Maia, very good,' he praised her even as he had mercy on her by slipping almost all the way out of her mouth.

She sucked gratefully on the tip of his shaft, grasping it with one hand for the purpose of stroking it, but also to keep it out of her throat for the moment. She pumped him passionately in her fist while twirling her tongue around his head, feeling a bit self-conscious about her oral skills or lack thereof. It made her wonder how many women had been in her position, and she was afraid most, if not all, of them must have done a better job at pleasing him this way than she was doing.

'You have a lot of energy and enthusiasm, Maia,' he said, sounding insultingly unaffected by how hard she was working on his penis, 'the skill will come later with practice, and believe me,' his chuckle was intensely sexy, 'I'll let you have lots of practice.'

Rituals of Surrender

Already she both loved and hated the way he seemed able to read her mind as she concentrated on the challenge of properly stimulating and intensifying his erection. The pleasure she took in her efforts was different from his, and this morning she imagined her satisfaction was even greater than the one he experienced fucking her mouth simply because he had enjoyed himself this way before but she never had; this was the first time she felt an inexplicable but very real sense of fulfillment going down on a man. Until now it had always seemed like a lot of effort for nothing, but the sensation of Chris's hard-on sliding gently yet relentlessly in and out of her inexperienced mouth was mysteriously stoking her pussy too, making her receptively warm and wet between her legs.

She was growing tired from the subtle strain of this novel exertion even as she relished the exercise, which would have been made somewhat easier if he had let her know how she was doing, but he was silent as a standing stone towering above her. He didn't make any sounds of pleasure, but his rock-hard cock told her she must be doing something right. She wondered if he was planning to get off in her mouth and was a little worried about how she would deal with that honor if it came. She had never brought a man to his climax with her lips and tongue and so had never been forced to swallow frothing mouthfuls of cum. She needn't have been concerned, however, for Chris slipped out of her abruptly and mussed her hair affectionately again as though her devoted licks had merely been those of a naïve kitten. 'That's enough for now,' he said like a school teacher addressing a student. 'You need to shower and dress. Our guest will be here any minute.'

Sir Eric Wolfson looked slowly around the living room, and his luminous gray eyes brought the overcast day's cool depths into the small space. They alighted on Maia, and remained fixed on her as he peeled off his black leather gloves one by one. He then gracefully draped them both over one slender but muscular thigh, revealingly clad in skin-tight black leather. 'Lovely,' he said, his quiet, lazy voice a seductive contrast to the thick brown hair waving passionately around his fine-boned face.

'What's lovely?' Chris asked, smiling. 'Are you referring to my work or my girlfriend, sir?'

'Both, naturally,' was the languid reply as he kept his eyes on Maia the whole time.

'Have a seat, please,' Chris said briskly, 'and I'll pour us some tea. Maia, dear wait for me upstairs, please, I won't be long.'

Eric turned and walked slowly over to the love-seat, his apparent lethargy actually only enhancing his obvious fitness and almost cat-like grace. 'Must she leave us?' he asked as he dropped onto a cushion, his knee-high leather boots looking even blacker against the light-blue cloth.

'I'm afraid she must,' his host replied sternly. 'We have business to discuss and she would only distract us.' Chris looked over at her, and then glanced significantly at the steep little staircase leading up to his bedroom.

'I beg to differ,' his guest disagreed politely, crossing his legs and resting his limp gloves over his crotch. 'To say that beauty can distract is to imply there is something better worth doing than enjoying and appreciating it.'

'It was a pleasure meeting you, Sir Wolfson,' Maia said quickly, and ascended the steps with her pulsing fluttering like a bird's wings as she obeyed the invisible current of Chris's will. She did not find his dismissal humiliating, on the contrary. It was extremely flattering to know her presence affected him enough that he was obliged to ask her to leave so he could concentrate. The way two highly attractive men had determined her actions between them, as though she had absolutely no say in the matter, might have offended her if it had not made her feel so beautiful and desirable. The moment he walked through the door, Eric Wolfson's wicked aura of fame and fortune made her feel as nervous as a mouse spotted by a dangerous black cat. He was so intensely sexy, her heart caught in her throat looking at him, another reason she did not mind leaving the room. It disturbed her to realize she had been staring at him the whole time instead of at Chris, her wonderful new lover who until a few seconds before she had never dreamed could be rivaled by any other man in Stoneshire or beyond.

It was impossible to resist the temptation to crouch in the grass-green carpet at the top of the stairs in order to listen to what was being said downstairs. As

Rituals of Surrender

she held her breath and strained her hearing, both hoping and strangely dreading they might still be talking about her, all the unpolished wood surrounding her felt like the roots of an ancient tree...

'Vines and serpents it is then,' she heard Chris say, and his voice seemed to be coming from deep underground. 'How many bottles would you like it to hold, sir?'

'A great many,' Eric replied laconically. 'As many as possible.'

'That's not very specific.'

'Specifics bore me.'

Suddenly ashamed of eavesdropping, Maia stood up and stepped into her lover's bedroom, where she dove restlessly onto the bed and crushed handfuls of painted leaves in order to smooth them out again. She frowned, burying her face in the mattress and restlessly kicking her feet as she fought the nearly irresistible current of her curiosity. Finally, she couldn't stand it anymore and she found herself perched at the top of the stairs again listening.

'Naturally...' Eric drew the word out languidly. 'Now, may I at least bid farewell to that lovely creature you're foolishly attempting to hide from me?' The heel of a boot struck wood as she pictured him rising from the loveseat, and the sound kicked her heart out of Chris's orbit for an exhilarating yet also terrifying moment. She could scarcely believe this intensely sexy man wanted to see her again when it was obvious from his attitude that he could have any woman he wanted.

'No, you may not bid her farewell,' Chris replied.

'You can't keep her from me forever,' Sir Wolfson warned mildly.

'The hell I can't.' Her lover almost sounded amused by his quest's arrogance. She couldn't be sure, but she thought she detected a confident smile in his voice.

Chapter Seven

'**D**ear, I never wanted to tell you this, but I only belong to this... this *cult* to indulge you.' Peter's thick silver hair gleamed like armor against his skull as he smoothed it firmly back with both hands away from a face nobly scarred by the years.

'What?' Stella was literally beside herself where she stood before an ornately framed mirror in a corner of their library. She clutched the back of a large chair upholstered in burgundy leather as though needing to steady herself against the shock of her husband's revelation.

'I didn't see any harm in it at first,' he added morosely from where he sat slumped in his favorite chair, 'although Carol certainly didn't approve of my becoming involved, even when I told her that some of the rites are quite lovely...' He stared down at the red and gold rug embroidered with stylized dragons that had been his aesthetic pets for years, yet ever since Maia's accident he suddenly saw them for the fierce ugly creatures they actually were.

'Peter,' Stella said desperately, 'look at yourself... this isn't the man I love, this isn't-'

'No, the man you really love is upstairs, isn't he?' He glared up at her. 'Isn't he?' he repeated, surging angrily to his feet. 'But he doesn't want you, Stella, he wants our daughter.' He grabbed both her upper arms and shook her roughly, as though trying to dislodge all the pagan ideas in her head by way of physical force since reason had failed. 'He wants Maia, do you hear me, that's why he's here, that's why he's helping us, because he wants her for himself afterwards!'

'Let go of me!' she gasped as strands of hair escaped the fiery ball at the nape of her neck. Static electricity from the rug made them cling to her pale cheeks, where they resembled a pattern of very fine cuts inflicted by her distress. 'Peter!'

'I'm sorry,' he breathed, and suddenly gentle, he urged her to sit down in the chair she had been holding onto. 'Please forgive me, Stella,' he begged miserably, sinking to one knee before her.

'Oh my love, why are you fighting me?' she asked wearily, gently resting one of her hands on his tormented head. 'I didn't do this to our daughter. I'm not responsible for her accident and neither is Drew. Maia isn't being punished by God because her parents belong to a pagan cult, as you put it.'

'But you heard what he said.' He stared up at her imploringly. 'You heard him!'

She sighed. 'Would it make you feel any better if there was absolutely no mystical reason for what happened to Maia?' She sat back in the chair as he stood up. 'Would it make you feel better to think that she's completely unconscious, trapped in a lifeless, mindless coma? If Drew is right, then at least there's some hope he can bring her back to us.'

'Oh yes,' he scoffed, 'it's quite magical that Maia is lying in a hospital bed now, not to mention that she'll be barren for life. We'll never have grandchildren, do you realize that?'

'She was struck across the womb by the branch of a centuries-old oak tree just after it was struck by lightning three times,' she reminded him patiently, as though it was a word-problem they were both assigned to solve in a class on metaphysics.

'It truly distresses me, Stella, how easily you can accept the fact that Maia was perhaps chosen by natural forces as some sort of sacrificial victim to appease the world's violated soul. Isn't that how he put it?' Peter now avoided his favorite chair like the throne of a kingdom in the throes of a bloody battle where rational strategies were completely useless. 'Maia is an embodiment of the modern world... that's essentially what he said, isn't it? She's innocent in herself, but born of poisoned roots, unable to conceive life in her body now just as our technology-worshipping society keeps taking and taking from nature without giving anything back. We're incredibly honored to be her parents, don't you think, since according to that fire-breathing dragon upstairs our daughter ... please, what was it he said?'

Stella gripped the arms of her chair as though it was moving at the speed of light and only appeared motionless. 'He said that Maia has the power to appease nature's violated forces with her profound sensuality…'

'That's it!' He laughed bitterly. 'Oh I love that, that's rich.'

'She's a grown woman now, not just your daughter,' she reminded him, folding her hands in her lap now and sitting straight-backed as a Victorian matron, but her chest heaving with emotion brought to life the marble-white perfection of her cleavage.

'I know she's a grown woman. That is not the issue here.'

Her face was hard. 'Yes it is.'

'For Christ's sake, Stella,' he gripped the fireplace mantel with both hands and leaned forward with his arms fully outstretched, 'have you taken leave of your senses?' He stared down at the cold gray hearth.

'No, I have not taken leave of my senses, but I also haven't merely been playing an eccentric game as you apparently have been. I know we can't really call ourselves Druids since there aren't any written records describing what their rites were actually like, but the rituals we do practice mean something to me and nature is my church, not some—'

'You're grasping at straws, love,' he cut her off, 'straws that come straight from the wicker man. What was it your chain-smoking high priest said about love being the only thing that can save Maia? In heaven's name, Stella, if *my* love can't bring her back, the love of a father for his only daughter, what makes you think she'll respond to some strange man's crude psychic pawing? You're letting him run around in some other dimension with our little girl doing—'

'You see, that is the issue here.' It was her turn to interrupt him angrily. 'I think you would almost prefer it if Maia died and took the sweet Virgin by the hand. You hate the idea of her naked energy joining with Drew's so he can help her slip her body back on like a dress. You hate thinking of his feelings caressing hers and of his thoughts penetrating her desires, you hate—'

'Forgive me for being so dense, dear.' He straightened up, but continued gazing down at the cold hearth. 'I think I understand now, please correct me if I'm wrong. What this twaddling bastard means is that Maia's soul is mysteriously making love to the sacred spirit of the oak tree that nearly killed her, and that she's having such a bloody good time she doesn't feel like zipping back into her body just yet.'

'It's not that simple and you know it, Peter,' his wife said desperately.

'No, it isn't that simple,' he echoed, staring at the woman he loved as though he had never seen her before in his life.

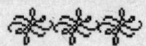

A faint cloud of smoke hovering above him, Drew Landson tucked his head into the crook of his arm and wiped an intangible perspiration of concentration from his brow. The white wicker chair that matched the delicate glass-top dresser was stronger than it looked, for it was managing to hold his weight without the slightest whine of pain.

Avoiding his reflection in the oval mirror, he picked up Maia's brush with his free hand. Dark strands of hair wound between the black bristles in a maze of tangles that made absolutely no sense; they lacked the purposeful order of a loom or the precise hunger of a spider's web. Nevertheless, he found that holding the brush helped him untangle some of the threads in the mystery surrounding its lovely owner.

He set it down again after a moment, and caressed the long crack running down the dead center of the egg-shaped mirror-glass dividing his reflected face in half. An intrigued smile lit the five-o'clock shadow surrounding his lips. This young woman had more power than he would ever have believed possible, more power than he cared to admit to her mother, much less to her totally distraught father. From the terrible tangle of her feelings at the accident on that stormy night, Maia had fashioned such a tight imaginative knot that even his fine comb of metaphysical logic was having a tough time with it. He was beginning to realize that unless he was a firm as he was gentle with her in her dream, there was a good chance she would end up cutting off her whole life by never returning to her body.

He hoped Stella would be able to keep her husband under control long enough for him to do his work. He had been about to drive home to pick up some of his things when he discovered that he could not just slip casually out of

Maia's personal space. He had taken possession of her bedroom with the intention of guiding her back into her body as swiftly as possible, yet now he found himself inclined to linger with her in another dimension...

He smiled at the reflection of her blue-and-white comforter flowing at the level of his gaze in the mirror's frozen surface, his imagination gliding like an ice-dancer as his mind warmed to its arousing choreography. Even Stella might turn against him if she grasped the full nature of his intentions. He couldn't risk slipping up, yet her parents should have realized his head-on battle with unknown forces would inevitably have serious consequences if he succeeded in winning Maia back for them. If he helped Maia's soul back into her body, she would be his forever.

The bedroom door opened silently behind him, but he pretended not to notice as he gazed into the cloud of smoke veiling his features from the cigarette hanging languidly between his lips.

'Drew?'

'Mm?' He shot Stella's reflection a look that would have burned through her heart if he had exposed her to it directly.

'Do you know what Peter just said to me?'

She sounded unnaturally calm and he noted that her lovely face was even more pale than usual. As always, he had to resist the urge to take her in his arms because the way he desired to make her feel better would only make them both feel worse in the end. 'What is it, Stella?' he asked gently.

'Peter says he only belongs to indulge me, and he called it a cult!'

'Leave him,' he suggested lightly.

'What?'

He half turned towards her on the wicker chair, resting an elbow on Maia's glass vanity while idly stroking a denim-wrapped thigh with the back of her hairbrush.

'Stop that,' she snapped, the tide of her grief receding beneath a violent wave of jealous guilt.

He obeyed her, and added yet another butt to the ashtray's crude stone altar. 'I have to go now.' He stood up.

Rituals of Surrender

'Where? Where are you going? You're not abandoning us, are you?'

'Of course not, Stella.' He paused before her to gaze tenderly down at her frightened face as he slipped on his jacket. 'I'm just going home for some of my things. I'll be right back.'

'Oh... thank you.'

'Don't worry about Peter. You know he's not himself right now.'

She frowned. 'I'm beginning to think he's more himself right now than ever.'

'He's battling all his demons at once, Stella. His contentment's castle is under siege and he either surrenders to all the doubts and fears in his subconscious moat, so to speak, or he wins a greater understanding and mastery of himself. You can only do so much to help him. After all,' he caressed fiery strands of hair away from her cheek and lowed his voice, 'you have your own weaknesses to fight.'

She closed her eyes as he moved past her on his way to the door. 'Hurry back!' she sighed.

Maia dreamed that Chris gave her two large tombstones as gifts, but they were really bookends, and she chose the summit of a hill as her shelf. She placed the tall stones a few yards apart to make sure the sun would set between them, and then sat down at the base of a tree, leaning comfortably against the trunk. She was enjoying the spectacle of the twilight when a man she vaguely remembered having seen somewhere before strolled into view. He was walking up the steep hill wearing a black leather jacket staring down into his cupped hands as though he had just caught a butterfly. He looked up as he released his invisible captive, and he didn't seem at all surprised to see her sitting in the grass beneath the deep shadow of an oak tree. She gazed up at him in curious wonder, unable to understand why she felt she knew him. Suddenly, one of the tree's dark limbs came to life and slithered down towards her in a menacing way. She could not find her voice to cry out, but she did not need to. The handsome stranger grasped the threatening branch firmly in one hand, and she watched in grateful amazement as in his grip it transformed into an ornately carved sword tarnished by centuries. She tried to sit up, but all she could manage was to catch her breath as he pierced the flesh directly over her heart with the sharp point of the ancient blade. A perfectly round drop of her blood ascended against gravity towards the sky and merged with the glowing red sphere of the dying sun perched on the horizon. The man then reached down for her hand, and pulled her to her feet beside him. A row of dark coffins standing upright were now neatly arranged between the tombstones like books.

'Maia,' he whispered.

She felt her pulse flutter strangely beneath the warm breeze of his breath, and she was more than willing to let his lips rest against hers for an instant in the lightest kiss imaginable.

'Come back with me,' he urged.

'No,' she said stubbornly, tilting her face up and closing her eyes in the hope that he would kiss her again. 'You stay here with me.'

He did not respond.

Chapter Eight

Maia opened her eyes and for some reason was intensely disappointed to find herself lying beside Chris in his bed. The moon was gazing possessively down at him again tonight, and his nocturnally muscular body looked strangely unreachable in the ghostly light.

She had just been dreaming about a man she had never met. This was not unusual; she often dreamed with people she did not know, but he felt different, she was sure she had seen him somewhere before… in fact, it might even have been his body lying beside hers right now, his dark hair and broad shoulders illuminated by the moon's romantic reflection of the sun's often disenchanting clarity. It was truly strange how different Chris's naked body looked at night, thicker and more muscular, and with the sheet caught around his thighs, she could see the tight white cheeks of his backside tempting her to caress them…

She bit her lip in frustration. Was she going to have to wake him up every night so he would pay attention to her sexually? After Eric Wolfson left, he had called her back downstairs, but only to tell her he was off to his workshop for the day. 'Make yourself at home,' he instructed, then added with a teasing glint in his eye as he kissed her good bye on the cheek, 'and feel free to play around in the kitchen later.' Maia still could not believe he had gone to work on their first day living together. She kept telling herself she was being unreasonable. A man could not be expected to totally rearrange his schedule just because he was in love… if he was in love. They had only just met. How could they really know if they loved each other or not?

She turned restively over onto her side and deliberately closed her eyes. She had to stop waking up in the middle of the night. She had to stop letting the moon illuminate all the disturbing thoughts lurking in the dark depths of her emotions, which seemed so much more straightforward and positive during the day. The moon had millions of years of experience gazing down at men and women and so couldn't help being somewhat cold and cynical about the concept of love. From the moon's perspective, one human soul's attraction to another was no more eternal than the minds and bodies that fell into sexual orbit around each other and thought of it as a special, magical thing called love...

The cool silver light kissing her eyelids inevitably forced them open again. Sighing, and giving up on sleep for the moment, she gazed pensively out the window again. The moon was not the best friend a hopeful young woman could have; she knew too much. Maia suspected the moon was also mysteriously jealous of the human body's ability to feel and touch. The moon made naked skin look so good beneath her caressing light because she wanted this sensual experience for herself... and in the end, all lovers become a part of her timeless desire... for if there really is such a thing as life after death, flesh absorbs and reflects the spirit's energy just as the moon is made visible and tangible by the sun...

Maia sighed again and rolled over onto her other side, turning her back on the window and the earth's disturbingly eloquent satellite. At least this way she could enjoy the sight of Chris's moonlit skin arousing her even while taunting her with its unavailable proximity, because he was fast asleep. She had prepared them a wonderful supper of Prawns sautéed in white wine and garlic, accompanied by a large garden salad. He opened a light red wine to go with it, and they ate informally in his tiny but well equipped kitchen. She felt wonderfully happy as he told her about the various projects he was working on for a handful of private clients like Sir Wolfson, yet her appetite had been somewhat compromised by how much she was anticipating what would happen afterwards when they left the kitchen...

Nothing had happened. Out in the living room, he opened another bottle of wine and sat beside her on the loveseat, where he regularly refilled his glass but not hers (she had had more than enough to drink with dinner) while he talked and talked about everything under the sun. She thoroughly enjoyed listening to him, she could not deny that. He seemed to know so much about everything, not just boring facts but the intriguing details of how things worked and were related to each other. He kept jumping from subject to subject as she did her best to keep up with him mentally, trying not to feel increasingly stupid because she could not think of anything to add to what he was saying. She was flattered he was opening up to her, yet also a little annoyed that he did not seem to care whether she added anything to the conversation or not. She felt peculiarly exhausted by the time he set his empty glass down and, grasping her hand, led her up to his bedroom. Yet it had been just like the previous night – they undressed in absolute darkness and then slipped into bed together like an ancient married couple.

'Is everything all right, Maia?' he asked her as he kissed her forehead good night.

Wanting to scream in frustration, she was afraid of saying too much. 'Yes, everything's fine,' she lied, too shy to beg him to make love to her; to prim and proper to beg him to fuck her as hard and selfishly as he had their first night together on his kitchen table…

Even though she was lying perfectly still beside him, Chris suddenly lifted his head from the pillow and looked at her. 'What's wrong, Maia?' he murmured.

She was impressed by the fact that her turbulent emotions had awoken him. 'I need you,' she whispered.

He rolled over onto his side and drew her gently into his arms. 'I'm here, baby.'

'That's not… that's not what I mean,' she dared to murmur against his chest.

'You want my cock, is that it?' He sounded wide awake now.

'I… I didn't say that, Chris.'

'Not in so many words,' he thrust a hand between her thighs, 'but your pussy doesn't lie.' He gently dipped the tips of two of his fingers into her sex. 'Does it?'

'No,' she sighed.

'Mm, you have such a sweet, tight little pussy, Maia.'

'Oh God,' she whispered, tilting her face up towards his lips, 'please make love to me, Chris.' She longed for the feel of his cock thrusting up between her legs as his tongue thrust between the lips on her face, totally possessing her and filling her with his desire.

Rituals of Surrender

'But I have been making love to you, Maia. We're living together, we're sleeping in the same bed together, we had dinner together, and afterwards we talked for hours together. Our lives are becoming one, and that's all part of making love, isn't it?'

'Yes,' she breathed, suddenly ashamed of herself for being so... so superficial, wanton, slutty... there was no end to the bad names she could call herself for craving rough sex more than the tender love she had been so miraculously blessed with. Here was a real man who cared for her and she was pouting and figuratively stamping her foot because he did not take enough advantage of her physically.

'But I suspect that's not what you meant by making love, is it?' He flung the sheet off them and spread himself on top of her. 'Be honest with me. We're never going to get anywhere if you conceal your true feelings from me. You don't just want me to make love to you, do you?'

'But it is what I want,' she protested weakly, spreading her legs for him.

'No, it's not.' He raised himself on his arms to separate his body from hers.

She moaned in sweet torment as the head of his erection kissed her labia and cruelly teased her with its firm fullness, making her sex lips ache to bloom open around his full length.

'Tell me what you really want, Maia,' he insisted quietly.

'I want you to fuck me!' she confessed abruptly, the words escaping her tense moral control as though mysteriously lubricated by her juicing pussy.

'See, that wasn't so hard,' he said, and entered her with a swift, hard thrust.

She gasped, 'Oh yes!' and gripped his firm ass with both hands as she raised her legs up around him, trying to shove his erection even deeper into her body.

Burying his face in her hair and neck, he pumped fiercely in and out of her, groaning with pleasure as her hands squeezed his tight buttocks and her pussy squeezed his cock.

She moved her hips up and down in rhythm with his, positioning her pussy in just the right place for his hard-on to sink into her as deeply as possible every time he rammed her with it. 'I want you to come inside me, Chris!'

He moaned and his body tensed against hers as his climax inexorably approached.

'Oh yes, come inside me!' she begged. 'Please, come inside me hard!'

He didn't interrupt his rhythm to ask her if it was safe; he simply reached down with one hand to grasp one of her soft ass cheeks for leverage as he relentlessly stabbed her tight slickness with his swelling cock faster and harder, pounding into her with all his strength as he ejaculated. Then he ruthlessly continued rending her open around his pulsing length as he milked every last drop of cum and pleasure from his cock with the fervent embrace of her innermost flesh.

'If I fail to observe my pledges to thee, may the sky fall and destroy me and the sea overflow and drown me, Maia dear.' Chris was quoting Celtic sayings to her in an academic tone that, in her opinion, deprived them of their profound poetic power.

'You've never mentioned your parents,' she said, wanting to know more about this man she could not resist, a man she occasionally found frustratingly cold and detached, but he was also capable of giving her the most intense pleasure she had ever experienced in her life.

'That's because my father was a mighty oak tree and my mother a vine of mistletoe,' he replied matter-of-factly, 'so there's not much to talk about.'

She frowned to herself in growing annoyance. He was being so deliberately evasive about his personal life that it was like playing tennis with a god who hit the ball so far she could not even try to run after it. 'Did you have a falling out with them?' she persisted.

'Yes,' he laughed, 'I definitely fell out of my mother!'

'Oh stop it,' she pleaded, but couldn't help laughing. The beautiful sunny day was cutting strangely into her vision as the bright sunshine outlined every leaf and blade of grass in breathtakingly sharp detail. It was also making her lover's blond hair almost blindingly bright, impressing upon her the fact that ever since she met him she could not seem to see anything except how much she desired him... or was it that she desired the incredible things he could make her feel? 'Are yours parents like mine, Chris, I mean... are they dead,

Rituals of Surrender

too?' The words felt like black bugs crawling out from between her lips.

'No, they're not, and neither are yours.'

'What do you mean?' She rose restlessly from the blanket they were sharing in the middle of his backyard, a small clearing surrounded by trees. But then she didn't know what to do with herself and so merely stood there ripping a blade of grass apart.

'Maia, there are endless wings in the Mansion and in one of them your parents are probably planning the next voyage together during which they can once again indulge in their love for each other. Yet instead of packing suitcases they're fashioning bodies and checking into hospitals as babies, so do them a favor and don't anchor them with your grief. They were given a great gift when they died together; they were allowed to enter the next world as one. What more could they have asked of Fate?'

She gazed down at his beautiful face in amazement, stunned by his logic. Ever since her parents' accident, she had perceived only her own terrible loss – a dead-end set up by the laws of reason she hadn't the profound courage to break.

Closing his eyes, Chris lay back across the blanket and flung his arms open at his sides.

She continued looking down at his slender body expectantly, but he was apparently through talking for the moment. She walked over to the nearest tree and yanked a leaf off a branch. She studied its veined body morosely sensing her lover falling asleep on her again.

'Hello.' Eric Wolfson suddenly strode into view, walking around the house from the front where he must have parked his car, obviously an extremely expensive vehicle with a nearly silent motor.

She was so surprised to see him she accidentally ripped the leaf in half as she echoed, 'Hello!'

'Is he asleep?' Eric whispered, treading as softly as a cat around Chris's inert body. Then he gracefully curled his long legs beneath him and sat cross-legged on one edge of the dark-red blanket. 'Come here...' He continued whispering as he patted the blanket between him and her sleeping lover. 'There's plenty of room for the three of us.' His gray eyes were so pale in the sunlight they appeared absolutely expressionless.

She tossed the leaf away and approached him, yet she couldn't just sit casually cross-legged beside him because her favorite cotton sundress decorated with tiny violet roses was much too short. Yet she also didn't want to stretch her bare legs out for his eyes to wander over casually, which meant she was forced to sink awkwardly to her knees beside him. Eric leaned back on his arms and closed his eyes, concentrating on absorbing the sun for a few long moments during which she was able to study his face unobserved. Faint lines branched around the delicate eggs of his eyelids like the imprint of crow's feet in his winter-pale skin, and a ghostly trace of long-ago acne on his cheeks made her think of a fragment of the moon impossibly fallen into the sunny yard. 'It's beautiful weather,' she said inanely, clutching the blanket on either side of her wondering how long she could tolerate kneeling like this.

'Yes, it is.' He sat up again and wrapped his arms around his knees as he stared over at her. His eyes narrowed, but whether it was due to the bright sunshine or to what he was thinking it was impossible to tell. 'I want you, Maia,' he informed her quietly.

She felt as though he had whipped out a knife and stabbed her in the heart merely to test the sharpness of his blade, and her helpless blush must have satisfied him she was vulnerable to him moving in for the kill.

'Well, hello there.' Chris woke up abruptly. 'May I ask what you're doing here, Sir Wolfson?' In his white cotton shirt and pants he evoked a ray of light alongside Eric's entirely black outfit – black leather sandals, black jeans and a sleeveless black silk T-shirt.

'I came to ask you for another piece.'

'I'll bet you did. Excuse me a moment.' He sat up by stretching his arms straight out before him as though he was diving up into the sky. 'As the mystics say,' he leapt lithely his feet, 'I must empty myself. I'll be right back.' He mussed Maia's hair affectionately (and it seemed to her reassuringly) as he walked away towards the house. She had no idea if he had overheard Mile's declaration and she wasn't sure whether she hoped he had or not. If he really had been asleep, then he was innocent of the position he was putting her in by leaving her alone with this dangerously sexy client of his...

'I have a proposition for you, love,' Eric informed her when they were alone with all the birds and insects working industriously but invisibly around them.

'A proposition?' she repeated blankly, her fingers embracing each other anxiously in her lap.

'How would you feel about starring in a music video, Maia?'

She glanced anxiously over at the house. 'A music video?' she echoed lamely, still not fully recovered from his blatant declaration of lust. 'You're a musician?'

'Yes, and it's the video for my latest hit song about the Druids and their fondness for human sacrifice.'

'Not today.' Chris was back again suddenly. He handed her a darkly glistening bottle of ale, keeping one for himself and rudely not offering his guest anything to drink.

'Eric wants me to be in his new music video,' she informed him, needing to know what her lover thought about it before she dared feel anything about it herself.

'Does he now?' He sat cross-legged beside her on the edge of the blanket.

'It's a video for a song about the Druids,' she added, anxiously studying his profile as he sipped his beer.

He gave her a sideways glance. 'Which means you'd be the lovely sacrifice?' he asked lightly, but his eyes and lips weren't smiling.

'It might be fun,' she heard herself say. 'Um, I really don't want anything to drink right now...' She offered her cold bottle to Eric. 'Would you like it?'

'Don't mind if I do,' he said, taking it from her, and the warm caress of his fingers was a delicious contrast.

'Well, I say we finish our drinks,' Chris declared, 'and then all go for a little walk in the woods to discuss this video.'

Chapter Nine

As they walked, Maia kept glancing up at the vein-like branches of the trees above them hoping to catch a glimpse of a cardinal's swiftly beating heart. She felt self-consciously sandwiched between two men who could not have looked more different except for how attractive they both were in their own way. Even their personalities clashed in an amiable but also seriously challenging way that made her feel they were both holding invisible swords. Chris made more cutting remarks than Eric, which she thought was understandable since he was on the defensive; he was defending his claim on her. She knew her lover was more than intelligent enough to sense the wealthy musician's personal interest in her, yet she also suspected he was confident enough not to feel too threatened by it. With her hand safely nestled in his as they walked, she was filled with feelings for Christopher Thorn – admiration, respect and gratitude – even while she found herself half hypnotized by the sound of Eric Wolfson's quiet voice as he described his creative project to her.

'What makes a good music video,' he was saying, 'is part planning and part chance, and in my opinion it's usually all the unexpected elements that crop up during filming that end up making it truly interesting.' He had tied his shoulder-length hair loosely back away from his face with a red band, exposing his beautiful high cheekbones. 'There's no reason for you to be nervous about it, Maia.' He gave her a brief, respectful glance. 'The production will be very intimate, involving only a few special friends I have in the industry.'

'What exactly will happen in the video?' she asked him, but it was Chris she looked at because his permission was the most important thing to her.

He squeezed her hand as though he approved of her dependence on his

Rituals of Surrender

opinion and answered her question before Eric had a chance to. 'I imagine Sir Wolfson is planning to re-create his fantasy of a Druid sacrifice, Maia, and I say his fantasy because there really is no way to know what Druid rituals were like. They didn't leave behind any written records, much less an official sacrifice manual.'

'We'll be shooting a great deal of raw material and editing it all together later,' Eric elaborated without offering anymore information on the video's actual plot and content. 'Intimate,' he stressed the word, 'low-budget productions are often the most powerfully atmospheric.' Chris's skeptical attitude didn't seem to bother him in the least.

'In my opinion,' her lover's mild tone paradoxically stressed how important his opinion was, 'you should focus on the experience of her soul after the sacrifice, not on the gruesome bloody details.' 'And how would we manage that, pray tell?' The musician followed Maia's eyes up into the trees. 'It's an interesting suggestion, but impossible to capture on film since the soul is invisible.'

'To the physical eye it's invisible,' Chris elaborated in his usual reasonable tone, 'but just because certain energies are invisible to the light receptors in our corneas doesn't mean they're insubstantial and formless. If you think of the soul as color and motion, as the human imagination turned inside out so feelings and desires manifest in a kaleidoscopic dance, so to speak, then you have a lot to work with. Magical transformations are relatively easy to express by way of visual metaphors. I'm sure you could find inspiration for your video in one of Maia's paintings, for example.'

Chris was the only person on earth besides Carol she had shown her work to, and his reaction to her surreal sensual landscapes had been much more gratifying then her aunt's. Seeing her paintings through his eyes had not only made her appreciate her talent more, it had showed her how profoundly erotic her vision was.

'I'm thinking especially of her painting of a woman lying across an altar,' her lover went on. 'Her arms are raised towards the heavens as they merge with the slender trunks of trees as her long red hair pours down the back of her stone bed and flows across the ground into the blazing sunset on the horizon. It's a powerfully sensual image I feel would work very nicely in your video.'

Eric gave her another narrow-eyed glance. 'She's an artist,' he said shortly, as though that explained everything.

'The video could visually express the mysterious fact that her soul is supernaturally the earth's body,' Chris added intently.

'Why do I get the feeling you want to direct the whole thing yourself?' Eric accused him mildly.

'I would love to.'

They came full circle along a path winding between the trees and leading them neatly back to the clearing behind Chris's house. He spread himself across the blanket again on his back, gently but firmly pulling Maia down beside him as Eric stretched out on his side facing her, behaving as innocently as a domestic cat the size of a black panther. She would much rather have sat up, but if Chris wanted her lying beside him she was not inclined to argue, even if she did question the wisdom of exposing the full length of her body like this to another man who was uncomfortably close to her. She bent one of her legs and rested her hands awkwardly over her womb as she turned her head towards her lover on the red cloth, but he was gazing serenely up at the heavens oblivious to any discomfort she might be feeling, in any sense. So, inevitably, she turned her head in the other direction.

Eric met her eyes boldly, and her breath caught as if his sharp stare had sunk like ruthlessly experienced fangs into her emotional jugular. She had no doubt that all she was to him was entertaining sexual prey, yet a blindly feminine part of her could not help but be flattered he found her desirable enough not to be deterred by the fact that she would be very hard for him to get his hands on since she was already taken. Turning her head again to stare neutrally up at the clear blue sky, she wondered if Eric knew she and Chris had only been together three days.

The three of them lay silently on the blanket for a while, and Maia found herself wondering at the ability of a perfectly beautiful day to empty the mind, as though thoughts had their origin in adversity and if the body could always manage to be happy and comfortable no concepts would ever be born at all...

Through the corner of her eye she was relieved to finally see Eric rolling lazily onto his back; his fixed regard had been making her extremely uncomfortable.

Rituals of Surrender

He raised his arms over his head, and the skin beneath them struck her as vulnerably pale and tender in contrast to his black silk T-shirt, making her think of a beached whale with a shiny oily back and a white underbelly. Then a faint buzzing sound told her to watch out for a bee headed towards one of her leg's smooth runways. She denied it permission to land by gently shooing it away, but she remained very much aware of the sexy and intriguing musician lying beside her. A quick glance at Chris told her his eyes were closed, which made her feel free to turn her head fully towards Eric again. She was fascinated by the way his sinewy muscles clung so tightly to his bones, like snakes wrapped tenaciously around tree branches, and suddenly she knew that her attraction to him could easily prove fatal to her newborn relationship.

He sat up without warning and yanked off the elastic band holding his hair back. He shook it loose around his face, glanced back at Chris, and gave one of her legs a swift, appraising caress from her ankle up to her knee.

She sat up in an instinctive effort to hide another man's caress from her lover, but now the singer's mouth was only a dangerous breath away as his eyes locked challengingly with hers. She had bent both her legs as she sat up, so it was easy for him to reach beneath them and squeeze one of her calves. She bit her lip to keep from crying out not sure whether she should stand up or lie back down again. As a result, she remained where she was, caught between a chilling fear and an insidiously warm excitement threatening to melt her cautious tension.

'I'll expect both of you at the small party I'm throwing Friday night,' he said.

'We'd be delighted to attend,' Chris replied, reaching up to idly stroke her back. 'Wouldn't we, Maia?'

'Yes...' she agreed uncertainly.

'Well, what is it you want?' Chris finally demanded of Eric, sitting up. 'You said you came to ask me for another piece, some original artwork to adorn your walls, perhaps? You would love Maia's paintings. She brought them all with her when she moved in with me, so perhaps you'd care to take a look at them and make her a generous offer on one or two.'

'It would be a real pleasure,' Eric declared, his eyes on her legs.

'But you might not like my paintings,' she protested shyly, somewhat embarrassed by all the attention she was getting, in every sense.

Chris laughed as though he found her modesty amusing. 'You know he'll love them,' he said, kissing her earlobe gently as he added in a private whisper, 'Use him!'

'I would love to look at them now,' Eric declared.

She blushed as though he had just asked her to strip for him. He and Chris were both ostensibly talking about her art work, but somehow she felt it was her body, and even her soul, they were discussing. 'I don't know…'

'Unfortunately, however, I have to run,' he added, surging gracefully to his feet. 'I'm already late for another appointment. But I'm very much looking forward to seeing your work, Maia. And remember, I'm expecting you both at my place Friday night.'

'How small is this small party of yours going to be?' Chris inquired.

'Oh it's to be a very intimate affair, only two-hundred of my best friends are invited.'

'Two-hundred?' she gasped.

'Yes, but never fear, you will be the most beautiful woman there, Maia.'

'Oh please, I doubt it.' She was a little annoyed by the excessive compliment, which implied she was either incredibly vain or insecure about her looks.

'Never doubt,' Chris whispered in her ear again, and then said in his sternest voice, 'Good afternoon, Sir Wolfson, we'll see you Friday night.'

※※※

'A rich and famous musician is probably going to buy one of my paintings, Carol, can you believe it? He might even buy more than one.'

'Certainly I can believe it, dear, they're… err, they're very interesting.'

'Chris said I could ask hundreds of pounds for each one, but I-'

'Speaking of pounds, dear, the solicitor's office called to ask when you would be going back to work.'

Maia stared at her aunt's face as though the woman had just spoken another lan-

Rituals of Surrender

guage she had to make an effort to translate in her brain. 'When I plan to go back to work?' she repeated blankly, and then shivered as shock drenched her psyche like an ice-cold ocean wave. 'I forgot all about my job!' she cried in disbelief. 'Ever since I met Chris, I haven't been able to think about anything else... I mean... I mean...' But it was no use, there was no sane excuse for how completely she had forgotten about something that been part of her life every Monday through Friday for nearly four years; it was impossible her job could have slipped her mind so completely if she wasn't losing her mind... she wasn't even sure how many work days had she missed... 'Oh my God, what did you tell them?' she asked desperately.

'I told them you hadn't been feeling well,' Carol replied calmly, 'that you had a very bad case of the flu. I apologized for not having called them, and said you would be back as soon as you were feeling better.'

'Oh God, thank you! I... I just don't know how...'

'Maia, dear, sit down, please, you're wearing me out pacing back and forth like that, not to mention what you're doing to my nice antique rug.'

'But auntie,' she dropped onto the edge of the couch, 'I completely forgot about my job!'

'It's all right, dear,' Carol patted her hand reassuringly, 'that young man has swept you off your feet, that's all. When you're in love, you're in a whole other world and it's easy to forget mundane things.'

Maia shook her head. 'Yes, I know, but-'

'Don't trouble yourself about it anymore,' the older woman said firmly. 'I took care of it. You rest up for a while and go back when you're ready, although sooner would be better than later as you don't want to try their patience too much.'

'But it's going to be such a long drive from Chris's place to the office,' she mused out loud, so utterly disturbed by her mental lapse she couldn't bring herself to truly face it.

'You should have thought of that before you moved in with him,' Carol replied tartly, but then added soothingly since she could see her niece was seriously distressed. 'I'm sure you'll work it out. The important thing is for you to come back to work soon and not dally too long in idleness. You know what they say about idle hands.'

'Maybe I don't need to... maybe I can start making a decent living off my artwork. If I can get at least seven-hundred pounds for each painting, and Chris says I definitely can, then-'

'Don't be foolish, Maia.' It was Carol's turn to look disturbed. 'You can't quit your day job! Please don't even think of it, dear, not yet.'

'No, I guess not...' She glanced out the window. 'But at least I'm not shy about my paintings anymore, not now that two other people besides me are interested in them.'

'Two other men, you mean,' Carol pointed out as mildly as she could bring herself to, 'one of them an eccentric carpenter, and the other one, God help us, a wealthy rock star.'

'He's perfectly nice,' Maia defended the sexy musician, 'a perfect gentleman.' The honest way he had declared his intention to seduce her could, she supposed, be interpreted as the act of a gentleman.

'Oh I'm sure he is,' Carol declared skeptically; Maia might as well have insisted the neighbor's dog was a brilliant scholar. 'I wonder...' She turned her head in the direction of the window and sunlight streaming in between the drawn curtains cruelly revealed countless wrinkles etched deep into her skin.

'You wonder what?' Maia stood up and began moving around the small living room again in an effort to assuage her restlessness; she hated being separated from Chris.

'I wonder why no one around here has ever heard of Christopher Thorn. Your charming carpenter seems to have sprung straight out of the ground like the trees he likes to cut up.'

'Carol, you've been gossiping about us? I thought you liked him!'

'Oh I do, dear, don't misunderstand me.' She rubbed her injured knee. 'I only wish you had gotten to know him a little better before you moved in with him, that's all.'

Maia went and stood by the window. The driveway looked achingly empty without Chris's bright red car parked in it. 'His house is very isolated,' she reasoned out loud, appreciating how patient and understanding her aunt was forcing herself to be with her. 'And we wanted to be together more than anything, so what was the point in waiting. Life's too short.'

Rituals of Surrender

'You only feel that way because you're young, Maia. Life is quite long, actually, and it's also like a recipe – you can't skip certain steps and ingredients and expect everything to turn out just the way you want it to. Well, perhaps no one in the neighborhood has heard of your handsome carpenter because they can't afford him. All his clients appear to be quite wealthy. You know, dear,' she tried to laugh, but failed miserably, 'if I didn't know better, if I hadn't seen Christopher with my own eyes, I could almost believe you were making all of this up, wealthy art patrons and music videos, indeed, all in quiet little Stoneshire! You always did have a marvelous imagination.'

'You and daddy thought it was a bit too marvelous sometimes,' Maia reminded her.

'Yes…' Her fond smile as she remembered dimmed sadly. 'I'll admit, I was a bit worried about how you'd turn out, but Stella always assured me you'd be fine.'

Maia perched on one of the couch's old arms. 'Chris is making frames for all my paintings, auntie,' she announced excitedly.

'Dear,' Carol avoided her eyes, 'has he mentioned marriage at all?'

'We're going to be together forever,' the young woman vowed fervently. 'I know we are. He's my soul mate, I felt it the moment I saw him in the cemetery.'

'Oh Maia, I wish you wouldn't…'

'Carol, please stop.' She leapt to her feet again impatiently. 'What's the matter with you, today? I've never seen you worry so much. You can't deny how wonderful Chris is. I mean, you've met all the pathetic sods I had to put up with before him. Chris is in a whole other class. He's the best thing that's ever happened to me. I've never been so happy.'

Carol winced. 'Please don't yell at me, dear.'

'Well then stop being so suspicious. I'm happier than I've ever been before,' she insisted. 'Can't you see that?'

'Yes, dear. Would you like some tea now?'

'Please, that would be lovely, but I'll make it. You stay here and rest.'

Carol sighed. 'I get frightfully bored if I'm not busy doing something,' she protested.

'Isn't there a book you're reading?' Maia glanced around the small living room. 'I'll fetch it for you.'

'You know I've never had the patience for books. I like to keep busy.'

'Oh all right, you make the tea if it'll make you happy.' She grasped both the old woman's hands and helped her up off of the couch before falling back across it herself. She was exhausted from the weight of minutes chaining her down while she waited for Chris to phone and tell her he was on his way over. It upset her she didn't know where his workshop was and that she had no way of reaching him there.

She was just drifting off to sleep when the phone on the table beside the couch rang suddenly, shocking her back into consciousness.

'God, I miss you,' Chris whispered in her ear.

'It's your fault for not taking me with you,' she retorted, because his sexy voice reaching her through the serpentine miracle of telephone wires was an agonizing tease. 'Are you on your way over now?'

'Yes. I'll be there in a flash.'

She sighed, 'Please!'

'Make some excuse for me. I don't feel like hanging out with your little old aunt this evening.'

'All right,' she agreed, and hung up only after she heard the clicking sound of the receiver being put down on his end. Then she got up and hurried happily into the dining room. Carol had just finished laying out tea. 'Chris is coming to pick me up now, auntie. He says he's terribly sorry he can't stay for tea, but one of his clients just called him and we have to go meet him somewhere.'

Carol looked distressed. 'Well, I hope you have time for at least one cup.'

'Of course.' Maia quickly sat down at the table. 'Oh, cucumber sandwiches, my favorites.' She poured the tea for them.

'The great oak is just a nut that held its ground,' Carol mumbled as she seated herself with a grimace of pain.

Maia laughed. 'What made you say that?'

'Dear,' there was a determined note in Carol's voice, 'it's time you knew something.'

'Knew what?' she asked with wary curiosity, somewhat worried by the intensely sober look darkening the old woman's eyes.

Rituals of Surrender

Carol took a deep breath. 'It's time you knew that your mother never really grew up, God rest her soul, and your father loved her so much he indulged her to the very end even though he never took the whole thing seriously himself. They might still be alive if...' Her lips set and she stared at the silver teapot as grimly as if was an urn containing her brother and sister-in-law's ashes.

'What...' Maia swallowed a lump in her throat. 'What are you talking about?'

'Peter kept assuring me it was all perfectly harmless,' Carol went on slowly. 'He knew I disapproved, and that the neighbors gossiped about it.'

'Gossiped about what?'

'Your mother was the priestess of a modern group of Druids that meets at the standing stones every week!' Carol blurted as though it was the only way she could get the truth out. 'There,' she sighed, 'now you know!' She carefully picked up her teacup between two gnarled fingers and took a long sip of the hot, fragrant liquid as if to get the strange taste of the words she had just uttered out of her mouth. 'Stella told me once that she believed in Christ,' she went on less urgently, 'but I never saw her enter a proper church. I suppose there was nothing wrong with her beliefs, and yet it was on their way to one of those pagan rites she was so fond of that they were killed at that intersection. It was such a horrible death, Maia, to be burned alive like that... like witches at the stake.' She shuddered and took another heartening swig of hot tea.

Maia was stunned, but before she could absorb what she had just learned, the warm bass note of Chris's car horn sounded outside, melting some of her shock and enabling her to get up. 'I love you, auntie, but I have to go now.' She needed to get away from the unbelievable fact Carol had just unearthed after all these years. Anger at the way her parents had kept her in the dark about their secret life was already spreading a thorny vine of hurt feelings and confused thoughts inside her she couldn't deal with just yet. 'We'll talk about this later.' She kissed the old woman's parchment-dry cheek. 'Thank you for telling me, it was the right thing to do,' she added, and then literally ran out of the dimly lit dining room into the afternoon sunlight's much more positive wavelength.

Chapter Ten

With the slowly setting sun playing in his hair and transforming his eyes into bottomless lakes, Chris looked much too good to be innocent of some kind of sorcery. The skin of his face and arms washed smooth of flaws by the fervent light of early evening, his profile resembled a molten hilt forged over the straight sword of his spine resting on the black leather seat. She could hardly wait to slip him inside her pussy's tight sheath.

He glanced at her, narrowing his eyes' shining fragments of the sky. 'I'm going to fuck you blind when we get home,' he warned quietly, 'so be prepared.'

'Mm,' she said, and caressed one of his hard thighs happily.

'Don't get me going.' He removed her hand from his leg gently. 'Not yet. Right now I want you to tell me what's troubling you.'

'I don't want to talk about it,' she said tightly. 'It's too unbelievable to even mention.'

'Tell me,' he commanded quietly.

'You're not going to believe it,' she warned.

'I said tell me, Maia.'

'Carol just informed me, after keeping it a secret all these years that my mother was the high priestess of a modern group of Druids that meets at the standing stones every week!' She got it all out in one breath thinking it curious how such a momentous discovery could fit into one casual sentence.

'Is that all?' He rested his warm hand on one of her cool thighs and pushed her dress up out of the way. 'Modern Druids are harmless enough. Their so-called rites are child's play, really; there's nothing truly ancient about them, but

Rituals of Surrender

at least most of them are avid environmentalists. God knows this planet needs as many environmentalists as possible these days.'

Maia stared at him in consternation. 'You're not at all surprised, are you?'

'No.' He glanced at her. 'Should I be?'

'Why aren't you a Druid since you're so interested in the standing stones and Celtic culture? I've seen all those books in your bedroom.'

'I don't belong to a group of Druids because all such contemporary cults are sanitized and essentially neutered, their beliefs and rituals conveniently and safely packaged for the modern sensibility, meaning there's nothing truly holy or pagan about them. They're like de-clawed cats that don't threaten to rip open the cozy fabric of the respectable, conventional life everyone is so deathly fond of nowadays.'

'Oh so you'd prefer it if they still practiced human sacrifice and things like that?' she challenged as a joke, but then gazing at his luminous profile she suddenly felt breathlessly worried.

'There are other much crueler ways of sacrificing people day in and day out, thousands, millions, at a time, Maia.'

'I don't know what you're talking about,' she declared, panicked by how sinisterly calm his voice was. She was appalled to feel herself close to tears, overwhelmed by everything she was discovering about her parents and now about her lover all at once.

'Relax, Maia.' He reached over to cradle her pussy possessively in his hand, pressing his hard palm against her soft panties as though this would help steady her emotionally. 'You're with me now.' He skillfully maneuvered his forefinger beneath the elastic of her skimpy undergarment and casually penetrated her with it, forcing his rigid finger up between the tenderly moist folds of her labia into her tight yet also welcomingly slick passage.

'Stop,' she protested even as she slouched lower in the seat so he could slip his finger even farther up inside her. She clutched the dashboard and closed her eyes as it wormed around in her hole, stirring up all sorts of subtle sensations. 'Stop,' she whispered again, 'please…'

'Are you sure you want me to stop, Maia?'

She moaned.

'That's right, you don't want me to stop.' He deftly added another strong and eager digger to her moistening shaft at the same time that his other hand turned the wheel sharply.

She grasped his wrist. 'Deeper...' she begged softly.

'That's it, sweetheart, give it to me, I want to hear you come.'

'Oh Chris, I can't, not so fast...'

'Yes you can, just relax...'

His confident encouragement stoked the climax simmering in her nerve-endings with miraculous swiftness. She ceased to feel the shell of the car around them as she pressed the heel of his palm directly against her clitoris and rubbed herself furiously, taking possession of his wrist as though it belonged to her. 'Oh yes!' she gasped as the pleasure ascended between her legs with devastating intensity. She spread her thighs as far as she could on the leather seat and shoved his fingers even deeper into her clenching pussy. Yet it was the heel of his thumb rubbing back and forth against her vulva's throbbing little heart that inspired her senses to rise up amongst the powerful trees flanking the road as she climaxed... the soul of her flesh soaring on the single wing of his hand with his fingers rooted deep inside her...

Her pulse beat gradually down to earth again as the car slowed to a stop.

'That's my good girl,' he said, slipping his fingers out of her panties and smoothing her skirt back down. 'You shouldn't doubt yourself, Maia.' He switched off the engine and the pregnant silence of the forest at twilight descended over them like a rich green cloak.

'What do you mean?' she asked languidly, open to anything he might have to say; to anything he might have to tell her about herself that would enable her to come like that again and again.

'I mean,' he held the keys in his hand where it rested between them on the seat, 'you're a sensual being. All you have to do to experience unimaginable pleasure is just let yourself go.'

She looked out at the trees. 'That's easier said than done... what exactly does it mean to let yourself go?'

'It means having faith in your divine nature and not letting doubts and fears clip your wings.'

Rituals of Surrender

'What exactly do you mean by my wings?'

'You spirituality and your sensuality. You literally can't get off the ground if they're both not working together.'

She looked at him, and his smile struck her as mysteriously luminous in the deepening dusk. 'Oh Chris,' she bent over and kissed the back of his hand, 'you're so wonderful.'

'I'd like to keep you here with me forever,' he said quietly, 'but whether you stay, or whether you go back, is entirely up to you, Maia.'

She sat up. 'I'm never going back.'

'It's your life,' he replied mildly. 'Now let's go have some wine.'

The following morning was dismally overcast and the sky opened up after Chris drove off to his workshop, leaving her alone in his home again.

Maia had no idea what she was going to do about her job. She never wanted to go back to the excruciatingly boring solicitor's office. It was very tempting to hope that from now on Chris could support her… and even more appealing was the dreamy possibility that she could make enough money to live selling her paintings, at first to some of his wealthy clients, and then perhaps to some of their friends, and their friends, until she was rich herself… the fantasies she indulged in while lying lazily in bed were endless. At first it was wonderful not having anything to do except daydream, but after she finally got up and showered and dressed, the day started crawling by more slowly than the occasional snail the pounding rain drove out of its murky lair. By the time she had gone down to the kitchen and fixed herself a cup of tea, the hours she had to wait for Chris to return in the evening already felt like a chain she was dragging around with her as she went and opened the front door in order to stand out on the small covered porch.

In the depressing downpour, amorphous fears she had been avoiding surfaced in her mind like worms rising out of the muddy ground, the relentless drumming of the rain on the roof echoing her own anxious thoughts clamoring for attention.

Her physical attraction to Eric Wolfson was just too much for her to handle right now. Her cup had been full with Chris, but now it was overflowing dangerously since there was a chance she could lose everything if she gave into the intoxicating lust the sexy musician aroused in her.

Then there was the skeleton Carol had unearthed in what she had believed was her parents' eternally locked closet. Learning about their secret life as Druids had ripped the healing scab of the years off her grief. Yet on the other hand, she no longer suffered that terrible, sinking despair when she remembered their coffins being lowered into the earth. When she pictured them now, they were walking hand in hand through the woods. Carol hadn't said as much, but Maia suspected it was her father who had forbidden Stella to involve their daughter in pagan pastimes. She wondered what the rites of this modern group of Druids was like, and found it impossible to picture her otherwise perfectly normal parents wearing formless white robes while chanting up at the moon.

At three o'clock in the afternoon the rain finally stopped for a little while as the sun's rays shoved the clouds away with slender but powerful arms. Maia gratefully watched them emerge from the sky's heavy gray cloak admiring the way they made the wet trees around Chris's home glimmer with gold.

She ached for a telephone to call him with. Her longing to communicate with him was so intense she felt it should at least take the form of a subliminal ringing in his ears.

She stood in the open doorway again for a long time inhaling the fragrance of wet grass and leaves and sipping yet another cup of tea. She sighed, wondering what she could do to keep herself from getting bored and depressed. No activity seemed able to contain her mood lately. Ghosts weren't bed sheets you could wash the soil off and rationally bleach away their darkly haunting nature. Ever since Carol's revelation, she couldn't seem to stop thinking about her parents. It was strange that her relationship with Chris had begun in the cemetery on the anniversary of their death. And she did not even want to remember how completely she had forgotten about her job at the solicitor's office. It was hard to believe, everything that had happened to her since her car stalled on her that night in the graveyard. Thanks to Chris, she was so unexpectedly fulfilled and excited about her sexuality and the future that the very atmosphere felt lighter. Yet it was impossible to deny her sexual attraction to Eric and that it threatened her new-found happiness like the veritable serpent in Eden.

'Oh God,' she muttered, caressing her long hair away from her face, too lazy to go back upstairs and brush it. Her hair provided an agreeably warm mantle in the winter, but it became unruly and tangled as the thriving foliage in summer.

Maybe if she pulled out a blank sheet of paper and stared at it long enough a drawing would take form and help her make sense of her emotions. She had all her art supplies with her; there was nothing stopping her from expressing herself creatively... nothing except the fact that she couldn't seem to focus here in Chris's home, not the way she had been able to apply herself to her artwork in the privacy and comfort of her own room. Yet she didn't want to go back to her old bedroom, not really...

She stood there a while longer gazing down at the dark dregs of her tea as though trying to read her future. She was about to turn back inside when the distant hum of a motor threaded itself through the sound of the renewed downpour. A moment later, she spotted Chris's small red car speeding towards her down the narrow road lined with trees like sentinels guarding the approach of their lord and master. She watched breathlessly as he pulled up, leapt out of the car and ran up onto the porch. Even though he was drenched, he smiled at her cheerfully. 'You called?'

She was feeling a little better. Chris had promised to come home and have lunch with her everyday, unless it was absolutely impossible for him to get away from the shop. This meant she would not be quite so lonely, because they had also discussed the matter of her position at the solicitor's office and decided there was no need for her to go back.

'I can find buyers for your work, Maia,' he assured her, sipping the hot tea she had made for him when they came inside. His hair and clothes were wet and she was afraid he would catch cold. 'You should concentrate on your creativity and stop wasting time in a dull little law office. You're immensely talented, there's no reason you can't devote yourself to your paintings from now on if that's what you feel like doing.'

'But Chris, it's not so easy,' she protested reluctantly, because in truth she was already seduced by his logic.

'Why not?' he countered, stoking the flames he had just brought to life in his tiny fireplace, brightening the cold gray day with warmth and color.

She shrugged, thinking she could have lit a fire for herself, but it would not have felt the same without him there. Nothing felt the same without him; everything felt different when she was alone, less uncomplicatedly beautiful and positive.

'You look great in my shirts,' he told her, setting down his empty tea cup. 'I love looking at you in my clothes.'

'I was too lazy to get dressed,' she murmured, gazing shyly down at her lap. She was wearing one of his long-sleeved forest-green button-down shirts, a pair of his black woolen socks, and nothing else.

'Come here.' He urged her to lie down beside him on the colorful Oriental rug softening the gray stones of the hearth.

Maia was distracted by the pleasure of his embrace as she wondered where she had seen this rug before with its vicious-looking stylized dragons…

'Come here,' he repeated gently, slipping one arm beneath her and gently pulling her onto her side so he could press the full length of his body against hers.

She sighed at once restlessly and contentedly. He was much taller than she was so her face was on a level with his chest. His damp slacks pressed against her naked thighs, and she shivered slightly as she reached up to caress his still wet hair before running her hand up the strong slope of his shoulder, her other arm pinned uselessly between them. He was a stimulating contrast of temperatures and textures – cold and warm, hard and smooth, tender and unyielding. She had never realized before how arousing a man's body could be whether fully dressed or naked.

He kissed the top of her head. 'I can't stay long,' he whispered, 'so I'll give

Rituals of Surrender

you a choice. Either you fix me so lunch or you let me eat you. After all, a hard-working man needs his nourishment.'

'Mm,' she murmured, 'I think I'm feeling too lazy to get up.'

'Not a problem.' He released her and she rolled languidly onto her back as he positioned himself between her legs. The fire crackled eagerly beside them, sending warm, caressing shadows across her pale flesh as he shoved the shirt she was wearing all the way up to her neck, exposing her sex, her belly and then her breasts, apparently too pressed for time and too hungry for her pussy to patiently unbutton it.

She raised her head slightly and gazed down the length of her fire lit body at his golden hair setting between her legs. Her breasts were pert mounds crowned with big puffy aureoles and long nipples begging to be licked and bitten. It was a sweet suffering that he concentrated exclusively on her clitoris and labia, his hands resting lightly on her inner thighs to hold them open around his intent face. He didn't caress her or penetrate her. All he did was lick her, deliciously tormenting her with everything else he wasn't doing to her while subjecting her to the sweet pleasure of his devotion to the heart of her pleasure, which he knew from experience was not easily seduced. Her clit had never before been treated with such respect and skillful consideration, and she realized her body's sensitive little button was very much like a queen who could not be approached directly, rather his tongue had to seek obsequious audience with her surrounding skin, first rousing her interest. He worked her up to a point where her clitoris was aching to grant his mouth a full, exclusive audience, and it felt almost too good when he at last focused all his attentions on the mysterious seed of her ecstasy. Her hips began writhing on the dragon-embroidered rug as she fondled her own breasts hungrily, her nipples longing for the same attention he was giving her pussy, but he was cruelly forcing her to choose between them. Then suddenly he penetrated her with his tongue, thrusting its surprisingly hard muscle as far into her juicing slit as it could reach, and its flicking thrusts stoked the delight smoldering between her thighs into an orgasmic fire.

'Oh God, yes,' she breathed, vaguely wondering why she could never think of anything more original to say as the need to climax inexorably possessed her.

Cat's Collar - Three Erotic Romances

Yet what more was there to say? Once he brought her this far, it felt like a matter of life and death to her flesh to achieve the release hovering so tantalizingly on the horizon of her nerve-endings. She simply had to come now, so when he abruptly sat up, abandoning his skilled tending of her growing ecstasy, a wordless wail of disappointment escaped her. Only the sight of him quickly opening his pants assuaged her disappointment. Then his thick and rigid cock was in his hands and all she could think about was how much she wanted to feel it stabbing her between the legs. But all he did was tower over her on his knees as he held his pants open with one hand and with the other hand swiftly stroked himself. She watched in frustrated fascination as the thick tip of his erection slipped in and out between his fingers, the sweet cleft in its head glimmering with semen.

'Touch yourself, Maia,' he commanded. 'I want to watch you pleasure yourself, and then I'm going to come all over you.'

'Oh Chris, please fuck me,' she begged. 'I want to feel your cock inside me, please.'

'You can feel it inside you later,' he teased soberly, 'right now I want to see you touching yourself. I want to see you enjoying your body.'

It was not what she wanted, but the tone of his voice and the look in his eyes told her she had no choice, so she decided to make the best of it… and discovered there was indeed something perversely enjoyable about teasing each other like this as he pumped his hard-on with increasing fervor, never once taking his eyes off her, and she fervently rubbed her clitoris with the fingertips of her right hand as her other hand played with the soft mounds of her breasts and pulled on the almost painfully stiff, rosy nipples crowning them. All she had to do to push herself over the edge was imagine his big hard dick sliding up inside her… she bit her lip to keep from crying out shamelessly as a climax broke between her thighs at the same time that he groaned and ejaculated, spraying her belly and breasts with the white foam of his cum.

Chapter Eleven

'You want me to tell you all about myself, don't you, Maia?' Chris asked her casually when he came home from the shop again later that evening.

'I do,' she admitted eagerly.

'Then let's have dinner out tonight,' he suggested. 'Go put on a nice dress for me.'

'All right,' she agreed happily. 'I'll go get ready.' She ran upstairs and emptied her bladder in the tiny bathroom toilet first, but she could not do the same with her heart, which felt almost uncomfortably full. Standing at the seashell-shaped sink, she cupped cold water in her hands and gazed down into the tiny pond formed by her palms for a contemplative moment before splashing it over her face. She dried herself off, ran a brush through her thick hair a few lazy times, and needlessly pinched some color into her cheeks. She had been blessed with a flawless complexion, long black eyelashes that never called for mascara, and her full rosy lips defied the need for lipstick. She was a little disappointed Chris did not appear to be into kissing, but he was definitely into fucking and that was more than enough for now. She had had her fill of necking in the front seat of cars; her new lover's confidence and sexual sophistication were infinitely more exciting and if kissing was the price she had to pay for his otherwise devastatingly thorough attentions, then so be it. At least that's what she told herself; she had too much on her mind to add one more uncertainty to the list.

Back in the bedroom, she slipped out of his shirt and socks before kneeling beside her suitcase to search for just the right dress. She had not yet unpacked her clothing; she was feeling remarkably lethargic these days. Also, she did not really care to admit it, but Chris's closet frightened her a little. She was not yet ready to hang all her clothes up across from his in that sinister space guarded by lightning-blackened oak wood. She spotted a simple, sleeveless red cotton dress at the bottom of the suitcase, wrested it out from the heavy pile of material on top, and wriggled into it, not bothering with a bra. She did, however, snatch up a pair of black bikini panties, also made of soft breathable cotton, and slipped them on before sitting on the edge of the bed to fasten a pair of black strap high-heeled sandals to her bare feet. She had never been so conscious of every part of her body; being with Chris was heightening all her senses to an almost unbearable point. Right now she was delightfully aware of her labial lips clinging moistly to her panties almost as if they resented being bandaged up like that, and her nipples also felt strangely confined where they poked against her dress, a sight she was sure her lover would appreciate.

He was already outside leaning against the car waiting for her by the time she hurried back downstairs. The sun was beginning to set behind the trees and she looked forward to enjoying the drama of the twilight on their way into town, which would take them right past the standing stones.

They rode in silence for a while, and during that time she determined that her mind would not be a courtroom in which her lover's history would be judged when he finally began telling her about himself. Her heart had to be the perfectly loving space in which all his past trials were soothed away.

When the standing stones came into view, he slowed the car down to give them both time to admire the dramatic tableau. The nine phallic pillars stood parallel to the sun that was descending amongst them like nobles at the bedside of their dying lord, some of them leaning forward slightly as though bowing respectfully. It occurred to her then that she had first experienced Chris (if not actually seen him) the evening he had been parked on the hill at exactly this time of the day. His red car had gleamed in the dying light like a bloodstained modern suit of armor protected by the small but powerfully concentrated force of the ancient stones...

'That's right,' he said abruptly as though reading her mind.

'That's right what?' she asked lightly, but for some reason she didn't dare look at him. Instead she leaned forward in her seat to gaze up at the deep blue color of the sky at the zenith peacefully ignoring the blazing passion of light and color on the horizon, where clouds had gathered like noble lords clad in richly dyed cloths accompanied by ladies wearing lovely pastel veils. And their undisputed sovereign the sun was a perfect drop of blood just as in her dream, the dream in which a mysterious dark-haired man had pricked the skin directly over her heart with the point of an ancient sword...

'The moon is our physical life,' Chris remarked matter-of-factly, 'the sun is the soul of experience, and our eternal being is the darkness itself. Matter is God's flesh, don't you think?'

'Yes, that makes sense,' she agreed casually, having entertained similar thoughts herself, thoughts she strove to express in her paintings. 'But I thought you were going to tell me about yourself Chris, not discourse on metaphysics.'

'What's the difference?' He smiled, his eyes fixed on the empty road.

The sun vanished behind the earth at last and Maia found herself wondering if the death of a loved one was a similar illusion. Wasn't it ignorant to believe that merely because the dead disappeared from view that they were lost in darkness? The sun kept burning and sustaining her life even when she could not see it, and in a similar sense she still felt some of her parents' love with her even though they were gone forever.

They didn't speak again for a while and she didn't suspect until too late where he appeared to be taking her. It wasn't until he had made disturbingly familiar turns down the streets of Stoneshire that she exclaimed without thinking, 'I don't want to go to The Phoenix!'

'Why not?' he asked, yet he didn't sound surprised by her passionate reticence.

'Because my parents and I ate there every Sunday night until they died. We have to go somewhere else, please.'

'No,' he said shortly. 'You have to face things, Maia. It's the only way to see where you're going.'

'Right now all I see is where I'm not going!' She crossed her arms defiantly over her chest feeling on the verge of a tantrum. 'Why are you being so cruel?'

she begged to know, a sob catching in her throat.

'You should honor your parents with a visit to their old haunt, Maia, excuse the pun. After all, you've just discovered something fascinating about them, something which leads me to believe they wouldn't appreciate such appetite-suppressing grief on your part. I imagine they find your sorrow much more distressing than being dead, a state of being that might be more enjoyable than you can possibly imagine.'

'Chris, please...' She felt helpless against his logic, which rolled over her like one of the ancient standing stones crushing any possible arguments against it.

'We're eating at The Phoenix tonight, Maia, and that's final.'

'I thought you were going to tell me about your life, Chris, not go back into my past!' She was furious with him now.

'Here we are.'

As ever, the intimate restaurant was only half full. She could scarcely believe it, but nothing had changed after all these years except for the waitress – a thin young creature who looked as though she never ate anything herself who darted from table to table like a robin in her brown-and-yellow uniform.

Maia seated herself in the chair Chris pulled out for her, and then stared at the candle burning steadily in the center of the small round table avoiding his eyes, not sure whether to be angry with him or grateful. The flood of memories overwhelming her was like sitting at the edge of a rushing river as vanished moments hit her chest directly over her heart like a cold spray... the red dress her mother had worn one night so similar to the one she was wearing herself now... her father discoursing on the fate of the candle flame... there seemed no beginning and no end to the nostalgic flow.

'See?' Chris winked at her over the black menu.

She raised her own menu in order to hide behind it.

'Not speaking to me, are you? Well, if you don't behave you might just find yourself in the kitchen helping with the dirty dishes.'

'I'll just have soup,' she stated, setting the menu down indifferently. If her appetite was a person, she would soon have to report it to the authorities as suspiciously missing.

He raised an eyebrow. 'Just soup, when you can have absolutely anything you desire?'

'All I want is for you to stop teasing me.'

'It's Eric who's teasing you, love.'

She was speechless for a guilty moment. 'I think he'd do a lot more than tease me if I let him,' she finally retorted.

'He'd only dump you in the end.' Setting his own menu down, he leaned over the table towards her, his face suddenly more intently beautiful than ever. 'He's nothing but a blind and selfish collection of hungers!' he whispered fiercely.

The waitress passed their table bearing two large grilled steaks on a platter.

He glanced in the direction of the fragrant meat. 'The only thing that motivates Eric is hunger for flesh!' He drew the word out in a disgusted hiss.

'Maia…' She felt a light touch on her shoulder and knew she had not only imagined hearing her name spoken. 'Maia Wilson, I believe.'

She stared at the man seated at the table with her and Chris. It was uncanny how clearly she remembered him even though she had glimpsed him only briefly years ago here in this very restaurant. Yet somehow it felt like yesterday as she re-lived her restlessness that evening, and then her disappointment when he got up to leave dressed all in black leather like the embodiment of her oddly pleasurable melancholy. She had watched the handsome stranger walk away as her father continued discussing the fate of the candle, not sensing the flames waiting to take both him and his wife into their violent embrace by way of a car crash only a few days later…

'But if you knew my parents,' she asked the man, 'why didn't they say hello to you that night?' She didn't want to sound suspicious, but she felt her self-control slipping. Too much was happening too fast and she was learning more than she had ever wanted to know about the past.

'Our friendship was not an open one,' Drew replied, gazing soberly but serenely at her face.

She noticed his eyes were the same deep blue color the sky had been tonight above the passionate sunset on the horizon. Then her awareness perched expectantly on his lips as she waited for him to say something more, and her pulse fluttered in a strangely wonderful way when he smiled slightly.

'Do you want the truth, Maia?' he asked, raising one hand to his heart as though about to swear on his honor. She didn't know whether to be relieved or disappointed when he merely extracted a pack of cigarettes from inside his black leather jacket. He had unzipped it but not bothered to remove it even though the temperature inside the restaurant was ideal.

'Yes, of course I want the truth,' she declared.

The skeletal waitress arrived to take their orders.

Maia still couldn't locate her appetite, but she quickly looked over the menu again compelled by Chris's pointed expression to order something other than soup.

'You're running out of time,' her lover warned her beneath his breath, and then smiled civilly at Drew. 'Can you give her any suggestions?'

'I'll decide for myself,' she said uncertainly.

Chris cheerfully addressed the waitress, 'We'll start with a carafe of the house red, please, love.'

'Very good, sir,' she chirped. 'I'll go fetch it and be back to take your orders.' She darted away, but not before smoothing her short skirt over twig-like thighs while holding Chris's eyes just a little longer than necessary.

'You were saying?' Maia addressed the dark-haired man even as she pretended to continue concentrating on the menu, yet the truth was that none of the entrees appealed to her.

'You wanted the truth,' he reminded her quietly.

'Yes,' she insisted, sensing he was giving her time to prepare herself for it, which made her nervous wondering what to expect.

'Maia,' Chris hooked her attention again, 'I suspect Mr. Landson here was part of your parents' secret life.'

She had already suspected as much herself. 'And my father didn't want me to know about it,' she mused out loud, 'so he pretended not to know Drew that night.'

'It was wrong of him to keep her in the dark, don't you think?' Chris asked.

'He had his reasons.' Drew leaned back in his chair and cradled his right elbow in his left hand to more easily draw the smoke from his cigarette. 'Does it bother you, Maia?'

'That my father-?'

'No, my smoking.'

'Daddy called them cancer sticks,' she informed him sternly.

'Yes,' a smile softened his firm mouth again for an instant, 'and he never stopped harassing me about my filthy habit.'

'And yet here you've outlived him by years,' Chris commented. 'Amazing irony, isn't it? Ah, we're saved.' The wine had arrived. 'Bless you, love.'

The girl preened. 'Are you ready to order now?'

'Maia?' Her lover's eyes commanded her to pick a dish whether she wanted it or not.

She quickly made a decision. 'I'll have the onion soup and a mixed green salad, please.'

Drew said he would have the same as the lady.

Chris suffered a peculiar lapse of imagination and ordered fish and chips. He then caressed Maia's knee beneath the table. 'It seems she's going to be hard to hold on to,' he remarked, and gave the other man an openly challenging stare.

'So you were a Druid too?' she asked quickly, and laughed a little from a build-up of tension, not because she thought the idea was silly. She fervently hoped Drew realized that.

'Were?' His lips puckered around the word as he stared at her with one of his dark eyebrows forming an incredulous arch at her choice of tense.

'Oh I'm sorry…' Her clumsy apology tripped over his sudden smile. 'You are a…' She found it impossible to bring the mysterious ancient term of 'Druid' into the casual present.

Drew gently killed his cigarette while Chris occupied himself with the wine's body, raising his glass and frowning when he discovered it had absolutely no legs.

'Is it all a secret,' she persisted, 'or can you give me some idea what-?'

'There's a time and place for everything, Maia,' Chris interrupted her. He had given up on the wine's body and was settling for the ghost of a bouquet. 'I'm sure Mr. Landson would rather not get into it right now.'

Drew fingered another tobacco shroud. 'It's not all a secret, Maia.'

'I feel I have a right to know... thank you.' She accepted a full glass of wine from her lover without taking her eyes off the other man.

'Yes, you do have a right to know.' Drew's low-pitched voice was almost hypnotically quiet, yet its timber made every word he said ring in her head. 'I'd like to tell you everything,' he added, continuing to hold her eyes.

'I'm sure you would,' Chris said agreeably. 'She'll hear the so-called truth about the Druids from you, and get to experience all the sensational fantasies about them through Eric Wolfson. A famous musician who recently commissioned a wine rack from me wants Maia to be in a music video he's producing that will essentially recreate an ancient sacrifice.'

When Drew abruptly glanced in the direction of another table, Maia realized it was the first time he had looked at anyone besides her. 'The standard sacrifice scene?' he asked.

'I assume so,' Chris replied, 'although we might be able to save it from total banality if he lets me direct the video. I doubt he will, however.'

Drew contemplated the flame of the match he lit before raising it to the fresh cigarette dangling between his lips, and watching him, Maia imagined an Indian woman tightly wrapped in a white shroud about to be burned with her husband. 'How do you feel about it?' he asked her, meeting her eyes again.

She felt as though he was inhaling her soul while he waited for her response. Looking down at the table, at once unnerved and reassured by his steady regard, she followed the snow-bound trail of a fold in the cloth with her little finger, which trembled slightly as she spoke. 'It might be interesting...'

'She's dying to say yes,' Chris rephrased her tentative reply.

Drew focused on Maia's restless hand. 'Maybe you can arrange for me to have a talk with Mr. Wolfson,' he suggested. 'After all, music videos are a powerful medium.'

She looked up again and was caught by the small silver earrings he wore, then by the thin silver chain describing a wide ark across his black shirt as her awareness seemed to fall into orbit around it...

Chapter Twelve

Maia had always considered pubs to be somewhat seedy places, but tonight she felt herself to be in an alchemist's basement where exotically labeled bottles and glasses of all different shapes gleamed an aura of dangerous enchantment... where the deep shadows seemed to orbit Drew's body sitting beside hers, intensifying his gravitational pull and making it difficult not to lean even closer to his mesmerizing voice.

After dinner, the three of them had walked a few blocks to a pub to continue their strange conversation, which couldn't seem to properly take off in the restaurant's more conventional atmosphere. But now, with countless bottles of spirits lined up before them like levers in a magical control panel, ideas could soar in any direction.

Maia took such comfortable root on her stool she almost grew fond of it. She began seeing it as a stem on which the full blossoming of her feeling depended, all the concepts contained in her mind like petals unfurling.

Chris had disappeared for the time being. Apparently, he had a number of casual acquaintances scattered around the pub's dim domain and he seemed intent on greeting all of them. She also suspected he was deliberately leaving her alone with Drew, which would have surprised her if she had expected her lover to behave normally. Whatever Chris's reasons, it suited her to have Drew all to herself for a while, and not only because she wanted to question him about her parents' secret life as pagans. He was dividing his attention between her and his drink, staring down into it as he spoke, and then up into her dark eyes as though to savor her reaction to his words. At first he leaned against the bar, but gradually he turned to face her, and she unconsciously reflected his movement like pure metal following the irresistible pull of a magnet.

'Are you confused?' he asked her.

'Yes,' she admitted.

'Why?'

Even in the dark space she could make out his vivid blue eyes. 'Because, just the other day I was wondering if anything exciting was ever going to happen to me…' She glanced down at the dark hill of his lap, and a sudden impulse to bend over and bury her face in it de-railed the train of her sentence for a breathless moment. 'Because my life was so drab and predictable,' she started over, 'and then all of a sudden so much is happening to me that my head is spinning!' She found herself relaxing as she could never remember doing with anyone before, not even (especially) with Chris. It was very nice the way Drew listened to everything she had to say, as if he had already guessed the words about to pass between her lips and yet still cared to hear her express them herself. He also seemed to enjoy watching her mouth as she talked. 'I mean,' she found herself looking down at his lap again, 'I met Chris in a cemetery. Can you believe it?' She laughed self-consciously, and then absorbed a little more courage by taking a quick sip from her glass of red wine. 'I drove to the graveyard to visit my parents' grave and my car stalled just a few yards from the gate,' she went on matter-of-factly, her casual tone striving to belie the strangely sinister event. 'I panicked. I don't know a thing about cars and I was out in the middle of nowhere. All I could think of to do was turn on my emergency blinkers, and before I knew it Chris had miraculously pulled in to help me. Yet there wasn't anything wrong with the engine after all, oddly enough.'

'No, there wasn't.' He touched her knee gently, but almost before her senses could register the warmth of his fingers, they were resting lightly on his glass again. 'I'm very fond of your mother, Maia,' he confessed, gazing down at the golden pool of his drink.

'You mean you were very fond of her.'

'No, I mean I am very fond of her. No one ever really dies,' he met her eyes, 'and I think you know that.'

Suddenly, all her hope of immortality seemed to hang from his silver earrings.

'Do you really believe that, Drew?' she asked him fervently, staring fixedly at his profile as he took another sip of his scotch 'Chris says he does, but do you, really?'

Once more he looked directly into her eyes. 'Absolutely.'

She felt more than heard his response, his whisper a gentle breeze in the pub's dark atmosphere storming with dozens of much more lively conversations than theirs. 'I'm so glad,' she whispered, and realized after it was too late that her hand was resting on one of his thighs.

Smiling, he spread his own warm fingers over hers. 'Do I feel familiar to you, Maia?'

'Yes,' she admitted, grateful to him for being able to sense how she felt. 'I don't know why, but you do.'

'That's what I have to talk to you about. You remember your accident, when an oak tree was struck by lightning three times and collapsed across the car you were in with your aunt?'

'Of course I remember. That's not the sort of thing you ever forget.'

'I helped bring you back.'

'What do you mean you helped bring me back? You mean you found our wrecked car and called the rescue and helped them–?'

'No, that's not what I mean. Someone else found the wreck and called for help. You're aware of the fact that you were unconscious for an entire month afterwards.' He added as if by way of an arcane explanation, 'For one full cycle of the moon.'

'I know I was,' she sounded impatient because she was getting nervous, 'but I still don't understand what you mean when you say you helped bring me back.' She knew, however, what it meant now when she saw him reach for his heart. 'Please don't,' she requested.

'You want me to stay, don't you, Maia?'

'Are you telling me you would get up and go because I don't want you to smoke?' She refused to believe he could be so rude and selfish.

'Trust me.'

Her heart burned with indignant disappointment when he lit the cigarette against her wishes.

'You see, to put it simply,' he went on, exhaling smoke across the bar away from her, 'you were having an amazingly good time away from your body.' He met her eyes again with this remarkable statement. 'You remember when you were a little girl playing in the yard how you resented going back inside when your mother called you in for supper, because you were in the middle of a really great game and you didn't want to stop playing?'

'Yes!' She laughed. 'All the time.'

'Well, you weren't listening to your mother or your father begging you to return to consciousness after your accident, therefore,' he tapped ashes into his empty glass, 'they asked me to run out and get you, so to speak. Although I'm afraid your father wasn't too happy with how I went about luring your soul home.'

Maia was amazed and enthralled by Drew's story. Strangely enough, it had never occurred to her to wonder why she had awoken from her month-long sleep in her own bedroom instead of in the hospital, which is where they normally kept people in comas. She was still disturbed by the fact that she had lost an entire month of her life, yet for her the time had gone by in the blink of an eye. Afterwards, her parents had done everything in their power to help her forget the unnerving experience as quickly as possible. Now Drew had given her an enigmatic sketch of physical facts merged with supernatural events in which possible and impossible merged like light and dark in his penetrating stare, and somehow the effect was realistic.

Chris finally returned to the bar to claim her, and she walked out of the pub pensively, as though her emotions were slippery stones emerging from a river she was being forced to cross in the dark, its dangerous currents the rushing sound of traffic on the street. It distressed her how hard she found it to part from Drew, a man she had only just met, and it was an effort not to let Chris see how she felt about her parents' old friend. The slight pain when Drew forcefully gripped her arm and whispered in her ear, 'We'll talk again soon' was the sweetest sensation ever.

Chapter Thirteen

During the long drive back to his house from town, Chris said, 'You fancy him.'

She quickly attempted to deflect his mild accusation with a revelation, 'He told me something I'm finding very hard to believe, and yet I do believe him, for some reason.'

'Maia,' his tone was indulgent, 'a woman always believes the man she desires no matter what he says.'

This blunt statement rendered her speechless for a long moment in which her guilt was loud as a scream. Chris was the man of her dreams, yet in the handful of days she had known him, he had already inadvertently introduced her to two other highly desirable men she found herself helplessly attracted to. 'I'm sure that's something you take full advantage of,' she retorted quietly, finally managing a swing at him, but her heart was heavy. What Eric aroused in her was uncomplicated lust she could get a reasonable grip on and fight against, but the feelings Drew inspired in her were at once too intense and too subtle for her to resist, at least not yet, she needed to see him and to talk to him again.

'Maia, I care about you very much.' Chris raised his left arm invitingly, steering with one hand so she could snuggle up close to him. 'What did he tell you, dear, you seem upset?'

'Oh Chris,' she sighed, taking comfort from his warmth and the already familiar feel of his slender yet muscular body. 'I can't believe that only a few days ago I didn't even know you! And now all this about my parents being Druids… that was hard enough to believe without everything Drew just told me.'

'There, there,' he murmured, 'you've been hit with a lot at once, but you don't have to think about it all right now. Relax and just let me hold you. Everything will be all right, trust me.'

'But I have to think about it,' she protested. 'I want to think about it.' She attempted to slip out from beneath his arm, which suddenly felt more like an oppressive weight than a comforting embrace.

'You want Drew, not an explanation, Maia. Desire is all you understand.'

'Let go of me, please.'

'As long as you realize you're already mine,' he let her slip away across the seat, 'I'll let you have your fun.'

'I think maybe I should move back in with Carol,' she said numbly.

'You're not going back, Maia,' he insisted pleasantly. 'You don't really want to. You know we were meant to be together, you felt it from the moment you saw me, didn't you?'

'Yes,' she confessed even though she was so distressed she couldn't think straight; she was too busy trying not to cry.

'And I can give you anything you desire, even other men, if that's what you want sometimes.'

'Oh God, no...' She suddenly wanted to die. How could he possibly love her if he felt that way?

'It's all right, Maia, I'm not the jealous type, and there's a world of difference between love and lust. I can give you everything,' he promised again gently. 'There's no need for you to go back to work. I want you to concentrate on your painting.'

His excessive generosity filled her with despair and threw her into a mysterious panic. 'But Chris, if I don't work-'

'I can give you anything you desire,' he insisted, 'there's no need for you to work.'

'But I have to earn a living for myself,' she said desperately, 'and I have no idea if my paintings will sell.'

'You can't worry about that, Maia you just have to follow your heart no matter what.'

The car sped around a sharp curve in the road and suddenly the standing stones rose up against the star-filled sky.

Cat's Collar - Three Erotic Romances

The awe-inspiring sight smoothed out her passionately tangled emotions like a hauntingly pleasurable caress. Impulsively, she rolled down her window and the cold night wind roared in like a black dragon impaled on the car's headlights – straight golden swords piercing the darkness, which seemed to emit a climactic scream of pain as Chris burned rubber to swerve off the road onto the grass.

'What are you doing?' she gasped.

'We're going for a little moonlit stroll.'

'But I'm tired,' she protested half-heartedly.

'I'm sure you can make it up the hill.' He turned off the engine, plunging them into darkness as he switched off the headlights. 'You won't be tired for long,' he promised in an almost reverently hushed voice. 'More energy than you can ever use is stored in these stones, Maia. All you have to do is open yourself up to it and let it fill you.' He reached over to squeeze her leg just above the knee. 'You're good at that.'

She felt herself becoming excited by the absolute stillness surrounding their small vehicle. Yet the darkness outside was also alive with the singing of crickets, a high-pitched energetic sound that seemed to communicate with the vibrant pulsing of the stars overhead. There wasn't a cloud in the sky. The moon was holding full glorious court in this once sacred place. Maia knew the luminous disc had to be gradually waning, she had been communing with it for several nights now, but so far the earth's shadow had not encroached upon it at all...

'Have you ever made love beneath the stars, Maia?'

'I've had sex in a car beneath the stars,' she replied tartly.

'That doesn't count.' He opened his door. 'Come on.'

She followed him out into the cool night air. The grass felt prickly against her bare toes and didn't inspire her to remove her high-heeled sandals even though it would have been easier to walk up the hill barefoot.

'Keep your heels on,' he instructed, as ever seeming to read her mind as he took her hand.

She let him lead her quickly up the steep slope. She had driven past the standing stones her whole life yet she had never stopped to walk amongst them, and it felt strange to be there now, as though she was crashing a party to which she had

Rituals of Surrender

not been invited; a gathering of spirits and forces beyond the comprehension of her excessively rational modern mind, which no longer knew how to understand this passionately simple language of nocturnal insects singing and of wind rustling through the grass. The stars were so bright, a part of her almost felt they were screaming at her on a frequency too high for her physical ears to register, but it was as though her soul could hear the cosmic symphony so that she didn't feel alone with Chris. It was as though they were entering an infinitely exclusive place very few people knew about or could gain mysterious admittance to.

When they reached the summit, he let go of her hand and she stumbled on the uneven ground as the full presence of the stones overwhelmed her. Now that she was amongst them, she could truly appreciate how tall and broad they were as well as how much individual space there was between them, each phallic column possessed of a private aura as it held its own special position in the group. The moon was intensely interested in Chris's white button-down shirt, which made him wonderfully visible to her as he strode into the open space between the stones. She thought about following him, but then decided not to. She didn't share his bold familiarity with the place and the pillar closest to her had captured her in its orbit. She found herself walking towards it as though it had silently commanded her to approach and reach out and touch its rough stone skin…

'Maia,' her name resounded amongst the stars and the moon suddenly seemed to be gazing exclusively down at her, 'take off your dress. I want you naked.'

She glanced self-consciously down the hill at the road, but there were no cars approaching from either direction. Part of her wanted to obey him, yet she hesitated to expose herself, not because it was a chilly night but because she felt surrounded by timeless elemental forces that would all be attracted to her vulnerable mortal flesh. She felt surrounded by ghosts, not so much of people as of the centuries themselves… if she took off her dress she would be exposing herself to the cold dark fingers of long-vanished decades to which her precious individual life meant nothing…

'I said take off your dress and your panties as well, Maia.'

It was impossible to resist her lover's command coming from the heart of an ancient stone circle. She grasped the hem of her cotton garment, took a bracing breath, and pulled it swiftly off over her head. She immediately felt her nipples harden beneath the wind's coldly moist lick as it forever blew between the erect columns of stone, and the way it wafted against her pussy as she slipped off her panties was almost too stimulating. Shivering, she abandoned her undergarment to the grass as she held her dress protectively over her breasts, thankful for the long hair cloaking her shoulders. Then she shivered again as Chris strode purposefully towards her.

He wrenched the dress out of her hands and flung it carelessly onto the ground behind him. 'Turn around,' he commanded. 'Brace yourself on the stone.'

She turned back towards the dark shape looming over her and bent at the waist to rest her hands on the rough surface, preparing herself for his thrusts. It turned her on how intensely aware she was of her warm pussy fully exposed to the cold night air. How available her tight little hole was intensified her appreciation of the phallic columns surrounding her, and imagining Chris's erection reflecting them thrilled her to the core as she felt him step up behind her. She didn't need to see him to know he was still fully clothed and that he was pulling his cock out like a weapon to stab her with. Then, waiting for his penetration, she suddenly caught herself thinking about Drew… picturing the way his dark-brown hair flowed back away from his high forehead and then curved gently around again to fall almost to his shoulders… remembering the cigarette burning between his firm lips and the crescent-shaped scar below them luminous in his unshaved chin as he looked into her eyes, listening… The napkin on which he had written his phone number down for her was folded carefully inside her purse resting on the front seat of the car. She hoped no one would steal it, but that seemed highly unlikely out here in the middle of nowhere…

She gasped when Chris clutched her hips with both hands, digging his hard fingers into her tender skin like a predator sinking its talons into unresisting prey. She thought of asking him to loosen his grip on her, but she didn't; she liked being roughly possessed like this by a man who knew what he wanted and wasn't afraid to take it. She moaned expectantly when he insinuated the full head of his erection between the moist folds of her labia, and then bit her lip as she endured the exquisite tease of him just resting there for a moment. She could feel the breathtaking length and girth of his hard-on poised at the entrance to her flesh ready to sink into her body's yielding depths, and she both loved and hated the way he made her wait for it, making her whimper and arch her back even more deeply to push her pussy back towards him invitingly. Without either of them saying a word he was making her beg him to fuck her. And the whole time she waited for his thrust she was aware of the moon looking down at her, like a haunting reflection of the tiny satellite of her clitoris needing his penetrating energy to come alive...

'What are you thinking, Maia?'

'I'm wishing you would fuck me.'

'Very good.' He shifted his hands down to her ass cheeks and squeezed them approvingly. 'You're learning to be more honest with yourself. A few days ago you would have said you were waiting for me to make love to you.'

Drew would make love to me, she thought, and then it was too late to take the feeling back and pretend she was really alone with Chris. Her heart began racing, but there was no way she could escape the conviction that Drew would be able to fuck her just as hard but that he would also make love to her.

'Mm, you're even more beautiful in the moonlight, Maia.' Chris ran his hands slowly up and down her back, his thumbs pressing into the sweet dip where her spine merged with her hips. 'I know you're thinking about that Druid priest. He's too late, of course, you're all mine now, but if you want to think about him, I don't mind, whatever turns you on.'

Protests perched on her lips, but somehow she never got around to uttering them. She couldn't quite reconcile how guilty she felt with how turned on she was until Chris at last condescended to stab her with his erection. He sank deliciously deep into her pussy, but then just rested there, tormenting her in another way; suspending her in a whole new dimension of mingled fulfillment and frustration. It seemed an eternity before he began driving his rock-hard cock swiftly in and out of her, slamming his body against hers as he banged her in rhythm with her cries of pleasure. She closed her eyes and braced herself for all she was worth against the stone, forgetting all about the moon and the stars, aware only of the earth beneath her sandaled feet as she dug her heels into it, keeping her legs perfectly so her hole was offered perfectly up to his filling thrusts. In this position he sank so completely inside her she almost couldn't bear the intense fulfillment, and yet she also loved it more than anything. His rigid dick stroking her most intimate depths felt better than anything, better even than his tongue teasing and licking her clitoris, or her own fingertips crushing her body's little seed so she could enjoy the beautiful sensation of an orgasm blooming between her legs. When he was fucking her like this she didn't care at all about coming; the overwhelming experience was an end in itself with psychological roots too profound to analyze as he rammed himself to the very soul of her flesh. There seemed no difference between her imagination and her skin while she was possessed by a handsome virile man, so even though it was Chris's hard-on in her cunt, she also felt as though Drew was there making love to her... as though he was there watching and appreciating her long legs and wantonly arched back and trembling breasts ... she could almost feel his penetrating regard mysteriously embracing her...

She knew when Chris began climaxing because the pleasure became almost devastating as he pulsed and swelled inside her clinging passage, relentlessly opening her up around him, and her cries of pleasure rose to the heavens where stars glimmered like divine sperm as he ejaculated deep in the dark space of her sex.

Chapter Fourteen

Maia felt as though all her turbulent emotions had become audible in the rumbling of thunder around Chris's little fairytale tree house. Images and events from the past few days flashed with a sinisterly vivid quality through her mind as she lay in bed without even the moon for company tonight. She could not shake the impression that the storm had its origin inside her, the almost continuous flashing and rumbling the generator of her own imaginative powers. She couldn't possibly sleep through it, yet Chris had drifted off peacefully a long time ago, essentially leaving her alone on the bed sheets' leaf-strewn shore even though his body was still lying beside hers. She could almost sense his adventuring subconscious floating somewhere in the night around her, anchored by his naked body. He lay on his side with his back to her, and the lamp she kept on for company evoked the setting sun at twilight behind the steep slope of his shoulder, smooth and warm as a desert dune.

Outside, lightning kept striking with a dangerous undiminished passion as the sky kept groaning...

She thought of Drew's black leather jacket... about the way it had gleamed beneath a street lamp like wet asphalt as he watched her walking away, disappearing into the darkness with Chris...

Careful not to wake her lover, she got up to use the bathroom and to attempt to relieve herself of fantasies for a few moments, fantasies that were at once exciting and tormenting. She told herself it shouldn't matter to her that Chris was just a bit odd. Everyone had quirks. Nobody was normal, not really. She had also read somewhere that nothing is known, only imagined, and lately she was feeling the truth of these words acutely. In any case, normal was synonymous with dull and she wanted no part of a mundane life.

She accidentally tugged out a long white carpet of toilet paper as a deafening clap of thunder made her jump. Her lover's house was surrounded by large old trees and she knew from experience how attracted lightning was to them.

As always, after washing and towel drying her hands, she paused to gaze at her face in the little oval mirror hanging over the seashell-shaped sink. Her sense of self perched proudly on the lovely branch of her smile, and then her pulse soared at the thought of Drew lying in his bed somewhere not too far away. If everything he said was true, they had somehow met in another dimension years ago when he succeeded in the haunting task of luring her soul back into her body. Was this why his slightest gesture was almost too intense for her, because the supernatural intimacy they had somehow shared still had a devastating effect on her sensual wiring even now?

Maia finally switched off the light in the tiny bathroom and slipped back into bed beside Chris. Even though she could scarcely wrap her brain around it, she had to admit part of her desperately wanted everything Drew had said to be true. Disturbing as his story was, she was determined to see him again and get all the details about their supernatural encounter. She also very much wanted to ask him about this modern group of Druids he belonged to, and why her father had not been at all happy with him even though he should have been grateful to Drew for awakening his sleeping daughter…

Reality was torn violently in half as a blinding bolt of lightning struck directly outside the window followed instantly by the deafening sound of the atmosphere being ripped open.

Chris rolled towards her and opened his eyes with a smile on his face…

She screamed as the night of her accident came back to her in full force recorded by the storm's photographic flashes in terrifying detail that made her relive all the shock and pain by way of a series of swift images flashing like a movie on her desperately closed eyelids… then dimensions closed up again just as abruptly and there was only the sound of the rain drumming on the roof and beating on the leaves of the forest and generally soothing the world…

'Lightning struck one of the trees outside,' Chris murmured sleepily, 'that's all, there's no reason to be afraid.'

She crossed her arms over her chest trying to breathe normally as she told herself she was only imagining the cramp-like pain in her womb, yet she suddenly couldn't understand what she was doing in this totally unreal bedroom. During the storm's endless eerie winks, the silhouette of the tree in the wall seemed to open all its dark arms just for her, and suddenly the sense of being trapped inside a huge tree trunk was more than she could bear. She flung the sheet off her gasping, 'I have to get out of here!'

'What's wrong with you, Maia?' Chris gripped her arm and effortlessly prevented her from rising. 'It's just a bloody storm.'

'Everything's wrong!' She almost hated him for not understanding how she felt. He knew her accident had happened on a night like this. She wanted Drew, he would understand. She needed Drew. She needed to talk to him again...

Chris sat up abruptly, and took her in his arms. He held her tightly, but to her horror the bed had transformed into the front seat of a car again from where she watched with hopeless fascination as the lightning's silver sword defeated the mighty oak tree's centuries-old armor with three swift slashes...

'Maia, what's wrong, sweetheart? You're trembling.'

She moaned and tried to push him away the way she had struggled to push open the car door, but there was no time. Sinisterly determined to get to her, the tree's gnarled old arms swooped possessively towards her and cracked the roof of the car as easily as an eggshell. One of the heavy limbs struck her directly across the womb, and then she was only vaguely aware of her body writhing beneath its weight like a fledgling fallen from its nest as the sky wept over her, mourning the death of the tree while baptizing her entrance into another world as her eyes closed...

The warm and comforting kiss of sunlight on her eyelids woke her to the loud hissing of the shower.

She lay staring up at the faraway ceiling impatient for Chris to leave for his

Rituals of Surrender

workshop so she could drive to Carol's house and use the phone there. Once again she looked over at her small snakeskin purse where it sat on his desk. Last night it had swallowed the napkin with the mysterious nourishment of Drew's phone number written on it and the hunger to get in touch with him was the only thing motivating her this morning.

Chris held her in his arms for a long time after rousing her from her nightmare. Her dream had felt so real she believed herself to be awake. Strangely enough, it was the first time she had ever dreamed about her near fatal accident and she sincerely hoped it was the last time. She had no desire to suffer through it again in such excruciating detail.

Her lover emerged from the bathroom with wildly towel-dried hair and his fine skin beaten rosy by the hot water. 'How are you feeling?' His usually smooth brow furrowed with concern as he gazed down at her.

'I'm okay, I guess.' Her gaze was irresistibly drawn down to his crotch. Even in repose his penis was impressively thick and long nestled against his scrotum. She had never realized before how luxuriously attractive a man's sexual organ could be, especially when framed by a tall and ideally proportioned body.

'That was quite a nightmare you had last night,' he commented, turning his back on her on his way to the closet.

She admired the way his broad shoulders tapered down to slender hips and the tightest, sweetest little ass she had never seen on a man, but then again she hadn't seen all that many naked male buttocks.

'Do you often dream about that night, Maia?' His question was muffled by the contents of his closet as he chose his outfit for the day.

'No, I don't, thank God.' She was trying to find the energy to get up and shower, but she had become lazy as a cat lately, lying around all day waiting for Chris to come back and doing nothing useful in the interim. But today would be different. She was going to call Drew, and she was going to see him again, she had to.

Chris stepped out of the closet tugging on a pair of tight black jeans and she wondered at how nicely he always dressed just to go to his shop, where he never seemed to get dirty. Come to think of it, she had ever seen him come home with even a speck of sawdust on his shirt...

'So, what are your plans for today?' He smiled brightly at her over the black T-shirt he slipped on.

'I'm going over to Carol's,' she replied, and guilt at her lie propelled her out of bed.

'Paying the little aunt a visit, eh?'

'Yes... I'm going to shower now.'

'Hey.' He grabbed her as she attempted to walk past him, and pressed her naked body against his fully clothed one. 'Don't I get a kiss goodbye first?'

He seemed to be looking down at her sadly, but she told herself it was only her guilty imagination imbuing his expression with such profound regret. He could not possibly know she was planning to call Drew, and even if he did know, all she wanted to do was talk to him again... She quickly reached up on tiptoe to kiss him on the lips, and as usual they were coolly unresponsive. 'Have a lovely day,' she said sweetly, wondering how Drew's mouth would respond to hers. She was sure he would kiss her back.

'Be good, Maia,' Chris said, letting go of her, and his quiet voice paradoxically rang in her head all through her shower, and as she dressed, and during the drive to her little old aunt's house.

※※※

'Maia, darling!' Carol looked infinitely relieved to see her. 'I should never have told you about your parents being Druids,' she chided herself. 'I should have left well enough alone and let them rest in peace and not broken their confidence since they obviously wanted to keep it a secret...'

'Carol, relax. You can't possibly be serious? Of course you did the right thing in telling me. I should have been told a long time ago.' She slipped into her usual seat at the kitchen table and carefully unfolded the precious napkin neatly stained with ink – the vital row of numbers that would enable her to get in touch with Drew again. She wanted to wait until at least ten o'clock to call her parents' old friend in case he liked to sleep late. 'Auntie,' she could make use of that time, 'did you ever meet a man named Drew Landson?'

Rituals of Surrender

Carol swiftly made the sign of the cross and nearly collapsed into a chair. 'How...?' She put a wrinkled hand over her eyes.

Maia couldn't help but be gratified by the dramatic effect her simple question had. 'I met him last night,' she added casually.

Her aunt looked at her in weary confusion. 'Last night?'

'At the restaurant where–'

'Oh my word!' She looked up at the blank white ceiling as though it was a Cathedral painted with angels who had all betrayed her.

'Then you have met him.'

'Oh no, I never actually him!'

'But you know of him, obviously,' Maia insisted.

'Yes, unfortunately I do.' She rubbed her bad knee fervently.

'Carol, what happened? He says that–'

'Don't listen to him, Maia, please.' She sounded a little calmer now and yet somehow even more desperate. 'Whatever you do, don't fall under his spell like your mother did.'

'Mummy was...?' Her stomach suddenly felt queasy; secrets were definitely not the best thing to have for breakfast. 'Mummy didn't–?' She could hardly think it much less say it.

Carol's eyes widened in horror. 'Never! How could you think such a thing about your own mother?'

'I didn't... Carol, remember when I was unconscious for a month after our accident?' She spoke carefully, afraid of further shattering her aunt's peace of mind with her hunger for information on the past, which had not been the normal domestic nest she had believed it to be. 'Drew said he helped bring me back... I mean, he said he helped wake me up from my coma. Is that true?'

'That's what he wanted your parents to believe, but as far as I'm concerned, it was that wonderful doctor who saved you, Dr. Christianson, Dr. Eric Christianson, a very handsome, hardworking young man he was. He stayed with you night and day, never left your side. The poor boy nearly died of exhaustion. All Drew ever did was sleep in your bed and fill your room with his foul cigarette smoke!'

'Really?' Maia realized she was smiling at the thought of Drew in her bedroom.

'And then...' Carol angrily caressed her bad knee again. 'To this day I cannot believe your father permitted it!'

'Permitted what?' Maia asked breathlessly, glancing up at the clock. It was ten o'clock. If she called Drew now there was still a chance she might wake him (he looked like the sort of man who liked to stay up half the night and sleep in) yet she didn't think she could stand to wait much longer and there was always the chance she might miss him...

'He asked,' Carol went on tightly, 'or rather he commanded that you be taken out of the hospital and brought back to your bedroom.' She shook her head, her disbelief and disapproval still as sharp now as they had been at the time. 'Even Stella finally hesitated to do as he said, but in the end she obeyed a relative stranger, simply because he called himself a high priest, instead of listening to her own husband. How she managed to convince Peter I will never know.'

Maia said in wonder, 'I do seem to recall a funny smell in my room when I woke up...'

'I'm sure there was.' She snorted derisively. 'That man smoked like a chimney.'

'Then it's true, he did somehow manage to bring me back.'

'Nonsense, you were in Doctor Christianson's hands for weeks and you were with that charlatan for one night. You would have come around in the hospital if Stella hadn't somehow convinced Peter to move you. It was only a coincidence you woke up when you did.' She frowned, and then blurted out the fact at the root of her indignation, 'You woke up in that man's arms! Thank God the neighbors never had any idea what your parents had permitted. I was even more thankful you didn't remember anything of the affair yourself.' She paused, looking more distressed than angry now. 'I shouldn't even be telling you any of this...'

'Oh please, Carol, go on, I have a right to know.'

'Hmm... well, he said to Stella that you opened your eyes for a moment at around one o'clock in the morning and smiled at him, but that you didn't come around completely for another three hours. Yet in my opinion, if it wasn't for that man none of it would have happened, not the accident, not any of it.'

Rituals of Surrender

'But Carol, how can you say that? It can't possibly be his fault that a tree was-'
'Oh yes it can.' She looked down at her bad knee as she intoned somberly, 'To this day I believe that man somehow had a hand in that storm!'

Chapter Fifteen

It was unusually cold for May, but the sun was shining as it rarely ever did in Stoneshire. However, Maia's conscience was nowhere near as clear as the sky. She was afraid Chris knew exactly what she was up to today, and she had always been a terrible liar. One way or another, she was destined to confess her indiscretion to him later, but she simply had to see Drew again, so here she was sitting in the front seat of his car.

His black vinyl jacket was mesmerizing, but everything about him seemed to have that effect on her. Swift silver snakes of light kept slipping up his arms and around his chest her eyes enjoyed following all over him as the sun played on the shiny material. It was only eleven o'clock in the morning, but he looked dressed for a nightclub in black wrap-around sunglasses. Even when his profile was turned towards her she couldn't see his eyes; all she could see was the reflection of trees flowing swiftly down a dark and narrow channel. Despite her shy efforts to concentrate on the colorful world flowing by outside the windows, she ended up staring at him most of the drive. She kept waiting for him to say something, but he seemed content to concentrate on the road. Like Chris, he paid absolutely no attention to the speed limit. They were going so fast, she was having a hard time holding on to any particular thoughts in the emotional rush and couldn't think of anything to say herself.

'You know, Drew,' she spoke up finally, 'my aunt is terrified of you.' She could still scarcely believe Carol's morally paranoid fantasy that Drew magically helped orchestrate the storm which caused their accident that stormy night when lightning felled an old oak tree. The idea was so ridiculous it was almost exciting.

'I know she is,' he replied placidly. 'Stella told me how Carol felt about me

Rituals of Surrender

and about the strange idea she got in her head that I had something to do with that storm, but I'm not Zeus or Thor, Maia. I can't command lightning.'

'I read somewhere once about a man who was struck by lightning years ago and hasn't worn a coat since then because he doesn't feel the cold anymore.'

'Lucky bastard.'

'Oh I don't know, I think it would be dull not to be able to experience contrasting sensations.'

'You're right, it would.'

She laughed. 'Make up your mind.'

'I made up my mind a long time ago never to make up my mind. A room that's too neatly arranged isn't lived in.'

'That makes very good sense, Drew.'

'You're a delightful young woman, Maia.'

'Thank you, but I wasn't fishing for a compliment. Where are you taking me?'

'I'm not taking you anywhere. We're both going somewhere together. Or do you prefer the idea of being taken?'

'I think most women do,' she confessed on behalf of her entire gender so it would seem less like a personal revelation on her part.

'I thought a picnic would prove a pleasant outing on such a beautiful day.'

'A picnic? You should have told me, Drew, I would have brought something...'

'I've taken care of it. We've got all we need in the trunk. Your aunt's opinion of me notwithstanding, I'm actually a pretty cool guy.'

'I believe you,' she murmured.

'Why?' he asked just as quietly.

'I don't know... I just do.'

'How do you know you're not just feeling what you want to feel about me?'

'I don't know,' she repeated, biting her lip uncertainly. She had been wondering that herself lately about Chris, the beautiful stranger who had saved her from spending the night in a graveyard and whom she had consequently knighted her true love as he knelt before the beautifully carved cabinet containing his spirits. She had only met Drew last night, yet already he was making her wonder if she was only imagining Chris was the prince of her dreams because he was like no other man she had ever met before... because he fucked her like she had never been fucked before...

'Think about it, Maia. How do you know when you're actually sensing what a person is like,' he sounded rather like a teacher privately tutoring his favorite student, 'as opposed to when you're just feeling what you want to feel about them?'

'Well...' She sought an answer in vain and concluded it had to be a trick question. 'But you can't draw a line like that, can you, since I can't ever really know you, can I? Who you are to me will always, in a sense, be part of my imagination, of my way of perceiving the world. So maybe there isn't only one you.' She warmed to the concept. 'It could be there's as many of each of us as there are other people to perceive and experience us, so even though the unique seed of our being is mysteriously inviolate, there are still as many variations of us out there as there are minds in which our existence is planted... Wow.' She smiled, impressed with herself.

'What you're saying then is that an aspect of my being or personality is in fact the evil sorcerer Carol perceives?'

'Oh no, I didn't mean that...'

He smiled.

She was dismayed. 'Okay, it was a stupid theory,' she conceded.

'Nothing you say is stupid, Maia. In a sense, you're right.'

She fervently wished they would get where they were going so he would stop concentrating on the road and look at her. 'Drew, are you going to tell me more today about how you... how you saved me?' she finally dared to ask.

'I'll tell you anything you want to hear,' he answered in a sexy voice that flowed like liquid gold down the center of her body and made her feel infinitely precious. 'Just don't believe all of it,' he warned.

'Why not?' she asked, and decided he was teasing her. Then she was distracted from pressing him for an answer when she spotted a lovely sapphire-colored lake set in the rough emerald of the forest. And apparently, the lake was their destination because he turned off the road onto a dirt path. Although it also made her somewhat nervous, she was pleased to see there was not another soul in sight as he parked at the edge of the clearing and switched off the engine.

Rituals of Surrender

Shivering in the cold breeze despite the protection of her red sweater, Maia watched Drew pull everything they needed out of his small black car – a red blanket, a large white wicker basket (both of which he handed to her) and a silver wine cooler that made her think of an ancient urn. 'You certainly come prepared,' she observed, setting down the basket and helping him spread the blanket out at the edge of the trees, as far from the chilling breeze blowing off the water as possible. She anchored the edges down with some rocks she found lying conveniently nearby, and then cursed herself for wearing a short white dress as she seated herself on the crimson sheet. Wanting to look casual and sexy for him, she had not had a picnic in mind when she dressed that morning. She also hadn't realized it was so brisk outside when she slipped on red strap sandals. She bent her knees and wrapped her arms around her legs trying to ignore how chilled her bare feet were already.

Drew was much better dressed for the elements in his black vinyl jacket, black jeans and a pair of black boots that looked like they could do serious damage if he decided to kick someone. He seated himself comfortably cross-legged beside her and gave her a look she couldn't read since only the lake was reflected in his sunglasses. She was about to ask him to take them off when it fully dawned on her that she enjoyed how mysterious he looked in them. It wasn't until she began seeing Chris, then was introduced to Eric Wolfson and after that to Drew Landson, that she had fully realized what an aphrodisiac a man's clothes could be for her. She wondered if it made her superficial that what a man wore affected her so deeply, and decided she didn't give a damn if it dead.

'I love your outfit, Drew,' she confessed. 'I wish all men dressed like that.'

'Let's make ourselves comfortable.' He unzipped his jacket, revealing the fine silver chain she had noticed resting against his chest last night. 'You might be in a lot of trouble,' he added quietly, and the old wicker emitted a high-pitched scream as he flung open the basket.

His sexy threat shifted her pulse into high gear and she shivered. Fortunately, there wasn't a cloud in the sky so the sun was able to rest a bracingly warm hand on her shoulders. 'It's cold,' she said, then coughed self-consciously. 'And I'm not just saying that so you'll feel obliged to keep me warm,' she elaborated, defending her virtue without much conviction. She was not surprised to find herself completely unable to resist when he placed one of his hands on the back of her head, and brought it gently down to rest against his chest, forcing her to shift her position on the blanket slightly. Her bent legs now rested against his as she awkwardly kept her hands clenched in her lap.

'Where should I begin, Maia?' he asked quietly. The wind was running curious fingers through her hair, and he smoothed it down gently across her back waiting for an answer.

'At the beginning,' she murmured, because already it was an effort for her to speak. Resting against his solid warmth made her feel so safe and relaxed it was almost like being drugged. Then she shivered again, but for a completely different reason, as she felt his hand slowly following the curve of her hip. 'No...' she whispered.

'It's all right,' he whispered back.

She watched the surface of the lake trembling as subtle waves of pleasure and contentment flowed through her beneath his light caress. Whatever he said now would feel as irrelevant as stones tossed into the water. All that mattered now was the power of his physical presence and the infinite promise of his touch. She couldn't tell whether the water was shallow or deep and she didn't care. She was curved like an embryo against him with her hands crossed at the wrists resting limply against her thighs.

'You know the story of Red Riding Hood, Maia?' he asked abruptly.

'Yes, of course I do.'

'Well, I'll tell you a secret.'

'Mm?'

'All fairytales are metaphysical lessons, equations summing up the magical relationship between energy and matter, soul and flesh. The wolf was actually a handsome man.'

'I'm sure he was.' She saw Carol's worried, wrinkled face in the rippling water lapping restlessly against the shore of the lake. 'I read somewhere that the story of Red Riding Hood is all about sex,' she added, staring down at her hands wondering when they would find the courage to move out of her lap and begin exploring him as gently and respectfully as his hand kept wandering up and down her back...

'Yes, but what is sex all about?'

'You tell me, Drew.'

'In sex, opposing metaphysical forces come together and create the dimension of experience. The wolf was wild and hungry, wasn't he? He thought only about himself and how he could get what he desired. In this context the beast is our own imagination, isn't it, Maia? We all know how powerful our fantasies can be, how swiftly and greedily they cross our minds without any consequences; we can sink our teeth into one pleasure after.'

'Mm, yes...'

'Now, that poor old grandmother's life was very limited, she was bedridden and dependent on Red Riding Hood for her nourishment, hence she stands for the boundaries of mortal existence and the grave we'll all rest in one day. But don't worry, the wolf devours her, which means that our imaginative powers can learn to use the limits of time and space in order to more fully appreciate and enjoy our mysterious nature.'

'If Carol heard you talking now she'd know she was right about you, Drew.'

'It's obvious Red Riding Hood's cloak is the blood-filled body,' he went on, clearly unperturbed by what Carol or anyone else might think of him, 'which her innocent energy slips on at the morning of every life, and the basket of fresh fruit she brings her grandmother every day represents all the pleasures of the physical senses.'

'But what does it mean that the wolf wants to eat her?'

He pulled gently on her hair to lift her face to his and looked silently down into her eyes, his own eyes still hidden behind the darkly reflective panes of his sunglasses.

'Tell me,' she whispered, but what she was really hoping for was the wordless explanation for everything that would be his lips moving against hers in a kiss.

'You tell me,' he said firmly.

'He wants to eat her because...' She felt she should be able to pluck the answer from somewhere inside her like a perfectly ripe apple juicy with meaning. 'He wants to eat her because if he eats her he won't be hungry anymore?'

'Why won't he be hungry anymore?'

'Because she's pure spirit, always skipping along and singing... to the wolf she's everything he could possibly desire, which is what fantasizing is all about... he wants to rip the flesh off her bones just as we long to wrest everything we desire from life's hard facts. What you said about her slipping on her red cloak like a body at the morning of every life, well, what the wolf, what our deepest self wants is this magical sensual power free of all responsibilities and consequences.'

'He's the devil, isn't he?'

'Yes, and he's so sexy...' She closed her eyes as his mouth finally opened over hers. His tongue was somehow both cool and warm, quenching her thirst and satisfying her hunger all at the same time, but the kiss did not last nearly long enough. She was too disappointed to protest when his lips abandoned hers as he leaned forward to reach for the wine. The dark bottle beaded with moisture from the melting ice in the cooler looked beautiful in his hand, as though it was sweating stars, and he suddenly seemed impossibly far away from her even though she was sitting pressed up against him. He removed his sunglasses, and without thinking she snatched them up curiously to slip them on. 'Wow,' she declared as the world was washed a brilliant violet color casting royal purple shadows.

'Careful.' He yanked the glasses off her and shoved them into an inside pocket of his jacket. Then he returned the wine to the cooler for a moment to slip out of the shining vinyl. 'You're just like a kitten,' he teased soberly.

'Why did you tell me all that about Red Riding Hood, Drew?'

'Why not?'

'Seriously.'

'What's the matter, didn't you find it seriously interesting?'

'Yes, but what does it mean, really... I mean to me, personally?'

'That's entirely up to you, Maia. Let's have some wine.'

She took this as a signal to reluctantly separate herself from him. But then

Rituals of Surrender

she was glad she did because now she could look at him in the sleeveless black leather T-shirt he was wearing. She had to agree with him, she was like a kitten, because she wanted desperately to run her nails across his pale skin, which looked fine as silk stretched over the smooth rocks of his muscles. She had to resist the urge to curl over his lap, impatiently peel away the tough shell of his black jeans, and begin licking him clean of any thoughts that did not revolve around her. She was eager to continue honing her oral skills and what better way than to practice on two men at once? There was also Eric Wolfson's potentially gorgeous cock to consider, for she was sure she could learn a great deal sucking him down…

Suddenly, Maia could not believe what she was thinking. She had never had such slutty thoughts in all her life.

'You called me so early, I didn't have a chance to have breakfast,' Drew said, handing her a lovely crystal wine glass. 'So let's indulge in some food and conversation first.'

'First?' she echoed haughtily, turning her back on the water as she slid farther away from him on the blanket, but it was really so she could face him as they ate and drank.

'After all,' he tossed a hunk of soft white cheese between them, 'there's a lot to talk about.'

'I'm listening.'

Chapter Sixteen

'Does Chris know where you are?' Drew asked her as he filled her glass with a beautifully clear white wine.

'No, he doesn't.' The stab of guilt she suffered somehow only sharpened her appetite for this other man. 'Actually, he probably does, even though I didn't tell him. I think he can read my mind.' She wasn't joking.

'Or maybe you're just not good at hiding what you feel.' He peeled the shining plastic skin off the cheese.

She considered this. 'No, I get the feeling he's a touch psychic.'

'We all are. It's a muscle everyone possesses, but which most people haven't learned to use, much less develop, yet.'

'He wasn't at all surprised when I told him about my parents being modern Druids. In fact, he looked rather pleased.'

Drew pulled a pocketknife out of his jacket and cut into the tender white block of cheese.

'He told me he wasn't, but is he... is Chris one too?' She cast a frightened glance at the interlaced branches of the trees above them as she suddenly thought she glimpsed a sinister sensual web being spun around her.

'No, he's not.'

The world shifted out of the painfully sharp focus in which only her feelings had been a confused, vulnerable blur. 'I want to trust you, Drew,' she said earnestly, 'yet you told me yourself not to believe everything you said.'

'Maybe you shouldn't believe that either, Maia.'

'Oh that's a good one.' She laughed. 'Talking to you is like being lost in a maze.'

Rituals of Surrender

'And you have to find your own way out.'

'Not necessarily. Didn't I need your help just to get in touch with my body again when I was in that coma? Wasn't that what we were going to talk about? Instead you give me a lesson on the metaphysical meaning of the Red Riding Hood fairytale.'

'I suppose in your case it was more like Sleeping Beauty.'

She smiled despite herself. She had always wondered what sort of dreams the sleeping princess lived in for a hundred years. Maybe Aurora dreamed the birth of her savior in a far away land, her eyelashes flickering as she slept brushing him like invisible wings were he knelt in the shadowy chapel of his castle, candles glimmering around him like the whites of her eyes, which had been veiled by the snow-covered hills of her lids for over a century...

'Come back to me, Maia and have something to eat.' He gently insinuated a piece of cheese between her lips. 'Come on,' he insisted, 'digesting is as vital as dreaming.'

'No, thank you, I'm not hungry.' She set her wine carefully down in the grass, planting the stem in the earth like a glass flower so she could bend her legs into a pyramid against her chest and wrap her arms around herself.

'You're completely fulfilled by fantasies, are you?'

'What do you mean?' She was both annoyed and intrigued by the question and his superior, almost taunting, tone.

'Wouldn't you like the real thing?'

'Of course I would.' She relaxed into a cross-legged position, but once more her fingers embraced each other with a nervous restlessness in the hollow of her lap.

'Do you want me?'

She quickly picked her glass up again to avoid his eyes, unsettled by his straightforward, almost brutal, honesty.

'Has it occurred to you, Maia that what you think is the past might really be the present in which you're imagining all this? You asked me how I brought you back into your body...' Their glasses chimed a pristine musical note in the beautiful morning as he touched his to hers in a toast, the atmosphere clear and taut as a string played on by the breeze. 'Maybe that's what I'm doing right now.'

In a burning flash of indignation she emptied her glass of wine across his chest like someone instinctively trying to put out a fire. 'You have no right to play with me like this, Drew!' she cried, then was immediately ashamed of her unbelievably rude gesture, yet she had had no control over herself for a blinding instant. 'Oh God, I'm sorry!' she said miserably. 'I don't... I don't know why I did that...' Her lack of self-control seriously worried her.

His only reaction was to glance down at his chest, glistening with wine like a divine perspiration. 'You'd better tell me how sorry you are for wasting perfectly good wine, Maia.'

For some reason his placid attitude roused a defiant response in her again. 'It's only fitting, isn't it? I mean, I wasted a perfectly good month of my life when I was asleep in the hospital, didn't I? What's a little wine compared to a whole month of my life?'

'There were years stored in that particular bottle, which was quite expensive, by the way. It contained months of ideal weather and soil conditions it was foolish to waste.'

'I'm sorry,' she declared, but she wasn't; she was angry with him for remaining so calm while managing to disturb her so profoundly.

'Too late,' he said coldly.

She lay her empty glass down on the blanket like a dead queen in Chess and searched the wicker basket for a napkin to dry him off with. She found one made of fine white linen, and kneeling beside him she quickly applied it to his chest trying not to let herself become distracted by the muscular firmness of his pecs almost completely exposed by his loose black T-shirt.

'That's enough.' He drained his glass, planted it upright in the grass, and stood up abruptly.

'Oh please don't be mad at me, Drew,' she pleaded in despair. Forgetting her pride, she wrapped her arms around his thighs and pressed her cheek shamelessly against his crotch. The fact that his hands came to rest gently on her head reassured her, and the hard-on buried in his jeans she could feel pressing against her soft cheek filled her with hope. 'I'm so sorry,' she murmured, 'but... but you scared me saying that. I won't do anything like that again though, I promise. I

Rituals of Surrender

want to keep talking to you. I need to talk to you, Drew, please don't leave me.'

'I wasn't planning to leave you, Maia. I just thought you might enjoy a little dip in the lake.'

She looked up at him in astonishment. 'But the water must be freezing!'

He peeled her arms from around him. 'Yes, it probably is,' he agreed, grasping her hands and pulling her to her feet. Then he turned her around and yanked her sweater off before she could even protest. She felt him grip the hem of her dress and still she didn't say anything. He paused a moment as if waiting for her to resist him somehow, but her body language must have told him he could go as far and as fast with her as he wanted to. She willingly raised her arms as he lifted her plain white dress up over her head, and then closed her eyes in anticipation as she felt him hook his thumbs into the elastic of her white cotton panties. She could scarcely believe she was letting a man she had only met last night take off all her clothes in the middle of the woods, and she shivered in the throes of an excitement that felt like the cold edge of a knife's blade licking up her spine and terrifying her even as it gave her the thrill of her life. Because of course he wasn't a total stranger, both her mother and father had known him, her parents had been his friends, and it was because she sensed beyond a shadow of a doubt that she was perfectly safe with him that it turned her on so much to pretend she was letting a dangerous stranger have his way with her. The truth was he was only doing what she wanted him to as he slowly slipped her panties down her legs while deliberately letting only the backs of his thumbs teasingly caress her skin.

She stepped gracefully out of her delicate undergarment. She was getting good at stripping outdoors, balancing on the uneven ground in her high-heels. She was also growing increasingly proud and fond of her body, which seemed to possess much more of a mysterious personality naked than it did clothed. The pert white mounds of her breasts looked so pretty crowned with pink nipples that relished the kiss of cold air so much they became almost obscenely long, and her labial lips also enjoyed being made even more acutely aware of her inviting, innermost warmth. She had been shaving her pussy for a long time, initially for aesthetic reasons, but now also because she knew Chris preferred her sex smooth and naked. As an artist, she had wanted her body to possess the sensual flawlessness of a statue's and she had shaved between her legs in order to better appreciate the sight of her full little pudenda in the mirror. She had even sat in front of the glass once with her legs spread wide open so she could gaze in wonder at the gently gaping mouth of her sex, the mysterious cleft in her flesh where so many aspects of the natural world metaphorically converged as the sight of her rosy vulva made her think of a seashell haunted by the ocean's wet and salty depths... yet it was also like the heart of an exotic orchid... or like the entrance to an enchanted cave glistening with bio-luminescent bacteria...

'You're so beautiful,' Drew whispered in her ear, 'and I mean that in every sense, Maia.' He was still standing behind her, still teasing her, this time with his lack of urgency to see all the most delectable parts of her body she had willingly let him expose. His warm heavy caress passed slowly down her arms. 'I want you,' he admitted, his fingers thrusting between hers, and she whimpered as he grasped her hands with all his strength. 'I want you all for myself, Maia.'

She longed to turn around and embrace him, but she was pinned helplessly back against him, increasingly tormented by the warm feel of his breath on her cheek and the knowledge that he was tall enough to be able to look down and see her breasts aching for his touch. She desperately wished he would stop talking, which kept forcing her to think, and she didn't want to think right now, not about Chris or about Eric or about anything. Yet she couldn't just beg him to fuck her like she begged Chris to fuck her. What she felt for this modern Druid priest was already too deep. It didn't matter that she was living with another man. All that had seemed to matter to her since she met him last night was what Drew wanted, what Drew thought about everything, what Drew thought about her and what Drew wanted from her...

'But before we can be together, Maia there's something you have to do for me first.'

She looked over at the lake. The water did indeed look cold, much too cold for a casual dip, and certainly much too frigid to play in for long. He abruptly let go of her hands and she dared to hope he would turn her around and do something to her, anything he wanted. She was not expecting him to literally

Rituals of Surrender

sweep her off her feet into his arms. The way he snatched her up was not romantic, it was sudden and urgent, as though he was pulling her body out of some imminent danger.

She gasped, 'What are you doing?' and then cried, 'No, put me down!' as he strode towards the water with her and she suddenly knew what a cat felt like when faced with a bath. Her skin was already covered with goose bumps in a useless evolutionary throwback to fish scales as it tried to prepare itself for the water's icy embrace. 'Drew, please, what are you doing?' she repeated, her arms wrapped around his neck, and it felt so good to be so close to him, to be holding onto him for all she was worth, that her body languidly surrendered to his superior strength without caring that her brain was seriously worried about what he was planning to do with her. Her ability to think was further undermined by a wonderful sensory overload... the soft caress of his hair falling over her fingers clinging to his firm neck... the sharp buckle of his belt giving her naked belly stimulating little nips... the warm tenderness of his flesh beneath the cool reptile skin of his black leather T-shirt... and best of all, the hard gravity of his arms surrounding her... 'You're not really going to throw me in, are you, Drew? I could catch my death in there.'

Her choice of words seemed to affect him because a faint web of frown lines formed between his dark eyebrows that captured all her attention as he paused just a few feet from the water. 'You'll catch your death,' he repeated, looking intently down into her eyes. 'That's not what you want is it, Maia?'

'Of course not, but that's what will happen if you let go of me, Drew.'

His smile was strange, a brief flash of upturned lips that did not send the slightest spark of amusement up into his eyes.

'What are you thinking?' she asked, abruptly wondering why she trusted this man so implicitly. Carol had warned her about falling under his spell the way her mother had, and yet here she was, naked in his arms in the middle of nowhere with absolutely no one around to help her should he desire to hurt her. She was lying to her lover, who believed she was innocently visiting her little old aunt today, and yet she was foolish enough to trust everything a stranger said to her even when he himself had warned her not to. Carol had verified the story of how

Drew exercised inexplicable supernatural skills to rescue her from a coma, and naturally she was grateful to him for that and intensely curious about how he had managed to meet her in another dimension, but his otherworldly sensibilities didn't necessarily make him a nice person in reality…

His whisper was barely audible over the rustling of the leaves, 'Are you frightened, Maia?'

'Yes, a little…' And yet she realized she was letting herself be scared only because she took a perverse pleasure in this fear, and this strange excitement was made possible by the fact that deep down she knew he would never hurt her, on the contrary.

'You should be afraid, Maia.'

'Why?' she asked, but her blood was purring through her body in a way that made it hard to think at all.

'Do you trust me?'

'Yes, Drew, I trust you.' Her eyes narrowed gazing up into his. Part of her felt languorous as a cat keeping the annoying nervous dog of her reason at bay, how profoundly peaceful she felt resting in his arms making it easy to ignore the protective barking of doubts and fears in the back of her mind.

'Will you do anything I ask you to do, Maia?'

'I… I don't know…'

He shifted her in his arms to bring her face even closer to his. 'Will you do anything I ask you to do, Maia?' he repeated urgently.

'Yes,' she answered fervently, and tried to kiss him.

He set her down abruptly. 'Then get your clothes back on.'

She swayed a little on her feet. 'What?' She was stunned. 'You're not still angry with me for-?'

'No, I'm not angry with you. I care about you, Maia.' He cupped her face passionately and possessively in his hands. 'Don't just give yourself away. You're worth a fight.'

'What do you mean?'

He pressed his mouth fiercely against hers and subjected her to a long, deep kiss that was exquisitely giving as well as demandingly forceful. Then leaving her

Rituals of Surrender

breathless, he walked back towards the blanket and picked her white dress up off the ground. 'If we stay here any longer,' he said, also snatching up her discarded panties, 'I'll do something we'll both regret.'

'I wouldn't regret it,' she said weakly as he approached her again.

'Yes, you would,' he insisted shortly, handing her back her clothes. 'You're not ready for me.'

She looked shyly down at her feet. 'Yes I am...'

He smiled as he gripped her chin and forced her to look up at him. 'Stop pouting and get dressed.' He ran the tip of his thumb teasingly between her lips. 'We'll talk again soon, I promise.'

Chapter Seventeen

Maia was sitting before one of Chris's wall-to-ceiling bookshelves, her thoughts flitting in rhythm with her pulse from one man to another making her feel light-headed as a butterfly wandering from stamen to stamen. But it was impossible to remain unaware of the danger lurking behind this uncontrolled blossoming of desire happening inside her, and of the evanescent nature of the stimulating situation, because eventually she would be forced to choose one man, and if she didn't choose soon, she might lose all of them.

She stared fixedly at the dark-green binding of a large volume without really seeing the title, only vaguely aware that it was a book about the Celts.

She didn't want to be forced to choose, not so soon. She was hurt and disappointed at the time, but now she was relieved that Drew had not immediately indulged her willingness to be unfaithful to Chris. He dropped her back off at Carol's house, and after she paid her aunt another brief courtesy visit, she returned home early in the afternoon in order to fix her hardworking carpenter a delicious supper. They ate in silence. She could barely swallow the sinfully rich cauliflower-and-cheese with her guilt like a poison concealed in the savory dish mysteriously killing conversation between them. Chris had smiled at her while he chewed as though nothing was wrong, but he had not said a word, and she was sure she could see in his eyes that he somehow knew everything about her day.

He was reclining naked in bed now reading a book that hid his face from her, but she did not doubt he was much more intent on her concealed thoughts than on the printed text and only biding his time before he confronted her about her day.

Rituals of Surrender

'What are you daydreaming about, Maia?' He finally deigned to address her. 'You've been awfully quiet this evening.' He looked down at her from over the black rim of his book. 'What's wrong, sweetheart, did you have a hard day?'

Lying felt like a piece of glass resting on her tongue she had to get the words around. 'It was all right,' she replied.

'Well,' he rested the book on his lap, 'judging by the wonderful supper you fixed me, you got what you wanted, and yet on the other hand the despondent way you're sitting there staring at nothing would seem to indicate that perhaps you didn't.'

'I spent the morning with Drew because I wanted to ask him about my parents.' It was an intense relief to confess at least part of the truth.

'I imagined that's what you were up to.' He didn't appear in the least bit jealous. 'Did you find out anything else?'

'Not really.' This fact had begun to bother her. She should have questioned Drew more thoroughly and demanded clearer answers from him, instead she had just let him go on and on about Red Riding Hood…

'I'm not surprised.'

'And why is that?' Anger at his condescending tone prompted her to pull out the book she had been staring at blindly. It was so heavy she could barely lift it, so she let it fall open in her lap.

'Why am I not surprised he didn't tell you more? Because I'm sure he had other plans for his tongue.'

'You have a filthy mind, Christopher Thorn.' She couldn't look at him.

'And you love it, so stop sounding like your dear old aunt.'

'Leave Carol out of this, please.'

'Gladly.'

'I asked Drew if you were a member of this cult,' she confessed. 'I asked him if you were a Druid, too.' She found herself wondering about how closely the word 'cult' resembled the word 'cunt', a harsh, cynical sound that seemed to deny a woman's inner self any sacred dimension.

'And what did he tell you?'

'He told me the truth,' she replied casually, hoping to trick him into revealing it, but all he said was, 'I see' and she felt a cold wave of dread wash through her. Desperately, as though it might offer her a life-line out of the terrible sinking feeling inside her, she focused down on a sentence in the book spread open across her lap.

It seems clear that this ritual involved a young woman passing from her husband to a lover and back again, just as nature passes from summer to winter and back to summer again, from a young man to an older rival.

'My God,' she whispered.

'Don't be so shocked, Maia. What's that Spanish expression... if it was a dog it would have bitten you. You gave this dog enough time to devour you.'

'Chris,' she looked over at him finally, 'Drew told me you weren't a Druid.'

'Then I'm afraid he didn't tell you the truth. You're mother was absolutely beautiful. She was a great loss to us.'

Maia slowly closed the book and occupied herself with the effort of slipping it back into its place on the shelf as her mind raced with the urgent efficiency of someone trying to dismantle a ticking time-bomb. She had made a mistake moving in with a man she didn't really know just because he was handsome and intelligent and sensitive to all her feelings and knew how to make love to her as no other man ever had... because he knew how to fuck her. Yet how could everything she felt be a mistake? And what did it matter that he considered himself a modern Druid if her parents had been involved in this cult, too? And calling it a 'cult' made it sound so negative and unhealthy. Why couldn't she think of it as a group, as a club, as something perfectly innocent? It was not innocent, however, that all she could think about was Drew and the way he had held her naked body against his... that all she could think about was the way she had felt with her head resting against his chest... that all she could think about was the way he had kissed her...

'Maia, I want you beside me, please. Why are you so far away?'

She got slowly to her feet, but then found she could not look at him again. He was so beautiful that resisting him was like trying to dance ballet on ice. It was possible to think clearly for herself only when she wasn't looking at him, when his penetrating stare wasn't weakening her own much too malleable willpower. She had to assert herself with him, so she stared courageously at the menacing silhouette of the tree in the wall. 'Why didn't you tell me before, Chris?'

'But I was telling you, Maia, in stages, in small, easy to swallow doses. I almost confessed when you told me Carol had revealed the secret about your parents, but I thought better of it. I didn't want to hit you with too much too fast. You seemed shocked, so I didn't dare add to your distress by saying "Oh by the way, I'm a Druid too". I thought it best to assuage your fears by telling you the truth, that these groups are really quite harmless. And contrary to what you might believe now, I hadn't planned on running into our amazingly talented high priest the other night at the restaurant.'

'But then why did he tell me you weren't...?' Maia realized she was more distressed by the fact that Drew had lied to her than by anything else. Exciting revelations and events were springing up around her lately as casually as dandelions, teaching her that the normal surface of life was actually sustained by deep, sensual roots that seemed to thrive in a secret darkness. The possibility that Drew might be lying to her threw dirt on all her most profound feelings and instincts and made her want to die. In twenty-four hours this enigmatic stranger had become the most important thing in her life. He was more important even than her ideal new lover, and she wasn't sure she could handle this turn of events. She had been so convinced she could be happy with Chris forever, but then this Druid high priest had come along with an unbelievable story about saving her in the past, and paradoxically killed her happiness and peace of mind in the present.

'Maia, didn't you hear me? I said I want you beside me. Come to bed, please.'

She turned slowly around to face him, but she kept her eyes downcast as she slipped out of one of his shirts. She let it fall to the floor at her feet and presented her naked, potentially unfaithful body up to his scrutiny as a form of penance, because it forced her to struggle against her natural shyness.

'Did you let him fuck you, Maia?' he asked quietly.

'No,' she replied firmly. There was no need to mention she had wanted Drew to make love to her. 'All we did was talk.'

'I don't believe that.'

She finally found the courage to meet his eyes. 'All he did was kiss me and that's the truth, Chris, I swear it.'

He smiled. 'What are you willing to swear by, Maia? Certainly not by the moon, "the inconstant moon that monthly changes in its circled orb, lest that thy love prove likewise variable".'

'"What should I swear by"?' She was proud to be able to quote Shakespeare right back at him, her head held high as she stood naked before him, the way his eyes caressed her making her thrillingly conscious of how desirable she was.

'"Do not swear at all",' his smiled deepened as he set the book he had been reading on the night table, '"or swear by thy gracious self…"'

'And you will believe me?'

'Probably not, but there's no need to torment yourself, my love. What we have together can last forever if you want it to. I'm not asking you to deny your desires, only to understand that love transcends them all. Love is not threatened by lust. Love is made even stronger by desire if you handle your thoughts and feelings properly.'

She went and crouched on the edge of the bed at his feet, unconsciously assuming a cat-like pose with her knees bent beneath her and her arms held straight in front of her supporting her while at the same time modestly concealing her nakedness. 'Chris, what do you mean by that?' She stared earnestly into his eyes in an effort to avoid the silent but indelible statement of his erection, which she couldn't quite bring herself to understand yet. As they spoke she had watched his cock swelling to life between his thighs, rearing its blind head and transforming the tender seed of his resting penis into a magnificent hard-on that told her more clearly than words how much their conversation excited him. She had not wanted to face it, but it was staring her so blatantly in the face now she had no choice. Her lover was aroused by the fact that other men wanted her and by her own guilty tormented longing to surrender her body to their lust.

He wasn't smiling anymore, but a spark of sinister amusement flashed in his eyes as he said, 'You'll come to understand it all in time, Maia.'

'But-'

'Stop thinking about it so much.' He grabbed one of her wrists and pulled her down into his arms. 'Just ride my cock like a good girl.'

'But-'

Rituals of Surrender

He gave her a quick, hard spank, but that was all it took to make her accept how wet and ready her pussy was for him. Her slick sex didn't care why she was so aroused. Her body didn't care whether it was thoughts of Drew or of Eric or of Chris that made her hole feel so achingly deep. All she wanted for the moment was relief from the emptiness this big, thick cock gave her as she grasped it by the base and guided it up inside her. Then she braced herself on his more yielding chest as she sank all the way down over his irresistible hardness.

'Ride me,' he commanded.

She sat up and flung her head back as she fully impaled herself on his erection challenging her deepest natural boundaries.

'Go on, baby, ride me,' he urged. 'Make yourself come…'

She wasn't at all sure she could bring herself to orgasm in this position, but she found herself more than willing to try as he supported her efforts to slide her pussy up and down his hard-on. She loved the feel of the thickest part of his rigid cock forcing her open around it, stretching the lips of her sex so her clitoris was forced to come out from hiding beneath its protective hood. Then she was surprised by how much her pleasure intensified when he reached up and trapped both her stiff nipples between his thumb and forefinger. He rubbed them slowly but firmly, giving them a hard squeeze occasionally, and it felt so painfully good she began stroking her clitoris with one hand while caressing his firm belly with the other. Her nipples felt like charged knobs directly connected to her cunt by a mysteriously sensual electricity because the instant he began turning them between his fingers, she felt a climax spark to life between her thighs she eagerly stoked into a blinding ecstasy with her fingertips.

'Mm,' he said when she finally grew quiet. 'Now it's my turn.' He eased her up off his erection and she rolled weakly onto her back beside him. 'Turn around,' he instructed, and she obeyed him languidly. 'That' it, just relax and spread your legs for me.'

She rested her cheek against the mattress and bent her arms around her head as she obeyed him. She moaned in trepidation when she felt his hard length brush the tender cheeks of her bottom, but thankfully it was the wet and welcoming mouth of her pussy he was after, and this time her moan was one of pure fulfillment as he thrust his cock into her from behind. The quality of the pleasure was different from every angle, and in this position she was able to fully experience and enjoy the feel of his erection pushing between her thighs and through the clinging folds of her labia to rend its way deep inside her.

'Oh yes,' she whispered, 'oh yes, yes…' She clutched the sheet to keep from sliding up the bed beneath the violent pounding of his hard hips against her soft ass as he climaxed, and she helped him milk every last drop of cum from his pulsing penis by squeezing him with her vaginal muscles. He spread his body breathlessly on top of hers, and she relished the feel of his heart beating against her skin. For a few timeless moments she was content, until thoughts began worming their way back into her brain and she found herself right where she had started – lying in bed with one man while thinking only of another.

Chapter Eighteen

'It might strike you as funny now, but it wasn't very amusing then, I can assure you.' Carol pulled her chin down against her chest in a stubborn gesture that always reminded Maia of Peter. 'Your father found that Landson fellow sitting on a red blanket spread out in the middle of your bedroom drinking a bottle of white wine with your favorite doll sitting across from him as though he was playing some sort of childish game. He had moved most of the furniture around in your room (without even asking your parents' permission I might add) yet Stella very calmly explained, as if it was the most natural thing in the world, that he had needed to reflect your entire bed in the mirror in order to use your blue-and-white comforter to evoke clouds reflected in a lake. You should have heard how matter-of-fact she sounded when she explained his actions. I loved your mother dearly, but she–'

'But she enjoyed her pagan games a little too much for your comfort,' Chris concluded for her.

Carol, Maia and Chris were all formally seated in the old woman's parlor. Maia and her aunt occupied the comfortable old couch, while Chris effortlessly dominated the small room from his position in a big old armchair facing them, almost like a witness on the stand.

'So, you were sixteen when you joined,' Maia addressed him, continuing the polite interrogation concerning his membership in a modern group of Druids as she tried very hard not to worry about Carol had just said... Drew must have deliberately driven her out to that lake yesterday so they could actually live what they had shared only as some kind of astral dream in the past... because obviously she was not lying unconscious on some hospital bed now dreaming, everything around her felt quite real and solid...

'Yes, I was sixteen when I joined,' Chris replied patiently, 'only a year before your mother left us, sadly enough.'

'When she was on her way to one of those...' Carol promptly brought up a fact she considered damning, but managed to stop herself from elaborating since she could offer no proof whatsoever to back up her suspicion.

'As I've tried to explain to you, Maia,' Chris went on serenely, 'your painful perspective of your parents' accident isn't the only one available to you. Dying together was a blessing for them. The pure force of their love ascended through the flames and left nothing behind for the worms. They were spared the slow decay of old age and the pain of separation.'

'I don't have to sit here and listen to this.' Carol attempted to rise, but her knee was bothering her more than usual today and Maia was easily able to hold her down by gently touching her hand.

'I apologize.' Chris bowed his head. 'It was not my intention to insult or upset you, Ms. Wilson, I was merely suggesting a more positive angle from which to view the painful matter of deceased loved ones.'

'My word, at least Peter still talked like a normal human being with real feelings! I ask you, young man, are you allowed to feel grief and remorse or can you always spin the cosmic wheel of fortune and come up with some winning formula to do away with such poor mortal reactions?'

Chris laughed, apparently genuinely amused, and the sunlight pouring in through a window formed a luminous aura around his blonde head that uncannily resembled a halo belying his devil-may-care attitude.

'If you two don't stop arguing,' Maia said impatiently, 'I'm never going to find out anything. I'm not interested in listening to a debate on Christianity vs. Paganism. That isn't the point here.'

'Well, if you manage to find a point,' Chris said, 'I'll sharpen it for you as best I can.'

Not permitting herself to be annoyed by his irreverent attitude, Maia tried to keep all the feeling out of her voice as she asked, 'What exactly are the duties of the high priestess in your... religion?'

'I'm afraid the term "exactly" doesn't apply as there is no exact division between the worlds and as high priestess Stella acted as a bridge between them.'

'And how did she become this... bridge between the worlds?'

'Be and come.' His smile deepened. 'Language often reflects metaphysical truths, doesn't it? To study the roots of words can be a very enlightening activity. To come is to be in the sense that at least one person had to come in order for you to be.' He stared coolly at Carol, who squirmed indignantly but could hardly deny the statement.

Maia felt as though she calmly pulled a trigger when she mused out loud, 'And Drew was the high priest.' Then all the implications of this fact hit her and nearly blew her mind.

'Drew is the high priest,' Chris corrected her.

'Do you mean to say that he and my mother...?' She couldn't possibly finish formulating the question in her head much less utter it out loud.

'No!' Carol gasped. 'Peter would never have-'

'Of course not.' Chris remained unperturbed by all the emotions he was stirring up, but he must have enjoyed shocking them with the assumption that the high priest and priestess formed a bridge between the worlds by way of sexual intercourse with each other. 'Our ancestors may have been so crudely literal, but the rituals of the group I belong to are all purely symbolic, purely being the operative word here.' He didn't sound entirely pleased about this himself.

I'm very fond of your mother... Drew's voice rang in Maia's head. I'm very fond of your mother... And what if Stella's daughter were to follow in her footsteps as high priestess? She realized the idea had been fermenting in her subconscious ever since she met Drew and discovered who he was, but it had only just now broken through her tense moral resistance.

Carol demanded to know in a tightly outraged voice, 'What exactly did Stella and that man do together while her husband watched?'

Chris sighed. 'There's that word again.'

'If their actions were symbolic, which they obviously were or daddy would never have been involved,' Maia heard herself speak with authority, 'there's really no need for us to pry, Carol.'

Chris rewarded her for taking his side with a smile that slipped straight between her legs and promised her whatever she desired when they were alone again.

'But Maia,' Carol gave her a betrayed look, 'I thought you wanted…'

'I got what I wanted. I think I know what's going on now.'

'Then would you mind terribly explaining it to me, dear?'

'Yes… I mean yes, I'll tell you, but first I want to know why Drew lied to me about your being a Druid, Chris.'

'It's very simple, my love, he respected my right to tell you in my own way and in my own good time. It was obvious I hadn't mentioned it to you yet, so he assumed I had my reasons and, very wisely, respected my deeper knowledge of your feelings. In other words, he left you in my hands.'

'I see.' Maia's outward smile was an intense inner frown as she reflected on this disappointing fact. 'Will you please assure my aunt, Chris, that Drew doesn't possess the ability to command lightning or anything fantastic like that.'

'I can only tell you that he would never deliberately hurt anyone, especially not the daughter and sister-in-law of his high priestess.'

Maia glanced at Carol and wasn't surprised to see the old woman's mouth hanging open in disbelief.

Chris crossed his long legs and gazed nonchalantly out the window.

'This is very strange,' Maia said carefully, making an effort to sound detached, but she knew her lover was contentedly picking up on her growing excitement. Drew's black vinyl jacket seemed to fill her mind glimmering with silver highlights like dark water reflecting flashes of lightning, his living chest beneath it the earth's atmosphere surrounded by the cold universe…

'Maia, dear…' It was Carol's turn to gently touch her hand. 'Don't fall into this like your mother did, please. I can't help but feel that these are evil games.'

'Miss Wilson,' Chris's voice rang clear as a bell, 'your irrational fears are the only evil in this room.'

'Dear, are you all right?' Carol deliberately ignored him as she focused on her niece. 'What are you thinking? I'd like to speak with you alone for a moment, if I may.'

'It's all right, auntie.' She relaxed against the soft old cushion, stretching her legs out before her as she met Chris's steady, challenging gaze. She was helplessly hooked by the erotic quality of his smile rather like a mermaid being dragged into a whole new world unable to distinguish between its pleasures and its dangers so soon.

'No, it is not all right,' Carol declared in her most authoritative voice, which means she only sounded desperate.

Chris rose. 'I'll wait out in the car, Maia. Good day to you, Ms. Wilson.'

'You may wait a long time, young man.'

'I don't think so. Try not to worry so much,' he advised. 'Your niece is in excellent hands.'

'Why is it so impossible for you to consider other people's beliefs?' Maia demanded once she and Carol were alone. 'How can you be so ready to think that you're own brother, who you loved so much was, involved in something even remotely wicked? You know daddy wouldn't have had anything to do with evil people.'

'Maia, what you don't know is that for the last few years of his life Peter did everything in his power to convince Stella to leave that cult.'

'Is that what they argued about in the library sometimes?' She was distressed by this bit of news. For some reason, proof of disharmony between her parents made her feel less sure of herself and of her ability to judge right from wrong. 'But they still loved each other, didn't they?'

'Yes, of course, dear, you know perfectly well they did. Peter positively worshipped Stella.'

'And I'll never believe she was unfaithful to him. Drew would never have-'

'Maia, you suffer from the same inexplicable faith in him your mother did. It's no use talking to you about it.' She sighed and rested her forehead in her hand for a resigned moment.

'Drew is a good person, Carol, I can feel it.' Stella's approval was more than sufficient evidence to back-up her own intuition concerning Drew's nature.

Rituals of Surrender

'Everyone dances to a different tune, so it's silly to imagine God only plays the organ in church.' She paused to let the metaphor sink into the old woman's resisting mind. 'The beat of their beliefs may be a little wilder than yours, the melody somewhat darker and the harmonies a bit more haunting, but the Spirit is like music, it's the same no matter how many songs or religions are composed from it.'

'But there are two Conductors, Maia,' Carol reminded her gravely, lifting her head out of her hand.

'You mean God and the devil? I don't believe in the devil, or even in God as a person.'

Carol automatically crossed herself. 'We're talking about good and evil, dear. You're very naive if you still believe there's no such thing as evil in the world, and everyone knows it always takes a seductive form. You know what they say, "the devil is a charming man". Please don't think I'm implying that your parents, God rest their souls-'

'Oh I hate that expression! Who wants to rest forever? I certainly don't.'

'Please, hear me out. I'm not implying that your parents were members of a Satanic cult, far from it, but there are different degrees of evil and it seems to me, as someone who has observed its effects, that this particular group did them more harm than good. Our souls are nourished by humility, by giving thanks for our blessings and enduring our sorrows with the knowledge that it is all for a higher purpose. These Druids feel they can ultimately control things through personal power. They're not humble, Maia, they imagine they can shape and influence events and nature, yet this is rightfully the domain of angels not of self-centered mortals who glorify their own basest instincts.'

'Carol!' Maia laughed despite herself. 'You certainly can raise hell when you want to.'

'I'd rather lower heaven and make it more a part of this world where there are too many other people raising hell.'

'You should have been a Minister, auntie.'

'That's what Peter always said,' Carol admitted, absently caressing her bad knee again.

'Believe me,' Maia said earnestly, needing to bring an end to a conversation that wasn't getting her anywhere, 'I intend to get to the bottom of this group of Druids. I don't want to call them a cult; it's too judgmental and I don't know enough about them yet. All I know is that I need to know why mummy was so into them and why daddy lost his faith in his involvement. I have to know, Carol or it'll obsess me for the rest of my life.'

'I understand, dear,' she agreed reluctantly. 'Just promise me you won't actually become a member yourself. Don't lose your objectivity. Stay detached. Chris is charming, I can't deny that, but he's also extremely arrogant. I suppose that's natural in a young man, and if you're happy with him, if he treats you well, then I'm happy too, but Drew Landson is over forty-years-old by my count, just a little too old to still be playing games.'

'It's not a game to him.'

'Some persons never tire of playing with other people's heads. You just keep that in mind, young lady and promise me you'll visit me regularly. I can't bear not having any way to reach you. Why can't he buy a telephone, for Christ's sake?'

'I promise I'll come by often.' She got up to go, but the only conclusion this lengthy conversation had given her was what she already knew – she wanted Drew. And then there was Eric Wolfson. The sexy musician was easy to forget when he wasn't around, but she already knew from experience that he was irresistible in the flesh. He had gone so far in his efforts to flatter her that he had bought one of her paintings sight unseen, and commissioned Chris to build a frame for it so she could have the pleasure of seeing her work displayed in public for the first time at his party.

Chapter Nineteen

Maia had never seen so many beautiful people in all her life. Try as she might, she could not find one unattractive person amidst all of Sir Wolfson's guests. When she and Chris arrived at the party, she had to force herself to cross the threshold, totally unprepared for the roaring crowd that greeted them in the vast entrance Hall. If Eric described this as an intimate affair, she could not imagine what one of his big bashes was like. Obviously, he had been teasing when he said only a few of his best friends were invited, and he had been especially sarcastic when he assured Maia she would be the most beautiful woman present. Her opinion of the sexy musician plummeted along with her stomach as Chris literally dragged her into the Hall, into a sea of glittering eyes, flashing white teeth and shining lips sipping expensively aged spirits on the rocks. She was so unsure of herself in the sophisticated cosmopolitan crowd that if Chris had not kept a firm grip on her arm, she would have walked right back out into the comfortably spacious darkness alive only with gently singing crickets.

Dressed entirely in black, her strikingly handsome carpenter fit right in with Eric's guests as he led her past smiling groups of breathtakingly attractive people towards the heart of the Hall – a large open bar. She felt painfully shy and out of place, but at least she had one good reason for being there. As she followed a few steps behind Chris, her hand imprisoned in his, she searched the crowd for Drew. Earlier that day, Eric had called Chris at his workshop to remind him that he was expecting them at his party. He had also mentioned they could bring whomever they like, and to Maia's astonishment and carefully concealed joy, Chris had chosen to invite Drew. She had believed his reason for asking Drew to the party had been to tease and torment her, until he explained that it was so he and the Druid high priest could have a little conference with Eric concerning his music video. She still didn't quite know how to handle Chris's lack of jealousy and so determined not to worry about it for the time being. The truth was she was thrilled that Drew would be here tonight. She had casually asked Chris what the older man did for a living (the fact that Drew had been asleep when she rang him at ten o'clock in the morning seemed to indicate he didn't have to get up to go to work) but Chris only laughed in response and she knew him well enough by now not to press him for an answer. She simply added the question of Drew's financial livelihood to the list she was determined to fire at her parents' old friend when she saw him again.

The moment she stepped in to the musician's mansion, she almost literally felt her elegant black silk dress turn to rags in a nightmarish reversal of the Cinderella story in the face of so many expensive designer creations. The idea of spending hundreds of pounds on a single outfit filled her with an almost existential terror, and she observed at once that almost all of Lord Wolfson's lady friends clearly starved themselves in order to maintain their runway figures. The ribs of one tall blonde were actually visible through her dress like the bars of a bird cage covered with a silk cloth.

By the time Chris found the modern open bar Eric had set up in the back of his Medieval Hall, she was already desperate to go home, and only the knowledge that Drew was also coming to this party in any way motivated her to stay. Electric light's cruel honesty had been banned for the affair. Black and violet candles had been set into ornate candelabrums placed on small antique tables along the walls. There seemed to be a flame burning for every person present, some of them pulsing gently beneath the arctic breeze of the central air-conditioning.

Drew was nowhere to be seen yet and neither was Eric.

She concentrated on sipping the red wine Chris procured for her as she wondered what on earth she was doing there. She especially wondered why, when he could obviously have any woman he wanted, Eric had chosen her to be in his music video. Perhaps she underestimated the sexy rock star; perhaps he enjoyed surrounding himself with model-types, but he actually had an eye for real beauty, the kind that shone from within. Maia was profoundly self-confident enough these days to believe that when her soul became visible in her eyes and radiated through her flesh she could easily be considered the most beautiful woman in any room, even if she would not qualify for that title with a measuring tape and a scale.

'Let's mingle,' Chris said cheerfully, and took off purposefully into the crowd without her.

She followed him desperately for a minute, but so many laughing and talking people came between them she finally gave up the pursuit, vowing never to forgive him for abandoning her like this. She was standing perfectly still listening to the roaring waves of conversation breaking all around her, pondering what to do with herself, when suddenly an idle comment hit her like a cold spray...

'I heard he wants a complete nobody to star in his next video, some local twit he seems to fancy.'

She forced her body to move even though she had no idea where she was going. Her nerves had already soaked up most of the wine in her glass and she dreaded the loss of this self-contained activity, so she turned back towards the bar.

Her slow progress towards the island of bottles and male bartenders in white jackets as immaculately pressed as idyllic Caribbean beaches obeyed the room's main current, and small eddies of people drifted along with her as she wished herself invisible while continuing to curse Chris for abandoning her. She was half hoping Drew wouldn't show up after all because she had no desire to fight the army of contemporary sirens Eric had assembled for the high priest's admiration. Her own unique charms felt powerless against the combined force of so much alluring female flesh, a veritable explosion of glossy hair and lips, deep cleavage and long legs in which her own body parts were nice but essentially insignificant fragments. She might be able to lodge herself in Drew's attention for a moment like a piece of shrapnel clinging to his suit on this sensual battlefield, but there was no chance in hell she could keep him focused entirely on her all night long. In this sea of femininity, she was just one deep little wave of sensuality.

Maia managed a refill for her empty wine glass and decided to remain close

Rituals of Surrender

to the bar for regular infusions of courage. The more fruit-of-the-vine she poured into her veins and mixed with her blood, the easier it was to objectively pluck herself from the scene and observe it with an invulnerable bird's eye interest. She chose to ignore the fact that below the frosty layer of her anxiety her warm body was growing hungrier by the second.

A handsome young man with short black hair smiled at her in passing, then one of the attractive bartenders took it upon himself to refill her glass again before she even asked, and suddenly she realized there were just as many good looking men milling around her as there were lovely women, which helped balance the scales a little and gave a bit more weight to her self-esteem.

Tentatively, she began walking down another distinct current in the crowd, reasonably assuming that if she followed other people who looked as if they knew where they were going she would eventually run into food.

The buffet tables in the dining room had been thoroughly attacked, but there were still so many gourmet finger foods left she didn't know where to start as she wandered alongside antique tables protected by golden cloths. The loudly muffled beat of rock music emanating from an adjoining room made her feel at once small and intensely alive like a single blood cell flowing inside the heart of a massive body as it expanded and contracted with people moving to and fro.

'There you are.' Chris abruptly materialized beside her and handed her an empty plate. 'By the way, Drew's here.'

'That's nice.' A slave to her appetite at the moment, she shamelessly stacked her plate with culinary treasures determined not to show how much this announcement affected her.

'He's upstairs examining the torture room.'

She barely heard him over the music pounding through the walls. 'That's nice,' she repeated with her mouth full, refusing to give him the satisfaction of reacting one way or the other.

'I'm surprised that particular room isn't the center of attraction.' Chris followed her along the table filling his own plate with delectable confections. 'But in fact, there's no one else up there at all.'

She was annoyed by how obviously he was baiting her, yet her pulse inevitably quickened at the thought of encountering Drew all alone upstairs. Resisting the urge to abandon her food, she bee-lined it towards some empty chairs, and he continued following her. It didn't take her long to devour the sumptuous repast she had assembled, and since she had somehow lost her wineglass along the way, it was time to procure another one. She was suddenly filled with a comfortable sense of purpose and direction independent of her lover's. She set her empty china plate on a side table, echoed his earlier words to her, 'Time to mingle' and took off for the bar alone.

Maia had grown quite fond of the young man who offered her a fresh glass of excellent Merlot, and her lips curved unconsciously upwards as she headed for the central staircase located in the center of the Hall. Maybe she would run into Drew on his way down or maybe Eric would finally appear on the landing…

The staircase wound up at forty-five degree angles so there was always a section of floor visible below her as she ascended. Yet oddly enough, every time she looked down during her careful climb (she was fearful of tripping in her highheels) no one walked across the floor below her. When she was nearly at the top, she leaned over the inner railing to try and catch sight of at least one body moving about in the subterranean roar, but all that happened was she suffered a strange vertigo. Her mind remained perfectly clear and she didn't feel in the least bit dizzy, yet she suddenly perceived the rectangular section of polished wood floor far below her as a coffin that had just been lowered into the ground. Her glass of wine tipped slightly in her curiously nerveless fingers as she suffered this disturbing impression and a dark red stream descended in haunting slow motion to baptize the coffin with blood…

'There you go again,' Drew steadied her against him, 'wasting perfectly good wine.'

'I didn't mean to…' Her voice died in her throat. Her memory had seriously underestimated the effect his physical presence had on her. Apparently her brain was capable of registering only certain amounts of sensual voltage, but now her body absorbed the real amount with a shiver as his touch burned all her thoughts away.

'How are you, Maia?' He kissed her cheek, leaving a cool wet spot on her

Rituals of Surrender

skin into which her awareness dove for a debilitating instant. 'Cat got your tongue?' he teased soberly.

'Yes,' she eyed his all-black attire, 'a big black panther.'

'Unfortunately they don't make very good pets. They're not content to sleep at the foot of the bed.'

'I would let him sleep right beside me.'

'That might not be wise. One night he might have a bad dream and scratch you up pretty badly.'

'He would never do that to me,' she said faintly, confused by how much it excited her to both trust and fear this man. 'Besides, I could always have him declawed.'

'If you do that you might as well kill him.'

'Well, they don't make flea collars that big anyway.'

'Are you enjoying yourself, Maia?'

'Not really. I've never liked parties much.'

'What *would* you like, princess?'

'More wine.' She drained what remained in her glass.

His mouth hardened as he looked at her in a way that mysteriously whipped her straight between the legs. 'Then shall we descend together?'

'Drew, Chris tried to explain to me why you lied about his involvement in your… whatever it is, and since you told me yourself not to believe everything you said, I don't have the right to be mad at you, but…'

'That's not why you're angry with me.'

Pride made her turn away from him so abruptly one of her high-heels snagged on the carpet. If he hadn't caught hold of her arm she would have tumbled down a dozen steps to the next landing. 'These damned heels!' she gasped, tears of frustration and embarrassment burning in her eyes.

'Death opens its arms for you when you run from what you really want,' he murmured.

She allowed her arms to slip around his chest as she enjoyed the soft material of his black shirt against her cheek. 'Why do you do this to me?' she was talking to herself as much as to him. 'There's so much I need to ask you, and yet when I'm with you I feel there's really nothing else that matters… when I'm with you there's only one thing I want… and yet I'm not sure what part of me wants it, because if it's only my body, I just can't…'

'You can't?' His hands rested heavily over each other against the small of her back.

'I can't give into it.'

'Why not?'

His whisper blew her mind as if it was only a candle flame burning from the wick of her spine. 'Because, I just can't,' she repeated desperately.

'Why not?' he asked again remorselessly.

'Because I don't want to ruin my chance of a long-term meaningful relationship with Chris…'

He brought one of his hands forward to finger one of her silver star-shaped earrings appreciatively. 'These are nice… I want you to live your life, Maia in whatever way feels right to you.' His eyes reflected two candle flames as they gazed down into hers. 'Let's be friends.'

The universe could not have been vaster than her disappointment. 'If that's what you want.' She dropped her eyes.

Without warning he slipped both his hands into her low-cut dress. 'Is that what you feel I want?' he whispered.

'Oh Drew…' At once she loved the feel of her breasts resting in his palms as though her sensitivity was perfectly equal to his ability to grasp and stimulate it. She had chosen not to wear the armor of a bra tonight so she was defenseless against his caress. 'I want to be your priestess!' she breathed, her heart beating the truth out of her even as her mind cringed with shame at the way she was throwing herself at him. Then she was glad to have confessed her deepest longing because the way he stared down into her eyes felt better than a sexual penetration. She could sense the power of his will and how firm it was without being at all cold or inflexible, and it aroused her as nothing else ever had.

'Tell me that again,' he said quietly.

His face was so close her breath grappled with his as she whispered, 'I want

Rituals of Surrender

to be your priestess, Drew.' The proximity of his mouth was torture, the teasing sight of it so close to hers like a whip lashing her soul.

'You want to be my priestess,' he repeated slowly, as though savoring her confession. 'Like your mother?'

'No.' She was thinking that with them the rites joining heaven and earth could cease to be merely symbolic. 'Better...'

His eyes narrowed. 'I've been waiting for you, Maia.'

Her sense of triumph was so sharp she had to close her eyes to endure the stab of desire she experienced as he squeezed her breasts possessively. It felt like her own life-force draining out of her when he slipped his hands out of her dress. She had to remind herself there were hundreds of people milling below them because the corridor behind him looked long and dark as a tunnel leading into another dimension not just to the other side of an old house. 'Has the position of your high priestess remained vacant all these years?' she asked with ill concealed jealousy.

'Yes, officially it has.' He reached for his heart.

'I see.'

He lowered his head to light a cigarette. 'Do you?' He glanced up at her over the small flame, and in her opinion the fire reflected in his eyes was hotter than the real thing.

'I think I'm beginning to.'

'Perhaps, but you still have a long way to go, Maia.'

'I know that.' As usual his cool patronizing made her a bit cross. 'But I learn very quickly and I'm sure you're an excellent teacher, Drew.'

'Have you seen all the goddesses down there?' he asked abruptly, leaning casually against the wooden railing as he smoked.

Immediately, Maia wondered if her eyeliner was smeared and realized she must have lost most of her lipstick to the unfeeling rim of two wine glasses, not to mention the fact that she hadn't bothered to comb her hair after the windy drive from Chris's house to Eric's mansion.

Drew chuckled to himself as he sent ashes down to the hall below as though hearing her thoughts.

'All those women down there look like they've been stretched out on the rack,' she declared cattily, self-consciously smoothing down her unruly hair.

'If you're going to be high priestess, Maia your self-esteem has to be as big as the world.'

'Oh it is, believe me, I'm not in the least jealous of any of those glamorous birds down there. I'm sure not one of them can fly as high inside as I do, so high you can't even imagine it!' The way he looked at her encouraged her to go on in this vein without holding anything back, so she did. 'I'm hungry, Drew, I'm so hungry for something! I don't know what it is only what it isn't, and it isn't just sex or money or fame as an artist. What I long for is to merge all these hungers somehow, all these separate passions into one glorious… something!' She sighed in frustration because there was no way to express how she felt in her soul. 'It's the sense I have when I'm painting that I'm revealing the world as it truly is, the way I know it to be deep down inside me where my desires are its only laws and where love is the atmosphere itself. I've never cared about money,' she shrugged, 'but it seems that if you don't have a lot of it then you also don't have the time or the energy to truly explore yourself. What do you do for a living, by the way?'

He studied his cigarette. 'Amazing.'

'What's amazing? I think it was a natural progression from those women downstairs to the topic of lots of money.' She couldn't prevent another catty remark from escaping her. 'You have the look of a man who doesn't need to get up at a certain time every morning. You're rich, aren't you?'

'Very.'

'Did you inherit your wealth?'

'No, I wrote myself into paradise and now I live like an ancient king on royalties.'

'You're a writer?' She was enthralled. 'What genre? Fiction? Non-fiction?'

'All of the above. Pornography. When I first started, whatever poetry I tried to slip between the sheets invariably got cut, so I divided myself in half and now I write under two different names. One of me makes ungodly amounts of money banging out smut, and the other me is spiritually fulfilled.' He killed his cigarette on the sole of his boot and tossed it away without any consideration for

Rituals of Surrender

their host's domestic staff. 'Wouldn't you like to inspire both sides of me, Maia?'

'Stop teasing me, Drew, please.' She had no desire to leave their shadowy privacy at the top of the steps, but there seemed no avoiding it as he offered her his arm. At least she would have the pleasure of making an entrance with him, before a group of models clad in colorful designer dresses surrounded his hot coal-black figure like hungry sparks. She fanned this depressing scenario with a hopeless sigh as they started walking down the stairs together.

'Why such a melancholy air?' he murmured against her temple. 'Careful with those heels.'

'When are we going to have a real uninterrupted talk, Drew?'

'Later tonight, I promise, after I've spoken with our host about this video he's filming. There's no reason why we shouldn't make it truly interesting.'

The roaring river of souls was drawing closer. 'But how can you pretend to use authentic details in this video when the Druids left absolutely no physical evidence behind as to the actual nature of their rites?'

'There are ways of knowing things that have nothing to do with shovels and carbon dating, but we'll discuss that later. Right now there's something you have to do to prove you can handle the position you desire as my priestess.'

'What do I have to do?' she asked eagerly.

'I want you to be unfaithful to Chris tonight.'

Her heart began racing for its life as she gazed incredulously up at his profile. 'What did you just say?'

'I want you,' he kept his eyes on the stairs, 'to fuck Eric tonight.'

'You... you want me to have sex with Eric Wolfson?' She couldn't believe what she was hearing. 'Why?' she asked desperately, forced by his uncompromising silence to accept the fact that he was serious. When he had said he wanted her to be unfaithful to Chris tonight she had dared hope he meant with him. 'Why Eric and not you?' They had reached the Hall and already she noticed several female gazes fluttering covetously his way.

'No more questions, Maia.' He still refused her even the small consolation of meeting her eyes. 'Just do as I say.'

She slipped her arm out of his, but it was like letting go of a life raft in the middle of an ocean rocked by the storm of her emotions. The music had been turned up to a deafening volume and she was glad she almost had to scream to make herself heard. 'Why are you hurting me like this?'

Turning towards her, he idly played with one of her star-shaped earrings again. 'I'm challenging you, not hurting you, Maia. You said you would do anything I told you to.'

She could only look beseechingly up into his eyes attempting to brace herself for his departure feeling like someone lost in deep space storing up enough oxygen to survive until she could safely dock with her ship again.

'Slip that tight moral leash off your inner wolf, Maia and spend some time with it,' he commanded quietly. 'Throw your wolf some raw flesh that hasn't been properly prepared for you over a romantic flame. Don't be afraid to surrender to lust and to just enjoy what your body has to offer without worrying about the consequences and your so-called meaningful long-term relationship with Chris. If you can't do this for me, then you can't be my priestess.'

'If discarding my moral sense is part of preparing myself to be the priestess of your so-called religion, then it's the devil you worship,' she accused him listlessly. 'I can't separate sex from love. I have no desire to.'

'Don't be a fool,' he said shortly, and she became aware of several people watching them as he slipped an arm around her waist while his other hand cradled the back of her head. 'You'll do as I say, Maia. Understand me?'

She closed her eyes. 'Yes, Drew.'

'Trust me this is for your own good.'

'I do trust you, Drew, I don't know why, but I do.' She felt irrationally humiliated by a sudden burst of laughter nearby just as she opened her eyes again and let her soul dive up into his unfathomable blue irises. 'Please tell me you're real and not like all these other people here, Drew, I mean truly real.'

'I'm real, Maia,' he caressed the back of her head gently, 'and I know that one of the hardest things in life is not belonging to a tradition and longing to fit into one. It took me a long time, but I finally realized the answer was not trying to belong anywhere anymore but just being myself. The only problem is new ideas and ways of being don't come with maps and safe comfortable little arrows pointing you in absolutely the right direction, it's the price you pay when you're forging your own way through life. You find yourself trying to unite paths that have been unnaturally split, forks in the road that lead to dead ends if you choose one over the other, which is why the devil carries a pitchfork, because evil lies precisely in this unnatural division. The truth is that your spirituality and your sensuality work together like your lovely legs, Maia, and tonight I want you to spread them wide for me. I want you to think about me while Eric is fucking you, and I want you to climax, I want you to come fully into your body for me. Will you do that for me?'

'Yes, Drew.'

'Good.' He let go of her. 'Now go find him. He's out by the pool.'

Chapter Twenty

Maia suspected she had been elaborately set up, but there was nothing she could do, or even wanted to do, about it. She was so profoundly excited it was impossible for her to pull out of the game now – a sinisterly seductive game in which her heart was the ball being tossed around by three men, and just how far she would spread her legs for all of them determined the boundary lines. The web spun around her had its dark heart on the evening she drove into the cemetery, yet she realized it had to stretch even farther back in time than that. If Drew was behind it all, which she was sure he was somehow, he must have known where she would be that night, which meant he had been secretly observing her. It would then have been a relatively simple matter to tamper with her car, although she could not help but be curious about how they had managed to rig it so it would stall exactly when it did. As she parted from Drew at the foot of the stairs, her frightened indignation was like a hand angrily sweeping away a spider's intricate work because of course she couldn't possibly be unfaithful to Chris merely because some arrogant so-called high priest had told her to. She had no proof whatsoever the three of them were acting together in a bizarre erotic play, but the instant the suspicion sparked in her mind it fanned into a blazing certainty as she thought about everything that had happened to her lately.

She had left her empty wine glass on the railing at the top of the stairs, and blind to the crowd now, she thought about making her way back to the bar and remaining there until Chris was ready to drive them home. But even as she considered this course of action, Maia found herself walking towards the back of the Hall. Naturally she had no intention of obeying Drew's immoral command, yet her body was making its way to the French doors reason told her led out to the pool he had mentioned, the host of contradictory emotions raging inside her buffeting her in this incriminating direction.

Part of her wondered furiously how these men dared play with her like this even as another part of her was so turned on by their intense, concentrated interest in her that she literally felt weak in the knees. Nevertheless, it was humiliating how easy it had been for them to trap her in their sensual web. Whatever it was they were up to, she must have been chosen because her mother had once been high priestess of their religion. It seemed obvious now that Eric was a Druid too, hence the theme of his music video. She reminded herself this was all a fantastic speculation on her part, but her intuition told her she was right to believe nothing that had happened to her since she drove into the graveyard on the evening of May 1st was a coincidence. From the moment her engine stalled, her life had been mysteriously choreographed.

As she made her way out of the Hall, Maia was deaf to the noise around her wrapped in a cocoon of fantasies her suspicious brain warned her were too good to be true, fantasies about Drew waiting for her all these years. She had always believed she was special, that she somehow rose above all the other young women in Stoneshire with her unusually deep thoughts and feelings and the intensely passionate nature she expressed in her paintings. Most of her school friends had dreamed only of becoming wives and mothers, and her co-workers at the solicitor's office were equally listless in their ambitions. She could easily believe Drew had been waiting for her all these years to succeed Stella as his high priestess. Or perhaps she had been chosen for this wicked sexual triptych because she was no naïve and easy to manipulate, because she was swiftly seduced and slow to become suspicious…

This disturbing possibility stopped her in her tracks, and once more she thought of turning around and heading for the bar. She could stick close to her handsome young wine-bearer and his reassuringly candid smile. She even toyed with the thought of leaving the party with him later and forgetting all about the self-centered Druids she had inadvertently become involved with. Yet of course she knew there wasn't a chance in hell of that happening because her misgivings were not as strong as how intrigued and aroused she was. And naturally she was flattered to be the center of three handsome men's attentions, how could she not be? Whether Eric was a Druid as well was the question it was seriously entertaining her to toy with at the moment like a cat tossing a tasty mouse around. Whatever the answer, the musician was definitely a savory dish and the truth was it would not be at all distasteful to her to obey Drew's command. Inexplicably, she still desired and trusted her parents' controversial old friend even though he had just told her to sleep with another man. She trusted him in the same way she knew the wine she had drunk was not poisoned but rather complex, delicious and intoxicating, just like this powerfully sexy high priest. She couldn't bring herself to believe he was intent on hurting her somehow, but she could easily bring herself to believe he was challenging her, testing her boundaries...

'There you are, my love.' Chris suddenly materialized beside her again.

'Where did you meet Drew?' she fired the question at him, but then found her body leaning comfortably against his.

'Mm, you're tipsy,' he observed approvingly. He himself did not appear to be drinking.

'I know he writes dirty books for a living,' she went on languidly. 'Is Eric a Druid too?'

He looked around them. 'Keep your voice down, Maia.'

'Stop squeezing my arm, please,' she demanded mildly. 'You know, Chris, I don't believe you love me.' She gazed regretfully up at his flawless features. 'I think I know what's going on now. I'm just a fly caught in a web, aren't I?'

'If you are, you're the most beautiful fly I've ever seen. But don't forget, pretty butterflies get caught in spider's webs too.' He essentially confirmed her ambiguous statement by not asking her what she meant by it. 'What did Drew say to you, Maia?'

She had never seen such a vulnerable expression in his eyes before and she savored it for a moment before replying. 'Everything that's happened to me since I met you is part of some mysterious rite, isn't it? It's all been planned somehow. Our relationship isn't real, it's just part of a play directed from day one, or more appropriately from night one, by Drew Landson. Someone tampered with my car so the engine would appear to die just a few minutes after I drove into the cemetery so you could pull in after me and pretend to rescue me. Am I right?' She knew she had every conceivable reason to be angry, and she was trying her best to be, but all she could still manage to feel was excited. Her response probably had something to do with the wine seducing her blood and dissolving all negative jagged emotions such as fear and resentment.

Chris smiled at her indulgently. 'You're definitely toasted, sweetheart.'

'Don't treat me like a fool, please.' She walked away from him confident he would follow her. 'I'll admit,' she went on almost contentedly, 'I've been naively blind to the obvious, but I think that's only because I've been having such a good time and I didn't want to see the fact that it couldn't all possibly be really happening. I mean, this is Stoneshire!' She laughed incredulously. 'What are the odds of meeting three sexy men right after the other and then have it turn out that they're all passionately interested in me as well?'

'Maia,' Chris turned her towards him and pressed her body against his, 'I love you. Never doubt that.'

She gazed up at his face almost indifferently, suddenly tired of his blonde buttery beauty which she now sensed was full of lies like empty calories. She slipped out of his grasp and began walking purposefully towards the French doors, eager to get out of the stuffy noisy Hall and out into the fresh night air.

She saw that torches in sconces had been set up along the veranda on which she stood and around the pool, where no one was swimming at the moment because they were all too engrossed in their host's unusual performance. Wearing a light-brown suit decorated with vertical ivory stripes, and a half unbuttoned white shirt exposing a vulnerable slice of his chest, Eric Wolfson was dancing with two flames. Relieved that Chris chose not to follow her outside, she nearly tripped down the porch steps she was so immediately enthralled by the musician's hypnotic hybrid of sophistication and savagery. He held two torches in his hands like SOS flags, and they even made a flapping sound in the strong breeze as he crossed his arms against his chest and let the hot tongues of fire lick up around him, his long brown hair whipping his neck as he flung his head back passionately, surrendering himself to this dangerously hot embrace for a breathtakingly long moment. Then he opened his arms wide and leapt over a plastic chair in which a coolly beautiful woman was reclining watching his performance. She screamed in fear and surprise, and then laughed self-consciously as he sprinted away from her around the pool, the torches in his hands sending luminous streamers behind him like the long red hair of Viking warriors. He ended up in his original spot, the skin of his face and chest gleaming with what struck Maia as a much purer, smoother energy than that of the raw, restless blazes he was commanding. When he suddenly looked her way, as if he had been aware of her presence for some time, every vein in her body ignited like fuses all coming to one explosive conclusion – she was going to obey Drew.

Bending lithely to one side, Eric swung a torch over his head in a fiery arch as he pointed the other flame at Maia as though symbolically offering it to her. He repeated this powerfully graceful gesture three times, surrounding himself with a burning halo as the other rigidly erect torch pinned her raptly to the spot watching him. He was basted in salty sweat and he looked so hot to her in every sense it was torture not being able to lick him and bite him right there and then.

The woman in the chair he had leapt over laughed again and applauded slowly, an oddly contemptuous sound that echoed over the pool like a dripping faucet.

Eric let his arms fall to his sides, pointing the dying flames towards the ground. He held them far enough away from his legs to keep them from charring his pants and yet close enough that he looked superbly cool and collected in the suit's expensive lines. He stared over at Maia, and her brown eyes absorbed the vision of him in their earthy depths as she sincerely hoped he would indeed make it possible for her to obey the high priest's command.

'That was fucking great, Eric!' someone declared as the lady in the plastic chair glanced over her shoulder to see who Eric was looking at so intently. Her expression when she noticed Maia standing there became an exquisitely made-up shield over her fierce jealousy.

'Who's that?' someone else wondered out loud.

Eric set the torches back in their sconces, smoothed sweat-soaked strands of hair away from his face with one hand, and extended the other hand towards

Rituals of Surrender

Maia. She noticed he had gotten some sun lately. Wet with perspiration, his skin gleamed like molten gold flowing over his ideal cheekbones.

'I'd like you all to meet the lovely star of my next video,' he announced in a deep relaxed voice that carried effortlessly.

Maia walked towards him, shyly ignoring all the speculative eyes on her, and tentatively accepted his proffered hand. His grip was so hot and hard it immediately melted all her thoughts into an incoherent jumble like candles left too long in the sun. Suddenly, all she could think about was his touch and the way her flesh fused with his as she distinctly felt him promise her the pleasures of his cock through his hard fingers. She ceased caring about anything except the lean strength of his body so close to hers and of how much she wanted to feel it against her skin.

'Excuse us, please,' Eric said to his other guests as he led her off the concrete halo surrounding the pool and onto the grass.

Maia couldn't resist casting a triumphant glance back at the gorgeous model he was casually abandoning, but then she forgot about everyone else as he led her away from the house across a closely cropped lawn in the direction of the woods surrounding his estate, the ancient forest where he planned to film his video.

'Ready?' he whispered, and keeping her hand firmly in his, he began running.

Taken completely by surprise, she surrendered to the strenuous exercise of sprinting in high-heels across uneven ground in nearly complete darkness, the blood surging through her heart thankfully drowning her brain's need to understand what exactly was happening as they careened between the trees. Her eyes gradually adjusting to the gloom, she miraculously avoided tripping over roots, but branches caught at her dress and she was afraid of ripping it beyond all hope of repair. Yet he completely ignored her breathless protests as he tugged her remorselessly along behind him.

When they at last burst into a clearing, it wasn't a moment too soon for Maia; the muscles in her calves had tightened almost beyond her control. The nocturnal woodland peace was broken by the sound of her labored breathing, and by the quietly urgent crackling of flames hungrily consuming their wooden hosts. Two torches burning on tall sconces thrust deep into the earth sent shimmering golden paths across a black body of water whose boundaries she could not make out, and the strangely eloquent sound they made seem to mysteriously communicate with the whispering of the leaves around them. The sconces rose straight out of the ground a few feet apart, forming a gateway between water and earth.

Eric stepped behind her.

'What are you doing?' she asked him even as she bent over to slip off her tortuous high-heels.

'What do you think I'm doing?' He drew the tiny car of her zipper slowly down its track.

With Drew's black-clad figure a haunting shadow across her mind she concentrated on the feather-light caress of the musician's fingertips. Because she was doing what he wanted her to do, she felt as though Drew was there with her... his will had penetrated deep into her heart and soul and he was there with her now even as she prepared to let another man enter her body...

Her silky black dress slipped easily down her legs and she stepped out of it gracefully in her bare feet. The lake looked as dark and menacing as a primordial pool before life came into being, and still wearing her black silk panties, she found herself walking bravely through the torches' burning portal towards the water's cold and unfathomable darkness. But then she paused, crossing her arms over chest as she stared at the forbidding black stillness. For some reason she felt that Drew would want her to enter it and she was trying to summon the courage to do so. Then added to the secret whispers of the trees behind her was the subtler yet even more significant sound of Eric slipping out of his suit, and suddenly she wanted to postpone the inevitable. She deliberately didn't look back at him, but it wasn't long before she felt him step up tightly behind her again. The tender head of his erection kissed the base of her spine and sent an invigorating shock through her whole body that propelled her away from him towards the lake.

The water was so cold she shuddered uncontrollably as it licked up around her ankles, then her knees, then her thighs, at which point she couldn't stand it anymore and forced herself to dive into one of the golden paths forged by the torches. She surfaced with every muscle in her body silently screaming in outrage, and felt literally impaled on the glimmering blade of light as she desperately hugged herself. Then she cried out when something gripped both her ankles and pulled her under again.

Eric's limbs entwined with hers beneath the surface, forming one writhing organism that might have been eons old, and during this silent struggle he managed to pull off her panties. They rocketed back out into the air together gasping for breath. Maia clutched herself for warmth, shivering to the core of her flesh as he swam elegantly over to stand in his own gilded path. The cool mud bottom sucked on her toes as she watched him dunk himself slowly over and over again, peacefully smoothing his dark hair back away from his face as he relished the water's cold embrace after his hot dance with flames. He was ostensibly ignoring her for the moment, so she sank back down below the surface again herself… down into a black space free of gravity… into an unrelentingly icy embrace in which she grew eerily languid…

When she shot back out into the air again, Eric was gone. She waited for what felt like a small eternity, and then nearly choked on a laugh as her mouth filled with water when he pulled her down into his arms again. This time when they emerged he was still holding onto her, and he answered her gasps for air with a violent kiss that doubled as mouth-to-mouth resuscitation. When he finally let her catch her own breath, she felt all her ability to resist him drown in the deep shadows masking his features. He kissed her again, boldly exploring her mouth as he pressed her body even more firmly against his. Then he thrust one of his hands between her thighs and clutched her pussy while his other hand cradled her from behind and she felt caught on an open shell in which her clitoris was the precious pearl. He gently rubbed her labia as his tongue kept playing between the lips on her face, and the pleasure was so delicate it felt like feathers brushing her veins as she mysteriously evolved into a higher form of life caught in the net of his fingers.

She was vaguely aware that the wind had dropped; the two torches were burning with concentrated control as he took her hand and led her back towards dry land. As he rose out of the water's dark mirror before her his naked body glistened beneath the flames, and his long narrow back made her think of a wild cat's spine magically learning to walk on two legs in the blink of an eye. His leanness was all muscle and his dark wet hair clung to his skull sleek as a panther's skin. He turned to face her beneath one of the torches, where they could absorb its warmth. His high cheekbones stood out dramatically, heightening the sensuality of his curving mouth, and the dark trees behind him were almost reverently silent as she slipped her arms around his neck.

The cold water had temporarily dissolved his desire, but she felt it quickly resurrecting against her belly. Yet she didn't want to make it too easy for him, so she pulled away and caressed his chest with her fingernails.

'Mm...' he said. 'Harder.'

She allowed her nails to rake down his body with a ferocious delight as she glanced up at his face to make sure she wasn't scratching him too deeply, but his gray eyes were a polished silver in the torchlight giving nothing away even as they let her catch an exciting glimpse of her true nature. Very carefully, she grazed the sides of his stiffening cock with two claw-like hands. It reared up stiffly in response and she let her nails stroke it a little more cruelly relishing the sight of its quivering response. His penis was not so very different from Chris's in appearance. They were both unusually fine examples of the circumcised male organ, the thick, straight shaft crowned by a head shaped like a mushroom cap, and the mere sight of it growing straight out from between the muscular trunks of his thighs was intoxicating to her. Curiously cradling the hard-on she was responsible for, Maia found herself giddily wondering if a great cock was a requirement for membership in this modern Druid cult, which naturally led her to try and picture what Drew's erection would be like... which proved a mistake since he was the man she really wanted inside her.

Eric sensed her hesitation and promptly dealt with it. He turned her around so she was facing the water and put a gentle but determined pressure to bear on both her shoulders.

She was at once stunned and thrilled by his absolute indifference to her thoughts. He didn't care about any moral battles she might be fighting inside herself anymore than a cat pays attention to the desperate beating of wings from a bird caught in its jaws. He did not actually force her down; she ended up on

Rituals of Surrender

her hands and knees on the ground because she wanted to. It turned her on that he said not a word and wasn't even bothering to tell her what to do. She knew how he wanted her because it was what her body wanted too. It was intensely relaxing how right and natural it felt to be on all fours in the grass as he positioned himself behind her. She imagined Drew watching her submissiveness to a man's will. For all she knew the high priest was standing in the darkness between the trees observing her obedience to a man's desires, and it was an intensely stimulating thought as Eric filled the entrance to her pussy, then paused to give her time to savor the anticipation of a cock she had never felt inside her before preparing to penetrate her. She moaned to tell him she was ready for the incomparable sensation as in her mind his erection transformed into much more. She felt herself opening up to the unknown as he sank leisurely into her, forcing her to dwell on the violation of her moral and romantic being as she let herself be filled with a complete stranger's hard-on. She felt herself opening up to her deepest feelings for Drew, letting go of her resistance to them and blissfully accepting them... the sharp pleasure she suffered amazed her as she allowed her willingness to do whatever Drew wanted her to do completely sink into her soul through another man's cock stabbing her body... a cock the Druid high priest commanded like a scepter with which he ruled her mind and heart as no other man ever had before or ever would again... she fully opened up to the mysteriously beautiful certainty that Drew Landson was her destiny as she let another man penetrate her in his name, as she let another man fuck her so he could know he truly possessed her... she was ecstatically filled with images of the high priest as Eric thrust himself all the way into her pussy, and it was the excitement she experienced in fulfilling Drew's desire that made this other man's vigorous strokes feel so impossibly good...

She was on her hands and knees for a long time as Sir Wolfson enjoyed indulging himself in her slick hole, and the whole time he said not a word. She kept her eyes open as he fucked her long and hard, until there seemed no end in sight to his driving energy and she almost couldn't stand how much she loved it. She was strangely proud of how wet and deep her pussy felt in response to her fantasy that Drew was watching her body being taken on his command.

Every beat of her heart and of Eric's cock said I love you, Drew, I love you, I'm doing this for you, I love you! as she sustained the submissive position enabling another man to plunge into her body with nearly vicious strength. She loved having a big hard dick inside her. Her innermost flesh felt achingly, meaninglessly empty when a man wasn't packing his rampant cock into her tight cunt and taking her feelings farther than they could ever go alone, and the thought of Drew was deliciously confused in her clitoris with the force pulsing between her thighs, the crackling torches perfectly reflecting the hot sensual rhythm of their coupling bodies...

'Oh yes, yes!' she pleaded softly, clutching the grass and concentrating on the exquisite quivering of her clit as Eric banged her with a casual fierceness that made how gloriously cheap she felt border on the mystical. Somehow managing to hold herself up on one arm trembling with the effort, she reached down to caress herself, and the sensation of his erection swelling to critical mass between her thighs easily pushed her over the edge into her own soaring climax.

Chapter Twenty One

Maia felt strangely like a ghost re-entering the festivities in the mansion after being magnificently stabbed to death in the woods. Only a quarter of an hour ago she had been a body crouched facedown in the ground, the dark hole between her legs the entrance to paradise even as her hair mingled with the dirt. Now she was wandering through a candle-lit manor house scarcely able to recall what had happened before her wonderfully rough encounter with Sir Wolfson in the forest. The walk back from the torch-lit lake to the French doors had felt curiously unreal to her as the tall trunks of trees all struck her as god-like shadows of a man's erect penis. Her pussy's longing to be filled by a big hard cock transcended the slight discomfort she was experiencing between her thighs as a result of how long and selfishly Eric had used her. He had relentlessly subjected her to his pounding rhythm, the shocks of his lightning-swift penetrations blinding her to everything but the searing pleasure they suffused her with.

He carried her shoes for her during their leisurely walk back to his palatial abode looking refreshed and devastatingly elegant dressed in his striped suit again. She had no idea how much time had passed since she parted from Drew at the bottom of the staircase. Every now and then the musician paused to kiss her gently, almost reverently, cradling her face in his free hand, and even in the nearly total darkness beneath the trees she could make out his gratified smile when she turned her head to suck hungrily on his thumb.

When they stepped out onto the open lawn leading up to the pool and the veranda, he gave her back her sandals and walked on ahead of her as she paused to slip them back on. She thought he was abandoning her until he turned around

Rituals of Surrender

and held his hand out to her. She took it gratefully, but when they reached the French doors he let go of her again and gave her a chaste kiss on the cheek. 'I'll catch you later,' he said. 'You're not leaving here tonight.'

'I'm not?' She was surprised, and then quickly decided this was merely a polite line he was throwing her before diving back into his sea of guests, at least half of whom were beautiful women.

'Don't even try,' he warned.

'Well, I may not even have a ride back if Chris suspects...' She wondered if Drew would drive her home, and yet she had no idea where home was anymore. She had just been unfaithful to her lover, the man she also lived with, in order to obey the desire of another man she barely even knew. It made no sense at all.

'I wouldn't worry about Chris,' he said lightly, turning away.

She caught him by his expensive sleeve and asked him quietly, 'You're one of them too, aren't you?'

He gazed soberly into her eyes, but a group of women had already spotted his return. They descended upon him, all laughing and talking at once, and Maia couldn't prevent him from being swallowed up by the carnivorous silk petals of their evening gowns. She found herself politely but determinedly elbowed away by the group of skeletal birds, and suddenly she was right back where she had started wandering alone through the party. However, she now desperately needed to use the bathroom, and the idea of finding an isolated space on the second floor – a little marble sanctuary cool and quiet and private as a tomb – appealed to her immensely at the moment. Safe inside there she would be able to relax and soothe her sore muscles, particularly the ones in her calves and thighs that ached like smoldering flames burning along the haunting sconces of her bones. She prayed she could find a bathroom all to herself; she desperately needed a haven in which to try and sort out the passionate mess of her thoughts and emotions.

This time she ascended the grand staircase in her bare feet, not giving a damn what anyone thought as she dangled her sandals by the straps in one hand while holding carefully onto the railing with the other. She scanned the Hall below her for Drew's dark figure, but to no avail. Now that she had actually gone and done what he had told her to do, she began to fear he had simply been testing her moral fortitude. If so, she had failed miserably. Yet perhaps all would not be lost if she could somehow manage to keep Chris from finding out about her infidelity.

At the shadowy summit of the staircase on the second floor of the mansion where Drew's aura still lingered to haunt her, she knew it would be impossible to lie to him about what she had just done for his sake, and if he knew, then so would Chris in the end. And if Eric was indeed a Druid, the pussy was already out of the bag.

Maia thanked whatever unseen forces watched over her that the upper floor remained deserted and she found what she was looking for just down the corridor. She locked the heavy door behind her and prepared to remain in the luxurious bathroom a good long time as she attempted to pull herself together. The shining metal fixtures were contrasted by large potted plants, and her bare feet (still aching a little from sprinting across uneven ground in high-heels) were grateful for the cool black marble tiles. She had lost her black silk panties in the lake, so all she had to do was lift her dress as she perched on the polished black toilet seat.

She still couldn't quite believe she had met Chris in a graveyard on the first day of May. 'On May Day,' she said out loud, and her quiet voice reverberated sinisterly in the pristine space. 'Jesus, I met him on May Day!' She laughed even though she was anything but amused. In fact, she was just a bit frightened, for one of the Druids' sacrificial victims had supposedly been the May Queen...

'I'm a loose woman,' she murmured, trying the old-fashioned label on for size, but it was too broad for her rather slender sin. After all, she and Chris were not engaged; they had only just met and she more than half suspected he and his friends were using her for their own bizarre purposes anyway. 'Oh mummy, I wish I could talk to you,' she sighed, and buried her face in her hands.

Drew's priestess... would she truly inherit this highly enviable position from Stella? Had her parents ever planned to tell her about their secret life as pagans? Neither one of them had died a natural, peaceful death; they had been killed together in a violent accident. They were killed... was it really a coincidence that a truck had swerved directly into their path on the icy road or had their hand-in-hand entrance into the next world been... arranged? They had burned like sacrificial victims in a cage, a modern cage made of metal and leather rather than the traditional wicker...

She raised her face from her hands and stared fixedly at the gleaming white oval bathtub surrounded by a small forest of potted plants. She stared at it without blinking until it began to resemble a magically gleaming dragon's egg...

'Stop right now,' she told herself firmly, at once unnerved and reassured by the sound of her own voice. 'These are crazy thoughts you're having, Maia. None of them can possibly be true!' If she took this train of thought any farther, she would plunge into a void from which she would not be able to save herself, because if she even remotely allowed herself to entertain the thought that Drew was evil, she would not wish to go on living.

She pulled out a long white carpet of sanitary paper and wiped herself clean with it. She stood up, her dress falling soothingly around her legs as she flushed the toilet and then turned to cling to the sink's comfortingly solid edge. Her reflection in the mirror above it shocked her. She had not expected her disheveled condition to outdo any professional hairdresser or make-up artist. Her hair was a tangled mass of dark coils with fiery highlights, the color of burned wood in which the sap is still smoldering. Her lips had lost their artificial gloss, but the wine and her recent exertions had kept them naturally rosy and they had been kissed into an even sweeter fullness. But it was her eyes that held her, their intensity the visibly smoldering core of this lovely package of flesh the immortal force inside her had sent to itself for its own mysterious pleasure, postmarked with her birth date. As she stared at her reflection, she saw both the divine shipper and the mortal receiver of the skin wrapped around her bones containing the gift of her life, and both were absolutely beautiful. It was no wonder Eric had fucked her for as long as he had and that Chris said he loved her, but only Drew looked into her eyes the way she was staring into them now, as though he could clearly see the power behind her vulnerable mortal self. And all of a sudden, Maia realized no one could truly hurt her anymore than they could steal her shadow. For even though her body seemed to cast it, her shadow was actually part of the unfathomable darkness between the stars. She truly seemed to see herself for the first time staring into her dark eyes in the bathroom mirror.

Reluctantly, Maia returned to the party. The huge noisy gathering made her feel insignificant as a single blood cell slipped out of the Hall's main artery through a wound. She wondered what the consequences of her actions tonight would end up being. She had to find Drew again and ask him what was really going on. It was entirely possible she was only imagining that all the men she was involved with were Druids seeking to use her for their own mystifying purposes. Chris was right, desire was all she understood, because the truth was that she desired Drew as much or even more than any explanations he might be able to give her. Yet the man she wanted had let another man possess her, and part of her was tempted to resent him for this and to regret her erotic encounter with Eric like a tumor subject to the anti-bodies of shame and guilt. At the same time, another part of her dared admit she had thoroughly enjoyed herself and that the only problem now was how dangerously the experience had sharpened her erotic appetite. Every muscle in her body had been tenderized by how hard Eric fucked her as though she was being primed for something or for someone, and she found herself daring to hope it was for Drew's even more devastatingly pleasurable penetrations. She felt ready for a prolonged sensual feast in which her juices would flow until there was absolutely nothing left of her. She knew this was what she wanted deep down and that only Drew could give it to her. Whatever it took, she had to have him. She had to be taken by him. Whether or not she could hold onto him afterwards was a battle she would fight when she came to it, once he was deep in her sexual territory.

People were dancing together in what Maia assumed was the living room, where all the furniture had been pushed back against the walls. The instant she walked in, an attractive young man tried to pull her out onto the dance floor, but she wrested her hand out of his with a smile, shaking her head. After what she had just been through in the woods she did not need to feel another man's body pressed against hers in a subtle simulation of sex. She searched the room for Drew even though she didn't actually hope to find him there. She was stimulatingly aware of having lost her panties in a dark lake as her tender labial lips rubbed against each other... and grew slick and warm as she wondered whether she was destined to feel another cock thrusting between them tonight...

'Our host seems to have gone missing,' a woman's lilting voice said in her ear. 'Would you happen to know where he is now?'

Maia turned and saw a pretty blonde wearing a challenging smile on her heavily made up face. 'I have no idea,' she replied sincerely.

'Where was he when you last saw him? Come, do tell, love.'

Before Maia could reply the girl suddenly cast a familiar shadow.

'Would you care to dance?' Drew asked the blonde as he claimed one of her bare shoulders.

'I'd love to.' She promptly handed Maia her empty glass. 'Be a dear and ditch this for me.'

Drew led the girl out onto the dance floor holding Maia's eyes.

She turned to discard the insulting glass on a table, but she could not escape the pain so easily, and she quickly realized her jealousy would only get worse if she didn't face it.

With the young woman's slender body clinging to his, Drew stared at Maia as he slowly wove the fingers of one hand through soft blonde hair as his other hand caressed a slim bare back.

Despite her indignation, Maia found herself breathlessly hooked on his smile as he deliberately held her eyes while fondling another woman's body. Her heart felt so painfully full she had to swallow a dry lump in her throat that felt as timelessly meaningful as the full moon outside. His partner almost looked unconscious she hung so limply in his embrace, her arms wrapped around his neck and crossed at the wrists evoking a white bow adorning his dark back as they turned around and around orbited by other slow-dancing couples. Maia experienced nothing but a cold rage during the few seconds Drew's gaze was directed away from her. His eyes had become the soul of her pulse and it seemed to flatline with fury until they looked at her again. In a form-fitting white evening dress, the slender young woman in his arms evoked a stream of smoke against his coal-black form, and Maia watched with pure murder in her mind as he whispered something in her ear and she kissed the side of his neck in response. She longed to turn away and run from the room, yet there was nowhere she wanted to be except with him, and the only thing that kept her from sinking into despair was the feeling that his true pleasure came from the fact that she was watching him. In her soul, Maia knew he was more aroused by the feel of her awareness embracing his actions than by the other woman's submissive body clinging to his. And somehow the way his naked stare spoke to her was more exciting than the casual way he whispered into the blonde's ear again and made her laugh.

Eventually, Maia did turn away. Enough was enough and she was too worn out by her encounter with Eric to endure the double-edged emotions Drew always seemed to bring with him like a sword. He was so kind and yet so cruel, so understanding and yet so perversely demanding, and suddenly she had lost the energy needed to deal with all these paradoxes.

'There's my little wandering pussy.' Chris grabbed her arm as she was about to leave the room. 'Enjoying yourself, my love?'

'Enormously!' She smiled up at him. 'And you?'

'Naturally I'm enjoying myself. Oh my, is that Drew dancing with someone else? Are you jealous?'

'I don't know, am I?'

'I believe you are.'

In an unconscious reflection of Drew's gesture with the girl, she ran her fingers through Chris's luminous hair. 'Why are you playing with me like this?' she sighed, feeling as numb as a mouse that has been under cats' paws for too long.

'Maia, take my advice and don't think about things so much.' He wrapped an arm around her shoulders and urged her towards the dance floor. 'Just go with the flow and relax and keep enjoying yourself. Everything will be all right no matter what happens.'

She rested her cheek on his shoulder as they began slow dancing, becoming one of the couples peacefully orbiting each other. She tried to forget that Drew was only a few bodies away. 'Chris, I don't believe you.' She sighed again.

'Maia, I love you.'

She closed her eyes. 'You do?' Then he couldn't possibly know about Eric yet...

'Yes, I do.'

She clung to him in desperation, her guilt and confusion suddenly so sharp it was almost a physical pain.

Drew's commanding voice slipped between her and Chris like a sharp blade, 'I'm cutting in now.'

'The hell you are,' Chris retorted mildly, holding her firmly against him.

'Let go of her,' Drew insisted. 'You had your chance.'

Maia kept her eyes closed. Her soul was already in Drew's hands and only a small frightened part of her continued trying to feel safe in Chris's potentially long-term embrace.

'Look, I don't know what you've been telling her behind my back,' Chris began, 'but you-'

'I said let go of her.' Drew's voice was harder than stone as his determination honed itself to a dangerous point, yet she was still surprised when Chris's arms slipped obediently from around her.

'Well?' Drew inquired, enveloping her in his arms with a tenderness that made them feel like the warm dark cloud of her own turbulent emotions.

'I did as you said.'

'Very good, Maia, I'm pleased with you. Now tell me how you felt.'

'Very good,' she echoed mockingly, hurt by his casual response to the intense effort she had made for him, but then smiled apologetically up into his eyes.

'Was he rough with you?' he asked quietly.

'Yes, a little... I wanted him to be,' she confessed.

He granted her the ghost of a smile in return for this admission. 'Let's go upstairs.'

Chapter Twenty-Two

A cloaked figure formed by a cloud stained red by the dying sun was reflected in a full-length mirror abandoned by the side of a road, its wooden frame carved with diamonds and crosses, and the mirror was in its turn framed by a car window. A woman's hands rested on the black leather wheel in the foreground, the golden ring on her wedding finger shaped like a serpent swallowing its tail forming the center of the painting as the black asphalt of the highway stretched straight as a sword into a point on the burning horizon. The distant cloud-figure in the bloody sky reflected in the mirror abandoned on the side of the road was beckoning to her across a darkening field of grass.

Maia regarded her work with a mixture of pride and dissatisfaction because it was so important to her that Drew like it. Chris had constructed a frame that matched the one around the mirror in the painting, and the effect was haunting as the imagined led out to the real and then turned back on itself again endlessly. Eric had hung her work on the wall just outside his 'torture' room.

'I painted it, but I don't get it,' she admitted as Drew continued studying it.

'Then I'll explain it to you,' he offered.

'Please do.'

'Twilight is a traditional crossover time,' he began. 'Dusk is neither night nor day and, therefore, offers a doorway out of the structure of time and space.'

'I sort of knew that much...'

'The cloaked figure is part of the sunset, which makes him magical... he has the air of a priest mediating between this world and the next.'

'Like you.'

Rituals of Surrender

He squeezed her hand. 'The priest-like figure is formed by a cloud stained a deep red by the dying sun, by its metaphorical blood, which can be interpreted as a union of the spirit's pure lightness with matter's heavier flesh.'

'Go on, please.'

'The woman's hands in the foreground resting on the black leather wheel express the fact that the soul is outside of time and actually controls it, the clock being circular and the universe black and the leather once living skin. The golden snake ring on your wedding finger is our immortal energy flowing from form to form, from body to body, and using each one as a vehicle for experience and growth, herein represented by the car. The empty mirror frame is a gateway between this dimension and another one.'

'Between the shipper and the receiver of this magical parcel of blood-and-bones,' she concluded, remembering her thoughts in the luxurious bathroom.

'Exactly.' He squeezed her hand again approvingly.

'But Chris said there couldn't be anything exact between the worlds.'

'Never mind Chris. The mirror in its turn framed by the car window reinforces the analogy of the body as the mysterious engine created and driven by our Spirit for the adventure of Self.'

'But what does the priest-like figure want? It's as though he made me paint him, and all these other images, without my even understanding them. Not even Chris was able to explain it all to me like this.'

'And he'll never be able to fuck you like I can either.'

'Is that all the cloud-being wants?' she demanded in order to cover up how her pulse took off in response to his sudden promise. 'Great sex?'

'I was coming to that.' He stepped closer to the painting. 'He's beckoning to you, Maia. He wants you to discover and fully explore your inner powers. He wants you to completely believe in them. He wants you to identify with the creative force of eternal blooming and not with the fragile petals it temporarily dresses itself in.'

'I wish it was so easy.'

'It is and it isn't, but then wherein would lie the pleasure if we climaxed in only a few seconds like animals? The sensual struggle is its own mysterious purpose and fulfillment.'

Cat's Collar - Three Erotic Romances

'Amen.'

'Let's have a look inside.' He opened the door to the room guarded by her painting.

In the center of the large space hung an enormous chandelier that came to splendid life when he flicked a switch. Apparently, the wall between two rooms had been knocked down to create one unusually large space, and the doors of what looked like two walk-in closets had been ripped off to form two cozy open alcoves, a black carpet soft and smooth as a layer of soot covering the entire floor. Directly beneath the chandelier, small wooden tables of varying styles clearly dating from different centuries were arranged in a circle, with a slightly larger space left between two of them to allow access to the pyramid of swords erected within them. The blades all pointed up at forty-five degree angles to each other, and it was impossible to tell that most of them were probably centuries old for they had been cleaned and polished until they shone as though freshly forged.

Maia watched as Drew was irresistibly drawn to the phallic blades. A ring of knives lying next to their scabbards decorated the little wooden tables, and nowhere else in the mansion was Eric's great wealth more apparent than in the ancient weapons he was able to afford. While Drew examined the swords, she found herself fascinated by the daggers, even though she had no idea what centuries they paradoxically represented. It was ironic how an instrument of death could so sumptuously evoke the life of its time. It was relatively easy for her to picture the men who had owned them because a few items of clothing, dull with age, were also laid out next to the virtually timeless metal blades. One black pair of gloves looked as though it had known at least a century of Time's merciless hand, ten decades for each finger, for only a thin shadow of cloth remained.

Drew held a sword admiringly out before him and she met his eyes over its fatal path for an instant before moving away from the gorgeous wheel of pain rimmed by the deadly clock of knives, exactly twelve of them. The room was laid out with an arcane significance that excited her in a way she was powerless to resist as she wandered through it, glancing back at the chandelier's luminous petticoats raised over so many phallic instruments of death. The edges of the room were in shadow as the objects of torture Eric had collected formed a loose cross-shape alongside one wall, in which an alcove black as a crypt contained a bed covered with white sheets. There was by far more empty black carpet than anything else in the room, a reflection of the universe itself that was not lost on her. She was pondering a scientific article she had read recently about dark-matter when she felt Drew walk up behind her.

'Are you ready to play now, Maia?'

'As ready as I'll ever be,' she replied in the same reverently hushed voice.

'The mistake everyone makes is not realizing that you have to know how to live in order to understand how to die,' he stated cryptically.

'They just expect death to happen,' she agreed, 'and that they won't have any control over it.'

'If that was how everyone felt about sex, we could never make love.'

She laughed out of nervous exultation as she turned to face him. It stunned her to discover that he had slipped on black leather gloves from one century and held a dagger with a jeweled hilt from another.

'I'm going to a lot of trouble for you, Maia.'

She somehow found her voice. 'I appreciate it, Drew.'

'You're beautiful soul is worth it.' He lightly traced one of her high cheekbones with the tip of the blade. 'You have such a stubborn skull,' he observed. 'How long is it going to take for you to fully realize and accept what's going on? Fear is the only thing that really hurts, Maia.'

'Yes, I know.'

'Then will you come with me?'

'Yes, I will, Drew.'

'Because you trust me?'

'No, because I have to.'

'That's not true, Maia, you have a choice.'

'No I don't... I love you.'

He glanced beyond her at one of the instruments of torture Eric had transformed to intensify pleasure. 'For years I sensed you were somewhere near,' he spoke as if to himself. 'I never dared dream you were Stella's own daughter.' He focused on her again. 'No other man would have been able to follow you into the fantastic illusion you conceived after that oak tree struck your womb, much less pull you out of it.'

She whispered, 'Because you love me, too?'

'As I love myself.' He smiled.

'Oh Drew…' She longed to throw her arms around him, but she was wary of the naked blade in his hand.

'However, I demand a lot from myself,' he warned, 'and I'm going to be just as hard on you, Maia.'

'But if you love me, how could you have told me to…? How could you have let Eric…? You're lying, you can't possibly really-'

'Stop giving into your fears so easily.' He clutched the front of her dress. 'You have to fight them. I'll help you.' He cut through the fine silk with one smooth motion to expose her breasts, and her pale skin was smoothly luminous in the shadows. 'No matter what happens, Maia, don't be afraid. This is your initiation into a new life. You know that nothing can happen to your divine shipper even if the body it sends itself is hurt, but it's a crime to return the gift unopened and unappreciated. Do you understand what I'm saying? Are you with me?'

Desire and doubt threatening to beat each other to the death in her pulse, she understood that only she could decide who the victor would be. 'Yes,' she said, 'I'm with you, Drew.'

Her dress hanging like bloodless black wings at her sides, Maia watched with growing excitement as Drew dramatically cut off his own shirt. She was surprised to see a silver cross hanging from a rough black cord against his chest as he tossed his ruined shirt away. She followed it with her eyes, not yet quite able to believe the sight of him half naked before her.

'Did you lock the door?' she asked anxiously.

Without answering, he pulled her against him.

She held her breath as she felt him rest the flat of the blade along her backbone.

'Relax,' he said firmly, and she knew he was slowly cutting her dress in the back, making her very much aware of the irreplaceable garment of her flesh the whole way down the seam of her spine. Her dress was now literally the rags she had felt it to be when she entered the festivities; there was no going back to the party for her now. 'This is your rite of way, Maia.'

Lightning flashes of desire as he pressed her hard against the bulge in his crotch clouded her awareness; they made her pussy so warm and wet she felt her thoughts slipping away helplessly. 'I want you,' she whispered, burying her face in the tender harbor formed by his neck and shoulder.

'You're not afraid of me?'

'No, I'm not afraid of you.'

'Good.' He released her and stepped back.

She stared worshipfully up at his face waiting to see what he would do next. He was not as pretty as Chris or as sensually arresting as Eric, yet he was the most handsome man she had ever seen. It had to be the personality shaping his features that appealed to her so much, the ability of his mind to formulate profound concepts expressed in his fine bone structure.

He shifted the dagger in his hand so that he held it by the blade and abruptly offered it to her.

She took it from him without hesitation, and before she even knew what she was doing, she had cut the cross from around his neck, the sharp edge easily slicing through the black cord. She then grasped the silver icon of Christianity so fiercely in her left hand the sharp metal bit painfully into her flesh.

After a slight flicker of surprise, his eyes challenged her.

She stared back at him, basking in having his attention focused so intently on her as she held his weapon in one hand and his cross in the other. Symbolically, his body and his soul were now hers to command, both his sexuality and his spirituality resting in her hands.

'Do you know what your name means, Maia? It means Daughter of the Earth.'

She struggled with her ignorance, desperate not to disappoint him during this arousing ritual. She had no idea what she was supposed to do or what he wanted her to do, yet she couldn't tie up her intuition wondering why he had chosen to thrust her into a play where she knew none of the lines.

She slipped out of the shreds of black silk he had left her wearing, shrugging them off like shadows at the sensual moonrise of her luminously pale skin. She was aware of the party's raucous energy still going strong beneath them, and the contrast of their two bodies silently facing each other in the utterly still room made her feel curiously empowered, as though their attraction to each other was the eye of the night's sensual storm.

She had taken drama class in school. Perhaps being in a ritual was like improvising a scene for which no script was provided, only a general theme. The cross and the phallic instrument she was holding were obvious clues… Conflict was the issue here, conflict on every level, all the contradictions that shape life, reason and intuition, fear and faith, pain and pleasure, the list was endless. And together they were standing on the fine line between the sacred and the satanic as he dared her to walk this metaphysical tightrope with him. They were acrobats balancing on the 'sword-edge bridge' from which she could easily fall into a soul-shattering decadence… or she could use it to achieve a greater mastery and higher understanding of herself…

'Take what is yours,' she heard herself say, and raising the cross she parted her lips in order to rest the cold metal on her tongue's warm bed.

His expression was all she had hoped for as he obeyed her. Tilting her face up to his, he thrust his tongue into her mouth so the arching wave of his lust caught the cross and returned it to him.

She slipped the knife back into his hand and sank to her knees before him. She was confident that with her he could explore a whole new dimension where rites no longer had to be purely symbolic, as they had been with her mother. She unzipped his pants quick as a lightning flash, gently wrested the soft seed of his penis out into her hands, and planted it reverently in her mouth.

He caressed her face with the cool blade as she sucked him, her fulfillment as great as though it was truly his soul caught between her lips like the rosy horizons of the world in which he buried himself only to rise again stronger and greater with every plunge in the rhythm of death and resurrection… but she knew he would not let himself come yet so she was not surprised when he stepped back and slipped his erection out of her mouth. She had been sure his penis would not disappoint her, but she could never have hoped it would look and feel so perfect to her. She had seen no less than three fully aroused cocks today, and this fact both worried and thrilled her as she sank contemplatively back on her heels. All she was wearing now were her high-heeled sandals as she watched him return the cross to the black cord around his neck, his eyes burning in a way that turned her on even more than the sight of his hard-on.

'Stand up,' he commanded.

She obeyed him, struggling with a strange weakness. Deprived of his creamy nourishment she felt mysteriously drained. She had actually relished the flavor of his semen in a way she never had before. For some reason his pleasure tasted better than any other man's and she longed to continue absorbing his intensity as her soul curled dreamily up in the lap of his personality, which was at once infinitely stimulating and profoundly restful. He had obviously appreciated the passionate effort of her lips and tongue, and she admired his control as she focused on the silver cross gleaming amidst the sparse black forest of hair growing between his muscular pecs. He was whole again with the savior resting against his heart and a weapon gripped in his hand, and suddenly she became fully aware of the sinister sensual instruments surrounding them, rising out of the sooty black carpet like charred tree limbs.

'I should have died that night,' she heard herself speak again in a clear, self-assured voice she barely recognized as her own. 'Lightning struck the oak tree, but it really wanted me.'

'Why do you believe that?' he asked very quietly.

'I don't know...'

'Dreams and fantasies are not as interesting as life's journey, Maia.' His voice was so gentle she felt as though his lips were moving directly against her heart in a profoundly sweet kiss of understanding. 'It's all what you make of it.'

'Yes... Oh Drew...' She was dying to fall into his strong arms.

'What have you learned, Maia?'

She was suddenly so inexplicably tired she felt as though a python was tightening remorselessly around her bones. 'I've learned that I have to take command of my body,' she began earnestly. 'I cannot allow it to rule me, yet I cannot ignore it either. I've learned that my body is like the horse my soul is riding through life and I need to have a firm but loving relationship with it. Part of me has to understand just how much freedom to give it and how much control to exert, because that's what's best for it and therefore for myself.'

'And who are you?'

'I'm Maia, the earth, and your wisdom is heaven to me, Drew, I mean the way you seem to understand everything I'm feeling…'

'What about Chris and Eric, how do you feel about them?'

'Oh God, they don't even seem real when I'm with you.'

'But they are real, aren't they?'

'Not like you are… they obey you.'

'That's right, just as they'll obey you when you're my priestess.'

'They'll obey me?' She couldn't quite picture this, but it was an exciting concept.

'Yes, they'll obey you, but only if you don't run away from life, only if you're strong enough to make them face each other.'

'Face each other? What do you mean, Drew? How-?'

'They have to face each other over your body.' The door to the torture room suddenly opened behind him. 'You're both the lion and its tamer, Maia, you can't let you're imagination run away from you and permit events to continue unfolding without your control. You have to take hold of matters.'

'What's happening?' she gasped, quickly rising so she could press herself against him and hide her naked body from whoever it was had entered the room. Then over his bare shoulder she glimpsed Chris's golden head along with Eric's unmistakable brown mane and she could scarcely catch her breath as the laws of gravity seemed to cave in on her with all her lovers suddenly in the same room. 'Why are you doing this, Drew?' she whispered desperately. 'What's going on?'

'Maia, I told you this is your rite of way. This is all happening on a metaphysical plain. Remember that and be yourself, your real self.'

She was saved from the distinct possibility of collapse when Chris very calmly took one of her hands and Eric gently grasped the other. Their faces were

Rituals of Surrender

devoid of expression as they led her away from Drew, and for some reason she didn't even think of asking where they were taking her. The truth was she had no desire to question whatever it was Drew had planned for her, and heavenly clouds could not have felt much softer than the mattress she willingly lay back across in one of the dark alcoves. Eric and Chris stood on either side of the bed and each took hold of one of her ankles to help her spread her legs for Drew as he knelt between them. The high priest had removed his pants and all he was wearing now was the silver cross.

Maia was barely aware of Chris and Eric stepping back into the shadows she was so enthralled by the sight of Drew's beautifully rigid cock about to slide into her pussy, which had been nicely primed for him by two other men. Her sex was deep and slick and just tight enough to passionately embrace his hard-on all the way down to its deliciously thick base as he slowly entered her, making her gasp with pleasure as he relished filling her with him. It was inconceivable anything could feel so good. It was almost unbearable how ideally the dimensions of his erection fitted those of her fervently yielding depths, and the experience of his penetration was made doubly intense by the way he stared down into her eyes. She slipped her hands beneath her knees, forcing her legs wide open and shifting her hips so he could sink into her completely, but then he held himself motionless as she moaned in an agony of anticipation for him to begin thrusting. His presence inside her stimulated her to no end and made his patience almost impossible to bear.

'Please,' she begged. Her voice was hoarse from the night's endless friction of emotional torment and physical ecstasy, guilt and delight, dread and exultation, fear and desire. It felt like undeniable proof of life's divine nature in the microcosmic world of all her blood cells when his hips finally began moving.

'Come, Maia, expand your horizons for me... that's it... see how good it feels?'

'Yes, oh yes!' The seed of her clitoris bloomed beneath his deep, hard, spade-like thrusts as she started coming almost at once, her enchanted nature fully unfolding around him and devastating her...

Chapter Twenty-Three

The sun passionately being born between the leaves in a quivering net of light tugged at her awareness with its beauty, the pricking shafts of illumination threading themselves through her veins until she became fully aware of her body and the chill morning air... yet it was also very pleasant the way the breeze sighed over her where she lay cradled in Drew's hard, warm arms. She couldn't remember falling asleep after they made love, yet she must have drifted off because the last thing she recalls is the nearly unbearable joy of ascending into his eyes as she climaxed. Then suddenly she was looking at blue fragments of sky between the branches of trees as he carried her across the forest floor.

It startled and worried her just a touch when he gradually genuflected and spread her body at the foot of a tree – an ancient oak very much like the one whose branch had rammed into her womb. He stepped away from her and she had every intention of getting up to follow him, but the hard ground felt so inexplicably comfortable she couldn't bring herself to move. For a brief instant she thought with distaste of all the insects crawling around in the dirt beneath her naked flesh, but this tense concern dissolved almost at once as she seemed unable to hold on to any negative thoughts. And as she gazed at the oak tree rising endlessly above her, she sensed that Chris and Eric were also somewhere nearby... she was surrounded by her own personal pyramid of men... but she was mixing religions and this was a Druid rite...

She arched her back so she could look up even farther in admiration of the ancient oak's phallic might. Then she rolled languidly over onto her stomach and grasped two of its broad roots thinking to brace herself on them as she stood up, because she couldn't just lie there forever... yet her physical strength had no more substance than mist and her body felt impossibly heavy as she struggled to her feet, supporting herself with helpful knots in the gnarled old trunk. It was an endless process pulling herself to her feet, but she made herself do it and then rested her cheek against the rough, unfeeling bark. That was when she saw the altar. Small shining crystals hung from the lower branches of the trees surrounding it, and as they swayed in the breeze, catching the intensifying light of the rising sun, they flashed lovely prisms across the dark-gray slab of rock. Drew had vanished. She seemed to be completely alone, yet her intuition told her she wasn't. She could sense her three men standing behind the black trunks of the crystal-jeweled trees and somehow she knew what they wanted her to do next. She had to lie down again, but not on the ground.

Unable to walk, Maia sank down onto her hands and knees and crawled towards the altar's stone bed. It was such an effort to move at all she felt almost as though she was underwater, the rustling of the trees at once deafeningly loud and so strangely far away the sound didn't even seem connected to the dreamily silent swaying of the branches in the wind's invisible currents. Birds had begun to sing and the chirping music was so beautiful it hurt like needles pricking the pores of her skin. She paused to catch her breath and to try and dim the acute receptivity of her senses to a more tolerable level, and noticed that the grass had left deep imprints on her palms, darkly tangled paths superimposed over the more subtle map of her lifelines. She could even smell the morning dew, which wasn't so much a scent as a pure sense of well-being. Her razor-sharp sensory perceptions seemed to be cutting straight through into another dimension in which the gravity of fear and worry played absolutely no part at all...

When at last she reached the altar, Maia rallied one final surge of strength from the utterly relaxed army of her muscles to hoist herself up onto it. Then it wasn't at all difficult to relax against the unyielding stone and to wait... wait for her dream of Fate. She had no desire to run from Drew. Life would feel meaningless to her if he was not the man she believed him to be. His sensual intensity didn't frighten her. On the contrary, it was the reason for his power over her that he could prove the truth of their shared beliefs through the force of their lovemaking. Her heaven was the love she felt for him, her hell was this constant burning desire for him, and there was no separating the two. The only way she could feel whole was to give herself to him completely, to not hold any part of herself back from him, ever.

She closed her eyes, her body languorous as a cloud held together by birdsong, and it was more of a relief than a surprise when she opened her eyes and saw Eric standing at her feet, his face once again absolutely expressionless. And even though she could not see him, she sensed Chris standing behind the altar just beyond her forehead. She licked her lips as she let her head fall to one side, and Drew was there standing parallel to her heart, a different dagger in his hand now. This particular knife boasted a golden hilt and a long, sinister blade. Looking at him she was half hypnotized by the rainbows of light appearing and disappearing and reappearing again in the shining black vest he was wearing, tiny prisms as evanescent and beautiful as life itself with all its emotional hues. He had stepped into the role of a pure power as high priest, and she fully acknowledged to herself now that this was what she had wanted from him all along.

He bent over to lightly kiss her mouth. 'Are you ready?' he whispered, his breath warm against her lips.

'You're never going to answer all my questions, are you?' she asked him, mildly surprised by her ability to speak.

'Don't you agree that our attempt to merge spirit and flesh is more interesting than anything else, more interesting especially than cut-and-dry answers you can never truly be sure of?'

'Yes, but you said they would obey me once I was your priestess,' she reminded him, referring to the other two men present. It worried her a little how unnaturally still and silent Chris and Eric were being.

Drew straightened up. 'They have come together and conceived your life, Maia.' He raised the dagger over his head so his muscular arms formed a pyramid framing his concentrated expression. 'Do you still feel torn between them?'

'No, I don't,' she replied serenely, 'because I know now that they're one inside me.'

'Amen, my priestess.' He shifted the dagger in his hands to get a firmer grip on the hilt. 'And this is your path into a realm where together we can command them at will.'

Rituals of Surrender

'Drew, what are you doing?'

'You want to live, don't you, Maia?'

'Yes, of course I want to live.'

'Then take the force of my spirit into your body, Maia, Daughter of the Earth, receive me willingly, in absolute trust and without fear, for as much as you can give me is as much as I am able to love you. Life is a single blade with two sides. Are you ready to accept this painful duality and to grasp your immortal nature's golden hilt in an effort to fight for what you believe and increase the creative power of your love?'

'Yes,' she breathed, closing her eyes, but not before she saw the flash of the blade descending over her heart...

She didn't want to open her eyes because the last thing she remembered was the first thing she became aware of – an almost unbearable pleasure. She moaned and bit her lip praying it would never go away even though she wasn't sure she could stand the divine sensation another second...

'Look at me, Maia.' A man's voice whispered and the warm breath against her mouth shocked her into forgetting the blinding ecstasy for a second, long enough for her to open her eyes. 'It's all right,' he said gently, 'everything's all right now, Maia.'

As she gazed up into the stranger's steady blue eyes, the physical joy playing so loudly in her nervous system began turning itself down into an acute but somehow tolerable delight in which she could begin to hear herself think... The man she had seen smoking in the restaurant the other night was in her room, in her bed! She remembered seeing him that evening and not wanting him to leave, and now he was here beneath her feather comforter with her as if she had dreamed him there... that was it, she was only dreaming, and in this dream her bedside lamp was still on and the sky had fallen impossibly close to her in his eyes, which narrowed as they stared down at her, making her heart contract in the most strangely wonderful way...

'It's all right,' he repeated quietly but firmly, 'you're awake now and everything is real, Maia. Do you hear me? Everything is real now.'

His statement contradicted what she had just concluded, but there was no mistaking the one very real fact of his cock buried inside her, of his erection thrust as deep into her body as a dream that was intensely real.

'Don't you know me, Maia?'

She was struggling to catch her breath beneath the flood of feelings and sensations he was arousing in her on every level. 'I saw you the other night at the restaurant!' she gasped, the silver cross hanging from his neck striking her as reassuringly familiar.

'Say my name,' he commanded.

She reached up to brace herself on the back of his neck as his body continued moving slowly but devastatingly against hers. 'Drew,' she sighed. 'Your name is Drew...'

'How much do you remember?' he asked, smiling, and suddenly he began fucking her in earnest, driving his cock in and out of her fast and hard, forcing her to experience his full rending length as his head kissed a blissfully sensitive spot deep inside her over and over again, until she thought she would die the pleasure was so intense. She didn't answer him because she couldn't hear her thoughts over how much it turned her own to watch her pert breasts bobbing up and down beneath his onslaught.

'Don't you remember anything, Maia?'

'Yes... yes, I do!' She suddenly suffered a landslide in her mind as the images of a fantastic erotic dream tumbled back into her memory and for a few wonderful moments buried her dull life beneath a gloriously seductive landscape.

'You remember?' he insisted a bit breathlessly.

'Yes, I think so... yes, yes, I do...' She glanced down the tunnel of their converging bodies at the dark point where his erection was digging into her as passionately as if her body held all the secrets of the universe. 'Am I still dreaming?' she asked anxiously, desperately wanting what was happening to be real.

'No, you're not dreaming, Maia.' Leaning on one arm he slipped a thumb between her lips, gently gagging her with it to muffle her cries as he drove into her. 'I'm your dream come true.'

Epilogue

Maia woke to the sun's rays flooding her bed. Her first thought was that she had left the window open and somehow managed to sleep through the storm that had devastated her bedroom. An amazingly powerful and disturbingly conscious wind had moved almost everything around, even going so far as to raise the lid of her old toy box (which hadn't been opened in years) and spirit her once favorite doll out of it. The poor thing was lying naked in the middle of the hardwood floor now, her long black hair an incongruously sinister halo around her happy smile.

She sat up in bed and rubbed her eyes with both hands feeling utterly disoriented. Her window, she carefully noted when she looked around her again, was closed. There was no way the wind could have gotten into her room and wreaked such havoc on her possessions. Then her hands flew to her mouth in astonishment when she realized that whatever force had rearranged her bedroom had also succeeded in stripping off her nightgown. Yet no matter how powerful it was, a storm did not have hands, only a person could have… only a man…

'It wasn't a dream,' she whispered. 'He was real and I knew him, I really knew him…' She looked around her room again in disbelief even as part of her began to understand the mysterious order behind the apparent chaos.

The clay ashtray she had made for her father such a long time ago was on her nightstand and it was full of cigarette butts. She knew right away they did not belong to her father since Peter hadn't smoked for years. The nicotine-stained paper had touched another man's lips, and suddenly she recalled the slightly bitter taste in his mouth when he kissed her…

Flinging the sheet off her to kneel on the mattress, Maia reached for the ashtray, but then she didn't dare touch it. An unpleasant odor like an evil aura surrounded this undeniable evidence that something very strange had happened in this room…

Rituals of Surrender

Very tentatively, she left the illusory safety of the bed she had slept in alone until last night.

She searched the floor for her nightgown. She couldn't find it anywhere, but in the process she discovered many other strange and interesting things. Black and violet candles were set in a bronze candelabrum on her window seat, from which the pillows had been removed and laid side-by-side at the dark entrance to her walk-in closet. An empty wine glass was reflected in her vanity mirror, and the protective glass pane over the woven wicker frame was covered with recent photographs of herself that had all been tampered with in some way. Her most recent portrait had been burned around the edges into an egg-shape and two small magazine images, one of a white bird in flight and the other of a black panther, had been glued to its sides like wings. Her dresser had been moved so the reflection of her bed stretched out behind her in the mirror, and a glimmer of gold emerging from beneath one of her pillows caught her eye.

She whirled around and confirmed the sight had not been a trick of the light; the smooth round end of an object was indeed protruding from beneath her pillow, and she knew what it was at the same moment that she fully understood what had happened to her. The man she remembered seeing in the restaurant had entered the intensely erotic dream she had been living, and he had even helped create it with her. Her room was cluttered with the toys he had used to evoke its images, which meant he had been telling her the truth when he helped her imagine they were sitting by a lake – that her accident and her coma had not happened years ago, that they were happening now and she was only dreaming they were distant memories. He deliberately had not picked up the mess he had made playing with her subconscious in order to leave her proof of their haunting game, and the glint of gold in her bed was the spark that brought it all back to her in one burning rush of amazement. Somehow, he had managed to pull her out of her incredibly vivid imagination and back into her real, living body, and marvelously wicked images began licking through her memory that caused her to sink weakly into the wicker chair in front of her vanity.

The door to her bedroom opened cautiously.

It was too late to run and put on some clothes, so fortunately it was only

Stella, who froze on the threshold as her hand flew to her throat.

'How long ago did Drew leave?' Maia asked her mother. 'I want to be a Druid, too. And by the way, I forbid you and daddy to drive anywhere on May Day!'

'Oh Maia...' Stella rushed over to hug her, and her mother's arms felt strangely soft and vulnerable to Maia after Drew's strong embrace.

'Mummy, lock the door please.'

'It's all right, dear, your father went over to Carol's house for a moment to check on her and see if she needed anything. The poor thing isn't used to walking around with a cane yet. How do you feel, sweetheart? Should you be out of bed?'

'There's a knife under my pillow.'

'A knife?!' Stella glanced at her daughter's bed as if it had suddenly caught fire.

'It's the kind of dagger the Druids used for their sacrifices. He left it for me.' Maia stood up and approached her bed. 'He used it in the dream.'

'He what?!'

Maia slipped her hand beneath the pillow, grasped the golden hilt and held the long blade up to admire it. 'He penetrated another dimension to come after me and to bring me back with him. He saved me.' She smiled. 'I woke up in his arms after he sacrificed me in my imagination just like in an ancient Druid rite.'

Stella stared at her with a dazed respect. 'You know everything now, don't you?'

'Yes. Is Carol all right?'

'She's fine. She was released from the hospital two weeks ago, but form now on she'll always need a cane to walk.'

'I know, she'll always have a bad limp, the poor dear.'

'Maia, how can you know that? I mean, you've been-'

'I've been in a coma for over a month, I know. Why hadn't you and dad ever told me you were Druids?'

'Because Peter has never been very comfortable with our involvement, or really trusted Drew.'

'Well he'll have to start trusting him now.' Maia walked over to the window and looked down at the quiet street. The freshly laid black asphalt looked impenetrably dark even in the bright early morning sunshine. Then her heart literally seemed to stop for an instant when she saw Drew leaning against a small red sports car, his arms crossed over his chest as he stood looking directly up at her bedroom. He smiled when he saw her naked figure appear in the window, and the blade he had left her rang against the pane as she began lifting it out of her way. She ceased her effort, however, when he shook his head and formed a silent message with his lips her heart understood perfectly. She would see him again later. This was only the beginning for them, and it was not a dream, it was real. She smiled back at him, and then watched happily as he slipped into the shining modern armor of his car and drove away straight into her heart forever.

The End

Cat's Collar

DEDICATION

For Stinger, the man I love. Thank you for always believing in me, and for giving me more than I can ever express no matter how many books I write.

And for Merlin, who always keeps me company while I write by passionately chewing his bone or by sleeping and dreaming curled up at my feet.

Author's Note

Last night the full moon felt like a spotlight shining in my brain and pulling on the wet strings of all my veins as if my mortal flesh is some kind of corset relentlessly being tightened by myriad efforts at self-improvement, so I can look and be my absolute best for that elusive man – that dream I had – of a life-long soul-mate.

I couldn't sleep. According to the flaming red numbers on my digital clock, I lay awake from about 2:29 to some time after 4:00 thinking and thinking; weaving thought after thought without coming to any wearable conclusions. Then I must have fallen asleep at last because I had a nightmare that the man I loved no longer loved me. He was featureless – his face was composed of all the photographs of us being happy together – and I was so furious and grief-stricken that I clawed viciously into these falsely idyllic images with my fingernails. He smiled placidly, maddeningly, and said, 'These things happen.' It was a profound relief to wake up again to the moon's unblinking glare like a divine hand shining a flashlight into the cobwebs of my thought processes as I thankfully remembered true love isn't a dream. The net of circumstances fashioning my life had indeed finally captured my heart's desire. Part of me still couldn't quite believe it (hence the nightmares) but it was true, and I smiled contentedly as I gazed at his naked body lying beside mine, long and sleek and relaxed as a big cat's on our moonlit bed.

Every day we spend together, all the words we say to each other, every thought, every feeling we share, every experience, every hope, every sadness, every dream is part of the fabric of our love, of our life which has become magically one. Sometimes the emotional fabric of our relationship is as mysterious-

Cat's Collar

ly stimulating as black leather; often it's as cozy and comfortable as a cotton throw on a cold winter night; and always it makes even the roughest circumstances feel smooth as satin, rich as velvet and warm as silk-lined wool. Whatever the emotional fabric of our love, I know in my soul that it's woven with an unbreakable and somehow eternal thread. Maybe one day I'll learn how to sew a dress, but for now I'll stick to what I do best and tell the story of how two other lovers met...

Prologue

"And as she worked, gazing at times out on the snow, she pricked her finger, and there fell from it three drops of blood on the snow... Not very long after she had a daughter, with skin as white as snow, lips as red as blood, and hair as black as ebony..."

Once upon a time – right now, actually – there lives a beautiful young woman named Mira. Her last name doesn't matter, but if you must know it's Rosemond, inherited from her father like half the genes in her pool, although 'microcosmic sea' would be a better analogy for the depth of thoughts and feelings composing her unique personality. Nevertheless, it was the sensual hum of 'Mm' and the buzzing energy of 'ee' and the profoundly joyful sigh of 'ra!' that greeted her when she entered the world, cradling her soul in consonants and vowels forming a special sound to make her feel at home in her individual mystery. You might argue that children's names are picked at random, but it can also be said there is no such thing as coincidence, and in Mira's case the name given her at birth truly suited her. In Spanish 'mira' means 'look' and look she did from day one, avidly studying her surroundings from the moment her eyes opened, and it wasn't long before she was curiously touching and assessing the shape and texture of everything she could get her pudgy (and already passionately possessive) little hands on. Her parents fondly brag to friends that their daughter was born an Interior Designer. From a very early age, Mira frowned severely, scrunching her face up in warning that a fit of outraged howling was imminent, if whatever they hung up over her crib didn't please her. Plastic toys and mobiles painted in garish primary colors were at

Cat's Collar

once banished from her bedroom, and silvery, lavender-colored wallpaper glimmering with hints of forest green in the sunlight soothingly surrounded her as she was growing up, having immediately replaced a terrifying décor of painted teddy bears and other zoologically unrealistic nightmares.

Mira grew up a child of the four seasons – fall, winter, spring and summer were all clearly defined in her psyche. If she had any complaint it was that it didn't snow quite enough to get her out of school. The white-washed dullness of public school classrooms was an affront to her senses, including her sixth sense – from a very early age she sensed that learning about the world was supposed to be a lot more fun and entertaining in the sense of involving her whole being, which consisted of her feelings and imagination as well as her fact-filled brain. Fortunately, the world outside was glorious, and when the weather was nice she liked taking her Barbie's camping down by the creek. She loved seeing their colorfully made-up and perpetually smiling faces contrasted against dark, hard, threatening rocks. It was unbelievably exciting to Mira that her surrogate selves actually got wet, and that there was real danger of them being carried away by the current, the dirt tainting their pure, plastic skins making it look vulnerably alive. She almost ecstatically enjoyed exposing her sensual dolls to the elements. She loved seeing the sun shining on the different colors of their hair, and the water lapping around their stiffly swimming arms and legs. Her own large, living hands were in control of their fate, holding and maneuvering their bodies the way the laws of the physical world she was learning about in science class surrounded her. This childish perception eventually led her to conclude a part of her was a vast, immortal awareness expressing Itself through the laws of manifestation – an eternal consciousness enjoying endless experiences of Itself through the dolls of its incarnations. But at the time she was still much too young to entertain such profound metaphysical thoughts. She simply relished the feel of the cool, rushing water contrasting with the warm caress of sunlight on her skin, and the dark thrill she experienced as she subjected her numerous pretend bodies to the sucking depth of the mud between the slick rocks on which they perched as lovely as mermaids. Her mind had not yet so defined it, but in her soul she knew all the world's elements were there for her soul to be creative with. Even before she could express the concept, she knew her spirit was immutable in essence no matter what happened to the forms through which it adventured and however much it loved them. That's not to say she wouldn't have been seriously upset if she had lost any of her dolls in the creek because in a sense they *were* her. Her Barbie's were still the only way she was able express the invisible, yet all-consuming intensity of her feelings, symbolized by the water threatening to carry her heroines away and by the dark mud sucking on their daintily arched feet, which were designed to wear only sexy high-heels.

History was Mira's favorite subject; she read about it voraciously, lying awake well into the night, fascinated by the different styles of life people had enjoyed throughout the ages – different clothes and food and homes and ways of expressing their thoughts and feelings. She was horrified to learn about the Oriental custom of binding women's feet, blithely unaware that the dolls she played with were having a similarly binding and shaping effect on how she perceived herself. She clearly remembers the first time she watched the Miss Universe pageant with her father. She enjoyed the spectacle of living dolls clad in the magnificently colorful costumes of their native cultures, until it dawned on her that they were competing against *her* too, which seriously offended her. No one had asked *her* to be in the pageant. The only thing that assuaged her wounded pride was the knowledge she was still too young for other people to see the woman who looked back at her from the mirror through her glowing, honey-colored eyes. So she grudgingly forgave the world its blindness even as she ran upstairs to the bathroom to gaze at herself, thinking, *I'm more beautiful than any of them...* Mira didn't realize it at the time, of course, but it was her soul talking. Even when pimples bloomed like poisonous red flowers across her face, and braces imprisoned her smile behind iron fences, she never lost sight of who she really was deep down or gave up hope that her flesh-and-blood would eventually catch up.

It amused her doting father to no end that Mira, at the tender age of six, declared herself more beautiful than the reigning Miss Universe. He smiled. 'Whatever you say, dear.'

'Or at least I will be when I grow up!' she insisted fervently.

Cat's Collar

'Mira, my love, there's more to beauty than meets the eye. Remember, beauty is not just skin deep.'

Subconsciously, she pondered her father's words for years, because it was the eyes that beheld beauty, she knew, yet she also sensed there was a deeper part of her that responded to it. And this reasoning led her to conclude so-called good taste has invisibly deep roots like the big oak tree in the front yard. It was this tree that first aroused in her an appreciation for clean and hard but also organically supple lines. Yet serious as this impressive life form was, she sensed it enjoyed being decorated by the elements. It looked absolutely splendid in the fall – a living palette of red and gold and oranges she struggled to capture on paper with her crayons. Then in the heart of winter the ancient oak was either hauntingly naked, its dark, open arms reaching for the heavens, or it was cloaked in snow and making her feel as if the silence around it was communicating a mysterious secret to her straining senses. For her the spirit of the tree was best revealed in the bold black-and-white lines with which it impressed itself on her vision after a snowstorm, much more so than during its lush abandon in the spring, when it was just another guest at the wild party nature threw every year at the same time.

Mira was the apple of her parents' eyes, and if as she grew older some of the things she said caused a shocked retort to stick in their throats, they only loved her all the more for it. A mild couple, they never rocked anyone's boat, including their own, so perhaps that was why they so enjoyed the heady wind of their daughter's exuberant imagination. Mira transformed the sedate sheet of their marriage bed into a sail swollen with promise as from the moment she was born it seemed she directed the course of all their lives.

Like any healthy girl, Mira had friends while she was growing up, but none of them could match her intense creative energy, and one fine summer evening she walked out on her best friend. She had gone over to Anna's house to spend the night, and eagerly began suggesting fascinating games they could play, beginning with Barbie's in the den using all the paper tombstones she had made for the graveyard and all the individual portraits of each doll she had drawn to hang inside the haunted Mansion.

'No,' Anna said placidly.

'Okay, how about Arabian Nights?' Mira went on, undaunted. 'We could set up your dad's camping tent in the back yard and pretend we've been captured and are being held prisoner in an oasis by handsome-'

'No,' I don't feel like it.

'Okay, then how about Mission Impossible? I brought my tape recorder to record the mission.'

'No.'

'Well then how about Go-Go Dancers? We can stand on chairs in the basement and pretend that upstairs is the hotel where we go-'

'No, I'd rather just watch TV, okay?'

'What?!' TV, her perennial enemy swallowing all her wonderfully exciting ideas and reducing her best friend to a zombie staring glassy-eyed at the screen. She left in a rage, infinitely proud of herself as she stomped the three blocks home. It caused quite a scandal, Anna's mother calling Mira's mother to find out what had happened, and Rose tactfully trying to explain to her that Mira had concluded her friend's inertia was dangerous to her health.

It was especially wonderful for Mira when she could manage to organize a war in her neighborhood. She divided all the kids up into two armies, always making sure to make the best looking boys her enemies so she could enjoy being shot by them. And the most fun part of the game for her was spreading herself out as seductively as possible on the grass to experience their reaction to the sight of her lovely, vulnerable body as they ran by. Unfortunately, they usually reacted with indifference, but the rare joy of having one of them bend down and mourn her loss, then perhaps risk his life to remove her from the battlefield and give her a proper burial, was worth all the usual frustration. And after a while, she automatically came alive again, which set her to thinking that the dead must feel similarly neglected if their living relatives cease to pay any attention to them just because they happen to be dead. They're just in a different stage of the game, that's all, and after a while they'll be reborn again as naturally as she got up from the battlefield of her yard and ran back into the fray. That's how it seemed to her, anyway, which may explain why she was never able to find any truly interesting playmates.

Cat's Collar

To her mother's carefully concealed chagrin, Mira pointedly ignored any baby dolls unsuspecting relatives chose to give her for Christmas or her birthday. She made it quite clear from the time she was very young that she had no intention of growing up and becoming a mother just to watch someone else grow up and become a mother to watch someone else grow up and become a mother in an endless vicious cycle. She planned to live her life to the fullest even when she still didn't have a clue what that meant. Rose didn't know how to embroider (she had a hard time just sewing the buttons back on her husband's dress shirts) so it wasn't likely she had pricked her finger while she was pregnant with Mira and wished for a baby with lips as red as blood, skin as white as snow and hair as black as ebony, but that's what she got anyway. Mira's coloring was a mystery – her mother's hair was blonde and her father's was light-brown – as though some anonymous relative from generations past had sought to be reborn through her. Mira secretly believed she wasn't related to anyone except herself, really.

Does anyone ever really enjoy being a teenager? It was hell giving up her Barbie's, but her body increasingly demanded to be the star of the show, no longer tolerating symbolic understudies. This terrible transition between the beautiful freedom of her imagination, and the struggle to embody it so she could make all her dreams come true in reality, is one Mira (like many other one-time adolescents) prefers to forget. Ever since she could remember she was grateful her parents had not condemned her to an all-girl school, for as she told her best friend in third grade, 'I would die if I couldn't be around boys all day.' Mira was also grateful she was only forced to attend Catholic school for two years before graduating to the licentious freedom of High School, although in many ways she enjoyed her uniformed stint in St. Leo's. All the classes went to church every Friday morning, a ritual that united her religious sensibilities with those of her heart and body – she loved glancing at the boys and seeing them glance at her while they did enigmatically attractive things like kneel and pray and take communion. For her there was no sight more devastating on the planet than seeing the boy she had a crush on wearing an immaculate white shirt and black tie sinking to his knees after receiving the Body of Christ in his mischievously smiling mouth. Oh, God, I love him! she thought. *I love him! I love him! I want him, please, God, I want him so much!* Some of her conversations with Jesus weren't exactly eloquent. And this delicious smoldering attraction to the opposite sex had been fanned by her hormones to a painfully raging fire by the time she turned fifteen. Even though she couldn't resist exploring the bases, she never went all the way, stubbornly saving herself for her soul mate. However, when the man of her dreams still hadn't shown up by the time she turned nineteen, Mira at last surrendered the ruby-red jewel of her virginity, which really wasn't worth anything in the 20th Century anyway.

Chapter One

"How can a silly beast give one any rational advice?"

Mira very reluctantly opens her eyes.

Big glowing irises the color of newborn spring leaves gaze back at her intently. 'Merr,' says Stormy, and butts his soft gray forehead against hers.

In all her twenty-seven years, Mira has never known such an affectionate cat. If her friendly feline doesn't realize that his weight on her chest is making it difficult for her to catch her breath, and if he's infinitely ignorant of the fact that he murdered a beautiful dream, the loving 'good morning' he always gives her more than makes up for his innocent transgressions.

'Stormy!' she gasps, lifting the padded pressure points of his paws off her chest and diaphragm. 'You're such a silly, stupid cat!' she coos.

A rumbling purr courses through his languid silver-gray body hanging over her like a storm cloud.

'Mami was having the best dream you silly, stupid pussy!'

'Purr... purr... purr...' The tone of her voice translates the insults into loving compliments inside his blessedly small brain.

Mira sets him down on the lavender sheet beside her, but he promptly leaps off the bed, his mission to awaken her accomplished. He will be off in search of his black sister; they cannot long be parted. Sekhmet – named after the ancient Egyptian goddess of strength and aggression – would never dream of saying good morning, and if she did consider it her greeting would undoubtedly take the form of a calculated swipe of her sharp claws.

Cat's Collar

Mira lingers languidly on her feather mattress. One of the many virtues of being self-employed is that she sets her own schedule. She scarcely remembers the last time she was forced to get up at the crack of dawn, which always made her feel there was a fatal crack in her psyche through which her soul was seeping away and leaving her with an empty, existential anxiety only the sunrise cured her of. Having spent most of her life (ever since she learned how to read) devouring books, Mira is aware of the ancient Celtic obsession with thresholds and crossover moments. In her opinion, rising before the sun places you in one of those powerfully vulnerable moments when the line between dimensions vanishes and the darkness outside is indistinguishable from the darkness within, in which the cold fear of death can be soothed only by the sun's rebirth.

Throwing her arms luxuriously over her head she stretches the rocky path of her spine against the thousands of feathers cushioning her skeleton, wrapped in silky-smooth flesh like a haunting present from her eternal spirit to her sensual soul... One of the few drawbacks of being self-employed is the temptation to indulge in poetic metaphysics in order to prolong the effort of dragging her body out of bed and starting a day she knows will not be half as stimulating as her sleeping and waking dreams. She always sleeps naked, loving the soft caress of Egyptian cotton sheets against her skin, and as she flings them off another temptation to linger on her cloud of feathers presents itself in the form of her very desirable body.

The sight of her firm, round breasts with their long, thick nipples never fails to excite her. She loves how small and tight and flushed with color her aureoles become when they're aroused, and it doesn't take much to raise erotically charged goose bumps on her bosom's rosy buds, sending her nipples thrusting up and out like hungry stamens. She usually can't resist cradling her soft tits in her hands, and squeezing them appreciatively. What she needs is the tip of a handsome man's tongue flicking across her tense peaks as lightly and swiftly as a hummingbird's wings awakening the sweet warm nectar between her thighs, the achingly tight bud of her pussy protected by thick and tender petals. It has been so long since she allowed a man to penetrate her, that the mere thought of her labial lips blooming open around a hard cock causes her sleepy clitoris to peer excitedly out from its fleshy hood. Knowing this almost painfully thick, long dick is only a figment of her imagination doesn't stop Mira's juices from flowing as she imagines it slowly filling her... and when this legendary erection begins thrusting, ramming violently into her, she gratefully surrenders to the invasion setting her on fire... deep moats and castles under violent siege fill her mind as she crushes her body's magically sensitive seed beneath two fingertips. She rubs herself furiously, igniting a beautiful conflagration in the nerve-endings piled so thickly beneath her clit a timeless blaze dedicated to the goddess of pleasure soon rages in her pelvis as she climaxes...

Afterwards, there's no excuse left for not getting out of bed and abandoning the mattress she knows is stuffed mainly with the small black feathers of anonymous winged creatures, because every now and then one of them stabs her painfully in the middle of the night by way of revenge.

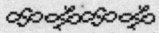

Mira owns several lovely hand-painted teapots, but they serve primarily as decoration in her kitchen as every morning she simply fills a mug with water and micro-waves it for a minute before adding her Organic Earl Grey teabag and a little of her favorite soy milk creamer. Usually by now she has already gone for a jog through the neighborhood and dressed for the day, but on this particular morning she is in the grip of an irresistible ennui. If she had a morning meeting scheduled with a client she would fight the mild depression fogging her positive energy by applying a light layer of make-up to her face – seductively blending black eyeliner with the shadow of sadness in her dark-gold eyes – and by dressing professionally, but also with an eye to looking sexy; no boring corporate suits for her, thank you. She got her fill of polyester-cotton blends working for a large interior decorating firm that hired her fresh from college, principally for her looks, although she hadn't realized that at the time. The ink on her degree had barely dried before she found herself questioning her choice of profession. Selecting the right table and chairs for corporate boardrooms from a list of pre-approved suppliers

Cat's Collar

was not her idea of being creative. She felt like a cog in a machine that would run more smoothly without her; her imagination kept having the disruptive effect of a mote of dust on a programmed computer chip. The CEO's of banks, chemical companies, and other multi-million dollar corporations failed to appreciate the colorful, life-affirming changes she suggested they make to their abstract decorating schemes. She lasted thirteen months at her first job because she was beautiful enough to express her unorthodox concepts to men who enjoyed watching her talk without listening to what she said, the Memo on their desk already having determined the acceptable look of their new offices. Mira's role was to be decorative and to stroke their egos while making sure the right tables, chairs and abstract paintings were delivered.

The view outside the many windows of her small house blatantly defies her dark mood. Another glorious May day has dawned in northern Virginia. Maybe how unconsciously happy and fulfilled nature is in the spring is what's getting on her nerves and making her profoundly jealous. For Mira it's easier to be alone in the winter with the passionately warm flames of a fire keeping her company, her body hidden beneath cozy sweaters and black house pants not constantly taunting her with the knowledge that her youth and beauty are flowing by unappreciated; unpenetrated. But whether she likes it or not, it's springtime now and she keeps her windows open night and day to catch the cool breeze and to avoid awakening her central air conditioner – the evil Freon-eating dragon living in her utility room breathing out poisonous fumes. Her open-window policy has her parents seriously concerned about her safety, but she enjoys the deeply soothing and strangely stimulating sound of leaves rustling in the wind too much to worry. Dad leant her half the money she needed to buy these three acres of tree-filled land, and her 'doll's house' as he fondly nicknamed it is the best thing that has happened to her in her adult life so far. At least she isn't condemned to an apartment's cage, where she might or might not be allowed a single pet. Her two beloved cats, and all the life growing around her, help keep her soul company while she waits...

Still wearing her violet silk robe – a skimpy affair from *Victoria's Secret*, her favorite multi-billion dollar corporation – Mira sips her hot tea as she unlocks the kitchen door and steps out into nature's delightful rush hour. Three stone bird baths and six wooden feeders hanging from the strong branches of several oaks and maples make her yard a favorite pit stop for countless birds, and many of them even seem to call it home. A double flash of red in the corner of her eye signals the flight of two cardinals from one spot in the treetops to another, and she takes another sip of tea pondering the mystery of birds' flight patterns. How do they determine where they soar to next with such energetic purpose? The branches of trees all look pretty much the same to her, and yet these light feathered beings always seem to know exactly which one they want to land on next.

Caffeine's chemical coach urging her brain cells to wake up and begin exercising themselves again, Mira wishes all the possible courses her life might take were as visible as a tree's branches, and that in one of them she could spot what her soul longs for, her heart soaring on the wings of relief and joy as she flies straight into his arms...

She sighs and walks barefoot towards her garage, enjoying the slightly rough texture of the cool gray stones in such contrast to her warm and tender flesh... flesh that has not been caressed by a man's hands in how long? She has lost count of the months and suspects enough have passed to make a whole year, a long time, and yet apparently not enough time for her loveless curse to end, because the divine blessing of true love still remains only the dream of a girl raised on fairytales. After she had her pussy pricked by more rejected suitors than she can count, she became totally disenchanted with the so-called dating scene and unofficially swore a vow of celibacy akin to sleeping away her youth and beauty waiting for her soul-mate. Yet are these tales of 'once upon a time' that always end 'happily ever after' in true love as bad for a woman's soul as eating fast-food is for the body? Certainly feminists want her to think so, but Mira loves her red leather-bound book of *Grimm's Fairytales* rather like a good Christian loves his bible. In her opinion, it is utterly simplistic to consider fairytales part of society's millenniums' old attempt to suppress the independent spirit in women. Anyone with half a brain not lobotomized by excessive social consciousness can see that fairytales are metaphysical equations involving the opposing yet complimentary

Cat's Collar

forces of man and woman, fire and water, sun and moon, nature and spirit, matter and energy popularly referred to as ying and yang, a concept she knows a good deal about as a casual practitioner of *Feng Shui*. Mira suspects that a prince and princess living happily ever after is an esoteric way to describe a person initiated into the mystery of his or her existence who is at one with the forces shaping all of life. And this is pretty much how she feels about true love… she and her other half will come together as one fulfilled whole that will be infinitely wiser and more beautiful and creative than they can ever be apart…

'Meow!' Sekhmet's preemptory tone rouses Mira from her Grim reverie as she fishes a key out of the pocket of her thigh-length robe to open the garage door.

'Good morning, my lady.' She smiles affectionately at Stormy's sister where she sits in the grass in the regal pose of her ancient Egyptian namesake, her lovely face held perfectly straight over her long legs, her slender haunches sleek black pyramids behind her.

Sekhmet's yellow eyes glare up at her with an expression that clearly tells Mira she has just exceeded the level of clueless stupidity her haughty feline expects from people.

'What?' Mira snaps, arrested by the glassy stare that invariably makes her feel like Sekhmet's pet human.

The black cat does not deign to reply but simply sits there, her whole body strangely taut and transfixed with purpose, as if she is trying to communicate something vitally important…

Mira gasps.

The sound of glass shattering against stone harmonizes with the chirping of birds.

She dropped her cup of tea only half drunk at her feet. She is accustomed to Sekhmet occasionally bringing home a boyfriend or two, but this time she has wandered as far as the zoo and scored the supreme catch of a big black panther… then her vision shifts into focus and she sees a man kneeling in the grass wearing skin-tight black leather pants. The instant her brain registers his true form he seems to suddenly appear before her and she cannot for the life of her understand how she failed to perceive his presence before. He is wearing an equally tight long-sleeved black leather shirt and black boots. Sekhmet rubs against them passionately, purring wantonly and further astonishing her owner, who has never seen her display such affection for anyone except her brother.

'I'm sorry,' the man speaks in a deep, quiet voice as he rises, 'I didn't mean to frighten you.'

Mira just stares at him as he walks towards her. Her heart is still pounding between her breasts from the shock, which won't seem to comfortably ebb as the sight of him rushes into her visual cortexes like a high tide filling all the sad, empty spaces inside her.

Following him, Sekhmet sniffs disdainfully at the spilled tea.

'Stay back, sweetheart,' the stranger urges gently, genuflecting before Mira's bare feet, and the cat and the woman both watch him intently as he picks up the pieces of broken glass and collects them in his other hand. Mira thinks of saying, 'You don't have to do that' but the polite words can't seem to get past all the emotions in her throat. Her view of his broad shoulders in slick, gleaming black is having a vertiginous effect on her ability to think straight, as though she is falling into a black hole that suddenly, impossibly, formed in the middle of her backyard. His hair is cut short and the same shining black as his clothes, as is the goatee framing his smile when he glances up at her... a smile that dims significantly as his eyes fall back down to her naked thighs...

She lifts one foot to step instinctively away from his open appraisal of her naked flesh, but he suddenly grasps her ankle. 'Don't move,' he commands his fingers warm and hard against her skin. 'You'll cut yourself,' he explains, releasing her leg to snatch up the offending shard of glass. 'There, I think that's all of them.' He straightens up.

'Thank you,' she declares stupidly, since it is his fault she dropped the cup and broke it in the first place.

'My pleasure...?' He arches a questioning black eyebrow above eyes the same color as the stones beneath her feet.

She breathes her name, 'Mira!'

'Phillip.' He holds the palm filled with broken glass up between them.

Cat's Collar

She wonders if he is offering the broken fragments to her, but then her brain shifts into rational gear. 'My trashcan is over there,' she says, and watches, focusing on his tight ass and long legs, as he strides over to the grey metal canister concealed behind a trellis gloriously overgrown with a wisteria vine in full bloom. He lifts the lid, and deposits the shards in the empty bin with a musical clangor mysteriously echoed by all her nerve-endings as he approaches her again.

She is torn between clutching her robe tightly closed over her breasts and making sure her thighs aren't too exposed. Okay, so *Victoria's Secret* doesn't make the most practical garments on earth; the slippery silk seems designed to fall open in all the right, or under certain circumstances all the wrong, places. And there is another way she feels compelled to defend herself. 'Why are you in my yard?' she demands mildly, because another part of her really can't resent such a striking intrusion. 'And why are you dressed like that at nine-thirty in the morning?'

'Please forgive me.' He picks Sekhmet up by the scruff of the neck like a kitten and cradles her slender buttocks in his other hand. 'Your lovely animal here tempted me into taking a short cut home this morning, and I dared to assume if I had her permission it would be all right with her owner as well.' His ink-black goatee makes his grin seem bright as the crescent moon causing serious tidal waves in her heart. *Feng Shui* understands that the moon affects the human body, which is made primarily of water, but nowhere in any of her textbooks on the ancient art of controlling the flow of energy has she ever read about the possible effects of a handsome stranger dressed entirely in black cutting through her yard.

'You know, it's much better to meander than to cut a path straight as an arrow,' she informs him, vaguely aware she is rambling inanely, because her pulse is telling her quite clearly the energy this man has brought into her garden is not negative. The sun could not be shining more brightly, yet Sekhmet is filling the atmosphere with a thunderous contentment, and Mira realizes with a start that this is the first time she has ever seen her proud cat so unselfconsciously relaxed.

'So, should I consider your land off limits in the future?' he asks, his carnivorously civilized white teeth no longer visible, but the ghost of a smile lingers in the dimples defining the corners of his slender mouth.

'Um, I didn't say that,' she stammers, mentally cursing herself for her submissive response even as the look in his eyes thrills her. She has never seen such irises... like the stones beneath her feet at different times of the year they look at once shockingly cold and painfully hot to the touch of her soul staring deeply into them, unable to look away. 'Where do you live?' she demands a bit breathlessly.

He pretends to glance over his shoulder. 'Oh, just across the way.'

'Just across the way where?'

He smiles. 'You know, over the river and through the woods...'

'Those directions lead to grandma's house,' she retorts, but can't resist returning his smile. 'You look more like the wolf.'

'I was on my way home from work.' At last he deigns to at least partially explain his intensely sexy attire.

Her mind races trying to come up with professions which require a man to wear skin-tight black leather, and suddenly a fear sharp and cold as a knife stabbing her in the gut wrenches the dreaded question from her like a cry of pain before she can stop it. 'You're gay?!'

His laughter feels like church bells ringing and announcing the end of the plague. 'No,' he says firmly, setting Sekhmet gently down at his feet, 'but I certainly appreciate your fervent curiosity.'

Abruptly, he reaches for her right hand where it is clenched over her heart holding her robe modestly closed, and this time she doesn't step back away from him. As she returns his penetrating regard, the thought crosses her mind that she didn't get out of bed after all; that she is still lying on her feather mattress wrapped in lavender sheets, dreaming. On the other hand her vision is strikingly clear and telling her that even his hand is attractive, with long, strong, fingers that are neither too masculine or too effeminate, his fingernails neatly trimmed but not obviously manicured. Maybe she notices these details to distract herself from the fact that she is letting a complete stranger grasp her hand and wrench it gently free of her robe, which faints dangerously open. Glancing down at her chest, Mira becomes self-consciously aware of her hard nipples impressing themselves on the fine fabric.

Cat's Collar

'Relax,' he whispers. A soft smile never leaves his mouth, as if he is privy to an infinite number of profoundly amusing secrets. He gently pries open her fingers, clenched into a fist around a key that has left an imprint on the map of her palm intersecting with all her life-lines. She gazes at the living bas relief in her skin as he unlocks the garage door for her.

'I owe you a cup of tea, Mira.' He slips the key back into the pocket of her robe with a swift, light caress she can neither take offense to or appreciate.

The knowledge that he is about to be on his way is intolerable. Outwardly, he will only be a minor disruption to her morning, but in truth his slender black form has already had the devastating effect of a tornado on her thoughts and feelings, which she knows will keep revolving obsessively around him. 'You can cut through my yard any time,' she says fervently, and is rewarded by the sight of his smile fully reaching his eyes for the first time.

'Thank you, Mira, you have a beautiful garden. But if I may observe, although I have absolutely no complaints about your attire, you hardly look dressed to drive anywhere.' He glances at the screen door leading into her kitchen. 'And didn't I see a car parked out front?'

She is overjoyed to realize he is fishing; he wants to know if that was her car he saw in the driveway or if she has someone – a man – in the house with her. For half a heartbeat she considers keeping him in suspense, but it's not in her nature. 'I use my garage for storage,' she explains.

'So, you're not one of those women who judges a man by his vehicle?'

He seems to be teasing her, his smile blooming briefly into a grin again, yet looking at it feels strangely like studying a flower up close while behind it she never ceases to be aware of the storm-grey, threatening horizon of his eyes. Yet the quality of his stare is not threatening in the sense that it frightens her; it is threatening in an exciting way, like lightening striking so close to home all the lights go out and force her to light candles, that kind of threat. 'Well, I wouldn't say that, exactly... Phillip.' She tastes his name on her tongue and feels warm all over for an instant as if she just downed a shot of hard liquor. 'I admit I often judge a man by his vehicle, the fleshly kind, the one with four wheels isn't that important.'

'Then what do you keep in your garage, Mira? You don't strike me as a pack-rat.' He glances at the garage door. 'Is it full of gardening tools and boxes of old clothes and books? Yet you're also not exactly dressed for gardening right now, are you. And if you only use the place for storage, what was it you so desperately needed to get at nine-thirty in the morning before you'd even finished your cup of tea?'

She likes the way his mind works too much to be offended by his intrusiveness, because obviously none of this is any of his business. But of course nothing is really obvious except how attracted she is to him, which places the conversation under the jurisdiction of entirely different laws than those which operate in normal polite society. 'Well, as a matter-of-fact, Phillip, in the Chinese horoscope I am a Rat.'

He crosses his arms over his chest. 'And I'm a Dragon.' He is at least six-feet-two inches tall, which combined with his attire makes his imperious stance quite effective.

She opens the garage door. 'This is my treasure room,' she confesses proudly, switching on the overhead light and stepping into the cool, temperature-controlled space. She hears the sound of his boots following her inside and triumph, pure and absolute, fills her to the very roots of her being for a timeless moment.

Chapter Two

"That is a wonderful animal, with most singular ideas."

The stranger's high-pitched melodic whistle threads itself through the room like an audible lasso as he takes in the contents of her garage. 'Oh, Mira, Mira,' he says quietly.

'I'm an Interior Designer,' she says as if it explains everything.

'Does that mean if I hire you to do my place I can buy anything I want from your collection here?'

'No, this is all mine!' She knows she sounds like a selfish little girl defending her enormous toy box, but she doesn't care, and the nipples practically poking through her robe certainly don't look childish; they belong to the full breasts of a grown woman who loves all the objects surrounding her as dearly as children who are a part of her and enrich her life in different ways. Not wanting to continue prudishly holding onto her robe, she slips her hands into the pockets and says a silent prayer for it to stay modestly closed. But apparently the only word her guardian angel hears is 'closed' because right on cue Phillip closes the garage door behind him. The lock falling into place only makes a small harmless clicking sound, but it has an explosive effect on her psyche. Suddenly, she is seeing a whole different world as her handsome, charming neighbor is transformed into a threatening stranger inexplicably clad in sadistic black leather on a sunny weekday morning in rural Virginia, and she is trapped inside her garage with him. More than one of her ex-lovers warned her she was entirely too sweet and trusting for her own good, but she supposes it is entirely too late to heed this warning now. Only the fact that he doesn't approach her in a threatening way, but instead walks over to another side of the garage, diffuses her anxiety somewhat.

Cat's Collar

'Exquisite!' he exclaims beneath his breath, reverently caressing a few inches of the hand-woven tapestry covering half the western wall of her treasure room. 'Where did you find this?'

'At an antique flea market, of course.'

'And here I thought flea markets were just full of junk.'

'Well, mainly they are,' she agrees, 'but they're like thrift stores – you never know what treasure you might just find that was meant just for you to find and no one else. The thing is, people can be so stupid, they don't even realize what they have.'

'I won't ask you what you paid for this, Mira, because that's rude,' he speaks with his back still to her as he studies the pagan hunting scene depicted by the multi-colored threads, 'but what you're telling me is that you essentially robbed this masterpiece from its unsuspecting previous owner?'

'I didn't rob it, I paid for everything in here! If they were too stupid to realize how much their possessions were worth, that's not my problem, and I see no reason why I should have enlightened them, especially since they were getting rid of these beautiful objects in the first place, which means they didn't really love and appreciate them-'

'Like you do.'

'Like I do,' she echoes, edging back towards the door as he turns towards her again. Then the next second she is ashamed of her cowardly and suspicious brain when he changes course to admire the ivory-skinned doll perched on top of a pile of small Oriental rugs that in turn rest on an antique dresser. 'She looks like you, Mira,' he comments, stroking the doll's long raven hair, and then he runs the ball of his thumb along her pouting red mouth in a light, sensual caress that parts Mira's own lips as her breath catches watching him. 'You have excellent taste, my beautiful neighbor.'

The compliment literally makes her feel weak in the knees, which in turn forces her to question her disrespect for clichés, because obviously some of them obey real physiological facts she is amazingly finding herself the victim of on this dream-like morning. 'You still haven't mentioned what you do for a living, Phillip.' The question is an effort to root herself in reality and to assuage her reason, which keeps insisting she is a fool to be alone with a total stranger who could easily overpower her physically.

'I'm a Master,' he replies, casually moving on to another aesthetic object in her collection that catches his eye.

She laughs, but hardly because she thinks his response is funny; it is the only way to vent the rush of emotions inside her. 'You're a Master,' she repeats in the hope he will elaborate on his unusual and intriguing profession, but all he says is 'That's right' as he admires her small painting of a handsome Native American Indian man. She tries another approach, 'Do you dominate men or women?'

'I told you, Mira, I'm not gay.'

'I never thought you were... I mean, it's just that when you said...'

'No need to explain.' He turns to face her again, and this time walks straight towards her.

The garage door is right behind her, she can easily turn and run, but instead she doesn't move a muscle as he comes and stands a mere hand's breadth away from her.

'You have some beautiful things here,' he says quietly, 'but you're the real treasure, Mira.'

'Thank you,' she whispers.

'My pleasure.' He caresses her hair just as he did the doll's raven locks. 'I love your hair. Most women cut it stylishly short these days, unfortunately.' He also traces the shape of her lower lip with the ball of his thumb, and it stuns her how hard it is to resist the impulse to take it in her mouth and suck on it like a baby at last offered a bottle containing the mysterious formulae of all she desires...

'Do you get paid to beat women?' she asks faintly, and he completely takes her breath away with his reply.

'Sometimes.' He pauses as if aware she needs time to remember how to breathe. 'But usually it's much more complex and subtle than that, as I'm sure you can imagine.'

'Can I? I'm not... I'm not sure I can.'

'And I'm sure you can,' he insists, no trace of a smile softening the firmness of his mouth. 'For instance, I think that if I tell you to untie the sash holding your robe closed, you'll obey me, Mira.'

Cat's Collar

'Oh, right!' She laughs, and once again takes a step back away from him, but for some reason only one step, not the three or four steps that will actually get her to the garage door and freedom. She reasons he can easily stop her if he wants to, yet she knows this is just a flimsy excuse concocted by the Catholic school girl inside her seeking to defend her virtue. The naked truth is she has absolutely no desire to escape his penetrating stare.

'Untie your sash, Mira,' he commands in a soothing, almost gentle tone. 'Trust me, I won't hurt you.'

'Isn't that what they all say?' she demands.

'Maybe, but you know I'm telling the truth.'

'How can I possibly know anything about you when we just met?' She is desperately buying herself some time before succumbing to the inevitable. Yet why it should be so inevitable she has no idea since most women in her situation would undoubtedly make a run for it and call 911.

'A man and a woman can know the most important things about each other the instant their eyes meet if they're really looking and listening with their souls, Mira.'

It is the incredible fact that he reasonably acknowledges the existence of her soul as no other man has done that undoes the sash of her robe as her fingers do exactly what he said they would and obey him.

He wrests the sash out of her hand.

Only her tense nipples keep the silk cloth from fainting open and exposing her. Mira considers certain types of clothing constrictive. She would never consider owning a pair of tight jeans, the only pants in her wardrobe are comfortable cotton leggings; she only tolerates cotton bikini underwear because occasionally they make sense and are necessary; and the countless sexy lace panties she owns are primarily designed to be ripped off. Beneath the robe she is completely naked.

'Are you seeing someone?' he demands quietly, wrapping the ends of the sash once around both his hands and stretching it taut.

She stands motionless as a statue, as if emulating a work of art will transform what is happening into something less shamefully sinful; as if it will protect her from the hot touch of his eyes as she pretends he is only objectively admiring her figure. 'No, I'm not,' she answers just as softly, as if they both know a loud, normal-sounding voice will break the spell she is in, a spell that is allowing the inconceivable to take place.

'You shave your pussy for your own pleasure?'

The undisguised admiration in his voice relaxes her a vital degree. 'Yes, it feels nicer that way...' Nothing like this has ever happened to her before, yet it feels strangely familiar, and as he steps behind her, the violet sash looking almost sacredly beautiful against his pitch-black leather, she remembers... it's like being in confessional and speaking about her most intimate transgressions to a nameless man just because he calls himself a priest. 'What are you doing?' she gasps, but the question is rhetorical since he is obviously tying her wrists behind her back.

'Everything you want me to.'

'But... but I don't want you to do anything,' she lies.

'I'm betting you were raised a Catholic.'

'How did you know that?' His powers of perception please her, and mysteriously make her feel less guilty about what is happening by confirming her instincts that she is surrendering to a man who appears to be worthy of having both her body and soul in his hands.

He steps around in front of her again. Her eyes are wide and trusting and only a little afraid as she gazes up at his face fully acknowledging that what he said was true – the wordless script of his features told her profoundly important things about him the second she saw him. What is transpiring now is her response to this knowledge by her intuitive self, which always works much faster than her reason, anchored as it is in the highly conflicted society that programmed it.

'You're so beautiful!' he whispers almost angrily, and the passionate compliment deepens the thrill of his hands slipping into her robe. Her chest heaves beneath a flood of feelings as he cups her naked breasts in his hands. 'Do you trust me?' he asks, looking down into her cleavage as he squeezes her soft mounds and grazes their exquisitely sensitive peaks with the balls of his thumb.

'Yes and I have no idea why!' she confesses all in one breath.

Cat's Collar

'I work three nights a week at a BDSM club in D.C. It's a private venue; you won't have heard of it.' He squeezes her bosom appraisingly. 'I dominate successful business women and even a few politicians, women with power who are otherwise in complete control of their lives.'

Mira senses he is telling her more about himself and his exotic profession to help her relax, and she finds what he is saying so fascinating she can almost forget to be afraid. His fingers kneading her tits might as well be directly massaging her brain as the deep pleasure makes her feel thoughtlessly warm all over. 'These women willingly submit to you?' she asks, part of her jealously resenting she isn't the first one to fall under his assertive spell.

'They become my slaves, Mira.'

She gasps, 'Your slaves?!' as he pinches both her nipples between his thumb and forefinger, and suddenly she is sure she is dreaming as she watches the tip of his tongue flicking swiftly and lightly, like a hummingbird's wings, against one of her breast's rosy buds. She moans with a satisfaction that goes much deeper than the mere physical sensation, because it was this very tongue she saw in her imagination as she was masturbating in bed this morning; it looks exactly like the image she had in her mind of a man's tongue as she stroked herself. And if his tongue lives up to the fantasy concocted by her brain, it seems very promising that his penis, and its skill, won't disappoint her either. The mere thought of being so fulfilled so soon – when she thought she would be celibate for many more months to come – makes her pussy juice with longing to be opened up by a big, hard cock. When he transfers the attention of his agile tongue to her other jealous nipple, she becomes fully conscious of her hands tied behind her back and the fact that she has no power to control his actions, yet the heat of desire is melting the coldness of fear and replacing it with an entirely different tension. Her cunt is tightening with anticipation not trepidation, and suddenly the only thing she is afraid of is that he won't actually fuck her. Then in the next heartbeat she can't believe she so desperately wants a man who just admitted to being a kinky gigolo, and her offended pride stiffens her back… or maybe it's just that she wants to push her breast deeper into his mouth.

'Mm!' He sucks furiously on her nipple.

His fingers digging almost painfully into her tender tits squeezes the question out of her, 'Do you sleep with all your slaves, Phillip?'

He glances up at her face, amusement flashing in his grey eyes like distant lightning. 'I always sleep alone, Mira.'

'I mean... do you fuck them?' She resents that he forces her to say the word.

'Rarely.' He straightens up. 'Only if I'm seriously inspired.' He slips his hands out of her robe. 'When I am inspired, it's always free of charge, and right now, Mira, I'm immensely inspired. Can you handle it?'

'Yes...'

He yanks her robe open, fully exposing her breasts and belly and the tender mound of her freshly shaved pussy. She knows from looking at herself in the mirror that there is an almost heart-shaped gap where the top of her thighs open up and merge with the tender bulge of her pudenda, which makes her think of a dolphin's smiling face.

He steps back to admire the view, and how hard his mouth suddenly looks tells her more clearly than words how beautiful she is. Everything about him suddenly seems harder, the look in his eyes especially, and there is a distinct bulge in his tight pants that wasn't there before. She holds her head high, proud of her body and of the obvious effect it is having on him. He tied her wrists against the center of her back, thrusting her breasts forward, which in turn arches her spine and pushes her buttocks out in a way that makes her feel dangerously vulnerable. If it wasn't for her robe covering the cheeks of her ass, all her orifices would be exposed to him.

'You're lucky I had a long night, Mira, otherwise you'd be in serious trouble right now, but never fear,' he unzips his leather pants, 'you'll still get as much as you're ready for.' His cock springs out towards her fully erect, and if it does not possess the damaging dimensions of her imagination, it is still more than big enough to safely satisfy the profound cravings of her flesh. 'Do you like chocolate?' He pulls a condom out of his back pocket.

'I love chocolate...'

'Good, because I'm going to treat you to a nice big chocolate cone this morning for breakfast. On your knees, sweetheart.'

Cat's Collar

She sinks to her knees on the garage floor with more gratitude and hopeful reverence than she ever felt at church. The cement is unyieldingly hard against her skeleton, but she doesn't care. All she cares about is proving to him, showing him, what a good cock-sucker she is so he'll want to come back to her, and next time they can forgo the chocolate latex frosting.

He threads his fingers firmly through her hair. 'I'm going to fuck your mouth like a cunt, Mira,' he warns, yet just as in Stormy's brain insults are transformed into compliments by the tone of her voice, Phillip's threat feels like a wonderful promise to the blood pounding through her heart as she prepares to take his chokingly large penis into her mouth. 'I'm going to fuck your beautiful face, Mira, because you're so fucking beautiful!'

He penetrates her mouth slowly at first, giving her orifice time to adjust to his dimensions; letting her tongue and teeth get a feel for what they're dealing with, giving her time to make her mouth an utterly smooth, yielding hole. With her wrists tied behind her back and his hands gripping her skull, all she has to do is tolerate the strain on her legs, keep her mouth wide open, and relax the muscles of her throat, the hardest task of all, because even though he starts with slow, half strokes, his head is soon grazing the back of her throat... and then more boldly caressing it, filling the darkly sensitive entrance to her neck. She closes her eyes and concentrates on not gagging as his hips pick up speed. The condom really does taste like dark-chocolate, and despite how completely fulfilled she is in a physical sense, the chemical flavor leaves her feeling strangely empty; mysteriously hungry for the unique taste of his semen, and, eventually, for the heady rush of his cum drenching her tongue. Naturally, she has given blow-jobs before, but no man has ever used her mouth so roughly. She discovers just what it feels like to really have her mouth fucked as hard as a pussy. There is no physical pleasure in it for her whatsoever, only effort, but for some reason she loves every breathless second.

He slides his full length in and out between the devoted ring of her lips faster and harder, and then he keeps her face pressed firmly against him, making it even harder for her to breathe as he moves her skull very subtly back and forth, caressing his head with the infinitely sensitive flesh of her neck. Mira has never been deep-throated before, not like this, and she imagines there is something to be said for his skill that she somehow resists the urge to gag around him; nevertheless, it's a huge relief when he slips out of her and she is able to take a deep, shuddering breath, her cheeks flushed with pride at her skill as much as from the strain.

'Very good, Mira.' He releases his cruel grip on the roots of her hair and strokes it gently with both hands. 'But you didn't expect me to come like that, did you?'

She hears herself whine softly, 'My knees hurt.' Suddenly, she is confused and a little frightened again, unable to rationalize why she so enjoyed his oral selfishness.

'I know they do,' he says mildly. 'Would you like to stand up or lie down?'

For some reason being given a choice when it is turning her on so much to feel helpless makes her want to cry. 'Please!' she whispers, casting a pleading glance up into his unreadable eyes.

'Please what?' He strokes her hair again soothingly, smoothing it back away from her face as if his caress will help untangle her thoughts.

'Please!' she repeats, a sob catching in her throat.

'You want me to fuck you, is that it?'

She closes her eyes in mingled relief and shame at the idea of having to beg him to fuck her. Isn't she beautiful enough that he can't resist her?

'On your feet!' he commands, and yanks her up himself before she has a chance to obey.

She doesn't know whether to be relieved or disappointed as he quickly frees her wrists. Then excitement overwhelms all other emotions as he pulls her robe off.

'God, you're magnificent,' he says through clenched teeth as he leads her by the hand over to where her doll is sitting, innocently observing the erotic proceedings. He grips her waist to lift her onto the dresser, and clutches the bottom of her thighs just above her knees to hold her legs open around him. She is torn between the vision of his erection poised at the entrance to her flesh and the proximity of his face, the magnetic pull of his hard mouth parting her own lips in a silent plea for a kiss. Yet there is something intensely arousing about the fact that he is about to thrust his cock into her cunt before their tongues have even

Cat's Collar

politely touched. She wraps her arms around his neck, and the sweet sensation of her labia blooming open around the thick head of his penis makes her moan in anticipation of the rest of him completely filling her.

'It's been such a long time,' she tells him, not because she wants him to be gentle but because she wants him to look forward to the tight fit he can expect from her pussy.

'It was worth the wait,' he says, and penetrates her both with his eyes and his hard-on.

She cries out as she feels her tight cleft clinging to his rigid length like a silk glove shaping all her innermost contours to his, and she wonders how she could possibly have survived for so long without experiencing this glorious fullness in her pelvis. He lodges his penis deep in her vagina, and then holds perfectly still.

'Oh, God, please...' She presses her hot vulva against the cool leather enclosing his scrotum, clinging to his shoulders as her hips writhe desperately around his cock planted deep inside her. It is absolute torture how patiently he waits to begin stabbing her into a higher form of life in which their bodies will beat together like a single heart... 'Oh, God, fuck me,' she begs, 'please! I can't bear it!'

His tongue thrusts between her lips as he pulls his erection almost all the way out of her, threatening her with its loss for a terrible second before he rams it back in.

Mira is only vaguely aware of her cries filling the garage like an intangible but priceless treasure, her nerve-ends close to short-circuiting with pleasure from the combined motion of his tongue in her mouth and his penis in her pussy, both of them thrusting and dipping and swirling and opening her up until she feels ecstatically bottomless. He fucks her with such force the black leather sheathing his naked flesh begins to feel like much more than just a sexy outfit, and there is another benefit to it as well... with only his driving erection rising out of the zippered crotch her clitoris comes into direct contact with the small metal tongue, and its cold, hard licks merging with the sensation of his head kissing her cervix is stimulating the very real possibility of an orgasm inside her.

'Come for me, Mira...'

'Oh, yes, I want to... I want to...'

Cat's Collar - Three Erotic Romances

'Then do it. I can feel your pussy tightening, you're almost there… come for me!'

Her brain doesn't think it's possible, usually she can only climax by touching herself, and she is astonished when her body quickly succeeds in obeying him.

'Oh, yes, yes…' She hears him whisper as she comes around him, her sweet hot juices wasted on latex and leather as she breathlessly buries her face in the hard space of his chest.

Once her pussy stops pulsing around his dick, he pulls out of her. 'Come here.' Her legs unsteady beneath her, he leads her to a faded gold antique chaise lounge. He doesn't need to tell her what to do; she reclines gratefully across it, bending her arms over her head as she absorbs the magnificent sight of his fully erect cock free of the condom. Dazed and relaxed as she is by her powerful orgasm, she still does not fail to notice and appreciate that he discards the semen-filled plastic carefully at his feet, making sure not to let it touch any of her beloved antiques.

'I'm going to come all over your beautiful breasts, Mira. Play with them for me.'

It is her pleasure to oblige. She is so aroused, her nipples look carved out of rosy marble in the soft golden light designed to show off all her precious possessions. She watches the slick, pumping violence of his fist in wide-eyed fascination. She has never seen anything so arousing as this man stroking his erection in front of her.

'What are you saving all these treasures for?' he asks abruptly, the almost indiscernible breathlessness in his voice the only sign he is close to coming. 'Not enough room for them in your doll's house?'

'Oh, my God, how did you know that's what I call it?'

'Because it's small and you're a doll, Mira.'

She would laugh if it wasn't for his intensely serious expression, to which she responds instead by arching her back and thrusting her breasts up towards him. She moans in the grip of an indefinably pure sensual pleasure as his cum begins raining down on the soft hills of her bosom, vanishing like snow into warm ground against her skin. He flings his head back as he ejaculates and her breath catches in sympathy watching him force every last drop of pleasure from his erection, which shows absolutely no sign of diminishing, and the staying power

Cat's Collar

of his hard-on has her pussy juicing in selfish admiration.

'Jesus,' he whispers, and this slight crack in his masterful aura makes him look even sexier to her as she sits up, compelled by years of hygienic indoctrination to find something to clean herself off with. 'Oh, no you don't, you're leaving my cum all over your breasts,' he says as if reading her mind, or perhaps just her eyes, which she has been told are very expressive. 'You're not showering until my sperm has completely dried on your skin.' He smiles as he reaches for both her hands and draws her up into his arms. He kisses her forehead, and it feels as though he is rewarding her for not letting her cowardly reason ruin what just happened between them. Then he takes her hand again and leads her towards the door. She stops with the intention of picking up her robe, but he says, 'No, I want to see you walking naked through your garden.'

Stepping outside ahead of him, Mira feels transformed from the woman she was only just a little while ago, sipping her cup of tea in the grip of a mild depression, into a wildly sensual nymph who, for once, spent the morning the way it should be spent, fucking shamelessly.

Stormy and Sekhmet are sprawled directly in her path on the gray stones leading to the kitchen door in what she thinks of as their ancient Egyptian brother and sister pose – various limbs entwined with their regal heads together. For once Sekhmet is gazing up at Mira with a mild, almost approving expression.

She crouches down to pet them, as always the urge to do so proving irresistible. 'This is Stormy, Sekhmet's brother,' she tells Phillip, smiling at him over her shoulder.

There is no one there.

Chapter Three

*"Even if the world is coming to an end,
I must go out for a little relief."*

Mira unlocks the door and walks into another empty space. She is concentrating on her work as never before, the only way she can keep at least a small part of her brain from thinking about Phillip night and day; he has even penetrated her dreams, usually an inviolate space where she can always count on finding solace from any problems and disappointments besetting her. For hours after he vanished, she had refrained from showering, very glad for the sensation of his cum drying on her skin that proved he had been real and not just an intensely vivid figment of her overactive imagination.

At the moment, Mira is glad her sandals make an efficient clicking sound on the hard-wood floor, helping to keep her focused on the objective physical reality surrounding her that is her responsibility to bring to life. Usually stepping into a virgin space she knows is all hers to decorate is exciting, but on this gloomy morning the blank white walls depress her like the sight of bleached bones in the desert of her loneliness. The sharp corners of the empty rooms feel like knife cuts to her soul, and naked windows looking out on a gray sky evoke dead, unblinking eyes from which color and hope have been forever leached.

Mira knows she is deliberately stoking her dark mood with these melancholy mental images, but she cannot resist indulging herself while she does a slow walk-through of the Arlington condo she has been hired to decorate, and which undoubtedly cost its new owner a small fortune. At least he had enough good

Cat's Collar

taste to choose a place with natural wood floors instead of carpeting; the sophisticated dimension of crown molding; a lovely island kitchen with real granite countertops and stainless steel appliances suited to a masculine owner; ceramic tiled bathrooms (linoleum floors and wall-to-wall carpeting are on the top of Mira's undesirable list) and best of all, a gas fireplace big enough to warm all the rooms in winter without having to resort to the flesh drying misery of central heating. Also an added bonus is a tiny balcony opening up off the living room, although why anyone would want to sit out there just looking at other tall, architecturally uninspired buildings while listening to the traffic on Fairfax Drive is beyond her comprehension. When she steps out onto her porch she is surrounded by nature, but she supposes that at night so high up the glowing red-and-gold flow of traffic below, and lights coming on in the neighboring buildings, will be lovely in the sense that luminosity is aesthetic to the human psyche's innate need for life and warmth and the sense of hope they provide. Nevertheless, she much prefers living on ground level surrounded by trees, whose company she generally prefers to that of people.

Her slow, brooding walk-through of the condominium completed, she has no excuse not to get to work. She sets her heavy purse down next to the front door and fishes her electronic tape measure from its malleable black leather depths. Her purse proves some of the new theories in physics about space folding to create other dimensions, because it usually takes her a small eternity to find anything in it.

She is willing to bet a considerable chunk of her fee that, as a general rule, architects who design million-dollar condos are not Chinese. Everywhere the laws of *Feng Shui* are so blatantly violated the architects were either in gleeful league with the forces of evil or had no idea what they were doing. Sometimes she feels as much like a spiritual fire-fighter in charge of damage control than an Interior Designer. The first problem she makes a note of concerning Ian McFarland's new home is the fact that his front door is directly across from the elevator shaft. Whenever he lets himself in and out, a stream of unfiltered, and potentially hostile energy will flood his living space while at the same time any positive energy accumulated inside rushes out. She will have to soften the entrance into the living room from the small foyer with a curtain that will serve as an energy dam to keep the home's positive *chi* inside and help block any negative *chi* pouring in from a hallway traveled by countless strangers, each one a unique universe of energy.

Fortunately Ian (who called her last week after being referred to her by one of her satisfied former clients) sounded ideally submissive to her designer's will. She only spoke to him for a few minutes, but she sensed he was wealthy and wise enough (in that order) to agree with most, if not everything, she might suggest for his new living space, which will, of course, make her job a lot easier. It is also much more fun for her when she is given the freedom and the power to exercise her talent and imagination without too many restrictions. She loves a client with a big budget, no doubt about it, and yet working for people with financial constraints affords her a different kind of challenge she also enjoys, being a firm believer in the magic of thrift stores and antique flea markets, where treasures can be found that don't cost an arm-and-a-leg. (If this saying was literally true, Ian McFarland, like many of her former clients, would be crippled for life.)

Mira begins her measurements with the living room. Its best feature are the three six-foot-high windows to the west of the gas fireplace; however, at a certain time of day they will let in too much light, making the room hot and uncomfortable during the warmer months of the year. Brief as her conversation with Ian was, she hung up feeling quite positive about her new client's amiable and open disposition. He won't consider his manhood threatened by the feminine detail of curtains supplementing more masculine blinds.

The kitchen won't require much work on her part since all the appliances are in place. She suspects the architect did not choose to position the stove away from the refrigerator because it is good *chi* to keep these opposing forces apart, nor did he or she give a thought to whether or not the stove was placed against the wall on the other side of which the occupant will be sleeping. She makes a mental note to position Ian's bed away from the spot on the wall where the stove sits so the active energy of heat will not disturb his sleep.

She will have to decide, after she actually meets him in person, whether or not she should share her thoughts on *Feng Shui* with him. She has learned from

Cat's Collar

experience that human beings can be strange creatures. If when she is determining the placing of individual pieces of furniture in each room she happens to mention, for example, that the foot of the bed cannot be directly facing the bedroom door because that's known as the 'death position' she can never be sure how a client will react. Once a woman was so disturbed by the image that she promptly fired Mira, as if getting rid of the source of the thought would dispel the fear it consequently haunted her with. That, of course, was an extreme case; most people are not quite so melodramatic. Nevertheless, she has learned that discussing a home's *chi* can make its owner uncomfortable, as if she is trying to see through their clothing by talking about something as mysteriously intimate as the direction and flow of their personal energy. Some people become almost embarrassed, as though she is casually stripping their clothes off to comment on the positive and negative way the skin flows over their bones and helps shape who they are and how they feel. Of course, other people merely smile condescendingly at the concept that an invisible energy has the power to affect their emotions and circumstances, although, fortunately, most of her clients possess at least a modicum of imagination.

Feng Shui means 'wind water' which she thinks is a lovely way to describe the flow of thoughts and feelings, at once spiritually abstract and sensually incarnate, that compose her unique personality. Nevertheless, it is sometimes best not to tell the people she is working for why she makes the decorating decisions she does, why she wants the desk in that particular corner of the study or why the walls should be the colors she selects, etc. With knowledge comes responsibility, and many people don't really seem to desire conscious control over the powerful energy of their feelings. They don't want to think they might be at least partially responsible when bad things happen to them; taking perverse comfort in believing everything is random chance and they are only hapless victims. Mira finds such profound spiritual laziness appalling, and such clients make it hard for her to be inspired about her work knowing it will only be appreciated on the most superficial level, at best. But a job is a job, and she is lucky to have one she enjoys so much most of the time, a job that enables her to be creative and to shop for a living. What more can a girl ask for?

Cat's Collar - Three Erotic Romances

Usually the first items on her shopping list, especially when she is working on a condominium and not a house, are plants, and lots of them. In her opinion, if you can't be around trees – prized for their power to block negative *chi* and attract good luck by providing fresh oxygen, making it easier and more pleasant to breathe and therefore to live – then you must absolutely possess as many indoor plants as possible.

Mira thanks all the Powers-that-Be for her electronic tape measure, which makes the task of recording a living space's dimensions much easier. Apart from the fact that she cannot understand why anyone would buy an apartment when they could afford a house, by the time she finishes her measurements she has concluded that her new client is a lucky man. There is only one serious structural poison arrow to deal with in his new home – the front door directly facing the elevator. Apart from that, especially since she will be supplying all his furnishing and lighting needs, the *chi* should flow quite nicely for Ian. Especially beneficial are the north and south facing windows that will let a breeze in from both directions. Although the quality of the air might be dubious, a slightly tainted wind is better than no wind at all.

The *Feng Shui* issues momentarily settled to her satisfaction (and she in no way pretends to be anything other than an inspired amateur, not actually having a degree in the ancient art form) Mira glances at her watch, and with the choreographed precision she is increasingly coming to expect from life, she hears the front door open behind her. Ian is right on time for their lunch appointment, where they will discuss in detail what he imagines his new home looking and feeling like, i.e. where she will seek to seduce him into believing that his heart's decorating desires are flatteringly synonymous with her own excellent professional tastes.

'Hello,' she says brightly, turning to face her new client, and a fist of *chi* hits her straight in the womb as she watches him step into the empty room. Ian McFarland is a strikingly attractive man, and it is immediately apparent that he has splendid taste in clothes. One look at him tells Mira designing his living space is going to be an exciting challenge the pleasure of which might, hopefully, eventually, enable her to forget the man in black leather who cut through her yard and her life with such devastating consequences to her peace of mind. Before Phillip, she was contentedly, positively, waiting for her soul-mate. Now, even though she feels she has met him at last, she still doesn't know where he is and can't find him. Approximately seventy-three hours ago he ejaculated all over her naked breasts and she has not seen or heard from him since.

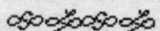

Mira has never managed to develop a taste for the business lunch. Apart from the fact that she prefers not to eat too much during the day to keep her energy level up, she doesn't like mixing business with pleasure. It's not because she is afraid her business will suffer, but because she resents wasting even a few minutes of her miraculous incarnation, and discussing a financial arrangement with a total stranger feels like deliberately stirring chalk into her food. She loves eating too much to relish having her attention distracted from the pleasure of its consumption, except by someone she is actually attracted to, in which case the conversation provides an additional stimulating spice to the dining experience. During business lunches, she is careful to order only a soup or a salad or a vegetarian sandwich – as much as her sensitive system can handle in tandem with the vital tension of getting to know new clients and what they desire. Maybe it's because she doesn't really care about their feelings and yet is forced to swallow and digest an entire open buffet of their thoughts and opinions that her dessert often consists of four citrus-flavored Tums.

Decorating your home is a very exciting task, and Mira doesn't blame her clients for being eagerly and anxiously talkative. She responds with a calm smiling assurance she wears like a mask to soothe their flighty energy like a bird's ruffled feathers as their untrained imaginations soar from one stylistic branch to another. While she pretends to be casually enjoying her soup she is intently absorbing her clients' personality and mentally designing their new nest in the hope that she can lure them into it with a minimum of effort, although usually she has to cast a complex net of designer terms over an erratic flock of ideas that would never succeed in settling down to a livable aesthetic without her firm guidance. Mixing bad taste with her meals is another reason she dislikes business lunches. The mere mention of leopard skin bedspreads, bear rugs and glass coffee tables ruins her appetite.

Lunch with Ian McFarland is one of those blessed exceptions to the rule deepening Mira's belief that there is no such thing as coincidence only choreography if you keep your positive outlook in shape and follow the subliminal music of your intuition. To avoid the often hellish traffic on Route 666 (as her environmental consciousness likes to think of it) she took the train into Ballston, secure in the knowledge that her new client would drive them anywhere she desired for lunch. She gleaned this much just from the quality of Ian's voice when they spoke on the phone, and the moment her eyes met his, her instincts were confirmed. First she assured herself he was indeed hers for the rest of the afternoon; that he wouldn't have to run back to the office for a last minute meeting. Thank God he wasn't a doctor, and not only was he not on call, he said, his cell phone was turned off. The hasty note scribbled in her Day Calendar in a skeletal scrawl – *Take I.M. shopping after lunch* – promised to flesh itself out into a highly enjoyable afternoon... an active, busy afternoon that would keep her brain cells occupied, diverting their obsessive focus from... but she doesn't even want to say his name in her head!

Much as Mira enjoys specialty shops and antique markets, she never minds a quick trip to *Crate & Barrel* with new clients – the ideal generic place to start out as she gets a feel for their tastes, or lack thereof, not to mention a feel for how much they're actually willing to spend as opposed to how much they say they are. With that plan in mind, she has Ian drive them to *Café Deluxe* in Tyson's Corner, also a good place to enjoy one of her favorite light lunches – a roasted vegetable sandwich with Goat Cheese on toasted whole-grain bread. Yet much as she intends to keep busy and stop thinking about Phillip, details seem to keep cropping up everywhere that remind her of him, for example Ian's stunning black Ferrari. Okay, so it doesn't really matter to her what kind of car a man drives, but it certainly doesn't hurt either when his vehicle feels like an extension

Cat's Collar

of her sensuality as they fly down the highway together at the speed of daydreams all promising to become very pleasantly real in the form of the driver behind the wheel.

Mira and Ian don't talk much during the drive to *Café Deluxe*, but it isn't because they don't feel comfortable, on the contrary; they keep casting smiling glances at each other amidst sporadic light conversation secure in the knowledge that they're already in a relationship. He is a wealthy, successful man, and she is his talented (high-priced) Interior Designer. The fact that they are both attractive, young and single gives their professional relationship potentially exhilarating dimensions. For years he will have to live with the furniture she helps him choose and how she arranges it for him, traditionally the role of a girl-friend or a wife... and with this thought the watch-dog of her reason reminds her with an annoyingly trite bark that just because he isn't wearing a wedding ring doesn't mean he's not attached.

'You come highly recommended,' he says abruptly, keeping his eyes on the road. They are a remarkably vivid green that remind her of Stormy's eyes mysteriously deepened by the shadow of a soul perceiving itself in the reflective surfaces.

She smiles. 'I'm glad to hear it.' She likes compliments as much any girl.

'How long have you been in the business?'

'About six years now, but only four-and-a-half working on my own.' She tells him about the decorating firm that hired her right after college, and it's a good sign that he doesn't appear to question her reason for leaving and adventuring out on her own at the risk of losing a cushy annual salary in order to fully exercise her creativity. Perhaps it is only her own stubborn hopefulness, but she gets the feeling he understands where she's coming from, and his mild expression (at least what she can see of it in profile as he drives) hovers encouragingly between serious attentiveness and smiling relaxation without obviously approving or disapproving of anything she says. Living in D.C., it makes her wonder if he is some sort of diplomat, but she concludes that he is much too at ease in his own skin to be a government employee. At least that's her opinion and she has been wrong before, but not often.

'So, may I ask what you do for a living that you can afford my services, Ian?'

He laughs. It is the first time she hears his deep, almost silent chuckle, and it makes her feel good all over, like a big cat purring just for her.

'You may.'

She waits, but the only response she gets is an adorable dimple carving a hole almost as deep as her curiosity into his visible cheek. 'Well?' she demands.

'I'm Regional Director for the Salvation Army.'

'Get *out* of here!' Now it is her turn to laugh, in amazement. She is delighted to have her powers of perception excelled, a rare enough event to excite her with the sense that the world is a much more wonderfully complex place than she can imagine. 'That's the last thing I would have guessed,' she declares, her sharp surprise feeling rather like a cosmic spank she finds at once stimulating and reassuring.

'I know,' he says simply, 'and I know what you're thinking.'

'What?' She holds her breath, turned on by having her perceptions penetrated by a man skilful enough to do so.

'You're thinking that I didn't exactly find the suit I'm wearing in the bargain bin of one of our local thrift stores.'

'Well, yes...'

'I was born with a comfortable Trust Fund I've since invested in the Stock Market,' he confesses, 'which supplements my modest salary, but I feel I know you well enough already, Mira, to guess that you can appreciate it's the satisfaction I get from my work that's important.'

'It's much easier to feel that way when you have a lot of money in the bank,' she points out with uncharacteristic cynicism.

He takes his eyes off the road to look directly into hers for an instant. 'Yes, it is,' he admits.

'I'm sorry!' she apologizes fervently, 'I didn't mean to imply that I don't believe you, because I do, and I feel the same way about my work... although obviously I'm not helping people the way you are...'

'There's no need for you to explain, Mira, you make a valid point.'

'You must have women swooning at your feet,' she teases, subconsciously defending herself from his charm by divorcing herself from the rest of woman kind. 'A selfless philanthropist and a successful player all rolled up into one sexy package. How can any girl resist you?'

'They can't,' he concedes mildly, but he takes the right turn into the *Crate & Barrel* parking lot with such speed she has to cling to the seat to keep from falling into his lap.

Chapter Four

"And in the despair of her heart she jumped down into the well the same way the spindle had gone. After that she knew nothing; and when she came to herself she was in a beautiful garden, and the sun was shining on the flowers that grew around her."

The gloomy clouds have parted, the sun has come out, and it is now one of those glorious Virginia days that people who live in other states can only dream of. The sky is a vibrant blue softened here and there by fluffy white clouds like cotton balls from the Goddess' cosmetic jar. A cool breeze, with just the slightest edge of a chill to it, gently caresses goose bumps across her skin so she can better appreciate the warmth of the sun penetrating it. There is no humidity to speak of, making the air so crisp that colors and shapes cut into her vision with a sense of significance transcending mere aesthetics. And everywhere birdsong punctuates these sweet, illusive instants of inspiration when pleasure in the physical world and a belief in life's divine soul come joyfully together inside her. This sensual communication with nature is still wonderfully possible in Fairfax County where Mira grew up, one of the richest counties in the nation, and to her its wealth is indeed summed up in green – the green of leaves, leaves belonging to the big old trees that are still there, protected, not plowed down as they are elsewhere with a murderous lack of respect for life and the environment.

As they stand before the café's hostess and her pulpit – red crosses bloodying the seating chart of hedonistic parishioners come to worship the delicious mystery of taste buds and a digestive track – Ian asks Mira where she would like

Cat's Collar

to sit, and she requests a table out on the balcony. They are led to a choice spot next to the open glass doors leading in and out of the restaurant, protected from the sun by the edge of the one of the large red-orange umbrellas. The round café-style table is delightfully intimate because it is Ian sitting across from her. If she was with a normal client she would have requested a big booth with plenty of personal space.

Their waiter brings them two menus and walks leisurely away again with their drink order. She already knows what she wants, but she pretends to peruse the selection because it affords her a good opportunity to surreptitiously study her client while he is engrossed in the task of making his choice. Usually such fair skin on a man doesn't appeal to her, and she wonders why now confronted with such a fine specimen of the type. Perhaps it is because she likes a touch of forcefulness (okay, yes, masterfulness) in a man, the arousing illusion of which would be harder to maintain if she could tell what he was feeling, and Ian possesses the kind of skin that blushes easily; she would be too easily able to gauge his emotional reactions. Yet looking at him now, she can't help but think this is a misguided assumption on her part, and that she has very foolishly been limiting her love-life to more olive-skinned partners. She has also never been attracted to a man with red hair, yet perhaps it is time to reprogram her erotic software with some new sensual input.

He looks up from his menu and catches her staring at him. Inside, Parisian cabaret-style posters decorate the walls of the restaurant in primary reds and yellows on a black background depicting long defunct actors and exotic liquors, and in an ad for the mystical drink, Absinth, the bottle is the same almost unreal green color as his eyes.

'What were you thinking just now?' he asks, smiling as though whatever she says will please him.

'I was just wondering what it would be like to drink Absinth,' she lies truthfully by only sharing a portion of her thoughts with him. She sets her menu down, and he immediately places his on top of hers. 'Not that I'm into drugs or anything.'

He stands up, and for a terrifying moment he seems to be walking out on her, but he merely shrugs off his jacket, and then drapes it over the back of his chair before resuming his seat, and it is enough time for her to be very pleased with what she sees. His shoulders are not as broad as... never mind, they're broad enough, and he possesses that wonderfully lean build that actually looks good in a white dress shirt stuffed into silky slacks held up by a brown leather belt. His suit isn't exactly olive-green, it's more like the color of leaves deep in a forest on an overcast day, a soft, muted green at once soothing and stimulating to her vision draped on the haunting branches of his skeleton... and his tie is almost the same greenish-violet as the wallpaper of her childhood bedroom...

The waiter returns with their drinks – bottled water for Mira, ice tea for Ian – and to take their orders.

'The Roasted Vegetable Sandwich is delicious here,' she tells her handsome new client, but he opts for the Turkey Club instead, and then they're alone again. Even here on the balcony of a restaurant overlooking a busy street she can rest her eyes on trees every now and then as they converse. She can almost distinctly feel his interest and curiosity taking strong, deep root in her, and in response she finds herself blooming trustingly in his company. She finds herself opening up to him, talking to him about everything and nothing, as they say, and the time goes by quickly. Then suddenly they hit a snag in the conversation, and the fantasies she was weaving about their future together snap free of the metaphorical loom to whip her heart painfully. They are discussing the layout of his new condo, and for some reason she happens to mention that she has the perfect corner set aside for his wine rack.

'I won't need a wine rack,' he says firmly, and abruptly drains his glass.

She sits in silence attempting to absorb this statement, but being an avid disciple of Dionysus, she clings stubbornly to the lost promise of their perfect compatibility for a few more desperate seconds.

'I haven't had a drink in over five years,' he adds, studying the check the waiter placed on the table between them as intently as a fragment of the Kabala containing vital esoteric information. He slips a platinum Master Card into the appropriate slot in the black leather folder, and slides it half over the edge of the table. 'I'm an alcoholic.'

Cat's Collar

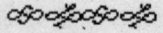

Ian graciously drops her off at the Vienna metro station where she left her car. The chemistry between them fizzled out before it even had a chance to overflow the test tube. All that's left is the professional shell of their relationship. She will do a fabulous (even if not a passionately inspired) job on his living space, and he will fill her checking account with a nice big fee for her services, and that's it. Nothing was said about his revelation, and for about half a second that split her personal universe painfully in half, she actually considered becoming intimately involved with him anyway and forsaking her devotion to Dionysus. After all, her potential soul-mate was more important than a glass of wine... more important than all the warming, inspiring, relaxing, food-enhancing glasses of a divine beverage as old as civilization she would be giving up for the rest of her life... No. She couldn't do it. Her soul-mate couldn't possibly be a recovering alcoholic. Her guardian angel often appears to have a sense of humor, but it has never been so cruel.

As the waiter returned to collect their payment, Mira had time to rise from the ashes of the possible burning love between her and this red-headed man that had fired her imagination. 'Oh, well, that's all right,' she said lightly, 'there are plenty of other things we can put in that corner besides a wine rack... it was just a thought...'

His strained smile made her think of a pink Band-Aid uselessly placed over a fatal wound. For a second she felt horrible, guilty and afraid that she was making a big mistake. How could she possibly judge such a kind, intelligent and attractive man by the fact that he would never be able to share a glass of wine with her by the fireplace? One minute they were talking as happily as birds chirping at the beginning of spring, the next it was the dead of winter and all the lovely fantasies swirling around in her head had fallen like dead leaves buried beneath a sudden frosty silence. But Mira has always dared to be selfish in order to remain true to herself. Even as Ian rose, and graciously helped pull her chair out for her, she decided there was no reason for her to give up something she desired simply because, for whatever reason, he hadn't possessed sufficient self-control over his own appetites.

'I'll be out of town for the next couple of weeks,' he says as she steps gracefully out of his Ferrari. 'I'll call you as soon as I get back.' He smiles just as he did when they first met in his empty condo, and she sincerely appreciates the clean slate he is handing her.

'I'll look forward to it, Ian,' she replies, but once inside the comfortably familiar interior of her old candy-apple-red Camaro (a gift from dad for her high school graduation) she heaves a deep sigh and rests her head back against the bone-colored leather, closing her eyes and regrouping her energies for a minute before switching on the ignition. She has to face it – part of her is relieved Ian is no longer a candidate for her life-long affections. She is relieved because it means she can stop pretending not to think about Phillip. She is relieved because it means her intuition about the mysterious stranger in black leather might be more than just her imagination. She is relieved because she doesn't have to stop thinking about him anymore, which is hopeless. He is *all* she has really been able to think about since they met.

She turns on the engine, and drives gratefully home to Falls Church following a series of back streets to avoid the beginnings of rush-hour traffic on the more major roads.

An old white pick-up truck is parked in her driveway filled with a motley assortment of gardening utensils so old and well-used they look more like archaeological relics themselves than tools used to dig. She smiles. Ramon is here, although she has secretly nicknamed him Ra after the ancient Egyptian sun god. She glances at her watch. He will just be finishing up, making his seemingly effortless magical touches to her lush and extensive garden. She gets out of the car and walks around the side of the house in search of him. Ra likes to work wearing only skimpy cut-off shorts that conceal the bare essentials required by modern social conventions, another reason she gave him an ancient Egyptian name, because his work shorts are so ancient, loose and frayed at the edges they very much resemble a loin cloth from a distance. And the Pharaohnic look is delightfully complete whenever he wraps an old white T-shirt or towel around his head to keep sweat from dripping into his eyes. Unfortunately, it's not hot enough for that in May, but she still pauses to enjoy the picture of his lean brown body bent over one of her white stone vases as he tends the sublime explosion of violet petunias overflowing its borders.

'*Hola*, Ramon!' If she calls him Ra she will have to launch into a historical explanation that could take a very long time since she suspects his brain is not much bigger than her two cats' combined.

He looks up, and his smile of pure, unfeigned pleasure in her presence never fails to flatter her.

'*Hola*, Mira. *Como estas?*' He walks towards her in his usual slow, unhurried way, and as he approaches her, she admires his broad shoulders, hard pecs and ribbed abs with the same superficial pleasure she sucks on a Hershey's Chocolate Kiss.

'*Bien, gracias. Agua?*' she asks quickly, because engaging in conversation with Ra is like deliberately wading through quicksand; his thought processes aren't the fastest in the land.

'*Si, porfavor, gracias.*'

'With lots of ice!' she adds cheerfully to cover up the fact that she is bee-lining it for the kitchen door, only there is something blocking her way inside. She stops and stares at the obstacle, unable to make sense of it as her pulse accelerates from the effort. She feels Ra step up behind her, and then walk past her to pick up the object of her contemplation – one of her empty half-gallon low-fat milk cartons with the top cut off to accommodate a bouquet of violet roses just beginning to bloom. He smiles at her again and stands there holding the impromptu vase as reverently motionless as a living relic from purer centuries visiting a temple to make an offering. And apparently Mira is the very reluctant goddess. She loves what Ra does for her garden, she has no desire to let him go, but if he begins exhibiting a more than extremely casual personal interest in her the sacrificial axe will have to fall...

He looks down at the house keys in her hand, glances at the lock on the kitchen door, and then looks back at her face, the glint of a question sparking in the dark depths of his eyes.

She realizes he is waiting for her to open the door so he can carry the roses inside for her. 'Ramon, you shouldn't have…'

His brow furrows slightly as he translates her words into Spanish in his mind, followed by the much longer process of trying to figure out exactly what they mean. The revelation of comprehension is beautiful to behold as his eyes ignite like hot coals and he grins at her, displaying all his perfect white teeth. 'Ah, no!' he says, laughing and shaking his head. '*Estavan aqui cuando llege.*' He glances down at the step leading up into the house, gesturing with his free hand. 'Here… found I.' Next he indicates her recycle bin and caresses the carton. 'I put in water so would not die.'

'You found these roses on my doorstep?' she cries, the concrete step leading up into her kitchen suddenly looking as beautifully significant as an altar.

'*Si*, someone left for you.' He reaches between the thorny stems and extracts a small white card.

She takes it from him and turns it over, her heart in her throat. She is reminded of the large, beautifully ornate capital letters that begin each chapter in her book of fairytales. There is no name on the card, merely the exquisite calligraphy of the letter *P*

'Phillip!' she breathes.

∞∽∞∽∞∽∞

The big, black, beautiful *P* with its elaborately curled ends has Mira riding a wave of euphoria all evening. There can be no doubt that the dozen violet roses are from Phillip, and the first thing she does before she gets Ra the glass of ice-water she promised him is rescue the beautiful blooms from the milk carton. She arranges them in a vase made of tiny multi-colored pieces of glass and places them in the center of her little living room just as all her thoughts center around the man who gave them to her. She is at once supremely happy and bitterly disappointed. Phillip was here, he came to see her again and she missed him, a terrible fact that takes the form of a physical tightness in her chest that is almost painful. Ra is standing in her kitchen,

Cat's Collar

patient as the life-sized statue of an ancient Egyptian worker. She is sorry he found the roses before she did, but she is grateful he saved them from wilting.

'*Agua o cerveza?*' she asks brightly.

He smiles as though catching a glimpse of paradise.

She returns his smile, and offers him one of the bottles of *Sam Adams* that has been sitting on the bottom shelf in the back of her refrigerator for so long they date back to the Boston Tea Party in her personal history. She never drinks beer, and has no idea why she bought that six-pack in the first place. Some man she dated briefly probably left it there, and now she's glad he did because it enables her to offer her messenger of happiness a small reward. Ra heads back outside with his beer to finish what he was doing before he goes, and at last she is alone with her joy. The relaxing sensuality of solitude is deepened by the promise of highly desirable company in the future... and by the slapping sound of the cat flap rocking gently back and forth as Stormy slinks inside. 'Merr!' he exclaims in mingled pleasure and protest that she is finally home after being gone for so long.

'Stormy, baby, come here, sweetie!' He is a more than willing victim of her rapture as she cradles him like a baby against her chest. His eyes narrow into ecstatic slits, and the vibration of his purr feels like a warm, relaxing massage to her soul.

The cat flap rattles again and Sekhmet makes a loud, yowling entrance. She pointedly dips her face into her empty food bowl, and then glares up at the spectacle her silly brother and their pet human are making of each other.

Mira laughs and sets the limp gray rag of Stormy down beside his contrastingly tense sister. 'You're in luck tonight, Sekhmety-poo, because mommy's in a very good mood!'

'Mreow!' Translated, 'Don't you ever dare call me that again!' and 'Yeow!' clearly says, 'Bring my food out now! Why are you keeping me waiting?'

Stormy contently licks one of his paws, and then rests his head on Mira's sandaled feet. His roughly soft cheek doesn't graze her toes in the possessive act of scenting her and claiming her as his territory; it simply rests there for a long moment in a beautiful gesture of affection that takes her breath away with love and respect for this creature born on her doorstep three years ago. Once their mother – an all-black stray who has haunted the neighborhood for over a decade – finished nursing them, and was sure Mira would take care of them, she vanished and was never seen again, but she could not have left her children in a better home. Mira regularly drives all the way to *Webber's Pet Supermarket* to buy the healthiest, most nutritious cat food money can buy, and occasionally she supplements their gourmet diet with cans of Salmon, Tuna and Crab meat. Tonight definitely qualifies as a special occasion, and whenever she celebrates so do her pussies.

As she pours herself a glass of Chardonnay (figuratively shuddering at the mere thought of giving up this ritual of a relaxing glass of wine in the evenings after a long hard day) Stormy and Sekhmet dig away at the tender pink meat of an Alaskan Salmon. Their bowls are on opposite sides of the kitchen. When they were kittens, Sekhmet would quickly devour her food, and then promptly begin devouring her brother's portion. She eats more slowly now, but she is still in the bad habit of stealing from her mild-mannered sibling, who steps meekly aside and begins licking his paws. Mira never ceases to be amazed at Stormy's gentle selflessness, and she keeps a watchful eye out for him, making sure he doesn't fall victim to his sister's greed as she leans against the counter sipping her wine and unwinding from the stress of three long days trying not to think about Phillip. Now at last she allows the memory and feel of him to fill her whole being with a deep, wonderfully promising warmth as the fruit of the vine branches through her veins and relaxes her into daring to feel nothing but hopeful...

All waves crash, some dashing themselves passionately against rocky shores while others gently surrender to the soft caress of white sand on a paradisiacal island. When Mira's euphoric wave inevitably begins to ebb, she finds herself in a place she has never been before – in an exotic world ripe with dangerously sinister terms like Master and slave, dominance and submission... suddenly she is afraid and in need of another glass of Chardonnay.

She takes her wine into the living room, kicks off her high-heeled sandals, and curls her legs beneath her on the black leather sofa in front of the violet roses – his second gift. His first gift was the powerful climax he gave her, and it seems she hasn't been able to think straight since then. The unexpected, violent

Cat's Collar

pleasure she gladly suffered that morning was like the shipwreck of all the normal, comfortable beliefs about love and sex she was sailing through life in. Now she finds herself curiously dazed and wandering a timeless realm deliberately left off all conventional maps as though it is located where dragons once dwelled at the ends of a flat world.

Dreaming of the man who calls himself a Master in a sexual and psychological subculture she knows next to nothing about, hints of oak and tropical fruit awash on her tongue as she sips her wine's liquid sunshine, Mira is possessed by the image of a proper young English woman – her white shirt and long skirt torn and soiled – stranded on a beach surrounded by a wild jungle, and she is destined to fall in love with a handsome barbarian king despite his humiliating harem and his fierce, arrogant ways. And Ian McFarland is the captain of the ship that fatally crashed into rocks and drowned, leaving her to fend for herself… leaving her alone with Richard, a man she knows essentially nothing about except that he frightens her a little… and turns her on a lot. Stormy leaps onto the sofa, and she gladly lets him curl up on her lap. 'How can I possibly get involved with a man who spends at least three nights a week with other women?' she asks him, and he stops purring abruptly, picking up on her distress. 'Yet he says he rarely sleeps with them, and if we become involved *rarely* will have to become *never* and carved in stone forever!' He begins purring again. Not knowing when she will see him again is torture, and yet it also turns her on in a perverse way; the fact that he might show up at any second keeps her in a heightened state of arousal. 'Stormy, I have to get up, baby,' she tells him reluctantly, and he jumps off her lap obligingly. The pussy between her thighs is silently but inexorably demanding her attention.

In her bedroom, Mira flings off her dress, which leaves only the black lace panties she chose to wear this morning for luck. She slips the delicate fabric slowly down her legs, the shimmering pearly drop of sweet-smelling juice crowning the cotton crotch testifying to how wet she has become thinking of Master Phillip. This is the first time she actually dares call him that in her mind, and a thrill of trepidation only stokes the warmth between her thighs. Now that she is free to think of him, she wonders exactly what he does when he dominates women. She sincerely hopes flavored condoms are not involved!

The few sex toys she possesses are housed in a red velvet box, and now she pulls out her favorite dildo – a firm but tender white cock with life-like ribbing, a realistic curve and a pronounced head rising from the shaft. At last she can admit to herself how erotically charged her body has been since a man she didn't know commanded her to open her robe for him. But as she lies back across the bed, it doesn't feel right to believe she didn't know him. Even though they had only just met, he still felt mysteriously familiar to her in a way she can't rationally express but which is nevertheless unquestionable.

The cool and lifeless plastic is no substitute for a warm, living erection, but her pussy is crying to be filled, and this thick pacifier is better than nothing at the moment. The dildo may possess a life-like appearance, but it in no way feels like a real penis. The experience of Phillip's hard-on opening her up was effortlessly pleasurable; her innermost flesh embraced him lovingly, gratefully. Not so with the dildo. Her tight hole resists the invasion of the plastic organ, refusing to bloom naturally open around it. She has to gently and very slowly force the surrogate penis into her vagina. She lodges it halfway up inside her with one hand, rubbing her clit with the other, and soon the rubber cock is able to slide all the way into her juicing slot. Only the red cap (which she has never unscrewed to insert batteries to active the vibrating mechanism which only annoys her) is visible between her labial lips at the heart of her vulva. Her eyes are open, but she is not seeing the blank white ceiling... she is seeing a tall, broad-shouldered figure dressed all in black standing before her pumping his glorious erection... she climaxes immediately, almost too quickly, and the relief is only briefly physical, the rest of her is more turned on than ever.

Anxious to avoid the mild depression using a dildo tends to fill her with, Mira quickly rinses it clean and places it back in the red velvet box. She then rescues her remaining half glass of Chardonnay and takes it into the bathroom, intent on the simple pleasure of a long hot shower to slough off the day's disappointments, and to baptize a fresh new self ready for everything.

Chapter Five

*The magical staff used by magicians may have been
camouflaged as a broom in the Middle Ages to hide it from
agents of the Inquisition, hence the legend of witches
flying across the moon on a broom...*

In the middle of the night a storm rolls in. A flash of lightning illuminates Mira's full-length mirror and transforms it into the silver sheet of a moonlit lake from which Richard emerges, his black leather outfit gleaming wetly; clinging tightly to his body as he steps into her bedroom from another dimension, using the mirror's wooden frame like a doorway. In the impenetrable darkness that follows, Mira tells herself it was only her dream-drenched brain imagining what her eyes just saw as the pounding of her heart merges with the rumble of thunder outside. It seems a flash of her own subconscious brilliance when lightning strikes again and reveals the impossible truth of her vision. She sits up in bed with a cry, clutching the violet sheet to her breasts as Stormy and Sekhmet greet the man in black like their long lost big brother, purring joyfully around his boots.

'Oh, my God!' she whispers, thrilled to the bone by this casual display of unfathomable powers proving what she has always believed – that life possesses much more interesting sensual dimensions than her frigid reason can even conceive of...

There is a crashing rumble directly outside the window as a divine flash captures the shape of everything inside the bedroom while leaching it of all living color. Her senses are thrown into a confused panic as a forceful gust of wind snatches the sheet away from her naked body. Her scream is drowned out by

Cat's Collar

another earth-shattering boom that sounds just like one of the old oak trees outside collapsing across her roof.

'Don't be afraid,' a man's voice whispers, carrying effortlessly over the storm's audio and visual chaos. 'It's all *us*, Mira, can't you feel it?'

At once she remembers, and it is with the bittersweet sense of falling back in time that she falls back across her violet bed sheets in Phillip's arms…

And suddenly wakes up alone in the dark to the ringing of her cell phone on the nightstand, its preemptory electronic bid for attention rising above the sound of wind-lashed rain beating against the window panes. She cries out in pain as Sekhmet leaps onto her legs and sinks the claws of her front paws into her thighs through the bed sheet. Stormy is right behind his sister, but he prefers the safety of Mira's chest where he perches Sphinx-like, staring earnestly into her eyes to let her know he wants her to exert a calming influence over the atmosphere.

'Mreow!' Sekhmet is more skeptical about Mira's powers and digs her claws into her skin again in furious denial that she is afraid.

She gently flings Sekhmet to the foot of the bed and cradles Stormy in one arm as she reaches anxiously for her cell phone. Her red digital clock brands 2:09 a.m. into her brain, signaling either a crank call or a life-threatening emergency on the other end of the virtual line. The few seconds it takes her to reach the phone feel like a much longer amount of time as her mind races… there aren't even any actual phone wires stretching like haunting black veins between her house and her parents' home; their voices have to journey up into space, all the warmth and meaning behind them disembodied for infinitesimal seconds before being bounced back by a satellite to enter a body again through the vehicle of the ears, just one miraculous sensory control in the complex adventure of physical incarnation…

She thanks God for the luminous violet display that enables her to find the 'Answer' button in the dark as she registers with relief that the number calling her is not familiar. 'Hello?' she says breathlessly.

'Don't be afraid,' a man's voice says quietly.

She sets Stormy down on the floor and gets out of bed, needing a solid surface beneath her to convince herself she isn't still dreaming.

'I hope you don't mind I looked up your number.'

'Of course I don't mind.' Her cellular is both her home and her work number; she got rid of her landline ages ago.

'Are you alone?'

'Well, not exactly…' She glances down at Stormy and Sekhmet circling her ankles, their ears thrown back anxiously. 'And if Sekhmet keeps sinking her claws into me, I'll need to call 911 and can get some handsome paramedics over here.'

The effect his laughter has on her is in no way diminished by the fact that it has to travel up into space and then back down through the atmosphere again; it still makes her feel weak and warm all over.

'I just find it hard to believe a woman as beautiful as you isn't taken.'

'Oh, I've been taken alright, the only problem is no one's been able to hold me.' She is amazed at the light-hearted banter she is managing, and wonders if it's a symptom of sensual disorientation caused in part by being awakened in the middle of the night during a thunder storm that penetrated her dreams along with the man calling her, and in part by a relief so deep she feels herself falling and falling, waiting for him to catch her in his arms and hold her forever… but unfortunately it's only his disembodied voice flowing through her blood like the warm, spiced wine they used to drink in Medieval times she has always been meaning to try.

'That's going to change, Mira.'

Once again her feminine brain translates his sexy threat into a sublime promise as she doesn't so much sit as collapse onto the edge of her bed. 'It already has changed,' she confesses to this black leather-wearing priest speaking to her through the passionate veil of the storm. 'You're all I've been able to think about for the last three days, Phillip. Why did you just vanish like that?'

'You just answered your own question.'

She feels hurt by the way he deliberately tormented her, and then reluctantly remembers what he calls himself – a Master – and that his profession (or isn't it more like a lifestyle?) occasionally involves beating women, and apparently not just literally, because for over ninety hours (even while she was asleep, it seems) the thought of him, the memory of him, the longing to see him again has whipped her soul even as she struggled to resist the thought of him; as she struggled to escape her painful obsession with him while at the same time dreading a return to her former freedom in which he did not exist, an existential pain far worse than the suffering of wondering if she would ever see him again. 'You didn't have to disappear for me to keep thinking about you, Phillip.'

'I know I didn't.'

She can't help it, she respects him for not indulging her, either with an explanation or with a justification for his actions. 'I guess you're not at work tonight,' she observes as neutrally as she can manage.

'I told you, Mira, I only work three nights a week.'

Considering what his work consists of (the excruciating details of which she has yet to try and picture) 'only' seems a rather unsuitable qualifier, but she keeps her catty claws sheathed, not wanting to frighten him away with a jealousy she has no right to feel yet. Or does she? 'Do you cut through lots of other women's yards?' she demands mildly.

His laughter is the best answer he can give her. It's the same way he laughed when she asked him if he was gay. 'No, that's the first time a pussy's ever tempted me into trespassing like that.'

Now it's her turn to laugh. 'I'm so glad she did, but then I don't believe in coincidence.'

'What do you believe in?'

'I believe in choreography, Phillip.'

'Mm, and judging by our first *pas de deux* together, the universe is more inspired than I ever dared hope.' He speaks so quietly her ears have a hard time capturing his voice over the sound of the rain beating against the window panes, but her heart hears him loud and clear. 'And if our first dance together is any indication, you don't have a problem with me leading, do you?'

No, I love it, she thinks, but is not ready to admit it yet. 'I don't know what you mean ...'

'Yes, you do.'

She wonders if she only imagined the slight note of disappointment in his voice that sears her soul like acid.

'I'll use an analogy I imagine you can relate to, Mira. Think of Ice Dancers… when the man throws his partner up in the air, she has to trust him to catch her and not let her fall. When he sends her into a spinning death spiral, it's a combination of her own submissive grace and his skill and strength that keep her safe and make the dance between them truly beautiful. Do you understand?'

She has never understood the dual nature of her heartbeat until now – hope and dread, excitement and fear – they are who she is and there is no distinguishing between them, until she makes the conscious choice to do so and whispers, 'I think so…'

'Good, then I'll be in touch again soon. Be ready.'

'When…?' But there is only empty space paradoxically ringing in her ears. She holds the phone away from her face, and sees the words printed in indelible black *Call Ended*. Thunder rumbles, farther away now, but her cats still leap shrilly onto the bed beside her. 'Oh, God, what am I getting myself into?' she asks them.

Stormy purrs, Sekhmet yowls, and somehow their reply is just how she feels inside. Despite what she must admit is a rather stimulating anxiety akin to stage fright before a major performance (she was in the Drama department all through high school and college) she is happier and more thrilled to be alive than she can remember being in all her adult life. She worries it's too soon to feel this way about a total stranger, but he ceased to be that the instant he penetrated her, and it's too late to go back now. What he made her feel is part of her forever, and yet only the beginning of a relationship that promises to challenge and fulfill her as she has never been challenged and fulfilled before.

∞∞∞

'Mira, why don't you ever call?'

Oh, Christ, this is the last thing she needs – to talk to her mother the morning after the night she agreed to become a man's sex slave. She didn't actually say so, but it was clearly implied when she essentially agreed to do whatever he said. 'Hi, mom, I'm sorry, it's just that I've been so busy lately.'

'Well…' A deep sigh. 'I suppose that's a good thing.'

'Yes, it definitely is, it means I won't ever have to ask you and dad for money again.'

'Oh, Mira, dear, you know we don't mind-'

'No, but I do. I actually have money saved and business is great.'

'I'm so happy to hear that, dear.'

'You don't *sound* happy.'

'It's just that we never see you…'

'Mom, that's not true.' At least not from what Mira admits is her own decidedly selfish perspective. She hasn't had her cup of tea yet this morning, and this phone conversation with her mother is making the one she had last night with a man feel increasingly like a dream as thunder rumbled and lightning flashed outside indistinguishable from her tumultuous emotions.

She remains on the phone chatting with her mother with only a fraction of her mind engaged in the conversation as she microwaves water for tea, and slips some high fiber whole wheat bread slices into her toaster. She is not yet awake enough to juggle her anxious anticipation concerning the intense sexual relationship she is embarking upon, with her sweet and comfortable love for her parents and the guilt she feels at not spending enough time with them. Rose's affectionately worried and needy voice makes Mira feel as if she is standing on a wharf about to deliberately board the ship flying a black flag painted with a white skull and crossbones while her parents watch, incredulous and horrified, as their innocent little girl willingly sells herself into slavery…

The microwave bell chimes just as Rose asks with a similarly high-pitched indignation, 'Have you even heard a word I said, Mira?'

'Mom, I have to go now, I'm meeting with a client this morning,' she lies. 'I'll call you later, I promise. I love you. And tell dad I love him, too, and that I'll come over for dinner again soon.'

'You promise?'

'I promise.'

'We love you too, dear, take care… and keep your windows closed at night, please!'

'Uh-huh. Bye.' She gently tosses the phone down on a black potholder. She wonders vaguely what it would be like to leave the house and be unreachable by anyone, interacting only with people she actually meets in the flesh. Her cell phone's technological butler is always with her, announcing in clear black letters or numbers who is seeking an audience with her. More often than not she sends everyone to the Drawing Room of her voicemail to await her pleasure. Phillip's number is stored in memory under Received Calls, yet these coordinates to his soul are absolutely useless to her because she would never dream of calling him. He said he would be in touch again soon. All she can do is wait.

As her tea steeps and she is spreading organic strawberry jam over the hot slices of bread, it dawns on Mira – with a sense of wonder much sharper than the butter knife – that her attitude has always been naturally submissive. The man makes the first move, and keeps making them while she either submits to his attentions or rejects them.

'I'll be in touch again soon…' The memory of his sexy, threatening, promising, everything-she-could-ever-have-hoped-for-in-a-man's-voice, is affecting her appetite. Suddenly she isn't interested in breakfast, but she makes herself eat, and drink her tea knowing caffeine withdrawal and hunger pangs will interfere with the smooth flow of her creative energies. She needs to enter the measurements of Ian's condo into her computer; the monthly bills are due to be paid; she should renew her ad in a local paper, and make an appointment for Stormy and Sekhmet at the Vet for their annual shots. She doesn't want to do any of these things. All she can do is wonder when Phillip will decide to get in touch with her again, what form his touch will take, what he will tell her to do, where they will be… All she can do is wonder if she'll be able to let go of her fears and dance the mysterious *pas de deux* of dominance and submission with him. Only time will tell, and right now every minute feels like an hour she somehow has to get through waiting for him to enter her life again.

Forget work and finances; all she is good for this morning is cleaning her little doll's house from top to bottom while doing all her laundry, including bed sheets, towels, bathroom rugs, everything!

Cat's Collar

※※※※

The doorbell rings at the worst possible moment. In the process of cleaning her doll's house, Mira has made an absolute mess of herself. Her hair is half up and half down (the hazards of a too hasty pin-up) and deep in the midst of mopping her kitchen floor she can't be bothered to do anything except curl it impatiently behind her ears. She is wearing old white socks, and a very skimpy pair of grey terrycloth shorts that tie closed in front with a delicate white bow adorning the bare skin just below her navel. And there is lots of skin to be seen, because the only other thing she's wearing is an old violet sport's bra to avoid the slight muscular ache in her chest caused by allowing her breasts to swing freely back and forth as she mops and vacuums. Cleaning is a full-body workout, involving lots of bending and squatting, lifting and folding, reaching and running back and forth, especially if you've decided to cook at the same time. She has allowed herself to be fully possessed by domestic demons today which ground her firmly in the present and keep her from anticipating and worrying about the future... except for in the very back of her mind, which is always filled with thoughts and images of Phillip no matter what she is doing.

The doorbell rings again as Mira stands, mop in hand, paralyzed with horror. It can't be! It just can't be him, not when she's in the middle of two loads of laundry on top of making split pea soup on one burner and Garbanzo and Chorizo stew on the other; not when she looks like something the cats just dragged in.

'Coming!' she cries, propping the mop up against the counter. Wresting the remaining pins from her hair, she shakes it loose over her bare shoulders. 'Please don't let it be him!' she prays beneath her breath. 'Please, please, Lord, don't let it be him!' Yet, naturally, deep down she desperately wants it to be him, so it is a hot and cold slap of mingled relief and disappointment when she opens the front door and sees only the lumpy blue-clad form of a female Federal Express courier standing out on her front porch.

'Package for Mira Rosenthal,' she says with the briefest of glances at the purported recipient; she keeps her eyes fixed on her electronic screen as if avoiding the sight of the half naked beautiful woman she is serving.

'That's me,' Mira claims the feather-light box and dutifully signs her name on the virtual line.

'Have a nice day,' the courier addresses an oak tree as she quickly takes her leave.

'You too,' Mira recites automatically, but in her case she sincerely means it. She is not expecting anything from anyone that she can remember, and it is with a fun, Christmas-like feeling that she takes the box inside and sets it down on the kitchen counter, pulling eagerly on the cardboard tab that slices it conveniently open. The package is so light she wonders what could possibly be inside it – probably a fabric sample she forgot she ordered – and her guess appears to be confirmed when she spots the shimmer of blood-red satin... except it is no boring square fragment, instead flows on and on as she pulls it gently out of the box. The piece of cloth is approximately three inches wide and not quite long enough to be a belt. She rifles through the file cabinets of her mental synapses trying to remember when she ordered this. She is already sure she didn't, but she is compelled to try and make sense of this unexpected special delivery. She turns the box over and hastily searches the Airbill for a clue, but there is no return address.

Phillip said he would be in touch again soon, and the fabric's coolly sensuous caress is telling her without words that it's from him... and that she knows what it is...

The cat flap rattles, announcing the entrance of one of her non-human roommates, but she scarcely notices, too intent on identifying the origin and purpose of the lovely length of fabric... which suddenly jerks as if alive and begins slipping out of her hand.

'Sekhmet, no!' She rescues the fine cloth from the damagingly curious swipe of her feline's claws. 'This isn't for you, it's for me!' she adds cattily, and Sekhmet walks away indifferently, pretending she was never really interested in it.

Mira has not forgotten what Phillip did with the sash of her robe (she will never forget) but this burgundy-colored cloth is broader and not as long... and soft enough to make an ideal blindfold. She tips the box over and shakes it, hoping something will fall out as if from another dimension in the cardboard invisible to the naked eye that will explain where the suggestive piece of fabric comes from and exactly what she is supposed to do with it. There is no note, nothing

Cat's Collar

except her intuitive certainty the 'gift' is from Phillip and his way of preparing her for what he plans to do to her next.

She has been blindfolded once or twice during sex, but it was always done in a fun, playful way. She knows in her bones that with this man it will be very different, more serious and meaningful, challenging and fulfilling. For the first time in her life, she is sure beyond a shadow of a doubt that the depth of her imagination and the intensity of her desires are not going to be left wanting, not if the erotic appetizer they shared in her treasure-filled garage is any indication.

She folds the sash reverently into the red velvet box in her bedroom, safely away from curious kitties. She then returns to serving the domestic demons she is willingly sacrificing herself to today. It is time to let the finished soups cool before she ladles them into individual portion-sized plastic containers to freeze for easy lunches and dinners in the future. She is in the middle of enough chores to keep her busy until late afternoon, at which point the promise of a shower and a glass of Chardonnay beckon her like the Holy Grail hidden beneath a gloriously hot waterfall.

※ ※ ※

Mira has just finished lathering herself up with her fluffy lavender sponge and favorite milk soap when her cell phone rings.

She quickly shuts off the water and reaches for her little metal butler where it is lying on top of her towel just within reach of her dripping hand. It crosses her mind that he told her to be ready, yet she seems to have done everything in her power not to be prepared for anything today – a subconscious form of resistance at odds with her excitement. She has only seen this series of numbers once before, but it is already branded into her heart. 'Hello?' she answers as calmly as possible considering her drenched state, both physically and emotionally, for no man has ever inspired such a flood of feelings in her before.

'Did you receive the package?' he asks quietly.

She suffers a thrill of secrecy and danger. 'Yes, I did,' she replies, shivering for more reasons than one.

'I'll teach you the correct response later, Mira, but since you're a virgin to

Cat's Collar - Three Erotic Romances

B&D I'm taking it very slowly with you. I noticed the secluded arbor out in your garden. At exactly eight o'clock this evening if you happen to be wearing any clothes you'll take them all off, everything, including your shoes, and you will wait for me there naked, wearing only the contents of the package. You know what to do with it. You will wait for me lying on your back with your arms over your head and your legs spread. You may bring a towel to lie on if you prefer.'

'You want me to lie naked out in my garden blindfolded?' The incredulous question escapes her before she can stop it.

'I won't repeat myself. If you're not there waiting for me exactly as I described, then I'll assume you've changed your mind about us.'

'I'll be there.'

'Then I'll see you then.'

He leaves her to wonder whether or not a pun was intended as the display on her phone once again announces Call Ended.

She scarcely notices the rest of her long-awaited shower. Her property is blessedly private – three full acres of big old trees, flowering bushes and vines, almost all of which are in bloom now and providing a natural protection from neighbor's prying eyes. Nevertheless, she does have neighbors, and it makes her anxious to imagine lying naked outside vulnerably blind. Only the fact that her little arbor is wonderfully private – a horseshoe of bushes over six-feet tall, two of them Rose bushes – assuages her nervousness. Chances are no one will see her, but that of course means there is also the chance someone might, yet because she is probably not in any real danger in the privacy of her yard, how vulnerable she will feel serves to excite her more than frighten her.

Chapter Six

> *"Don't settle for the one you can live with,*
> *wait for the one you can't live without."*
> Anonymous

Eight o'clock arrives and brings with it those cool, lovely, and sadly evanescent moments just after the sun dips below the horizon when the beauty of the dying day is both softened and intensified – a classic crossover moment. Mira has a feeling there will be many such moments with Phillip, and her anticipation is so intense it has the power to slow time down to a miserable crawl. The evening seems endless as one glass of Chardonnay flows into another. She is sitting with her legs curled up beneath her on the couch wearing her violet robe and gazing at the violet roses left by the man she has agreed to meet naked and blindfolded out in her garden. Part of her feels like a little girl playing a really exciting game with the new boy next door, who at last seems a fit match for her imaginative energies.

'Eat your heart out, Anna,' she murmurs, smugly taking another sip of wine. Her parents are still in touch with Anna's parents, which is why she knows that her ex best friend from long ago married a stock broker and is getting ready to pop her third baby, in Mira's opinion a nightmare scenario if there ever was one. Suddenly she feels sorry for women whose circumstances prohibit them from doing such simple sensual things as lying naked out in a garden waiting for their lover. The blindfold seems symbolically appropriate since she has not been able to truly see anything lately except her thoughts of Phillip.

When the clock on her cable box reads seven-fifty-four, Mira slips out of her robe,

Cat's Collar

picks up a burgundy towel with the red satin blindfold resting ready on top of it, and heads outside wearing nothing but the black hair waving gently down her back.

Being naked out in her yard feels utterly natural to her; she doesn't experience any of the awkward sense of exposure she feared. On the contrary, she feels like a special guest, the center of attention in a wild yet sophisticated celebration serving the heady cocktail of flowers in bloom, each color intoxicatingly lovely in its own way. And even though most of the lively guests are invisible, her naked flesh clearly senses their presence in the prickly grass, in the dark earth, and in the sap-filled barks of old trees. She is surrounded by the cool, shadowy peace of evening... and of life speaking to her through a silence punctuated by the sound of leaves rustling in the breeze...

Dusk, when the sun has set but night has not yet fallen, the ultimate crossover moments when the sky is an indescribable color – a deep, haunting blue that can never be mixed on an artist's palette occasionally deepened by an erratic black streak. The bats are out. She sometimes enjoys sipping her Chardonnay out on the porch watching them, twilight's haunting window between night and day the only time they're visible to the human eye... evoking legends of vampires rising from their coffins the instant the sun sets, vulnerable for a few moments before they blend into the darkness to begin wreaking their deadly sensuality...

The red and white roses that will adorn her bower have not yet bloomed, so it is in a deep-green well of darkening foliage that Mira spreads out her towel and kneels naked in the center of it. She has never tied a blindfold over her own eyes before, and she takes great care to get it just right so there aren't any cracks she can cheat and see through. Beneath the slick cloth absolute darkness reigns as she secures it in a firm knot at the back of her head, unable to avoid tangling a few of her hairs in it. Then she lies on her back, bends her arms over her head, and spreads her legs just as he instructed her to do.

For the first minute or so she wonders how long she will have to wait for him like this, but gradually her mind relaxes along with her body, and like the loud, clattering engine of a train slowing down at a major crossroads she stops thinking to just listen. It's true that not being able to see the world magnifies the sounds around her. The soft rustling of leaves seems to grow louder and louder until it becomes a veritable symphony rising in tempo the more she focuses on it. She won't be able to hear Phillip's approach on the soft carpet of grass so well-tended by Ra. Will she be able to sense him? She is glad he gave her permission to spread a towel between her naked skin and all the creepy-crawly creatures living in the dirt, because though she doesn't mind them every now and then accidentally landing on her arms and legs, but her pussy is another matter altogether, a sacred shrine off limits to all biological riffraff. And right now her fleshly temple doors are wide open waiting for the man her soul has already dared to identify as the exciting high priest she has been waiting for since she knew how to daydream.

The wind lightly caressing her skin makes her think of the words, 'You know not whence it comes or whence it goes' a metaphor for the spirit as an invisible force that nevertheless has the power to touch us... but not like that... there is something warm and decidedly substantial moving slowly up her legs...

'Phillip?' she whispers, but does not really need to hear him reply. Her body knows those are a man's hands caressing the infinitely sensitive flesh of her inner thighs even as she senses the deepening of the air above her. Suddenly, she longs to rip off the blindfold to see him. Desperate to look at him, to fill all her senses with him, she arches her back beneath the delicious torture of only being able to experience his ghostly touch. She can't even be sure it truly is him. The wild thought crosses her mind that Ramon forgot one of his gardening tools, and that those are actually his hands moving ever so lightly up towards her eagerly waiting breasts, but she immediately dismisses the notion. She doesn't need to see to know that is not her gardener kneeling between her legs; she recognizes the almost palpable magnetic current flowing between Phillip's skin and hers as his fingertips just barely brush her skin. She sighs with pleasure as a cool, warm, firm and moist sensation engulfs one of her nipples, instantly hardening it into a pebble sending ripples of delight into the depths of her sex.

It doesn't take long for a sublime anarchy to reign in her other senses freed from the tyranny of sight. He works on both her nipples with a skill that has her nerve-ends smoldering with a desire that keeps intensifying the wetter her pussy gets. It is too much for her, she has to touch him, she has to feel him, her arms

Cat's Collar

refuse to remain resting passively over her head...

He grasps both her wrists with a swift strength that makes her aware of how delicate her bones are. She moans, knowing she has done wrong, and senses him move away from her as he stretches her arms up over her head again. Tears of frustration and regret that she has failed to submit gracefully to him threaten to dampen the blindfold. She has to bite her lip to keep them in check. The loving way his fingertips caress her open palms soothes and forgives her. Then she senses another welcome disturbance of the air around her and knows he is moving again. Her suspicions are confirmed when she distinctly feels his presence once more concentrated between her legs. The tongue she fantasized about that morning as she touched herself becomes real, and miraculously even more skilled and sensitive to her slightest reaction than she could ever have dared hope.

Small, whimpering sounds of disbelief and gratitude well up from within her, released into the cool evening as he goes down on her with a precision that is almost surgical in its power to cut through her defenses, yet there is nothing cold and passionless about the way he eats her. Her pussy is juicing helplessly, gushing like another small organic fountain added to the three already gracing her garden. The tip of his tongue circling endlessly makes her clitoris feel like a priestess coaxed all the way out of her fleshly temple for the first time by the quality of a devotion at last worthy of her sensitive spirit. In the past so many men simply attacked her clit with all the finesse of farmers trampling on a seed expecting pleasure to just naturally bloom between her thighs as a result; sucking on her body's mysterious seed as though it was a simple sugar-based candy, making it defensively hard and producing the opposite effect of melting her in their mouth. Some of her lovers were a bit more circumspect, but there was not enough passion in the almost mathematical application of licks, sucks, laps and nips they patiently subjected her to, seeking her sexual response like the answer to an almost impossibly complex equation.

As she hoped and suspected would be the case, being orally pleasured by a man feels stunningly different with Phillip. The muscle of his tongue is so firm and thick that when it works its way up between the folds of her labia, opening her up as he savors the nectar of her arousal, her back arches with longing; with the blind need to be penetrated by his cock or his tongue or his fingers, she doesn't care which, she just has to feel a part of him inside her before she completely loses her mind wanting him. Yet she doesn't dare speak; she doesn't dare beg him to fuck her. Already she has learned enough to suspect pleading with him will only delay her fulfillment, so she submissively endures the divine torment of his features burying themselves in her sex. He uses his whole face to arouse her, not just his tongue, working her pussy up into a drenched frenzy that will suck him down to the very hilt of her incarnation when he finally penetrates her.

Her nipples are so hard that when he reaches up and begins firmly stroking them between this thumb and forefinger a climax blooms between her thighs like a hot house flower, with time-lapse explosiveness, her clit abruptly dissolving between his lips like a drop of dew reflecting all the heat of the sun. Her brain is not prepared for the intensity of the orgasm that takes root in her pelvis and blossoms with devastating beauty in all her nerve-ends and she hears herself cry out as if in pain. The pleasure is so powerful she needed to prepare herself for it, but it's too late as she comes in waves that just keep deepening and deepening rather than ebbing. She has never climaxed like this before without touching herself, with only a man's face buried between her thighs. Her most vital muscles contracting, it takes all the willpower she possesses not to reach down and grab his head, whether to push it away or drive his face deeper into her pussy she cannot say.

'Very good, Mira.' He finally lets her hear his voice.

'Oh, God, Phillip, I've never-'

'Did I give you permission to speak?'

'I'm sorry,' she whispers, and then bites her lip fearing she has further compounded her transgression by speaking again. It feels as much reward as punishment when he abruptly turns her over onto her stomach and spanks her. She has been spanked before, but never like this, and she gasps beneath the impact of a sensation that prepares her for the even more welcome experience of his erection thrusting into her pussy from behind. The soft cotton beneath her is cushioned by lush grass but it does not give way like a bed. The earth beneath her feels rock-solid as he pounds his cock into her slick hole at an angle that leaves nothing to her imagination, his balls slapping her labia as his head vio-

Cat's Collar

lently kisses her cervix. She rests her cheek on the towel and clutches it to brace herself even as the rest of her body rests limp as a beached mermaid beneath his plunging dives. There is nothing passive about her on the inside, however; her pussy is actively, greedily grasping his erection, pulsing open and closed around him like a hungry anemone feasting on his totally fulfilling dimensions. He is so hard she suspects his relentless penetrations would almost hurt if her sex wasn't so wet and relaxed from the orgasm he gave her with his mouth, and when he spreads his body on top of hers it feels like the full, wondrous weight of the universe falling on her as his warm breath caresses her cheek, 'Oh, Mira!'

She moans in response, engrossed in the profound thrill of caressing and squeezing his cock with the most special muscles she possesses. This time he isn't wearing a condom and she is very glad of that, because not being able to see him as well as not truly feeling him inside her would have been unbearable. In her mind's eye she pictures his erection stabbing her and visualizes the walls of her innermost flesh wrapping around it, squeezing his shaft from the base to the head in a continuous rippling motion even as the rest of her flesh remains utterly submissive beneath him. She relishes every second of his beating as he packs the full, rending length of his penis into her pussy with every stroke. She is going to make him come inside her. She will make it impossible for him to pull out of her at the last minute. She is determined to have the impenetrable darkness behind her eyelids illuminated by the exploding stars of his cum surging into her innermost space in an erotic Milky Way. She longs to beg him to come inside her, but he hasn't given her permission to speak. So she begs him silently, with the part of her made especially to coax everything she desires from a man. For years she has been exercising her vaginal muscles in the hope of one day using this sensual skill on her soul-mate, and his breathless groans speak to the effectiveness of her self-training, as does the way his hard-on begins pulsing inside her, further intensifying the pleasure bonding them, until she has to break her silence by crying out as his cock reaches critical mass and he ejaculates deep between her thighs.

Afterwards, they lie still for a few moments. She can tell he is still fully dressed and that he isn't wearing black leather. His shirt is soft against her skin, and before fucking her he pushed his pants down far enough for her to be able to feel his naked hips and scrotum as well as his condom-free dick. She is almost sorry when he lifts his weight off her, and sudden panic prompts her to raise herself up onto her elbows. She is afraid he will walk silently away again while she isn't looking, once again disappearing from her life for an intolerably long time. This nightmare scenario almost makes her speak, but she retrains herself with a monumental effort of will.

'Thank you, Mira,' he says from somewhere above her. 'You may sit up now, which means you may kneel.... no, not like that. We *are* in a temple of sorts, but it's not a Catholic church, so spread your legs more... that's good. Now sit back on your heels and rest the backs of both your hands on your knees... very nice... keep your head lowered... beautiful.'

She is grateful for his firm commands, which offer a civilized contrast to how uncontrollably wet her pussy is. Not being able to see her juices mingled with his sperm trickling down the insides of her thighs causes it to assume embarrassing, almost geographical dimensions in her mind... the tributaries of a river flowing from a temple as old as life... Holding herself perfectly still, she sighs with contentment that her quest for a truly virile man is over at last.

'Did you enjoy that?' he asks, his voice sounding a little closer now and coming from somewhere to her left. 'You have permission to speak.'

'Yes,' she confesses softly.

'The correct response is "Yes, Master".'

Her back stiffens.

'I told you to keep your head down.'

She obeys him tensely, her lips sealed like a tomb behind which all her self-respect is buried as she remains stubbornly silent for a few seconds. 'I refuse to call you what countless other women call you,' she informs him tightly; proudly.

'The women I work with address me as Master Phillip. Did I ask you to call me Master Phillip?'

The beautiful hope and happiness that spark in her heart is fanned by her whispered submission, 'No, Master.'

'I want you to understand, Mira, that only you have the right to call me Master.'

'I hope so...'

Cat's Collar

'Which means I already care about you, and want you, more than any other woman I've ever met. It means I want you to be my real, one-and-only slave.'

Her joy at his words is compounded by the sensation of him untying her blindfold. She holds her breath, scarcely able to believe she is about to see him again after so long, not to mention after how blindly intimate they just were together. The satiny blackness slips away and is replaced by a slightly less absolute darkness. Night has fallen. All she can see of him at first is his white shirt, lovely and luminous as moonlight. His features are distinguishable only as infinitely intriguing shadows when he kisses her, threading his fingers through her hair and tilting her head back to part her lips so he can tongue her deeply, reminding her of how selfishly his cock used her throat.

'Are you cold?' he asks, crouching before her.

'Not at all... I mean, no Master.'

His smile is a subtle light in the darkness. 'You may rise now,' he says, straightening up and offering her his hand so she can brace herself on it as she obeys him. 'Shall we adjourn to your doll's house?'

'Yes, Master,' she replies happily, and bends over to pick up her towel.

'No, leave it there,' he commands. 'Lots of intense, positive energy was just absorbed by that fabric. I want you to leave it there for at least twenty-four hours to remind you of this special night, Mira.'

'Yes, Master,' she agrees, but makes no move to walk towards her house, afraid he will vanish if she doesn't keep her vision fixed directly on him.

'Come on,' he says gently, and once again his smile hits her retinas as a subtle glow in the darkness. He takes her hand and leads the way to her kitchen door. Somewhere along the way Stormy and Sekhmet join them, doing everything in their power to trip them up as they insist on purring passionately around their ankles.

'I don't know what it is about you, Phillip, but Sekhmet has never reacted to another human being like this before. She adores you!'

'She has profoundly good taste, just like her mistress.'

'Yes, we're both very particular.'

'And I'm grateful for that. You could very well be married and pregnant with your second baby by now.'

'Right!'

He opens the door, intuitively aware she didn't lock it, or rather he commanded her to lie out in her garden wearing nothing but a blindfold so he knew there was no place for her to keep a key.

The doll's house is dark except for a lamp in the living room illuminating the bouquet of violet roses. She automatically switches on the overhead light in the kitchen.

Pressing his body up against hers, he promptly flicks the switch back down. 'Do you have any candles?' he asks in a voice soft enough to be her own imagination, except that his presence is more real than anything she has ever experienced; it makes her heartbeats feel like hammer blows erecting the glorious edifice of their future together in the form of a temple dedicated to love and sex and ancient erotic rituals without end...

'Of course I have candles,' she retorts breathlessly. 'As a matter-of-fact, there are two candles on the fireplace mantle in the living room.'

'Matches?'

She opens the small drawer beside which they're standing and extracts one of her many little boxes of wooden matches.

'Light the candles for us, Mira,' he caresses her hair as he speaks, 'then go find the highest pair of heels you own. Put them on, and walk slowly back into the living room.'

She does not need to clearly see his eyes in the dim light to be hopelessly caught up in the gravity of his regard; nevertheless, the correct reply to his command sticks in her throat, battling decades of feminist indoctrination. 'Yes, Master,' she whispers at last.

He kisses her forehead as if rewarding the supreme mental and emotional effort she just made for him. 'And while you're doing that for me,' he adds, 'I'll open a bottle of wine.'

'How did you know I drink wine?' she asks happily.

'The same way I knew you would let me fuck you ten minutes after we met.'

'Oh...' She escapes into the living room and lights the two candles on the fireplace mantle as he instructed her to do, wondering which high-heeled sandals he would prefer of the many pairs she owns. Then she hears the lamp click off behind her. He is completely banishing the easy comfort of electricity in favor of the warm illumination provided by the two flames flickering in the breeze from an open window, and giving off a surprising amount of light even while deepening the shadows. Her modest wine rack remains in darkness, but he walks straight towards it as though he possesses a built-in honing device for the fruit-of-the-vine. She watches him, mentally thanking her guardian angel for finally coming through. 'Shall I get us two wine glasses?' she asks.

'I told you what to do, Mira.'

She hurries into her bedroom feeling almost literally shoved into its refuge by the tone of his voice, which brooks no argument whatsoever. Almost inevitably, she selects a red pair of sandals from *Victoria's Secret* with stiletto heels and thin straps designed to show off the shapely curves of her feet. Then she cheats and sneaks a quick peak at herself in the bathroom mirror, only to discover there is nothing she can do with her appearance to improve it. Her cheeks are attractively flushed from having her pussy very properly fucked, and her eyes are shining with a happiness she has not seen reflected back at her for as long as she can remember. The slightly humid evening air has given an even fuller wave to her hair, and the contented smile on her lips feels like the new natural setting for her facial muscles. She also takes a moment to clean her excessively moist slit and the insides of her thighs with a tissue. His cum trickling slowly out of her is a distracting sensation, to say the least. Yet suddenly part of her feels guilty about wiping her skin clean of the evidence of his pleasure. She knows she will have to confess doing so to him to find out if he considers it a transgression, and this thought process astonishes her more than anything that has happened between them so far.

She practices a sexy walk from the bathroom to the bedroom door, where she pauses like an actress about to step out on stage for the second act of a performance that, so far, has totally captivated her, and gotten rave reviews from even the most critical parts of her mind. The sight of him sitting casually on her black leather couch, his right ankle resting on his left knee, nearly arrests her progress towards him it has such an impact on her. The white button-down shirt open halfway down his chest and tucked into silky black slacks becomes him just as much as tight black leather, the slightly full sleeves evocative of a prince's romantic garment. Sekhmet is nearly invisible curled up on his lap, obviously well aware of the fact that she has secured the best seat in the house. Stormy is lying on the floor at Phillip's feet, his head resting on his left foot clad in a polished black shoe. Two half full glasses of red wine wait beside the vase veritably exploding with roses.

The penetrating gravity of his stare draws her to him like an invisible leash, making it hard for her to walk slowly, as though she could possibly be indifferent to how soon she reaches him.

He smiles. 'Mm...'

She proudly tosses her hair back over her shoulders. Her breasts are round and firm, responding to how aroused she is in every fiber of her being.

'A black cat is a very interesting form for Cupid to take,' he remarks.

'Well, you know what they say – dogs think they're humans, cats think they're gods.'

'Come here.' He extends his right hand towards her. She reaches for it with hers, and as their fingertips touch she thinks of the Sistine Chapel's bearded old patriarch in a hospital gown offering the spark of life to a grotesquely muscular young man. Michael Angelo's talent and perseverance notwithstanding, she has never liked that fresco, and she understands why now as electricity literally crackles between her flesh and Phillip's – because the spark of life can only be ignited between a man and a woman no matter what any religions or alternative lifestyles preach. 'Stand right there,' he instructs gently, directing her slightly to one side of him. 'I want to look at you... you have the most beautiful pussy, Mira.' He idly strokes her sleeping feline's sleek fur as he speaks. 'And you know how to use it, too. You pleased me very much out there.'

'Thank you... Master.' Every time she uses this title to address him, Mira feels as though she deliberately shoots up a powerful drug which is making her feel better and better the more she surrenders control of herself. She never realized (although intuitively she suspected) that submitting to the right man could be so intoxicating.

'You may hand us our wine and sit down beside me now.'

She obeys him gracefully.

Cat's Collar

He chimes his glass against hers. 'To us.'

'To us,' she echoes, and they each take a sip of the Australian Zinfandel.

'Very nice,' he compliments her taste in wine.

'It's okay for the price,' she replies humbly.

'Do you drink wine every night?'

'Yes, with dinner, and usually I have a glass or two of Chardonnay before that, to relax.' She knows she sounds defensive, but she can't help thinking of Ian, and shuddering inwardly at the mere possibility of a universe in which she never saw Phillip again and ended up settling for a handsome recovering alcoholic.

'My parents own a vineyard,' he tells her.

She laughs. 'What?'

'A small vineyard in Washington State just big enough for uninhibited personal consumption and to give away cases as gifts every year.'

'That's wonderful!'

'And you're luscious.' He tilts her face up to his and kisses her on the lips, his mouth moving directly against hers as he whispers, 'I think you may be the one...'

'You think?' she breathes, and feels him smile.

He thrusts his tongue into her mouth and wrestle hers into breathless submission for a moment. Then he sits back comfortably and takes another sip of wine. 'I *know* you are,' he adds soberly. 'And to think I had almost given up hope.'

This admission of vulnerability makes him even more stunningly attractive in her eyes.

'But I don't think we should talk about the past tonight, Mira. Tonight is about the present, and everything the future holds for us.'

'Amen,' she whispers, and takes another sip of the young vintage.

'Not that I have any frightening skeletons in my closet,' he teases.

'Except for your job,' she points out quietly, glancing down at her naked breasts.

'You have an amazingly beautiful body, Mira.' He changes the subject.

'Well, I don't exactly have washboard abs,' she observes, patting the little round belly she gets when she sits down.

'And what makes you think fucking a woman with washboard abs appeals to all men? I much prefer a softer cushion. You're toned and yet soft all over. In my eyes you're perfect.'

She smiles. 'My dad used to tease me when I was little because I thought I was more beautiful than Miss Universe.'

'You're the most beautiful woman in my universe, and that's what counts.'

She sighs. 'You say all the right things, Phillip.'

He laughs. 'That's the first time a woman has ever said *that* to me.'

'But how is that possible?' She is genuinely indignant, and has to take another sip of wine to wash away the bad taste of other people's limited perceptions.

'I've never said such things to a woman before, Mira.'

'I believe you...'

'And you trust me.'

'Yes, Master.'

'Then we have all we need to embark on a very exciting life-long journey together.'

'I've been lied to before,' she confesses abruptly, setting her glass down on the table in front of them. 'I'm very trusting.'

'I know.' He places his glass beside hers. 'But you're safe with me now. I'll never lie to you, Mira, and I'll never do anything to hurt you.'

Annoyed by the motion of her warm bed, Sekhmet jumps off his lap.

'Come here.' He slips an arm around her shoulders while his other hand gently urges her cheek down against his chest. 'You believe me when I say that I'll never hurt you, don't you?'

'Yes, Master.' The sound of his heart beating has a profoundly soothing affect on her; a deep, steady rhythm she mysteriously knows she can trust for as long as they live.

'Good, and now I want you to go put on something nice. I'm taking us out to dinner.'

Chapter Seven

*"Do you love me because I am beautiful, or am
I beautiful because you love me?"*
Charles Perrault, Cinderella

The good thing about being self-employed is that no one can force you to work if you don't want to. In some universe that might be considered bad, but not in Mira's. Her office assistants consist of two cats whose only priority (when they aren't napping on her desk or file cabinet) is to sensually enjoy every second they're awake. In the three years she has known them they have had a very positive effect on her disposition. Once again in an alternate universe the effect her felines have had on her might be considered deleterious, but even medical science is on her side now – tests have proved cat owners suffer considerably less stress than non-pet owners. And today she fully shares her pussies' attitude that there is absolutely nothing wrong with the world (except perhaps the inability to refill their own food bowls) and everything exciting about it. She also seems to have adopted their fondness for curling up wherever she happens to find herself in the doll's house just to daydream for a while…

Snippets of the conversation she savored with Phillip over dinner last night keep drifting through her mind. In retrospect, it amazes her how many serious thoughts and feelings he managed to express while all the time maintaining a teasing, light-hearted attitude. For instance, when she described to him how sometimes she is possessed by demons of domesticity, he remarked, 'You can't be possessed by them ever again because you're possessed by me now.' In that other objective universe so many people seem to be trapped in, such a remark

Cat's Collar

might be considered a joke, but it thrilled her like the most serious declaration of commitment. And don't 'they' also say that 'in every joke is a hidden truth'?

Perhaps this morning she is so concerned about what 'they' say because she is defying that 'they' with which she was raised by willingly becoming a man's love slave instead of just calling herself his girl friend, or eventually (hopefully) his fiancé. Frankly, she would let him call her anything he wanted to just for the pleasure of his company. It surprised her (although it shouldn't have) that she enjoyed talking to him as much as she loved being fucked by him. Dinner passed in a dream of fulfillment – excellent food, good wine, and (in her opinion) the best company imaginable. They dined in a French restaurant on Maple, an obscure little culinary jewel hidden away in a strip mall. They both ordered seafood, which presented no conflict with the wine he selected for them, a lovely Italian Frascati.

'Purr…' Stormy jumps onto the sofa beside her. 'Mreow,' he adds, and she understands he wants her to settle down somewhere so he can either curl up on her lap or at her feet and take his morning nap.

'Sorry honey,' she strokes him, 'mommy's very distracted today, but she's also very happy, so very, very happy!'

'Purr… purr… purr!'

She remembers walking into the living room with the intention of changing the water in which her roses are thriving almost obscenely (they could not have bloomed more beautifully if they tried) but then another memory from last night deliciously felled her and she lay back on the sofa to gaze unseeing out the window at the branches of one of her old oak trees. 'Your flesh is bonded to mine now,' he said as they shared a sinfully creamy chocolate mousse for dessert. They did not discuss his work. She made it a point not to bring it up, and he did not volunteer anymore information, but he had said they wouldn't be talking about the past and she was content to let his employment fall into that category for the moment. She learned he was a single child and that his parents were both retired human right's attorneys. Normally, she doesn't much care for lawyers, but there are always exceptions to the rule, and she is willing to give this couple the full benefit of the doubt because they produced her soul-mate. And to think she has Sekhmet to thank for her happiness, a truly humbling thought that leads her to wonder if perhaps she isn't her cat's pet human after all.

She cannot possibly recall everything she and Phillip talked about, all she knows is they were in profound accord over most things, even if they had some superficial differences that only made their growing mental and emotional bond more stimulating. He drove her car to the restaurant. She also discovered that she has his old white-and-gold Jeep Wrangler to thank for putting him on the sidewalk were Sekhmet found him. His one-and-only vehicle is currently in the shop receiving a new engine mount, and as a result he has been taking a cab to work at nights. On impulse the morning they met, he had the driver drop him off a few miles from his house because he felt like walking, Sekhmet found him, and the rest is history. All the little, seemingly unrelated details some people might call coincidence resulted in the most important choreography of her life.

Mira is glad she has some pre-made soup for lunch as a hunger pang tells her it's past noon and she hasn't accomplished anything useful yet; however, that is another erroneous perspective of the alternate universe she doesn't live in. She can't remember a more vitally fulfilling morning, during which she has crossed off her To Do list such things as *Meet a man I can finally respect; Meet a man that really knows how to give oral sex; Meet a man I can enjoy talking to as much as I'm physically attracted to him*; etc. etc. on the top of the list of course being, *Meet my soul-mate*. In this light she has gotten a lot done today, indeed.

A bowl of home-made split pea soup and a cup of Chamomile tea later, Mira feels able to partially concentrate on more mundane tasks. There is no housework to be done, of course, and her computer lures her into her study with the promise of being able to relax on the pretext of getting some work done. She deliberately didn't check her e-mail when she got up this morning, usually the first thing she does as she sips her tea and eats her toast. Phillip was the last person she communicated with, and she wanted to savor that for a while longer. But now with a second cup of tea steeping beside her keyboard, she opens the door on her electronic postman who never rings twice – the sound of her incoming mail is a bird's lovely chirping. She has an efficient junk mail filter, so there's never too much annoying spam crowding her Inbox, making it easy for her to discern at a glance whether she has any important or potentially interesting messages. Today she hits the virtual jackpot.

Cat's Collar

The name 'Phillip Montaigne' registers in her brain like the notes of a melody heard in a dream. He always manages to get in touch with her in an unexpected way. First, after not hearing from him for three days, he takes the form of a dozen violet roses on her doorstep. Then, during a thunderstorm in the middle of the night, he phones her when she least expects it. Now it's obvious he went to her Interior Design website and obtained her e-mail address. The affect of never knowing just how and when he will communicate with her is both arousing and unsettling, like abruptly feeling him slip his hand up her skirt even though she knows she is alone. Mira opens the e-mail and forgets to breathe as she reads it:

I had a wonderful time. I have to work tonight, but I'll be thinking of you.

Short, sweet and to the point. No mention of when he will call her or when they will see each other again. She clicks on Reply and quickly types:

I'm thinking of you, too... Her fingertips hover over the keyboard a moment before tapping on the appropriate keys to spell, *Master*.

Before she can write, *When will I see you again?* she quickly hits Send, and sits back in the chair, her heart pounding as though she just launched a guided missile full of desire... and of something else... an emotion that leaves her figuratively reeling, because it's not possible so soon and yet it's true, she already loves this man.

※

In a way Mira is glad she knows for sure she won't be seeing Phillip tonight, because the uncertainty and anticipation of not knowing is worse than the sweet ache of missing him and longing to be with him again; however, it also leaves her with entirely too much time on her hands. She can't possibly concentrate on work, there's no more laundry or cleaning to be done, and it's too late to exercise; if she doesn't work-out first thing in the morning she simply can't bring herself to do it. She could conceivably call her parents and invite herself over for dinner, but her restless arousal immediately kills that option. She makes herself comfortable on her sofa and tries to lose herself in Nevada

Cat's Collar - Three Erotic Romances

Barr's latest novel, but solving a murder committed in a National Park does not have the power to engross her today despite the heroine's engaging personality.

She tosses the glossy mass market paperback onto the table beside Phillip's roses, and contemplates the sharp silhouettes of thorns partially hidden behind deep-green leaves like the approach to Sleeping Beauty's castle... a nice long cat nap is the only activity that seems to appeal to her at the moment, perhaps because it affords her the possibility of dreaming with Phillip. The only problem is she's not tired, on the contrary; she has never felt so invigorated. This leaves only one other possible option – shopping. Fortunately her refrigerator, vegetable, and fruit bowls are less than half full, justifying a trip to her favorite grocery stores.

A bird chirp's loudly in her study.

She can't help running to her computer even though Mr. Spock would have to calculate the odds the message is from Phillip, which is why she can hardly believe her eyes when she sees his full name written across her screen again in bold black print. She plops down in her chair and once again forgets to breathe as she reads:

I've ordered you some real high-heels along with something else very important I want you to have.

He doesn't sign his name, simply attaches a link to a website. She clicks on it. Thanks to her high-speed internet connection, only two seconds pass before an image appears on her screen of shoes from some wild and impossible dream – black vinyl strap pumps with heels that look at least half-a-mile long, although the description indicates they are actually only six inches high. It seems Phillip was in a shopping mood this afternoon, only he stayed home to do it.

'I can't possibly walk in those!' she declares out loud, addressing the invisible, all-pervasive 'they' her brain has been conditioned to believe in. Another challenge has presented itself that makes a small part of her anxious while exciting the rest of her. 'But I suppose I'll have to learn...' She does not doubt many more challenges are headed her way, and a positive attitude towards them is essential if she is to be a good slave. She has already learned that pleasing this man is totally fulfilling to her in mysterious ways she can't explain, and she doesn't want to; she just wants to keep feeling the way she does, more beautiful, desirable and appreciated on all levels of her being than she has felt in her life.

Mira studies the image of the shoes in morbid fascination. They are strikingly different from anything in her closet. She wonders what else he ordered for her, but apparently he only cared to share the high-heel link with her. The other item is to be a surprise, and if the results of this surprise is anything like it was with the blindfold he shipped her via Federal Express, she can scarcely wait to receive it.

Somewhere in the doll's house her cell phone rings.

She literally leaps out of her chair and runs into the living room, but it's not there. She listens to it ring again, and sprints into the bathroom, but it's not there either. Naturally, she finds it in the last room she looks, lying on her nightstand where she left it all night.

'Hello?' she gasps.

'Do you like the shoes?'

She spreads herself belly-down on the bed loving the way he is coming at her from all angles today. 'Yes, they're stunning, Master, but I've never worn such extremely high-heels before. Can women actually walk in those?'

'Strippers dance in shoes like that every night.

'Well, I wouldn't know, since I've never been to a strip club,' she retorts.

'And why is that?'

'What do you mean? Why should I want to go to a strip club? I'm not gay.'

'Stripping is an art form like any other, Mira. Some strippers are actually very talented dancers. Just because so many bad novels have been written and so many bad movies have been made doesn't mean all books and films are worthless, and just because there are a lot of seedy strip joints doesn't mean there also aren't some classier establishments worth visiting every now and then.'

'I'm sure that's true,' she sits up defensively, 'but I wouldn't enjoy watching a woman ing naked in front of me, it's not my thing.' She is beginning to he doesn't understand how she feels and because they seem to rst major disagreement. It worries her that his world is not one in while remaining true to herself.

Cat's Collar - Three Erotic Romances

'How can you say you wouldn't like it if you've never experienced it?' he asks reasonably. 'You don't have to be gay to enjoy the sensuality of the experience. Think of strippers as priestesses of the Goddess, Mira. The power women have over men is not debasing, it's just that, power. A woman worshipping the metaphysical forces expressing themselves through her body is not something you should be ashamed to watch; it's beautiful, and should be empowering to you as a woman, not humiliating.'

'Well, if you put it that way...'

'I'll take you to a very nice place one night when you're ready.'

'I *have* heard of a new aerobic exercise that's all the rage now, pole dancing, or something like that,' she concedes. 'Apparently strippers get a very good workout every night.'

'As will you, so keep your pussy nice and warm and wet for me.'

'It already is...'

'I don't want you to masturbate. Promise you won't touch yourself until I give you permission to do so, Mira.'

'I promise, Master.'

'Say it.'

'I promise I won't touch myself without your permission, Master.'

'What are you planning to do today?'

'I have no idea. So far I haven't done anything useful at all. I already miss you so much...'

'I miss you, too. Are you free tomorrow morning?'

'Yes.' She would cancel an appointment with Jesus Christ Himself.

'Then how about if I come over for breakfast.'

'I would love that!'

'I'm warning you, I don't do low-carb, low-fat or the too-healthy anything so no cottage cheese and fruit, please.'

She laughs. 'I don't do any of those either. How do eggs-over-easy with bacon, whole-grain toast and fully caffeinated coffee with real cream sound?'

'I'm there.'

'What time do you work till?' she dares to ask.

Cat's Collar

'I'll be there by nine,' he replies.
'Alight.'
'I'll see you then.'
'Okay... have a good night at work.'
He laughs softly. 'Sweet dreams, Mira.'

Chapter Eight

> *"I do not wish [women] to have power
> over men; but over themselves."*
> Mary Wollstonecraft

She is tempted to have breakfast ready at exactly nine o'clock so she won't have to concentrate on cooking in Phillip's presence, coordinating frying eggs, toasting bread and sautéing bacon while distracted by his penetrating stare. But if for some reason he's late, she'll end up serving him cold, unappetizing food, a risk she cannot take. She settles for having everything ready to go at her fingertips like a cooking show. She will simply have to be careful not to allow how hot she is for him burn everything.

Her small wooden dining table is visible from the open kitchen and looks exceedingly fine set with burgundy place mats, violet cloth napkins and bone-white china. She thought of pulling out her silverware, but it would have required polishing, and she is only preparing breakfast after all; the silver will have to wait for a candle lit dinner.

Sekhmet is either possessed of feline extra-sensory perception and knows the man she set Mira up with is planning to visit this morning, or she is unable to tear herself away from the enticing smell of bacon lying on the kitchen counter. Whatever the reason, she is dangerously haunting her pet human's ankles.

'If you make me trip over you while he's here,' her mistress says sternly, 'I'll never feed you canned Salmon again.'

Stormy has taken an unobtrusive position directly between the kitchen and the dining room, where he is contentedly licking himself, apparently indifferent to the smell of raw bacon. Mira knows better, however, for once his sister has procured the prize he will promptly join her in devouring it. For some inherently male reason, he is much more passionate about food that is not officially presented to him on a plate.

Cat's Collar

For her breakfast date, Mira has chosen an innocent little sundress, the off-white cotton printed with tiny red roses. Spaghetti straps are attached to a bodice-style top, the skirt flaring gently over her hips down to mid-thigh. And on her feet are the red high-heeled sandals she wore for her 'Master' the other night and which match the roses, as do her silver stem-shaped earrings blooming with tiny red ruby blossoms, one of the few expensive gifts she has treated herself to as a financially independent adult; she cannot resist beautifully crafted organic jewelry. Since it is early morning, her make-up is light enough to be non-existent. The blush on her cheeks appears perfectly natural, as does the rose tint of her lips and the dark line of her lashes.

She props the kitchen door open with a brick so she can see her very special guest arriving through the screen door, which he does at three minutes after nine, heralded by Sekhmet's uncannily joyous yowl.

'Please!' Mira chides her cat proudly for daring to express what she herself is feeling but has to politely conceal. Of course, she knew he would still be dressed for work; nevertheless, the sight of his tall body suddenly appearing on her threshold all in black blows her mind as it turns her on in that inexplicable but totally intense way.

He lets himself in without bothering to knock, which would be silly considering the liberties he has already taken with her body. They have known each other hardly any time at all, yet they have long since left such formalities behind. He does not verbally acknowledge Sekhmet's passionate greeting, he simply he picks her up by the scruff of the neck and bangs her forehead gently against his while Mira watches, the pussy between her thighs feeling wonderfully jealous.

'Good morning.' He addresses the two purring cats and the silent woman at the same time, and as he gently drops Sekhmet at his booted feet, his smile draws Mira to him with a magnetism as irresistible as his arms coming around her. Then dimensions are effortlessly crushed and time and space cease to exist except as the warm space of his mouth. Their tongues dance together like pure energy in the arousing process of becoming embodied as he separates his face from hers again.

'Mm,' he smiles, 'that's what I call a good morning kiss.'

'It feels like it's been years since I saw you!' she gasps.

He laughs in that deeply quiet way of his that somehow makes everything amusing and yet beautifully serious at the same time; already she loves the steady, penetrating expression in his eyes more than anything on earth. 'Tell me you haven't made breakfast yet...' His tone somehow manages to make the mundane statement sound sexy.

'No, not yet.'

'Good, because I'd really love to borrow your shower.'

Only then does she notice the small black bag at his feet that Stormy and Sekhmet could not be sniffing more fervently if it contained a batch of fresh catnip. She ignores a stab of disappointment that he will be removing his black leather outfit, yet it might be a good thing since it arouses a very different appetite in her than the kind she can fulfill with bacon and eggs.

'You look absolutely lovely,' he adds, 'so I won't ask you to join me, this time.' He releases her and picks up his bag.

'Let me get you a towel.' She is conscious of every sway of her hips and click of her sandals on the hard-wood floor as he follows her to the linen closet next to her bedroom door.

'Very nice,' he comments.

She is confused as to what he is referring to until she turns and sees him smiling at the neatly folded towels, bed sheets, table cloths, extra curtains and assorted linens stored on the shelves.

'Beautiful, smart, sexy, talented and a domestic goddess as well. You're going to make some lucky man a very nice slave, Mira.'

'*Some* lucky man?'

He laughs. '*This* lucky man.' He takes the towel from her. 'I'm starving. Go start breakfast.'

Without thinking she returns obediently to the kitchen. Soon she hears the shower turn on in her bathroom, and the whole time the water is running and the bacon is sizzling and the coffee pot is gurgling she feels utterly, mindlessly content. She is so happy she doesn't even notice it; she is purely in the sweet, sensual grip of these special moments in which the past is the ground in which they're rooted and the future is the open sky.

When she hears the shower turn off all her senses come to attention because it never seems to take men very long to dry themselves off and dress. His timing is

Cat's Collar

flawless – she has just set the hot plates she had warming in the oven on the table when he appears looking casually resplendent in blue jeans and a forest-green short-sleeved cotton t-shirt. The symmetry of his broad shoulders, narrow hips and long legs strikes an ideal chord inside her. When her DNA was being mysteriously arranged by the Powers-That-Be, she was designed to feel this was the perfect man's body, and she can scarcely believe it's casually sitting down at her table for breakfast.

'This looks wonderful,' he declares, 'and it smells even better.'

She brings the coffee pot over and carefully fills his cup, leaving enough room for the cream she took the trouble to pour into a porcelain pitcher. As usual, she is having Earl Grey tea.

He smiles up at her. 'But you didn't have to go to quite so much trouble.'

'It was my pleasure,' she says truthfully, with a quick glance assuring herself everything they need is on the table.

'Well, next time we can go out for breakfast.' He rises again to pull her chair out for her. 'I don't want my slave working so hard all the time.' His tone is teasing as he resumes his seat, but his smile is in striking contrast to the serious glint in his eyes. 'Not in the kitchen anyway.'

She spreads the violet napkin across her lap, shyly avoiding looking at him.

'Mreoow!'

'Sekhmet, go away,' she says without conviction, for she knows there is no banishing her greedy feline from the smell of cooked bacon and fresh cream.

'I think you've spoiled them just a little bit,' Phillip observes.

Looking up from her plate, Mira is startled to see he has already finished his eggs. 'My God, you eat fast!'

'I was hungry.'

'Another hard night at work?' she asks sourly.

'Very.'

His response paralyzes her – she can't decide whether to hate him for it or to respect him for not indulging her jealousy, which she knows is quite unbecoming considering everything they have said to each other so soon in their relationship. Yet there is no denying her happiness is painfully tempered by fearful suspicions she has to struggle to keep in check. Until she knows exactly what goes on at his 'job' she won't be able to fully relax, and yet she doesn't dare openly ask him about it. She is afraid of what she might find out and that she won't be able to handle it. She is terrified of ruining the feelings growing between them.

He wipes his mouth with the napkin and grasps her left hand where it rests limply on the table. 'What are you thinking?' he asks soberly.

She sips her tea to consider her reply.

He squeezes her hand so hard the slight pain tells her the gesture is a reprimand. 'I asked you a question, Mira.'

Her breath catches and makes it even harder for her to speak. She can't really put her amorphous fears into words. 'I guess…' she clears her throat. 'I guess the thought of you spending three nights a week with other women is just… just a little hard for me to deal with.'

He gently lets go of her hand and spreads some wild blueberry jam across a slice of toast. 'You're deliberately tormenting yourself by putting it that way,' he says quietly. 'I don't spend my nights with these women, they just happen to be there. And did you really think I planned on doing this forever? It's only a temporary gig while I finish my thesis.'

'Your thesis?' she breathes.

'If all goes as planned, I should have my PhD in six months.'

'Your PhD?'

Sekhmet reaches up to plant her front paws on his denim-clad thighs and meows plaintively.

He picks up a piece of bacon. 'May I?'

'Yes, go ahead. What are you getting your PhD in?'

'Guess.'

'I have no idea!'

'That's the nature of guessing.' He picks up his empty coffee cup and gazes down at it for an instant before meeting her eyes again.

She quickly takes it from him, gets up, and pours him another cup.

'Thank you.' He rewards her with the smile that reaches his eyes in that special way that seems to melt her bones and make her grateful there's a chair directly beneath her.

'I can't possibly guess,' she insists.

Cat's Collar

'Well, then, I'll let you think about it for a while.'

'Phillip!'

'Eat your breakfast, Mira, you need your strength.'

She has no desire to argue with such a promising threat and obeys him, relishing her eggs-over-easy, which she actually fried in Canola oil this morning, throwing fat and calories to the wind. Her first breakfast with her soul-mate is a special occasion immune from her eternal health-conscious diet.

'Do you like to cook?' he asks.

'Yes, I suppose I do. I can't say I love it, but I do insist on enjoying my meals every night, and since I can't afford to eat out all the time, I cook. Also, I could never maintain my weight or my health if I ate out all the time. This way I know exactly what I'm putting into my body.'

'You're in full control.'

'Yes.'

'I'll allow you that control in the kitchen, and in your work, and in your domestic chores,' he states as casually as if they are merely discussing the weather, 'but when it comes to us, you will surrender that control completely and absolutely without question.'

She takes a breath as if to protest, and then realizes with a shocking thrill that the only words lined up in her head and lodged in her throat ready to emerge are, 'Yes, Master.' Yet she does not allow herself to speak them; she cannot possibly agree to such a thing. She clutches her cup of tea in both hands and stares down into it, but since she uses a tea bag there aren't any leaves on the bottom to be read. 'Yes, Master,' she whispers, divining her future not by any outward signs but by how she feels inside whenever she is with him, or even just thinking about him. She cannot apply normal rules of relationship to this man, and she has no desire to do so, especially considering how unfulfilling she found all her other liaisons before him. Her shipwrecked reason is deep in the sensual jungle following a mysterious path to a dark and ancient realm and there's no turning back now… the Catholic school girl has boarded the pirate ship and is surrounded by the sea of her sexuality and only the sinisterly handsome captain can help her navigate it, her concerned parents no longer visible on the safe, rational shore... there *is* no rational shore when she is looking into his eyes, all that exists is how intensely drawn she is to him.

'You haven't finished your breakfast, Mira.'

'I'm not that hungry right now...'

'Are you finished then?'

'Yes.'

The ensuing silence is so pregnant it only takes a few seconds for the realization to be born inside her (amidst screams of protest from her feminist brain) that she made a mistake he is waiting for her to correct.

'Yes, I'm finished, Master.'

He pushes his chair back and stands up so abruptly her heart takes off in response, but all he does is take her hand. 'Come,' he commands.

He leads her into her bedroom. 'Since you're not hungry for food, I'm going to feed you something else.'

She licks her lips in anticipation of really tasting him for the first time.

He seats himself on the edge of her bed, and with a tilt of his head indicates he wants her to kneel before him. Already he does not need to speak for her to sense what he wants and obey him. 'You're going to spend a lot more time on your knees as a woman than you ever did as a Catholic school girl.' Another sexy threat that thrills her to the subconscious core of her being. 'But trust me, you're going to enjoy it a hell of a lot more.'

They smile at each other for an instant like two kids playing a very exciting game they never want to end. And gloriously enough, it doesn't have to end since 'they' don't exist in this world that magically opened up around her the instant she saw him kneeling in the grass next to her black cat.

He opens his pants – button-fly jeans beneath which he isn't wearing any underwear – and releases his semi-erect penis. Then he reaches in and lifts out his scrotum, those two heavy, luscious balls pushed up at an unnatural angle by the crotch of his tight pants offered up to her as if on a platter. He is as smoothly shaved as she remembers, which makes obeying his next command a pure pleasure. 'Suck my balls, Mira... that's right, don't be afraid, you won't hurt me.'

She takes one of his tender sacks more boldly into her mouth.

Cat's Collar

'Mm, now the other one... that's good. Now suck my cock.' He grips it at the base and slides it between her lips, pressing its rigid length against her tongue. 'You just had some food, so I won't deep-throat you. I want you to suck my cock however feels good to you. I want to see how skilled you are at pleasing a man with just your moth and hands, and how much it will be my pleasure to have to teach you.'

She hasn't felt this safe and excited and eager to learn since they got to the ancient Egyptians in third grade history class. Then she suspects her oral vocabulary is not as sophisticated as she believed as she is confronted with the intensely eloquent statement of this man's erection. She forms a tight ring around his cock with her lips and twirls her tongue around it, searching for the most sensitive spots on his hard length as she swallows him. He does not react like other men, with grateful groans and helpless pulses that warn her a premature release of sperm is imminent. Phillip reacts not at all to the increasingly fervent ministrations of her mouth, tongue and hands, which she brings energetically into play, pumping him hard with one fist while delicately caressing his balls with her fingertips. She knows she must be pleasing him because he couldn't possibly be harder, yet it's also obvious he is nowhere close to coming and she begins to despair.

'Mm...' he says at last, 'very nice, Mira.'

His praise frees her from purgatory, and she groans with gratitude and pleasure when he grasps the hair at the back of her head. He plunges her face down around his towering erection with a swift, steady rhythm she passionately sustains even after he releases her.

He strokes her hair. 'Would you like me to fuck you?'

With her mouth full of his cock she looks up into his eyes.

'Stand up.'

She obeys him as quickly as she can, her knees a little stiff.

'You look so sweet in that dress, I don't want to muss you up. Bend over the bed and brace yourself on it... no move back a little... that's right.' He lifts her skirt. 'These are very sweet,' he says and she knows he is referring to her white-lace panties as he hooks his thumbs into the elastic, and yanks them roughly down to her knees. 'But your pussy should always be exposed and ready for me. From now on you will have to ask my permission to wear panties. Do you understand?'

Her head spins as a lifetime of being warned about germs ties her tongue. 'Yes, Master.'

'The only exception to this rule is, obviously, when it's that time of the month,' he steps up tightly behind her, 'and when you wear pants. I don't want you chafing this pretty little labia of yours, which you will always keep shaved for me, naturally.'

'Yes, Master!' she gasps as the thick head of his cock lodges itself in her vulva's hungry mouth. She didn't realize how starved her body was for him until the lips of her pussy once again tasted his tender firmness and the promise of so much more of him to come.

'Do you want my cock in your cunt, Mira?'

'Oh, yes, Master...'

'Beg me for it.'

'Oh, God, please, Master... please fuck me...'

His head stops teasingly kissing her sex lips. 'You don't sound like you want it enough.'

'Oh, my God, yes, I do, please... please put your cock in my cunt, Master, please, I want it more than anything!'

'Arch your back,' he commands, and pressing his hand down on the base of her spine, he penetrates her.

His thrust has the rending effect of a weapon at the angle she is offering her pussy to him. 'Oh, God, Master!' Under the circumstances it feels perfectly natural to be calling him that because at the moment he has complete mastery of her flesh. Even though his erection is only coming into contact with her vaginal walls, it feels as though he is stabbing himself to the very core of her physical being. The intensity of the experience makes up for the slight discomfort; her pussy has never felt so open and so tight at the same time, and she can sense how good her tight slot feels to his hard-on – slick and soft and deep and clinging, the cushion of her cervix kissing his head and welcoming him into a hot, wet harem of sensations as she consciously milks him, tightening and relaxing around him.

'Oh, yes,' he whispers, and a profound triumph deepens her cunt's ability to absorb his relentless strokes as she suddenly (more with the combined power of her senses than her mind) becomes aware of just how much power she actually has over him even in her vulnerable position. Closing her eyes, she clamps her pussy muscles around his erection, squeezing him gently at first and then harder and harder, until it's as if there is no limit to how tightly she can grip him. Her sex is a cosmic black hole sucking him into the ever diminishing singularity of her innermost being, and the bigger and thicker his penis gets, the closer he comes to the event horizon of his pleasure, the more she tightens her hold on him. In her mind's eye she can see the shape and length of his cock wrapped in her hot flesh. No other man has ever inspired her to such visualizations before, much less filled her with the mysterious ability to tighten endlessly around him. She knows when he starts coming because of the quiet, breathless sounds he makes and because he gets so hard she almost can't stand how good his increasingly violent penetrations feel.

'Oh, Mira...'

She cries out in triumph and pleasure as her awareness of everything is momentarily laid waist by the explosion of his pleasure deep in her sex. His throbbing cock fills her almost to bursting as she relishes the sinful baptism of his cum drenching her insides.

Even after he has long since finished climaxing he remains buried peacefully inside her for a minute, giving vital parts of her time to come back down to earth, which in turn enables her to straighten up with casual dignity as he pulls out of her.

'Did I say you could move, Mira?'

She moans and plants her hands on the bed again, hiding her face behind her hair, half ashamed she is proving to be such a sloppy slave, and half hurt by his reprimand after the transcendent orgasm she just helped him achieve.

Her panties have slipped down to her ankles. He helps her step out of them. 'Okay, now you may get up.'

She turns towards him, and rests her head gratefully on his chest as he takes her in his arms.

'That was amazing,' he whispers into her hair.

'Thank you, Master,' she whispers back, and wonders why human females weren't born with the genes that would enable them to purr, because that's exactly what she feels like doing in those moments. All words are inadequate to how she feels with his arms around her and his heart beating in her ear.

Chapter Nine

"The girl answered, 'I do not know where your house is' then he said, 'My house is a long way in the wood'."

Phillip leaves not long afterwards. Mira isn't surprised, she knows he worked all night, and even though she'll miss him, he has left her feeling languidly fulfilled and utterly at peace for a while.

Stormy and Sekhmet materialize from out of nowhere to see him off.

'Is your car still in the shop?' she asks.

'Yes.'

'So you're walking home from here?'

'Yes.'

'May I walk with you?'

'No.' The small black bag containing his leather outfit and boots already in hand, he slips his free arm around her waist and gently kisses her lips. 'I'll talk to you later.'

'But why don't you want me to walk you home, Phillip?'

'No whining, Mira.'

'I'm not whining, I just don't understand why you don't want me to walk you home.'

He opens the screen door, but pauses on the threshold as Sekhmet scents one of his big toes, visible through his leather sandal. 'Do you trust me, Mira?'

'You know I do, Phillip.'

'Then when you ask me a question, you shouldn't question my answer. Just trust me. We'll be walking home together soon enough.'

Cat's Collar

If he had shoved a piece of rich dark chocolate in her mouth he couldn't have silenced her more effectively or filled her with a sweeter happiness. She says nothing as he kisses her lightly on the lips again, and steps outside.

'Is it all right if I cut through your yard again?' he smiles.

She laughs. 'Yes.' She holds the screen door open so she can watch him disappear around the back of her house. 'Go follow him, Sekhmet!' she whispers, and her black cat races after him as though she truly is Mira's intelligent familiar. 'Oh, God, Sekhmet, come back!' She regrets her impulsive command. 'Oh, well, maybe she'll bring us directions to his house,' she tells Stormy, who remains sitting faithfully at her feet.

She sighs and turns back to face the elegant devastation of her dining room table, and another long day awaiting her. 'I have to get some work done,' she says firmly.

Stormy does not comment on this announcement. He is staring intently out the screen door as though expecting his sister to return at any moment.

Yet how can she possibly concentrate on anything with the distraction of her Master's cum trickling down the insides of her thighs again? She forgot to mention wiping herself clean the other night, and now she postpones doing so because it will eliminate one of the traces of his presence, the same excuse she uses not to clean up the breakfast dishes right away. For a little while longer she wants to savor the knowledge and evidence that he was here with her.

∽∽∽∽∽∽

Everyone knows physical exercise produces endorphins that make you feel really good about life, at least for a little while, and every woman knows the same is true of shopping. It doesn't matter what you're shopping for; there's just something about walking leisurely through stores with countless items theoretically available to make you and your living space more beautiful and desirable, which will (once again theoretically) make you happier. Mira does not hesitate to admit to herself that shopping is the opium of her feminine psyche. The only problem is she does so much of it in her line of work she has built up an annoying tolerance to the soothing consumer endorphins. It's different when you're shopping for someone who isn't intimately related to or involved with you.

She knows she should be thinking about the contents of Ian's condo, but her guardian angels appear to be paying special attention to her these days and have given her a two-week reprieve from her current project. She needn't waste time feeling guilty about wandering around the Ballston Mall, exclusively with an eye to pleasing the other, and only truly important, man in her life – Master Phillip. The extreme high-heels and the other mysterious item he ordered for her on the Internet have not yet arrived, but there's always something she can buy that will make her feel even more desirable than she already does. Lingerie is the icing on the rich sensual cake she suspects will be a part of her daily nourishment from now on, yet even though she owns more baby dolls and sexy satin slips than she knows what to do with, Mira cannot resist a quick tour of *Victoria's Secret*. Their current pink look does not in the least appeal to her, but she is rewarded in the back room with a rack where already radically reduced items are an additional fifty percent off. In her opinion, a woman can never have too many thigh-length short-sleeved cotton shirts to hang around the house in, especially when they're marked down to what is probably their actual cost at six dollars, and there's even one in her size and favorite color – violet. She also buys a white sleeveless T embroidered with a glittering red heart reflecting how big and full hers has felt since Sekhmet brought her soul-mate home instead of a dead mouse.

On her way out of the store she casts a rather forlorn glance at all the tables neatly covered with sexy panties. No other man has ever told her she needed his permission to cover her pubes with cotton or silk or any other material. It is going to take some getting used to; nevertheless, even now she is obeying him and not wearing any panties beneath her innocent sundress, the same outfit she had on this morning when he fucked her from behind, except that she exchanged the red high-heeled sandals for comfortable white socks and sneakers. She loves shopping for high-heels but not shopping *in* high-heels. She respects the health of her spine and likes being comfortable when she's shooting up her relaxing consumer drug.

Cat's Collar

Mira likes the Ballston Mall because it's small and manageable, not overwhelming like Tyson's Corner, and it is also more suited to buyers who don't want to spend their entire paycheck on one or two items. Fortunately, she has never suffered from the delusion that more expensive means better quality. Her self-esteem has always been deep and rich enough not to need the psychological bandage of designer labels to make her feel she is truly worth something in the mysterious scheme of things. Good thrift stores and consignment shops are still her favorite place to buy things.

She avoids *Hechts* because it takes too much energy and instead makes her way to the comfortably intimate *Rainbow* to see if there are any cotton treasures buried amidst all the cheap polyester. Most of the cute colored T's she wears around the house have come from *Rainbow*, and she can never have too many lounging around outfits since she spends most of her time at home either working or relaxing.

She guardedly embraced the trend that swept the nation a few years back that replaced bars with major bookstore chains as a place to find a more fulfilling relationship than the one-night-stand available at eighty-proof watering holes. Yet she never managed to meet a man at *Borders* or *Barnes and Noble*, perhaps because she always became too engrossed in whatever book she wasn't only pretending to be reading and forgot to look up to see if there were any eligible bachelors milling around her. Mira knows her parents are proud of how particular she is about potential suitors and of her financial independence, but she is also aware they keep glancing at her biological clock wondering if she'll ever produce a grandchild for them. She does not have the heart to tell them as a grown woman what she made clear as a child – that she has no desire to have a baby or babies, much less an adolescent or two clipping her sensual and emotional wings. And even though they have not yet discussed it, she suspects Phillip shares her sentiments regarding offspring.

There is no pot of Egyptian cotton gold at the foot of the *Rainbow* this afternoon, so Mira wanders back out into the carpeted mall towards *Parade of Shoes*. Even though she has never seen anything she liked there, they get new stock in all the time and there's always hope.

'Hello.' The sale's girl smiles at her dutifully.

'Hello!' Mira replies cheerfully.

'Is there anything I can help you find today?'

'No, thanks, I'm just looking.'

The usual array of questionably aesthetic and decidedly uncomfortable looking sandals and shoes meet her eyes, but she doesn't know when she'll be seeing Phillip again, so she has all the time in the world to wander around aimlessly. Her cell phone is on and in her purse; he can reach her wherever she is, so there's no need to hurry home to Stormy and Sekhmet.

Mira finds what she didn't even know she was looking for in a pair of black high-heeled sandals with two straps in the front covered with diamond-like rhinestones. The heels are only two inches high, but that makes them ideal for sexy around-the-house shoes, and somehow she knows Phillip will appreciate them. Best of all they're half off – reduced from forty dollars to twenty. She slips off her sneakers and socks, tries them on, walks around in them for half a minute gazing at her sexy legs in the mirrors, takes them off, returns them to the box, slips her socks and shoes back on, and buys them. They are the climax of her shopping day; she knows she won't find anything else she wants or can afford, and suddenly she feels a pressing need to check her e-mail to see if Phillip communicated with her again that way.

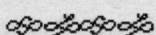

When Mira lets herself into the doll's house, as usual through the kitchen door, Stormy and Sekhmet are nowhere to be seen. She misses their warm purring greeting, but there's still a chance the electronically caged bird of her e-mail will welcome her home with a note from Phillip.

Her Inbox is empty.

Sharply disappointed, she stares at the screen as if the intensity of her desire alone will produce and incoming message, but it doesn't work any better than rubbing a bronze lamp did in ancient Sumeria. She has his number stored in her

Cat's Collar

cell phone, yet like a powerful Gin being released she cannot be sure if it will grant her wish of hearing his voice again, or if her desire will be trapped in a voicemail box, or if a woman will answer instead. She really doesn't believe the latter scenario is a possibility. The real reason she doesn't call him is because she does not wish to disturb him. He is probably still sleeping off his hard night at work, not to mention the very fulfilling breakfast they shared.

Mira knows the social 'they' might categorize her as a bit of a control freak. Her doll's house is always clean and neat; both her hard-copy and electronic files are organized in folders; she has a notebook in the kitchen filled with all her favorite recipes she types out on the computer as she comes across them, then prints out and tapes onto the ruled paper divided into different sections – Sandwiches, Seafood, Chicken, Pasta, etc.; Phillip himself already admired the organized fullness of her linen closet; all her clothes are arranged by season and color; her kitchen invariably looks good enough to be the set of a cooking show; she writes everything she needs to do in her Day Timer; all her bills are paid long before the due date, and she never fails to have stamps on hand for those she can't dispose of online; as a member of *Netflix* she always has DVD's available to entertain her at night; her wine rack never has less than five bottles in it, and there are always two vintages of Chardonnay chilling in her refrigerator.

Obviously, she likes to be prepared for things, because in her opinion that's the best way to enjoy them to the fullest. Unlike the infamous Blanche, she has no desire to rely on the kindness of strangers, feeling she can do a better job of most everything herself. She doesn't trust most people to be as intensely discriminating as she is. Mira believes that, in general, people are good, but she is more skeptical about them as individuals she can relate to for a prolonged period of time, hence her marked lack of any close friends. Not since college has she been able to bond with anyone in that way, and the truth is that most days she doesn't miss it. She has Rose to talk to whenever she needs a woman's perspective and sympathy, for she has always valued her mother's innate wisdom. This afternoon, however, with Stormy and Sekhmet gone missing for an unusual amount of time, and Phillip asleep somewhere like a prince in a reversal of the traditional fairytale, she admits it would be nice to have a female friend close to her own age she could confide in about her new exciting yet also intensely challenging relationship. She cannot talk to Rose about Phillip, not yet, and to be honest probably not ever, although obviously she wants her parents to meet him one day, and vice versa. A trip to a private vineyard in Washington State would hardly be painful.

Mira unpacks her small treasures, eager to show her sexy new sandals to Phillip… that's the hard part, not knowing when she'll see him again. It's like floating in the vacuum of space trapped between two worlds – the one behind her when she last saw him, the one before her when she'll next see him. There's nothing for her to control except her impatience and longing, and her growing anxiety the more time passes and she doesn't hear from him. It doesn't matter that only six hours have ticked by since they were together. Every woman knows time can become painfully relative when a man is involved… when you're in love… the speed of light, the speed of love… metal spaceships will never travel through the universe to distant worlds, yet the soul already does so through the vehicle of imagination, and she has already imagined countless ways in which they will meet again and myriads of futures together, lifetimes lived in the few languid blinks of eyes gazing dreamily out at nothing and everything at the same time…

Mira glances at her watch. It's only four-thirty, too early for a glass of Chardonnay; she has to wait until at least six o'clock on spring evenings when the days are impossibly long. She opens her refrigerator and stands there for a while pondering dinner, but the big breakfast she prepared this morning has exhausted her culinary self; time to rely on the frozen piece of home-made vegetable lasagna in the freezer. She places it on the counter to defrost and once more finds herself at a loss.

Where are her cats?

Chapter Ten

*"They came to the wood, and the way grew
more and more familiar."*

Careful to bring her cell phone with her, she steps outside. The sight of her blooming wisteria vine always pleases her, as do the white stone vases overflowing with violet petunias, and soon her red and white rose bushes will also be in glorious bloom. The towel on which she lay naked and blindfolded while Phillip ate her pussy and then fucked her violently from behind is still lying on the grass, a bittersweet reminder of how pleasurable his company can be that deepens how lonely she already feels without him.

The temperature is ideal, somewhere between sixty-eight and seventy degrees by her estimate, and wandering down one of the curving stone paths of her expansive garden, Mira wonders why she should feel compelled to find something better to do. She pauses beside one of her stone fountains to enjoy the tinkling music of water flowing down from the iron flower growing in its center. Running water and *Feng Shui* are inseparable. For her, the fountain's lovely design justifies the major headache it proves to Ramon at least once a month, because the spout from which the water flows out is so narrow it is constantly clogging up.

Through the branches of a maple tree she can just barely discern the distant outlines of one of her neighbor's homes. Phillip does not live in either of the two houses directly to the north and south of her, she knows that much. To her east is the street, where she assumes Sekhmet found him after his cab dropped him off, and to her west stretches one of the many wooded areas Virginia is still

Cat's Collar

miraculously full of. More than once she has glimpsed a deer grazing on the outskirts of her yard. Perhaps he wasn't just teasing her when he told her he lived over the hill and through the woods... suddenly she's worried Sekhmet took her command to follow him seriously and got lost, and that Stormy went in search of her and got lost himself.

'Stormy! Sekhmet!' She walks westward, looking around for them anxiously. 'Stormy? Sekhmet?' There is not the slightest breeze and the stillness assumes a sinister quality as no reassuring rustling response emanates from the foliage. She begins to worry in earnest. It is close to dinner time, the landmark event of Sekhmet's day she has not once failed to miss. This is the risk people who own outdoor cats take – that one day they might never come back. She lived in a constant state of worry the first year, but lately she has taken it for granted that her felines are smart enough to take care of themselves. She firmly tells herself it is too early to worry even as she keeps heading towards the western border of her property, the direction she assumes Phillip took this morning when he began walking home.

A loud flapping sound to her left makes her cry out, and her heart beats harder than its wings as she watches a goose take flight. It's not the first time she has seen one in her yard, but how abruptly it shattered the stillness is unsettling and contributes to her growing unease. It is only half-past-four, but the sunny, passive afternoon is being overthrown by an aggressive storm front. The sun is suddenly imprisoned behind a wall of grey clouds and the world darkens as though three hours pass in the blink of an eye. She has reached the cross-over place where her well-maintained lawn ends and the untamed woodland begins. This small patch of forest may be surrounded by civilization on all sides, affected by the myriad environmental ills of urban sprawl in ways invisible to her untrained naked eye; nevertheless, in the abrupt gloom the close-growing trees fill her with a series of anxieties programmed into her primordial genes... She slips her cell phone into the pocket of her sundress, no longer clinging to it and to the chance Phillip might call at any moment. A deepening concern for her missing cats is merging with a need to follow the path her lover took away from her this morning. There is no official trail as such that she can see, but like a female egg that can only be penetrated at one specific point by a single sperm, there is a subtly discernable gap in the line of trees a person journeying into the woods would naturally take advantage of. She doesn't think it is her imagination the grass looks slightly more trampled there ... as if by heavy black boots, the kind of boots her Master wears...

She glances up at the sky. The overcast afternoon feels even more oppressively still. There is no warning flash of lightning or grumble of distant thunder, yet every fiber in her civilized being wants to turn back to her doll's house, appalled by the mere thought of getting lost in the woods during a storm. But her purring, loving companions are missing; there is nothing for her at home except a lonely glass of Chardonnay, and suddenly a few yards ahead of her amidst the lush chaos of the forest floor she glimpses movement – a patch of sleek grey streaking from behind a tree trunk and vanishing behind some bushes.

'Stormy?' she cries. 'Stormy, come back here!' She starts after him, only now she isn't so sure that was Stormy; it could easily have been a big squirrel or some other form of woodland creature she can't identify. It shames her how ignorant she is of native Virginia wild life. 'Stormy?' Upon receiving no reassuring, rustling response from the foliage, she pauses, preparing to turn back, but just then sunlight finds a gap in the brooding armor of clouds. A big black-and-gold dragonfly takes flight along a luminous runway, while still in shadow a pair of white moths spiral upwards in an ethereally energetic mating dance.

She starts walking again, every few seconds looking down at her feet, not so much to watch her step across the uneven ground as to avoid stepping on anything beautifully alive. Sure enough, a metallic-blue beetle shining like a precious gem is granted a few more minutes, weeks or months of life as she steps aside to avoid casually crushing it. It is vaguely shaped like an Egyptian scarab, yet its color is almost unreal.

'Stormy? Sekhmet?' she calls, but with less concern in her voice as she makes her way between flowering trees. Glancing over her shoulder, Mira makes sure she can still see the reassuring order of her garden and the landmark of one of her stone fountains. It seems impossible to believe that in all the years she has lived here, this is as far as she has ever ventured into the woods flanking her home. What was she afraid of, becoming lost in a patch of forest probably less than a mile square? Is she such a pathetic creature of civilization that she must have a safe, accepted path laid out for her because she dare not venture into the unknown on her own? The six o'clock news with its endless stories of female bodies found buried in the woods doesn't help, nor did her maternal grandmother's stern warning that a little girl wandering alone into the forest would be easy prey for hungry wolves. Granted, she has not exactly been conditioned to be brave, but what she is truly afraid of is modern society and the unusual amount of psychopaths it seems to breed. The only snakes or wolves she might encounter in northern Virginia are of the human variety.

Fortunately, an amazingly big orange butterfly, with a design on its wings that looks freshly drawn by a black magic marker, distracts her from her morbid thoughts and enables her to rest comfortably in her senses again as she keeps walking. The soft, stubborn light makes it appear as if the storm might blow over after all, and a large yellow-and-orange mushroom made of sci-fi suede fascinates her enough to crouch down beside it and contemplate its impressive fungal dimensions. She strokes it tentatively with a fingertip and wonders if the striking looking thing is edible. Then something between a startled laugh and a squeamish shriek escapes her lips as a spider appears between her sneakers. Its eight legs are at least three inches long and as thin as black needles arching out of a heart-shaped orange-and-black body that manages to look sinister despite it miniscule size.

She quickly straightens up again, but now that she has become aware of them, these delicately massive arachnids appear to be everywhere; she has to consciously avoid stepping on them as she moves deeper between the trees. It is not obvious now that someone else (much less a number of people) have walked this way before, and glancing behind her again, Mira's pulse accelerates as she realizes she can no longer see her property.

'Stormy, Sekhmet, I want you both to come home right now!' She strains to make out another mischievous streak of grey or black as her felines play hide-and-seek with her, but what she sees instead is a flash of red hanging from a tree branch. There are no flowers such a deep crimson color, and closer inspection reveals a piece of cloth that appears to have been torn off something even though it is too high to be a fragment of clothing ripped off a hiker by a thorny branch. The piece of red fabric is dangling exactly at her eye level as though deliberately placed there. She reaches up to lightly finger the cloth with the same respectful reverence she caressed the mushroom. Both are mysterious in their own way, except there must obviously be a human, not a divine, hand behind this particular phenomena. The miniature red flag is approximately six inches long and three inches wide and made of a very fine, shining silk. Possibly a woman out for a stroll was wearing a red scarf over her head that got tangled and ripped in the low-lying branches, only the cloth was deliberately impaled on the tree's thing young arm. The length of fabric makes no sense at all except as a rather expensive trail marker, because it is definitely no cheap drugstore ribbon.

The day has darkened ominously again as her friendly light loses its battle with the moody atmosphere, yet Mira tells herself that if it begins to rain the trees will protect her from the full force of the downpour, because another reason to continue her nature trek has presented itself in the form of an enticing gleam of violet a few yards away and slightly to her left. She hurries towards it, forgetting to watch for spiders and other vulnerable forms of life. The fabric riddle continues. Both pieces appear to have been torn from some fantastic multi-hued garment. This second raggedly rectangular piece of cloth is a lovely lavender color and the richest, softest velvet she has ever had the pleasure of touching. It hangs impaled on a branch that pierced it as neatly as a needle, and she stares keenly ahead of her between the trees, no longer searching for her missing felines, who have temporarily wandered out of her mind. Sure enough, another flash of unexpected, if not unnatural, color meets her eye about the same distance away – another few yards ahead and this time slightly to her right. The fabric trail is meandering through the forest in true *Feng Shui* fashion. The third piece of cloth is the same length and irregular rectangular shape as the first two and a bright dandelion, buttercup, yellow that flows soft as satin against her fingertips.

She turns a full three-hundred-and-sixty degrees looking around her, half expecting to glimpse a woodland nymph wearing a multi-colored skirt sewn

Cat's Collar

magically together of autumn leaves beneath a naked torso white as moonlight coalesced into flesh, like an illustration of Daphne from one of her old mythology books... but she appears to be quite alone with the deepening shadows, in which the winding trail of colorful cloth fragments becomes even more intriguingly visible, glowing as if with its own significant light in the gloom. The threat of rain is no longer reason enough to stop her from wandering deeper into the woods, and the next marker on the gradually lengthening trail is silver mesh reminiscent of a spider's web, only the weave is much tighter, and all it has managed to trap in it so far is Mira's imagination.

She is entertaining the wild thought that Phillip left this trail for her, the black overnight bag he was carrying when he left containing more than just his leather outfit and heavy boots. The idea is utterly fanciful, but there has to be an explanation for everything, and these beautiful lengths of fabric have clearly not been exposed to the elements for very long. Why should it strike her as so hard to believe he marked the path between his home and hers? It makes a certain amount of sense. What she's not convinced of is that he did it for himself; this spectrum of colors and textures seems especially designed to lure her deeper and deeper into the woods with the promise of being able to find her way back so she needn't be afraid to explore and enjoy the adventure. If she knows anything so far, it's that her lover is creatively unpredictable, and that everything he does seems orchestrated to evoke an intense emotional as well as physical response from her.

Mira has counted nine lengths of fabric impaled on branches when thunder rumbles a traditional menacing warning overhead. Time for her to listen to reason and turn back and stop behaving like Alice in a wonderland growing increasingly dark and dangerous with threats of lightning – the violent electric union between heaven and earth particularly attracted to the sensually open arms of trees. The woods are not a good place to be during this passionately charged communion between the ground and the atmosphere, yet she cannot resist continuing to follow a trail that somehow feels made for her. It's entirely possible that Stormy and Sekhmet have already found their way home and are waiting for her by their food bowls. It probably *was* just a big squirrel she saw earlier, not her cat's sleek gray back. Stormy would have answered if he had heard her call his name, she is sure of that. She really should turn back...

She can't possibly turn back, not if there's any chance Phillip made this trail for her. It's too expensive, too lovely, too intriguing to be mere coincidence – it's impossible so many different types of fabric were all accidentally ripped off unwary hikers at the exact same height and neatly threaded through each branch. This is the work of one man, or of one person, possibly some anonymous female neighbor who shares Mira's trepidation about becoming lost in the woods. Whoever created the trail, she cannot resist continuing to follow it to its end or until she runs out of markers. Colors have inevitably begun repeating themselves, but they are never exactly the same and their texture is always different. Naturally there are no green strips of cloth, which would be virtually invisible against the leaves. Nor are there black or grey or brown strips; only bright-hued colors tempt her along a gently meandering path. And in her eagerness to follow it, she walks straight through a spider's web. She shrieks in disgust as the sticky threads cling to the bare skin of her arms and legs and tangle with her hair. She is conscious of behaving just like a stereotypical girl as she desperately seeks to caress her flesh free of arachnid secretions, dreading that any little dark bugs the spider might have caught for its dinner are now hopelessly lost in her hair. Thunder rumbles again overhead. If she didn't know better she would say the sun had already set it is so dark beneath the trees. She looks anxiously behind her. The cloth clues she has been following are barely discernable in the premature dusk.

'Oh, my God,' she says out loud, and her voice sounds uncannily loud to her in the pregnant stillness before the storm's water breaks and drenches her like a new-born baby just emerged from the womb. That would be the best case scenario. The worst case scenario would be the umbilical cord of a bolt of lightning seeking to reunite with her. She could very well die less than a mile from her doll's house. In a flash, all her unique memories, hopes and dreams could be reduced to another meaningless statistic on the six o'clock news. Actually, she probably wouldn't make it until the eleven o'clock local

Cat's Collar

broadcast right before Jay Leno, depending on when someone happened to find her body.

She is despairing about what to do – turn back or go forward – when searching for another flash of color she glimpses the mysteriously reassuring geometric lines of a roof and a house beneath it. A moment ago it wasn't there, now she clearly makes out the shape of a house beyond the trees. The cloth trail has led her safely to the other edge of the woods.

Chapter Eleven

*"She wandered about into all nooks and corners, and into
all the chambers and parlours, as the fancy took her,
till at last she came to an old tower."*

Mira emerges from the miniature forest and stands at the fringe of a tree-filled lawn gazing up at a Gothic dream. The structure crowns the top of a hill overgrown with a civilized extension of the woodland she just traversed and which conceals any possible neighbors so completely the house feels utterly isolated. Nathaniel Hawthorne and Edgar Alan Poe come to mind as a flash of lightning illuminates a gabled roof cutting sharply into the sky. She catches a tantalizing glimpse of grey stone overgrown with ivy before the strangely featureless light of a prematurely murdered day descends again. She looks nervously up at the threatening heavens, and a cool raindrop baptizes her forehead. Her brain warns her it is starting to rain, but her heart is so full of other much more exciting perceptions it doesn't care and her pussy knows getting wet never hurt anyone. She has come upon what could very possibly be her Master's house, and there's only one way to find out...

She is about to run in search of the front door when a light suddenly goes on in the tower room. A tall, broad-shouldered silhouette imprints itself on her retinas, and her right hand falls over her heart in an unconscious parody of romantic heroines everywhere as her breath catches watching the slender shadow of her lover undressing. Every cell in her body recognizes him as he pulls his shirt up over her head and tosses it away. A disappointed moan escapes her lips as he walks deeper into the room, out of her line of sight. His silhouette was magically gild-

Cat's Collar

ed by the light he was standing in front of – a sensual halo that has made her warm all over with the longing to take his already beloved form into her arms.

More wet kisses landing on her chest and arms gently urge her to seek out what she desires. Feeling like Dracula's Mina in her innocent white dress, she runs around the left side of the house in search of the front door, and in the process she discovers that the eccentric structure's square footage is mostly vertical. The wooden front door is almost twice as tall and wide as she is and looks scavenged from a fifteenth-century Portuguese castle. She has to stand on tiptoe to reach the large bronze knocker, which is not shaped like a lion's head... a beautiful pagan face gazes down at her, and what at first appears to be thick, wavy hair is actually bunches of grapes. It is the head of Dionysus. She bangs his thick metal 'necklace' against the dark wood three times, but an almost deafening clap of thunder drowns out her plea for admittance as a bolt of lightning brings the sensual deity's eyes to life. This is no classical portrait with empty sockets; the visage is more ancient and vivid, and Mira suffers the distinct impression her favorite god is challenging her.

Her emotions are cursed to uncanny synchronicity with the elements, because once again an unnervingly loud explosion of thunder drowns out the sound of bronze striking wood. She cannot be sure if Phillip heard the knocks on his door through the storm, but at least the covered porch is keeping her dry. His property is even more private than hers; behind her no street lined with parked cars is visible... she is beginning to feel as if she traveled decades through a time tunnel disguised as a brief patch of woodland, each colorful strip of fabric a subtle magical shift in dimensions leading her into this unreal realm of Gothic facades, gabled rooftops and pagan accents. The sound of the rain is becoming almost deafening magnified a thousand fold by the leaves of all the trees it is beating against. She has her cell phone and his number stored inside its electronic bowels. She could call him and tell him she is standing on his doorstep like a stray cat desperate for his caress, but that seems a ridiculous course of action when the iron doorknob is already turning in her hand. He forgot to lock the front door behind him. Or perhaps men who think of themselves as Masters aren't afraid of dealing with intruders.

Cat's Collar - Three Erotic Romances

Mira is both relieved and terrified that the door is unlocked and she is stepping unannounced and uninvited into a dark house. What if she is wrong and that wasn't Phillip she saw undressing in the upstairs bedroom? Tall, broad-shouldered men are not all that uncommon after all, yet it's too late now; she's inside and the door closes of its own weight behind her. She tells herself she should call his name and make her presence known to him, the only problem is her voice is cowering in her chest and refuses to cooperate with her good intention. The silence is so deep it would be like trying to yell under water; she can't do it. She is too busy fighting a powerful undertow of fear mixed with the current of excitement washing over her mind and nerve-endings. Then another feeling grips her almost as forcefully as a hand luring her deeper into the house across a darkly polished wooden floor. The front door led her directly into an open hall lost in shadow to her right, but to her left a soft golden light reveals a wondrous fireplace the Interior Designer inside her is covetously drawn towards.

Mira finds herself in the kind of space she has always dreamed of decorating; the kind of space in which all the treasures buried in her garage would come to glorious life again; the kind of space that makes a modern high-rise condo feel like a prison cell to her senses and imagination; the kind of space she could live in until she died peacefully in her sleep of old age with a smile on her lips, her body an almost centuries-old vintage her soul finally finished sipping and enjoying...

She cannot believe it, but her caressing fingertips tell her it's true, the mantel is made entirely of marble – a polished black stone threaded with rosy veins – and the grate is large enough to burn half a small tree a night, at least. The room is not vast as in story book descriptions of mansions and castles, but it is sparsely enough furnished to give the impression of great space. At the same time there is nothing ascetic about the minimal décor. A comfortably large chair sits at an angle to the hearth made of deep-red leather softened by decades of bodies reclining gratefully against it. A lamp with a black wrought iron stand shaped like a slender bark overgrown with a leafy vine sits next to this consummate reading chair, and by its light she is able to make out floor-to-ceiling shelves filled with books...

She would love to explore the rest of the first floor, but her nerves are silent-

Cat's Collar

ly screaming at her like a crowd made hysterical by the paranoid dictator of her brain insisting she really has no idea who the man upstairs is and that she's only imagining it's her lover. She could very well be trespassing, a criminal offence punishable by arrest, not the sort of bondage she imagines Phillip has in mind for her. Ludicrous as her overly cautious reason seems to a part of her, Mira cannot ignore it. She either has to make her presence known to the owner of this wondrous home, or she has to leave as silently as she arrived.

There is no grand central staircase; an archway opens up onto a narrow stairwell ascending at a steep angle. A dim light in the shape of a candle in its sconce illuminates the landing, but where the steps curve to the left they vanish into darkness.

'Phillip?' Her call possesses less substance than a moth hovering around the light; no one upstairs could possibly have heard it. 'Phillip?' She winces at how loud her voice sounds to her, and she didn't even raise it above a normal conversational level. She has to take a deep breath and muster all her courage to call out as loudly as she possibly can without yelling, 'Phillip?'

The sound of quiet footsteps she imagines being made by bare feet answer her almost immediately, reeking havoc with her heartbeats as whoever she saw up in the tower room begins descending.

'Mira?'

The sound of her name affects her like a blessing descending from above and saving her from all her fears. The warmth in his voice melts her dread just as a figure appears at the curve of the steps – her Master wearing a dark robe tied loosely closed around his waist and exposing most of his chest.

As usual, the sight of him feels like a divine fist hitting her in the womb. 'Phillip!' she breathes.

'I see you found your way to me.' He smiles. 'Come,' he extends his hand, 'I've been waiting for you.'

Chapter Twelve

"She climbed the narrow winding stair…"

Mira feels as full of questions as there are steps leading up to Master Phillip's tower bedroom. 'Did you leave that beautiful trail for me?' she asks breathlessly. She's in very good shape physically, but the stairwell seems to wind up and up endlessly.

'No questions right now.' He leads the way, her hand grasped firmly in his, forcing her to follow at his pace.

'Well, you certainly don't need to go to the gym,' she pants. 'You get a workout at home every day! Who designed this house anyway? It's amazing.'

He stops dead, causing her to collide with his soft cotton back in the ankle-length robe.

'Sorry,' she says quickly, and from that point forward concentrates on expressing her remarks as statements rather than questions. She is aware this might be a slightly deceptive way of obeying him, but thoughts and perceptions keep pouring out of her as freely as the rain beating down on the roof outside sounding louder and louder the higher up they climb. 'I imagine you decorated the downstairs room with the fireplace yourself, Phillip.'

No comment.

'But you couldn't possibly have known I would find that trail…'

Silence, unbroken even by heavy breathing and it annoys her that he is in even better physical shape than she is.

'Some of the treasures I have stored in my garage look made for this place,' she dares this radical observation as they finally reach a landing. 'I found the trail only because I was looking for Stormy and Sekhmet. I was worried about them.'

'I'm sure they're fine.'

She has to bite her lip to refrain from asking, 'How do you know that?' as she steps into the sacred domain of his bedroom.

The masculine décor is just right. Nowhere in evidence, she is pleased to see, is the popular minimalist metal style, nor is his private space taken straight out of a *Pottery Barn* catalogue with its excessive reliance on heavy wooden furniture and its perverse obsession with paisley. A king-size bed with a Shaker-style oak-wood headboard is softened by a divinely thick mattress covered with white cotton flannel sheets and an almost feminine profusion of large fluffy pillows. The single nightstand is also en elegant Shaker-style table with a single drawer, its timeless look complimented by a futuristic conical lamp burning a bright red color. She counts three separate Oriental rugs adding warmth and softness to the wooden floor, the darkly vivid colors matching splendidly with a polished black hardwood desk placed beneath one of the windows. The room is a *Feng Shui* master's dream for there are no sharp angles; the walls all curve gently in a cozy egg-shape. And the apparent lack of closet space is more than made up for by a huge antique wardrobe that must have cost a small fortune.

'This is perfect,' she says, thinking out loud.

'Nothing in this world is perfect,' he replies, shedding his robe and standing naked before her as if to deliberately belie the cynical statement, because in her eyes he is absolutely perfect, and the fact that his cock is already almost fully erect is only part of it. 'I very much enjoyed fucking you in that cute little dress, Mira, but now it's time for you to take it off.'

She reaches behind her to unzip it, and careful of the weight of her cell phone in one of the pockets, she slips the dress down her hips and steps gracefully out of it.

'Very good...' He is gazing at her naked pussy lips. 'I was afraid I might have to punish you for wearing panties when I expressly forbid you to do so without my permission.'

'I would never disobey you, Master.'

He smiles. 'Perhaps not consciously, but you will, and often, and I'll deal with it. You'll get better with time.'

She is hurt by how little faith he seems to have in her.

'It has nothing to do with you personally.' He reads her petulant look. 'This is just a new world to you, and you'll inevitably stumble as you learn the rules.'

'But you're supposed to teach me the rules...'

'I will, but some things cannot be taught; some things you have to discover on your own.'

She very much wants to ask him what he means by that and to give her an example, but she expects the ban on asking questions is still in place.

'Take off the rest of your clothes.'

She quickly removes her sneakers and socks.

'I suppose I can't expect you to go trekking through the woods in high-heels,' he remarks wistfully. 'Oh, well.' He smiles again, this time playfully, and surprises her by drawing her into his arms and holding her close, her cheek pressed against his chest.

'I really am worried about Stormy and Sekhmet,' she confesses.

'I told you, Mira, they're all right.'

'You can't know that for sure.'

'I sense they are.'

She is careful to avoid a questioning inflection, 'So you believe in what is traditionally known as woman's intuition.'

'Of course, women possess qualities any intelligent man would rely on to enhance his own abilities.'

She laughs because his answer is so perfect it makes her feel strangely giddy.

'It's a gut feeling I have that Stormy and Sekhmet are fine, although the gut has nothing to do with it. Just because intuition is a form of knowledge that transcends the physical senses doesn't mean it isn't a very real perception, and that it won't continue developing in human beings just as walking upright was latent in our ancestors.'

'I hope you give me permission to ask questions soon, Master, because there's so much I'd like to know about you and this house.'

'It was left to me by my great grandfather. I couldn't possibly afford it on my Master's salary.'

Cat's Collar

She pulls away from him to look up at his face. 'That's funny,' she says, reflecting his smile, 'because this house was made for a Master. I thought your family lived in Washington State.'

'They're originally from Virginia. They worked in D.C. for years until they could finally afford to buy their vineyard and get the hell out of here.'

'I suppose you have a cleaning lady,' she remarks cattily.

'Nope, can't afford one, not yet.'

'Oh, so is that why you want a slave, because she'll cook and clean for free?'

The glint in his eye tells her she has fallen into the trap despite all her careful effort and asked a question. He grabs her hand and pulls her over to the bed. He sits down on its edge, and instructs her to kneel. 'No, not in front of me, like this… that's it, I want you over my lap.' His legs are breathtakingly hard against her belly as he drapes her across them. She whines, bracing herself against the floor with her bare toes on one end and with her fingertips on the other. 'Regular discipline is a very important part of a slave's life,' he informs her, 'but right now I'm not going to spank you as punishment; this is purely for pleasure, my pleasure and yours.'

'But how can pain be pleasure?' The words have barely escaped her lips before a sharp, hot blow to her ass cheeks makes her cry out indignantly. 'I'm sorry!' she gasps.

'That's all right; any excuse to spank you is a good one. You have the most beautiful ass.' His amazingly hard palm lands across it again with a loud smacking sound.

Mira moans, and continues to moan as he spanks her, yet after a while she is no longer sure the sounds she is making are actually ones of protest, because beneath her hotly outraged nether cheeks her pussy is getting so hot and wet her perception of what is pain and what is pleasure is flowing together into one intensely indistinguishable sensation. She was never spanked as a child, and apart from a few playful slaps on the ass delivered by a handful of former boyfriends who didn't last, her buttocks have never been the subject of so much passionate attention.

'Are you enjoying this, Mira?'

'No, Master! I mean... I don't know...'

He strokes her burning cheeks, and then squeezes them each appreciatively. 'Mm,' he insinuates the tips of two fingertips between her labial lips, 'I think you are enjoying it.'

The teasing dip of his digits makes her aware of how wet she is. Her pussy's traitorous response to the humiliation of being spanked is a smoldering need totally at odds with her reason. She is both disappointed and relieved when he urges her gently off his lap and onto her knees on the rug before him. He opens his legs, and she braces her hands on his inner thighs as she bends her head and slides his erection between her lips. She loves how tender his skin remains over his rock-like hardness beneath it, and his semen tastes wonderful to her. She twirls her tongue around his head, gripping the base of his shaft with her left hand while her right hand gently cradles his balls.

'Oh, yes,' he whispers, encouraging the swift bobbing of her head up and down his cock. Blowing him is a totally engrossing experience, a way of wordlessly praising how thick and hard and long his penis is; a way of worshipping his erection while also claiming it as hers. She is pleasantly possessed by a feeling of timelessness, of an endless, sensual continuum as the scepter containing all the power of his pleasure slides in and out of her mouth... into darkness and back out into light... into warm, wet, sucking depths and back out into cool, caressing air... she can almost taste intoxicating secrets of life and creation as she sucks her Master's cock forgetting everything else in the world, all her senses and attention concentrated on his beautiful hard-on.

'Oh, yes...' he says again so softly she barely hears him over the lusty slurps of her tongue as she savors him even more fervently. The more she swallows of his sweet pre-cum the more mysteriously hungry she gets for more of him. She has no idea, nor does she care, how much time has passed before he says, 'I'm going to fuck you now.' He moves farther up on the mattress and spreads himself out on his back, watching as she crawls onto the bed with him.

Cat's Collar

'Oh, my God, this is a feather mattress,' she exclaims as she molds herself to his side, her cheek resting between his shoulder and his chest as she caresses the sparse black hairs providing a pleasant contrast in texture to his tender skin. 'You have wonderful skin,' she tells him.

'So do you. I love everything about you, Mira.'

It is the first time she has ever heard him say the word 'love'. As far as she can remember she has never heard him casually say he loved anything. He enjoys. He likes. He appreciates. He does not *love*. 'I love everything about you too, Phillip... except your job,' she is honest enough to add, and is rewarded by the gentle vibration of his chest as he laughs beneath his breath.

'I told you not to worry about that.'

'I know.' This is also the first time they have just lain peacefully in each other's arms. They are silent for a few minutes, during which she feels absolutely no need to invite any words into the room.

'I love listening to the rain,' he murmurs.

'Me too... sometimes I think it sounds like a huge cat curled around the house purring.'

'Mm, I like that.'

'I'm falling in love with you, Phillip,' she whispers.

His silence seems to extend beyond the edges of the known universe. She is beginning to drift off into a numbing despair when his voice finally rescues her from a hopeless void, 'Part of me keeps thinking it's too soon, but it's true... I love you, too, Mira.'

She closes her eyes and sighs as deeply as if she's been holding her breath all her life.

He rolls on top of her, thrusting a knee between her thighs, and she gladly spreads her legs for him. He pins her hands up over her head, raises his hips, and enters her.

She cries out beneath the wonderful shock of his abrupt penetration. She loves the feel of being pinned down by him – by his weight, by his hands, by his stabbing cock, and by his tongue plunging into her mouth. She responds to his savage kiss submissively, raising her legs around him, opening them as wide as she can to offer her pussy to him at the most deeply inviting angle, loving the experience of his hard-on plunging into the ultimate depths of her flesh. He buries his face in the side of her neck, and bites her, groaning.

'Oh, yes, yes!' she whispers, loving the experience of being absolutely possessed by him; of her body offering no resistance to his driving, biting, sucking, thrusting energy. Her clit quivers with pleasure as he bangs her, but how good it all feels has little to do with her body's temperamental seed. She has heard of the mythical G-spot, like the X on a treasure map that's only a fantasy, or at least it was... this evening her cervix feels full of subtly priceless sensations she never knew it was capable of, so much so that a clitoral climax seems almost superficial by comparison. She must be in love because the missionary position never felt so good. She is purely the vessel of his pleasure lying utterly pliant and submissive beneath him, until he starts coming, then her pussy begins deliberately milking him, her innermost flesh contracting and relaxing and deliberately prolonging his ejaculation. No military general could ever have felt more triumphant than she does as he collapses against her, his penis pulsing deep between the slender borders of her thighs. She lightly caresses his back with her fingernails, moving both her hands up from the base of his spine to the back of his neck slowly and gently, directing the energy concentrated in his groin back up to his consciousness.

After a few minutes he rolls onto his back beside her and she snuggles beneath his arm, her cheek resting contentedly against his chest and shoulder again.

He announces quietly, 'I think I'm going to call in sick tonight.'

She raises her head to look up at his face. 'Really?'

'Really.'

'You don't have to...'

'I know I don't *have* to do anything.' The Master is back in his eyes.

'Of course not, that's not what I meant...'

'I know,' he relents, gently forcing her head back down against his chest. 'I *want* to.'

'You still haven't told me what you're getting your PhD in, Phillip.'

'You still haven't guessed.'

Cat's Collar

Suddenly she remembers her concern for Stormy and Sekhmet.
'What's wrong?' He senses her body tense against him.
'I'm sorry, but I'm still worried about my cats.'
'Well, then, we'll just have to walk over there and make sure they're all right.'
'Could we?'
'We can do anything we want to, Mira.'

Chapter Thirteen

*"That which thou hast promised in thy time of necessity,
must thou now perform."*

Now that Phillip has promised her they will soon be leaving to check on Stormy and Sekhmet, Mira relaxes enough to inadvertently fall asleep in his arms...

When she wakes, she has no idea how much time has passed, and except for the increasingly vague anxiety about her cats – who have always been able to take care of themselves – she really doesn't care how many hours, weeks or centuries have elapsed. Phillip's eyes are closed, and the deep, even rhythm of his breathing beneath her cheek tells her he too has fallen asleep, which for some reason makes her inordinately happy. She gazes up at his face, and as though sensing her dreamy gaze, he opens his eyes and smiles at her.

'Sorry, I must have drifted off,' he murmurs.

'So did I.'

'It was nice.'

'Yes.' Curiosity and excitement have completely replaced the anxiety that drove her out of the doll's house and into the small forest between their homes. She can't wait to see the rest of his place.

The downpour outside has spent itself and it has either stopped raining completely or there is a gentle, silent drizzle falling. They get out of bed and dress as companionably as if they have been living together for years. It feels pleasantly natural to be slipping back into her dress as she watches him pull on a pair of black jeans, and then slip a simple short-sleeved cotton shirt over his head. Its neutral faded burgundy color goes strikingly well with his black goatee and hair, but then she seems to feel that way about everything he wears.

'Are you going to show me your castle now, Master?'

'I think you probably saw most of it.' He smiles up at her from where he's sitting on the edge of the bed slipping on his brown leather sandals. 'It's not as big as it seems. It extends higher into the sky and deeper into the earth than it actually takes up space on the ground.'

She sits down next to him, pressing one of her arms against his to absorb his strong warmth, which already she hates being separated from. 'Don't tell me you have your own private wine cellar.'

'All right, I won't tell you, but I do.'

'Oh, my God.' She lets her face fall into her hands as if her skull suddenly weighs too much for her to hold up, but it's really all the doubts and frustrations other man have forced it to contain she is letting go of now.

'But that's not all I keep down in my basement.'

She looks up and opens her eyes again as she feels him get up off the bed.

'Come.' His eyes and mouth are hard again in that way that helplessly arouses her, but she discerns the ghost of a smile buried in the deep dimples on either side of his firm lips.

'I'm not sure I'm ready for this,' she admits even as she lets him take her hand.

Trent Reznor and *The Downward Spiral* come to mind as they descend the tower staircase. 'Whoever designed this place was either a sadist or a masochist or both,' she remarks.

'You think so?' he replies neutrally.

Even in her sneakers and walking down she has to make an effort to match his pace until they reach level ground. 'I love your living room,' she declares. 'Have you really read all those books?'

'I inherited some, the rest are mine. I'm working on it. The kitchen is on the other side.'

'Oh, may I see it?'

'Not tonight.'

Cat's Collar - Three Erotic Romances

She follows him to a narrow door hidden in shadow, and does not need to ask to know it leads down into the cellar. Suddenly, all her nerves stand on end like a cat's back arching, and she hesitates. He opens the door and switches on an electric bulb no brighter than moonlight diffused through heavy cloud cover, but at least he doesn't expect her to descend into the terrifying unknown in total darkness. It's not much of a relief, however, and she continues to hesitate, afraid of seeing something down there she won't be able to live with. 'You don't have a torture room down there, do you?' she asks tightly, forgetting all about the ban on questions.

He turns towards her. 'No, Mira,' he answers gently, stroking the length of her bare arms lightly with his fingertips, a gesture that has a deeply soothing effect on her taut nerves, 'I have a play room. There's a big difference. You should know there can be a world of difference between S&M and B&D.'

'You mean between sadomasochism and bondage and domination?' she asks urgently, feeling as if she missed a vital course in college.

'Precisely. When you think of extreme pain and distasteful activities, those are the most radical manifestation of S&M, while normal vanilla couples playing at blindfolding and tying up is the mildest form of B&D, and there's a whole spectrum in between. Sometimes the two merge, but never anymore than you want them to. Do you understand?'

'So... experiencing severe pain all the time is not part of being a sex slave?'

'Not at all.'

She sighs, 'Well that's a relief!'

'Did it hurt when I spanked you?'

'Yes.'

'Would you say it was painful?'

'In a way, yes, and no...'

'Did you enjoy it?'

She suddenly appreciates the expression 'cat got your tongue?' when she finds herself unable to respond. The truth might incriminate her and get her into a world, a lifetime, of trouble.

Fortunately, her silence appears to be answer enough for him, because once

Cat's Collar

again he says, 'Come' in that quiet but inexorable way that has her feet obeying him before her mind has given them permission. She finds herself walking down the stairs in front of him as though she is not at all concerned about what she will find at the bottom.

This time the descent is relatively brief, and with the flick of his wrist he reveals the wine cellar of her dreams. 'Oh, my God, look at all this wine!'

'A lot of it is accumulated Christmas, birthday and Thanks Giving gifts from mommy and daddy,' he explains. 'It's not as varied and exciting a collection as it might seem, but I haven't really started working on it yet. I have to pay off my student loan first.'

Perhaps it is the fact that her soul is somewhat intoxicated by the sight of so much wine – so many bottles full of sunshine and rain, earth and air and fruit ripening beneath the full moon, growing older and wiser, more intoxicating to the palate and the psyche – but she suddenly feels so relaxed that she boldly sweeps aside the black velvet curtain herself.

The same switch that revealed the wine cellar apparently also illuminates the play room, after all, you have to be able to see what (and who) you're doing to truly enjoy all the subtleties of the experience. She appreciates the archaic touch of electric candles in their sconces lining the traditional gray stone walls, and she discovers the lighting can be dimmed or brightened as Phillip turns a circular knob all the way to the right, making the forbidding space as bright as possible. He is flooding her visual cortexes with light, as if this will help clear the spider webs of negative preconceptions out of her brain while she takes in all the arcane furniture and equipment.

Almost inevitably, the first object that captures her Catholic school girl's attention is a wooden cross shaped like a large X placed against the back wall. What appear to be black leather straps are attached to the four corners… her vivid imagination immediately pictures herself naked and spread-eagled against it while he fucks her from behind for as long and as hard as he wants to without her being able to resist him, as if she would want to.

There is what could pass for an innocent black leather weight bench except for all the miscellaneous straps and chains dangling from it, and a red leather chair that looks as though it was stolen from a Victorian gynecologist's office. But what really interests her is the adult 'swing set' – an iron frame with what looks very much like a black cloth swing hanging from its center.

'That's used for suspension,' he tells her, following her eyes, a smile on his lips as he reads her expressions.

She is relieved not to see any iron maidens, or racks on which people are stretched until they look like refugees from an El Greco painting. And even though there is an entire wall devoted to such items even her inexperienced eye recognizes as whips and riding crops, there is nothing that looks as if it would inflict permanent damage – no needles, no nails, no clamps, no evil-looking vices, nothing that causes her flesh to shudder and cringe.

'So these are your toys?' she speaks at last.

'Yes, I guess you could call him that. Not very frightening, are they?'

'No, not at all, they're very intriguing, actually.'

His smile deepens. 'Come on. Let's go find your missing pussies.'

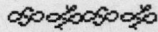

Left to herself, Mira would have taken a cab home, but she has no qualms about crossing a dark patch of woodland with Phillip along. With him – and a flashlight big and heavy enough to double as a weapon – to help guide her way, what would be a frightening prospect turns into an exciting adventure as they find their way back to her doll's house through the toy forest. She preserves the sense of mystery by not asking him again if he left the fabric trail for her. This man is teaching her to put into practice on a daily basis what she already understood conceptually – that she does not need to give her mind one-hundred percent evidence of something to know in her heart and soul that it's true.

It has stopped raining but all the leaves are wet and cool, and moist drops kiss her bare shoulders whenever she brushes against a damp branch in the darkness. She is content to let Phillip lead the way while she walks right behind him and slightly to the right, following his silhouette and the beam of the flashlight. It

Cat's Collar

comforts her that he seems to know exactly where he's going, and it further lifts her spirits whenever she catches a glimpse of cloth – little beacons of color lighting their way.

'I've always been a coward,' she muses out loud, thinking of a line from an old Kate Bush song.

He stops dead in his tracks as if she stabbed him in the back. 'How's that?' He turns to face her, holding the flashlight down so the light pools at their feet – a tiny yellow sphere with no true power to stave off the night.

'It means I'm scared to be out here at night even though there's nothing around that can actually hurt me. It's a primal fear of the dark, I guess, and of forests.'

'You're right, there's nothing out here that can hurt you,' he agrees mildly.

'The fear isn't rational,' she defends herself.

'Is any fear rational?'

'Well, yes… I mean it's perfectly natural to fear you'll be hit by a car if you step out into the middle of traffic. It's perfectly reasonable to be afraid of cancer, or something.'

'Why stop there? The list goes on forever, doesn't it? If you give into one fear you inevitably fall victim to them all. It's common sense not to walk out into traffic. It's a death sentence not to overcome the paralysis of fear.'

It's disturbing not being able to see his face or his eyes as he speaks, and she wishes they would keep walking. The pool of light revealing a patch of ground at their feet is making her feel strangely claustrophobic, as if her awareness is being forced to take refuge inside it – a small constricting cell of visibility protecting her from the amorphously threatening darkness surrounding them. 'But there's a place for fear just like there's a place for pain,' she insists half-heartedly. 'Pain is the body's way of telling you something's wrong. Fear is the way to realize you're in danger and vulnerable so you need to protect yourself.'

'Yes, but that's different than being afraid even when you're not immediately threatened by anything.'

'Yes, okay, I get it, can we keep going now?'

'Why, are you still afraid?'

'No, not with you here, Phillip.'

'But if your fears are insubstantial how can I possibly protect you from them?'

She laughs. 'You have a point there,' she admits, and the sound of her laughter somehow lessens the oppressive weight of the darkness. Because she can't see the individual trees, they have become a single essence weighing on her psyche with their almost depressingly patient and indifferent presence. Laughter feels like a charm holding all evil forces at bay, and it also seems to satisfy Phillip because he starts walking again. The random way the flashlight beam picks out branches and trunks and roots and the ground covered with a soft carpet of dead leaves is at once hypnotic and slightly dizzying. When the light at last flows across smoothly mowed grass, and then spotlights one of her white stone vases so it glows bright as a chunk of the moon fallen into her yard, Mira almost feels as if they journey millenniums in the seconds it takes them to step out from between the trees onto her lawn.

It is dark in her garden, but Phillips switches off the flashlight as they walk hand-in-hand towards the doll's house. She didn't leave any lights on or even lock the kitchen door behind her, yet much to her parents' chagrin she has never much worried about intruders, for up until now hers has proven to be a safe neighborhood. The sound of the cat flap rattling is music to her ears.

'Stormy!' she exclaims as his sleek, purring body wraps around her ankles. She scoops him up into her arms. 'Where have you been you silly, stupid pussy?' She is glad Phillip refrains from laughing at the silly sing-song tone of her voice, which she has allowed few other human beings to hear. Sekhmet is already proudly perched on his forearm, her lean black body resting across it as though it is a pedestal made especially for her, one paw curled up on his palm while her other front leg hangs elegantly straight. And thus encumbered with purring cat fur, Mira and Phillip enter the doll's house.

Despite how much she enjoyed her Gothic adventure this evening, she is glad he doesn't turn the light off in the kitchen after she switches it on. Part of her needs the steady passionless glow of electricity; candle light is sensually demanding.

Cat's Collar

'Would you like a glass of Chardonnay?' she asks, seriously craving one herself and eager to share.

'I would love one, but first I'll need to use your phone.'

'To call in sick?'

'Yep.'

She gladly fishes the phone out of her dress pocket for him.

He carries it over to her couch, where he seats himself with his left ankle resting on his right knee. Apparently, there is a limit to Sekhmet's devotion to Master Phillip – the sound of the electric can opener. While he makes his phone call, Mira busies herself feeding her pets. She scoops the gourmet food into Sekhmet's bowl first, and then feeds the more patient Stormy before rinsing two wine glasses and filling them generously with one of her favorite California chardonnays, *Chateau St Jean*. Phillip's voice is so soft it is impossible for her to make out what he is saying, and by the time she carries the wine into the living room, he has finished his conversation. Now her electronic butler has the number to his job stored in its memory, not that she'll ever dare dial it.

'Thanks,' he says, accepting the glass from her.

'My pleasure.' She sits down right beside him on the comfortable black leather cushion.

'The roses are still looking good,' he observes.

'Yes, they're beautiful!'

He spots the remote control on the side table beside him, picks it up and turns on the television, without asking her permission she observes, smiling to herself as she sips her Chardonnay. He begins flipping through the channels in traditionally annoying male fashion, never really pausing long enough on one scene to determine what is happening or if it might be interesting.

'I have over two-hundred channels,' she warns, wanting to save herself from becoming aggravated with her beautiful Master.

'And how many of them do you actually watch?'

'Less than ten, I think, but that's cable companies for you, they make you choose packages; you can't just pick individual channels.'

'Hey, the sci-fi channel!'

'One of my favorites. Don't you have cable?'

'Nope, can't afford it. I spent too much on my toys.' He winks at her. 'Here's to real-life entertainment.'

'I'll drink to that.'

For lack of anything better to watch, he leaves *Stargate-SG1* playing on low volume, sets the remote down, and slides a little lower on the cushion, making himself comfortable. The digital clock shows half-past-nine. 'So, where would you like to have dinner tonight, my lovely slave?'

'You're taking me out to dinner?'

'Didn't I just ask you where you wanted to go for dinner?'

'Well, as long as you let it be my treat this time...'

'Mira,' he grasps her free hand with his, 'I'm only teasing you a little about my financial straits; I'm okay, and I can't think of anything I'd rather spend my money on than us.'

Chapter Fourteen

"Beauty is eternity gazing at itself in a mirror."
Kahlil Gibran

Mira regrets having taken Ian McFarland on as a client, not because she has anything in particular against him; she simply cannot concentrate on work. Her sample books are figuratively gathering cobwebs like ponderous stones from an abandoned temple. The only fabric swatches that interest her are the ones hanging from trees in the patch of woodland behind her doll's house. Ever since she left the big interior decorating firm and struck out on her own she has not taken what can be considered a real vacation – two or three continuous weeks of work-free relaxation. The time seems to have come to draw a red line through at least seven blank white plots on her calendar, preferably more. When Ian gets back into town and calls her, she'll tell him some white lie about a minor family emergency. She doesn't doubt he'll give her all the time she needs to straighten out her personal problems. The red pen she fishes out of her desk drawer takes on all the properties of a sword in the constant battle to make money as it spills its blood in a straight line across two whole weeks, and gains that much neutral ground for her where she can relax away from the financial fray.

'There!' she says to Stormy where he sits perched on her desk next to the calendar watching the progress of the thin red thread with great interest. 'Mommy's taking her first real vacation ever!' She smiles at him, and he bangs his forehead approvingly against hers. She feels like applying the principals of *Feng Shui* to her own life for a change. She feels like meandering lazily and contentedly through

Cat's Collar

each day instead of cutting a straight path from one professional or domestic goal to the next. Without realizing it, her need to be in complete control of her life has had a negative effect on her ability to truly relax and simply enjoy who she is and how far she has come and how far she can go. Ever since she met Phillip, his actions have seemed designed to eliminate this *shar-like* patch in her emotional being. It is daunting to realize just how many fears from her subconscious basement were cluttering the otherwise lovely and luminous space of her psyche like ugly Victorian knick-knacks she should have consciously rid herself of years ago.

'I've lived a very sheltered life,' she tells Stormy, who is now reclining on his side directly over the red line she drew across the calendar whilst cleaning his whiskers. 'Apparently you don't think that's a problem, but then you have a lot more adventures than I ever do. God only knows what trouble you and Sekhmet get into when you vanish into your jungle bushes.' He pauses in his ablutions to look straight into her eyes for a long, disturbingly intelligent moment which is abruptly destroyed when he furiously attacks an itch in his buttocks with his teeth. She laughs. 'Come on,' she commands, and he leaps off the desk to follow her out of the office.

⁂

One of Phillip's presents arrives. This time it comes via U.P.S., delivered by a handsome young man dressed all in brown and full of such good cheer it makes her happy to know he apparently loves his job. After she dutifully signs for the box on the virtual line, he deposits it in her arms with a smile that promises she will love its contents even as it renders them unimportant in comparison with the free and priceless gift of his positive energy.

'Have a great day!' he says, literally leaping off her front step and running jauntily to his waiting truck.

'You too!' she calls after him.

Still smiling, she sets the box – which does not weigh very much – on the table in front of her couch, where it is instantly joined by Stormy. Then Sekhmet appears out of nowhere to inspect what in her opinion is obviously *her* package and she is simply allowing Mira to open it for her. The haughty tilt of her chin clearly says, 'I have people for that!' as she waits for the cardboard portals to open and admit her.

Mira fetches a knife from the kitchen. 'Get back,' she says firmly, not wanting to accidentally cut one of her cats as she slices through the tape, and she is also careful to put the knife away again before dealing with the utterly annoying Styrofoam eggs concealing the box's contents. Sekhmet and Stormy are not so patient. Already they are batting a few of the environmentally evil little balls across the coffee table and playing their own version of feline soccer. 'God, I hate this stuff,' Mira mumbles, struggling not to let anymore of the filling spill out as she reaches into the depths of a material that will survive until the sun goes nova. She finds another smaller box within the bigger box, and manages to extract it without getting kitty soccer balls all over the living room. She then takes the time to toss the box and its contents in the trashcan outside, safely away from covetous cats, deliberately prolonging the suspense... or deliberately postponing the moment when she will have to face the mythical shoes her Master expects her to walk through the real world in.

The high-heels are terrifyingly beautiful. The black vinyl shines in the sunlight pouring in through the window like some space-age material, a 'normal' curved shoe with a closed toe and a buckle strap perched on a platform three inches high to accommodate a slender six-inch heel that tapers open slightly at the end. Mira has no idea how she will ever be able to balance her weight on them, much less walk, but she quickly kicks off her black leather flip flops and prepares to make the attempt. Her Master accurately guessed her shoe-size, for the supernatural heels fit like a glove. She finishes strapping them on, and tentatively pushes herself up off the couch.

'Wow...' She towers over all the familiar objects in her living room which suddenly appear made for very short people. It dawns on her that this is the lofty angle from which a tall man like Phillip perceives everything. She puts one foot in front of the other, and is amazed when she manages to sustain her center of gravity and take another mincing baby step into her new life as a sex slave.

Mira makes it all the way to the full-length mirror in her bedroom, where she promptly pulls off her little cotton housedress and stares at herself in the mirror.

Cat's Collar

'Wow...' she says again, and understands. What the astronomical heels do for her legs is unbelievable. Their shapely curves are breathtakingly lengthened, and the shoes have an equally appealing effect on her upper body, pushing her ass out and curving her back so her breasts jut forward, enhancing her natural desire to have them kissed and caressed and fondled. The extreme heels perform a subtle but stunning magic with her figure, the way her legs 'go on forever' also making her curvaceous torso appear more slender, which in turn makes her breasts look fuller. Wearing only the long black hair flowing down her back and the black 'stripper' heels, Mira gazes at herself in the mirror in awe of her beauty. She has never looked as good as she does now, and she never will. This is the ultimate 'outfit'... although something tells her there's something missing...

There is a loud, urgent knocking on her front door.

'Oh, Jesus!' she gasps. She is too high up off the floor to just casually bend over and pick up her dress. 'Just a minute!' she cries, and bending straight from the waist makes use of her years of stretching and exercising to brush her fingertips against the cloth and snatch it up. 'I'm coming!' she yells as she slips the dress back on over her head. There's no time to take off the shoes. She walks as quickly as possible across her hardwood floor, and opens the door.

'Sorry miss, there were actually two packages for you.' The U.P.S. guy is back, his smile apologetic now. 'It was so small I didn't see it.' He hands her the light little package, caressing her legs with his eyes. 'Nice shoes!'

She smiles. 'They were in the other box you brought me.'

He grins. 'I wonder what's in this one,' he says, but doesn't stay to find out, nor does he redundantly wish her a great day again since obviously, in his opinion, she is having a very good day, indeed.

The second mystery gift from Master Phillip is a black leather collar about two inches thick set with tiny faux ruby hearts.

'Mreow!' Sekhmet is clearly of the opinion that this second delivery is also meant for her.

'Your neck is much too small for it,' Mira snaps, her emotions in turmoil. If she were to show her parents the first three presents from her lover, only the violet roses would fail to raise their blood pressure. How could they ever condone their precious daughter being collared like a cat; like just another mindless sensual pussy? Obviously, they can never know about it.

She carries the collar into her bedroom. Already she feels quite comfortable walking in impossibly high-heels, but all her life she suspected she was never normal, and now at last she feels as though she's entering a realm where she can truly be herself.

Standing before her full-length mirror again she slips on the collar, adjusting it so it fits snugly but still lets her breathe and swallow freely. She then twists the buckle to the back, and once again gazes at her reflection. There is absolutely nothing missing now.

'Mirror mirror on the wall, who's the fairest slave of all?'

'Mira-ow!' the glass replies as Stormy steps out from behind the wooden frame and fervently begins scenting her new shoes.

Her phone rings on the nightstand.

She teeters sexily over to answer it, but when she sees 'Caller Unknown' written across the display, her elation ebbs. 'Hello?' she answers in her sexiest voice.

'Mira?'

'Yes?'

'This is Anna, Anna Bianco, remember me?'

'Oh, my God, Anna?'

'Hi.'

'My God, it's been…. forever!'

A baby wails in the background. 'Just a minute, Mira, duty calls, but I'll be right back, don't hang up.'

She is sorely tempted to do just that, yet part of her is thrilled to hear from her old best friend again, frustrating as their relationship was. It did not survive the sheltered confines of Catholic school; once they hit Fairfax High they drifted apart almost at once.

'Okay, I'm back. I asked my mom to get your number from Rose. I hope you don't mind.'

'Of course I don't mind,' she lies blithely. 'It's great to hear from you. I heard you were pregnant…' She bites back the word 'again'.

Cat's Collar

'Eight months.'

'My God.' Her vocabulary has seriously degenerated. It's very odd talking to her childhood friend wearing nothing but six-inch heels and a black leather collar, especially knowing the woman on the other end of the line would not be able to wear such an 'outfit' at the moment and look, much less feel, desirable. 'How many children do you have?' she asks carefully, having discarded less flattering nouns such as 'kids' and 'brats'.

'Two at the moment, can you believe it?'

'No!' It's the most honest thing she has said so far. 'How do you do it, Anna?'

'Some days I really don't know.'

"Do you have... help?'

'Oh, yeah, mom and dad are great. When I can't take it anymore, it's off to grandma's house they go.'

Mira suffers a queasy sense of déjà vu.

'So what's up with you?' Anna interrogates cheerfully. 'I hear you're running your own company.'

'Yes,' she laughs, 'my one woman and two cat company.'

'You're an Interior Designer?'

'Yep.'

'That must be exciting work.'

'It can be. Sometimes it's just work.'

'You don't sound too thrilled with your successful career, Mira.'

'Oh, I am, it's just that I'm on vacation right now and I don't really feel like thinking about work.'

'Vacation, really, where are you going?'

'Nowhere.' She winces at how lame that sounds. 'You see, I just met someone...'

'Oh, that's great.'

'And I really can't concentrate on work right now, if you know what I mean.'

'Well, how would you feel about getting together one afternoon and catching up on things? Evenings are for hubby and the kids, but I can get away during the day.'

She thinks fast, but can't come up with a gracious way to extricate herself from this completely unexpected invitation. 'That would be great.' She is somewhat morbidly curious to see Anna again, whom she suspects could never understand why Mira is standing in the middle of her bedroom wearing nothing but shiny black vinyl heels even their Barbie's would have hesitated to slip on, and a black leather collar marking her as a man's slave.

'How about tomorrow? I know mom can take the kids then.'

'Sure. Okay.'

'This place is a mess. Would you mind if I drove over to your house?'

'No, I'd love you to see my doll's house. Would you like to come by for a light lunch and some tea?' They giggle as the formal tone of her voice suddenly transports them into the past.

'Oh, I would simply love to come over for some tea, darling!' Anna declares in her best British accent.

Phillip is working again tonight and tomorrow night, and for once she knows exactly when she will see him again – not for forty-eight hours. She invited him over for dinner, but he declined the invitation, saying he would rather take her out afterwards. He did not clarify on this 'afterwards' nor did she bother asking what he has planned; she is coming to enjoy the mystery.

Chapter Fifteen

*"If you want a drink, you may get it yourself;
I am not going to be your slave."*

'Anna!' she exclaims, schooling her voice so it doesn't sound like the gasp of shock it is; her old friend is obviously indulging the infamous food cravings pregnant women suffer from.

'Sorry, Mira, mom wasn't feeling well enough to take care of both Lizzie and the baby this afternoon, so I just left her with Brad junior and brought his sister along. I hope you don't mind.'

'Of course I don't mind, come in.' She refrains from offering Anna help in crossing the threshold lest the gesture insult her. 'Hi Lizzie.' She grins stiffly, eyeing the little girl like an explosive with legs walking into her neat little home. Through the corner of her eye she sees Stormy and Sekhmet dash into the kitchen, and a second later the cat flap rattles as they quickly make their escape. *Smart cats*, she thinks. *I'll get you for abandoning me!* It seems to her that time thickens and slows down as Anna makes her way over to the couch. Lizzie clings to one of her mother's hands and never takes her eyes off Mira, an ominous calculating expression in her huge blue-green eyes. When Anna finally makes it to the couch and gingerly seats herself, Mira sinks with sympathetic relief into the chair across from her.

'Twins,' Anna says proudly, patting her planet-sized belly.

'Twins? Oh, my God, congratulations!'

'Brad's happy too, although at first we were a bit overwhelmed. We weren't planning on four kids, you know.'

Cat's Collar

'I can imagine.' Mira can see the girl who was once her surly playmate haunting the pudgy features, and the light-brown hair she always envied so (because it was perfectly straight, never curling wildly out of control like hers always did) is still the same, only shorter now, neatly cropped around her face. She knows next to nothing about being pregnant, but clearly water retention is an issue. 'What's it like?' she asks curiously. 'Being pregnant, I mean? Oh, but I'm sorry,' she leaps to her feet, 'I should offer you something to drink.'

Lizzie is perched on the edge of the cushion right next to her mother, her hands clasped primly in her lap, her disturbingly conscious gaze never once leaving their hostess' face.

'Would you like something to drink, Lizzie?' she asks, addressing her as an adult because her silly cat voice doesn't feel appropriate; she really has no idea how to relate to children.

'Mira asked you a question, honey.'

'Honey' is wearing a pink little dress with pink little socks and Dorothy's ruby-red slippers Mira belatedly envies. *She* would have liked a pair of ruby-red slippers. She also would have liked a video of all her favorite Disney cartoons, but no, she had to settle for picture books.

Lizzie tosses her head back as if arrogantly aware of how superior her wish-fulfillment capabilities are compared to what Mira's and her mother's once were. 'I would like a coke please, madam.'

Mira bristles inwardly at the 'madam'.

'In a glass with ice not in the can.'

'I'll have the same.' Anna smiles proudly at her offspring.

'Oh, I'm sorry, I don't have any coke in the house,' Mira announces in a falsely apologetic tone.

Mother and daughter glance at each other.

'I don't drink soda.' She is compelled to explain her lack of sugary and nutritiously empty liquids. 'All I have is water and tea, wine and beer.'

'We'll both have some ice water then,' Anna says quickly as Lizzie's eyes narrow threateningly.

At least the little demon appears to be well behaved, Mira thinks.

Two hours later she has cause to regret the fact that she forgot to knock on wood.

'Sorry,' Anna apologizes for the umpteenth time. 'I should have brought her toy piano or computer with us. I don't know what I was thinking.'

'It's okay,' Mira lies, also for the umpteenth time. 'I don't mind her playing with my lap top.' She grits her teeth and smiles. 'How old is she again anyway?'

'Four-and-a-half.' Anna sounds disgustingly proud of the little devil she spawned.

'Four-and-a-half... computers didn't even exist when we were that age, did they?'

Anna laughs from where she is progressively sinking deeper and deeper into Mira's couch looking as if it will take a crane to lift her off it. 'Yes, they existed, we just didn't know about them, much less know how to use them.'

'I guess it's true what they say that kids grow up a lot faster these days.'

'So, tell me more about this man you're seeing now. All I know is his name is Phillip and that he's strikingly handsome and that his parents own a vineyard and that apparently he's the boy next door.'

Mira has to laugh. 'There's not much else to tell, really,' she says evasively, wishing she hadn't finally been forced to throw out the violet roses that looked so beautiful for an almost supernaturally long time. 'He's like no man I've ever met.'

Anna's delicate mouth looks even smaller in her puffy face as she gives Mira another one of her pregnant Mona Lisa smiles. 'It's always that way in the beginning,' she states with smug cynicism.

Mira keeps an eye on Lizzie where she's sprawled out on her stomach gazing intently at the lap top screen while manipulating the mouse across the Oriental rug and looking for all the world as though she's completing one of Einstein's unsolved equations. 'She seems like a very smart little girl,' she observes, trying to change the subject. She doesn't have to worry about her young guest stumbling upon any rape and torture scenes because she's not connected to the Internet; she's playing in *Adobe Photoshop*, a program that took Mira months to master. She remembers when crayons were all the rage, in fact, she still has to suppress the desire to buy a box whenever she sees one. She almost surrendered to the impulse recently when

Cat's Collar

Michael's was having a sale of sixty-four colors for ninety-nine cents.

'Have you introduced Phillip to your parents yet?'

She tries to determine whether her friend's innocence is genuine, and generously concludes that Anna is simply clueless. Two babies, and two more on the way, is bound to wreak havoc with a woman's sense of subtlety. 'No, not yet, it's too soon. We only just met.' She wants to ask her old friend all sorts of improper questions such as, 'Is your vagina as tight as it used to be?' But maybe Anna had C-sections, which appear to be all the rage these days, and maybe a small scar is preferable to a distended pussy. Unfortunately, everything she wants to know is inappropriate for polite conversation. At least lunch was an entertaining and tasty affair of grilled cheese with tomato sandwiches accompanied by reduced fat Cape Cod potato chips and iced tea. But what she enjoyed most about it was being able to chew and sip and refrain from trying to make conversation with someone who was essentially a total stranger to her.

'Is there some reason you don't want to talk about him, Mira?'

She remembers clearly now (how could she have forgotten?) the infuriatingly superior way her friend could sometimes behave, and now, ensconced in her couch like a female Java the Hut, she is making Mira squirm like Princess Leia dressed in a skimpy slave outfit. The subconscious weight of 'they' is embodied in Anna's matronly virtue; she rules supreme in the middle of a beautiful single woman's living room. Mira's life may be clean and orderly and hedonistically pleasurable, yet Anna's timelessly fecund presence makes it seem to be lacking in something vital.

'Why don't you tell me about Brad,' she counters. 'All I know about him is that he's a stock broker with excellent sperm.'

Anna has the good grace to laugh.

Fifteen minutes later, Mira is figuratively squirming in her chair regretting how successfully she managed to shift the conversation from her Master and soul-mate to Anna's financially successful husband.

'Look, mommy!' Lizzie scrambles to her feet lap-top in hand, and Mira holds her breath as she totters across the living room with the thousand-dollar notebook held proudly out in front of her.

'It's lovely, dear,' Anna coos, 'now go show Mira.'

Lizzie gladly complies with this request.

'Wow!' Mira exclaims. 'That's *very* good.' She has seen a lot worse on museum walls.

Satisfied with the praise, Lizzie resumes her belly-down position to begin creating another masterpiece.

'I remember you said you never wanted children,' Anna comments, stepping energetically back on memory lane since she doesn't have to physically move to do so. Her tone implies she's waiting to hear that Mira has changed her mind.

'That's right, and I still feel that way. I'm just too selfish. Two cats and a man are my idea of paradise.'

Anna's complacent little smile stiffens almost imperceptibly. 'For now, anyway.'

'Forever.' She clearly remembers now what was blessedly forgotten – the dead-end arguments they used to get into to the tune of 'Is so!' 'Is not!' 'Is so!' until one of them just gave up in exasperation. *Where the hell is Stormy?* she wonders. She could really use a warm, purring body on her lap to soothe her bored tension. It is unpleasantly dawning on her that her old friend is trying to use her to feel good about her conventionally fertile life by getting Mira to admit she is dissatisfied and lonely, that she's missing something. Anna appears to be getting increasingly (although always politely) miffed that her single female specimen is refusing to be poked and prodded into confessing that what she secretly wants deep down is a house and children and a husband, necessarily in that order. She wants her ex best friend to admit that this career girl thing and living on her own is not what her heart and soul truly crave.

'Phillip is a Master,' Mira hears herself announce happily. 'He dominates women for a living.'

'Excuse me?'

'You should see him when he's dressed all in black leather. Sometimes he beats women, and they love it.'

Both of Anna's hands come to rest on her belly as though to shield her unborn babies' ears. 'Mira, what are you talking about? Did you just say your new boyfriend beats women for a living?'

Cat's Collar

Mira smiles; she can almost see the smoke emanating from her old friend's traditionally programmed brain. She is deliberately setting out to short-circuit it, but the way she sees it, Anna has only her own insufferable smugness to blame. 'Well, sometimes, usually he just dominates them with his intensely sexy will power.' She has no idea exactly what Phillip does on those three mysterious nights a week, and right now she doesn't care; Anna's expression is just too entertaining. 'You see, he's my Master and I'm his slave. I'll show you.' She exits into the bedroom, and returns carrying her new black leather collar in one hand and her six-inch black heels in the other. 'He bought these for me,' she says proudly.

'Jesus Christ, those aren't real shoes, are they?'

'Oh, yes they are, very real, and you can't believe what they do for my legs.' She glances down at Anna's swollen extremities. 'Would you like to see.'

'Um, no, thank you... mom wasn't feeling well, I really should get going.' She struggles to stand up as quickly as possible.

Mira sets her treasures down and walks over to help her. 'Are you sure you can't stay a little longer?

'I'm sure. Lizzie, honey, let's go.'

'But mommy, I was just–'

'I said let's go!'

Mira suppresses a grin as she escorts them to the door. 'This was fun, Anna. We really should do it again soon. Good luck with the twins.'

Anna mumbles a polite inanity, but it's obvious she can't get out of there fast enough.

The minute Mira closes the front door behind her guests – cutting off the sound of Lizzie shrilly complaining about the loss of her latest masterpiece – the cat flap rattles, announcing the return of her cowardly felines.

'You two suck!' she says fondly. 'I can't believe you made me go through that all by myself.'

Sekhmet inspects her food bowl even though she knows perfectly well it's not dinnertime yet. Only Stormy has the good grace to purr around her ankles by way of apology.

Chapter Sixteen

> *"'Oh dear!' said the princess. And the three*
> *drops of blood heard her, and said, 'If your mother*
> *knew of this, it would break her heart'."*

Mira should have foreseen the consequences of her impulsive honesty, but she didn't, and it's too late to take it all back now. Rose is at the other end of the virtual line demanding to know what Anna's mother was raving about.

'She said you told her daughter you were a man's *slave*?'

Mira is tempted to exclaim, 'I did not!' but the fact is she did, and now she somehow has to make the sensually exciting world of B&D palatable to her sedately conventional mother.

'Mira, talk to me honey, what exactly did you say to Anna?'

At least Rose is giving her the benefit of the doubt, undoubtedly remembering all the times Mira came home disappointed by her friend's lack of imagination. Yet the opposite seems to be the case now and Anna is guilty of an overactive imagination, hopefully as a result of hormones gone out of control in her pregnant brain.

'Mommy, I'm in love.'

'Oh, my… I see… well, that's wonderful, dear, but…'

'I have no idea what Anna told her parents, but I'm sure she exaggerated, or at least tried to make it sound negative. She hasn't changed a bit. I really got the feeling she was trying to make me feel bad about my life; trying to get me to admit I couldn't possibly be happy if I wasn't married and pregnant. It really pissed me off.'

Cat's Collar

'But it's-'

'The man I'm seeing is much more interesting than her stupid stockbroker husband, Brad, will ever dream of being!'

'I'm sure he is, dear.' Rose's voice is placating, the audio equivalent of a hand smoothing ruffled feathers; it is how she has always dealt with Mira's intense and sometimes bristling temperament. 'But why hadn't you mentioned him before?'

'I wasn't ready yet. I'm sorry you had to find out about him this way, but trust me, you'll love him. He's a wonderful person.'

'What's his name?'

That's a safe place to start at least. 'Phillip.'

'Well, that's a very nice name!' Rose declares inanely, but she is genuine enough for it to come out sounding charming.

'Yes it is, a very nice name, but he's even nicer.' Mira laughs wondering how long her mother will allow her to continue skirting the issue of whatever it was Anna said to her parents. 'So, what exactly *did* Anna say to her parents?' She grabs the bull by the horns.

'Well, it made absolutely no sense to me, some nonsense about indecent shoes and dog collars and sex slaves...'

'She was referring to the high-heels Phillip bought for me, and to the black leather... um, necklace.' She is allowed some poetic license. It's rather like trying to feed meat to a vegetarian by calling the chopped bacon in the stew diced tomatoes. 'Remember how I used to love to play fantasy games when I was little, mommy? Well, Phillip and I are sort of playing a game together; playing at being Master and slave, and it's really a lot of fun for us. But just because we choose different terms for our relationship doesn't mean our feelings for each other aren't as loving and as caring as Anna's are for Brad, and vice versa.'

'Mira, you're a grown woman,' her mother reminds her sternly, 'life isn't a game.'

'That's not what I mean! You shouldn't take me literally, mommy. I said its *like* a game, but that doesn't mean it's not serious. What I mean is that it's fun and healthy, not negative and scary like I'm sure Anna tried to make it seem because that's the way she perceives it. She's even more intolerably dull now than when we were kids.'

'You sound very defensive dear, as though you're trying to prove something to yourself.'

'I don't need to prove anything to myself, I'm just trying to get you to understand, but there's really no point in continuing to talk about this over the phone. You just have to meet Phillip, that's all, and see for yourself.'

'Your father and I would love to meet him. What does he do for a living?'

'He's getting his Ph.D.'

'So he'll be a doctor...' A note of approval softens her concerned tone. 'A doctor of what?'

'Viniculture.' Mira finally takes her guess. If she's wrong, Phillip will simply have to be getting two PhD's.

'Viniculture...' Rose searches her mental files, but clearly she has never met such a doctor.

'A doctor of winemaking.'

'Winemaking?' Clearly it never crossed Rose's mind that something as culturally rich and healthy as wine ever required the services of a doctor.

'His parents own a vineyard in Washington State.'

'An entire vineyard?'

'Yes! And he has a wine cellar in his basement.' Absolute honesty is as impossible as zero gravity beneath the complex layers of the earth's atmosphere – her parents can never know what else Phillip has in his basement.

'And how did you meet this wine doctor?'

'Sekhmet brought him home, can you believe it.'

'Sekhmet? Your cat?'

'Yes... mom, I have to go, I have another call coming in.'

'Phillip?'

'Yes, I love you. I'll call you later.'

'Mira-?'

'Don't worry, mommy. Forget whatever Anna said, the truth is much more complex, and wonderful, trust me.' She disconnects her mother and quickly lets Phillip in through the virtual portal. 'Hello?'

Cat's Collar

'Hello. Were you on the other line?'

'Yes, how did you know?'

'It took you a while to answer, and you sound a little breathless, as if I interrupted something.'

'Not really, I was just talking to my mom.'

'About?'

'About you, actually.'

'I see.'

'Are you getting your PhD in viniculture?'

'Very good, Mira. You finally guessed it.'

'I don't believe it! You are, really?'

'Really. What else did you tell your mom?'

'I told her I was in love with you...'

'That's nice.'

'You see, my ex childhood pregnant friend was here today and she annoyed me so much I sort of felt like shocking her, so I showed her the shoes and the collar you sent me and told her the truth – that you're my Master and I'm your slave.'

'Very good, Mira, I'm pleased.'

'Only problem is, she told her parents, and her parents called my mother, and you get the picture.'

'I see,' he says again.

'I tried to make her realize that terminologies are irrelevant and that what matters is the depth of feeling between two people in a relationship. She knows I've always been rather unusually intense, and I tried to let her know, if not in so many words, that I'd finally met a man who could handle that. But, of course, all you have in your basement is wine.'

'Of course.'

'You don't have a problem with meeting my parents soon, do you?'

'Why would I have problem with that, Mira? Call your mom back and tell her we can all have dinner together soon, but not tomorrow. Tomorrow you're coming over to my house for a slumber party so we can play with all my toys.'

'*All* your toys?'
'Well two or three of them, at least.'
'Ok.'
'Ok?'
'Yes, Master.'
'Your lack of discipline has just introduced a new toy into my planned play, Mira. I've been very lenient with you, but the more time passes, the less excuse you'll have to be so sloppy.'

She closes her eyes. 'Yes, Master.'

'I'm proud of you for being honest with your mother, and I'm happy you trust me enough not to feel you have to keep our relationship a dirty little secret. We're just at the beginning of our journey, but over time your parents will see that no other man could love you as I do, or will, because it'll only get better.'

'I believe you, Master.'

'You have my permission to touch yourself this evening. It sounds like you've have a hard day.'

'Oh, yes, Master, thank you, I have... but, God, I'm sorry, I forgot to thank you for your gifts!'

'You showed them off to another woman and proudly told her you were my slave. That's thanks enough.'

'No it's not. I really love them, thank you.'

'And I'll bet you love how great you look in them, too?'

'Yes...'

'When you touch yourself this evening you will be wearing your collar and your new heels and nothing else. Understand?'

'Yes, Master.'

'What will you be thinking of as you touch yourself, Mira?'

'I'll be thinking of you, Master.'

'And what else?'

'I'll be wondering which of your toys you're planning to play with tomorrow.'

'Yes, you will.'

Cat's Collar

༶ཽ༷

Mira has an entertaining, if also somewhat nerve-racking, evening cruising some of the most tasteful kinky sites on the Internet. She learns there is a very powerful fashion element to BDSM she was only vaguely aware of. Black leather is hardly the only fabric of choice, in fact, vinyl and rubber and latex seem to be even more popular – extremely shiny black latex, or candy-apple-red latex, and even purple latex a slightly darker shade than her favorite color. She lingers longest at a web site devoted to kinky couture. Her metaphysical side is immediately captivated by images of beautiful women clad in skintight reflective black latex wearing high heels even more extreme than the ones Phillip gave her... heels in which it would be impossible to do anything except lean against the stone balcony of an old mansion overgrown with ivy... and certainly a woman wearing such shoes could only crawl across the grass towards an old tombstone growing amidst the trees... crawling like a cat is definitely the best way to get around in nine-inch stiletto heels. And yet it seems to Mira that the women in these photographs are more than sex objects. Power and vulnerability are combined in them in a totally stimulating way. The high-heels they are wearing are not meant to get around in, not in any normal sense; they are for taking mysterious root in while being violently fucked, for holding erotic sway in. When a woman wears shoes with heels as sharp as knives she is offering herself up as a sacrifice, and yet they are also the weapons she wields to conquer the man whose erection sinks into the hole in her shiny black latex as if into the haunting heart of the universe itself...

Mira is fascinated by the shiny black latex fabric that reflects the whole world off a woman's figure. She loves the juxtaposition of innocently lush nature with this unnatural material clinging to a woman's curves like a second, magical skin. Some of the photographed latex suits cover an entire woman's body except for her face and her feet; even her hands and fingers are sheathed in built-in gloves, with a zipper strategically placed over her ass and crotch so it isn't necessary for her to strip to be fucked. All a man has to do is skin the cool black peel away from her pink pussy and thrust into the warm and tender depths within. Mira feels that to wear such an outfit would be to assume the profound power of the energy-filled darkness of space containing the sensuality of all the worlds and of life itself. Shining black latex is a fabric she would definitely like to explore, and the artistic quality of the photographs she admires reassure her. They offer a necessary antidote to all the crude amateur images the Internet virtually bombards her with that are, at best, good for masturbation only.

Stormy leaps onto her desk and stares at the computer screen while she is studying images of naked women in bondage. Perhaps it is all the string-like rope that appeals to him, but she suspects it is her aura of intense concentration that attracted him into exploring the source of her focused attention. She doesn't want to admit it, but there is something perversely stimulating about pictures of helpless naked women, especially ones involving suspension, where despite how bound and immobile a girl is, all her orifices are still available for use. Mira is not entirely sure how she would feel finding herself in such a position, but she suspects she will find out soon enough. She also suspects that if she asks her Master to get her a shiny black latex bodysuit for her birthday that he will be happy to comply with her request. At least she already has the opposite end of the kinky spectrum covered, because she is the genuine item – a Catholic school girl. It is also flattering to note that Egyptian-style bangs and long black hair like hers possesses a timeless appeal transcending the traditional blonde bimbo.

'What do you think, Stormy, would you like to see your mommy dressed as a black cat?'

He quickly licks his right paw, ignoring the question as utterly ridiculous.

'I'll bet Sekhmet wouldn't like it.'

Windows keep popping up on her screen seeking to lure her into virtual worlds all promising to be the most extreme, graphic, shocking, etc. etc. for a small membership fee. Phillip's toast of the other night comes to mind, 'Here's to real-life entertainment.' When only the visual cortex is engaged, all the other senses are left out, which in Mira's opinion creates a dangerous imbalance, because real life is so much more than just what you can see. She can't taste, touch, smell, or otherwise interact with any of the men and women virtually crowding her study, much less have any affect on them either physically or emotionally.

'I don't know how far I can go in this world, Stormy. I guess I just have to trust Phillip to know, and especially I have to trust the fact that as far as I desire to go is how far he desires to go, too.'

Stormy finishes cleaning his right paw and begins industriously working on his left one.

'Come on.' She pushes her chair back and gets up. 'Let's go have some dinner.' She has had her fill of kinky images for one evening. In school she never used to get nervous before a major test, but she is nervous tonight because her whole body will be involved in the test tomorrow, not just her mind. And if she doesn't pass, she will, more likely than not, lose the love of her life…

She needs some wine.

Chapter Seventeen

*"That is an art that pleases me well; if thy daughter
is as clever as you say, bring her to my castle tomorrow,
that I may put her to the proof."*

She arrives at her Master's house at exactly six o'clock as he commanded her to. She does not knock; he indicated the front door would be unlocked. She is carrying a black bag with two changes of outfit – one for playing in, the other for dining out in later. Per her Master's instructions, she walks straight to the door leading down into the basement. The light illuminating the steps is already on and she quickly descends. In the wine cellar she sets down her bag, and proceeds stripping off the sneakers, socks, shorts and tank top she wore to follow the colorful fabric trail through the forest. Beneath them she is wearing thigh-high black stockings that don't require a garter belt to stay up, and her new black leather collar with the faux rubies is already around her throat. All she needs to do now is slip into her extreme high-heels. The knowledge that her Master is waiting for her behind the black velvet curtain sends a warming rush of adrenaline through her naked body in the chilly basement, and the wine bottles around her seem to offer their mysterious support as she walks carefully across the stone floor. She is carrying nothing now except her pride and her beauty and her love for the man she is confident is about to use her as she was made to be used.

Outside it is still daylight, but inside the earth it always feels like night. Perched on the erotic pedestals of her extreme high-heels, completely naked except for the stockings and her Master's collar, it seems to Mira that her senses are coming fully alive like never before; her fingertips have never felt anything so luxuriously soft as the black velvet cloth she parts to reveal the scene from a nightmare, or a dream... definitely a dream. Along with the three dimensions all her perceptions, both physical and conceptual, seem to orbit the figure standing there to greet her. Phillip is dressed entirely in black again, but with a breathtaking difference – his shoulders and arms are bare, his torso hugged by a tight black latex T-shirt reflecting the artificial candlelight. On a normal day, she would do anything he wanted her to, but when he looks like this, heaven and hell are the limit. For the space of a few accelerated heartbeats they simply stare at each other. Mira is not sure how to proceed now and waits for his direction.

He approaches her, the sound of his boots eloquently taking the place of words. 'Good evening, my beautiful slave,' he says formally, but a subtle smile shines in his eyes.

'Good evening, Master.'

'You look absolutely beautiful in your slave uniform, Mira.' He lifts the weight of her hair with the backs of his hands and tosses it over her shoulders to fully expose her breasts.

His physical proximity makes her weak; in the towering heels it's as if she weighs less than normal. She will do anything for him. Her body was made for him. This is not a figure of speech or a metaphor; as he takes her arm and leads her deeper into the room it feels like the literal truth. The pages of the haunting exam she must take to graduate into her new life as a sex slave are opening up and she is facing her first challenge. It is no normal black leather weight bench, but it looks comfortable enough sitting in the heart of a minimalist metal structure from which hang four chains and buckled straps.

'Lie down on your back, Mira.'

She obeys him as gracefully as she can, her backside making rather swifter contact with the cushy leather than she intended; she is still getting used to her new center of gravity in the extreme shoes. It feels very nice to stretch out on the comfortable platform, and she is only vaguely wondering what he has in mind, content to savor the mystery like a rare vintage. There is also a little bit of 'ignorance is bliss' in her current submissive attitude, although she knows that will change soon enough; soon she will know whether or not she can remain so pliant, whether or not her flesh can pass all he has in mind for it. And there's no way she can cheat because the only way she can pass is to truly enjoy the challenge.

'Are you frightened, Mira?'

'No, Master, I'm not.'

'Good, because there's no reason you should be.'

The 'bench' is just the right height to put her hips on a level with his. 'Raise your legs and spread them,' he commands.

She obeys him naturally, her pussy lips parting as if in wonder, and the slick sound her labial lips make as they open speaks loudly of unconfessed hungers. Suddenly, Mira realizes he is going to force the truth out of her, and that she won't be able to lie to herself or to the world anymore about the dark depths hibernating in her libido. She has never had her legs spread and suspended like this. The gynecologist's office was just a terrible tease that did not even hint at how gloriously vulnerable this position would make her feel. Her arms suffer the same fate as her legs, spread open over her head with her wrists resting in what feel like fur-lined straps he buckles just tightly enough that she can't wriggle her hands free. The final touch comes as a surprise. She gasps when her head is thrown back as he bends over to release a lever beneath the cushion. Immediately she worries that if he forces her to sustain this pose for too long the blood will rush to her head and she won't be able to bear it.

'Master...' she says, a tremor of uncertainty in her voice.

Darkness fills her vision as he comes and stands directly over her prone face. The universe is divided in half in his gleaming black thighs, and it feels like the hand of God descending over her features to gently caress her cheek and part her lips with the tip of his strong, demanding thumb.

'Mira, the first and the last and the most important lesson a slave has to learn is to trust her Master. You're worried I'll leave you like this for too long?'

'Yes, Master,' she admits, intensely grateful for his perceptive understanding.

'Very good, you were honest with me about it. But you came here of your own free will, Mira, which means you trust me. Yet clearly that trust still has its limits, and these limits are the only things in the room that are going to cause you pain and discomfort. There can be no limits to how much you trust me. The trust must be absolute and include the largest and smallest of your fears and anxieties.'

'Yes Master, I understand.' Her world is literally upside down. Pleasing him is all that matters to her now, and yet she knows that in doing so she will also mysteriously be fulfilling herself. This is the dance he mentioned, the beginning of the death spiral – the death of the doubts and fears limiting her experiences. She is in absolutely no physical danger, she knows this, yet being completely bound and helpless is still an unnerving experience. Part of her is desperate to feel anxious. Another part of her is so excited she has to close her eyes as he cradles her head in both his hands and lifts it, stopping the flow of blood to her skull. He massages her scalp with his fingertips, and for an instant she can almost imagine she is at the beauty salon getting her hair washed, her head tilted back into the sink.

'Would you like to suck my cock?'

'Oh, yes, Master.'

He gently lets go of her head again, and she opens her eyes to try and get a glimpse of his penis as he unzips his tight pants. She needn't have worried. Soon his erection is all she can see, taste, smell and feel. He sinks to his knees and begins fucking her face. His hands caress her throat on the outside while the engorged head of his cock strokes it from the inside. Her wrists and ankles jerk in their straps in sympathy with her gag reflex, but whether she likes it or not the slender shaft of her neck remains completely open to him. The cool pillows of his balls press against her features in breathless contrast to his hard-on filling her mouth and throat like porous stone stiffening and swelling against her wet tongue. Dimly colorful lights flash behind her closed eyelids as the intoxicating smell and taste of him act like a powerful drug lessening her discomfort. Her pussy cries hotly at being so left out of the action; at feeling so empty compared to her mouth, which technically wasn't even made for his penis the way her cunt was. Her nose smothered in his scrotum, Mira breathes in the scent of his skin like an elixir. She swallows his erection's tender sword, and the point metaphorically pierces her heart – the excruciating experience is thrilling because she truly loves him.

When his penis slides out of her mouth she gasps to fill her lungs with air, surprised and rather awed by her ability to swallow him whole without choking.

Cat's Collar - Three Erotic Romances

He slips out of her slowly, allowing her time to savor the full length of his cock caressing parts of her no man has ever reached before. She sees him stand up, but before she can begin to feel abandoned, he adjusts the lever beneath the cushion and raises her head level with her body again. Her cheeks are flushed, and her awareness of everything feels relaxed and open in an arousing way. It seems right that her hands and arms are raised as if in supplication or worship or both, because she just worshiped him and now a part of her is silently pleading with him to reward her efforts. Her pussy is open and aching for him. Her cunt's juicy feast is offered up for his cock to begin carving her up and serving them both the pleasure she can't get enough of. On the other hand, she suspects it is too soon in the test for him to reward her by making a hot little red star of her clitoris. He has moved out of her line of sight, and she is just beginning to seriously miss him when he appears again, but only for an instant.

'Oh, no,' she moans as a blindfold falls over her eyes.

'Oh, yes.'

As always the caress of his deep, quiet voice assuages her ruffled emotions. If he says 'oh, yes,' then 'oh, yes' it is. Another small eternity seems to pass as she lies there in her supplicating pose, and the position turns her on so much she feels as if she is begging all the angels above to follow Lucifer down and fuck her one by one...

As if in response to her sacrilegious fantasy a flaming kiss suddenly lands on her skin over her heart. She cries out in confusion, not sure if what she just felt was pain or intense pleasure. Then it's as if she is surrounded by falling angels planting hellishly hot kisses on her naked breasts. Crying out again she arches her back in an effort to throw off their demonic attention, but all she succeeds in doing is offering one of her hard nipples to the concentrated attention of a burning tongue.

'Oh, my God, Master, Master!'

'I'm here, Mira.'

'What *is* that?'

'What does it feel like?'

'Hot wax! Is it wax, Master?'

Cat's Collar

'Yes, it is. How does it feel?'

'It feels like beautiful demons kissing and licking me, Master!'

He laughs. 'I like the way you think, Mira.' Then he ceases to speak as the wax rains swift hot kisses along her body down to her navel. She emits a little shriek as the tiny crater in her flesh fills with molten liquid, making her vividly aware of the fact that it's the center of her body as a sweetly debilitating warmth radiates up into her breasts and down into her sex.

'Oh, no, no, please...' The painfully hot pecks are making their slow way down to her pudenda as everywhere the flame shed its burning tears her skin is tightening beneath a stiffening armor of wax. Her sensitive clitoris cannot possibly handle such an ardent kiss, she couldn't possibly bear it, and yet she holds her breath anticipating the terrifyingly intense sensation. She does not know whether to be disappointed or relieved it when it never comes. Instead she suffers the sweet, deep relief of his cock suddenly sliding into her pussy. She moans in gratitude, and then again in frustration desperately wishing she could see him. She could never have foreseen what an exciting new dimension would be added to the pleasure of his penetrations by the straps and chains holding her legs wide open. She cannot defend herself from his thrusts; she cannot control the angle or depth of his penetrations; her hole is forced to absolutely accept his relentless strokes, and the sensation is devastating. She is vaguely aware of her hands fluttering like wings as her cries rise eloquently around them, letting him know how much she loves being violently stabbed by his erection, and especially how much she loves the excruciating fact that she cannot defend herself from it. Once again relief and disappointment define the nature of her heartbeats as he pulls out of her almost immediately, letting her know there is much more to come and that her first major test as a sex slave has only just begun.

Mira makes a mental note to add more inner thigh exercises to her workout as he releases the straps around her ankles and she has to very gingerly close and lower her legs after their long suspension. Her arms, strengthened by weightlifting, are not as affected. She is hopeful the blindfold will come off next. She should have known it was too much of a reprieve to expect so soon as he grasps both her hands and helps her sit up, keeping her blind and vulnerable while he urges her gently to her feet. He lets go of her hands, and she resists the temptation to cling to his arm as she relocates her center of gravity on the six-inch black pedestals. She has a vivid picture in her mind of the other 'toys' in his play room, and wonders where he will lead her next. Then a strangely sharp, clinging sensation beneath her chin makes her tilt her head back proudly.

'This way, my slave.'

'But I can't see...'

'That's right, you have to trust me. Follow the directions of the riding crop and don't be afraid, just concentrate on its touch.'

This command would not be half as daunting if she was barefoot or wearing normal shoes, and if she was more familiar with her surroundings, but she supposes that's the whole point – to intensify how vulnerable she feels as anxiety and arousal battle each other in the core of her being, which he so effortlessly reaches with his penis when he fucks her. It is much harder for her to access this haunting sensual core of herself merely with her willpower; she wouldn't be able to do it if the desire to trust him, and to show him that she trusts him, wasn't intricately woven into the exercise. She hesitates as the tip of the crop snakes out from beneath her chin, and a moment passes before she feels it again at the base of her spine. She moves tentatively forward, pausing in confusion when she feels the tip of the riding crop press against her left thigh.

'Turn a little to the right, Mira.'

She obeys her Master's voice, blindly following his lead. She can't be sure, but she suspects the wooden cross in the back of the room is their destination. Naturally, she knows better than to ask. She hesitates again as the crop comes to rest directly behind her knees. A few seconds later, a fiery lick across her ass cheeks comes as a shock. She gasps, and tears spring into her eyes beneath the blindfold.

'You're not listening with your body, Mira. Stop thinking and start feeling.'

'Yes, Master, I'm sorry!' The flesh of her buttocks is burning in silent in sympathy with horses everywhere. She takes great care to keep her skin soft and supple using all the latest fruit-based products, but she never realized just how incredibly sensitive her glove-like organ can be.

'Stop right there,' he commands.

Cat's Collar

She gladly plants her towering heels together and stands with her arms relaxed at her sides, her breasts and ass thrusting out into the chill air of the cellar, her nipples straining for his attention.

'Spread your legs.'

It seems a simple enough command, but when she slipped on the extreme high-heels she stepped into another dimension where gravity became more severe. She manages to shift her feet apart, having no desire to feel the hot snaky reprimand of the crop across her buttocks again. His warm hands grasp her wrists to lift her arms over her head, and then he presses the full length of his body against hers so she has no choice but to fall forward into the void.

'Master!' she cries, but already her cheek is resting safely against cool, smooth wood as once again he secures her wrists over her head, and then firmly manacles her ankles to keep her legs spread.

She has been fantasizing about this position and this cross ever since she saw it; however, she couldn't have imagined the intense gratification of his hands parting her ass cheeks so he could thrust his tongue up into her pussy from behind. His skilled oral devotion comes as a blessing to her overwrought senses. She is deliciously aware of her lush labial lips as he takes them in his mouth, alternately sucking and feasting on the sweet and tender crack in her flesh. Tendrils of pleasure indistinguishable from pure, hot energy are slowly unraveling deep in her pelvis, snaking down to meet the tip of his licking, flicking, thrusting tongue, and the subtle, exquisite conflagration is concentrated in her swelling clitoris. Everything is so hard – his fingers digging into her nether cheeks, the wood pressing against her nipples and belly, the stiff leather cuffing her wrists and ankles – and she is so soft and yielding and helpless.

'Oh, Master, please, please…'

He shoves his face into her vulva with a ravenous growl.

'Oh, God, please fuck me, Master, please!'

His features cease to imprint themselves on the haunting clay of her hotly juicing sex. 'I suppose I could do that,' he says. And he does.

Being nailed to the cross takes on a whole different meaning to the Catholic school girl inside Mira. Her breasts are no longer crushed against the wood because they're in his hands, his fingers pressing cruelly into her tender mounds. He braces himself on their soft fullness as his cock surges into her cunt over and over again in a tight, pounding rhythm. It seems to Mira that her whole life was leading up to these moments when absolute fulfillment pushes all the thoughts out of her head. She is at peace as she never has been before and not despite the violence trapped between her thighs but precisely because of it. No man has ever fucked her so selfishly. No man has ever banged her from behind when she was bound and helpless to defend herself. No man has ever driven his erection so deep into her pussy. He stabs her with increasing force in between pausing to circle his hips and grind against her ass cheeks, forcing her to savor the sensation of his hard-on packed into her hole; intensifying her awareness of his cock remorselessly rammed up into her body as he stirs her juices up with spiraling motions, making a hot cauldron of her cunt. The darkness behind her blindfold is black magic – a staggeringly powerful spell is being worked by the controlled confines of her limbs and senses and transforming her into the pure, unresisting vessel of his pleasure. Her sex, her breasts, her legs, her ass, her neck, all of her was designed with his lust in mind. Ground into the palms of his hands, her nipples are hard as diamonds refracting pricelessly sharp sensations through her flesh as his penis seems to drive deeper and deeper into her pelvis. He flings her hair over one shoulder and bites her neck with such vicious abandon that she grows limp as prey in a predator's jaws, allowing herself to be absolutely possessed and loving it even as she marvels at the paradox that his giving no thought to her comfort and pleasure pleases her more than anything.

He comes inside her with a vengeance, as if drowning all evidence of any man who has been there before him. Afterwards, he remains buried inside her, the weight of his body pressing her against the cross, and she is so stunned and fulfilled she is glad of its support. Surely this was the climax of her first test as a sex slave. She hopes it was because her senses and emotions are completely spent for the moment, as spent as his penis, also only for the moment, thank the Lord.

'Mm,' he says at last, his voice vibrating deliciously down her spine. Then he steps back, and yanks her blindfold off.

Cat's Collar

She opens her eyes but all she can see is her left arm bound above her and a portion of stone wall.

'I'm tempted to leave you like this for a while, Mira. You're such a lovely sight.'

'My ankles, Master…' she whispers.

'I know, they hurt, but you're doing very well in your new shoes, my beautiful slave.'

She is afraid he really intends to leave her there for awhile and her feet literally couldn't stand it. She is very glad when he begins freeing her ankles.

'You did very well, Mira. Did you enjoy yourself?'

'Oh, yes, Master!'

'I want you to share everything you felt with me over a bottle of wine. How does that sound?'

'That sounds divine, Master.'

※

Mira is very glad to sit down on a padded black leather surface as she slips off her black magic heels. She feels as beautiful and timeless as a priestess who just performed a sensual ritual deep in the heart of a temple with the high priest who watches her now as she divests herself of ritual attire.

'I've never felt so happy and so relaxed, Phillip,' she says even as she groans with relief to be standing up on her bare feet.

'You'd better get used to it, my slave.' He smiles and allows her to slip her arms around his neck.

'My God, you're so tall,' she exclaims. When she was wearing the heels her face was nearly on a level with his, now she has to look up at him again.

'You're so small.' He kisses the tip of her nose.

She giggles. The evening has been full of unexpected sensations so intense they nearly defy her ability to rationally remember them. 'I brought a change of clothes as you instructed, Master.'

'That's nice, but for now you're remaining naked.'

Before they leave the room she turns and looks at all the arcane objects it contains, and the space fills her with a sense of reverence mixed with gratitude that her guardian angels at last led her to this dark church, and to this man with whom she can worship her sensuality as never before.

In the wine cellar, Phillip picks up the black bag with her change of costume in it, and she follows him up the stairs.

Chapter Eighteen

"We don't see things as they are, we see them as we are."
Anaïs Nin

Mira cannot seem to get enough of Phillip or his cellar. What she once almost dreaded she now looks forward to with a thrill of anxious anticipation she likens to an athlete struggling to reach the top of her form. During her demanding sensual encounters with her Master she is obviously not trying to set any kind of record, and there are no invisible judges to give her a perfect 10 as a sex slave, more and more what she fervently desires to do is transcend her limits, emotional, mental and even physical. She has come to appreciate her threefold nature as never before. She is more aware than ever that often what excites her feelings makes her brain anxious, and her body is caught in the middle. It was much more difficult for her to have an orgasm before she met Phillip. Her sensual wiring is not as moody and difficult to turn on as she had believed it was with other men. Every time she says 'Yes, Master' a switch is thrown inside her between the tense career woman in full control of her life, and between the sensually submissive slave in love surrendering all doubts and fears into the hands of her love and lord. And it is almost as if Sekhmet has noticed the changes in Mira because lately she behaves a bit more respectfully (if not affectionately) towards her pet human. Of course this change in her cat could simply be Mira's imagination, but who is to say how many aspects of the world aren't as well; therefore, she chooses to believe that she and Sekhmet are growing closer as she achieves a mysteriously higher status in her feline's mind as a pussy with a Master whose lap they both love resting on (although Sekhmet clearly considers herself superior for being able to curl her entire body up on his thighs whereas Mira can only rest her stupidly heavy human head on them.)

Phillip at last gave her a tour of the rest of his miniature castle. The square footage is indeed primarily vertical; nevertheless, there is more than enough space for a single man, and for a loving couple. The kitchen left Mira speechless. 'Food and wine go hand in hand,' he said, and she nodded in stunned agreement. Apparently he really was teasing her about his financial straits because no expense was spared on his kitchen that she can see. Black granite counters speckled with white like a starry night as seen now only from remote places on earth free of light pollution, and stainless steel appliances, were offset by polished oak cabinets, many of which were graced with stained-glass doors through which she could see an assortment of stemware worthy of a man who would one day inherit a vineyard.

'But you said you hate to cook, Master,' she reminded him.

'Yes, I don't much care for it, I'll admit, but my slave happens to be an excellent cook, and she deserves the best tools, and the nicest atmosphere to work in.'

She didn't point out that he designed this dream kitchen long before they met because she suspects that the foundations of his entire home have much to do with belief in Choreography as opposed to coincidence, and with his aggressively positive nature. He mentioned when they first met that he had begun losing hope that he would ever meet the right woman, but he had set the stage as though he never doubted it. There are a myriad of things she loves about him, especially the way his intelligence and his imagination work together, and how he can make what to her appears to be a mountainous obstacle feel like a challenge she can easily conquer with the right attitude. He is actively reinforcing her life-long belief that how you perceive things, and how you structure and illuminate your thoughts makes all the difference in the world. If you're climbing a mountain and deliberately choose cheap, poorly made equipment you can get yourself killed; you should always bring the best attitude along no matter what it costs you in courage.

Mira loves everything about Phillip's home, but his back porch holds a special place in her heart. In nice weather it is a haven of ivy-covered trellises surrounded by flowering plants and flanked by big beautiful old trees. There is an outdoor fireplace, and of course a hot tub that will make it a cozy and stimulating place to be even on cold winter nights. Black wrought iron chairs surrounding a table with a glass top, and an abundance of gas lamps, also make his porch a beautiful place to dine. It was where they enjoyed the first dinner she prepared for them, and for which he opened a special bottle from his cellar – a thirty-five year-old vintage from Portugal his parents had given him for his birthday five years ago.

Mira should not have been surprised that Phillip effortlessly charmed her own parents. To see the three of them conversing pleasantly, and generally getting along splendidly, was such a relief she had to excuse herself and savor a moment alone in her old bathroom. They had stopped by her childhood home for a social drink before going out to dinner, by themselves; she had felt it was too much to ask of her lover that he dine with Rose and John so soon in their relationship. Her mother clearly felt there was nothing wrong with having a doctor in the family, even if all he did was preside over healthy grapes and the bottles convalescing in his cellar, and Mira's good-natured father had grown even mellower with age; it would not even occur to him to pass negative judgment on a man his daughter so thoroughly approved of, for he had always trusted her demanding taste in everything, men included. Once again Phillip reduced the mountain in Mira's psyche to a pleasant little hill they soon got over together. Before she knew it, Rose and John were standing in the front door smiling and waving goodbye as she and her Master drove off in a cloud of love given a silver lining by her parents' blessing.

'The Catholic school I went to is just two blocks away down Old Lee Highway,' she informed him.

'A genuine Catholic school girl...' He shook his head as if he couldn't believe his luck, yet whether it was good or bad luck she couldn't tell by his grin, which always made his goatee look even darker and more sinisterly arousing. 'I'd like to see the church where you used to kneel and pray wearing your little plaid uniform.'

'Are you serious?'

'Why not, it'll be fun.'

'If you say so, Master.'

St. Leo's had not changed a bit. The church was as ugly on the outside as she

Cat's Collar

remembered it, plain and modern in a completely uninspired way. This late on a weekday there were few cars in the parking lot; school had long since let out and apparently no masses were scheduled. Phillip's jeep had successfully survived its engine transplant, but they still preferred getting around town in her Camaro (which boasted the luxury of air-conditioning) and his driving skills (like many of his other skills) took her breath away as he pulled into a spot directly in front of the church with effortlessly controlled speed.

'We'll have to come back here after I buy you a new uniform,' he said.

Laughing, she let herself out of the car, not sure if he was serious or not.

'Mm, I'm getting hard just thinking about you in a little plaid skirt and white socks.' He gripped her ass with one hand and squeezed it so hard she cried out in protest.

'Are you really sure you want to go in there, Master? There's nothing to see except an ugly old church.'

'Yes, I'm sure.' He grasped her hand, and the firmness of his grip told her there was no arguing with his decision.

It had been years since Mira was inside a church, and she was surprised by all the emotions that swept over her as she stepped into the stone-paved foyer. She would never forget standing there as a little girl craning her neck to see inside the church. She had been part of a crowd of people bundled up in dark winter coats attending candlelight Mass on Christmas Eve, snow falling like a blessing behind them in the night – like infinite fragments of the Virgin's pure veil – while inside the church hundreds of phallic candles burned, the flames reflecting off the handsome priest's gilded vestments. Cold darkness behind her, warmth and light before her, and all around her a comforting mass of humanity made special by her parents' beloved faces, and by the distant, rather bored profile of a boy she thought she was passionately in love with...

Memories brushed her like invisible wings as Phillip pulled open the door leading into the church itself, and waited for her to precede him into the empty silence. The time when churches offered a peaceful, compassionate refuge to people living in the brutal chaos of the Dark Ages had long since passed, but Mira's psyche could still sense the relief of finding sanctuary in a way that made her seriously wonder whether the concept of racial memory wasn't more fact than fiction. As if with a life of its own her hand reached up so she could dip her fingertips into the well of holy water and make the sign of the cross. Phillip wasn't watching her; he had his eyes fixed on the pristine white altar, and then he was studying the narrow booths in which Mira had confessed to a hidden priest about yelling at her mother and lying to her grandmother – the extent of her sins at so young an age. It was also where she had smoked her first cigarette with a group of the school's more daring girls who, for some reason, had welcomed her into their exclusive fold one day. She had done her best afterwards to hide how much she had hated the smell of chemically processed tobacco and the nauseous experience of nicotine contaminating her bloodstream.

The church was completely empty. Not a single soul knelt in the pews silently praying to God or the saints or whatever.

'Come here,' Phillip whispered, and took her hand again even more firmly.

She was not surprised that he led her directly to one of the confessionals. At least there was no one around to see when he opened the narrow wooden door, and shoved her gently into the dark interior. Then he joined her, and she didn't care about anything except the feel of his body pressed hard against hers and the sensation of his teeth biting into the side of her neck as his swelling erection dug into her womb.

'Oh, my God!' she breathed as he sucked on her flesh with the fierce hunger of a blood-thirsty vampire. He had given her a hickey before, but he had never used his teeth quite like he did in the house of God that evening, as though he truly meant to tear open her skin and drink her blood. 'Oh, Master...' There it was again, her brain being afraid while the rest of her was so turned on she never wanted him to stop; she longed for him to truly possess her body and soul. Images of vampires sleeping in a crypt beneath the church flashed on the screen of her closed eyelids as he reached down and yanked her dress up around her waist, never once loosing his vicious grip on her neck. He was going to fuck her in a confessional, and her pussy felt as deep and dark and wet as the crypt in her imagination. All she desired was the stake of his cock plunging deep into her body. She clung to his shoulders when he thrust his hand between their bodies

Cat's Collar

to unzip his slacks. The angle was wrong so she lifted one of her high-heels onto the padded bench where she had once sat as a little girl confessing her innocent sins. She couldn't remain silent as he stabbed her with his erection and she was afraid her cry could be heard throughout the whole church, yet it didn't matter; nothing mattered now except the fact that she was going to die from the dark joy of being his willing victim. His confidence and intelligence, his masterful personality, had hypnotized her into absolute submission, and the more she gave him, the more selfishly he used her, the more she longed to give him and the more she surrendered all resistance and grew absolutely languid against him.

Her brain forced her to gasp, 'What if someone comes?!' but the most important parts of her weren't at all concerned, and soon how violently he brought himself to a climax banging her and sucking on her seemed to blow her mind so she was aware only of their mutual fulfillment.

Unbelievably, their violent love making was not sensed by any of the priests or nuns living in the residences adjoining the church. Mira's knees were literally week as she stepped out of the booth where she had just confessed her deepest, darkest desires with her whole body. She didn't need a mirror to know he had marked her, and even though she was proud, she was also glad of her long hair which would hide the evidence of his vicious lust during dinner in a restaurant. She smiled to herself. At least she would never hear him quote Dracula and say, 'I don't drink... *wine.*' She did not cross herself leaving the church. Her pussy was so warm and wet that immersing her fingertips in the cool holy water would have felt like the ultimate hypocrisy.

Back in the comforting confines of the Camaro, she rested her head against the seat and gazed at her Master's handsome profile as he started the engine and sped out of the church parking lot.

'I... I really liked that,' she confessed.

'I know you did. We'll be exploring more of that in the future.'

She chose not to ask him what he meant, content to savor the frightening, thrilling promise.

Chapter Nineteen

"Time spent with cats is never wasted."
Collette

Because they live so close, just a quick walk through the woods, Sekhmet and Mira both have to wait for the special treat of Phillip spending an entire night in their home. Mira has yet to stay at his place from sunset to sunrise because she doesn't want to leave her cats alone all night, although if the truth be told she would probably miss them more than they would her. Phillip is a very tall man, nevertheless, she is astonished and dismayed that his feet hang off the end of her queen-size mattress. Her bed, which always felt so big and luxurious to her when she was sleeping in it alone, suddenly seems very small. Her Master is a slender man but his shoulders are broad, and even when he rolls over onto his side his powerful body dominates most of the mattress. She is willing to give up a good night's sleep for the pleasure and emotional comfort of his presence, but come morning she has reconciled herself to the fact that she will have to detach herself from her felines somewhat so that she and her Master can enjoy the luxury of his king-size feather bed.

'We should bring them over to my place,' Phillip says over breakfast as they are discussing Stormy and Sekhmet.

'I'd have to put them in their carrier and drive them over.'

'Then I suggest you do so.' He pours himself another cup of coffee. 'They need to begin getting used to my house and to their new territory.'

They're sitting in the *Pan Am Family Restaurant*, which as far as Mira can tell is actually family owned. Blue plastic booths and white walls covered with sketchy uninspired paintings of Greece somehow manage not to offend her

Cat's Collar

aesthetic sense, perhaps because of all the dark-brown wicker baskets hanging from the ceiling overflowing with healthy plants. The service is so pleasant and efficient, and the diner-style food so abundant and delicious within it's traditional unhealthy parameters, that she and Phillip have taken to having either breakfast or lunch their on Saturdays. She has lost count of how many cups of coffee her Master has already had this morning. She is still slowly sipping her second cup of Earl Grey tea (she appreciates a management that doesn't mind her bringing her own gourmet blend) but what she is truly savoring are the last words her sexy, commanding, tender, intelligent, funny, infinitely wonderful companion just said. He just let her know, with a sweet subtlety wafting over her soul like an angel's perfume, that they will be living together soon. The slight hangover she was suffering from this morning vanishes in a rush of euphoria. Ever since she met her Master the endorphin count in her blood has skyrocketed, and these very special endorphins don't just vanish thirty minutes to an hour after their sensual workouts but remain as a deepening contentment in her emotional system.

'Well, you let me know when would be a good night for you, Master, and I'll bring them over.'

'Tonight would be good.'

'Okay.' And the matter is settled with the relaxed ease she is growing more and more accustomed to the more time she spends with him. If she wasn't so happy she might be a bit disturbed by how much energy she once wasted worrying about both big and little things without even realizing how tense she allowed things to make her. That's not to say that everything is perfect now, after all they're still living in the real world. For instance, they occasionally tend to indulge their love of good food and wine a little too much, hence the slight fog in her skull this morning. Yet other than that there are no flaws in their relationship that she can see – it is a beautifully cut diamond that demands much from both their mental and emotional synapses, but in her opinion this is a good thing.

'So, what would you like to do today, my beautiful slave?'

'A trip to a grocery store would be nice,' she replies, and as usual feels guilty about dragging him shopping with her, an activity he has made it clear is not on the top of his favorite's list. Yet he always seems to enjoy himself (thanks in part to how well his willpower and his positive attitude work together) especially when they visit *Super H-Mart* which is like teleporting to a huge fish and farmer's market in Hong Kong for an hour. 'We really have to stop eating out to all the time,' she adds, striving to justify her love of food buying.

'And why is that? Don't you enjoy our dinners out?'

'Of course I do, Master, but it's very expensive; just one meal at a decent restaurant with a bottle of wine costs my entire grocery bill for a week.'

'That's true,' he agrees, pouring himself yet another cup of coffee.

'We're also going to gain weight if I don't start watching our fat and calorie intake.'

'Now we wouldn't want that, would we? I hereby command you, my slave, not to let that happen.'

She laughs. 'Yes, Master, it will be my pleasure.'

'Where exactly do you need to go?'

'*Super H-Mart and Trader Joe's.*'

'Okay. And then what?'

'Whatever Master desires.'

'Very good, Mira, but I think we'll have a quiet evening with the pussies tonight. We opened one too many bottles of wine last night, but of course it's your fault for making such a delicious meal.'

'Of course.' She smiles, and even though she does her best to hide it, she is relieved that another intensely demanding sojourn in the cellar is not on the agenda for this evening. Being fucked by her Master is a serious workout, and while she enjoys it like nothing else on earth – while the feel of his cock thrusting into her pussy mysteriously fulfills her on all levels of her being – the truth is her pussy sometimes needs a day or two to recover, as do other parts of her body if she has been in even mild bondage for a prolonged period of time. The more she gets to know her Master, the more she loves all the subtleties of his personality. She is surprised and grateful for the sense of humor she had not expected from the stranger dressed entirely in black who commanded her to take off her robe for him.

Cat's Collar

❦❦❦❦❦

Stormy and Sekhmet refuse to cooperate. Mira has locked the cat flap so they can't escape the house, but that doesn't make the task of getting them into the carrier any easier. Fortunately, Phillip is there to assist her; Sekhmet is much more likely to respond to his cajoling voice than to Mira's impatient, and increasingly frustrated, commands. When it concerns being imprisoned in a moving plastic cage is the only time Stormy ceases to be his usual compliant and amiable self. He hides so far under the bed there's no way she can pull him out, and she doesn't entirely trust him not to scratch her to defend himself from incarceration. If they can just get Sekhmet into the carrier she knows Stormy will slink out from his hiding place in response to his sister's yowls of protest, and she can catch him then.

'Sekhmet, come here sweetheart.' Phillip is kneeling in front of Mira's desk, beneath which Sekhmet has taken refuge. 'Come on sweetie, I've got a very special treat waiting for you at my place. Come on… that's a good girl, you won't be sorry.'

Mira watches in wonder as he straightens up holding Sekhmet by the scruff of the neck like a black rag that just cleaned two resentful yellow eyes up off the floor. 'I can't believe she listened to you!'

'Of course she did. She's a good little pussy. Aren't you sweetheart?'

Sekhmet may have yielded to his persuasion against her better judgment, but she is not about to purr now as she usually does in response to his voice. He urges her gently into the carrier, and quickly closes the metal door on her little black backside. Mira waits for howls of protest to ensue, but a miraculous silence reigns in the study. And apparently Stormy finds the stillness more disconcerting than his sister's screams because he peers out from beneath Mira's big comfortable reading chair.

'Got ya!' Mira snatches him up into her arms, but then holds him tenderly against her breasts. 'It's okay, baby, we're just going for a little ride.'

Phillip is crouched beside the carrier and effortlessly soothing Sekhmet by letting her smell and lick his fingertips through the bars. 'Ready?' he asks.

'Ready.'

He opens the carrier door.

Mira gently shoves Stormy inside next to his sister.

He quickly closes the door again before Sekhmet can escape.

'Wow, that was easier than ever.' She tosses her hair away from her face and steps into his arms as he straightens up. 'You have no idea what I go through every time I have to take them to the vet. This is the quickest I've ever gotten them both in there, thank you, Master.'

'You don't have to do everything alone anymore, Mira,' he says soberly.

'I know,' she sighs, and slips her arms around his neck so she can rest her cheek against him. 'I still can't quite believe it...'

'Mreow!'

'Merr!'

'I think we'd best be going,' he suggests.

'Yes, I think that would be a good idea,' she agrees.

He carries the passionately protesting felines out to the car while she does a quick check of the doll's house to make sure everything is turned off. Then she grabs her overnight bag and locks the kitchen door behind her. They did indeed go grocery shopping earlier in the afternoon; the trunk of her car is full of plastic bags. She insisted on paying for the groceries, but they decided to keep them all in Phillip's kitchen since they seem to be spending more and more time at his place.

'I'm glad were not driving to Florida with those two in the backseat,' he remarks as she slips into the car.

'I think they must have some Siamese blood in them.'

'No doubt!'

Even though it is a blessedly short drive, by the time they reach his house Mira's nerves feels as frayed as a delicate cloth subjected to a cat's sharpening claws for a month.

'Okay guys,' Phillips declares as he sets the carrier down in his entrance hall, 'time to explore.'

Cat's Collar

'And to shut up!'

The second he opens the cage Sekhmet shoots out like a fur-covered bullet, moving fast enough to prove all the supernatural tales of black cats appearing and disappearing as if at will. In contrast Stormy steps out of the plastic cell with painstaking slowness, one tentative paw emerging at a time, all his whiskers extended to their full, quivering reach sensing the atmosphere of a whole new world surrounding him. Sekhmet has vanished into the living room and Mira can only pray she won't do anything damaging by way of revenge.

'I'll start bringing the stuff in,' he says.

'I'll help you.'

'I'll get the bags. You set up the litter box, please.'

'Okay... I mean, yes, Master.'

They smile at each other.

Chapter Twenty

> *"Surely something resides in this heart that is not*
> *perishable – and life is more than a dream."*
> Mary Wollstonecraft

A few hours later Stormy and Sekhmet have explored Phillip's house from top to bottom several times, not including the cellar, from which they are forever banned. The evening is unnaturally cool for early August in Virginia, and it is all the excuse Phillip and Mira need to strip naked and step into the hot tub where they sit across from each other. A filet mignon roast and too large Idaho potatoes are cooking in the oven, and the cold white wine flowing onto her tongue is a delicious contrast to the embracing heat of the water. The sun has sunk below the horizon but it isn't dark yet, and the sight of her Master's handsome face framed by the beauty of his yard at twilight is all she can possibly ask of life as she takes another inspiring sip of Chardonnay. Every relaxing moment she spends with him is promisingly pregnant with all the sensual feasts they will share in every sense.

'I'm so glad you're here,' he tells her quietly. 'You make me very happy, Mira.'

The deep, penetrating look in his eyes is the very heart of the universe for her; everything lives in and for him. His awareness, his soul is the reason she was born and took form and developed a visual cortex so her being could gaze into his like this. Together they are the reason for everything mysteriously delivered in an envelope of flesh, and the closer they become, the more they open up to each other, the more every day and every night feels like a love letter written in blood from the heart of the cosmos. 'Do you believe in the soul, Phillip?'

'You know I do, Mira.'

'I just can't imagine dying and never seeing you again...'

'Then don't imagine it.'

She smiles, sadness and happiness battling in her pulse. 'Yes, Master.'

'I've had certain... experiences that can only be explained by the possibility that I've lived before,' he confesses.

'Really? Such as?'

'I'll tell you about them some other time, not tonight. Suffice it to say that I definitely believe there's such a thing as a soul that survives the death of the body.'

As if in response to his assertion of immortality two black streaks soar erratically over their heads. 'Oh, look, bats!' she exclaims happily. It is much darker now; the leaves of the trees are almost indistinguishable from the sky, and soon only the porch's halo of light will reveal individual flowers and bushes. Mira took it upon herself to light all the gas lamps so the night would not swallow them up as they sat in the hot tub. A powerful jet of water is massaging her lower back, and she lifts her right foot in search of some aquatic reflexology, all the time holding her glass of Chardonnay above the frothing water. 'Mm...' The hard bubbles beating against the sole of her foot somehow help relax her entire body. 'I understand now why Chinese concubines were treated to foot rubs with little circular mallets,' she muses out loud, 'but only on the night their lord had chosen to spend with them as a reward for being in his favor.'

'Tell me more.' He sounds intrigued.

'I don't know much more really, I've never particularly cared for the Chinese culture; I much prefer the Japanese and the Hindus.'

'Oh, yes, Tantric sex... that's something else we should explore in the future, not anytime soon, though; we're not ready for that yet.'

'It's wonderful having things to look forward to, isn't it?' She sets her glass down on the tub's wooden platform in favor of sinking even lower into the hot foam and subjecting her other foot to a jet's teasingly inconsistent massage. 'I could never be just another concubine,' she continues thinking out loud, something she can do with her Master she was never really able to do with anyone else. 'I could never share your love and attention with other women, but then love has had very little to do with marriage throughout most of history.' She glances at him uncertainly, regretting her use of the word 'marriage' afraid he might take it personally. They have known each other less than three months; it is definitely too soon to even discuss such a possibility.

'I understand you couldn't share my love with other women,' he says, and pauses to drain his glass, 'but what about occasionally sharing my body?'

'That's different,' she replies, too busy riding a wave of relief that he didn't even blink at her Freudian slip to think about it. 'In ancient Egypt there was only one wife and all the other women in the household were either servants or concubines... not that I would like that either; I wouldn't want other women around all the time.'

'That's perfectly understandable, and there never will be, but I'm very proud of you for grasping the difference between loving someone and fucking them.'

'When we first met, I was very jealous of the women you dominate, but I'm not anymore, not like I used to be, anyway. I know they don't mean anything to you, not like I do.' She sits up and reaches for her wine again. 'But are you saying that sex and love have nothing to do with each other?' The darkness around them suddenly feels threatening rather than promising.

'Not at all, when you have sex with the person you love, you're making love, not just fucking.'

'Then why was the Chief Wife in ancient Egypt not allowed the same sexual freedom as her husband?' she demands, centuries of oppression fueling her retort.

'Because he had to make sure those were his babies she was breeding, not some other man's. It had everything to do with preserving the bloodline and the political power that went with it. In the ancient Egypt of the future, things will be different.'

She laughs. 'I like that, an ancient Egypt of the future... it would be a wonderful place to live.'

Cat's Collar

'And we've already begun laying the foundations for such a sensually enlightened society, my beautiful slave.'

'But it would also have to be an intensely spiritual society,' she points out, shying away from the glorification of superficial hedonism. 'And I'm not talking institutionalized religion here.'

'Mira,' he sets his empty glass down on the tub's wooden lip, 'to be enlightened implies a certain depth of mind and spirit. When I say "sensually enlightened" I'm not talking about the Playboy castle, I'm talking about integrating all aspects of our being, which is a sacred art and the only true pleasure to be had in life as we know it.'

She carefully discards her own glass again, and wades across the waves into his arms. 'You are the smartest, wisest man I have ever met, Master.' She plants her lips against his. They taste better to her everyday as a result of all the fascinating thoughts and concepts he expresses with them, and tonight they're slick from being kissed by hot foam as well as tartly sweet from the Chardonnay. She loses herself in his mouth for timeless moments, playing contentedly with his tongue, and then wrestling with it more urgently as she feels his penis hardening between her thighs.

She pulls back. 'Do you love me, Master?'

'You know I do, Mira.' Beneath the water his hands wrap her legs fully around his hips. 'I love you more than anything,' he adds intently, positioning the swollen head of his cock at the entrance to her flesh. 'You're the most important thing in the world to me, never forget it.'

'But what about when I'm old and ugly?' she asks breathlessly as his hard-on slips into her cunt and fills her up as only he can.

'You'll never be ugly!' he says through his teeth, jamming his cock even deeper into her pussy and leaving no room inside her for doubts.

'But I'll be old,' she insists, 'and how can I be a beautiful sex slave when I'm old?' She knows she is being perversely needy and begging for his reassurance, but she doesn't care; she needs him more than anything and she is afraid her growing happiness will be cruelly cut down one day for some reason or other.

'We'll both be old,' he points out, 'and you'll be even more beautiful in my eyes than ever, and I'll still be your Master and the love of your life, won't I.' His fingers gripping her ass are silent, indelible statements she has no desire to argue with as he holds her down around his erection and thrusts urgently up beneath her. 'For a deep and intelligent woman, you can be very silly sometimes, Mira.'

'I didn't say that,' she moans as his hands now clutch her hips and force her pussy up and down his rigid length.

'Yes, you did say that.'

'Oh, God, no, I didn't!' she cries, holding on to his slick shoulders. She resents the rushing heat of the water that does not allow her to fully feel him, and the chemically-treated foam is competing with her vagina's natural juices and winning. Their genitals are completely underwater yet his greedy shaft has to ram past her dry opening into the moist interior.

'Are you arguing with your Master?' he demands.

'No, Master, I'm sorry...'

'What's wrong?' He studies her face. 'Don't you like having my cock inside you?'

'I love your cock inside me, Master, but... it doesn't feel as good in here.'

He slides her tight hole off his dick. 'Come on.' He takes her hand, and side-by-side they climb the steps out of the hot tub.

The porch is a dry golden haven of gas lamps and candle light and a large wicker couch covered with water-proof cushions. He seats himself, and she knows he wants her to keep riding him, but she isn't yet wet enough on the inside.

'May I touch myself, Master?' she asks, standing before him.

'Yes, you may,' he replies.

She shivers. The night feels even colder than it really is to her flushed skin, but the tremor that courses down her spine has much more to do with the look in his eyes and with the sight of his hands cradling his generous balls and stroking his ideal erection as he looks at her. She doesn't feel at all shy tonight. With her hair half dry and half wet, black tendrils clinging snake-like to her taut breasts, light-jeweled drops of water caressing her body all the slow way down her belly and legs, the candle light gilding her smooth skin to a flawless, ageless perfection, she feels timelessly beautiful as she crushes her clit beneath her fingertips and firmly coaxes her pussy into juicing. Her clit is another wick coming to warm life on the porch and igniting that sweet, greedy tension in her pelvis which can so easily lead to the devastating conflagration of a climax. In a matter of seconds, she is ready for him. She straddles him, her knees sinking into the cushions on either side of him, and takes possession of his erection to guide it slowly inside her. She wants to savor the experience of his hard-on's demanding dimensions opening her up, and she also wants him to watch his cock parting the folds of her labia and slowly disappearing into her warm, embracing slot. Only when his penis is packed inside her to the hilt does she brace herself on his shoulders – as straight and broad as any pharaoh's – and begin massaging his cock with her pussy muscles as she rides him, working her cunt swiftly up and down around him.

'Keep touching yourself,' he commands.

She moans, only interested in pleasing him at the moment.

'I told you to touch yourself, Mira.'

She obeys of course, and forgets her reluctance, wondering why she ever felt it in the first place as her fingertips work her clitoris like the magic button of her sensual wiring. Her hips selfishly orbit the climax building inside her, his rampant penis the motionless center of the beautiful storm in her nerve-endings.

'That's it, make yourself come,' he urges quietly, caressing her breasts and gently pinching her nipples.

Up until that moment she was concentrating on the pulsing wick of a candle burning in a bronze lamp hanging from the ceiling, but now she looks down into his eyes, and ecstasy mysteriously unravels her from the inside out as she sees all the flames reflected back at her in his penetratingly dark irises.

'Mm,' he says after she finally descends from the blindingly beautiful realm of her orgasm. 'Get up.'

She is literally weak in the knees, the warm glow in her sex relaxing all her other muscles so that it takes her longer than it normally would to lift herself off him, stand up, and then position herself on her hands and knees on the cushions. He kneels behind her, and she tosses her head as he penetrates her, flinging her hair across her back so he can grab its mane as he swiftly rides her to his own pounding climax.

'Mreow!' Sekhmet materializes from the shadows. She assumes the statuesque pose of her namesake and stares up at the two naked human bodies pretending to be cats with eyes the same burning yellow of the flames illuminating her like a sacred icon.

Mira returns her stare, not sure if her feline's eyes are blazing with jealousy or cold with contempt or if her regard is, somehow, fiercely approving. She sits down beside her Master on the couch and rests her head on his chest, cuddling up against him for warmth as they both gaze back at the cat.

'Well, Sekhmet,' he says, 'do you and your brother approve of your soon-to-be new territory?'

She turns her head.

Stormy slinks out from the cover of another shadow and rubs his purring body up against his sister's.

She hisses and swats him with her paw, but her claws are sheathed, betraying her secret fondness for him.

He removes himself to a safer distance and begins licking his penis, his hind leg thrust comically straight up into the air.

'They love it,' Mira translates. 'I'm getting cold. May we go inside, Master?'

'Yes, we may.'

'I'll get the wine glasses.'

'No, just leave them. I have plenty more, and there's still some wine left in yours that will serve as an offering.'

'As an offering to what?' she asks, intrigued.

He shrugs as they get up. 'Whatever's out there... there are unseen forces all around us, Mira, best to keep them on our side.'

'Yes!' she agrees, and walks gratefully into the warmer embrace of the house as he opens the screen door for her. 'Dinner should be ready soon. May I put something on to serve, Master?'

'Yes, I suppose you may. It's getting chilly and I'd like to eat outside, if that's

Cat's Collar

all right with you. We'll be cooped up inside long enough during the winter.'

'I love eating outside.'

'Mm... and I love eating you.' He pulls her into his arms and kisses her. 'But I suppose that will have to wait until later.' He lets go of her just as abruptly. 'I don't want you burning our dinner.'

She follows him upstairs. The climb to his tower bedroom never fails to leave her a bit winded, and she wonders if she'll ever get used to it. He heads for the shower to rinse off, but she contents herself with the soft hug of a large Egyptian cotton towel before slipping into a pair of black cotton house pants, and a violet shirt with long sleeves that end in tulip-like ruffles that cover her upper hands Medieval-style. And because he has given her permission to wear clothing, it means she does not have to wear high-heels while moving about in the kitchen and carrying a heavy tray out onto the porch. Soft black 'ballet' slippers are just what her feet need to hurry back down the tower stairs, at the bottom of which Stormy and Sekhmet both greet her vociferously.

'Yes, yes, I know, it's past your dinner time,' she apologizes happily. 'But don't worry, I brought your bowls and your favorite canned tuna.' Her devoted (hungry) entourage follows her into the kitchen, which still takes her breath away with its utterly efficient beauty. She knows where everything is already, and has not quite gotten over marveling at a straight man with such excellent taste in plates and stemware. The stainless steel side-by-side refrigerator was going sadly to waste before she came along, but now its clean white plastic bowels are at least modestly filled with food. Once she and her Master live together, and she is not dividing groceries between their two homes, this dream refrigerator will be bursting with cheeses and condiments and fruits and vegetables and meats and everything else needed for a sensually enlightened existence, which naturally includes regular orgasms of the taste buds by way of excellent nutrition.

She takes the roast out of the oven, and thrusts the metal tip of an electronic meat thermometer into the thickest part of the filet, watching anxiously as the temperature on the display escalates. She sincerely hopes she did not overdo it, but sometimes it's hard balancing gourmet cooking with great sex, a demanding task she is more than happy to live with.

'Meow! Meow! Meow!' Sekhmet is letting her know *she* is always supposed to come first.

'I'm coming!' The temperature of the roast is perfect. She tents it loosely beneath tinfoil so it will finish cooking while releasing more of its delicious internal juices. 'Okay.' She quickly opens two cans of tuna, and quickly dishes the feast out into two separate bowls. 'See, it's just like we're at home,' she says, and as she straightens up from feeding her cats, Mira realizes it's true, they are at home, in her Master's castle, and as long as they live she'll never feel that cold, paralyzing loneliness in her soul again. 'You have no idea how lucky we are, babies,' she says, but her words fall on ears deafened by the greedy smacking of the jaws beneath them.

She has just finished loading the large wicker tray with plates, napkins, glasses, forks and steak knives when her Master enters the kitchen, as usual looking intensely sexy even though he's very casually dressed in black slippers, black sweat pants and a black sweatshirt. He steps up behind her and slips his arms around her waist as she lifts the foil off the filet mignon.

'Mm!' He buries his face in her damp hair. 'That looks fabulous.'

'Thank you, Master, but timing is critical here; I really need to serve this right away.'

'Which means I'd better hurry down to the cellar for a bottle of wine.'

'Yes, and please hurry, Master. I'll meet you out on the porch.'

'Want to just have one of mom and dad's bottles tonight?'

'Sure, that would be great. I love your parents' wine.'

'And they'll love you, my slave. I've already told them I'm getting married.'

She nearly drops the tray.

'Not any time soon, mind you, I want to get my PhD first, and continue your training before we take that conventional step, but it *will* happen Mira, you know that, and when the time comes, I'll ask you properly.'

They both stand perfectly still gazing at each other while she holds the tray up between them like an offering, and the longer they just stand there lost in each other's eyes, the more the silver and the crystal and the fine fabric placemats and napkins begin to feel like symbols of everything they can possibly desire together. There are only two words she needs to speak, only two words she needs to utter to express everything she has always believed deep in her soul and everything she is daring to feel, only two words which say it all and which no one can prove untrue in the universe that is all theirs, 'Yes, Master.'

The End

FOOTNOTE:
Unless otherwise indicated, all the quotes at the beginning of each chapter are from Grimm's Fairy Tales.

AVAILABLE FROM
MAGIC CARPET BOOKS

The Story Of M... A Memoir
by Maria Isabel Pita

The true, vividly detailed and profoundly erotic account of a beautiful, intelligent woman's first year of training as a slave to the man of her dreams. Maria Isabel Pita wrote this account of her ascent into submission for all the women out there who might be confused and frightened by their own contradictory desires, just as she was. Her vividly detailed story makes it clear we should never feel guilty about daring to make our deepest, darkest longings come true, and serves as proof that they do.
0-9726339-5-2 $14.95

Beauty & Submission by Maria Isabel Pita

In a desire to tell the truth and dispel negative stereotypes about the life of a sex slave, Maria Isabel Pita wrote *The Story of M... A Memoir*. Her intensely erotic life with the man of her dreams continues now in Beauty & Submission, a vividly detailed sexual and philosophical account of her second year of training as a slave to her Master and soul mate.
0-9755331-1-8 $14.95

The Collector's Edition of Victorian Erotica
Dr. Major LaCartilie, Editor

No lone soul can possibly read the thousands of erotic books, pamphlets and broadsides the English reading public were offered in the 19th century. In this comprehensive anthology, 'erotica' stands for bawdy, obscene, salacious, pornographic and ribald works including humor and satire employing sexual elements. Included are selections from such Anonymous classics as *A Weekend Visit*, *The Modern Eveline*, *Misfortunes of Mary*, *My Secret Life*, *The Man With A Maid*, *The Life of Fanny Hill*, *The Mournings of a Courtesan*, *The Romance of Lust*, *Pauline*, *Forbidden Fruit* and *Venus School-Mistress*.

0-9755331-0-X   **$15.95**

Guilty Pleasures by Maria Isabel Pita

Guilty Pleasures explores the passionate willingness of women throughout the ages to offer themselves up to the forces of love. Historical facts are seamlessly woven into intensely graphic sexual encounters.

Beneath the cover of *Guilty Pleasures* you will find intensely erotic love stories with a profound feel for the different centuries and cultures where they take place. An ancient Egyptian princess… a courtesan rising to fame in Athen's Golden Age…a Transylvanian Count's wicked bride… and many more are all one eternal woman in *Guilty Pleasures*.

0-9755331-5-0   **$16.95**

The Collector's Edition of The Lost Erotic Novels
Dr. Major LaCartilie, Editor

The history of erotic literature is long and distinguished. It holds valuable lessons and insights for the general reader, the sociologist, the student of sexual behavior, and the literary specialist interested in knowing how people of different cultures and different times acted and how these actions relate to the present. They are presented to the reader exactly as they first appeared in

print by writers who were, in every sense, representative of their time: *The Instruments of the Passion & Misfortunes of Mary*–Anonymous; *White Stains* - Anaïs Nin & Friends; *Innocence* - Harriet Daimler
0-9755331-0-X $16.95

The Ties That Bind
by Vanessa Duriés

The incredible confessions of a thrillingly unconventional woman. From the first page, this chronicle of dominance and submission will keep you gasping with its vivid depictions of sensual abandon. At the hand of Masters Georges, Patrick, Pierre and others, this submissive seductress experiences pleasures she never knew existed. Re-print of the French bestseller.
0-9766510-1-7 $14.95

Cat's Collar - Three Erotic Romances
by Maria Isabel Pita

Dreams of Anubis – A legal secretary from Boston visiting Egypt explores much more than just tombs and temples in the stimulating arms of a powerfully erotic priest of Anubis who enters her dreams, and then her life one night in the dark heart of Cairo's timeless bazaar.

Rituals of Surrender – Maia Wilson finds herself the heart of an erotic web spun by three sexy, enigmatic men – modern Druids intent on using her for a dark and ancient rite…

Cat's Collar – Interior designer Mira Rosemond finds herself in one attractive successful man's bedroom after the other, but then one beautiful morning a stranger dressed in black leather takes a short cut through her garden and changes the course of her life forever.
0-9766510-0-9 $16.95

Available January 2006

Monique, Blanche & Alice

ALICE: When innocent young Alice goes to live with her uncle, she has no choice then but to suffer all the deliciously shocking consequences...

MONIQUE: A mysterious Villa by the sea is the setting for dark sexual rites that beckon to many a lovely young woman, including the ripe and willing Monique...

BLANCHE: When young Blanche loses her husband on her honeymoon, it becomes clear she will need a job. She sets her sights on the stage, and soon encounters a cast of lecherous characters intent on making her path to success as hot and hard as possible.

0-9766510-3-3 $16.95

The Collector's Edition of the Ironwood Series by Don Winslow

The three Ironwood classics revised exclusively for this Magic Carpet Collector's edition.

Ironwood

James Carrington's bleak prospects were transformed overnight when he was offered a choice position at Ironwood, a unique finishing school where young women were trained to become premiere Ladies of Pleasure.